THE SCHOOL OF THE REGIMENT;

or,

LIFE AT BANGFIRE BARRACKS.

"What the dickens are you grinning at? Do you see anything in me to laugh at, you grinning apes?"—See page 6.

CONTENTS.

CONTENTS—*continued.*

THE

SCHOOL OF THE REGIMENT;

OR,

Life at Bangfire Barracks.

By the Author of "Our Boys in the Army."

CHAPTER I.

PREPARING FOR A LARK.—THE PUNISHMENT OF A SNEAK.

BANGFIRE BARRACKS.

If our readers were to search the most complete map of England that has ever been published, they would fail in discovering a town of that name, and yet it is not many miles from London.

If you were to ascend one fine morning to the top of St. Paul's, when there is no fog to intercept the view, you might, by looking to the eastward, catch sight of the chimneys and church-steeples of Bangfire, and, possibly, the clock-tower and weather-vane which decorate the front of the block of buildings which forms part of the barracks.

Beyond this, we do not intend to furnish you with further particulars respecting the whereabouts of this town; but will at once begin the recording of the incidents which gave a local celebrity to "Our Boys in the Army," who formed the scholars of the School of the Regiment—the Royal Regiment of Artillery.

The school-house stands just outside the western end of the barracks, close to the granary and forage stores.

It is a large building, divided, internally, into three principal rooms—the school-room and two others.

The latter are furnished, in every particular, as barrack-rooms, and contain twenty-five beds each.

Early one summer's morning, several years ago, an amusing scene was being enacted in one of these rooms.

The reville had just been beaten by a little drummer, under the school-house windows, and all the boys, with one exception, were busily engaged making their beds.

This boy was displaying his talent for drawing, by sketching the caricature of the Sergeant Schoolmaster, on a long piece of white paper, with a piece of charcoal and red chalk.

To accomplish this with the greatest convenience, he had fastened the paper against the wall by the fireplace by means of a fork, and he seemed to be enjoying his performance with as much zest as the boys who were watching him.

"How am I getting on, chaps?" he asked, stopping to contemplate the degree of success he was attaining. "Have I caught the expression?"

"First-rate, Dick," said one. "It's exactly like him."

"You haven,t got the moustaches quite large enough, Dick," observed another; "they want curling up more at the ends."

",Yes," remarked another," and the squint in his left eye don't show enough."

"Don't forget to give him plenty of red on the nose, Dick," laughed another. "He won't be satisfied with his likeness if the tip of his nose isn't made as natural as life."

"I should make the nose to turn up, if I were you, Dick,' put in a little fellow, with a fat, round face, small, black, mischiveous-looking eyes, and a nose so "puggish" that it seemed as though the point of it had been cut off directly after his birth.

"I am not drawing you, Dolly," returned Dick, with a good-humoured laugh, in which all the others joined.

"But you are drawing a caricature, ain't you, Dick?" said Dolly, joining in the laughter. "The Sergeant's always twitting me about the shape of my nose, and I should like too see how he would look with one like it"

"It won't do, Dolly," said Dick, as he resumed his sketching; "I must stick to nature."

As Dick progressed with his work and produced, in exaggerated outline, the characteristic points of the Sergeant's figure, the satisfaction of the boys was expressed in delighted caperings and complimentary remarks.

"There!" exclaimed Dick, as he gave the finishing touch, and stepped back to admire his handiwork. "That's worthy of being hung on the walls of the Royal Academy. I think I was born to be an artist! What do you say, Shepherd?"

"Oh, of course you were, Dick!" laughed the lad addressed. "It's a first-rate production, but it's more worthy of being hung on the Sergeant's back. Speaking of that," he added, "how are you going to manage?"

"I can't think there will be much difficulty about it, Tom. I shall put a piece of string through the top of the paper, with a pin bent like a fish-hook fastened to the end of the string, and hang it on to the collar of his jacket."

"Yes. But when will you do it?"

"Before we go down for inspection parade, if I can. If I can't get the chance, I leave it to you."

"How am I to do it, Dick?"

"I will roll up the picture, and tuck it under your jacket behind. You must fall in on the left of the rear rank, and when the Sergeant turns the left of the front rank, to inspect it in rear, you must slip out the paper, just straighten it, and hang it to his collar. But I don't think I shall fail."

It is almost needless to say that as this was a practical joke, proposed to be carried out at the expense of the personal feelings of the Sergeant Schoolmaster, proper precaution was not neglected to prevent a surprise during the process of sketching the caricature.

Double sentries had been posted at the door, one inside, and two out.

The duty of those outside was to watch for the sudden appearance of the Sergeant, and give the alarm.

This was always managed so as not to arouse the suspicion of the Schoolmaster.

The dodge was to take their boots, or gloves, into the passage, and keep close to the door, and, whilst appearing to be engaged in polishing one or beating the pipe clay out of the other, to give a couple of sharp kicks on the pannel, by way of signal.

The sentry inside, who kept intently on the listen, then gave a low whistle, or cry, as he thought proper on the spur of the moment.

As a rule, it was only the prying of the Sergeant the boys had to fear.

Among themselves there was very little sneaking carried on, as everyone knew that any attempt on the part of any boy to tattle would be sure to be followed by summary punishment, either by being held face downwards on a table and well "larruped" with a strap, or "tossed."

By this means, a feeling of good-fellowship and honour was engendered in the breasts of the boys, and a case of peaching was seldom known.

A yob who did it once was never very likely to do it again.

When it did occur it was generally a new boy who was the culprit.

It so happened this morning that it was necessary to teach a "raw," as a new arrival was called, a sharp lesson.

At the moment that Dick and the other boys were admiring the caricature, a boy named Dawson, the son of a sergeant-major, who had only been in the school a few days, came out of the opposite room and advanced towards the two sentries.

Dawson was not much liked.

Being the son of a non-commissioned officer of such an exalted rank as the sergeant-major, he was rather inclined to be "cockey," and give himself superior airs.

"Hallo, Harry!" said one of the sentries, hastily; "here's that upstart Dawson coming."

"All right, Bob," replied the other, planting himself against the door, and at the same time giving the signal. "Where are you going?" he added, as Dawson pushed past Bob and put out his hand to lift the latch.

"Where am I going?" asked Dawson, in a contemptuous tone. "Can't you see where I am going? In this room, to be sure."

"No, you are not," said Harry, coolly.

"And why not, pray?" said Dawson, as his face flushed with anger.

"Because we won't let you—that's all."

"Won't let me!" exclaimed Dawson, indignantly. "Don't you know that my father is a sergeant-major, and yours is only a common gunner?" he added, haughtily. "I call it precious cheeky of you to talk to me like that."

'Oh!" retorted Harry, sneeringly. "I suppose you think because your father is a sergeant-major, that you ought to be 'cock-of-the-walk' and do just what you like?"

"Of course I do," returned Dawson.

"Then you are just mistaken, my young 'raw,'" put in Bob, who had been calmly listening to the colloquy. "Just take yourself off, or you'll get what you don't like."

"What have you to do with it?" asked Dawson, pompously "Your father is only a 'driver,' and your mother does washing for the men. The idea of you interfering!"

At this insulting speech, Bob's eyes flashed, and his face flushed with anger, and, suddenly dropping his boot and polishing-brush, he let fly his left hand full on Dawson's nose.

"That's what I have to do with it!" said Bob, between his clenched teeth. "And that, too," he added, following the blow with another stinger from his right hand.

Dawson's face turned awfully white, and, as he staggered back, holding his hands to his bleeding nose, Bob continued squaring up to him.

"Now then, Dawson, if you're game, we'll just have it out. Come on!"

There was very little difference between the size of the two; but, if any, Dawson was the heaviest. He was not inclined to fight.

Like all bullies, he felt cowed at an unexpected exhibition of pluck, and felt faint-hearted at the sight of his own blood.

"I won't fight with an inferior," he said, retreating before Bob's uplifted fists and determined attitude. "But I tell you what I will do. There's something going on in there you don't want the Sergeant to know of, and I'll go and tell him."

He had scarcely uttered the threat when Bob and Harry were upon him.

Seizing him by the arms and ears, they dragged him, despite his struggles, to the door, and, throwing it open, Bob shouted—

"Blankets! All hands to punish a sneak and a coward!"

This cry acted on the feelings of the boys like the thrilling notes of the trumpet-sound to "Charge" on a body of cavalry!

"It's that cockey Dawson!" shouted Dick, jumping on to a form. "Fall in boys! Toss him! toss him!"

The process of tossing was well understood.

It took four boys to a blanket, one at each corner, and, with a rapidity that showed how well they could act in concert on such an occasion, five blankets were held in readiness in as many seconds.

"In with him!" cried Dick. "That's the style!" he added, encouragingly, as Harry and Bob, assisted by two others, lifted Dawson into the first blanket.

Dawson struggled and floundered about, like a person suddenly dropped in the sea unable to swim.

"Now, then!" continued Dick. "One! two! three! Out!"

At each word of command the victim was tossed into the air; and at the word "Out!" he was thrown into the next blanket.

The tossing and throwing out was then repeated until the last blanket had been reached.

To be whirled about in this fashion, like a leaf before the wind, with a sense of utter helplessness, with the brain in a state of confusion, with everything around performing fantastic, topsy-turvy dances, the arms and legs flying about, and falling in all kinds of crumped-up positions, was enough to take the pluck out of the pluckiest boy.

But no mercy was ever shown towards a coward and a sneak.

Dawson by this time had ceased to cry out, which he had done at first—but Dick was inexorable.

"Back with him, boys! Give him enough of it. Death before dishonour in the School of the Regiment! One! Two! Three! Out! That's it! Keep it up!"

By the time Dawson had been tossed in the last blanket he was utterly exhausted.

He was then laid on a bed, and when he had recovered himself sufficiently to speak, Dick said—

"Look here, Dawson, that's how we serve all sneaks and cowards the first time. The next time you go sneaking, you shall be mounted on a table and get two or three dozen over the seat with a strap."

"Or if he refuses to fight," said Bob.

"Did he do that, Bob?" asked Dick.

"Well, it was worse than that, Dick. I gave him two cracks on the nose for telling me that my father was only a 'driver,' and that my mother did the men's washing, and then challenged him to have it out. But he said he wouldn't fight with an inferior, and threatened to go and tell the Sergeant that we were up to something we didn't want him to know."

"That's true," said Harry; "I was present all the time."

"That's very bad, Dawson," remarked Dick. "You musn't turn up your nose at everybody as you have done, and make such insulting remarks, because your father happens to be a sergeant-major. This is the School of the Regiment, and we are all equals here."

"I call it cowardly for so many to attack one," said Dawson, sullenly.

"You may, but we don't," returned Dick. "A fellow who insults his mates, refuses to fight for it, and threatens to tattle into the bargain, deserves to be taught an exceptional lesson. I hope this will prove a lesson to you. The best thing you can do is to be jolly, and make yourself one of us. What do you say? Shall we shake hands over it?"

Dawson hesitated for a few moments.

He saw plainly enough that Dick's advice was the best thing for him to follow, but he did not relish being pulled so suddenly off his "high-horse," and it was a touch-and-go with him as to whether his common-sense or his pride should win the day.

"Come, Dawson," said Dick frankly, and extending his hand. "It will be best to be friends. You will never be twitted with what has passed."

Dawson's better spirit triumphed.

"Very good," he said, as tears stood in his eyes. "Here's my hand upon it. I don't think I shall be a coward or a sneak in future."

"That's the style!" said Dick heartily, and wringing his hand.

Dawson then shook hands with Harry and Bob, and left the room amidst a loud clapping of hands.

CHAPTER II.

THE LARK—WHAT IS IT EVERYBODY'S LAUGHING AT?

WHEN Dawson had retired the boys set to work with alacrity to finish the making up of the beds, an operation which the tossing punishment had considerably interrupted.

The lost time, however, was soon pulled up.

In a few minutes the beds were made according to the regulation form. The blankets, sheets, and rugs were first folded, the palliasse, or bed, rolled into a circular form, and strapped on the iron bedstead, after the latter had been turned up.

The blankets, sheets, and rug were then neatly laid on the top of the bed, and when this had been accomplished, the boys commenced the process of polishing boots jacket-buttons, and beating the pipeclay out of their gloves.

To this followed the morning ablution in the lavatory, which was carried on amidst much larking and boisterous laughter.

Then came breakfast.

There was no difference between the meals of the boys and those of the regular soldiers.

The breakfast consisted of a pint of hot coffee and bread, a pound being served out to each boy every morning.

For dinner, as growing lads, they were allowed the same quantity of meat as the men—three quarters of a pound.

This was cooked in various ways—sometimes made into soup, sometimes stewed, or made into pies.

This, with potatoes and other vegetables found, out of the mess money, afforded them an ample and substantial meal.

The third meal of the day consisted of a pint of tea and more bread.

Butter and other aids to get down the bread they had to find themselves, by purchasing them at the canteen.

Supper was made up of scraps left from the other meals.

The cooking of the meals was not left to the boys.

As the school had been instituted for th

double purpose of instructing the boys in the usual branches of knowledge and military drill, two old soldiers, one to each room, were appointed as " standing cooks."

Breakfast over, the boys dressed in uniform, and got themselves ready for inspection, previously to being marched into school.

Inspection parade was a most important item of the daily routine.

To be clean and smart are two soldierly essentials, and on these points the Sergeant Schoolmaster was most rigorously particular.

We shall see presently that such was the case.

The " warning " for parade and the " fall-in " were always given by beat of drum, to distinguish them from the trumpet-calls of the regular soldiers.

As the boys were giving the finishing touches to their uniforms, the rattle of the drum was heard.

" There goes the warning," cried Dick. " Tumble down, boys."

" I don't see the Sergeant," said Dolly, who had been watching for the Schoolmaster's figure with his " pug " pressed against the window-pane. " You'll catch him yet, if you ain't got a ' muff,' Dick."

" Be off with you, you young monkey ! " said Dick, laughingly, and pretending to throw a brush at him which he held in his hand. " And mind you have your nose clean this morning."

It was the custom of the Schoolmaster, Sergeant Dennis O'Shehe, to descend to the square before the beat of the warning for the purpose of setting an example of punctuality to the boys, and keeping his eye on them as they came from the school.

But this morning he was late.

The Sergeant had stayed late the previous night at a convivial party, and it took him longer than usual to open his eyes and get his head off the pillow. The Sergeant's personal characteristics may be summed up in a few words.

He was of medium height, and supposed himself to possess a splendid figure.

With this idea he always padded the breast of his jacket with, at least, two handkerchiefs, to make it full and round, to match with the deep bend of his back.

He wore a huge pair of moustaches curled up at the points, to soften the outline, some said, of an unusually large and red-tipped nose, and hide a red patch on each cheek.

The Sergeant squinted in the left eye—a defect which, as he affected a look that was intended to be very awe-inspiring and piercing, imparted to his features a very disagreeable expression.

Being a clever and learned man, in his own estimation at least, Sergeant O'Shehe thought " no end " of himself, and was very pompous and self-conceited.

To give ease and gracefulness to his movements, the Sergeant always carried a whip—silver-topped—which he made good use of in the way of swishing and flourishing.

Altogether he was a great buck and a very important man.

After making this impudent remark, Dolly, who was the last in the room save Dick, rushed off at full speed, darting through the door into the passage just in time to dash full butt against the Sergeant, who was hurrying past.

" Confound your awkwardness ! " cried the Sergeant, savagely, whom the force of the contact had sent staggering against the wall. " I'll shake the inside out of you, you little whelp ! " he added, seizing Dolly by the collar and shaking him until he looked as though he had been suddenly attacked by the St. Vitus's dance.

" Oh ! don't Sergeant," cried Dolly. " I—I couldn't he—help it."

" Couldn't help it ! You're always running that nose of yours against something or somebody," returned the Sergeant, still shaking him.

" Please, Sergeant," pleaded Dolly, " it was my head."

" Your head or your nose, it's all the same," said the Sergeant, with a fierce look. " Take yourself off ! " he added, giving Dolly a kick behind that propelled him out of the passage; " and just mind, but I'll be down upon you this morning."

As Dolly disappeared the Sergeant muttered—

" A nice mess I'm in, I'll be bound, with whitewash, and no one to brush it off."

" I will give you a brush down, Sergeant," said Dick, who, hearing the row, had come to see what it was about.

Dick still had the brush in his hand.

" You ought to be in the square, Everett," said the Sergeant, sharply. " Look sharp about it, or the ' fall in ' will beat before we get outside."

" Just the very opportunity I wanted," thought Dick, as he began to brush away vigorously.

At the same time he slipped out the paper with the caricature from beneath his jacket behind, and, whilst working away with one hand, dexterously hung it on to the Sergeant's collar, unrolled it, and tucked the end of it under the bottom of his unsuspecting victim's jacket.

" That will keep the wind from blowing it about," thought Dick. " You are all right now, Sergeant," he said, aloud; " as clean as a new pin ! "

" Thank you, my lad," said the Sergeant, as he squared his shoulders, placed his whip under his arm, and, with a satisfied smirk, marched forth to exhibit his paces.

Dick tossed the brush into the room, and immediately followed, squaring his shoulders and mimicking the pompous walk of the Schoolmaster.

It was a lovely, sunshiny morning—calm and bright.

The drum-and-fife band belonging to the school was drawn up in a circle, playing very sweetly, " The Last Rose of Summer."

The morning parade of the boys always attracted a certain number of sight-seers, and this morning there was no falling off in the usual numbers.

The Sergeant was always gratified to see a goodly sprinkling of spectators, especially if there was a corresponding proportion of ladies, before whose admiring eyes he could strut and swagger, and then exhibit his elegant person.

The expected lark had been confided to the boys, who were ignorant of what had been going on, and they all awaited the appearance of the Sergeant in a considerable state of excitement.

No sooner had he advanced among them, and they caught sight of the caricature, than they began grinning.

The spectators were also affected in the same manner, not only at the ridiculous figure the

Sergeant cut, but also at the comic mimicry of Dick.

The Sergeant had never seen so many laughing faces, and he took the circumstance as being complimentary to himself.

"I suppose I must look more fascinating than usual," he thought, as he strutted about, swishing his whip; and occasionally he stopped to place himself in an elegant pose. "I'll be bound to say now that the ladies are all desperately in love with me!"

Entertaining this fond delusion the Sergeant's antics became each moment more extravagantly ludicrous, and the smiles and grins changed to open laughter.

As the Sergeant did not for a moment dream that he was the object of this demonstration, he looked wonderingly about to see what had caused it.

But in every direction he gazed he could see nothing but laughing faces; and the more he twisted and turned and looked about, the greater became the general amusement.

"This is very strange," he muttered. "What is it everybody's laughing at? Everybody seems to be grinning but me!"

Suddenly a dreadful thought flashed into his mind—a thought, the bare possibility of which brought the blood with a rush into his florid face.

"Can it be me they're laughing at?"

The thought had no sooner suggested itself than the Sergeant began to examine his person, scanning himself from his breast downwards, and twisting his body first one side and then the other, in his endeavour to get a glimpse behind.

But he could see nothing, whilst his movements, which denoted to the on-lookers that he was getting suspicious that the laughter was directed towards himself, only increased the hilarity and amusement.

At this moment there seemed to be something the matter with the band.

The drummer seemed to be beating time irregularly, whilst the fifes gave forth disjointed and jerky notes.

The bewildered Sergeant turned, with the quickness of lightning, and directed such a look of wonder on the band that the boys could stand it no longer, and fairly burst into a roar of laughter, in which they were loudly joined by the boys of the school and the other spectators.

The Sergeant, feeling now convinced that he must be the object of the laughter, strutted up to the laughing drummers and fifers in a towering passion, demanding savagely—

"What is the meaning of this—this outrageous conduct? What the devil are you all grinning at? Do you see anything in me to laugh at, you grinning apes?"

But this only made the boys laugh the more; a result which so increased the Sergeant's rage that, losing all control of his temper, he rushed amongst them and commenced lashing away with his whip, right and left.

The boys of course scattered in all directions, with the Sergeant dodging first after one and then another, whilst the laughter continued to increase.

Almost mad with rage at the peals of laughter which rang on every side, even from the verandahs of the barrack-rooms, where many of the soldiers had collected, the Sergeant would willingly have made free use of his whip on the shoulders of all around.

There is no knowing what his temper might have urged him to do had he not at this moment been recalled to himself by the beating of the "fall in."

Suddenly desisting in his pursuit of the drummers and fifers, the Sergeant walked to the spot where the school usually paraded with as much dignity as he could assume, and stood awaiting, sternly and silently, the falling in of the boys, who were biting their lips with suppressed laughter.

"I'll find out what all this grinning's about, before the day's over, I'll take my oath!" he muttered.

The usual formation of the parade for inspection was in two ranks, the rear rank standing three paces from the front rank to admit of the Sergeant passing between them.

Each boy, as he fell into his place, stood at "ease."

This position is attained by crossing the right hand over the left in the front of the body, at the same time drawing the right foot six inches in rear of the left heel, and bending the left knee.

When this had been done the Sergeant proceeded to "dress" and "tell off" the ranks.

At the word "Attention," the boys sprang up into an erect position, with the heels close and toes slightly turned outward, the arms brought straight to the side with the palms of hands to the front: head erect, and eyes looking straight to the front.

"Now," said the Sergeant, in a tone of caution and an ominous frown, "at the words 'eyes right—dress!' just see that the order is executed properly, and let me have none of that nonsense that was carried on yesterday—mind! Let me see the heads and eyes turned sharply to the right like one man. You have been at it long enough to do it correctly. I'll show you once more how it ought to be done. Look at me!"

Here the Sergeant, standing rigidly to attention, turned his head quickly towards his right shoulder, his eyes taking the same direction.

"You see which way my eyes are turned? Well, let there be no mistake about it."

As the Sergeant stood in front of the boys, his right shoulder, of course, pointed to the left of the rank, and then his eyes, though turning to his own right, turned towards the left of the squad.

"Now, eyes right—dr——'"

The Sergeant stopped abruptly; a look as black as a thunder-cloud darkened his face.

He had scarcely got out the words "eyes right," when, as though each head had been attached to one piece of wire, the whole turned simultaneously to the left, whilst a tittering ran through the spectators.

"I tell you what it is," said the Sergeant, choking with passion, "I won't stand here to be made a laughing-stock of! I'll resign my appointment if this kind of thing goes on! I'll report this deliberate attempt to bring me into ridicule, to the Commandant, and see if you can't be brought to your senses!"

The Sergeant, bestowing a malignant scowl at the boys, and at the amused spectators, resumed his unpleasant task.

The boys' heads and eyes were still rigidly turned to the left.

"Eyes front!" commanded the Sergeant, sharply. "Eyes right!—dress."

This time the order was obeyed, and all heads and eyes turned properly to the right.

The ranks were then "dressed" by the Sergeant, and the squad told off.

Slipping to the front, he gave the following command—

"From the right, tell off by fours."

"In telling off by fours, the first file calls out "One," the second "Two," the third "Three," and the fourth "Four," and so on from one to four along the front rank.

When this had been gone through, the several tellings-off were proved thus :—

The Sergeant gave the command—

"Flanks of four, prove."

On this order, the boys who told themselves off, one and four quickly stretched out their right hands, their arms being on a level with their shoulders.

The Sergeant cast his eyes along the ranks to see that this had been properly executed, and saw two arms outstretched touching each other elbow to elbow.

This had been caused by Dolly putting out his left arm instead of his right, and being the flank of a section his arm touched that of the right flank boy of the next section.

"What are you doing with your left arm stretched out, sir? demanded the Sergeant, fiercely.

"Please Sergeant, I am left-handed," replied Dolly, with an assumed innocence that caused a titter to pass along the ranks.

"Oh, you are! Then I'll see if you can't make use of your right hand when you are in school presently," said the Sergeant, significantly.

Then, addressing the squad, he gave the words—

"As you were."

At this command the boys dropped their arms to their sides.

They were then proved in "Even numbers," and put through various movements of "Fours," wheeling to "Fours Right," "Four Left," "Fours about," and "Fours left about."

When they had repeated these movements of fours several times, they formed again to the front, and the personal inspection began.

Beginning at the right of the front rank, the Sergeant closely scanned each boy from his forage-cap to his boots, making such remarks that he deemed necessary.

As the annoyance to which he had been subjected was not calculated to induce a particular amiable frame of mind, the Sergeant vented his temper by being more than usual critically.

There was not a boy that he did not find some fault with.

The buttons of some had not been polished, and the boots of others were in the same condition ; the uniforms were generally dirty, and their appearance was slovenly.

He was particularly down on Dolly.

"I never saw such a dirty-looking cub," observed the Sergeant, after he had looked at him from head to foot. "Your uniform has not had a brush near it ; buttons black, boots not touched, hair just as you got out of bed. You have not put a bit of soap or a drop of water near your face. Your eyes are full of dirt, and the condition of your nose is sickening to look at!" concluded the Sergeant, with an expressive look of disgust.

"Please Sergeant," said Dolly, innocently, "I can't help it. My nose is too stumpy to keep clean. It's no use wiping it. If it was like yours—Oh!"

This cry was elicited from Dolly by a sudden box on the ears from the enraged Sergeant, accompanied by the words—

"Silence, you impertinent young whelp! My cane and your back will make acquaintance when we're in school—mind that!"

He then continued his inspection until he came to Dolly in the rear.

"You are as bad behind as you are in front. You look as though you had jumped into a sack. What have you been doing to the seat of your trousers? It's baggy enough to hold a half-quartern loaf!"

"Please Sergeant," said Dolly, followed by a good deal of tittering, "that's where your horse 'Rasper' caught me with his teeth yesterday and carried me round the square."

"Pity 'Rasper' hadn't caught hold of something more substantial!" remarked the Sergeant. "We'll try if the cane can't make a better catch in that region by-and-bye! Where did you get all that dirt from? Where have you been sitting?"

"Nowhere, Sergeant ; it's the dirt off your boots when you kicked me this morning."

"Well, as I put it on, I'll take it off for you when we come to settle up."

When the Sergeant had completed his inspection he took up his position again in front of the parade, preparatory to forming the boys into fours, and taking them for half an hour's march with the band.

As he was on the point of giving the word of command his eyes fell upon Dolly's legs, which had suddenly left the perpendicular and assumed the position called "knock-knee'd."

"What do you mean by standing in that awkward manner?" demanded the Sergeant.

"I can't help it, Sergeant," said Dolly ; "you shook me so just now that it's made my knees loose."

This speech was followed by a general titter, which so enraged the Sergeant that, addressing Dolly, he said—

"Come this way. Six paces to the front—March."

To the amusement of everyone Dolly, instead of stepping up to the Sergeant, coolly marched along the front of the rank and took up a position immediately behind the right file.

"What do you mean by that?" asked the Sergeant. "Do you call that six paces to the front?"

"No, Sergeant," called out Dolly, in a loud tone ; "but owing to the defectiveness of your eye I thought you could see me better round the corner?"

An irresistible burst of laughter from the boys followed this speech.

The Sergeant flushed with anger.

"Step this way?" he roared. "I'll show you whether I have a defective vision! Now, sir!" he continued, as Dolly rolled up and stood to attention before him, "Right about face! Bend forward. More still!"

Dolly obeyed these orders, but he had no intention of waiting for the crack if he could help it.

He had watched the Sergeant sideways under his arm, and just at the moment his trousers had nicely tightened, and the whip was about to descend Dolly ducked his head and began rolling away heels over head, and head over heels, like a ball.

This dodge was so dexterously accomplished, and was so unexpected, that it sent everybody off screaming with laughter—everybody except the Sergeant.

The latter, if possible, was more enraged than ever at this scurvy trick, and uttering a cry of rage he started in pursuit, slashing away with his whip at the rolling Dolly, indifferent as to what part of the body it descended on.

It must be acknowledged that the Sergeant had the best of it.

It would have been much wiser on the part of Dolly had he stayed to receive the punishment on one spot.

As it was, he caught it on every part of his person, and he was compelled very soon to bring his acrobatic career to an end.

"I thought I'd soon stop your tumbling, my young buck," said the panting Sergeant, with a sarcastic grin. "Have you had enough, my joker, eh ?"

"I think I've had enough of it this time, Sergeant," said Dolly, as he got up and returned to his place, rubbing his smarting arms and legs and seat, and with an expression on his face which seemed to indicate that he was undecided whether to cry with pain, or laugh at his discomfiture.

The Sergeant, somewhat mollified at having been enabled to vent his rage on some object, once more took his place in front of the parade.

The band had taken up position on the right of the boys, and the Sergeant at once gave the orders for marching.

"Fours—right, quick—march !"

The tune to be played had been suggested by Dick Everett, and as they stepped out, the band struck up, "A Perfect Cure," the Sergeant little dreaming, as he stalked along the side of the column, that it had been selected to do him special honour.

The practice of the school of the regiment, taking a short morning's march with the band, was well known to all the boys who lived in the immediate neighbourhood of the barracks, and a crowd of them always collected to witness the scene, and usually accompanied the embryo soldiers out and home.

As a matter of course, the trick that was being played off on the Sergeant was immediately discovered, and also, as a matter of course, was immediately appreciated.

There was no mistaking, either, the appropriateness of the tune to the occasion.

Sergeant O'Shehe was well known as an eccentric character, and broad grins and loud laughter greeted his appearance.

The urchins fairly capered with delight, accompanying their demonstrations with sundry remarks.

"Oh, my eye, what a jolly lark !"

"Ain't it a famous trick ?"

"What rum fellows them boys is !"

"I say, Sargint, 'ow much did yer pay fur yer portrit ?"

"Where did yer hev it took, Sargint ? I'll hev mine done hat that fertografer's !"

"Dosen't yer feel orfully proud hon it ?"

"I should think he do, jist !"

Never was a man more bewildered than the Sergeant, at these incomprehensible remarks, and he muttered as he stalked along, trying to look unconscious of their utterance—

"What the devil is the meaning of it ? Curse them !"

In this manner—the laughter and joke increasing, and the Sergeant almost bursting with pent-up rage—the procession passed along the road which skirts the boundary of what is known as the "Repository Grounds" until it came to a lane which divides the grounds from a gentleman's park, and leads in a circular direction on to the Bangfire Common.

It was the Sergeant's custom to take the boys across this common, and march them past the quarters of the General commanding the garrison.

"Now," said Dick to Tom Sheppard, as they were passing along the lane, "mind, when we're marching before the General's house, we must all suddenly join in the chorus, and bring the old fellow to the window if we can."

"All right," returned Tom, grinning.

"Pass the word along the front section, Tom. Directly we begin to sing, the rest will be sure to join in."

This was done, and each boy promised to rap out lustily.

This morning the mentally disturbed Sergeant would have given anything not to pass the General's quarters; but to change route was more than he dared to do.

It was a standing order, and must be obeyed.

"I hope the row of the cursed rabble won't reach the General's ears," groaned the Sergeant, inwardly. "He'll go mad with rage at such a disgraceful scene."

General Shoot was a short, fat, red-faced, choleric man, with a voice as deep and gruff as a bear's growl.

He was a tremendous stickler for discipline and order, and the slightest breach of the one, or disturbance of the other, would set him off into a towering rage.

At the moment the strains of the band caught his ears, the General was seated at breakfast with one of his aides-de-camp, for, being a bachelor, his table was not graced by the presence of ladies.

At first the shouting and laughter of the rabble were inaudible in the distance; but gradually, as the band drew nearer, the commotion became very pronounced.

At the unusual noise the General pricked up his ears, growling out—

"What on earth's that ?"

"It sounds like the shouting of a mob, General." replied the aid-de-camp.

"Go and see what it is," ordered the General, irritably.

By this time the band had come under the windows, and just as the officer was rising to obey the order, Dick gave the signal, and the next instant the General jumped off his chair as though he had been shot, as the voices of the boys rose on the morning air, singing—

" A cure, a cure, a perfect cure,
        He is a perfect cure !
   A cure, a cure, a perfect cure,
        He is a perfect cure ! "

For the General to rush to the window, and throw it open, was the work of an instant.

What a sight was that to meet the eyes of a general !

There, in front of his quarters, were the boys of the regiment, actually roaring out the chorus of a comic song, with two or three hundred boys joining in, and dancing to the tune !

For a moment or two he stood glaring on the scene, speechless with rage and indignation.

Was this audacious demonstration intended as a personal application to himself ?

As the possibility of this bein the case

rushed into the General's mind, he became almost black in the face with rage, and stretching forth both his clenched fists, he cried in a voice of thunder—

"Halt! Halt! Ha—a—lt!"

At the sound of the General's voice, the boys came to an instant stand; the singing was dropped, and the band ceased playing.

The poor flabergastered Sergeant, whose knees actually shook with shame and apprehension, stood rooted to the spot.

"What is the meaning of this disgraceful uproar, Sergeant O'Shehe?" demanded the General. "Speak, sir!" he added, with angry impatience, as the Sergeant, unable to articulate a word, and the perspiration pouring down his face, remained staring stupidly at the General. "Speak, sir! Where's your confounded tongue"

The Sergeant was trembling like an aspen leaf, and at last stammered out—

"I-I-do-don't know, General. I—"

"Don't know, sir! You dare to tell me you don't know!"

"Up-up-on my sou—my word I-I-don't, General!"

"Why, damme sir, do you mean to say you don't know that that insulting song was intended to apply to me?" shouted the General, shaking his fist at the Sergeant.

This question was followed by a shout of laughter from the crowd of boys, and one little fellow called out—

"The Sargint's been an' had his pictur painted, Gen'r'l, and he's a hexibbittin' of it on his back!"

"Jist turn him round, Gen'r'l, an' hev a look!"

The Sergeant could scarcely believe his ears, and an indescribable sensation passed through his frame as he instinctively put his hand behind him and felt the paper.

He was in the act of pulling it off, when the General cried—

"Attention, Sergeant O'Shehe! Right-about-face! Oh!" added the General, as he saw the caricature, "that accounts for all this disgraceful hubbub! A pretty guy you've allowed yourself to be made, sir! Take that outlandish figure off your back, sir, and march the boys off at once! You shall hear more about this, I can tell you!"

The expression of feelings that had been wounded, to a degree that was impossible to be described in words, that came into the Sergeant's face as he snatched off the caricature and gazed at it, was most pitiable to behold.

Tears of deep mortification filled his eyes.

To think that he, the smartest man in the regiment, the very beau-ideal of a soldier, should have been selected as the victim of such a practical joke, was something dreadful to contemplate.

He felt bewildered, stunned, knocked all of a heap, crestfallen, humiliated!

But what pained his mind more than the derision he had been subjected to was, that the discovery should have been made before the very eyes, under the very nose, of the General!

And yet nobody pitied him!

Everybody was laughing and chaffing, except the General and his aide-de-camp.

"Now, then, sir!" said the General, sharply, "don't stand there looking like a fool! March!"

Mechanically saluting the Generl, and tearing off the horrid caricature, the Sergeant, in a voice that had lost its metallic ring, gave the words—

"Quick—march!"

And once more the boys stepped off to return to the barracks, the band playing "Cheer boys, cheer."

CHAPTER III.

IN WHICH THREE INDIVIDUALS GET PUNISHED —DOLLY SWAPS, GENERAL SHOOTS, AND DICK EVERETT.

SERGEANT O'SHEHE knew that it would be a long time before he should hear the last of this practical joke.

But he had one reflection to comfort him.

He was sure of punishing the perpetrator.

He guessed who was the originator, and who it was that had so cleverly pinned the caricature on his back.

"If it was Dick Everett—and I believe it was" —muttered the Sergeant, as he entered his room, after dismissing the boys, "he will be sure to confess it. He is the instigator of all the mischief that is carried on in the school; and I know him well enough to be certain that he won't allow the whole lot to be punished to escape punishment himself. And, by Jove! he shall catch it smarter than he ever has in his life! If he is able to sit down comfortably for a week to come, it won't be the fault of Sergeant O'Shehe."

Before entering the schoolroom to begin studies after the morning's march out, the boys were always permitted to go to their room for ten minutes' rest, and to brush the dust off their uniforms.

This morning they all rushed with one accord into Dick's room to give expression to their feelings of delight at the success of his trick, and speculate upon the possible consequences:

"I say, Dick," said Dolly, who mounted a table, and sat with his legs doubled up under him, "you have got up many larks, but this beats all! Ha! ha! ha! It was jolly! But I say, won't you come in for wollops!"

"Dick need'nt unless he likes," said Tom Sheppard. "He's only to say the word, and we'll prevent the Sergeant punishing him."

"To be sure!"

"Of course we will!"

"What do you say, Dick?"

"I know you are all game enough to do it," said Dick, in reply to their unanimous offer, "and it's jolly good of you, But it won't do to go in for wholesale opposition. I'll take the punishment, whatever it is."

"Two dozen, at least, on your 'right about face,'" said Dolly, making a comical face. "That's what you'll get, Mister Dick."

"Never mind, Dolly," laughed Dick; "I'll be revenged for it—never fear."

"I am very sorry to see you cherish such a wicked spirit of revenge," said Dolly, with a sad shake of the head. "It's very shocking! Look how patiently I take my whackings!"

"You deserve all you get, you know, Dolly," returned Dick, with a laugh, in which all joined.

"Oh, do I though!" replied Dolly, protestingly. "That's good, that is! What a lot of exemplary youths you must be! Dear me! Oh, you to be sure! Poor suffering innocents! Just see, Dick, if I don't volunteer to give you the two dozen! Be quiet now!" cried Dolly, as Dick rushed at him, "I'm too sore to be rolled!"

"Roll him! Roll him! Take the cheek out of him!" cried Dick, as, with half a dozen others, he seized Dolly, and began to roll him on the table. "Make a pudding of him!"

"Just see if I don't be revenged on you," said Dolly, shaking his fist at Dick, when he was released, with assumed anger. "Oh, my beauty! look out!—that's all!"

As the ten minutes' grace had nearly expired, the boys dispersed to brush up, and then they repaired to the schoolroom, and took their places at the desks.

They had no sooner entered than the nature of the punishment to be inflicted was made plain.

Near the Sergeant's desk, at one end of the room, was placed a table—one of the ordinary barrack-room tables, consisting of a flat deal top, six feet by two, resting on iron trestles.

The process of castigation was the same as that which has already been explained—the culprit being hoisted on the table and held by the arms and legs face downwards, by four persons, whilst the fifth administered justice with a strap.

"There's the altar ready for the innocent sacrifidge,'" said Dolly, turning on Dick with a delicious chuckle, and an excruciating squint. "Won't you "bellow" presently—oh, my goodness!"

"Take that, and shut up!" laughed Dick, giving Dolly a tremendous dig in the ribs that almost knocked the wind out of that facetious young scamp's body.

Dolly's chuckling anticipations were, however, brought to an end sooner than he expected.

He had scarcely regained his wind when the Sergeant, with a majestic mien, and a set and stern expression of features, entered, and taking his stand in front of the boys, said,—

"Adolphus Swaps! Attention! Step over! Quick march; Left turn! Forward! Left half turn! Halt! Front!"

These movements were necessitated by the position of the desks and forms.

At the first word of command Dolly sprang into that position. At the second he stepped over the form and remained stationary. At the third he marched forward till he reached the end of the desk. At the fourth, and fifth, he advanced till he came abreast of the front desk. The sixth caused him to make a half-turn to bring him into the centre of the floor. The seventh brought him to a stand, and the eighth face to face with the Sergeant.

The latter held his whip in his hand.

"Now, Dolly Swaps," he said, facetiously bending forward, fixing his defective eye on Dolly, playfully touching the turned-up surface of his nose with the whip, "I suppose you know what's going to happen—hey?"

"No, Sergeant," said Dolly, putting up his hand to rub his nose, into which the thong of the whip had brought a tickling sensation —"I don't."

"Keep your hand down," said the Sergeant, "and stand at attention."

"But you tickle me, Sergeant," returned Dolly, screwing up his face. "I shall sneeze if you do that."

Amongst a number of boys there is sure to be one, or more, conspicious for peculiar personal characteristics.

Some are densely stupid, others possess an easily irritated temper, and become, in consequence, the butts of the school.

Others, again, are constitutionally comic, and make fun for everybody.

To this class belonged Dolly Swaps.

Dolly had not only a physically comic person, but he possessed a comic turn of mind, aided by the most imperturbable good temper, and perfect indifference to any amount of whacking.

Dolly had a keen perception of the ridiculous, and whatever the consequences to himself, he never hesitated to make the most of every opportunity to create a laugh, and he did it in a naive manner that was perfectly irresistible.

Dolly was favoured with such an opportunity now, and he scarcely uttered his last remark when it was greeted with a general grin.

"I'll give you something to sneeze at presently," said the Sergeant, nodding his head slowly, "Answer me, Dolly Swaps. Do you know what is going to happen?"

"Perhaps you are going to give me a reward for good conduct, Sergeant," said Dolly, looking up and opening his eyes, as though he suddenly hit upon a bright idea.

This wilful misconstruction put upon the Sergeant's facetious question sounded so absurd, and so tickled the fancy of the boys, that it added considerably to the giggling, which Dolly had already aroused.

"No, Dolly swaps! No, no, Dolly Swaps!" continued the Sergeant, ironically; "I'm going to take the dust out of your trousers. See, my Dolly—hey—um?"

"You have done that already, Sergeant," said Dolly. "Once is quite enough, you know!"

"I don't think it's quite out, Dolly. I think there is a little bit left—hey?"

"I don't think there is, Sergeant," said, Dolly, argumentatively.

"We'll put it to the proof, Dolly," returned the Sergeant. "We'll just put it to the proof, my little man. So I'll just trouble you to place your head under my arm. 'Come to my arms, my bundle of charms.' There shall be no rolling away this time. Come," added the Sergeant, with affected politeness, and opening his arms, "three steps forward. March!"

Amidst much tittering, Dolly advanced, and placed his head in "chancery."

"That's it!" said the Sergeant, closing his arm round Dolly's body. "You made a mistake, Dolly, I never saw a boy's trousers in such a dusty state. One!"

The next instant, the whip descended on Dolly's 'right about face,' with a swish that sent the dust flying in a cloud.

"Two! three! fo—Oh, Lord! Oh, you young devil! Leave go, you young bull-dog! I'll murder you!"

These cries of agony and rage were drawn from the Sergeant by an unexpected and clever invention on the part of Dolly for returning his castigator as good as he gave.

As Dolly's body protruded through the Sergeant's arm, he found his mouth close to that individual's thigh in the rear.

Dolly was immediately inspired by a happy thought.

"What a tempting bit for a bite!" thought Dolly.

Dolly had good teeth, and he had scarcely received the third application of the whip, when he opened his mouth to the fullest extent and made a grab at the Sergeant's leg, as though he were taking a bite at an apple.

Dolly's jaws closed with such good effect, that the Sergeant fairly yelled with pain and rage.

Directly the boys perceived the state of affairs, they burst into convulsions of laughter.

The uproar was deafening.

"You young cannibal!" roared the Sergeant. "Leave go! I'll flay you alive!"

These exclamations were received with frantic lashings of the whip.

Dolly, however, could not be shaken nor whipped off.

He had got his arms and legs entwined round the Sergeant's walking member, and he kept his grip with the bloodthirsty instinct of a leech, whilst he was encouraged to hold on by the cries of the boys.

"Bravo, Towser!"

"Hold on, good dog!"

"Shake him, then!"

"Stick to him, my beauty!"

"Ha! ha! ha! ha-a-a-oh!"

"Sis! Sis! S-i-s-s-s-s!"

Fuming and swearing, lashing away with the whip, the Sergeant staggered about, striving in vain to dislodge the young cannibal; and it was not until Dolly's jaws ached to an extent that prevented him holding on any longer, that he relinquished his grasp, and rolled on to the floor.

The moment Dolly let go, the Sergeant, who was worked up to a pitch of ungovernable rage, turned his whip, and began belabouring him with the butt end, exclaiming—

"You young vampire! Take that!—and that! —and that!—and that! D—— you! I'll beat you to a jelly!"

Dolly's anatomy would certainly have been reduced to a very pulpy condition had not the infuriated Sergeant been restrained from the further infliction of punishment by the indignant cries of the boys—

"Shame! Shame!"

"Brute!"

"Coward!"

"Sish! Sish!"

Recalled to himself by these unmistakable evidences of disapproval, the Sergeant desisted— and only just in time.

In another minute he would have the boys upon him like a pack of hounds!

Most of them had started to their feet, with the intention of rushing forward.

The Sergeant, panting from his exertions, glared upon them with a glance full of fiendish passion—a glance that was met by the boys with glances of defiance and firm resolve.

At that instant, a hasty word from the Sergeant would have caused an outbreak; but, happily, this was prevented by Dolly himself giving a comic turn to affairs.

After letting go of the Sergeant's thigh, Dolly rolled over and over a few turns to dodge the whip, but do what he would, he received two or three sounding cracks on the head, and at the moment the Sergeant and the boys were glaring angrily at each other, he was sitting up, looking like a fowl that has had its feathers rumpled, and rubbing his bumps—bumps unknown to the phrenologist—with both hands, and presenting a face with a rueful look that was exceedingly comic in itself.

In the midst of the profound silence, the voice of Dolly became suddenly heard.

"Confound it!" muttered Dolly, with a half-grin on his features; "I believe I've got the worst of it, after all!"

It was impossible to resist the impulse to laugh, and Dolly's lament was followed by a unanimous roar from the boys.

This little diversion gave the Sergeant time to recovery his dignity, and, putting a great restraint upon his feelings, he resumed his ironically bantering manner.

"So Dolly Swaps thinks he's had the worst of it—hey?" he asked, looking down upon Dolly.

"I think I would rather have had the bite, Sergeant," returned Dolly, looking sideways at the boys, and giving a wicked wink that called up more grinning, and made the Schoolmaster bite his lips with passion. "You won't want to take any more dust out, I hope, Sergeant," added Dolly, with provoking innocence.

"Not at present, my Dolly," said the Sergeant, resuming his bantering tone with an effort. "But the programme is not quite complete. I so much admire the gracefulness of your form, Dolly, that I am going to make a statue of you, and exhibit you to the admiring eyes of your schoolfellows."

"I shall like that exceedingly," said Dolly. "My mother always said I was a perfect little model—Hercules in miniature! Shall I take off my uniform at once, Sergeant?" added Dolly, beginning to unbutton his jacket, amidst great amusement.

"You'll do very well in your present drapery," said the Sergeant.

"But I'm afraid the bagginess of my trousers will mar the rounded outlines of my figure, Sergeant," returned Dolly.

"The chaps are awful art-critics, especially of statues—and portraits!" he added, slowly, and with great emphasis.

At this obvious allusion to the trick played off upon him, the Sergeant turned pale with passion, but, mastering his feelings, he said—

"I am sorry you are not in better trim for the occasion, Dolly, so, as time passes, and I have some one else to touch up, I will just trouble you to mount that form," pointing to one that stood by the door, and about eighteen inches from the wall. "Right about face! Quick march! Halt! Step up! Front!"

Dolly went through these movements with the greatest promptness and gravity, and faced the school without his features rippling into the faintest of smiles.

His appearance, however, was most provocative of mirth.

His little podgy body was fully exposed to every eye; but if Dolly had been a real statue stuck up there for exhibition, the sculptor would not have reaped golden opinions, or received unqualified praise, on having turned out a first-class, elaborately-executed piece of art.

The shape of Dolly's nose, in the first place would certainly not have called forth expressions of admiration. It was not a classical nose; nor, though of the "celestial" order, could it be angelic.

Though Dolly's cheeks were chubby enough, they did not entitle him to be a cherub—they were much too red; whilst his eyes and lips were more impish in their expression than otherwise. Had anyone been asked to candidly give an opinion as to the class of expression in Dolly's features, he would instantly have pronounced it as cheeky."

Dolly hair was the reverse of an Apolo's, being cropped short, and sticking out in all directions like the pricks of a hedgehog.

His body may have been beautifully modelled, but, as his trousers were five or six inches too short, and bagged at the knees and seat; his arms too long for the sleeves of his jacket, the body of the latter tucked up in wrinkles, exposing his braces on the nether garment, the graceful outlines of Dolly's form were completely destroyed.

Looking at him as he stood there—at the figure he presented—no one could have believed his mother's assertion that he was a "perfect little model."

But, although standing there under these disadvantages, Dolly seemed unconscious of the fact, or was perfectly indifferent thereto.

"Now," said the Sergeant, "as you possess such a nicely modelled form, let us see how gracefully you can pose it in various positions. You will remain there until school is over, and during that time you will practise the 'Extension Motions!' first, second, and third practice —beginning again at the first when the third is done, and keep on at it.   Begin!"

As it is probable that very few, if any, of our readers are acquainted with the movements constituting the "Extension Motion," it will be advisable to explain them.

By practising the motions, the task that Dolly had to perform will be clearly understood, and the incident which resulted therefrom fully appreciated.

First Practice.—On the word "One" bring the hand, at the full extent of the arms, to the front, close to the body, knuckles downwards, till the fingers meet at the points. Then raise them in a circular direction over the head, the ends of the fingers still touching and pointing downwards so as to touch the head, thumbs pointing to the rear, elbows pressed back, shoulders kept down.

On the word "Two," throw the hands up, extending the arms smartly upwards, palms of the hands inwards. Then form them obliquely back, and gradually let them fall to the position of attention, elevating the neck and chest as much as possible.

On the word "Three," raise the arms outwards from the sides without bending the elbow, pressing the shoulders back, until the hands meet above the head, palms to the front, fingers pointing upwards, thumbs locked, left thumb in front.

On the word "Four," bend over until the hands touch the feet, keeping the arms and knees straight: after a slight pause, raise the body gradually, bring the arms to the sides, and resume the position of attention.

Second Practice.—On the word "One," raise the hands in the front of the body, at the full extent of the arms, and in line with the mouth, palms meeting, but without noise, thumbs close to the forefingers.

On the word "Two," separate the arms smartly, throwing them well back, slanting downwards. At the same time raise the body on the fore-part of the feet.

Now, on the word "One," bring the arms forward to the position above described, and on the word "Two" back again, and so repeat the motion.

On the word "Three," smartly resume the position of attention.

Third Practice.—On the word "One," raise the hands with the fists clenched, in front of the body, at the full extent of the arms, and in line with the mouth, thumbs upwards, fingers touching.

On the word "Two,", separate the hands smartly, throwing the arms back in a line with the shoulder back of the hand downwards.

On the word "Three," swing the arms round as quickly as possible from front to rear.

On the word "Steady," resume the second position.

On the word "Four," let the arms fall smartly to the position of attention.

It will be seen from this, that the "Extension Motions" are not of a particularly graceful character, and that, even if Dolly could have gone through the several movements, under the condition in which his mother had been enabled to pronounce her hopeful boy a "perfect little model," they would not have helped to enhance the graces of his person.

Dolly was perfectly aware of the fact, nor would he have had it otherwise at that moment.

He knew he should cut a most grotesque figure, and so secretly chuckling at the fun he was sure to cause, he set to work with the regularity of a machine, adding to the ridiculousness of the scene by working his features into all kinds of comical contortions, whenever he saw that the Sergeant's eye was not upon him.

Having wound Dolly up, as it were, and set him going, the Sergeant proceeded to carry out the second act of punishment.

Giving a preliminary "Hem!" he looked fixedly at Dick, and, after a moment's pause, gave the usual words of command to bring any boy to the front,

"Richard Everett! Attention—step over, right turn, quick march—left turn, forward—left half-turn—half-front!"

Dick never hesitated for a moment, and, when he had come to the "front," stood looking calmly at the Sergeant.

There was now a silence of breathless interest in the school, and not even Dolly's monkeyfied antics could produce a smile on any face.

"Everett," began the Sergeant, sternly, "I am not going to ask you who drew that wretched caricature. It was you!"

"It was, Sergeant," replied Dick.

"It was you who pinned it on my back?"

"Yes, Sergeant, it was."

"Then I'll teach you," said the Sergeant, with a malicious look, and nodding his head slowly, "that Sergeant O'Shehe is not an individual you can play off your tricks upon with impunity! You see that table?"

"Yes, Sergeant, and understand what it's for."

"Just so," said the Sergeant, "and as you've done me the honour of practising on my back, I'll return the favour by practising on yours."

Then turning towards the boys, he called out the names of Sheppard, Smith, and another named Fogle, and ordered them to the front in the usual way.

"I suppose it's to hold Dick down," thought Sheppard, as he obeyed the order; "but he won't get me to assist."

"Now, Master Everett," continued the Sergeant, addressing Dick, "Mount! "And you," he added, turning to the four boys, "will perform the duty of holding him down. To your places."

"I, for one, decline to do so," said Sheppard calmly.

"What!" cried the Sergeant, in astonish-

"Oh—o—oh!" moaned poor Dolly. "This is AWFUL! Everybody's enjoying the fun but me!"
See page 18.

ment, whilst the blood rushed into his face, "you refuse to obey?"

"I refuse to make one to hold down Dick Everett," replied Sheppard, resolutely.

"So do I," said Smith.

"And I," echoed Jones.

"And I, too," followed Fogle.

These refusals were received by the rest of the boys by cries of approval and clapping of hands, whilst the Sergeant, scarcely crediting the evidence of his ears, glared at them with the veins of his forehead swollen with passion.

Suddenly he seized the strap that was lying on the table, and making a rush at Sheppard, exclaimed—

"You insubordinate cub! You won't, won't you!"

The next instant and the strap would have descended on Tom's back, and the blow was prevented by Dick quickly stepping between, receiving it on his shoulder.

"You needn't punish Sheppard, nor any of them, Sergeant," said Dick. "It's quite natural that such a duty should be repugnant to their feelings, but I don't require to be held. I will take the thrashing without."

Dick's plucky conduct elicited murmurs of admiration, adding, if possible, to the Sergeant's anger.

"Stand aside!" he cried, furiously, pushing Dick roughly away; and, seizing Sheppard by the collar, he was in the act of applying the strap, when his uplifted arm suddenly became stationary, and gradually dropped to the side, whilst the inflamed look of passion on his face gave place to a look of awe.

What was it that suddenly caused the Sergeant to arrest his hand, and brought that scared look into his face?

Some supernatural occurrence?

No! It was something of a very tangible nature!

Nothing less than the sound of footsteps, with jingling spurs, and the rattle of sword-scabbards in the passage!

"It must be the General," thought the Sergeant, listening intently to the fast-approaching sounds.

Yes, it was the General, accompanied by two of his aides-de-camp, on his way to give the boys and the Sergeant a bit of his mind respecting the disgraceful proceedings of the morning.

Those disgraceful proceedings were rankling in the General's mind, and had more than usually upset the equanimity of his temper.

The Sergeant, releasing Sheppard, put on as calm a demeanour as he could under the emergency, and stood ready to receive the dreaded visitor, by calling the boys to attention.

The General's reception, however, proved to be of a kind which neither he, nor the Sergeant, nor anyone in the school, for one moment expected.

During the scene we have been describing Dolly Swaps had been working away at the "Extension Motions" with great patience and diligence, trying all he knew to create a smile in the midst of the excitement, but without success.

His time, however, was at hand.

Dolly had repeated each practice several times, and, at this moment was going through a third, by swinging his arms round and round like a couple of wheels gone mad.

To assist the swing of his arms, Dolly had got hold of a pair of dumb-bells which, with other articles, such as fencing-sticks and baskets and masks, were kept on a shelf which ran across the school-room.

It will be remembered that Dolly was standing on a form close to the door.

The General, bent on relieving his mind as quickly as possible, came clattering into the school-room with the headlong recklessness of an enraged bull.

Dolly's arms were revolving away at a tremendous rate, and, before a word of caution could be given the General was sent staggering into the arms of his aides-de-camp by a terrific blow on the nose.

The state of terror, confusion, consternation, bewilderment, into which everybody was thrown, and the rage of the General, is almost indescribable.

Such parts of Sergeant O'Shehe's face as were capable of undergoing a change of hue turned as white as a sheet with fear, whilst he stood speechless and trembling.

The boys were thunderstruck.

The aides-de-camp, supporting the General, looked at his bleeding nose, and didn't know what to make of it.

But Dolly was the most flabbergasted of any.

With a look of dismay that, at any other moment would have caused roars of laughter, he stood gazing at the gasping General with staring eyes and open mouth.

What had he done?

Knocked out the General's brains?

Good Heaven!—what a horrible thought!

What would be his fate?

Should he be hanged, or blown away from the mouth of a cannon?

These fears and surmises, which passed rapidly, and yet confusedly, through his brain, were soon solved.

The General's brains were right enough: they had not been scattered, but only knocked into temporary confusion.

In ten seconds he knew what kind of misfortune had overtaken his nose, and who it was that had given the blow.

His eyes fell upon Dolly with a baleful glance, and, uttering a howl of rage, very much like a wounded tiger, he sprang towards that young gentleman with a fulness of intent that caused him to cast away the dumb-bells, jump off his perch, and dive under the desks and forms, and between the legs of his schoolfellows for shelter, more rapidly than he had ever moved in his life before.

Quick as Dolly's movements were, the General would have had him before he had disappeared beneath the desk, but for a circumstance that, for a moment or two, checked his pursuer's advance.

One of the dumb-bells which Dolly threw away in his haste, alighted with great force on the General's left shin bone, eliciting a cry of pain, and causing him to peform a war-dance on one leg.

This accident only served to increase the General's anger, and added to his determination to capture the daring offender, at all hazards; and so, after two or three hops, he dropped on his hands and knees, and started in pursuit, with the avidity of a ferret after a rabbit.

By this time, Dolly, aided by the boys, who opened their legs to allow him to pass, had made good headway, and the chase became exciting.

Once under the desks, the General found that he had undertaken a task beset with serious difficulties.

Being hampered with his sword, that warlike instrument was continually getting between his legs, whilst his spurs pertinaciously insisted on stopping his progress by catching in the bottoms of the legs of the boys' trousers.

Furthermore, the legs of the boys became obstinately stiff, and refused to part on the approach of the general, without a vigorous push, or a telling pinch.

On the other hand, every encouragement was afforded to Dolly by his chums.

"Well done, Dolly!"

"Keep it it up, old chap!"

"Here you are—this way! Through my legs—that's it!"

"Make for the far corner, Dolly!"

But the General knew that the capture was only a matter of time, and puffing and growling and overcoming all obstacles, he kept up the chaise.

The General, however, was not entirely without assistance.

Whilst the Sergeant went beween the desks ahead of Dolly, to turn his course, the two aides-decamp stationed themselves outside to prevent his escape in that direction.

At length Dolly was captured.

Finding his progress stopped by the Sergeant, he turned to make his way to the outside of the desks, but, he had scarcely advanced a foot when he felt his legs seized by the General, and the next instant he was being dragged out, face downwards, on the floor.

This process did not end immediately he was clear the desks, for the General continued to drag him up the room towards the front.

As this was anything but an agreeable and comfortable mode of progression, being eminently calculated to scrape the skin off his chin, lips, and the flat part of his nose, Dolly wriggled and turned his head and shoulders like a snake, when being hauled along by its tail, accompanying his struggles with cries of—

"Oh, my! Oh, dear! Please, sir, leave go! I'll come quietly! You're taking all the skin off my face!"

"I'll take all the skin off your body, you young rascal!" exclaimed the tugging and panting General, without desisting in his efforts.

Suddenly, Dolly bethought of an expedient to checkmate the General.

With a desperate effort, he seized one of the iron supports of a desk, and held on like grim death.

But the dodge proved almost as painful as being dragged, for the sudden pull-up nearly dragged his arms from their sockets.

"Let go, you young villain!" cried the General, savagely, "or I'll pull you limb from limb!"

But Dolly held on with the desperation of a drowning man to a floating spar, and the General was at length compelled to try another plan of getting his victim to the front.

"Unclasp his hands, someone!" he shouted.

The Sergeant, who was standing by, rapidly obeyed this order, when the General, dragging Dolly away from the desks, suddenly caught him by the baggy part of his trousers, and, lifting him up, carried him off amidst great tittering.

The triumphant General now proceeded to inflict summary punishment.

First dropping the "perfect little model" on to the floor as though he were nothing better than a sack of oats, the General seized him by the back of his coller, and, lifting him on to his feet, said savagely as he shook him violently—

"You young vagabond! How dare you have the audacity to strike a general on the nose with a dumb-bell?"

"Ple-ple-ase-sir-I-I-cu-cud'nt-hel-help it! I-I——"

But the General was not in a state of mind to listen to reason, and, being too irritated to listen to Dolly's attempted explanation, he began inflicting a succession of slaps on his right ear that echoed throughout the schoolroom, and caused Dolly to imagine that a thunderstorm had broken forth in his head.

Having battered Dolly's right ear until his arm ached, the General commenced operations on his left, with a similar sensational result.

"There!" cried the General, as, tired with his efforts, he gave Dolly a final shake and sent him staggering to the floor, "that will teach you to be careful how you play off pugnacious tricks on a General again! The next time you shall be shot, sir! Do you hear that? Shot!"

It was not the first time that Dolly had had his ears boxed.

Perfect little model as he was, he had many times been subjected to that process by his admiring mother.

But he had never met with anything half so severe as the General's boxing, and, as he sat on the floor with his ears burning, he began to wonder whether they would ever get cool again, or the storm that had been raised in his head would ever cease.

The General now turned his attention to Sergeant O'Shehe.

His anger had been in no way appeased by the gratification of having inflicted punishment on Dolly.

In fact he was more angry than ever.

He was conscious that the whole proceeding had not added to the dignity which one of his elevated rank was called upon to enhance, rather than decrease.

"I have a great mind to try you by court-martial, sir," snarled the General, bestowing a fierce look upon the trembling Sergeant.

"I am very sorry, Ge——"

"Silence!" snapped the General. "Don't talk to me, sir! You're a disgrace to the regiment, sir! Of what use are those stripes on your arm, sir, if you cannot keep a lot of scamping boys in order? Hey, sir?"

"They're such a lot of young dare-devils, Gen——"

"Hold your tongue, sir!" shouted the General, stamping his foot. "Don't tell me about dare-devils, sir! Thrash them, sir! Thrash the young rascals, I say, sir! Give them a taste of the strap!"

"That is just what I was doing, General," replied the Sergeant, eagerly, and brightening up, "when you came in."

"Just what you were doing, sir!" growled the General; "do you call sticking a misshapen, ugly young imp on a form to break people's heads with dumb-bells, giving the strap, sir? You're a fool, sir! Yes, sir—a fool!"

"Beg your pardon, sir," said the Sergeant, "I meant to say that I was just going to mount Richard Everett—that boy there, sir—on this table, and touch him up—I mean, give him two dozen with a strap."

"That's a different thing," returned the General, a little bit mollified. "You were going to do it. Very good, sir; I'll stay and see it done. What is his crime?"

"That's the boy, sir, that drew the caricature and pinned it on my back," answered the Sergeant, casting a malicious look on Dick.

"Ho! hoh!" ejaculated the General, with something approaching to a gleam of satisfaction in his eyes. "That's the young rascal, is it? Then he deserves all you can give him! All you can give him, sir! Let him have it! On to the table with him! He! he! We'll teach you how to draw caricatures, my young scamp!"

The General actually rubbed his hands in pleased anticipation of the coming sight.

"Hoist the young rascal up!" he chuckled.

"I don't want any hoisting," said Dick, contemptuously, springing on to the table, and placing himself in position.

"We'll soon take the bravado out of you, my cub!" sneered the General. "Hold him down, some of you!"

"No!—I don't want holding down!" said Dick.

"Oh, you don't, don't you? Very good! Very good! Proceed, Sergeant; where is the trap?"

The Sergeant was already standing ready with the strap, and, as the General spoke, he brought it down on Dick's person with an effect that elicited an admiring exclamation from the great officer.

"Good!"

Two.

"Beautiful!"

Three.

"Capital! Capital!"

Four.

"Splendid!"

Five.

"Very good! But give it to him harder, if you can. Make the young villain cry out!"

But the Sergeant wanted no inciting to put his utmost strength into each blow.

He was doing that for his own personal satisfaction—his revenge.

But severe as was the punishment, Dick was determined not to gratify either of them by his cries, if he could help it.

He clenched his teeth, and neither moved nor whimpered.

Stroke after stroke fell until the first dozen had been given, when the General lost his patience.

"Confound the obstinate young dog!" he exclaimed. "Here, give me the strap! He shall squeal, if there's any feeling in him!"

And, seizing the strap, the excited General was in the act of giving it a preliminary flourish over his head to add force to the stroke, when he was arrested by a loud explosion, which shook the building, followed by a shower of broken glass, and a cloud of something that enveloped all in the schoolroom in almost total darkness.

———

CHAPTER IV.

"THE ROGUE'S MARCH."

THE phenomenon with which the last chapter ended was not occasioned—as doubtless our readers will be cute enough to guess—by a miraculous intervention of supernatural agency to prevent the further punishment of Dick.

By no means.

It was certainly the work of an imp, but not an imp of darkness.

The inventor of the expedient was a tangible personage in the shape of Dolly Swaps.

For a minute or two, after receiving that tremendous banging, Dolly sat still, wondering, as we have said, if the burning sensation in his ear and the deafening noise in his head would ever cease, and finding that neither seemed inclined to lessen in intensity, he resolved to slip out into the open air, and subject his head to a watery process by placing it under the pump.

So, taking advantage of the attention that was being bestowed upon the punishment of Dick, Dolly crept beneath the desks, and from thence succeeded in reaching the door unperceived by any except a few of the boys, and darted into the yard.

Making straight for the pump, Dolly seized the handle, gave two or three vigorous pumps, and then popped his hot and throbbing head under the spout.

"Ah!" said Dolly, "that's beautiful, that is! I'm blowed if the water don't almost hiss! Shouldn't I just like to serve him out!"

After a couple more sousings, which had the effect of reducing his head to a comparative state of coolness, Dolly left the yard and made his way into the square.

Standing in position on the gravel, about three yards from one of the school-room windows, was a six-pounder gun, with its limbers complete, kept there for the purpose of teaching the boys gun-drill.

As Dolly was passing the gun, with the intention of leaving the square, and making his a roaming excursion on his own account, his eyes fell upon a bag of soot lying by one of the wheels, where it had been deposited by the sweep who had the contract for sweeping the barrack-room chimney.

Dolly stood for a few moments eyeing the bag, in deep cogitation.

"By jingo!" he exclaimed, "what a jolly lark it would be to charge the gun with soot, and fire it through the window! I know there's some cartridges in the limber-boxes, and I know where the key is kept."

Dolly's eyes fairly sparkled at the idea!

Should he, or should he not do it?

The opportunity of paying out the General in such a novel manner was too fascinating to be resisted.

"I'll do it—hanged if I don't!" chuckled Dolly.

To rush into the school-house, upstairs to the servants' room, take the ammunition key from its peg, and back again to the gun, did not take Dolly more than two minutes.

Hastily unlocking one of the limber-boxes, Dolly extracted a flannel cartridge, popped it in the muzzle of the gun, unstrapped the rammer from the gun-trail, and rammed home the charge.

Then dragging the bag to the muzzle, he put in handful after handful of soot, until it was filled to the very mouth.

His next proceeding was to take a detonating tube from the leather pocket attached to the trail, and put it in the vent.

Then taking the lanyard from another pocket,

he hooked it in the eye of the tube, and—pulled.

Bang! and away sped the black cloud.

As the report reverberated through the square, and he heard the immediate smashing of glass, and saw the dense cloud go pouring through the window, Dolly for a few moments stared aghast at what he had done.

It suddenly flashed across his mind, that everybody in the room was sure to be smothered, and his terrified immagination conjured up a dreadful scene.

In those few terrible moments, Dolly saw, in his mental eye, a confused mass of human beings, with their eyes, noses, and throats, crammed with soot, struggling and rolling in the agonies of suffocation.

How could it be otherwise.

Dolly's sensations, at having struck the General on the nose with the dumb-bell, were nothing in intensity to those he was now experiencing.

He had, without doubt, committed wholesale murder.

He saw, in his imagination, the blackened bodies of his victims lying in heaps on the floor of the schoolroom, and yet again another horrible sight arose before his mental gaze.

He saw a little figure hanging by the neck to a gallows, with a white cap over its face, which he knew to be himself!"

This vision was more than his horrified imagination could endure, and, with a cry between a sob and a shriek, Dolly turned to make a bolt of it.

But, to his consternation, he had not run half a dozen paces when he rushed into the outstretched arms of some black-looking object, and heard the words—

"No you don't, my beauty! Oh dear no! I've just nabbed yeh in time, have I?"

The speaker had folded Dolly in his arms, and held Dolly's face pressed against his body with such force that, for the moment, that little boy could neither cry out nor look up, and was, in fact, in danger of being smothered.

When he did, after a frantic struggle, succeed in regaining his breath and looking up, Dolly discovered that he was firmly held in the embrace—the sooty embrace—of the sweep.

It so happened that the latter gentleman, having been to the canteen to sweep his own chimney, or throat, with a drink of porter, had returned for his bag of soot, and had caught Dolly in the act of firing the gun.

"You're a pretty chap, don't you think?" continued the sweep, "to go for to blow my sut hout of a cannon? and right bang through the schoolroom windy too! Well, I'm blest!"

"You just let me go!" cried Dolly, struggling desperately to release himself. "What do you want to stop me for? I'll bite you and kick your shins if you don't!"

And forthwith Dolly began to use his teeth and feet in a manner that taxed all his sooty captor's ingenuity to keep possession of his prisoner.

But after a desperate struggle, the sweep got Dolly on the ground face downwards, and there held him.

"There, my dear," said the sweep. "Now, if yeh want to kick and bite, just have a go at the pebbles. Peg into 'em. I know which'll be tired fust."

Dolly, who now felt himself conquered and helpless, was compelled to have resource to persuasive measures.

He was nearly mad with fear.

"Oh, please to let me go," he cried, in a supplicating tone. "How would you have liked being stopped when you were a kid, and up to your larks?"

"Ho, ho, ho! that's werry good, that is!" laughed the sweep, highly tickled at the naiveness of the question. "That's wot I calls a very hinnocent and touching appeal to the feelings! He, he! I don't suppose I should have liked it, but, you see, this is a werry different case. I've been hup to a many larks in my time, when I used to climb chimbleys, but I never fired sut hout of a cannon through people's windies. Why, I shouldn't wonder if the boys is all choked 'an dead by this time!"

"That's where it is!" whined Dolly. "It ain't only the boys, but the General's in there too."

"What! The General?"

"Yes, and two aides-de-camp," replied Dolly, as though that were a conclusive reason why he should be released.

"Whew! The doose!" exclaimed the sweep, "this is wus than I thought! Hoh, my eye! No wonder you wants to cut and run! Let yeh go, hey?—not if I knows it, you young wagobone! You just come with me," he added, lifting Dolly up by his collar, and dragging him, despite his struggles, towards the schoolhouse door, "and let's see wot's going on in there. Come hon, come hon—it ain't no use a strugglin'!"

Fortunately for the General, and all affected by the sooty discharge, their condition was more calculated to produce mirth than alarm.

When the sweep, with the struggling Dolly, reached the schoolroom door, he could scarcely believe the evidence of his senses.

The occupants were all alive, sure enough, but as black as the sweep himself—blinded, choking, spluttering, sneezing, and coughing, were groping, wriggling, and jostling each other in their endeavours to find the door, in a state of the utmost confusion.

Some, energetically engaged in the hopeless task of clearing their eyes of the soot, were seated on the forms and desks, or on the floor: others, with their eyes smarting with pain, and half-choked, were rolling frantically about, uttering inarticulate sounds.

But the most side-splitting sight was the unfortunate condition of the General.

In his struggles to get out, the General had tripped over one of the boys and fallen with his face downwards, and, in that position, Sergeant O'Shehe had unconsciously made a cushion of him, and was now seated on his hind-quarters, busily at work clearing his optics.

The General had fallen close to the opposite wall, and, as the Sergeant was leaning with his back against it, he was struggling in vain to throw off his heavy burden.

The sight so tickled the sweep's fancy, that, unable to resist his sense of its ridiculousness, he leant against the door-post, and gave himself up to a fit of exhaustive laughter.

Dolly, at first, afraid to look into the room, lest his gaze should encounter the horrifying sight of heaps of dead, had resolutely kept his eyes shut; but hearing the explosive burst of laughter from the sweep, instead of, as he expected, a series of alarmed exclamations, he summoned up courage to look upon the scene.

So comical was the sight, and so sudden the revulsion of his feelings from deadly fear to happy relief, that Dolly instantly went off into the same state as his captor, and sank down against the opposite door-post, doubled up with hysterical laughter.

The unusual circumstance of a gun being fired in the square and, as a matter of course, brought all the men rushing from the barrack-rooms, and by this time the foremost of them had traversed the passage, and come to a stop at the threshold of the schoolroom door.

There was no need to ask what had happened.

One glance was sufficient to show them that.

Not knowing that the General was there, and, unable to recognise him and the other officers in their sooty and begrimed condition, the soldiers joined in the laughter with the sweep and Dolly, with unrestrained heartiness and gusto.

As others came up, those in front were pushed into the room, and the hilarity and amusement became general.

The laughter and jokes continued for some minutes, and would have lasted much longer but for the accidental discovery of the General.

"Sergeant O'Shehe has found a comfortable seat at any rate," said one. "It's as good as a spring sofy!"

"I wonder who the poor fellow is?" observed another, bending over to look at him. "Hanged if he isn't an officer!" he added.

"And a General Officer, too, by George!" exclaimed a third.

"It's the Commandant himself!" cried a fourth.

This discovery had the effect of subduing the mirth, and those near speedily rolled the Sergeant from his perch, and assisted the poor General to his feet.

The two aides-de-camp were discovered at the same moment, doubled up behind the Sergeant's desk, and, with the General, led to the Sergeant's room, where they were provided with soap and water.

In the mean time, the Sergeant and the boys were taken into the open air.

Buckets of water were brought, and the process of clearing eyes, noses, and mouths proceeded, amid much excitement and merriment.

A good deal of this was attributable to the comical behaviour of Dolly Swaps, who, now that his fears of being hanged for wholesale slaughter had been removed, was in a state of great exultation at what he had done, and openly declared himself as the hero of the daring deed.

Anticipating nothing but two or three dozen with a strap on his "right about face," Dolly rolled about amongst the men and boys, cracking jokes, and holding his sides with immoderate laughter.

Dancing and twisting himself about in all kinds of fantastic contortions, Dolly chaffed every one of his schoolfellows, especially Dick Everett, whose good temper he knew he could safely assail.

"Oh, don't you look a guy—just!" said Dolly, stepping in front of Dick, with a broad grin on his face, and pointing derisively; "blowed if your own mother would know you hardly! Ha-ha-ha-ha!" laughed Dolly.

"You'll laugh the other side of your mouth presently, master Dolly," laughed Dick. "Your 'right about face' will be jolly hot before you go to bed to-night."

"I don't care!" returned Dolly, recklessly. "It's about the rummiest go that ever was, and I don't mind a whacking for it! You didn't think it was in me to do such a thing, Dick, I suppose?" added the little shrimp, with great self-satisfaction.

"Why I didn't think you could have come out so strong, Dolly, I must say," returned Dick; "there's something in you, little as you are. I must make you my Lieutenant, I think, after this—unless you are too conceited, and would like to be Captain."

"No, no," returned Dolly; "I've no wish to supersede you, Dick. I'm too little to take the lead. I don't care so long as none of you fellows can crow over me—that's all, you pretty-looking guy? Ha-ha-ha!"

And Dolly once more began capering and chuckling, and looking as pleased as a baby with a new toy.

At this moment the General, followed by two aides-de-camp and Sergeant O'Shehe, made their appearance at the schoolhouse door.

"Look out, Dolly!" cried Dick, "here's the General!"

With a scowl on his face as black, metaphorically speaking, as it was with soot a few minutes since, the General advanced towards the boys and, in spite of his boasted bravado, Dolly's heart sank within him, and he came over very "queer."

He would have made a bolt of it, but for the fear of drawing upon himself the contempt of his schoolfellows.

After all, corporal punishment was better to endure than scorn.

"Don't show the white feather, Dolly," said Dick, who had noticed the alteration in his manner. "Face it out, old chap."

"Oh, I'm not afraid, Dick!" returned Dolly, in a tone that belied his words, which were spoken as though they stuck in his throat. "He can't hang me!"

"Of course not, Dolly. He can scarcely do more than order you two or three dozen. That's nothing more than a fleabite, you know, and will soon be over."

As the General appeared, the soldiers became silent, and quietly and respectfully retired to the verandah in front of the barrack-rooms, and stood waiting to see what he would do.

After glaring round for a few moments, the General turned to Sergeant O'Shehe.

"Call the drummer!" he commanded, in a harsh voice.

The order was promptly obeyed, and, as the little drummer came up, the General continued—

"Beat the Fall-in."

The next moment, the rattle of the drum resounded through the square, and in obedience to the call, the boys fell in, in the usual formation of two ranks.

And a very curious spectacle they presented.

Having been in school when the gun was fired, the boys were bareheaded, and although they had succeeded in washing their eyes and mouths free from soot, their faces were still in a very grimy and smeared condition, whilst their uniforms were black as the sweep's bag.

Dolly's appearance was still worse.

As Dolly's time had been occupied in indulging in his triumphant demonstrations, he had given no thought as to the advisability of washing his face, and he now stood in the front rank, a conspicuously dirty-looking object.

Standing by the side of the General was the sweep who had captured Dolly, and, having an eye to his own interests, he had volunteered to point out the culprit.

"Now, my man," said the General, "Do you see the one who perpetrated this outrage?"

"That's him, General," replied the sweep, pointing to Dolly. "That little 'un there with the black face."

"Do you hear that, sir?" asked the General, sternly, addressing Dolly. "Step forward! Quick—march!"

Dolly obeyed mechanically, but not very quickly.

He felt very shaky all over, especially about the legs, which trembled and wobbled about as though they were made of indiarubber.

"Why, you are the young villain that struck me on the nose with the dumb-bell," growled the General.

"Ye—ye—yes, sir," faltered Dolly.

"Ugh! and it was you who fired the gun, was it?"

"Ye—ye—yes, sir," said Dolly, still more falteringly. "Ple—ple—please, sir, do—o—not ha—ang me!"

"Hang you!" snarled the General, "I'll give you a lesson that will be worse than hanging! Sergeant, mount the rascal on a boy's back, and march him three times round the square to the tune of the 'Rogue's March,' and each time I give the word 'halt', let him have half-a-dozen with the strap!"

To the General this seemed a tremendous punishment, but to Dolly it was an immense relief.

It was much more satisfactory to be whacked than hanged, and there was a spice of novelty in the mode of receiving it that tickled Dolly's fancy.

To enable our readers to fully understand and appreciate the scene that followed, we must give a brief explanation.

The "Rogue's March" is a tune played when a soldier is drummed out of the regiment.

Two ranks facing each other, making a kind of lane, are formed along the parade or front of a barracks, or in the barrack-square itself.

The band is placed at one end of this lane of men, with the man to be drummed out in front.

The prisoner, who is always one who is a disgrace to the regiment, is then stripped of his facings, that is, the coloured cloth on the cuffs and collar of his jacket, and the stripes on his trousers, and band and button on his cap.

All the lace and buttons are also cut off his jacket, and when this has been done, and the crime of which he is guilty and the sentence upon him have been read out by an officer, the band plays the "Rogue's March," and marches him between the ranks, stopping some three or four times to repeat the reading of the crime and sentence, until he is finally kicked out at the gate.

Though Dolly was not drummed out of the School of the Regiment, the mode of punishment intended was sufficiently like the drumming out process, to render it extremely novel.

Instead of the boys being formed into a lane, they were formed into column of fours.

The band was placed at the head of the column, and Dolly, riding "pick-a-back" on Dick, who had been selected for the purpose, in front of the band.

The Sergeant then took up his position near Dolly with the strap in his hand, awaiting the signal of the General to commence operations, whilst a drummer stood ready to beat time.

When all was ready, the General gave the word—

"Begin! and let him feel it, Sergeant O'Shehe, or by heaven! I'll reduce you!"

The Sergeant glanced at the drummer, who immediately tapped "One" on his drum, and down came the strap.

Then followed in succession, until the six strokes had been given, the tap—whack—tap—whack—of the drum and strap.

And then, to the no small amusement of the soldiers who crowded the verandah, the boys stepped out to the tune of "The Rogue's March."

"How did you like the first half-dozen, Dolly?" asked Dick, as they marched along. "Pretty stiff, eh?"

"Awful stiff, by jingo, Dick!" replied Dolly.

"Do you think you will be able to take the lot without whimpering?"

"I don't know, Dick. I'll try."

"That's the style! Let the old General see that if you are little you've got some pluck."

"I'll do my best, Dick."

"Don't you hold me so tightly round the neck next time; you nearly choked me just now. Are you grinning, Dolly?"

"No."

"Then do grin, and let them all see that you enjoy the fun as much as themselves."

In obedience to this, Dolly's face immediately burst into beaming smiles, and further determined to let everybody see that he fully appreciated the novelty of the situation, took his right arm off Dick's neck, and began imitating the actions of a jockey.

"That will make the General savage!" thought Dick, as a ring of laughter ran round the square at Dolly's pantomimic motions.

And Dick was right.

The next moment there was an angry roar, followed by deep growls from the General.

"Halt! Give him a dozen this time, Sergeant O'Shehe, and make him cut some different kind of antics!"

Tap—whack—tap—whack, a dozen times repeated, made poor Dolly quiver with pain, and caused him to hug Dick round the neck till he was almost black in the face.

"Oh, my!" moaned Dolly. "That was awful! I can't take much more of it!"

"Don't give in, Dolly," said Dick, encouragingly. "Grin and bear it."

"It's all very fine to say that," returned Dolly. "I wouldn't care if the Sergeant would strike fair all over, but he gives it me all in one spot."

"Never mind," replied Dick, shaking with laughter. "We'll pay the Sergeant out for it to-morrow. I've got a nice little plan in my head."

Off again at the quick march, with the band rattling out the tune at a famous rate, and the Sergeant stepping pompously along, with a gratified grin on his face!

Oh, he thoroughly enjoyed it, did Sergeant O'Shehe!

So did the General.

Not one stroke of the punishment would he abate!

Though all the laughter and liveliness were taken out of Dolly, encouraged by Dick, he managed not to cry out—an exhibition of endurance and pluck that called forth the admiration of the soldiers, and the delight of his schoolfellows.

But the General was not satisfied even now.

When Dolly had received his three dozen, and the procession stood ready to move off once more, the General cried—

"Now give the stubborn hound a night in the Black Hole. Bread and water, mind, to cool his courage? Off with him! Quick—march!"

Once more the "Rogue's March" echoed through the square, and Dolly was marched off to the guardroom, amidst a scene of great excitement and merriment.

CHAPTER V.

PREPARING FOR "GUN-DRILL."—DOLLY SWAPS HAS AN ADVENTURE.

THE events of the day formed inexhaustible topics for conversation amongst the soldiers of the regiment.

There was not a barrack-room where they were not freely discussed, with much zest and great gusto.

It was confidentally predicted that, if these kind of larks were carried on much longer, the school, which had only been instituted as an experiment, would be broken up.

But if the men were excited, in what state of mind was it to be expected the boys themselves would be found?

We need scarcely say that they were nearly mad with excitement.

Their tongues went nineteen to the dozen.

The great point of the fun was the General being mixed up in it.

If it had been the Sergeant only, that would have been a good thing.

But, to think of the General! Oh, that was tremendously fine!

Dolly Swaps was voted no end of a hero, and, in future, he would take rank next to Dick Everett.

When bed-time came, they all lay awake, talking and laughing, and nearly drove the Sergeant frantic, going from one room to the other, making himself hoarse, in the vain endeavour to command silence, until past midnight.

Our readers will remember Dick having hinted to Dolly, during the ceremony of the "Rogue's March," that he had a plan in his head for serving out the Sergeant.

That plan, whilst the row was going on, Dick communicated to Tom Sheppard.

Tom slept next bed to Dick, and so they could talk without restraint or interruption.

"Look here, Tom," said Dick, "I've got another lark on way. What do you think it is?"

"Oh, I can't guess!" replied Tom. "Something good, no doubt. Has it anything to do with the General?"

"No, not this time," laughed Dick, "only the Sergeant!"

"I would rather it was the General, Dick! It would cause such a sensation!"

"We can't get at the General so easily as the Sergeant, Tom. So we must be satisfied with game nearer to hand."

"Well, what is it, Dick?"

"I told Dolly I'd serve the Sergeant out for letting him have it so hot on his 'right about face, and I'll keep my word too!"

"Well?" said Tom, impatiently.

"It's our turn for gun-drill to-morrow afternoon, and I intend to put a charge of powder in the gun, and fire it in the Sergeant's face!"

"What?" cried Tom. "I say, Dick, that will be rather a dangerous game, won't it?"

"Not as I've planned it, Tom."

"I don't see how you're going to manage, Dick. The Sergeant will be almost sure to see No. 7 take the cartridge out of the limber-box, and pass it on till it reaches No. 3, and it is impossible for No. 3 to put it in the muzzle without the Sergeant twigging him!"

"Of course. But then, you see, I'm not going to try it that way. I shall slip down presently, when all is right, take a cartridge from the limber-box, and put about half of the powder loosely in the gun, and sponge it up under the vent. Won't that do, old fellow—eh?"

"Capitally!" exclaimed Tom. "I see the dodge! When the detonating tube is put in the vent and fired—"

"Off will go the powder!" interrupted Dick. "It will only cause a smother, and won't hurt the Sergeant, if he is not too close to it."

"It's a famous idea, Dick. Are you going to tell the boys what you are up to?"

"Yes; I shall tell them in the morning; half the fun will consist in their knowing what is coming."

"I suppose it was Dolly's trick that gave the notion; was it, Dick?"

"Not at first; my idea was to get up a ghost and frighten the Sergeant that way. But when he broke off the 'Rogue's March' procession, I saw the key of the limber-box on the ground, where Dolly had dropped it, and then it flashed into my mind that a charge of powder would frighten him more. You know he's always boasting about his nerve, and coolness under fire. So we will see how he will stand it to-morrow."

"We will drive him mad before we have done with him!" chuckled Tom.

"It won't be my fault if we don't," said Dick.

To put the powder in the gun, Dick knew, would not be a very difficult matter.

There were only three persons who would interfere with him if they were on the lookout.

Two of these were the Sergeant and the picquet sentry over the stables near the schoolhouse.

The other was one of the two cooks, whom we have mentioned elsewhere, and one of whom slept in each room as a check upon the boys.

Dick concluded that, when the row was over, and the Sergeant had retired to bed, he would not be likely to leave it again, unless upon a cry of alarm.

And as the cook was one of those old soldiers who manage somehow to always go to bed with a good allowance of beer, it required something more than the noise of lifting the latch of the door to wake him.

So Dick had little apprehension of being discovered so far as those two were concerned.

The real danger lay with the picquet sentry, and, to avoid his vigilance, Dick trusted to the darkness and the quickness of his action.

Dick and Tom lay awake, conversing in whispers, for some time after the other boys had gone to sleep, and profound silence, save the breathing of the sleepers and the stentorious snoring of the cook, reigned in the school-house.

The sonorous "All's well!" of the sentry had twice echoed through the silent precincts of the square before Dick judged it safe to make a move.

"I'll be off, now," he whispered.

"All right," returned Tom. "Success to you."

Dick had got into bed with his overalls and socks on.

So, quickly getting out, he slipped on his jacket, and groped his way to the door.

The cook, whose bed was next to the door, was sleeping sound as a top, and Dick lifted the latch, and passed on to the landing.

It was pitch dark, and hearing no one stirring, he felt his way downstairs into the passage, noiselessly opened the front door, and peeped out.

He could see nothing, not even the gun, which was only about three yards away from him.

But, listening attentively, he could hear the slow tread of the sentry as his heavy boots came into contact with the stones.

"I wonder whereabouts he is?" thought Dick. "Not far off, as I can hear."

He waited a minute, still on the listen.

The footsteps were retreating.

He could not have a better opportunity, he thought.

"Here goes!" muttered Dick; "hit or miss! He can't see what I'm up to, at any rate."

Knowing exactly where the gun stood, Dick had no difficulty in finding it.

But the task of getting at the cartridges proved a slower process than he anticipated.

He had to grope his way to the limber-boxes, and then feel about for two or three minutes before he could get the key into the lock.

When he had succeeded thus far, he had to cease his operations.

He could hear the footsteps of the returning sentry.

Crouching down against the inside of one of the wheels of the limbers, he waited quietly until the sentry, who passed within a foot of the gun, had again retired, as he imagined, to a safe distance, and resumed his task.

"I must be quick about it," muttered Dick; "or he'll be back again before I can get the powder in the gun."

Turning the key in the lock, he threw up the lid of the box, hastily felt for a cartridge, and drew it forth.

Placing it under his left arm, Dick was in the act of stretching forth his right to lower the lid, when the latter, which he had thrown sufficiently back, came down with a bang that could be heard in every part of the square!

The noise was immediately followed by the quick and peremptory challenge of the sentry—

"Who goes there?"

"Confound it," muttered Dick; "What am I to do!"

For a moment or two, Dick felt too flurried to decide how to act.

Whilst he stood hesitating, there came the second challenge, in a still more peremptory tone.

"Who goes there?"

This was followed by the quickly approaching footsteps of the sentry.

If Dick didn't wish to be discovered, he must now make a move of some kind.

The necessity restored his presence of mind.

Darting to the schoolhouse, he threw himself down at full length close to the wall.

Dick had scarcely gained this position, when the sentry came up, and he heard him mutter—

"What the deuce was it? It sounded like the banging of a door."

He could make nothing of it, however, and after looking about for two or three minutes he resumed his walk, much to Dick's relief.

Then he got up and proceeded to put the powder in the gun.

Tearing open the flannel cartrige, he emptied about half the powder loosely in the tube, and placed the remainder in his jacket pocket, mentally observing that he might want it some day.

He had now to get the sponge to ram home the powder.

Considering that he was working in the dark, and had two straps to unbuckle to get the sponge off the trail, he succeeded much more quickly than he expected, and in less than a minute he stood at the muzzle of the gun.

"I shall do it now, before the sentry returns," thought Dick.

Feeling for the muzzle with one hand, he was in the act of raising the sponge with the other, when he was startled to find the end of it come into contact with something, followed by the cry of—

"Oh!"

Dick, thinking it was the sentry who had come up without his hearing his footsteps, was on the point of making another bolt of it, when he was arrested by hearing words uttered in a voice which he thought he recognised.

"Crikey-jimmy! what an unlucky beggar I am! I am always getting into the wars! Oh, lor! I believe my nose is flatter than ever!"

"Who is it? Is that you, Dolly?" asked Dick.

"Yes it is," returned Dolly, spitefully; "and I wish it had been somebody else! That's all! Who are you?"

"I'm Dick Everett. What are you doing here, Dolly? I thought you were safe and snug in the guardroom!"

"It's what are you doing here? I should think," grumbled Dolly. "Do you know you have knocked my nose out of all shape?"

"Never mind that now," said Dick, with a laugh.

"Tell me quick, before the sentry comes back, what brings you here?"

"I'm escaping for my life."

"What do you mean?"

"I've killed the General and a lady?"

"Nonsense!" said Dick. "Where? How?"

"In the Officers' Mess-room. I—"

"Stop!" whispered Dick. "Here's the sentry coming. You can tell your story presently. Come with me and lie down against the wall."

When the sentry had again retired, Dick proceeded to finish his task, whispering Dolly to lie still till he called him.

This time Dick succeeded in ramming home the powder; and, replacing the sponge, and taking away the key of the limber-box, regained his room, accompanied by Dolly.

"I've done it, Tom," said Dick.

"That's the style! But I say, what a time you've been over it."

"I was interrupted by the sentry, and had to be cautious—see?"

"Yes. Who have you got there?" asked Tom, as Dolly gave a sudden sneeze.

"Only Dolly Swaps!" laughed Dick.

"Dolly! Why, how did you get out of the Black Hole?" cried Tom.

"I hardly know," returned Dolly. "I hardly know what has happened. One of the soldiers, who was in the Hole with me, lifted me up and helped me to get through a small opening in the wall, just large enough for me to squeeze through. He told me there was some litter underneath, and I need not mind dropping. Oh, lor, I wish I hadn't tried it, though!"

"Did you hurt yourself falling?" asked Tom.

"Hurt myself!—with my usual luck I dropped on to the farrier's bulldog, that had got loose, I suppose, and was sleeping on the litter. The brute seized me behind, fortunately only by the seat of my trousers, and began growling and shaking away at it at such a rate, that he almost frightened the life out of me."

"What did you do?" laughed Tom.

"Do! why I cut off as fast as I could, with the brute hanging to my tail, until I got to an open window, where I could see a light, and scrambled up, as well as I could for the weight behind, on to the window-ledge, and tried to get into the room."

Both Dick and Tom were now shaking with laughter.

"Didn't you manage it then?" asked Dick.

"Oh, yes, I managed it!" returned Dolly. "You see the dog was too heavy to drag over the window-ledge, and, as he wouldn't leave go, I tugged and tugged until the cloth suddenly gave way, and I pitched head-foremost into—you'd never guess what!"

"Into a bucketful of water?" said Tom.

"No—a large pan of jam, and jolly nice it was, too!"

"Quite a lucky tumble, Dolly, eh?" said Tom.

"Only for a little while," returned Dolly. "The place I'd got into was a sort of pantry, belonging to the kitchen of the Officers' Mess. There were lot's of tarts about, and as I was safe from the dog, and wasn't in any particular hurry and was awfully hungry, I set to work upon some lemon custard cheese-cakes. But I hadn't got through more than one and a-half, when I was dropped on by one of the men cooks, landed into the kitchen, and kicked by nearly a dozen of 'em from one end to the other, as though I were only a football, and bundled into a passage."

"Well?" said Dick, who with Tom was thoroughly enjoying Dolly's adventures, "what came next?"

"I didn't know where the passage led to, of course," continued Dolly; "but I could hear music somewhere, so I thought I'd try and find out what was up. There was a light at one end of the passage, and when I got to it I saw a flight of stairs. Up I went, and found myself on a landing with a conservatory at one end, and I could hear the music quite plain now, and concluded there must be a ball going on in the Officers' Mess-room. As I'd never seen the swells dancing, I thought I'd just take a peep.

"The door of the conservatory was open, and in I went as bold as brass.

"I was too short to look through the glass into the room, so I climbed up on to the top step of the flower-stand, all amongst the pots and flowers.

"It was such a jolly sight.

"But I hadn't been there a minute before I saw the General coming with a lady on his arm.

"I had had enough of the General for one day, you know, and thought it best to be off.

"But I found it wasn't so easy to get down as it had been to get up, and before I could get one foot on the next step of the stand, the General and the lady came in.

"And there I had to stick, trembling, and watching them spoon."

"Spoon!" said Dick. "By Jove, should have liked to have seen that!"

"I should just think they did spoon!" said Dolly. "The General was awfully tender and nice! I wouldn't have believed he could be so polite and soft, if I hadn't seen it. I began to be awfully tickled at his goings on, and felt inclined to laugh outright. Presently he began to kiss her, and then I couldn't stand it any longer, and, forgetting my fear, I called out——

"Bravo, General! That's the style! Go it! Oh, my, ain't it nice!"

"You should have seen their faces as they looked up and saw me! The General looked at me like he did when I knocked him on the nose with the dumb-bell. He would have made a rush at me, but the lady was fainting in his arms, and he couldn't let her go. I thought I'd better cut and run whilst there was time.

"So I made a desperate spring to jump off the stand; but, with my usual luck, my toe caught against one of the flower-pots, and I pitched head-long right on their heads, and down they went, with an awful crash, with me on the top of 'em.

"I didn't get up and bolt, you may suppose! Oh, no, of course not! I was off like a shot; but how I escaped I don't know. There were so many passages, and stairs, and turnings, that I thought I should never get out of the place. But I did, somehow, at last, and got here, after no end of dodging the sentries, just in time to get a crack on my nose with the end of the sponge."

Dick and Tom laughed to such a degree at Dolly's misadventures, that there was considerable danger of their awaking the boys.

"Don't wake 'em up," pleaded Dolly; "or they'll kick up such a row, and bring in the Sergeant, and then I shall be walked off to the Black Hole again."

"You will be sure to be taken there in the morning, anyway," said Tom.

"Unless we can hit upon a place to hide him," observed Dick.

"I know a capital place," said Dolly. "I'll slip out at daylight, and wait about till the granary's open, and then hide in the top loft in the corn. The men will be sure to let me up."

"Just the very place," said Dick, "and now let us turn in, and get some sleep."

CHAPTER VI.

"GUN-DRILL," AND WHAT CAME OF IT.

THE delight of the boys, when Dick made known the trick he had prepared for the Sergeant, was unbounded.

They laughed and shouted, and capered about to such an extent, that they brought the Sergeant amongst them in a towering rage, threatening them with all kinds of dreadful punishment.

But even his awe-inspiring presence, conmands, and threats, had very little effect upon the boys' spirits.

Figuratively speaking, they "smelt powder," and, like true warriors, eager for the fray, they gave full expression to their feelings, and could not be easily restrained.

The escape, too, of Dolly from the Black Hole, with this adventure with the General, and his safe retreat to the top loft of the granary, had contributed to increase their excitement, and, between the two events, they were as wild as March hares.

The Sergeant, seeing it was useless trying to enforce his commands, at length retired to his room in a high state of choler, and left the excitement to die out.

And so it did, so far as noisy demonstrations were concerned; but though these became subdued, the excitement of anticipation was none the less great.

Drilling the boys in the open square was always a pleasant duty for the Sergeant, more especially when there were plenty of spectators, as it gave him the opportunity of not only showing off the graces of his fine figure, but exhibiting his proficiency as a drill-instructor.

The boys were well aware of these pardonable weaknesses, and nothing pleased them more than to make the Schoolmaster an object of ridicule.

Gun-drill took place three times a week, in the afternoon, and whilst one squad was at the gun, the rest of the boys were divided into squads and exercised in marching, sword, or carbine drill, or the extension motions, and so on, by non-commissioned officers of the regiment.

Gun-drill was always taken by the Sergeant.

He was considered to be A 1 at it.

This afternoon the Fates were propitious for the full development of his great points—the consummate mastery of his subject, and the exhibition of the unrivalled elegance of his person.

It was a delicious afternoon.

The sun shone brightly, but its heat was tempered by a gentle breeze.

There was a goodly group of spectators, with a due proportion of the fair sex, within the gate.

The Sergeant looked his best, and was in high good-humour.

The boys never looked smarter, nor in better spirits.

After the usual parade and inspection, the boys were told off into squads, and handed over to the various non-commissioned officers.

The Sergeant, full of the impression which his performances were sure to make on the minds of the spectators, marched his squad to the gun, numbered it off from one to nine (the usual number to work a gun) and stationed each at his allotted post.

Conscious that the eyes of the ladies were concentrated upon him with an admiring gaze, the Sergeant disposed his person in the most graceful pose he could assume, and began—

"Now, boys, let me see you go through the respective motions with smartness and spirit. Try and imagine that you are in the presence of an enemy, and that you are called upon to fire away like blazes. Such an enemy, for instance, as the British artillery had to encounter at the battle of the Alma. Splendid affair that was! I wish you could have seen the magnificent style in which we worked our guns on that glorious day! You would never have forgotten it! I never shall! Think of the charging squadrons of the enemy's cavalry—the murderous fire of the infantry—the awful thunder of the guns—the lightning flashes—the smoke—the clashing—the smashing—the cheers—the maddening excitement! By Jove!" continued the Sergeant, extending his arm, and holding aloft his whip as though he were an officer, sword in hand, leading on his men, "it makes my blood boil to think of it! How I went through it all I don't know! If I hadn't been a very devil to stand fire, I couldn't have done it!"

(As a matter of fact, the Sergeant was not in the battle. He was sick with the white-liver complaint.)

He paused here, to notice the effect of his fiery eloquence upon the spectators, and was rather nettled to see that they were laughing.

But he continued—

"Now, let me see that you have caught some of my enthusiasm! Each of you knows his duty, so I needn't repeat it! I would only caution numbers 2 and 5. Ram home number 3 as if you meant it! and let number 5 fire smartly! Now mind, all of you, 'Quick's' the word and 'sharp's' the motion! When I give the word 'Load!' go at it as if you meant it! Just fancy that I am a Russian, and that you are trying to 'bowl' me over! Stead—"

The Sergeant stopped abruptly, and addressing number 5 said, sharply—

"What are you laughing at, Sheppard?"

"Was I laughing, Sergeant?" replied Tom. "I thought I experienced an involuntary movement about the mouth. It must have been the outward expression of the enthusiasm you have kindled within my breast."

"Then confine the expression of your enthusiasm to your hands, sir, by firing smartly when I give the word."

"All right," said Tom, in a significant tone, that made it difficult for his chums to maintain composed features.

"Now," resumed the Sergeant "Steady! Load!"

In a moment the boys began to go through the movements with an alacrity and smartness that not only surprised the unsuspecting Sergeant, but charmed him excessively, and drew forth approving comments.

"Very good indeed! Capital! Sponge smartly pitched, number 4! and well caught, number 2! Numbers 6 and 3—movements very active. Couldn't be better! Vent!—excellently served, number 4. Now, number 2, ram home steadily. That's it!"

As number 2 was Dick Everett, in ramming home he was brought into a side position that enabled him to tip Tom a knowing wink, unseen by the Sergeant, who stood about four yards in front of the muzzle of the gun.

Tom returned the wink with an expressive look, as he hooked the lanyard on to the tube in the vent.

When the various movements had been gone through, and the gun stood ready to be fired, the Sergeant said, approvingly—

"Very well executed! Quite equal to the working of my gun at the Alma! Steady. Now, number 1, you know what you have to do. Give the word in a commanding tone!"

At this moment the pitch of excitement of the boys was intense.

The Sergeant had scarcely ceased speaking, when number 1 issued the command.

" Fire ! "

The next instant the powder went off with a dull puff.

There was a bright flash, accompanied by a huge cloud of white smoke, which for a few seconds hid the Sergeant from view as completely as though he had been suddenly transformed into the sulphureous vapour.

If the possibility of such a transformation having taken place suggested itself to the minds of the spectators, it was speedily dispelled.

As the smoke cleared away, the form of the Sergeant was disclosed to view.

But what a sight !

What a lamentable transmogrification !

In place of the elegant figure, with its graceful motions, which a moment since had charmed all eyes, was now seen a confused heap, writhing, and rolling on the ground, like a cat in a fit.

Such an extraordinary incident could not occur without causing intense excitement.

Immediately the spectators recovered from the first stunning effect of the shock, they rushed forward to the scene of the tragedy.

At the same moment the other boys, who had been anxiously awaiting the climax, broke off from their drill, and came doubling up like a pack of hounds.

All those who were not in the secret looked on with pale and horrified faces, giving vent to numerous exclamations of alarm and pity.

" Dear, dear ! What a shocking accident ! "

" Shocking indeed ! "

" Dreadful ! dreadful ! "

" Oh, poor man ! poor man ! "

" His features must be frightfully disfigured ! "

" Such an extraordinary accident, you know."

" He seems in dreadful agony ! "

And, indeed, the Sergeant's condition seemed pitiable enough to draw forth all these feeling remarks ; for he not only rolled about, but his cries were heartrending.

" Oh, Lord ! Oh, Lord ! I'm killed ! ! I'm killed ! I'm shot ! The young devils have done for me ! My head's blown all to pieces ! Send for the doctor ! Take me to the hospital ! I'm dying fast ! "

To tell the truth, however, the sympathy of the crowd was being bestowed upon an undeserving object, for the Sergeant was more frightened than hurt.

Dick and his chums knew this, as he had been too far off the muzzle of the gun for the flash of the powder to reach his face.

The result was that the boys, much to the indignation of the Sergeant's sympathisers, stood yelling with laughter at his extraordinary antics and frightened exclamations.

The indignation, however, soon subsided, to give place to a high degree of amusement.

For two or three minutes, the Sergeant had rolled about in such a frantic and lively manner, that it had been impossible to get near him.

But when he had so far cooled down as to be enabled to sit up, holding his hands before his face, rocking and moaning, Dick, bestowing a wink on those near him, approached, saying—

" Come, Sergeant, show up. You are not half a dead man yet."

' " But I soon shall be ! " moaned the Sergeant. ' Ten thousand curses on you all, you young villains ! "

" It would be better to forgive, rather than curse us, if you are in your last moments," said Dick. " But I don't think you are. I expect

you are only burnt a little about the face. Let me look."

But the Sergeant only replied by a deep moan.

" Don't give way like this," continued Dick, lowering his tone. " Let everybody see that you can stand fire better than this. Think of what you endured at the battle of the Alma. Thinking you might be burnt a little, I got some ointment ready to put on your face. Take away your hands, and let me see the extent of the damage."

Whether it was owing to Dick's appeal to the Sergeant's vanity, or to the immediate prospect of having his fancied pain relieved by the application of the ointment, we cannot say, but he slowly removed his trembling hands from his face, and, keeping his eyes shut, sat awaiting the verdict.

As Dick had anticipated, the indignation of the spectators underwent a sudden change.

The Sergeant's features were not only uninjured, but the skin was as clean as when he appeared in all his glory on parade.

It immediately became plain that his fears were purely imaginary, and that his idea of being on the point of departing this life on the spot was due to his heart having sunk down to an unmentionable part of his trousers.

The indignation changed to titters, which soon expanded into open laughter, as Dick carried on the joke.

" Dear me ! " exclaimed Dick, in assumed surprise, this is much worse than I thought ! "

" What—what—am I like ? " said the Sergeant, faintly.

" I scarcely like to tell you ! " replied Dick. " Dear, dear ! "

" Am I—I—so—so dreadfully disfigured ? "

" I shall never forgive myself for this ! "—in a tone of self-reproach, said Dick.

" Good Heavens ! " cried the alarmed Sergeant. " Tell me what has happened ? "

" You're as black as a nigger, and I'm afraid your skin will always be tattooed with the powder ! "

" Black as a nigger, and my face tattooed with powder ! Oh, Lord ! Oh, Lord ! Oh, Lord ! " moaned the Sergeant, dropping his arms by his sides, and letting his head fall forward in helpless despair. " Disfigured for life ! Shoot me ! Put me out of my misery ! "

" But that is not the worst of it," continued Dick, winking again at the grinning spectators.

" Not the worst of it ? " cried the victim, actually shuddering with apprehension.

" No ! " said Dick.

" For Heaven's sake, let me know the worst ! " again cried the Sergeant, rocking himself more than ever, and still keeping his eyes closed.

" I'm almost afraid to tell you, Sergeant,' returned Dick, in a pitying tone. " You had better remain in ignorance, I think."

" Tell me ! Tell me ! For Heaven's sake tell me ! " screamed the poor victim. " I shall go mad ! Is it my moustache that's blown off ? "

" No, no. I wish it *was* only that ! " said Dick, in a solemn voice.

The Sergeant wondering what fearful disfigurement had overtaken him, groaned aloud.

" Is it my eyebrows ? " he asked, in a broken voice.

Dick gave another wink around, and, making a sign to the spectators to be prepared for what was coming, stooped over the Sergeant, and asked—

"You are resolved to know?"

"Yes, yes!" murmured the Sergeant. "Let me hear the worst and have it over!"

"Will you promise not to give way to your feelings?"

"I do. I can bear anything now!"

"I hope so, indeed!" said Dick. "You haven't the slightest conception of what has happened. Be calm now. Listen. The tip of your nose is blown clean off!"

"What! My nose! Blown off! O-o-h!"

And uttering a shout between a yell and a sob, the Sergeant once more clapped his hands to his face, and began rolling about, whilst the spectators tittered, and all the boys twisted themselves into all kinds of contortions expressive of the delicious nature of their enjoyment.

The fun, too, was thoroughly enjoyed by the non-commissioned officers who had been drilling the other squads.

Had they done their duty they would have arrested Dick and the other boys who formed the squad at gun-drill, and marched them off to the guardroom.

But Sergeant O'Shehe was no favourite with them, and so, glad to see his bounce brought down a few pegs, they allowed Dick to have his own way.

That the latter had not done with his victim soon became unmistakably evident, his proceedings taking a turn that at once placed him, in the opinion of everybody, in the front rank amongst mischievous and humorous young scamps.

Having all along suspected that the Sergeant was a coward at heart, and that his boasting on the score of bravery was nothing but sham, Dick had fully expected to witness this paltry exhibition of fear, and had come prepared to take the utmost advantage of it.

Unknown to his chums, Dick had mixed up a thin paste of blacking and oil in a flat tin blacking-box.

This he had placed in the breast of his jacket to be used as an unction for anointing the Sergeant's face—a soothing remedy which he flattered himself would prove more efficacious for the purpose than any other salve or specific that had ever been, or could by any possibility be invented.

Having brought the Sergeant to this abject state, Dick once more set about reducing him to a condition of comparative calmness, and brought him round so far as to keep still enough to allow the ointment to be applied to his face.

"You see," said Dick, as the Sergeant rested his head against the knees of Tom Sheppard and Bob Jones, "this will afford you a temporary relief, and then we will take you to the hospital. One of the men will carry you there on his back, I have no doubt. Here, Jock Jameson will do it, I know. Won't you Jock?" asked Dick, tipping a wink.

Jameson was a big gunner, as strong as a horse, who, with others had come up to see what was going on.

"Oh, yes, I'll do it!" said Jock, with a broad grin.

"That's all right," returned Dick, "and now I'll apply the ointment. Keep your eyes quite closed, Sergeant, and don't wince more than you can help. Your nose isn't so bad as I thought it was, after all," continued Dick, beginning to spread the black ointment. "It's only a little shrivelled at the point. It looks like a bit of

cinder. Oh! that's nothing! It will come all right in time," he added, as the Sergeant gave a moan. "The ointment will work wonders!"

Whilst the Sergeant was rolling on the ground the second time—Dick had whispered to Harry Smith—

"I say Harry, I want a strong cord. Just see if you can get one. I expect you'll find one in the gymnasium. And when you've done that, tell the band to get the drums and fifes, and be ready to fall in when I give the word."

CHAPTER VII.

RETALIATION.

THE process of applying the ointment to the Sergeant's face was a sight to see!

No hospital dresser could have applied it with greater *sang froid* and tenderness than Dick, and, as his victim's skin gradually assumed a hue of greasy blackness, the effect of the metamorphosis on the bystanders was almost side-splitting.

By the time that Dick had put the finishing touch, Harry Smith came up with the rope.

"You feel much easier now, Sergeant?" asked Dick.

The reply to this was a feeble, "Yes."

"I thought you would," returned Dick, with a squint. "And now you are ready for the hospital?"

"Yes."

Beckoning the old gunner, Jock Jameson, Dick said—

"Now, Jock, mount the Sergeant on your back, and mind you go very carefully. Don't shake him more than you can help."

Dick said this with a comical grimace that caused more titillation amongst the crowd, and then, helping the Sergeant to his feet, he guided him to the old gunner, and, in another moment, he was mounted.

Dick then took the rope, and began to bind the Sergeant's arms and legs to Jock's body.

At this proceeding the Sergeant entered a feeble protest.

"It's really necessary," said Dick. "You are so weak, you see, you may not be able to hold on until you reach the hospital."

The Sergeant groaned, and resigned himself to his fate.

The tying-on process was quickly accomplished, and then, with a look of exultation at the success of his project, Dick suddenly assumed the voice and manner of the General.

Drawing up his body into a stiff attitude, he issued the following commands in gruff, pompous tones—

"Gunner Jameson, six paces to the front! March! Halt!"

Then after a moment's pause—

"Band! Fall in! Fours left! Quick-march."

Grinning all over their faces, the band-boys advanced until they came within a few paces of Jameson and the Sergeant, when Dick called—

"Halt!"

By this time the rest of the boys, who had soon "twigged" what Dick was up to, had fallen in, in two ranks, ready for the word of command.

"I like to see soldierlike promptness," said

Dick; "though you young beggars wouldn't have been so fast at falling in, if you hadn't smelt mischief. I hope you'll show the same degree of alacrity when you've a chance of smelling powder! Silence! No laughing on parade! Attention! Fours left! Quick-march! Halt!"

When these movements had been accomplished, Dick unbuckled a stout strap which he had concealed beneath his jacket, and was on the point of ordering Tom Shepperd to fall out and perform the duty of executioner, when, who should present himself on the scene but Dolly Swaps.

It will be remembered that Dolly had taken refuge in the granary, to escape the immediate consequences of the General's anger at being so inconveniently interrupted whilst paying marked attension to a lady in the conservatory of the Officers' Mess-room.

Dolly's hiding in the granary had been connived at by the men of the regiment whose duty it was to serve out the oats and hay for the horses, and they had left him there after the duty had been performed.

Dolly ascended to the top loft, where he found himself in very snug and enjoyable quarters, and with the means of rendering himself invisible at a moment's notice.

The floor of the loft was covered, several feet deep with loose corn, and so, all that Dolly had to do, if his retreat were invaded by enemies, was to dive headlong into the corn, and bury himself *pro tem.*

Dolly, too, had a good look-out from the door of the loft over the square. From here he could see all that was going on without himself being seen.

Stretched on his stomach, ready for a sudden dive into the corn, if necessary, Dolly had been passing the time, and watching the proceedings of Dick and the others at gun-drill, and enjoying the scene immensely.

At the firing of the powder, and the annointing of the Sergeant's face with the black ointment, Dolly rolled over and over, and fairly screamed again with laughter.

"What a jolly go!" muttered Dolly. I wish I was down there!"

Presently the wish to be present was turned into the resolve to join in the fun.

When Dolly saw the Sergeant mounted, and tied on to the gunner's back, he could no longer contain himself.

"By jingo! if Dick isn't going to whack him round the square to the 'Rogue's March!'" exclaimed Dolly, excitedly. "Blow'd if I don't have a cut at him!"

No sooner said than done.

There was a crane affixed to the loft-wall, and it took Dolly but two or three minutes to lower the chain, seize it, slip down, and dash up to Dick.

"Hallo, Dolly Swaps!" said Dick, with assumed severity and ominous frown, "what do you want here, sir? Back, sir, to your loft!"

"Not if I know it, Dick!" said Dolly, his still sooty face expanding into a broad grin. "I say, you're going to give him (here Dolly went through the pantomic performance of whacking the Sergeant's right-about-face with a strap) eh?"

"Well," said Dick, with difficulty maintaining his gravity. "What is that to you, sir?"

"Retaliation," returned Dolly. "That's what

it is to me. Just you give me that strap, Mister Dick, and see if I don't tip it into him fine with the buckle end! Oh, my goodness!" added Dolly, with a chuckle, capering about as Dick gave him the strap, "Here's a jolly go!"

Dolly took up his position amidst much laughter, the latter being caused by the delighted little fellow passing his hand over that part of the Sergeant's anatomy which was destined to taste the strap with facetious tenderness.

By this time the Sergeant had an inkling of the trap he had fallen into, but it was too late to extricate himself.

He was in an awkward fix.

Tied to the gunner's back, he could make no effectual efforts to release himself.

For the time being he was blind as a bat, as the ointment effectually prevented him opening his eyes.

He could do nothing but use his tongue, and with that he freely threatened his tormentors with condign punishment.

"You young villains, I'll have every one of you shot!" he cried, with an oath. "I will! Every mother's son of you! D'ye hear that?"

But the Sergeant's threats were cut short by Dick giving the word of command—

"Attention! To the 'Rogue's March.' Quick march!"

As the drums and fifes struck up, Dick, as the Sergeant had done, took up his position in the centre of the square, whilst Dolly Swaps marched alongside the Sergeant, eagerly waiting the order to halt.

Presently it came.

"Halt! Now then, Dolly Swaps," said Dick. "let him see you do your duty. Give him half a dozen well laid on. Smart with it! Drummer beat time. Begin."

"Now, you beggar!" chuckled Dolly, flourishing the strap; and at the first tap of the drum, down came the buckle with a whack that made the Sergeant wince again.

"Ah, you felt that, did you?" chuckled Dolly. Tap!

Down again came the buckle with marked effect, producing another wriggle, and eliciting a savage oath.

"That touched your feelings, did it?" grinned Dolly.

Tap!

The third application of the buckle elicited a groan from the Sergeant, not so much of physical as mental agony.

The disgrace of his position was weighing heavily upon his mind.

Though he could not see, he knew that he was the centre of attraction—that hundreds of his comrades were rejoicing in his discomfiture.

"Oh, you young devil, you shall suffer for this!" he growled.

"Don't be unreasonable, Sergeant," returned Dolly; "you had your go at me, you know, and now it's my turn. Tit for tat's only fair play!"

Tap!

"Four!" cried Dolly.

Tap!

"Five!"

Tap!

"Six!"

As Dolly delivered the last stroke, Dick cried—

"Very well done, Dolly Swaps! Quick March!"

This process was repeated four times, and then Dick was struck by a bright idea.

"I've a great mind," thought Dick, "to take him on to the front parade and march him up a few times up and down. It would be a lark. I will, too!"

Having come to this determination, he gave the word of command accordingly.

"Column, left wheel!"

Next moment the procession was passing through the gates of the square, followed by the cheers and laughter of the soldiers and other spectators.

A couple of minutes more, and the head of the column turned the angle of the barracks, and advanced boldly, the drums and fifes rattling away with great energy, on to the front parade.

CHAPTER VIII.

A PRIVATE VIEW OF GENERAL SHOOT.

WE must retrace the course of this narrative a few hours, and take a look in upon General Shoot.

The General is at breakfast, looking as savage as a bear with a sore head.

He is savage, too, and no wonder.

The manner in which he has been victimised by the boys of the school is enough to ruffle the sweetest temper.

The more he thinks of the indignity to which he has been subjected, the more savage he gets, and each sip of coffee washes down a growl, or a muttered oath.

"If this goes on much longer I shall have to break up the school," muttered the General when he had nearly finished breakfast; "and a nice thing that will be—to confess that my scheme is a failure. I shall be looked upon as a visionary old fool?"

The latter contingency was a sore point with the General.

The institution of "The School of the Regiment" was a pet scheme of the General's.

He had succeeded in carrying it out in the teeth of great opposition.

The idea of such a scheme proving a success had been scouted and laughed at by many of his brother-generals, and now it really seemed as though their prognostications were in a fair way of being fulfilled.

The very idea of failure and becoming a laughing-stock, to one of the General's mercurial temperament, was awfully exasperating.

Never before had Private Patrick O'Down, the General's servant, who now stood behind his chair, seen him in such a continuously irritable state of mind.

"It's the brain fever he'll be getting prisintly," thought Pat, "if he goes on like this much longer!"

Pat had scarcely made this reflection when the General, turning suddenly round upon him, demanded—

"Where's the 'Morning Report?'"

"It's not come yet, sur," said Pat.

"Not come! How the devil's that, sir?"

"I don't know, sur. I suppose the Orderly Serjint hasn't come with it yit, sur!"

"Suppose!—what business have you to suppose, sir?" growled the General, "The duty of a soldier is not to suppose, but to say 'yes' or 'no.' Do you hear, sir?"

"Yis or no, Gineril?"

"Why, confound your impudence! what do you mean by that?" demanded the General, turning purple in the face, and glaring at Pat.

"Sure you told me to say 'yes or no,' Gineril," returned Pat, with affected innocence.

The General eyed Patrick for a moment or two with a doubtful expression, and then said abruptly—

"You're a fool! Go downstairs and look for the 'Morning Report,' and send the Orderly Sergeant up with it."

As Patrick left the room, the General, who could not sit still, jumped up and began pacing to and fro, clearing the way by upsetting two or three chairs, and kicking a hassock into the fire place.

In the meantime, Patrick, proceeding on his errand, encountered the Orderly Sergeant in the hall, and greeted him with pursed up lips and ominous nods of the head.

"Is that it?" said the Sergeant. "Tantrums?"

"It's worse than tantrums, Sergeant," replied Pat. "It's the wrong side of the bed he's got out of this morning, an' he's in the divil's own temper! It's nearly kilt I am with the things he's pitched at me. He's mad about the 'Report,' an' ye'd better take it up at once."

"Take it up?"

"Yes. That was the order."

"Phew! Then I'm in for a jackoting, eh?"

"Ye may say that, Sergeant."

"What's the meaning of this delay, sir?" growled the General when, a minute later, the Sergeant entered and, with a salute, handed the "Morning Report."

"An extra number of prisoners, sir; report took longer to make out."

"Prisoners! So it seems. It's disgraceful! The regiment is going to the dogs!"

Here the General began reading the various crimes.

"'Sergeant Dubbin, absent without leave three hours—came in with a black eye, three teeth knocked out, and drunk.' That's a pretty blackguard to be a Sergeant," muttered the General. "Dubbin shall be tried by court-martial, and reduced."

The next on the list was

"'Corporal Spunger, drunk at stables. Supposed to be mad, as he insisted upon calling General Shoot a "dashed muff," and wanted to punch his head.' 'Pon my soul," exclaimed the General, the blood rushing into his face with anger "if discipline isn't coming to a pretty pass! Such disrespectful language towards a General I never heard! Is this true, sir?" snapped the infuriated Officer, addressing the Sergeant.

"Quite, sir; I heard Spunger say it with my own ears."

"Then it's time, sir," snarled the General, "when an Officer of my rank is spoken of by one of his soldiers in such language, for that officer to resign, sir. Is it not, sir?"

"Yes, sir," replied the Sergeant. "If I was in your place I should throw up my commission."

"Oh you would, would you?" thundered the General. "I dare say you'd all like me to do so! But I shan't, sir! I'll stay until I haven't a leg to stand upon, and work you all up—a lot of drunken, mutinous, disgraceful blackguards! Yes, sir!" he reiterated, striking the table between each word. "A—lot—of—drunken—

"Good Heavens! Can I believe my eyes—Sergeant O'Shene! This is worse and worse!"
See page 28.

No. 3.

mutinous—disgraceful blackguards! Here's a pretty list of crimes," holding up the "Morning Report." "Nothing but drunk—drunk—drunk —absent without leave—insubordi—"

"By jingo!" thought the Sergeant: "if he's got his eye on Oilrag's crime, he'll go mad! It's true, too, that's the worst of it.'"

The cause of the General's abrupt pause was as the Sergeant suspected. He had got his eye on Oilrag's crime, and was reading it, too, with mingled feelings of anger, annoyance, and shame.

It ran as follows:—

"'Gunner Oilrag confined for being drunk, and swearing that he carried home General Shoot from the Officers' Ball on his back, the General being in a beastly state of intoxication.' Good heavens!" muttered the General, sinking into a chair. "I shall go mad! Leave the room, sir!" he added, in a voice husky with passion.

The Sergeant disappeared, and the General sprang to his feet, and began tearing about the room like a madman, and threatening the unfortunate Oilrag with all kinds of punishment.

This indiscretion on the part of Oilrag was bad enough, but there was a last straw to come.

Glancing once more at the report as he continued his excited perambulation, his eyes fell upon the following—

"Master Adolphus Swaps, of the School of the Regiment, escaped from the Main Guard Room.'"

This brought to the General's memory the little episode in the conservatory of the Officers' Mess room, where Dolly had interrupted his gallant attentions to a lady, and, dashing the Report on the floor, he rushed from the room, commanded his horse to be brought round, mounted and galloped off to the Commandant's Office in a state of frantic passion.

CHAPTER IX.

AN EXCITING CHASE.

FOR the information of the reader, we may state, that the Commandant's office is an office appropriated to the use of the General Officer commanding the garrison.

It is here that the General transacts his official duties, such as issuing the programme of the drills, &c., for the troops for the ensuing day, approving of the sentences awarded by court-martial, and other items.

The General's temper had by no means improved as he dismounted, and made his way to his official sanctum.

As he clattered up-stairs—his spurs jingling and his sword rattling—his face was as black as a thunder-cloud, and he snapped and snarled at everything and everybody.

The cause of the General's mental disturbance was pretty well known by the non-commissioned officers and others on duty this morning, and knowing winks were exchanged behind the General's back, and the ominous word "Oilrag" was whispered with a chuckle from one to another.

But the General was destined to have his temper much more severely tried presently.

He had scarcely taken his seat at the desk, and proceeded to sign some papers, when his ear caught the sound of music.

Pausing, he asked one of his aides-de-camp, in an abrupt manner—

"What the devil's that?"

"Sounds like drums and fifes, General."

"Drums and fifes! What the deuce do drums and fifes want playing this time of day?"

"Can't say, General. It's strange; and the tune is the 'Rogue's March.'"

"It sounds like the band of The School of the Regiment," observed another aide-de-camp.

"It's coming along the front parade, too," said a third.

Dashing down the pen, the General, his face glowing like a red-hot coal, rushed to the window, threw it up, and thrust forth his head.

The sight that met his gaze absolutely took his breath away with astonishment.

There, marching along, with all the cheek of the world, was the School of the Regiment with the band at its head, rattling out the "Rogue's March," with great gusto.

But that was not all.

What was that at the head of the band?

"What the devil does it mean, gentlemen?" gasped the General, when he at last found his tongue.

"They appear to be playing somebody about to the 'Rogue's March,'" answered the senior Aide-de-camp.

"Who is it?"

"He looks like a black man, General."

"A black man! The young scoundrels are up to another of their tricks!" said the General, in a tone of compressed passion. "They'll drive me mad! Mad, I say, gentlemen! Follow me!"

The next moment the excited General rushed from the room, down the stairs two at a time, his sword dashing against the baluster and wall with a wild clatter, along the passage, until he reached the top step of the vestibule, when his mad career was brought to a sudden stop.

"The more haste, the less speed," sayeth the proverb.

This proved true in the General's case.

At this moment, the sword, that had been cutting no end of eccentric capers, got between the General's legs, precipitating its master headforemost on to the gravel of the parade.

Gravel, composed for the most part of tiny pieces of sharp flint, is not a pleasant thing for one's nose to scrape acquaintance with, and is not calculated to mollify one's temper.

And so the General picked himself up, his nose burning with pain, and began stamping and swearing with rage.

This incident was not unobserved by Dick and his fellow "chums," and a general titter testified the enjoyment felt at the General's discomfiture.

The band broke down, and the procession came to a sudden halt.

The sudden silence recalled the General to himself.

Hastily soothing his smarting nose with his pocket-handkerchief, the General, looking like an enraged bull, advanced to the head of the column, and stood contemplating the disconsolate figure tied to the gunner's back.

Despite the change of hue his skin had undergone, the General had no difficulty in recognizing the features of the Sergeant.

"Bless my soul;" muttered the General, "things are getting worse and worse! What is the meaning of *this*, Sergeant O'Shehe?" he asked, in a severe tone.

"It is those young demons again, General," whined the Sergeant. "They've disfigured me for life!"

"And serve you right too, for letting them make a fool of you," growled the General.

"I couldn't help it, General. They—"

"Silence, sir! Don't tell me you couldn't help it! You should keep your eyes about you, sir, and then you couldn't be made a fool of! These proceedings are disgraceful! If you can't curb the young rascals better than this, I'll reduce you to the ranks and break up the school! You are making me the laughing stock, sir, of the whole garrison. Silence, sir!" continued the General, as the poor victim again began to justify himself; "who are the ringleaders of this outrage?"

At the moment the General made his appearance on the scene by diving on to the gravel, Dolly Swaps, thinking that discretion would prove the better part of valour, had made his way to the side of Dick, ready to act as circumstances dictated on the spur of the moment.

That the General would endeavour to secure and punish the ringleaders, Dolly had no doubt.

It was but the natural sequence to be expected.

But Dolly wasn't going to allow himself or his fellow-sinners to be taken without a chase and a siege.

He had a plan which he hastily communicated to Dick, whilst the foregoing dialogue between the General and the Sergeant was proceeding.

"I say, Dick," said Dolly; "I suppose the General will be down on the leaders, eh?"

"For certain, Dolly."

"Then I know what to do."

"What?"

"You know the top loft of the granary?"

"Well?"

"It's such a stunning place to hide."

"But how are we to get there?"

"Climb up the crane-chain."

"That might be done if we could reach it in time."

"Oh, we'll manage it right enough, Dick."

"But can't they get in by the door?"

"Not without breaking it open. I've put up the oak bar inside."

"All right, Dolly. Keep yourself ready for a bolt."

It will, then, be seen that our young rascals were fully prepared for the General's demand, and which had no sooner been made than they conceived it time to "bolt."

Before the Sergeant could answer the General's question, Dick and Dolly, giving the signal to the School to break off and disperse, set off with the nimbleness of deer for the granary.

The General, who was unprepared for this move, once more burst into a terrific passion, and, forgetting the dignity attached to his rank, started in pursuit, calling on his aides-de-camp to turn out the main guard to assist in the capture.

The scene which followed was one of considerable excitement and amusement.

Besides the soldiers who had accompanied the procession on the front parade, were a goodly number of civilians, and from these last, having

no fear of the General's wrath before their eyes, came cries of encouragement to both parties.

"Go it, boys! Keep it up!"

"Well done, little 'un; work your stumps !'

"That's the style, General! You'll ketch 'em, if you have luck."

"Undo your straps, General, or you'll split your breeches."

"Go home, General, and put on your seven-league boots."

Presently the excitement of the chase was added to by the appearance of a dozen file of the main guard following up at the double, with carbines at the trail.

At sight of these, the crowd cheered lustily, and shouted its encouragement to Dick and Dolly.

By this time, Dolly was getting hard pressed. The pace was beginning to tell upon him.

Looking round, Dick perceived that his little chum was in difficulties.

"Keep up your pluck, Dolly," cried Dick.

"The pluck's all right, Dick," puffed Dolly, "but my wind's giving way."

"Give me your hand, old chap," said Dick. "That's it."

This action on the part of Dick elicited a cheer from the crowd, and his schoolfellows.

"Bravo, Dick!"

"Don't give in, Dolly!"

"We'll all stand between you and the General!"

Dick and Dolly had now reached the gate of the square, and passing through, made for the granary, from the top loft of which the crane-chain was hanging.

The pace now, owing to Dolly's dragging, was much slower, and the General was perceptably gaining.

The general sympathy, however, was with Dick and Dolly, and the boys of the school contrived to keep themselves in front of the General, and considerably retard his progress.

The distance from the gate to the granary was about forty yards, and just as Dolly seized the chain and began his ascent, the General made his appearance.

"Go it, Dolly," cried Dick; "here's the General!"

"Oh, lor! I'm pretty near done up," puffed Dolly. "I don't think I can get up."

"You *must*. Don't give in!"

Thus encouraged, Dolly persevered; and when he had reached about half-way up, Dick essayed to try his luck.

This was a most exciting moment.

The General was within ten yards, and the cries of the crowd became deafening.

"He'll be too late; the General will win!"

"Up the chain, you young goose! Quick!"

"Ten to one on the General!"

This was followed by ironical cries, and great clapping of hands.

Dick had coolly waited till the General had come up close, and then, with a spring, he seized the chain, and pulled himself out of reach, hand over hand, with the nimbleness of a squirrel.

But though Dick and Dolly were out of reach, they were not out of danger.

Though for the moment baulked, the General was determined to persevere.

"You villains!" he panted, seizing the chain, and shaking it vigorously; "I'll have you, dead or alive!"

This was a tremendous trial of the tenacity of Dick and Dolly, especially the latter, who, being nearly exhausted, and not quite up to the foot-board of the loft, felt as though he must be shaken off.

The danger of both was seen by the crowd, and once more cries of encouragement reached their ears.

"Hold on! Hold fast!"

"Stick to the chain!"

"Bravo, little 'un! On to the board!"

"That's it!"

"He's done it!" came the general cry, as Dolly, after a desperate effort, rolled on to the footboard.

This was all Dick was waiting for.

No sooner had Dolly landed in safety than, putting forth his strength, he shot up the remainder of the chain, despite its shaking, and stepped nimbly on to the board, followed by ringing cheers, and loud cries of—

"Bravo! Bravo! Bravo!"

CHAPTER X.

GENERAL SHOOT GETS A LIFT, BUT NOT IN RANK.

THE rage of General Shoot, at the temporary escape of Dick and Dolly, will be easier to imagine than descrbe.

The manner in which he stormed and raved, and shook his fist at them was particularly edifying to everybody, especially Dolly.

That provoking young dot, now that he found himself safe for the present, suddenly recovered his usual buoyancy of spirits and characteristic "cheek."

Dolly had no sooner recovered his wind than he determined to indulge in some "chaff."

For this purpose, Dolly cast himself on his stomach, and, protruding his comical-looking head over the edge of the foot-board, began grinning with all the assurance of a monkey out of reach.

Dolly's face was still almost as black as a sweep's, and, as his hair was "nohow," and still sticky with jam, he presented a most rakish, and, to the General, most saucily-provoking appearance.

At the sight of Dolly's sooty, grinning phiz, the General was almost choked with passion, and, whilst growling out threats, shook his fist in accompaniment.

"Oh! Ah! I dare say!" said Dolly, resting his face in his hand, and showing his white teeth. "You're in an awful state of mind, I've no doubt! Ah! Yes, to be sure! You'd just like to get at us? To be sure you would! Yes, yes, I know, it's awfully tantalising! It's like the Fox and the Grapes, ain't it? Why don't you try a jump? Nothing venture, nothing win, you know, General. Ha, ha, ha, ha!"

This laugh was called forth by a little incident by way of diversity to the scene.

The General, during his manifestations of anger, had kept his look fixed on the object of his wrath.

Stepping back at this moment to command a clearer view of the loft, his spurs crossed, and he suddenly found himself seated on the stones, with a bump that caused him considerable pain.

"Nebber mind, General," said Dolly. "Did it hurt him den? Ups 'e get. Don't cry! I

say, Dick," added Dolly, "the General will half kill me, I expect, when he gets the chance."

"You are certainly adding fuel to the fire, Dolly," said Dick, laughing; "and I shouldn't be surprised if you get jolly well warmed."

"I don't care, Dick, now that I've touched up the Sergeant, and dodged the General. Here comes the aides-de-camps, and the main guard, and the Sergeant himself. By jingo!" chuckled the hardened scamp. "What a cure he does look!"

"He's an awful coward, and I'll frighten the life out of him, before I've done with him," said Dick.

"What is that black stuff on his face, Dick?"

"Blacking and oil."

"What a rum idea!" laughed Dolly.

"I used it as an ointment, to assuage the pain."

"Was he burnt with the powder, then?"

"No. I made him imagine so, however; and also," laughed Dick, "that the point of his nose was blown off. You never saw a man in such a funk."

"Oh, you beauty!" said Dick, apostrophising the Sergeant.

Their attention was now attracted by the proceedings of those below.

As the officers and the escort came up, the General began to vociferate his instructions.

Retaining the chain with one hand, and stretching forth the other, like a gallant General leading on his men, he exclaimed—

"Captain Sloper, prepare to storm this granary! Those young villains must be captured!"

"Dear me!" was Dolly's comment. "How brave we are! We must be captured, must we? Storm away! Oh, you're done, my beauties, are you, eh?" added Dolly, with another chuckle, as Captain Sloper, after unlocking the padlock, found that the door would not open.

"There's an obstruction inside, General," said the Captain.

"Then batter down the door," thundered the General.

"Ah!" observed Dolly. "I didn't think you had so much good sense, General. That'll do it, and then you'll be satisfied. But I don't think I'll cry about it. I say, Dick," continued Dolly, who was watching every movement of the General; "do you feel inclined to catch a fish?"

"What do you mean, Dolly?"

"Just look down at the General."

"Well?" said Dick, complying.

"Do you see where the hook of the chain is?"

"Hook of the chain? Ah! I see, it seems to be under the General's coat-tails."

"Right you are, Dick. Turn the handle and see if we can fish him up. What a lark it would be!"

Dick immediately seized the handle.

"Gently," said Dolly. "Go slowly. That's it. Now it's got it. Turn away! Up he comes! Oh, lor! ain t he shouting? Ha! ha! ha!"

General Shoot had experienced a variety of sensations during his lifetime; amongst these was that of being frequently elevated with port wine—his favourite drink.

He had more than once been elevated, when in a state of happy unconsciousness and help-lessness, on someone's back, as he had been on the back of Oilrag last night.

But these sensations were different to that which he now experienced.

At first he could scarcely realise what was happening, but imagined he must have been seized with giddiness, and was gradually falling forward on his nose.

But when he found that his feet were slowly leaving the ground, and that he was being drawn upwards by some mysterious agency, a dreadful fear seized him.

Where was he going?

Was he in the body or out of the body?

He was rising faster now.

He could see the hundreds of upturned faces below him, and could see the astonishment depicted thereon.

Suddenly it burst upon his mind what had happened.

The hook of the chain had got under his coat-tails, and the young rascals above were drawing him up!

He was conscious, too, of presenting a most absurd figure.

His arms, legs, and head hung downward in the most helplessly idiotic fashion.

The gallant General was in a state of utter physical collapse, and he could make use of nothing but his tongue.

The manner in which he raved, swore, and threatened the awfullest of punishments on Dick and Dolly, was of too wild and dreadful a character to be recorded here.

It was now that Dolly came out strong in the way of chaff.

Dolly knew that his punishment was sure to be the heaviest the General could give him, so he may just as well be "hung for a sheep as a lamb," he thought.

When the General had been drawn up to within a few feet of the foot-board, Dolly said—

"You don't seem to like your rise in the world, General, eh?" It don't add to your dignity, I suppose, you think? Well, I must say you don't look at all graceful or pretty!"

"You young dare-devil!" gasped the General; "I'll——"

"Come, come, General," grinned Dolly, in a cautionary tone. "Don't give way to your temper, or——down you goes again by the run, and you won't like that, you know."

The General groaned.

"Yes, it's awful, I know, continued Dolly. "You never were in such a fix before. It's a dangerous one, too. Just suppose your coat was to give way behind! I say, General, what a buster you'd go down! Why you'd be smashed all abroad like an egg!"

Another groan from the General.

"Ah! a smash like that is awful to contemplate, I expect! I shouldn't like to be in your place, General—that's all I know!"

Whilst Dolly was indulging in this unlicensed impudence, great efforts were being made by the officers of the main guard to force an entrance into the granary.

The position of the General, in spite of its ridiculous aspect, and the amusement which it caused, was very critical.

He had now ceased to cry out, and was hanging in an apparently insensible condition.

Fortunately for the General, the door was at last broken open; the officers and men rushed up to the top loft and, in two or three minutes, Dick and Dolly, who could not help themselves, were captured, and the General delivered from his perilous position.

Dick and Dolly were marched off prisoners to the main guard room, followed by an admiring cheer from their schoolfellows, and a scowl of hate from Sergeant O'Shehe.

CHAPTER XI.

THE STORY OF THE HAUNTED CELL—DOLLY PERSONATES THE GHOST, AND GETS HIMSELF AND TWO OTHERS INTO A "PICKLE."

THERE are two individuals whose minds were so perfectly disarranged by the tricks to which they had been personally subjected, as to cause their actions, for some time, to assume the most eccentric vagaries.

These were General Shoot and Sergeant O'Shehe.

The General's tongue went at a terrific rate in the way of growling, bullying, and swearing, when he reached his quarters.

His legs and arms, also, kept pace with his tongue.

He first swore at, then "punched," and then kicked his Irish servant, for keeping him too long at the door.

After this energetic performance, the General metaphorically worried his domestic household "out of their lives," and turned the house "inside out."

He broke nearly all the bell-wires with furious tugging; threw aside his sword with such violence as to smash a splendid collection of Indian and Chinese works of art, which decorated a sideboard; pitched one book through the window, and splintered the panel of the door with the other; hurled his cocked hat at his valet with such force as to seriously damage the sight of that individual's left eye; and, finally, after drinking three bottles of port wine, and smoking no end of cigars, retired to rest, to sleep himself in a calmer state of mind.

Sergeant O'Shehe was no less violent in his demonstrations.

He gave way to the most terrible ebullition of passion as he contemplated the blackened state of his features in his glass, and then mentally reflected on what a fool he had made of himself by his paltry exhibition of fear.

"May the devil fly away with me!" he exclaimed, shaking his fist at his own reflected "mug," "if I don't pay the young villains out for this day's work!"

The Sergeant was in such a state of mind that, had he not been too fond of his life, he would certainly have dashed his brains out there and then.

As it was, he scattered his things about the room in impotent anger, presently got some hot water from one of the cooks and washed his face, and finally, like the General, got drunk to to assuage his chagrin, and went to bed in a state of mental obfuscation.

In this state we must leave the two great men, and return to Dolly and Dick.

The cell in which those young gentlemen found themselves shortly after their capture was not the same as that in which Dolly had been placed the previous night.

It was one of the series of cells, however, of which the main guard-room consists, and was by no means a cosy little place.

In the first place, it was almost pitch dark, the only light admitted into it being through a square aperture in the wall near the ceiling.

In the second place, it was very small—a size larger, perhaps, than a rat-trap; and in the third place it struck damp and cold,

"I've never been in this cell before, Dolly," observed Dick, looking curiously around as the door was bolted upon them.

"Nor I, Dick," replied Dolly. "I wonder where it overlooks!"

"Why?" asked Dick.

"Why? Because I intend to escape, if I can, to be sure. Don't you?"

"Of course I do!"

"Then, look here, Dick, let's settle the whereabouts of the drop outside at once. Just get on this wooden bed, and I'll climb up on your shoulders and have a peep."

Dick immediately put himself in position, and, the next minute, Dolly was mounted and had his head and shoulders protruding through the aperture.

Dolly took a hasty look round, and then descended from his perch.

"Where does the cell overlook, Dolly?" asked Dick.

"A jolly awkward place," said Dolly; "we're at the east end of the North-east Avenue, and the only way we can get out of the barracks is by passing the sentry at the gate."

"Bother it!" said Dick. "What a nuisance!"

"Ain't it!" returned Dolly.

"Is the drop easy?" asked Dick.

"Jolly easy, Dick. There is a large barrel, or tub, just underneath, and we shall only have about a six feet to drop."

"Then all we have to do, Dolly, is to dodge the sentry?"

"That's all, Dick!"

Though Dick and Dolly, from long practice, were adepts at dodging a sentry, such a feat was only fairly possible on a dark night.

This happened to be about the time of the first quarter of the moon, which would afford, if not obstructed by clouds, sufficient light to render dodging a sentry a rather uncertain game.

"What are we to do, Dolly, if the moon shines?" asked Dick.

"You mean about dodging the sentry?"

"Yes!"

"We must trust to luck, Dick,"

"Your luck is generally bad luck, Dolly," laughed Dick. "The last time you dropped from the Black Hole you came down on the farrier's dog, you know."

"So I did, and lost a piece of my overalls in consequence," returned Dolly, with a grin. "But the farrier's dog can't get this side, Dick, and so we shall be safe from his fangs."

"But you may drop on to something quite as inconvenient, Dolly."

"There is nothing beneath here but a tub, Dick, and that has a cover on it. It's safe enough. I'll go first to try it."

"All right, Dolly, and I wish you luck."

As luck would have it, Dolly was presently furnished with a magnificent idea for dodging the sentry.

When tattoo had been sounded, the roll called, and the picquets posted, Dick and Dolly were invited by the Sergeant of the Guard to take a seat by the guard-room fire.

"It's rather cold in the cell for youngsters like you," said the Sergeant, "so just post your-selves by the fire for an hour or two, and then I will let you have a couple of cloaks to wrap yourselves in."

Though Dick and Dolly felt anything but grateful to the Sergeant for this kindness, they made a show of seeming so, and seated themselves by the fire as though they thoroughly enjoyed the privilege.

They wanted to make their escape, and did not relish their detention, kindly as it was meant.

A guard-room by night is not an unpicturesque sight.

The one in which our embryo soldiers, Dick and Dolly, now found themselves, though much against their wills, was not devoid of fascination, even to them, in their present mood.

The furniture was not of the most luxurious description.

Heavy wooden forms with iron legs formed the only seats.

There was a small barrack-room table for the accommodation of the Sergeant of the Guard, and which he used for making out his "Guard Report," and checking off the men's names as they returned to barracks "off leave."

The beds were simply wooden platforms, with a wooden step at the top, close to the wall, to serve as a pillow.

These platforms occupied one end of the room, one being placed over the other, looking very much like a gallery to which access was gained by a flight of wooden steps.

The walls were merely whitewashed; and the grate was large enough to hold two bushels of coal.

The hearth was protected by a huge fender; and the fire-irons were large and heavy enough for the use of Hercules himself.

But for the presence of the soldiers, this room would have looked bare and dreary enough.

Stretched at full length on the guard-beds, wrapped in their thick cloaks, were some of the men of the day guard, and the night picquets, trying to snatch "forty winks" ere their turn came for "sentry-go."

Others, wakefully inclined, were seated on the forms smoking, or carefully cutting up their "negro-head" to indulge in a quiet whiff.

To all this, though it was summer time, a fire lent an appearance of snugness that completed the military charm.

This is better than the cold cell, my lads, I guess—eh?" said the Sergeant, presently.

"Yes, Sergeant," replied Dick; "no doubt of it. I hope you won't get into trouble for letting us out."

"I should be sorry if you did, Sergeant," added Dolly, inwardly wishing the non-commissioned officers were at Jericho for spoiling his fun.

"I will take that with a grain of salt," grinned the Sergeant. "Youngsters who fire soot at Generals and suspend them at the end of crane-chains, are not likely to feel much sympathy for a Sergeant getting into a scrape —eh?"

Dick and Dolly grinned also, but the former remarked—

"A general is a diffent animal to one of the rank and file. General Shoot is fair game, you know!"

"You don't confine your hunting to generals," said the Sergeant. "How about Sergeant O'Shehe?" he added, with a wink.

At the mention of O'Shehe's name, there

was a general laugh, whilst the Sergeant continued—

"Between the lot of you, you'll drive the General and O'Shehe mad. You'd better take care; I heard something to-day that will astonish you."

"What was that?" asked Dick, eagerly.

"Why, the General swears, if these tricks go on much longer, he'll pack the whole School off to Gibraltar!"

"What!" came the simultaneous exclamation from Dick and Dolly, whilst their eyes opened indeed with astonishment. "Send us to Gibraltar?"

"Yes."

"By jingo!" exclaimed Dick. "I only wish he would!"

"Oh, what a jolly lark it would be!" cried Dolly, fairly hugging himself at the very thought.

"It strikes me, the General is one to keep his word, too," said the Sergeant.

"It won't be my fault if he doesn't!" said Dick.

"Nor mine, either!" added Dolly.

There was something so fascinating in this idea, that, boy-like, Dick and Dolly wanted to talk it over "all to themselves," and Dick proposed their retiring to the cell.

"You may stay here all night, if you like," said the Sergeant, good-naturedly: "and have a shake down on the guard-bed. It's better than a cold cell, and one that is said to be haunted, too."

"Haunted!"

Dick and Dolly pricked up their ears at this.

What boy is there who will not, at any time, listen to a ghost-story?

What boy is there who, if circumstanced as were Dick and Dolly, would not have demanded the story of the Haunted Cell?

The Sergeant, who was really a good-natured fellow, and wished to keep them out of the cold cell, complied with Dick's and Dolly's request to hear the story.

"It's not a long one," begun the Sergeant, "but it's a melancholy one enough. Part of it I know to be true, but I won't vouch for the ghost. There are some who believe in ghosts, and some do not. I belong to those who don't, though what I am going to tell you may have happened.

"It's many years ago, now—before the Battle of Waterloo was fought—that a young fellow presented himself in the East Square for enlistment.

"He was a handsome fellow, and not only handsome, but, as every one could see, was a gentleman born.

"It isn't often, you know, that a gentleman enlists, unless he's down on his luck in the matter of scarcity of 'tin,' or, perhaps, has lost his head for a time owing to his sweetheart giving him the 'right about face, quick march' for some other fellow who has tickled her fickle fancy!

"But in the case of Dick Newton—for that was the name he went by—it was neither want of cash nor a jilting by his lady-love.

"Dick had naturally a martial spirit, a thorough love for the profession of arms, not as an officer, but as one of the rank and file.

"'I want to be a soldier in the ranks, sir,' said Dick, in reply to the Adjutant's remark that a commission was more suitable to one who was evidently a gentleman. 'I could buy a commission to-morrow; but I want to learn what real soldiering is.'

"Well, there was not a merrier or more gallant fellow going than Dick Newton, He was a jolly comrade, a thorough soldier, and was liked by everybody.

"Dick had been with the battery about twelve months, when, one day, as he was passing through the gate, he was encountered by a lady whom he recognised to be his sister—an only sister too.

"Dick, who had studiously kept his whereabouts a secret from his family, was struck all of a heap at the sudden meeting, and not wishing that his sister should be seen in company with a private soldier, he hastily begged her to retire, when he promised to write to her and arrange a private interview.

"With this no doubt she would have complied, but that an officer of the battery, who had witnessed the meeting, and overheard the conversation, offered them his quarters for their accommodation.

"The brother and sister gladly availed themfelves of the offer; but, better had it been for both had they never done so.

"To cut the story short, I will merely say that from that moment an intimacy sprang up between the officer and Dick's sister.

"The officer was a bad fellow, a heartless libertine, and going through the ceremony of a sham marriage, effected the ruin of the poor girl.

"From that moment Dick became a changed character. From a gay lighthearted young fellow, he became one sullen and morose; and he swore he would have a terrible revenge for the evil wrought upon his only sister.

"The officer—I do not mention his name, for certain reasons—kept away from the battery for some time, not daring to encounter the young soldier whilst freshly smarting under the wound his honour had received.

"If the officer thought that Dick's feelings would be deadened by lapse of time, he was greatly mistaken.

"He had no sooner returned than poor Dick, in the presence of the battery and officers, approached him, and, deliberately striking him a heavy blow in the face, challenged him to a duel to the death.

"But, in giving that blow, Dick forgot that, although a gentleman, he was also a soldier, and that, in striking an officer, he had sealed his own death warrant.

"It is death, by the Mutiny Act, to strike an officer.

"Dick turned out to have influential friends, and efforts were made to induce the officer to meet him in fair fight, Dick to be discharged for the purpose of placing them upon an equality.

"But the officer refused.

"He was either a coward, or a man of such vengeful feelings, that he was determined Dick should have no chance of life.

"Dick was tried by a general court-martial, and sentenced to be shot.

"Pending the execution, he was placed in that cell, but he never came out of it alive.

"The poor boy went mad with the double disgrace brought upon his family—his sister ruined, himself to be shot for a breach of military discipline.

"On the morning appointed for the execucution, Dick sprang up to the aperture in the cell, forced his body through, and, falling head-foremost, broke his neck in contact with the stones.

"Whether such an occurrence really takes place I cannot say, but, it is asserted, that whenever a general court-martial is sitting on a man for striking his officer (they seldom shoot nowaday), the spirit of Dick is seen every night, until the court is closed, precipitating itself through the square hole."

"It's true enough, Sergeant," said an old Gunner: "I've seen it myself. I saw it when Jack Wilcox was tried, just ten years ago, and so did several others who were on sentry at the North-east Avenue Gate."

"In what dress does it appear?" asked Dolly, looking innocently at the last speaker.

"All in white."

"All in white? What kind of white? I mean, what kind of dress?"

"Why, I hardly know," said the Gunner; "it's so long ago, now."

"Was it a flowing garment it had on, do you think?"

"Well, now I come to think of it, I believe it was."

"Did the tails flutter in the wind?"

"Yes, I could swear they did."

"Then I expect the ghost had on nothing but its shirt?" suggested Dolly.

"That was it, no doubt."

"That's funny. I should have thought it would have been dressed in uniform."

"Oh, no! Dick Newton was in bed, and he didn't wait to dress himself."

That Dolly had an object in putting these questions, will presently be seen.

"I think we'll retire to the cell now, Sergeant," he said.

"Then you're not afraid of cold cells nor ghosts?"

"We are not afraid of either," said Dick. "Besides, there is no fear of the ghost appearing, as there's no general court-martial sitting."

"I'm glad you said that, Dick," chuckled Dolly, when they were once more locked in the cell.

"What for?"

"It will put them off the scent."

"What scent? What are you up to?" asked Dick.

"I am going to do the ghost, Dick."

"Do the ghost? What for."

"It's a dodge that struck me all at once—how to 'do' the sentry."

"You mean to frighten him?"

"That's it. I shall get out of the hole, in my shirt, with the tails fluttering like the real ghost's, you know, and drop down on to the tub; and I shall be jolly well mistaken if the sentry doesn't hook it like one o'clock when he sees me."

"All right, Dolly," laughed Dick. "I wish you success."

Full of his project, and thinking it a famous joke, Dolly slipped off his jacket and overalls, and, with his "perfect little model" of a figure, only screened from vulgar gaze by his shirt, mounted Dick's shoulders and crept into the aperture.

Before venturing forth in his capacity of ghost, Dolly thought it best to reconnoitre the position.

The moon was shining, but as she had got rather low towards the west, the Avenue was thrown into shadow by the barrack buildings forming the front parade.

This was rather disappointing to Dolly, as he wanted the moonlight to make his ghostly person as conspicuous as possible.

"Bother it all," thought Dolly, as he crouched in the aperture, his teeth almost chattering in a most unghostly manner, with cold; the beggared sentry won't see me drop, and that's the most important part of it! The ghost always throws itself out headforemost, and to see a ghost or anything else do that is enough to frighten anybody. I ain't going to do that, though—I'm not such a fool as to break my neck; but if he could only see the white shirt, he would be too jolly frightened to notice which way I got out."

This was 'cute reasoning no doubt, on the part of Dolly! but he ought also to have reflected that such a state of confusion on the part of the sentry was only to be produced under one condition—namely, that he was a man to be easily frightened.

The success or failure of Dolly's ghostly enterprise all depended upon the state of the sentry's nerves.

That the sentry, however, might prove a man of strong nerve never entered Dolly's head.

He had made up his mind that the guardian of the gate couldn't be otherwise than "jolly frightened"—if he could only see the white shirt.

Presently, as Dolly's eyesight got clearer, he observed the figure of the sentry, standing motionless with the point of his sword on the ground, and his hands resting on the hilt, gazing intently in his direction.

"That's capital!" thought Dolly. "If I can see him down there, I expect he can see me up here. I believe he sees me now, blowed if I don't, and he doesn't know what to make of it! Won't the beggar cut and run when he sees me drop!"

At this moment Dick, who was getting impatient at the delay, asked—

"I say, Dolly, why don't you go?"

Dolly turned his head inside the cell, and said, in a cautious whisper—

"Si-i-s-h! You'll spoil all if you talk, Dick. Here's the sentry standing stock-still, staring at my white shirt, and looking awfully funky! Have you tied my jacket and overalls into a bundle?"

"Yes."

"All right, you can pitch it after me. I'm going to drop now. Do you think you can manage to get up by yourself?"

"Easily."

"Then I'm off!"

Before Dolly drops we must pay a visit to the sentry.

That individual was the old Gunner, who had asserted that he had seen the ghost.

He had only been a few minutes on guard, and it being the first time he had been on the post since the imagined supernatural occurrence, he stood curiously watching the aperture.

Presently, as he gazed, he saw something white moving in the hole.

At first he could not believe the evidence of his eyes; but, after a steady gaze, he muttered—

"There is something there. What can it be? Not the ghost, surely! When I saw it it did not stick in the hole like that before it pitched itself out!"

Being considerably puzzled, the old Gunner put on his "considering cap."

"If it ain't the ghost, what is it?" he continued. "Something material. And if so, what kind of material?"

But before he could come to a decision, the something white slowly emerged from the aperture, unrolled himself, and gracefully developed itself into a little human figure in a white shirt.

The next moment it dropped, like a flash of white light, and disappeared in the tub!

The tub in question was one of large size, belonging to the Commissariat Department, and used for pickling meat.

Since Dolly had first reconnoitred the tub, the cover had been removed by some one, and not having been replaced, the young representative of the ghost suddenly found himself in "pickle," floundering and spluttering in the briny water, and battling with sundry pieces of beef and pork.

Hearing the souse into the pickle, and the splashing and spluttering, the sentry rushed forward and peered into the tub.

"By jove!" he exclaimed, as he saw Dolly struggling in the briny compound, "it's one of the youngsters! The young beggar will be drowned."

As he spoke, he stretched forth his arm to seize the unlucky Dolly, but, finding he was out of reach, mounted on the edge of the tub, and leaned forward.

At this moment occurred a sad calamity.

Anxious to follow Dolly as quickly as possible, that young adventurer had no sooner disappeared than Dick, pitching Dolly's bundle of clothes through the aperture, sprang up and followed it, and, without stopping to reconnoitre, lowered himself and dropped.

The bundle descended on the head of the sentry, who, losing his balance, took a sudden and unexpected dive into the brine, in which he was immediately followed by Dick.

Never before, surely, did three fellows ever get in such a "pickle!"

After a great deal of splashing and struggling, Dick was the first to scramble out. Then Dolly, looking like a young porker pickled whole, was handed out by the sentry.

The latter, who was already blind of one eye, had the other temporarily darkened by brine, and, thinking it best to attend to his only optic before attending to his legs, remained in the tub for that purpose.

Dick, being the last to fall in the tub, escaped with a salting about the overalls and part of his jacket, whilst the personator of the ghost—the "perfect little model" of a Dolly, was in a pretty plight.

"Oh, lor!" cried Dolly, as he sank on the ground in a sitting posture, and leaned against the tub. "This is a regular take in, and no mistake! I believe I shall be blind with this blessed brine! A pretty go that will be? Just fancy my sightless orbs, looking like a couple of pickled onions!"

"Don't talk nonsense, Dolly," said Dick, who was nearly convulsed with laughter at Dolly's comical appearance. "Your eyes will be all right in a few minutes. They are only smarting a little. Hadn't we better make a bolt through the gate?" he added, in an undertone, "before the sentry gets out of the tub?"

"But where are my clothes?" asked Dolly.

"Here they are," whispered Dick, taking up the bundle. "Come along."

"But I can't go out of the gate in only my shirt!" said Dolly.

"Yes, you can," returned Dick; "we will find a place near where you can dress. Come along!"

Thus urged, Dolly rose, and shuffled his way after Dick, feeling awfully chilly and dreadfully modest in his airy costume of the ghost.

CHAPTER XII.

WHAT HAPPENED IN THE SCHOOLHOUSE AFTER DICK AND DOLLY WERE SENT TO THE BLACK HOLE.—A WHOLESALE ESCAPE.—FIRE.

LEAVING Dick and Dolly to turn up presently, we must return to the schoolhouse, and see what happened there after these two young gentlemen were safely, as the General imagined, lodged in the Black Hole.

A decree had gone forth from the General, and there was much excitement amongst the boys in consequence.

The decree was simply this—that, for taking part in the outrage on the Sergeant, and giving expression to the satisfaction they experienced at the hoisting of the General, the boys were to be confined to the square for seven days, and to be kept at incessant lessons and drill.

There was much grumbling and a general inclination to mutiny—to refuse to do lessons and drill.

Now that Dick was out of the way, Tom Sheppard took the leadership of the School *pro tem.*, and in virtue of the authority which that position gave him, he summoned the boys to his room, and, mounting on a form, thus addressed them—

"Look here, chaps, of course you all agree with me that this decree is a precious jolly hard one?"

"We do!" came the unanimous response.

"Now just answer me a few questions. I ask, didn't the Sergeant deserve what he got?"

"Yes! Yes!"—with some laughter.

"Do you think Dick would have blown him away from the gun without a proper motive?"

"No! No!"—"Of course not!"—"Trust Dick for that!"

These expressions were rather ironically given, and caused much laughter.

"Very well, then," continued Tom, with a comical look of mock-gravity; "why did Dick blow our respected pedagogue from the gun?"

"For a lark!"

This was shouted out by a little boy with a very shrill voice, and was received with great laughter, which was continued as Tom remarked—

"No, no, youngster; that would constitute an improper motive!"

When silence permitted Tom to be heard, he proceeded.

"Dick's motive was to test the Sergeant's pluck. The Sergeant is always boasting how splendidly he can stand fire; you all know that?"

"Yes! Yes!"

"He's always at it!"

"Well, Dick resolved to test him; and he did. You all saw with what result."

The reply to this was a loud and continuous roar of laughter.

"We now know what the Sergeant's boasting is worth; and you will all acknowledge that Dick deserves our thanks?"

"Yes! Yes!" accompanied by laughter and clapping of hands.

"Again," continued Tom, "Dick had two motives for marching the Sergeant to the 'Rogue's March.' What do you think they were?"

"To warm the Sergeant's 'Oh, no, we never mention it!'" sang out the little boy with the shrill voice.

This poetical definition of the nature of the Sergeant's castigation was received with screaming laughter, in which Tom joined.

"The youngster is about right there," he continued; "and the objects of the warming were to punish the Sergeant for his paltry exhibition of fear, and to revenge Dolly Swaps. Then, so far, you all agree that our conduct has been praiseworthy rather than censurable?"

"Yes! Yes!"

"Oh—of course!"

"Then, with regard to the General. Who could have helped laughing to see him hanging in that ridiculous fashion to the end of the chain?"

"It was enough to make a pig laugh!" cried the boy with the shrill voice.

"So it was, my little squeaker!" said Tom, amidst great laughter; "and, therefore, I say it is a shame to confine us, metaphorically speaking, like pigs in a sty!"

"Yes!"—"It is!"—"It's a beastly shame!"

Here the little boy with the shrill voice caused more laughter by observing—

"I wouldn't care if we were treated like pigs, and had no lessons nor drill."

"Well, chaps," continued Tom, "I must say that all work and no play for seven days is jolly miserable to contemplate; but, although we don't deserve such punishment—as I think I have logically proved—I would not propose our sticking out and against lessons and drill."

"But why should we be punished for nothing?" cried one.

This question was followed by cries of—

"Hear! hear!?"

"Ah, why?"

"I don't see why we should!"

"I quite agree with you, chaps," said Tom, with a knowing wink, "and therefore, I propose that we do something to be punished for."

This was received with cries of approval, and more laughter.

"That's the style, Tom!" —"Bravo!" — "What's the lark?"

"To attack and burn the Chinese Pagoda!" said Tom.

This proposal was received at first with breathless silence and astonishment; but, after a moment there arose a clamour of excitement which testified the degree to which it had fired their imaginations.

To enable the reader to understand the daring nature of the proposal, it will be as well to afford an explanation.

At one side of Bangfire Common stands a building called the Repository.

It stands in the midst of beautifully kept grounds surrounded by noble trees, and banked by earthworks, from the embrasures of which bristle numerous heavy guns.

The place is rendered more picturesque by the presence of a large pond, crossed at one end by a graceful bridge.

This pond lies in a deep valley, the sides of which are carpeted with grass of beautiful dark green, and velvety texture.

On one side of this valley, near the bank of the pond, the General had taken into his head to erect a Chinese Pagoda.

Of this structure he was very proud, not only as a work of art of extraordinary merit, but as adding greatly to the picturesque appearance of the Repository grounds.

The General allowed no one but himself to enter this sacred place.

Woe be to the daring wretch, if the General only found it out, who dared to put even his nose within the door!

"Oh, lor!" as Dolly Swaps would have said, "Better for that poor covey if he hadn't been born!"

Not even the ladies had the privilege of an occasional peep.

The Pagoda was guarded day and night by a sentry.

From these circumstances, a certain air of mystery surrounded this gorgeous building; and many there were who were burning to fathom it.

The reader will now be able to comprehend why it was that Tom's proposal to attack and burn the Pagoda was received with such astonishment and wild excitement by the boys.

There would be one difficulty in the way, at starting.

As though the General anticipated an attempt to break out of barracks at night, he had given directions that an extra sentry should be placed over the school to give immediate alarm to the Sergeant of the Guard.

It was evident, therefore, that, as regards their chance of taking the sentry at the gate by surprise and forcing their way through, it was quite a forlorn hope.

This way being cut off, there was only one other way left, and that was through Sergeant O'Shehe's room.

The latter was at the back of the building, and overlooked the cookhouse and a wall, over which access could be had to a "range" or road which led to the open Common, and the Repository grounds.

The situation was fully discussed, and ended in the resolve to pass through the Sergeant's room by "hook or by crook."

Tom Sheppard undertook to get the Sergeant out of the way.

"How will you do it, Tom?" asked Bob Jones.

"Never you mind, Bob," returned Tom, winking knowingly. "I'll manage it, right enough. All you have to do, and all the rest of you mind! is to go to bed after out-lights with your uniforms on, and stick there until I give you the signal."

Tom here took off his forage cap, which he had stuck carelessly at the back of his head, pitched it into the air, and, catching it deftly, gave the crown a tap with his hand, and presented it to the nearest boy.

This happened to be Bob Jones.

"Gentlemen," said Tom, bowing with mock politeness, "being desirous of investing a small sum in the Post Office Savings Bank, as a provision for my old age, I'll just trouble you to con-tribute towards that worthy object to the extent of one ha'penny each. Bob, pop in your coin, and pass round the plate."

Bob, with a grin, did as he was desired.

Dropping a halfpenny into the cap, alias "plate," Bob passed it to the next boy, and so, amidst a chatter of laughter and jokes, it went round.

"And now, let's see" said Tom, receiving the cap from Bob, and turning the contents on the table with a rattle, "what you have the con-science to think is enough for me to live on at the patriarchal age of three-score and ten. Keep off, you beggars," continued Tom, holding his cap in one hand, and quickly counting the cop-pers into it with the other, as they all began to crowd round.

When he had finished, he once more mounted the form and began rattling the contents of the cap, amidst cries of—

"How much?"—"How much?"—"What's the total?"

"How much, indeed!" said Tom, with an affected expression of scorn and disgust. "Two 'Bob!'"

The announcement was followed by shouts of hearty laughter, and questions of—

"What's it for"

"What are you going to do with it, Tom!"

"Never mind," returned Tom, cramming the 'coppers' into his jacket pocket. "What's it for? You'll know in good time. I'll disburse it first, and account for it afterwards."

At this moment, the cook, Soaker by name, entered the room with the tea—contained in a three gallon tin—and there was a general rush for basins.

Whilst the tea was being served out and the row going on, Bob took the opportunity of sounding Tom as to what he was going to do with the money.

"It's for 'swipes,' Bob."

"'Swipes'? Who for?"

"Soaker and Gobble."

"What's the dodge, Tom?"

"I want the key of the cook-house, and I'm going to entertain our respected cooks with a belly-full of porter. See!"

"What do you want the key of the cook-house for, Tom?"

"I'm going to try and shut up the Ser-geant!"

"By jingo! I see," chuckled Bob. "Do you think you'll succeed?"

"It won't be my fault if I don't, Bob," re-turned Tom, with a wink.

When the tea had been ladled out, and the cook was at liberty, Tom, who had taken a seat at the end of the table next to that greasy indi-vidual, nudged his arm, and beckoned him to a whisper—

"I say, Soaker, don't be in a hurry to shut up the cook-house to-night."

"Why, what's up, Tom?" asked Soaker in the same tone, and looking askance at him with his moist and "fishy" eyes.

"Got a gallon of 'wet' coming," returned Tom, with a sly wink. "We've made a sub-scription to stand treat to you and old Gobble."

"All right, Tom, we'll be there."

"I say, you'll keep dark, you know—eh? It's only for you two."

Soaker gave an assuring nod, and asked—

"What time?"

"After roll-call."

Soaker gave another nod of intelligence and satisfaction, and then went into the other room to communicate the good news to his chum, Gobble.

Tom's plan was to get on the "soft side" of the two cooks, induce them to leave the key of the cook-house in the door, and, after check-roll —about midnight—to enter the Sergeant's room, wake the occupant, whom he guessed would be too "fuddled" to see through the trick, and persuade him to go to the cook-house on the pretence that he had discovered something mys-terious in the place used for gastronomic pur-poses.

Tom allowed his plan to leak out during the evening, and, as an inevitable consequence, there was plenty of speculative excitement amongst the boys as to the success or failure of the ruse.

The Sergeant had gone into the town to drown (as we elsewhere intimated), his chagrin and mortification in potent liquor.

A few minutes before roll-call, Tom, as he was not allowed to leave the square, bribed one of the men with a "pot" of porter to fetch a gallon of that beverage from the canteen; and, then waiting until the roll had been called, he slipped with it to the cook-house, where the cooks, called Soak and Gob for short, were eagerly waiting his appearance.

"Here you are," said Tom, shutting the door carefully and depositing the can on the copper range; "go ahead, my beauties."

Soak and Gob each filled a basin and tossed it off.

"Better have a wet, Tom," said Soak, as he wiped his moustache with his bare arm.

"No, thank'ee," said Tom; "I must be off. Here's some bacca," putting down an ounce of nigger-head, "and I hope you'll enjoy that and the swipes. I say," he added, in a confidential tone, before disappearing, "don't you chaps think you could manage to leave the key in the door to-night—eh?"

"I thought there was something in the wind," said Gob. "What's up, Tom?"

"Why, we're up to another lark on the Ser-geant, Gob—see?"

"You're not going to 'cook his goose' quite, Tom, I hope—eh?" said Gob, laughing at his own wit.

"No, not quite, Gob. Don't be afraid," grinned Tom.

"All right, then. Off you go."

It is needless to say how delighted the boys were at Tom's success thus far, or how eagerly they awaited the return of the Sergeant, and the result of Tom's experiment. Suffice it to say, they all got into bed with their uniforms on, as Tom had directed, and awaited the moment for action with as much patience as they could muster—and that was not much, you may be sure.

At length they heard the Sergeant open the schoolhouse door, and stagger along the passage to his room.

The excitement now became intense, all the more so from the necessity they were under of subduing it, as Tom's success depended in a great measure on his being undisturbed.

If any noise had reached the sentry posted under the window, the fat would have been in the fire immediately.

Allowing sufficient time to elapse for the Ser-geant to get to sleep, Tom quietly approached the room, opened the door and peeped in.

By the faint light of the moon, Tom could see that the Sergeant was asleep.

"Snoring like old boots," chuckled Tom.

Tom first of all opened the window and looked towards the cook-house.

The place was in darkness, but Tom fancied he could hear sounds proceeding from the building.

Tom listened.

"It's Soak and Gob singing, I do believe," muttered Tom; "I'd no idea they would stick there so long. However, it doesn't matter; I"ll leave the three of 'em to fight it out, like the Kilkenny cats."

Tom then approached the bed, and giving the Sergeant a preliminary crack on the nose, seized him by the shoulders, and whilst vigorously shaking him, cried—

"Hi! Sergeant! I say, Sergeant? Sergeant! Rouse! Rouse!"

But so successful had the Sergeant been in drowning his chagrin and mortification in the water of oblivion (rum was his favourite water) that Tom may just as well have shouted and tugged away at a block of wood.

"By jingo, he *is* awful 'tight,'" commented Tom, as he panted with his exertions. "I wouldn't have given those beggars the beer if I'd known he'd got so screwed as this. We can all get through without fear of disturbing his innocent slumbers."

"How shall I bring him to?" muttered Tom, looking round.

His eyes fell upon the water-jug, and, seizing upon this, Tom held it over the Sergeant's face, and allowed the water to run out slowly.

In a minute the effect was visible.

The Sergeant's features began to twitch, then his head to roll from side to side, accompanied by spitting puffs and half-choking gasps; then his eyes opened, but only to close again quicker than they had opened as the cold water splashed into them.

At last he sat up, feeling his saturated face, head, and shirt, and blinking his eyes in a state of drunken bewilderment.

"Wha the devil isht!" he muttered. "Rain! Splendish nisht when I come shin. It's cussed storm sposh, and water coming inst through the confouned roofsh!"

"Come, I say, Sergeant," said Tom, who thoroughly enjoyed his victim's bewilderment, "turn out quick, there's somebody kicking up a row in the cook-house. It's not raining. I was obliged to souse you, you slept so soundly."

"Wha's that shay? Shomsbody's kicking up rowsh in cook shoush? Confoun their impeshense! who ish it?"

"Soaker and Gobble, I think," said Tom, getting drunk. "You'd better come before the General finds it out."

As Tom imagined it would, the mention of the General had a magic effect upon the Sergeant's movements.

The latter had no sooner heard it than, rising to his feet, he asked for his trousers.

"Never mind dressing, Sergeant," said Tom, "There's no time for that. Come on as you are. This way,"—and seizing him by the arm, Tom began pulling the unsteady pedagogue towards the window.

In less than a minute the yard was crossed.

Opening the door of the cook-house, Tom gave the Sergeant a push that sent him sprawling on to the floor, banged-to the door, hastily locked

it, and, rushing back, gave the signal—three shrill whistles.

The signal was quickly answered.

"No noise about it," said Tom, when they had assembled in the passage. "Go quietly to the third embrasure in the Flag-staff Battery, and get into the Repository grounds that way."

Then commenced the exodus.

One by one the boys passed out of the Sergeant's window, along the yard, clambered over the wall which divided the school-house from the "range," crept quietly into the Flag-staff Battery, and then, slipping through the embrasure mentioned by Tom, and in which stood a powerful gun, glided towards the great Pagoda.

So quietly was this movement effected, that the sentry failed to detect their approach, and continued to perambulate his post with the usual slow steps, humming the tune of a popular song.

It was necessary, in order to effect their purpose quietly, that this sentry should be secured or silenced.

Tom did not wish to use violence in doing so, and so he thought he'd give the sentry a chance.

Passing whispered directions that no boy was to move until he made a signal, and that they all should be in readiness to pounce upon the sentry, he quickly advanced, and placed himself in front.

"Hallo!" cried the sentry, suddenly halting, and opening his eyes in surprise. "Who are *you?* and what do *you* want *here*—eh?"

The sentry clutched Tom by the arm as he asked these questions, presenting, at the same time, the point of his sword to his breast.

"We've come to assault and burn the Pagoda," said Tom, coolly.

"Come to assault and burn the Pagoda, have we?" returned the sentry, adding ironically, "Oh, indeed! we have, have we? And who may 'we' be, now—eh?"

"The School of the Regiment," said Tom.

"Oh, I see! Just so! You're a precious lot of beauties, no doubt; but it strikes me that you've reckoned without the sentry this time —eh?"

"No we haven't," said Tom. "The fact is, I've come to appeal to your common-sense. We've made up our minds to burn the Pagoda. The whole school is assembled behind there," pointing to the rear of the building, "and I've only to give the signal for them to pounce upon, disarm, and gag you. But we don't want to hurt you, so I offer you the chance of submitting quietly to be bound and gagged. What do you say?"

"Well, I'm blest!" exclaimed the sentry. "If this ain't about the coolest piece of cheek as Jack Oilrag's ever come across! Ho! ho! ho! Ha! ha! ha! Well, dash my wigs!"

Here the sentry dropped the point of his sword, and began shaking with suppressed enjoyment at the absurdity of the situation.

"Come," said Tom, "what do you say? The time passes. The moon is getting low, and the chaps are impatient."

"What do I say?" returned Oilrag, still chuckling. "Why, I say that you deserve to be allowed to burn the heathenish place, for the daring nature of your cheek! It beats the devil—he, he!—hanged if it don't! Well, I don't know that there's a fellow in the garrison would be sorry to see the outlandish concern down. It would knock off a sentry, and give an extra night in bed. Hang it all, whatever comes of it I don't care! Go a-head."

Tom then returned and reported the success of his negotiations to his companions, who immediately surrounded the sentry to witness the ceremony of his being voluntarily overpowered and bound.

The process was not accomplished without a good deal of laughing and chaff—the sentry seeming to enjoy the fun as greatly as the boys, his favourite ejaculation being—

"It beats the devil, hanged if it don't. He! he!"

When he had been bound hand and feet—straps being used for the purpose—he was deposited gently on the grass at a safe distance from the Pagoda.

"There," said Tom, "I hope you will enjoy the fun."

Having got over this preliminary so quietly and satisfactorily, the boys, headed by Tom, now proceeded to assault the Pagoda.

"Doors and windows," cried Tom. "Now we're about it, we must see the inside!"

The door and lower windows, however, were found fast and impregnable, and after a few minutes spent in endeavouring to enter, the first story windows were tried.

There were four of these, and the boys, not having a ladder they substituted their bodies.

From almost daily practice in the regimental gymnasium, they had attained the agility of monkeys, and in less than a couple of minutes they had erected what they called four "pyramids," by mounting on each other's shoulders.

Fortune favoured the pyramid, of which Tom formed the apex.

The window was open, and, with a triumphant shout, Tom slipped in, and found himself on a narrow winding staircase.

Groping his way down until he reached the floor, he hastily took some matches from his pocket, and struck a light.

A glance round showed him several elaborately-worked candelabra, with wax-candles.

Tom at once lit these, and then opened the windows to admit his companions, who immediately came swarming in, and began spreading themselves over the sacred place, peering about like a lot of rats.

The interior was very prettily decorated, the chief features being the panelling pricked out in blue and gold, with numerous small painted Chinese figures scattered about on brackets, and delicately tinted Chinese lanterns floating airily from the pointed roof, and the staircase that ascended in a gracefully diminishing spiral to the summit.

The boys were delighted, as a matter of course.

"I say, Tom," said Bob Jones, with a laugh; "we'd better take these images to decorate our rooms with."

"Or just to remind the General of his lost Pagoda, when he comes to inspect the rooms, eh? But there's an image worth taking away, Bob," added Tom, drawing aside some muslin curtains, which screened a large recess. "A Chinese idol! Hurrah!"

This discovery was greeted with loud shouts of delight, and much laughter.

"The secret's out now," cried Bob Jones. "The General's an old heathen, and that's the god he comes here to worship!"

"Not a bit of it," said Tom, who at that moment had opened a door in the figure's

stomach. "He comes here to worship Bacchus more likely. Look here! wine and cigars!"

This discovery was received with cries of—

"Loot! Loot!"—"Divide the spoil!"—"Fair's fair, Tom!"—"Pass the bottles!"—And the cigars!"

"We don't want the wines, nor the cigars,' said Tom. "I won't encourage intemperance nor smoking. But I tell you what we will do. We'll take possession of the idol, and have a lark with it."

"Bravo!"—"So we will!"—"Hurrah!"

"We'll set it alongside the figure of Victory on the front parade," said Harry Smith.

"With the General's cocked hat on," suggested Bob Jones.

"That would be a lark," said Tom; but what do you say to make a procession and play it round the town?"

"Capital! Capital!"—"Ha, ha, ha!"—"Jolly! Jolly!"

After more excited talking, the idol was taken from the recess, passed through the window, and tenderly—for it had now become a very precious prize in the estimation of the boys—deposited in the shrubbery, some distance from the Pagoda, and where it might chance to remain undiscovered until it was wanted.

The Pagoda having been now thoroughly explored, nothing remained but to set it on fire.

"It seems a pity, too," said Tom, "it's a jolly nice place."

"Much too jolly for such an old prig as the General," observed Bob Jones.

"It must be sacrificed now," said one.

"Yes, yes! Down with it!" cried another.

"All right," laughed Tom. "Fire away!"

They proceeded systematically, however.

The candelabra which held the wax candles were turned so as to bring the flames in contact with the woodwork.

This being done, they all bundled through the windows, and, encircling the Pagoda, awaited the result.

They had not many minutes to wait.

The woodwork, which consisted of delicate carvings—mere cobwebs comparatively speaking, so fine was the work—quickly ignited, and presently, the handsome building was enveloped in fire.

Then followed a grand sight.

Under the towering and leaping flames the Repository building and grounds, and the front parade and common, became brilliantly illuminated.

The sight was indeed grand and awe-inspiring!

The boys, appalled for the time at what they had done, stood looking on at the fiery work of destruction in silent contemplation.

For several minutes the whole extent of common and the front of the barracks seemed wrapped in a weird, mysterious silence.

But, suddenly the spell was dissolved by the quick, sharp, rattle of drums.

The alarm of "fire!" was being beaten in various parts of the garrison.

CHAPTER XIII.

IN WHICH THE USUAL COURSE OF THE PRO
VERB "JUMPING FROM THE FRYING-PAN
INTO THE FIRE," IS REVERSED—GENERAL
SHOOT, THROUGH RUSHING TO A FIRE,
JUMPS, METAPHORICALLY SPEAKING, INTO
A WARMING-PAN.

AT the moment the front of the barracks was illuminated by the flames from the burning Pagoda, General Shoot, with his household, was fast asleep, little dreaming of the catastrophe that had overtaken the fancy building.

From this happy state they were rudely roused.

No sooner did the sentry, who is stationed day and night over the General's quarters, hear the drums rattling out the fire alarm, than he began to arouse the General and servants by ringing frantically at the door-bell, and crying loudly—

"Fire! Fire!"

The sentry had seen the blaze in the Repository grounds, but, until he heard the fire-drums had refrained from giving tongue.

But now he did it so effectually as to bring a storm about his ears.

The General, it will be remembered, before retiring to bed, had indulged in potent measures to drown the remembrance of being made a laughing-stock to his men, by being hauled up at the end of the crane-chain, and being left suspended in mid-air.

This remedy for obliterating unpleasant reflections was successful, and he sank into a dreamless slumber.

By this time, however, it was now near morning—the effect of the potent draughts had somewhat evaporated—sufficiently for his half-obfuscated brain to be impressed with the fact that a most horrible din was being made by somebody, and that not far away.

He lay for a few moments trying to clear his brain, and satisfy himself that he was not asleep.

No—there was no mistake about it.

He was awake, and each moment becoming only too painfully aware of the fact!

Ring! Ring! Ring!

"Fire! Fire! Fire! F-i-r-e! F-i-r-e!"

Unable to endure it any longer, the General, with a stifled oath, sprang out of bed, flung up the window, and thrusting forth his head, exclaimed in a savage growl—

"What the devil's the matter? Who are you, sir? What are you making that infernal row about, eh?"

"I'm the sentry, sir," returned the man. "Th——"

"What if you are, sir?" interrupted the General, in a voice of thunder. "What the——"

At this moment the General caught the sound of the alarm drums.

"There's the fire-drum, sir," said the sentry. "That's what I wanted to let you know, sir."

"Let me know!" growled the General. "Take a different method of letting me know another time, sir! Where is the fire?"

"Yonder, sir, in the Repository grounds. Don't you see the blaze, sir? It seems like the Pagoda on fire, sir."

"What!"

This exclamation came from the General's lips, with a sound between a shriek and a bark; flames with a glance and expression of stupefaction.

The blaze was, apparently, in the exact spot where stood his much-prized Pagoda.

How long the General would have stood gazing at the flickering and waving pyramid of flame, at the same moment fixing his gaze on the it is impossible to say; but not many seconds had elapsed when he felt a sudden tug at his shirt-tails, accompanied by a shrill voice exclaiming—

"Whar is it? Whar is it? Oh, Lor' a mussy, we shall all be burned to death! Come in an' save me! Oh dear, dear!"

This assault and frantic appeal were most unexpected by the General; but his astonishment was something inconceivable when he found himself being forcibly dragged across the room.

But his astonishment was turned to utter confusion when, on turning his head to obtain a glimpse of his assailant, he found that the tail of his night-garment had been taken possession of by his cook!

The presiding genius of the General's culinary department—a lady of considerable fatty development—having been greatly alarmed at the ringing and cries of fire, had popped out of bed, tremblingly slipped on her petticoat, seized the first weapon that came to her hand—which happened to be a frying-pan—rushed upstairs, and into (by mistake) the General's bedroom.

Here, seeing the reflection of the fire, and a white figure leaning out of the window, the alarmed lady seized the loose drapery, and acted as has been described.

It was an unpleasant, not to say an embarrassing, position, in which to be placed. The General was helpless, too; that was the worst of it.

The cook was twice as heavy as the General, and he was compelled to succumb to the preponderance of weight.

"What the deuce—do you know what you are doing, woman?" cried the General. "Leave go!"

"Come along!" cried the cook, "come along, and get the fire-escape! I shall be burnt alive!"

"Fire-escape be hanged!" he yelled, "you must be mad! There is no fire-escape in the house! Leave go, I say!"

By this time the frightened woman, waving the frying-pan in her right hand, had dragged the General to the door, and, as he was passing through backwards, he caught at the doorpost and held fast.

The cook thus suddenly found herself suddenly pulled up, and turning, she screamed, at the same time tugging away with a strength that threatened each moment to carry away the tail of the shirt.

"Come on, if yer a man! Git the fire-escape!"

"But the fire's not in this house," cried the General. "Leave go, and go to bed!"

"Come along, you coward, an' git the fire-escape!" continued the cook. "You wretch, to want me to be burnt to cinders in bed! You cruel willin! Fire! fire!!"

It seemed now to the General, so frantically was the scared woman tugging, that his shirt-tail must inevitably give way.

To one of the General's naturally modest inclination, this idea was very distressing.

What could he do?

If he let go the doorpost, he would be dragged ignominiously downstairs, and yet, if he held on, the catastrophe he dreaded would certainly happen!

At this moment the linen began to tear.

"Confound it," muttered the General, breaking into a perspiration, "the tail's giving way!"

And then, in an agony of mind, he cried—

"Damme, you stupid old fool, will you leave go? Do you know who I am? I'm the General—General Shoot!"

But the cook's terror was, apparently, so great, that the name of the General failed to instil further fear in her mind.

She continued her tugging at the shirt-tail with unabated determination, whilst her screams and objurgations to "Get the fire-escape!" became each moment louder and more frantic.

The General could do nothing now but groan and await the inevitable.

Of the two alternatives, that of being dragged downstairs, or losing his shirt-tails, he preferred the latter.

A few seconds more and the struggle ended.

With a suddenness that took the General by surprise, he pitched head-foremost into the room, whilst the cook went flying down the stairs, with the shirt-tail fluttering in her hand, and uttering the most piercing shrieks.

Thankful for his release, and that his cook had not had time to witness the result—to himself—of the severance of his shirt-tail, the General hastily put on his uniform, had his horse saddled and set off at a gallop towards the fire.

But the General this night was destined to be unfortunate.

As he was passing under a wall, the summit of which was protected by formidable spikes at certain distances, the flying steed pulled up abruptly—so abruptly indeed, that, before the General could make an effort to prevent it, he was shot out of his saddle and sent flying on the top of the wall, fortunately alighting between two of the spikes, where he became a fixture for some hours.

What was the result of this untimely accident?

Unseen by the General, but startlingly plain to his charger, was a white figure under the wall.

This white figure was none other than that half-pickled young gentleman—Dolly Swaps.

Dick and Dolly had escaped just in time to witness the great blaze in the Repository grounds, and hear the beating of the alarm-drums, and whilst Dick went on to the fire, Dolly had remained to dress himself.

Hence the cause of the catastrophe that had overtaken the unfortunate General.

Now, Dolly had observed the maddened approach of the General, and was as much surprised as the General himself at his sudden ejectment from the saddle.

When Dolly was able to collect his temporarily obscured faculties, his first thought was—

"What's become of the General, I wonder?"

Looking up, Dolly saw something moving near the top of the wall.

Approaching for a closer inspection, he made out the "something" to be a man's legs in a state of violent motion, whilst the body of the man was fixed between the spikes, stomach downwards.

"By jingo!" chuckled Dolly. "Here's a go! The General's got into a jolly fix this time! Ho, ho, ho! He, he! Ain't his legs going it? And just look at his 'right-about-face!' My eye, what a jolly size! Oh lor!" continued Dolly; "wouldn't he feel a whacking on that ever. It's beautiful and tight!"

Full of the latter idea, Dolly finished dressing, and then sat down on the grass to keep watch over the General, who, struggle as he might, could not extricate himself from between the spikes.

"He'll keep till daylight," thought Dolly; "and then I'll bring the chaps!"

Dolly had sat thus, in delightful contemplation of the General's struggle, some minutes, when he was suddenly upset, and reduced to a state of suffocation by a heavy body falling upon him.

Fortunately, it lasted but a few moments.

As Dolly, almost black in the face from suspension of breath, sat up and looked bewilderingly about him, he saw a large, white figure—it had on a night-cap and petticoat, Dolly saw that—gather itself up, and dart away like a spirit, crying frantically—"Fire! Fire!"

It was the General's cook, who, afraid to stay in the house, had rushed frantically after the General.

In the meantime, Dolly kept watch over the General until daylight, and then, proceeding to the fire, where was a scene of great bustle and excitement—the grounds being filled with hundreds of soldiers, some looking on, others working the fire-engines, Dolly sought out Dick, Tom Sheppard, Bob Jones, Harry Smith, and others, and led them, in a state of high glee, to where the General was impaled.

Dick and his companions were not slow to appreciate this unexpected opportunity of retaliating on the General, especially as it could be done without the General twigging who were the operators, as his head hung over the other side of the wall.

Dick, making a sign for silence, was in the act of picking up a piece of stout stick, when his glance fell upon a large frying-pan, lying close to the wall.

It was the cook's frying-pan, which she had lost in tumbling over Dolly.

With a cry of delight, which he could not restrain, Dick seized with avidity on the flat, sooty-bottomed pan, and commenced a vigorous assault on the General's "right-about-face," which soon assumed the hue of the pan itself—a discolouration which sent the young rascals into fits of laughter, and almost took all the life and strength out of Dolly's body, causing him to roll about on the grass in contortions that rendered him anything but "a perfect little model."

CHAPTER XIV.

A LADY TO THE RESCUE. — THE GENERAL SUFFERS MORE AT THE HANDS OF HIS FRIENDS THAN HIS ENEMIES.

WHEN General Shoot found that he was so firmly fixed between the spikes on the wall, that, with all his struggling and wriggling, he failed to extricate himself, he came to the conclusion that he was the most unfortunate wretch in creation.

And, indeed, looking back upon what he had suffered within a few days, we are inclined to agree with him.

First, he had his nose nearly smashed with a terrific blow from a dumb-bell.

Quickly following upon this, he was nearly smothered with soot fired from a gun.

Next he was interrupted in a little tender

To the General's consternation the mad sergeant put himself in position for the cavalry sword exercise, and nearly cutting off the General's nose first go.—See page 45.

No. 4.

scene in the conservatory of the officer's mess-room by little Dolly Swaps, and narrowly escaped ending his military career by having his neck broken.

Then he was hoisted in mid-air on the end of a crane-chain, and exhibited to the public gaze a sorry and absurd specimen of utter helplessness and collapse.

"And now," groaned the General, "I have been roused out of bed by an alarm of fire, indecently assaulted by my own cook, pitched from my horse as though I were only a bundle of rubbish, and here I am, fixed between these d—— spikes! Oh, Lord? what an unfortunate devil I am!"

But the catalogue of the poor General's woes was, as we have seen, not yet complete.

Just as he came to the conclusion that his situation could scarcely be worse, commenced the assault on his person with an instrument, the nature of which baffled his comprehension.

That it came in contact with his seat with tremendous force, and that it covered a larger area than was compatible with the notion of its being a strap or a stick, he was painfully aware.

"What on earth could it be?"

And who was it wielding the mysterious instrument?

To satisfy himself, if possible, on these points, the General made frantic efforts to twist his head over his shoulder.

But, unfortunately for his purpose, the General possessed an exceedingly short neck, and, as his head hung over the other side of the wall, all he succeeded in accomplishing was, to bring the blood with painful effusion into his face—the whole effort ending in a hoarse and passionate exclamation of despair.

Finding it was useless to struggle against his fate, the General gave up the attempt, and Dick presently found the frying-pan descending upon a quiescent target.

There was no fun in this, however.

"How quiet he is," said Dolly, in a low tone. "You don't half lay it on, Dick. Give it to him hot, and make the beggar squeal!"

"I can't give it harder," returned Dick, panting. "Have a go, yourself, Dolly," handing him the frying-pan.

Dolly was nothing loth to try a "go," but Dolly was little, the frying-pan heavy, and the General's rear out of his reach, and so the first blow fell upon the wall with a metallic ring, whilst, at the second, the sharp edge of the pan caught the General on the calf of his leg, with a cut that elicited a deep groan.

This was greeted by Dolly with a grin and a dance of triumph, and he was about again to essay another "go," when a guardian angel, in the shape of the General's cook, appeared, to arrest the blow.

That lady was still habited in the costume in which she had seized upon the General's shirt-tails, but it was now a very seedy and dilapidated costume, indeed.

It had undergone a lamentable change.

From a pure white, it had changed to a muddy hue, and hung close to the lady's person limp, ungraceful, and saturated with water.

The lady's face was very blue, and her eyes were nearly started from their sockets, and, altogether, she looked the embodiment of misery and rage.

The cause of this sad change may be given in half-a-dozen words.

She had been pumped on by the soldiers engaged in putting out the fire.

As may be imagined, this treatment had not tended to cool her excitement and temper, and she was now returning, mad with passion.

For a few moments, the infuriated cook stood staring in profound astonishment at the scene before her.

In fact, it was a very interesting and novel tableaux.

There was Dolly Swaps, whose blow had been suddenly arrested, standing with the frying-pan poised at arm's length, and staring at her with a look of comic astonishment.

Around him, staring also in astonishment—"struck comical," as Dolly afterwards said, at the peculiar apparition—were Dick and his companions.

Dangling from the wall were the General's legs and hind-quarters, the latter presenting a very black appearance, looking exceedingly like a reflection from the bottom of the elevated frying-pan.

After a steady glance, the irate lady took in the meaning of what was going on—or rather, had been going on.

"It's them willainous boys of the School of the Regiment, taking liberties with the General's pusson!" she muttered: adding, indignantly, "and with my frying-pan, too!"

It was easy enough for the cook to recognise the frying-pan; she had used it often enough, and was well acquainted with the shape; but, from whatever indication she knew that the figure on the wall was the General (since there was nothing of him visible but his back parts), it is hard to say.

We only know that she did; that the treatment that the General had received filled her with indignation; and that, with a cry of angry reproach, she flew amongst his tormentors, making straight for Dolly Swaps.

"You young willain!" she exclaimed. "I knows you! I've heard of your tricks! And you're at it agin, are you! And with my frying-pan, too! I'll frying-pan you, you young wretch!"

Exclaiming thus, the excited cook, despite her saturated garments, kept close on the heels of Dolly, who, with the frying-pan sloped over his shoulder, was maintaining a good pace.

Seeing that all her efforts were directed to the capturing of Dolly, Dick and the rest stood watching the chase, and crying—

"Go it, Dolly!"

"Look out, Dolly! Round the tree!"

"That's it!"

"Double now!"

"Drop the frying-pan!"

"Ha, ha! By Jove, she's got him!" cried Dick.

This was true.

At this moment, Dolly's foot tripped in the exposed root of a tree, and down he went, and, before he could pick himself up, his pursuer was upon him, had seized the frying-pan, and commenced to inflict a similar punishment to that which had been inflicted on the General.

"Oh, lor!" cried Dolly. "What are you up to? Drop it, can't you!"

"Oh, yes; I'll drop it!" panted the lady. "Take that, and that. You'll go—a little shrimp like you—to beat the General with a frying-pan, ablackin' his trousers so as they ain't fit to sit down on anything with, will you?"

"What's that to you?" cried the wriggling Dolly. "What's the General's trousers got to do with you? Come, you just drop it, and leave go my ear; you'll pull it off!"

Dolly, no doubt, had got into rough and willing hands, and it is doubtful whether he would not have been beaten to a jelly if his chums had not interfered.

For a time they stood cracking their sides with laughter; but, when they saw that Dolly was being unmercifully pommelled, they rushed forward to the rescue.

By their united efforts, they succeeded in pulling the lady off her victim, but only to transfer her anger to themselves.

Enraged at being deprived of her prey, she darted after them, flourishing the formidable frying-pan, and vowing death and destruction to the first one she caught.

But the chase was in vain.

She might just as well have tried to catch so many monkeys; and, after a long series of dodgings and doublings, she gave up the attempt; and, returning to where the General was perched on the wall, sat down to recover her breath, and contemplate all that could be seen of the General's battered person.

Our young jokers, now relieved of the lady's immediate attentions, watched her further proceedings with great interest, taking care, however, to keep at a respectful distance from the terrible frying-pan.

If someone had whispered in the General's ear at that moment that a deliverer was at hand in the person of his cook, would he have felt greatly rejoiced?

We shall see.

Mrs. Macnamarrow, for that was the lady's name, sat for two or three minutes recovering her breath, and with her eyes fixed on the helpless form of her loved master.

At length, shaking her head sadly, she murmured—

"I never thought to see 'im in sich a degradin' persishin as that. He've a bullied me offen enough, an' we've had words that was putty stron'. Many's the time I've wished all the skin orf 'is nose and that a bone 'ud stick in 'is throat wen he've a called me an ole cat, but I didn't mean it really, an both on it would be better than this."

Mrs. Macnamarrow, much affected at the touching and melancholy spectacle before her, heaved a sigh, and wiped away a tear with the hem of her wet petticoat.

Then she continued, a change coming over the spirit of her feelings.

"Hif it was anybody else, I b'lieve I should larf, he-he-do look so redickliss! Oh, dear, I b'eve I'm goin' to. My goodness! Oh! he, he! O-O-h-h! Oh, de-e-ar! He, he! Ha, ha, ha-a-a-h!"

And Mrs. Macnamarrow, unable to shut out the ridiculous aspect of that portion of the General's anatomy presented to her gaze, sullied as the largest part was with the black off the frying-pan, gave way to the new feeling that had come over her, and fairly screamed with laughter, to the no small delight of Dick and his chums.

When the fit of laughter with which she was seized had exhausted itself, Mrs. Macnamarrow was struck with a bright idea.

Why couldn't she release the General?

"The spikes is ony caught in 'is tunic," she muttered, "an a few wigorous pulls, if he'll only 'elp isself, 'll do it."

Now it was that the General, who had long since given up all Hope of rescue, and had reached a state of mind which enabled him to calmly contemplate the prospect of a lingering death, heard a voice that brought back hope to his breast with a rush, and set his heart in rapid motion.

"Gen'ral, Gen'ral!"

Whose voice was that?

Surely he had heard it before?

"Gen'ral. I say, Gen'ral—can't you 'ear?"

There it was again!

"Yes," answered the General, "who is it?"

"Your Macnamarrow, your own Macnamarrow, Gen'ral. I've come to your resku; but you mus' 'elp me. Wen I pulls, you wriggle, an atween us we'll get you down. Now, Gen'ral, I'm goin' to begin."

The next moment the poor General felt his legs seized in a powerful grip by the ankles, and, immediately followed a vigorous tugging.

"Wriggle!" cried Mrs. Macnamarrow, "Wriggle."

It was all very well to say "wriggle," but the lady was tugging away at such a rate, that the General's legs were in danger of being pulled from their sockets, and his body was being drawn against the spikes, the points of which caused him excruciating pain.

The General couldn't wriggle.

But, exhausted as he was with his long impalement, the pain he was suffering restored his voice—

"Don't! don't! For Heaven's sake, desist, and get some one to assist you!" he cried, in a voice of agony.

"Nonsense!" returned Mrs. Macnamarrow, "we don't want no 'elp! Wriggle, I tells you, all you got to do is to wriggle, and down you comes."

"Oh, dear, dear!" groaned the General, as the lady continued to tug, accompanying her exertions with the advice to "wriggle," "this is dreadful!"

The General's sides were being excoriated against the spikes, and, at length, he wriggled to some purpose.

Unable to endure the pain any longer, by a mighty effort he extricated one of his legs from the grasp of his determined rescuer, and, striking out vigorously, gave the lady a kick in the face that sent her sprawling on the grass.

For a few moments Mrs. Macnamarrow was greatly bewildered by the sudden shock, and the fear entered her mind that she had pulled off one of the General's legs.

But, on recovering her senses, and observing that the General's legs were still complete in number, and dangling from the wall, the true state of the case flashed across her mind.

She had been subjected to an ignominious and vicious kick!

The thought of being kicked, under such circumstances, was too irritating to be borne quietly, and seizing the frying-pan, the indignant and angry woman commenced an assault on the General's person that was ten times more painful than the excoriating of the spikes or the castigation administered by Dick and his chums.

The General fairly roared with pain.

"Ah, roar away!" cried Mrs. Macnamarrow, "you're a ungrateful wretch! You kicked me, did you? and all becos I only wanted you to wriggle!"

It is needless to say how much Dick and the others enjoyed the scene.

They laughed till the tears streamed down their cheeks.

But they were destined to be laughed presently into a state of utter prostration.

The General's cries became so loud and continuous, that they were at length heard above the din of the soldiers, and the pumping of the fire-engines in the Repository grounds.

"Where does that row come from?" asked a Sergeant who was in charge of one of the engines.

"From the top of the wall yonder, Sergeant," said one of the men, "Don't you see that fellow's head?"

"What's the matter with him, I wonder!" said the Sergeant. "I never heard such a bellowing in my life."

"He's mad, I should think," remarked one.

"Or got the belly-ache, from the manner in which he's lying on his stomach," observed another, who was directing the hosepipe.

"Stop his row, Jack!" said the Sergeant; "turn the hose on him."

The next moment the General, amidst much laughter, was drenched with a strong jet of water, which, not only effectually silenced him, but, dashing over the wall, a second time deluged Mrs. Macnamarrow, and brought her frying-pan castigation to an abrupt end.

The boys now actually screamed, and rolled on the grass with hysterical laughter—all except Dolly, who was quite unable to roll, and sat with his back against a tree, his arms hanging helplessly at his sides, his "perfect little model" of a body shaking with inward convulsions, and his mouth wide open, gasping for breath.

"It's about the jolliest go that ever was," murmured Dolly, when he was able to articulate. "Oh my! Oh, dear, dear! I feel as flabby as a roley-poley jam before it's boiled!"

It was no laughing matter, however, for the General.

The Sergeant, noticing that the cries had not only ceased, but that the individual appeared to have become insensible, proceeded to the wall to see what had happened.

The result, of course, was inevitable.

The consternation that followed the discovery that the noisy individual was no other than the General, was intense.

Needless to say that, the unfortunate General was speedily released from his more than uncomfortable position, and tenderly carried to his quarters, in an insensible state.

Mrs. Macnamarrow accompanied the procession, loudly lamenting the sad fate of her dear master.

"If he'd only wriggled w'en I wanted 'im too, this wouldn't a 'appened;" she moaned, wringing her hands

———

CHAPTER XV.

DESCRIBES THE EFFECT WHICH RECENT EVENTS HAD UPON THE MINDS OF GENERAL SHOOT AND SERGEANT O'SHEHE.

THERE was plenty of noise and excitement, when the boys assembled in the schoolhouse that morning, after the events recorded in the two foregoing chapters.

And no wonder.

The Pagoda was entirely destroyed, and it was rumoured that the General had gone mad.

The story went that he recovered his senses for a few brief moments—just long enough to learn that his splendid Pagoda had been burnt by the boys of the School of the Regiment—and then he went off raving mad.

It was reported that he imagined himself still on the wall between the spikes, and that he had the Pagoda on the back of his head; whilst a lot of demons were banging away at him behind, with an instrument the nature of which he was trying in vain to discover.

The boys were willing to give credence to this report, as they thought that under the circumstances it was most likely to be true.

"I suppose the General will devise some kind of punishment for us, Dick?" said Tom Sheppard,

"That's already devised, Tom," replied Dick.

"What do you mean?"

"Exactly what I say, Tom. Dolly knows what the punishment will be, too; don't you Dolly?"

"Rather," said Dolly, with a chuckle; "Oh! my eye, don't I just!"

At these mysterious remarks, the curiosity of Tom and all the boys who were standing around Dick and Dolly became sharply aroused, and they loudly demanded an explanation.

"I'll leave Dolly to explain," said Dick. "Up you get on the table, Dolly, and proclaim the doom of the School of the Regiment."

But Dolly was not allowed to exert himself in climbing.

He was seized by a couple of chums, and in a moment was hoisted on the table.

Dolly's appearance was greeted with a loud clapping of hands, and much laughter,

As a model of elegance and symmetry, Dolly was much the same as when we had the pleasure of seeing him go through the extension motions, on that occasion which ended in such a disastrous collision between Dolly's dumb-bell and the General's nose.

His trousers were still too short, and just as baggy at the knees and the seat; whilst his arms, as usual, were much too long for the sleeves of his jacket.

After all his adventures, Dolly's cheeks were as chubby as ever, his nose just as much turned up, and his face, considering it had not been washed since he loaded the gun with soot, that his head had been in a pan of jam, and subsequently in pickle—his face, we say, was as clean as might be expected.

As Dolly stood smiling, and bending his ridiculous little figure with exaggerated empressment, he was again loudly clapped, and, amidst great laughter, requested not to be bashful, but to begin at once,

"Before making your hearts sink considerably below the waist of your trousers," began Dolly, "by telling you the punishment in store for you for burning that beautiful Pagoda, I must first congratulate you upon the able manner in which you carried it out. Tom Sheppard worked it out first-class. I didn't think his brain had so much——"

Dolly's remark was cut short by Tom's cap suddenly flying through space and alighting on Dolly's mouth.

"Take that!" cried Tom, "and let's have none of your personal remarks. I've sense enough not to do the ghost and vanish into a pickling-tub,"

Dolly's great ghost feat had rapidly got wind from Dick soon after he joined the boys in the Repository grounds, whilst the fire was raging, and a burst of laughter, in which Dolly joined with great unction, followed Tom's speech.

"Never mind, Tom," retorted Dolly, "if I hadn't acted the ghost, the General's horse wouldn't have been frightened and pitched him on to the wall, and we wouldn't have been able to pay off old scores with the frying——"

Imagine a pale face, staring eyes, open mouth, expressive of the most profound astonishment and consternation, and you will portray the expression of Dolly's features at this moment.

What was the cause of Dolly's abrupt stoppage, and his petrified, alarmed appearance?

Was it a ghost he saw before him?

Nay, something far worse, far more terrifying than a ghostly visitant.

It was the General!

The General, pale, haggard, wild-looking.

If ever a countenance portrayed mental distress, anger almost insupportable to the verge of madness, it was the General's at that moment.

As all eyes followed the direction of Dolly's, and fell upon that awful visage, an awe-struck silence replaced the noisy mirth.

When the General had recovered consciousness, and was informed of what had really taken place, he did not go mad, as was reported, but flew into a paroxysm of rage, that was akin for the time, to madness.

That story about the General imagining himself still on the wall, supporting his pet Pagoda on the back of his head, and surrounded by unseen demons assaulting his person with a mysterious instrument, was due to the excited imagination of the bewildered Mrs. Macnamarrow.

The poor General, beside himself with passion, would not be restrained.

He swore he would go to the schoolhouse and have summary vengeance on some one, and so, with his uniform still wet from the drenching of the fire-engine, and the black patch still visible on the back part of his trousers, he seized his cocked-hat, and rushed from his quarters.

As we have seen, the General reached the school, ascended quickly to the sleeping-room where the boys were assembled, and paused at the door, just in time to overhear Dolly's significant remarks.

To say the truth, the General had taken an inveterate dislike to Dolly.

Ever since the little fellow had witnessed and interrupted his flirtation with the lady in the conservatory, the General's heart was filled with an intense hatred of our little favourite, and he felt that, metaphorically speaking, nothing would please him better than to crush the obnoxious creature between his thumb-nails, like a chambermaid does a flea.

With such a bitter feeling raging in his breast, the General's sensations on beholding the object of his hatred cheekily perched on a table, glorifying in the part he had taken in the personal outrage, can easily be imagined.

The expression of deadly animosity in the General's eyes, as he fixed them upon Dolly, was plainly observable to all the boys.

The thought that passed through every mind was—

"If he isn't mad, he looks like it!"

Dolly seemed petrified, and felt cold as marble.

He didn't like the baleful light in the General's eyes fixed upon him with the fascinating glance of the rattlesnake!

And now came a few intensely sensational moments.

The General, keeping his eyes fixed upon Dolly, began to advance slowly, with the soft, gliding tread of a stage-ghost.

Dolly was conscious of the stealthy approach of his enemy.

He saw the General's gliding, forward movement, but, though he felt that peculiar creeping sensation of the blood, that deadened feeling of the brain, which we experience, at times, at the sudden approach of danger, Dolly was unable to make an attempt to fly.

He felt like one under the paralysing influence of nightmare.

Dolly would have flown, and been at that moment only too glad to creep into any hole that would admit his little body; but, in spite of his wish, Dolly stood staring, open-mouthed, and wide-open eyed at the stealthily approaching General.

The situation was intensely dramatic.

Would the General maintain his fascination over Dolly's faculties to the last moment? or would Dolly, at the last moment, shake off the fascination, and disappoint the General by a beautiful dodge?

These were interesting queries, but neither of them was destined to be solved.

Just as the General had reached half-way across the floor he was arrested by a wild, prolonged laugh on the landing, and the next moment the figure of a man, habited only in his night-shirt, displaying a pair of blackened eyes, with hair wildly dishevelled, entered the room with a drawn sword in his hand.

This extraordinary-looking figure was waving the formidable weapon over his head, accompanied by wild laughter, in a manner that instantly caused two-thirds of the boys to seek shelter under the beds, made the General involuntarily back against the wall, whilst Dolly, anxious to get out of way as quickly as possible, climbed on the bread-shelf, which, being just over his head as he stood on the table, he was able to reach.

From this perch, Dolly looked down on the scene which followed.

Who was this madman—for mad he was—who had thus so suddenly entered the room?

None other than the poor schoolmaster—Sergeant Dennis O'Shehe!

With his incarceration in the cook-house, the events of the past few days had turned the poor fellow's brain.

He was fortunate, in fact, that his brains had not been knocked out.

The Sergeant had no sooner been locked in the cook-house, and had regained his feet, than he found himself engaged in a desperate fight with the two drunken cooks, Soaker and Gobble.

The result was two fearful black eyes, and the loss of his reason.

After he had indulged in his laughter and waving of the sword for a couple of minutes, the mad Sergeant fixed his eyes on the General,

"Ah, ah, old cock!—my beauty!—my tulip

—my rose!—my old Rajah of Rumbletumble! How's your liver—eh? Ha, ha! How's your ——? I say" (suddenly lowering his voice, and speaking in a confidential tone) "would you like to see me go through the sword exercise? Cuts and points combined? Then stand where you are. Don't wince! There's no fear; I can deliver the cuts and points within a hair's breadth of your nose! Now!"

And, to the General's consternation, the mad Sergeant put himself in position for the cavalry sword exercise, and, commencing at the first part went through the whole, finishing with the "pursuing practice."

Never before was the General in such a dangerous position.

All he had gone through of late was trifling in the item of danger, compared to having a madman before him performing the sword exercise.

The cuts flashed every second within an inch of his nose, and each "point" he expected would pass through his body.

The perspiration poured off the poor General's face, with the agony of suspense.

By this time Dolly, being safely out of the way, had recovered his self-possession, and sat on his perch, enjoying the exhibition immensely.

"I say, my Jerusalem artichoke," exclaimed the Sergeant, when he had finished; "what do you think of that—eh? Say you don't think it first-class, and I'll run you through the liver! Ha, ha! Ha, ha! Hurrah! Can you dance, my old cock-a-lornm? Come on, my beauty!"

And seizing the General by the collar with one hand, and waving the sword in the other, he compelled him to perform a kind of wild Indian dance round the room.

The dance ended, the madman again indulged in a wild laugh, and wild waving of the sword.

The General was utterly unable to help himself.

His nerves had been already unstrung with his adventure on the wall, and he was as passive as a frightened child in the hands of the madman.

The General felt that if this continued much longer, he should himself go mad; and he inwardly hoped that he should, or that death would end his sufferings.

But the General was not destined to go mad just yet, and his release came from an unexpected quarter—the madman himself.

Turning suddenly to the General, the Sergeant asked in a deep tone :—

"Do you know General Shoot? Because, if you don't, let me tell you he's one of the greatest scamps, the most bloodthirsty, murderous villain, that ever wore her Majesty's uniform. What do you think he did? He blew me away from the mouth of a gun, and now I'm the ugliest devil in creation! Look at my nose! where is it? Do you know General Shoot? Speak!"

"Yes," said the General, faintly.

"Do you know where to find him?"

The mad Sergeant's eyes glared wildly as he asked this question.

"Yes," came the trembling reply.

"Then go and fetch him, that I may run him through his rotten liver!"

And before the General could have offered any resistance, had he been capable of doing so, the Sergeant caught him by the collar, turned him with his face to the door and, giving

him a tremendous kick on the black spot in rear of his trousers, sent him flying on to the landing, exclaiming in a voice of thunder—

"Go!"

CHAPTER XVI.

THE GENERAL ORDER—GOOD NEWS.

THE summary ejectment of the General from the room, as described in the last chapter, proved a dreadful blow, mentally as well as physically.

To receive a kick (though the madman had no boots on) in the region which had already suffered to an alarming extent from the free use of a fryingpan, was about the last spot on which he could have wished to receive so violent an application.

But the General did not care so much for the physical as the mental pain.

To be made the victim of a madman, to the evident delight of the boys (they were grinning to a maddening extent) was almost too much for the General's mental endurance.

He wondered why it was his brain didn't "turn" on the spot.

It did not, however.

The General strove hard (and pretty successfully) to maintain his dignity; remained until the mad Sergeant was secured and taken to the hospital, and then returned to his quarters, a sadder and a wiser man.

When the General came to calmly reflect upon all that had happened, with a view to devising what adequate punishment he could inflict upon the boys, he was greatly puzzled how to act and, at length, found himself philosophising—

"I doubt whether any punishment I could inflict upon them would be adequate to the offence of burning the Pagoda," he murmured, "upon boys who are so daring as to commit an act of that kind for a lark, punishment would have little effect. If I punish them in one way, they will retaliate in another. It's a most extraordinary fact that they don't seem to have the least respect for me or the Sergeant. I wonder how it can be accounted for?"

If the General had asked that question of the boys, there was not one, scarcely, but would have answered—

"Because, General, neither you nor the Sergeant possess the dignity of mind and character which are demanded in men holding high command, or set to train up the rising generation in the way they should go."

General Shoot was incapable of accounting for this fact, and so he continued—

"They are a set of incorrigible young devils, and I wish to Heaven I'd never established the school; I can't abolish it just yet; but I can get rid of it from here. I'll pack the lot of them off to Gibraltar. Not that that will be deemed a punishment, I'm afraid! They'll be jolly seasick, though; that's one comforting reflection—the young reprobates!"

Having come to this decision, the General issued a "General Order" to that effect, and which Dick, a few mornings after the scene of the mad Sergeant, read out to the boys—

It was just before morning parade.

The boys were just ready for turning out when Dick mounted the table—

"Listen, chaps," said Dick, "I've something

here that will make your eyes sparkle, and your hearts leap for joy. It's short and sweet—

"Commandant Office, ——18—.

"GENERAL ORDER,

"The General commanding the troops, having decided that the School of the Regiment shall be transferred from this garrison to the garrison of Gibraltar, directs that the students hold themselves in readiness to embark at the shortest notice.

"(Signed) JOACHIM SHOOT,

"General Commanding Garrison."

Dick had scarcely concluded, when the boys sent up a shout that made the place ring again.

"Three cheers for the jolly old General!" demanded Dolly Swaps, mounting the table by the side of Dick.

"Now then. Hip—hip—Hurrah!"

"Hip—hip—Hurrah!"

"Hip—hip—Hurrah!"

"Once more! Hip—hip—Hurrah!"

"Another for luck. Hip!—hip—Hurrah!

Scarcely had the last cheer died away, when, who should walk in, clothed and in his right mind, but Sergeant O'Shehe.

The Sergeant was looking almost his own self again, a little paler than usual, if anything, but looking very smart, and fit to try another tussle with "Our Boys in the Army."

He had just come out of the hospital, and his appearance was a surprise to the young gentlemen, who no sooner caught sight of him than he was loudly clapped (they would have clapped their greatest enemy at that moment), Dolly Swaps demanding—

"And three cheers for the Sergeant!"

The demand was responded to right heartily, and the gratified Sergeant retired to his room with the tears in his eyes, murmuring—

"I believe the young beggars like me, after all."

CHAPTER XVII.

THE GRAND INSPECTION.—A GENERAL OFFICER NOT ON THE ARMY LIST.

IT was General Shoot's intention to "pack off" the boys at the earliest opportunity, and, three days after the promulgation of his general order, directing the "students" to be in readiness to embark at a moment's notice, he had secured a passage for them in one of the Government troop-ships.

The steamer was to sail the next day, and the General was congratulating himself on the near approach of the moment when he should be well rid of his troublesome "bantlings," as Mrs. Macnamarrow called the boys.

"It will be good riddance of bad rubbish," chuckled the General.

But the boys had not gone yet, and the General's chuckling was somewhat premature, as we shall see.

People should never count their chickens before they are hatched, and the General should not have chuckled until the boys had actually sailed.

As we have done twice already, we must once more introduce the reader to the General at breakfast-time.

On this particular morning there was a happy smile radiating on the General's florid face, and he was eating his breakfast with a good appetite, and without the faintest sound approaching to a growl or a grumble.

The General had nearly finished when his servant Patrick O'Dowd entered and presented him with a large, official letter, saying—

"Sint by special messenger, Gineral."

As this was no rare occurrence, the General was in no way flurried, but, opening it leisurely, read, much to his surprise—

"Horse Guards,

"——, 18—.

"Sir,—I am directed by His Royal Highness the Duke of Cambridge, General Commanding-in-Chief, to acquaint you that His Highness will proceed to Bangfire Barracks to-morrow, at ten o'clock a.m., for the purpose of inspecting the scholars of the School of the Regiment. The troops in garrison will also parade at the same hour; the whole to be in full marching order. The troops to be supplied with five rounds of blank ammunition.

"I have the honour to be, Sir,

"Your most obedient humble Servant,

"RICHARD S. LEATHERSTOCK,

"Adjutant-General to the Forces."

As the General read this letter, the smile was chased away by a frown, and something very like an oath escaped his lips.

"Thundering nuisance!" he muttered. "I thought I'd done with these public exhibitions of the young rascals! What the deuce——! but there, it is no use swearing; the inspection must take place."

And it did.

The next day a very brilliant and martial display took place on Bangfire Common.

At ten o'clock all the available troops,—the Horse Artillery, with their yellow-braided jackets, and guns; the 97th Highlanders, in their plumed bonnets and kilts; and the noble regiment af Scots Greys, were drawn up in line.

The School of the Regiment was formed up a hundred paces in front of the flag-staff.

Extending right and left of the flag-staff were hundreds of carriages filled with gaily-dressed ladies, attended by gentlemen—the majority of them quite as curious to see the Duke of Cambridge as the inspection of the School.

The General placed himself in front of the boys, looking tolerably easy in his mind, as, up to the present, the boys had behaved well, and he saw no indication of a pending "lark," nor any other unseemly kind of proceeding.

Still waters run deep, General!

At that moment two of the boys, named Dick and Dolly, were hidden behind the front row of carriages, holding by the collar a huge specimen of the Newfoundland dog, and which was impatient to be off.

The dog was dressed in the uniform of a General—that is, the scarlet tunic and cocked-hat.

What the two boys of the school were "up to," the laughing spectators could not tell, nor were Dick and Dolly inclined to reveal the secret.

Presently the firing of a royal salute announced the approach of the Duke.

"Here he comes, Dolly, said Dick.

"I'm ready, Dick," returned Dolly.

"Come on, then."

The two then pushed their way through the carriages, and, letting the dog loose, the animal trotted forward and took its station immediately behind the General.

As the Duke, with his staff, galloped up to flag-staff, the General gave the command—

"Attention! Present arms!"

The troops and the boys went through these movements with fine precision, but, to the surprise and great amusement of the spectators, the Newfoundland dog, "Pomp," at the word "attention," rose promptly on his hind legs, and stood stiff and solemn-looking behind the General.

So utterly unexpected was this incident, and so absurdly comical did Master "Pomp" look in his scarlet tunic, cocked hat, and carbine, that the impulse to laugh amongst the spectators, despite the presence of the popular Duke, was irresistible.

At the same moment, the General observed a grin on the face of each boy in the front rank.

So much had the General been victimised of late, that this, together with the laughter in his rear, sent a spasm of suspicion through his mind that all was not right.

He was too close an observer, however, of military etiquette to turn his head, or drop the position of "attention" until addressed by the Duke, so still keeping his face rigidly to the front, he muttered—

"I wonder what devilment the young cubs have been up to now?"

Feeling conscious that something was "up," and feeling very warm in consequence, the General tremblingly awaited the approach of the Duke.

Now, there is no more affable and courteous gentleman in existence than the noble and Royal Commander-in-Chief of the British army.

But affable and courteous as he is, he is also a thorough-going soldier, and, consequently, a strict upholder of discipline, and one who does not look upon soldiering as mere child's play, and he can, therefore, be stern when necessary, where the honour or morale of the Army is concerned,

The Duke is one who looks upon the military profession as too sacred a calling, of too great a national importance to be made fun of, to be caricatured and brought into ridicule.

When, therefore, his eyes fell upon the figure of "Pomp" standing at attention in the uniform of a general officer, and immediately in rear of the General commanding the garrison, a frown clouded his usually open, smiling face.

The shocked Duke saw open laughter all round him, but he could not give it his approval by joining in.

His Royal Highness formed the immediate resolve to discover the originator of the insulting trick, and approaching the General, he demanded, sternly—

"Do you know anything about this wretched farce, sir?"

"Curse it! I knew there was something!" thought the General. Then added aloud, "What —what farce, your Highness?"

"Look behind you, sir."

The poor General looked, and—broke into a frightful perspiration.

Utterly astounded, he gazed at the horrible caricature for some moments in silence, then burst out passionately—

"This is another of their damnable tricks!"

"I'll thank you not to swear, General," said the Duke, "in my presence. It's a low practice, and, consequently, ungentlemanly. Pray, explain whom you mean by 'their'—you said 'their tricks.'"

The General, whose face had turned a dark red with annoyance at the Duke's rebuke, took out his pocket-handkerchief and, wiping the streaming perspiration, said in a nettled tone—

"I mean the School—the boys of the School of the Regiment, your Highness."

"You astonish me!" exclaimed the Duke. "I thought the boys of this school were under your particular — your own personal guidance, General!"

"Damn them!" inwardly swore the General, feeling ready to burst with rage at the depreciating and ironical tone of the Duke, but adding, aloud, "That is so your Highness."

"Then, retorted the Duke, sternly, "if this is the depth of the respect you have only succeeded in instilling into their minds for discipline—the only kind of love for the glorious profession of a soldier—the love of casting ridicule on the service, I cannot congratulate you upon the admirable result of your training."

At these severe comments, made, too, within the hearing of many of the spectators and young officers, the General was ready to sink into the earth with vexation and shame.

"Good Heavens!" thought the poor General, continuing to mop the perspiration from his face; "I never was so disgraced in my life!"

"But I hope," continued the Duke, "for the credit of your military reputation, that this is an unusual occurrence, and that the state of discipline is not so lax as this would seem to indicate?"

This was put in the form of a question, but as the General was only too conscious that suchlike occurrences had only been too frequent of late, he was much too embarrassed to reply, and as he remained mopping his damp face in silence, the Duke said—

"Let us proceed to the school, General."

The Duke turned his horse's head to move up to the boys, when his attention was arrested by a peculiar sight.

This was Sergeant O'Shehe in full chase of that "perfect little model" Dolly Swaps."

Here some explanation is necessary.

The trick of dressing up "Pomp" in the General's tunic and cocked-hat originated in the fertile brain of Dolly Swaps.

"Pomp" was what is known as a soldier's dog, that is, a dog which attaches itself to a regiment, belongs to no particular man, but is fed and sheltered as joint property of the regiment.

A soldier's dog is generally very expert in performing tricks, as is only to be expected, where it has so many men who take a delight in training it.

These tricks are often of a very curious nature.

We knew a soldiers' dog which was trained to take its turn at picquet and guard-mounting.

"Jim"—that was its name—never had more than four nights in bed, and then, when its turn came, "Jim" would fall in with the new guard, march as orderly and gravely as possible to the guard-room, and take its turn at sentry, walking up and down with the soldier, and return to the guard-room to the minute at the cry of "Sentry go!"

"Pomp" was a dog which had been taught a great number of tricks, amongst others being that of standing to attention when the word was called.

When it became known that the Duke was coming to inspect them, Dolly considered it necessary, in order that the General and Sergeant should reap as much credit as possible for the high state of discipline to which they had brought the school, that some trick should be played to demonstrate it in an unmistakable manner,

Dolly thought of "Pomp's" trick, and spoke to Dick.

The two put their heads together, and thought that something might be made of it with proper manœuvring.

They decided that "Pomp" should be dressed up as a General.

It was not difficult to procure a General's uniform,

There was more than one Jew's shop outside the barrack-gate, where one could be had on loan for a trifle.

A General's tunic and cocked-hat were borrowed, and smuggled into the schoolhouse, and, on the morning of the inspection, Dolly and Dick took "French leave," and absented themselves from parade.

About the hour of inspection, however, they turned up with "Pomp" in the spot where we have already seen them, and at the right moment they led the new General to the front.

It was fortunate for the success of their trick, that the word "attention" was called just as "Pomp" reached the rear of the General, for it no sooner heard the well-known command than up it sprang into position.

Having succeeded thus far, Dolly became anxious to join the ranks to share in any fun that might be going on, and also because he wanted to march past the Duke.

"You'd better not risk it, Dolly," said Dick. "The Sergeant will be sure to twig you as you pass over.'

"Not if I get on the blind side of him, Dick."

"You can try it, if you like ; but I'll bet you what you like that you're caught."

"Well, I don't care if I am, Dick. I'll have a go for it."

"All right," laughed Dick; "off you go."

And Dolly did go.

He first of all got as close as he could to hear what the Duke said, and then, passing round the group, made an extended half-circle to keep as much on the "blind side" of the Sergeant as possible.

But Dolly had underrated the visual power of the Sergeant's defective eye.

Dolly had no sooner stepped out from behind the group of officers, than the Sergeant twigged him.

"Oh! Oh! Master Doll, it's there you are, eh?" thought the Sergeant. " I know what you're up to, my dear! If you think you're just going to slip into the ranks, you're mistaken—just a *leetle* bit mistaken! "

Here the Sergeant's frame vibrated with a deep chuckle.

Dolly, too, kept his eye on the Sergeant.

"He don't see me," chuckled Dolly. "He's too much occupied looking at the Duke, and General Pomp! Blow'd if I shan't 'do' him! I wish I'd bet something with Dick! "

Dolly had now begun to draw near the ranks.

A few yards more, and then Dolly, feeling sure that he was all right, made a run for it.

But at that moment, like a tiger that had been waiting the approach of its prey, the Sergeant, forgetting the calls of discipline, in the anticipated triumph of spoiling Dolly's little game, suddenly broke away from his position, and darted towards Dolly like a shot.

Dolly was taken completely aback at this sudden manœuvre.

He stopped, looking very disconcerted.

"There's a sly beggar," thought Dolly. "He has had his blind eye on me all the time! What am I to do?"

Dolly didn't [know what to do, knowing that he had no chance in a chace with the Sergeant, so he naturally stood still.

The Sergeant, seeing that Dolly made no attempt to escape, and thinking he had surrendered at discretion, reduced his pace to a walk, muttering—

"It's about the best thing you can do, my Dolly! It's a 'gone case' with you, anyway!"

But no sooner had the Sergeant come to a walk, than Dolly thought of a plan to "do" him.

He suddenly turned, and began running, a movement which brought the Sergeant after him in double-quick time.

In a few monstrous strides, Dolly was overtaken; but, just as the Sergeant put forth his hand to secure him, Dolly dropped on his hands and knees, and the next instant, the schoolmaster, amidst much laughter, was stretched on the ground, stomach downwards, his nose coming in unpleasant contact with a large stone.

The discomfited Sergeant was up again, however, before Dolly had gained many yards, and chase was renewed this time, accompanied by the laughter and comments of the boys.

"Go it, Dolly!"

"Double! Double!"

"The Sergeant is sure to catch him!"

"Of course, but Dolly will give him a 'winder' first!"

Dolly, it must be observed, was very well skilled in the art of dodging—"doing the fox," as it was called by the boys, and his twistings and turnings, feints and baulks, elicited loud cries of admiration from his chums.

Though the incident was amusing enough, and the Duke could barely maintain a grave countenance, he was much annoyed that such a thing should happen at such a moment, with the Commander-in-Chief present, and the troops actually at "present arms!"

"Who is that Sergeant, General?" demanded the Duke.

"D—— it?" thought the General, "it's getting worse and worse!"

But he was obliged to answer, and he replied doggedly—

"The Schoolmaster-Sergeant, your highness!"

"Bless me!" exclaimed the astonished Duke, "this is a lamentable state of things! Discipline and respect for the presence of the Commander-in-Chief utterly disregarded! and who is that extraordinary-looking little boy, General?" he added.

Dolly certainly did present a very extraordinary appearance just now, and this was simply produced by the addition of a busby—the sealskin, full-dress hat of the regiment.

Dolly's busby was much too large and, in addition to its nearly concealing his eyes, and quite covering his ears, it rested on the back of his neck, and was merely kept from falling off by the chin-strap, buckled tightly, nearly to choking, under his jaw.

With Dolly's short-legged, and ample-spaced trousers behind he looked—all busby and bagginess—quite a laughter-provoking "little model."

The General was heartily ashamed of Dolly at this moment, and felt that he never hated a boy so intensely in his life, yet he answered the Duke with apparent calmness.

"Adolphus Swaps, your highness."

A faint smile crossed the Duke's features as he heard the name, and he expressed a desire to have a close look at Dolly.

In the meantime, the chase after Dolly had been progressing in a very spirit-stirring manner, and just as the Duke spoke, Dolly, after dodging the Sergeant between the ranks of the school and round the big drummer of the band of the regiment, was captured.

The Sergeant, in order to reduce Dolly's known propensity for kicking when in the hands of an enemy, to the lowest possible minimum, carried him by the collar of his jacket (Dolly hadn't put on his tunic) and that convenient holdfast, the baggy part of his overalls, and, as though he had divined the desire of the Duke, advanced, and dropping Dolly on his feet in front of his highness, said, as he saluted—

"He's worth inspecting separately, your Royal Highness, and I've brought him for you to look at."

"I wanted to have a close view of him," returned the Duke. "He's a very little fellow. How old is he?"

"That's more than I can tell, your highness," said the Sergeant in a significant tone. "But to go by the tricks he's up to, your highness, it's old enought to be my grandmother he is."

A suppressed laugh passed round the officers of the Duke's staff at this, what the Sergeant intended should convey the comparative degree of Dolly's mischievous inventiveness, whilst the General tried to catch the Sergeant's eye to sign him to be cautious in what he said.

But the Sergeant seemingly only had an eye for the Duke, who, smiling, asked—

"Master Swaps is fond of playing tricks is he?"

"Tricks, your highness! He's a perfect little devil—I mean imp, your highness—at 'em. It was only the other day—and the General will tell you the same, your highness—that the young scamp tried to break the General's nose with a dumb-bell" (the General flushed with annoyance, and tried again to catch the Sergeant's eye; but the Sergeant, looking straight at the Duke, continued)—"and then he loaded a gun with soot, your highness, and fired it into the schoolroom, nearly smothering us, the General included." ("What a fool the fellow is!" thought the General, as he heard titters around him. "I'll try the ass by court-martial for this!") "And then, your highness," the Sergeant continued, "nothing would suit his taste but fastening the General—he's here, and'll confirm what I say—to the end of the crane-chain of the granary, and hauling him up for everybody to grin at!"

"Oh, the consummate idiot!" groaned the General, inwardly, as the tittering increased. "I'll murder him!"

The Duke bit his lips to prevent a laugh; but Dolly, who was watching the General's embarrassment, was openly giggling.

The Sergeant, still looking fixedly at the Duke, continued, as though nothing should prevent him from unburdening his mind—

"And the same evening, your highness, he was one amongst them to burn down the General's fancy Pagoda, yonder in the Repository grounds."

Here the General, fearing what was coming, and getting hotter than ever in consequence, coughed, and tried to attract the Sergeant's attention.

But it was useless.

The Sergeant had made up his mind to make a clean breast of it, and not even the approach of the regiment of Scots Greys, at a flying charge, would have turned him from his purpose.

"The confounded idiot!" muttered the poor General, between his teeth.

"But that wasn't the worst of it, your highness," the Sergeant went on. "I didn't see it myself, but I'm told that the young villains found the General on the top of a wall, where his horse had pitched him through being frightened at a ghost—the ghost being this young devil—I mean rascal—roaming about in his night-shirt, and that they maltreated the thick part of his person behind with a dirty frying-pan——"

Here the General, who was nearly dying with shame and chagrin, and could endure the humiliating position no longer, called out in a thundering voice—

"Silence, you idiot! Good Heavens, sir, are you gone mad again?"

The Sergeant was about to make a reply, when the Duke interposed, saying—

"I have heard enough! I am afraid," he added, turning to the General, "that your experiment in training boys to become soldiers has not, up to the present, proved altogether a success. There is no regard for the mainstay of soldiering—discipline; and there is no respect for you or your Sergeant. I should advise you to abolish the institution. I will now inspect the troops."

As the Duke rode off, followed by his staff, the General bestowed on the Sergeant a malicious scowl, and, shaking his fist at him, growled as he prepared to mount his horse—

"You fool! I'll have a reckoning with you for this! Leave that young rascal and return to your position, sir."

The Sergeant dared not disobey; but, before going, he tightened his grasp on Dolly's collar, and, lifting him up, shook his fist in his face, saying—

"Oh, Dolly Swaps! Oh, Dolly Swaps! Oh, my beau-ti-ful little Dol-ly! It's a bad ending you'll come to, I'm thinking!"

"I say, don't hold me up like this, Sergeant," said Dolly, in a half-choked voice; "there's the ladies laughing at me. I ain't such a beautiful figure, you know, that I care to be exhibited like dead game!"

"I thought it was a perfect model you are, Dolly?" returned the Sergeant, in a bantering tone.

"That's only what my mother says," replied Dolly. "But I don't agree with her. Let me down Sergeant. You're choking me."

"I'll let you down by the run in a second, Dolly. I hope the spot is soft just under you. But before we part for the present, don't forget, my dear, that the blessed lot of you embark this afternoon for Gibraltar. Parade at four o'clock. Don't fail to be present, Dolly, for I wouldn't be without the pleasure of your company for a big trifle."

The Sergeant nodded his head significantly, as he said this, and then added, suddenly loosening his grip—

"Now, Dolly!"

The next moment Dolly became painfully aware that his body did not possess the buoyant properties of a filled balloon; as, instead of floating gracefully off into space, he dropped quickly towards the earth, against which he came into inelegant contact with a force that caused him to hold his hands to a certain part with sympathetic pressure, as he picked himself up and passed through the carriages to join Dick.

"Oh, lor!" muttered Dolly; "I wish I was made of india-rubber. I should have popped up again without being hurt!"

CHAPTER XVIII.

DICK AND DOLLY MAKE A NEW, AND THE READER AN OLD, ACQUAINTANCE.—HOW CHING - CHING - HANGHOO - FUNKY - BUNG MARCHED PAST THE DUKE OF CAMBRIDGE.

"I THOUGHT you'd get nabbed, Dolly," grinned Dick, as that vanquished little individual came up. "That was good generalship on the part of the Sergeant."

"He can see better than I thought out of that queer eye," returned Dolly. "He did me that time. Never mind, I'll owe him one for that, and another for dropping me down. I suppose he thought I hadn't any bones in my body!"

"I don't suppose he thought much about it, Dolly. But, I say, what was that the Sergeant was telling the Duke? The General seemed awfully waxy about something."

"I should think he was, too! He had enough to make him! Oh, lor! 'twas awful good!" chuckled Dolly.

"Tell us all about it, Dolly," said Dick.

"Why, in the first place, Dick, the Sergeant said that he brought me up because I was worth inspecting separately. See what it is to have such a graceful figure," added Dolly, placing his hands on his hips, twirling round slowly, and making an exaggeratedly affected bow.

As Dolly, with an equally affected movement, resumed an upright position, he became conscious that he was an object of special attention and admiration to a young gentleman who was standing a couple of yards distant.

This young gentleman's physical proportions bore a remarkable resemblance to Dolly's, and were "set off" to the same admirable advantage —his little trousers reaching only a few inches below the knee, and showing a large development of bagginess "behind and before."

He also wore a jacket, the sleeves of which had hard work to keep below the elbow.

On the back of his head was stuck a little felt "bowler" with scarcely any brim worth mentioning.

On all these nice points, this young gentleman certainly came out strong, leaving nothing to be desired in the way of additional picturesqueness.

But his face was the strongest point—or feature—about him.

Talk about the countenance being an index to the character of the soul!—you should have seen this young gentleman's countenance!

It was the very concentration of consummate impudence!

Ingrained rakish impudence actually radiated from his staring black eyes, played about his long slit of a mouth, with its thin lips, and had taken permanent lodgment in his little turned-up nose.

His features, generally, were as flat as a plate.

At the instant Dolly's gaze fell upon this young gentleman, he—the young gentleman— who was standing with his thin pegs of legs wide apart, and had his hands stuck in his pocket, favoured Dolly with a wink.

Dolly was so struck with the pleasant appearance of the young gentleman, and so gratified at the expressive manner in which he had conveyed his admiration, as, he imagined, of his figure that, without changing his attitude, he returned the wink.

The young gentleman, evidently gratified that his advances had been so promptly met, quickly winked again.

Dolly, not to be surpassed in politeness, also winked again in the most elegant manner he could command.

The young gentleman gave wink number three.

This was again returned by Dolly "to the echo."

Then, so fascinating appeared this dumb, but expressive manner of conversing, that the conversation was kept up for nearly a minute in the most animated manner imaginable, both maintaining a preternaturally grave cast of countenance.

But, at the end of the time mentioned, the young gentleman suddenly collapsed and, leaning against the wheel of a carriage, indulged in silent, chuckling, serio-comic mirth.

"Well," said Dolly, sarcastically, and still maintaining his attitude, "when you've recovered, perhaps you'll just say what it's all about?"

The young gentleman, apparently recovering without an effort, suddenly advanced towards Dolly, and, holding forth his hand as though he were going to let something drop, said with a comic look—

"I say young feller, he let yer down a pretty buster on your 'rum-ti-tum-tiddidy-i-do,' eh? Ha, ha, ha! Oh, lor!" continued the young gentleman, opening his eyes and grinning as though the recollection afforded him the most exquisite enjoyment. "That Sergeant did it fust rate! He's about as clever at that sort o' thing as Mrs. Rumball. She's a stunner at it, she is. Mrs. Rumball thought nothing o' ketchin' me by the leg or the arm, or the 'air, an' droppin' me inter the fust recep-tickle as was 'andy. Sometimes it was the washin'-tub, sometimes the copper, an' she hev dropped me, inter the flour-barrel, an' wonce it was the ash-pit! She got so used to it hat larst that she didn't know when she did it, and it took me all my blessed time to watch 'er an' dodge hout of 'er way! She suffers from habsense o' mind in that way, does Mrs. Rumball!"

This extraordinary young gentleman finished with another knowing wink, and both Dick and Dolly burst out laughing.

"You're a jolly rum 'un, you are!" grinned Dolly, "and pray, who is this dear lady—Mrs. Rumball? and who are you?"

"Who's Mrs. Rumball? I guess as you'll jolly soon find hout *that* my covies," returned the young gentleman with a nod and a wink; "you'll soon be brought inter close culinary relations with that hestimable 'ooman—don't you know that?"

"What do you mean by 'culinary relations'?" laughed Dick.

"Well, I'm bless'd!" exclaimed the facetious youngster, in a tone of assumed surprise. "Not know what 'culinary relations' means! I'm afeared as they aint hattended much to yer horfog-ra-ffaged eddication, hat yer preshus a-cademy! Oh, p'raps, as yer aven't hattended to hit yer selves—likes it better in the larkin' way, I hexpects? Yer know what cookin' is, I s'pose, eh?"

"I think we know what you mean," said Dolly.

"Then 'culinary' is the furren lingo for cookin'. It growed from a Greek root, I'm told! Did yer hever see yer mother peel pertaters or scrape carrots?" he added, looking fixedly at Dolly.

"I think I've witnessed those interesting operations," returned Dolly, gravely.

"Then them's two of the rudiments of the culinary art. I'm well up in 'em, I am. Mrs. Rumball put me at 'em wen I was only a little cove—so high"—holding his hand about two feet from the ground, "an' I've bin hat the rudiments hever since, an' a-tween you an' me, an' the everlastin' gate-postes, I'm blow'd if I thinks as I shall hever get hout of 'em!"

Here the young gentleman seemed so tickled at the notion of his passing a lifetime in practising the two "rudiments" of the culinary art—peeling potatoes and scraping carrots— that he threw back his head and indulged in a spell of laughter.

It was contagious, too, and Dick and Dolly catching the infection, joined in, in sympathy.

"Then, I suppose," said Dick, presently, "we are to understand that Mrs. Rumball follows the noble profession of cook, and that she is going to act in that capacity for our school?"

"'Zactly! Now you've a got hat it! You're hall a-goin' to Giberalter, ain't you?"

"Yes," said Dick.

"That's hit! An' Mrs. Rumball's a-goin' too. A Gen'ral of my hacquaintance 'eard of the sittivation, an' got it for 'er. She's a awfully clever one at 'er business, too, I can tell yer," added the young gentleman, with an impressive voice and shake of the head. "She's one o' them as knows the art o' keepin' hall the tasty bits o' meat an' the mealiest of pertaters for 'erself. Oh, don't she just!"

"That's a nice look-out for us, I must say," said Dick, laughing heartily, in which he was joined by Dolly.

"You're right, my covies, it just is. An' you'll have to watch 'er precious sharp, too, on the woyage to Gibber."

"Ah!—why?" asked Dolly.

"Oh, I knows her little games, an' I can tell 'zactly what she'll do as if I wos inside 'er werry own mind this blessed minute. She'll try an' keep yer hall jolly sea-sick by givin' yer nothin' but the fattest and turned orf bits o' pork, so as she can hev the best for 'erself and Rumball—that's 'er husband! See?" said the young gentleman, with an exquisitely knowing wink.

"Oh!" said Dolly, when he had recovered from another fit of laughter. "That's it, is it?"

"That's hit, to a jolly big T!"

"Well," returned Dolly, significantly, "I don't think she'll have the chance of 'doing' us that way, What do you say, Dick?"

"Wait till the time comes, Dolly; that's what I say," said Dick. "Mrs. Rumball won't find 'Our boys in the Army' fools quite!"

"Hit does my 'art good to 'ear yer say hit!" exclaimed the young gentleman. "I'm glad to find as yer, my kids, hev got some sperrit in yer buzzums. Ah, the school I've just left was the place for jolly larkin'."

"What school is that?" asked Dolly.

"Why, it's called 'Garrison House Academy,' where they trains the 'young hideas 'ow to shoot,' has Sergeant McWheltem ses. He's the perprie-ter."

"It's a military school then, is it?" said Dolly, feeling interested.

"Well, it hain't a milantery affair like as yourn quite. The chaps is ciwillians, an' they gees thur to be drilled an' learned to be sodjers. An' don't the Sergeant wheel 'em into line hever! Oh! but some of the chaps is more'n a match for 'im, though! Crikey, jimminy, what rum larks I've seen done thur, an' 'elped hin too! Oh, lor, oh, dear! I be orf!"

Here the young gentleman, overcome with the exquisiteness of the pleasing recollection, sank against the carriage-wheel and gave way to an exhaustive fit of laughter.

Dick and Dolly were reduced nearly to the same state—laughing till the tears streamed over their cheeks, and they could hardly close their mouths again.

"Oh, lor," said Dolly, in a weak voice, "if he ain't about the rummiest card that ever I've seen."

Dick conveyed a similar opinion by nodding his head, feeling too far gone to speak.

"Oh, lor!" sighed the young gentleman, as he languidly picked himself up, "Oh, lor! Oh, dear! I halways feels orful limp arter one o' these hattacks, an' it takes such a little to send me orf. The werry thort of a lark's enuf sometimes. Oh, lor!"

After a short rest he began again.

"As for myself, I do-no as I can 'ardly satisfy yer natral cooriosity has to my hindiwidooality. I'm a mystery, I am. The Rumball's called me Joey Pumps, 'cos I wos found wen a babby in the trof of a parish pump—wot parish I don't know, as Mrs. Rumball keeps it to 'erself, and swares as she don't know my mother. But Mrs. Rumball's a deep 'un, I can tell yer. She keeps the secret o' my berf to 'erself becos she knows as it keeps my cooriosity hon the key V, an' perwents me givin' 'em the slip. She knows the walue of my services does Mrs. Rumball, an she gets 'em cheap."

"What!" exclaimed Dolly, "don't you get any wages?"

"Wages!" cried Joey. Oh, lor! That's a good hidea, that is! Why, I've never had a blessed farden from 'er to call my hone, yet."

"You get thanks, I suppose, instead."

"Not a bit of hit," returned Joey. "Why I don't b'lieve as she knows what hit means. Hall I gits is lickins in a wariety of shapes. The rollin'-pin I makes hacquaintance with *hevery* day. Sometimes she picks hit hup afore I'm aware hon it, an' gives me a sounder hon the 'nut'; sometimes she sends hit arter me like one o' them bummyrangs what the haboriggin'ls of the Antipods is so clever in shyin'. She 'ardly hever misses. When the rolling-pin ain't 'andy, she shies anythink she can git 'old hon! She ain't hat all partickler—she don't wait to see what hit shall be. Knives an' forks is has sootable to the hexigency as the pepper-box an' salt-cellar. She's smashed no hend o' basins an' cups an' saucers at that fun. But I keeps as fur away from 'er as I can, becos I *can* dodge 'em sometimes. She's so werry hartful, that lots o' times wen she've bin dishin' hup the dinner, an' I've been standin' close to 'er a-sniffin' hon it, she've hintrodooced a 'ot tater hin my hi, 'an dropped the 'ot an' greasy puddin'-cloth hin my face."

Dick and Dolly felt that in Joey Pumps they had met a most eccentric character.

Indeed, Joey had proved so amusing, that they had forgotten they had to carry out another lark upon the General whilst the School was marching past the Duke.

Dolly now thought of it.

"I say, Dick, we shall hardly have time to bring up the Chinese image if we don't start."

"I forgot that, Dolly, in listening to our entertaining friend here," said Dick.

"Perhaps he'll come with us," suggested Dolly. "What do you say, sir?"—addressing Joey.

"Hallow me to hobserve," said Joey, "that amongst friends I don't stan' hon no ceremony, an' submits to be fameelar haddress'd as Joey. Has I shall hav the honner of haccompany-in yer to Gibberalter in the capacity of factotum to Mrs. Rumball, I trust as I shall stand hat 'Joey.'"

"Are you really going with us?" asked Dolly.

"Honner bright!" returned Joey.

"That's capital!" cried Dolly. "I say, Joey, what do you say to being my chum, and let us work together, eh?"

"Wot do I say, Dolly? Why I ses, 'eres my 'and hon hit, an' perpetool wor agin Mrs. Rumball!"

"That's the style," said Dolly, "and now come and see *us* carry out a lark!"

"I'm ready," said Joey. "Give me yer harms, gen'lm?"

And linking his arms in those of Dick and Dolly, Joey strutted off with a great assumption of pomposity, keeping them in roars of laughter with his recollections of larks, and the oddities of the Rumballs, at Garrison House Academy, until they reached the Repository grounds.

The reader will not have forgotten the Chinese image that was taken from the Pagoda (on the night the latter was burnt), and secreted in the shrubbery of the grounds?

It was towards this that Dick and Dolly and Joey were now proceeding.

Dick and Dolly had concocted a lark, if it could be managed to be played off, on the General, independent of the dog-trick, in which this image was to perform a prominent part.

The idea was to support the image between them on a pole run through the body, and, if possible, get between the front of the column and the Sergeant when the School was marching past the Duke, and, in order to make the scene as impressive as possible, an explosion of gun-powder in the image was to close the display.

Accordingly, the preliminary arrangements were made.

A mop-handle was procured, and fixed through the centre of the image's body.

The powder, consisting of the half flannel-cartridge that Dick had saved from the charge used in blowing away the Sergeant from the gun, was cleverly placed in the head of the image.

To ignite the powder, a hole was made in the mouth, large enough to insert a stick of portfire.

The latter, they calculated, would last five minutes—about the time that would be occupied in marching past the flagstaff.

From this lark they anticipated two results—the awful rage of the General, and the profound astonishment of everybody, from the Duke of Cambridge downwards.

The difficult part of the affair would be to avoid being stopped in carrying the image to the spot.

This they hoped to accomplish by creeping round the Common, keeping close to the hedge, and waiting in a small plantation, opposite to which the School would "form column" from "fours," and commence the march past.

From this plantation they were to rush at the "double," directly the boys stepped out, and place themselves between the front of the column and the Sergeant.

Before entering the Repository grounds, they found that they should have more time than they anticipated.

"The chaps are being put through the 'carbine exercise,' Dick," said Dolly, "and you may depend the Duke will want to see them go through a few evolutions. So we shall have time to get round to the plantation."

"Plenty," replied Dick.

When they reached the shrubbery and drew forth the image, Joey Pumps gazed at it in great admiration, exclaiming—

"Oh, lor, wot a beauty! Wen that ere stick's afire wot e's got hin is mouth, he'll look just as hif 'e wos a-smoking'! What a jolly big chap 'e is! Suppose I get inside?"

"There's plenty of room inside, but suppose your brains get blown out, Joey, as well as the image's?" said Dolly, laughing.

"Why, that's not a werry pleasant kon-tin-gency to look forward to," returned Joey, "I must say; but lor, I dono as hit signerfies much. I ain't got many brains to lose, an' I ain't got no relations as 'll mourn my sad fate, as I knows hon. So hin I goes!"

Joey's incarceration in the image was not effected without a great deal of laughter; and when a hole was made in the neck for Joey to breathe through and take an occasional peep, Dick and Dolly took each an end of the pole on their shoulders and marched off, whilst Joey entertained them by the way with no end of chaff.

"Ain't I jolly 'eavy?" asked Joey, when they had not got fairly on to the Common and under the hedge.

"Nothing much to speak of," returned Dolly, who was puffing and panting like a steam-engine; "but if you wriggle about so yo'll break the pole and upset the blessed thing!"

"That's werry good adwice to a outsider!" returned Joey; "but yer forgits as this ain't a armcheer, an' I'm pretty nigh squeedged to death by this 'ere same blessed pole!"

"Shut up," said Dick, "and let us get on!"

Five minutes more they entered the plantation, and then came to a rest.

It was not long, however, before the strange affair was twigged by some boys, who communicating their discoveries to others, a curious and laughing crowd was soon collected.

That some lark was up the crowd felt sure; but Dick and Dolly kept dark, only winking mysteriously in reply to numerous queries.

In the meantime Dick and Dolly anxiously watched the movements of the school.

After going through some manœuvres, and firing a few rounds of blank cartridge, they saw the boys formed into "fours" and march down the Common, wheel round the left flank of the "line," along the rear, then wheel round the right flank, and form from "fours" into "close column" for marching past the Duke.

The Sergeant, full of importance, sprang to the right of the column.

"Eyes right—dress! Steady—eyes front!"

Then taking his place in front of the column, he gave the further words of command—

"Fix—swords! Shoulder—arms! Quick—march!"

This was the moment for which Dick and Dolly were waiting.

Dick struck a fusee and ignited the portfire; and, just as the band of drums and fifes, which was stationed opposite the flagstaff, struck up "The British Grenadiers," and the boys stepped out at a rattling quick pace, Dick and Dolly once more shouldered the image, and emerging at the "double," took up their position just behind the Sergeant.

As the boys were unprepared for this trick, it came upon them with a suddenness that was almost leading to an outbreak of laughter.

A cautionary sign from Dick, however, restrained the impulse, and the march past proceeded without the lark being discovered by the Sergeant, who, although he saw the troops in line grinning to an unusual extent, was too intent upon showing off his fine figure before the Duke to turn his head.

What the Sergeant could not see, however, the Duke, with his staff, and the General, *could*.

"What on earth is it?" exclaimed the Duke.

"Oh, Lord!" thought the General, with an inward groan. "Here's another d——d trick coming!"

"It's not a Guy Fawks, surely!" said the Duke.

"Can you make out what it is, General? What is that burning? It looks like portfire!"

The General was not sure, but he thought it looked very like his Chinese image.

"It can't be, certainly," he thought. "The image was burnt with the Pagoda."

By this time the boys had got within a hundred yards of the flagstaff, and the General, dismounting from his horse, said hurriedly—

"I'll go and see what it is, your highness."

The Duke's curiosity was greatly aroused, however, and, determining to have a close view, dismounted also and followed the General.

Seeing this, the officers of the staff also dismounted, and, leaving their horses in charge of some soldiers who were keeping the ground, hastened after the Duke.

The excitement of the spectators became so great that hundreds broke through the line of sentries, and came crowding round.

"Here's a go, Dick," said Dolly. "Ain't the General working himself up?"

The procession had come to a halt, and at this moment the General, looking awfully wild, came up, stared at the image, and exclaimed.

"It *is*!"

"What is it?" asked the Duke, who was close behind him.

"The statue of my Celestial friend, Ching-Ching-Hangoo-Funky-Bung, that I thought was burned in my Pagoda, your Highness! You villains!" roared the General, rushing forward to seize Dolly, who was looking on with a grin of enjoyment. "I'll teach you——"

The sentence was cut short by a loud explosion.

A cloud of smoke for an instant seemed to envelop the image of Ching-Ching-Hanghoo-Funky-Bung; and, when it cleared away, what was that which now occupied the place of the head of the General's Celestial friend?

It was the head and shoulders of our friend Joey Pumps, who, looking sternly at the General, stretched forth his right hand, saying, in a melodramatic tone—

"Yer wicked old wretch ter keep me 'ere a starvin' hever since yer left Chiny!"

The roar of laughter that followed from everybody—the Duke included, who had to hold his sides—was something indescribable, and the General, unable to face the ridicule to which this last terrible masterpiece of a trick had subjected him, did a graceful faint, and was carried off the field—vanquished!

CHAPTER XIX.

SERGEANT O'SHEHE'S INDIGNATION.—HE HAS A PARTIAL RETURN OF MADNESS.—JOEY PUMPS COMES OUT "STRONG."—DICK EVERETT MARCHES PAST THE BOYS.—WHAT THE DUKE OF CAMBRIDGE SAID.—THE MARCH TO BARRACKS OF THE "CONQUERING HEROES."

"It is quite time," thought the Duke, as he returned to mount his horse, "that those boys were sent to Gibraltar. The very daring manifested in these tricks, proves that there is some splendid stuff in them, but they want some tight handling, and proper moulding, and the best thing is to remove them for a time from the home influences of the barracks."

The indignation of Sergeant O'Shehe at these outrageous proceedings was considerably above fever heat. It had reached the boiling point, and he was suffering great mental agony in being compelled to "keep on the lid," to prevent it boiling over in the presence of the Duke.

But, no sooner had his highness turned his back than, bestowing on Dick and Dolly that awfully scathing look which he assumed on such solemn occasions as the present, and which he flattered himself ought to, if it did not, strike the young souls of the daring culprits with terror, he shook his fist at them saying—

"You young devils! Oh, so help me ten men and a donkey, if I don't pay you out for this when we get to Gib! Stop till I get you on the top of the rock, my dears—Oh!"

Here the Sergeant slowly nodded his head, the more emphatically to convey the awful extent of the punishment they might expect at his hands.

"Hanging, skinned alive, burned at the stake," continued the Sergeant, "will be nothing to what you'll catch! Absolutely nothing to it, so help me ten men——."

"Come, come, Sarjint,' here interrupted Joey Pumps in a tone of admonition, and shaking his head. None o' that now! Come! Them 'ere threats ain't haccording to milantary, law yer knows. Yer hoversteppen yer hauthority. Jist mind what yer hup to! An don't call hon ten men an a donkey ter 'elp yer, 'cos yer won't find 'em hon the top 'o the rock. Thur's nothin thur but monkeys——"

Nothing could surpass the look of astonishment with which the Sergeant was regarding Joey during this speech.

His astonishment, in fact, took the form of temporary petrification.

He had been impressing his threats on Dick and Dolly with his body inclined, and his fist upraised; and, in this position he was struck motionless.

The Sergeant, we must say at once, was more touchy than ever since his attack of madness, and he experienced, even now, queer sensations in his upper regions.

Occasionally, he rambled in his speech, and uttered almost meaningless words.

The slightest thing sometimes would upset the equilibrium of his brain.

It was so just now.

There was a species of impudence in Joey's words and manner that touched the Sergeant on the, so to speak, rawest part of his dignity, and that was always raw and tender.

It was bad enough to be cheeked by his own boys, but they *were* his own boys, and had a greater right, if they had any, to cheek him more than anybody else.

But by what right did this little imp of a stranger dare to thus address him?

The Sergeant could scarcely articulate, so great was his indignant agitation.

At length he mastered his astonishment sufficiently to stutter out—

"Si—si—*si*-lence! Meh—meh—monkeys, yourself! Who—are you speaking to? Deh—deh—demme, who are *you?*"

"Well I'm blest," said Joey, looking round at the spectators. "Hif hewery body I comes across don't axe me that question! Why, I dono myself, I'm werry sorry to say I halways refers 'em to Dolly—I don't mean yer, Dolly Swaps—I means Dolly Rumball, which I'm afeared thur'll be a clash in the name, an' one hon 'em'll hev to change. So hif yer wants pertickler to find out the hindiwidooality of Joey Pumps, Sargint, I murs refer——Ah!—Would yer!"

At this moment, the enraged Sergeant making a sudden dash at Joey, that individual forthwith dipped and disappeared in what was left of the facsimile of Ching-Ching-Hanghoo-Funky-Bung.

This disappearance, and the haste with which it was accomplished, produced a roar of laughter, but the Sergeant, who was determined to inflict summary chastisement, placed his face over the aperture to ascertain the exact position of Joey's head, with the intention of hauling that young gentleman forth by the scalp.

It was a mad thing to do—quite as sane an act as putting one's nose between the bars of a monkey's cage.

The next moment the Sergeant staggered back, holding his nose—something hard had struck it from the interior of Funky-Bung.

"That wos a werry orkard an' painful collishun, I'm afeared Sarjint," said Joey, once more sparring up, placing his arms akimbo, and making a horrible grimace. "Yer looked down jist as somethin' took me hin the harm, an' I couldn't 'elp hit a-goin' out. In coorse, I'm werry sorry hif yer 'urt, but yer so——Oh—yer would!"

This second exclamation was caused by a second dash of the Sergeant at his impudent tormentor, who, a second time, sank out of sight with wonderful promptness.

What the result of a second assault on Joey's "castle" might have been, it is impossible to say.

It was prevented, however.

The Sergeant was in the act of laying hands on the headless trunk of Ching-Ching, when he was arrested by the voice of the Duke.

"Sergeant—attend to your duty, sir! Get the School in position to march past. It must be done over again. Quick, sir!"

The Sergeant heard the command, but he was so much bewildered that he spoke in a most extraordinary manner.

"All right, sir—I mean your worship—your highness—forgive me, and God bless you! Is it the image your Dukeship wishes to see over again? It's lost its head!"

"And so have you, sir," returned the Duke, followed by a burst of laughter, in which Joey not only joined with great gusto, but freely gave his approval to the Duke.

"Ha, ha, ha! Well done, yer 'ighness!" laughed Joey, clapping his hands. "That's won to yer, that is! That wos werry good, that wos! I wos just a-goin' ter say that myself! He wants wakin' hup, 'e does. 'E don't seem quite hisself—rather staggery jist 'ere," tapping his forehead, "don't 'e? Come, Sargint," he continued, winking at his highness, "'ere's the Dook awaitin' for yer to begin! Now then—right shoulder forrards and left shoulder backkards—quick—mar-r-ch!"

It was impossible to resist laughing, and a loud roar rewarded Joey's facetious remarks.

At the laughter, the Sergeant was more than ever bewildered; he had a singing noise in his ears, his brain seemed stunned, and a mistiness was before his eyes.

But, feeling that he was called upon to do something, he took up a position in front of the boys, and began—

"As his lordship wants it all over again, we'll begin at the 'Stand at ease.' What the devil are you all grinning about? 'Pon my soul, I believe everybody's gone mad! Now then, when I give the words 'Stand at ease,' the left foot will be carried forward six inches, toes to the left front——"

"Ha, ha, ha!" laughed Joey. "Bless'd hif 'e ain't puttin' 'em through 'cruties drill.' Ha, ha, ha! Oh, lor, I shall be orf agin in a minnet! That ain't wot the Dook wants, stoopid. It's march parst, 'e wants. I shall have ter come and do it myself, I can see! Ah—would yer?"

For the third time, Joey considered it expedient to disappear within the protecting shelter of Ching-Ching-Hanghoo-Funky-Bung.

The Sergeant, stung almost to mad passion by Joey's last insulting remarks, once more turned to rush upon his relentless foe.

It would have fared badly, too, for Joey, doubtless, but for the timely interposition of the Duke, saying—

"What is the matter with you, Sergeant? Will you attend to your duty, sir, and march-past the boys?"

The Sergeant halted, placed his hand to his

Dolly's aim was true. The old lady screamed, threw up her arms, tottered a step or two, and
sank backwards on the band-box.—See page 59.

forehead, and looked around like a man just awakened from a dream.

What between the chaff of Joey, and the stern calls to duty of the Duke, he seemed hopelessly bewildered.

At this juncture, Dick Everett came to the rescue.

Seeing the state the Sergeant was in, Dick, who was dressed in full uniform, and really looked a smart, soldier-like, intelligent young fellow, stepped up to the Duke, and coming to attention, and giving the salute, explained the illness under which the Sergeant had but lately been suffering, adding—

"I know my drill, your highness, and will march-past the School, if you will let me?"

"Do so," said the Duke, smiling, and evidently pleased.

Dick then saluted, turned smartly to the right-about-face, and, going up to the Sergeant said, kindly—

"You had better retire for a bit, Sergeant, until you recover. You seem quite out of sorts, to-day. I'll march-past the boys, and march them home."

The Sergeant, who seemed really grateful for the release, said—

"Very well, Everett. I'll go. I'm afraid I've made a d——d fool of myself!"

It was not without a feeling of elation that Dick took the Sergeant's place.

It was the first time he had ever attempted to manœuvre the School in public, but he had great self-confidence in his ability to do it; besides, he was stimulated by the presence of the Duke to acquit himself creditably.

Dick felt that all eyes were upon him; but this, instead of making him nervous, only made him the more resolved to be calm and cool.

His chums smiled, as Dick took up his position, and Tom Sheppard said, in an undertone—

"Bravo Dick! We'll do you credit, old fellow!"

Before taking the School round to the marching-past point, Dick put it through all the movements by "fours," which were capitally executed.

After getting them to attention, dressing, and telling them off into "fours," he began, in a calm clear voice—

"Fours, right. Fours, left. Fours, about. Fours, left-about. Fours!"

He then put them through, "Marches to the right," and "Marches from the Right to the Front," by "Fours." "Sections," "Half Sections," "Single File;" also "Marches from the Right to the Rear," with "Formations to the Front," "Flanks," and "Rear," from "Fours," "Sections," &c.

In fact, Dick put them through all the drill, comprising "Movements by Fours," and then, marching the School from the left flank of the line by the rear, brought it into position for marching-past.

Dick couldn't help smiling, as he thought of the last time the School stood there in position to march past.

Dolly and he were concealed in the plantation, ready to rush out with the complete and blooming statue of the poor General's Chinese friend—Ching-Ching-Hanghoo-Funky-Bung.

This time, however, the march-past was to be accomplished in decency and order.

Taking up his position, he gave the words of command.

"By the right! Quick march!"

Once more the band struck up "The British Grenadiers," and the boys stepped off.

They kept their formation well, too; marching, front and rear-rank, in unbroken line, like two walls.

As they approached the flag-staff, step after step, with the regularity of clockwork, they were greeted with cheers, clapping, and cries by the spectators—

"Bravo! Well done, School of the Regiment!"

"Regular troops couldn't march better!"

The Duke was very pleased, and showed that he was so by the constant smiles on his face.

It was a splendid sight to see Dick salute the Duke as he came opposite the flagstaff.

It was done with the greatest precision, eliciting an admiring exclamation from his highness, and the patronising approval of Joey Pumps, who still occupied the headless body of Ching-Ching.

"That's not so dusty, that ain't!" sang out Joey. "Werry well done, hindeed, Master Dick, werry well! I'd reck-kommend yer to 'Er Majesty, fur a commission, hif yer'd only lerve orf them larks o' you'rn!"

When the flagstaff had been passed, the Duke halted the boys, formed them up in front of the staff, and thus addressed them—

"Boys, I am much pleased with the manner in which you have gone through the various movements, and marching-past, under the direction of—your name?" addressing Dick.

"Richard Everett, your highness."

"—Your comrade, Richard Everett. From the two specimens I have seen of your propensities for larking, I did not expect to see you display so much knowledge of your drill, or perform it with such precision. It shows you can do something besides larking——"

"'Ere, 'ere!" cried Joey, accompanying his coincidence with the Duke's opinion with a nod and a knowing wink.

"Always remember," continued the Duke, "that the profession of a soldier is an honourable profession, and that you should strive to do it honour, by becoming honourable members of it. Your very larkishness prove to me that there is some sterling British stuff in you——"

"'Ere, 'ere!" again cried Joey. "Them's just my sentiments, Dook!"

"And I hope," concluded his highness, "that when you have sown your 'wild oats,' you will settle down to be good, honest, brave soldiers!"

The Duke then, taking off his plumed hat, demanded three cheers for the "Queen," which were given with rattling effect, and in which Joey Pumps, as a matter of course, joined his little voice, as he also did in three hearty cheers given for the Duke by the boys.

Dick then formed the boys into column of "fours," the band took its place at the head, and marched off the common, playing and singing—

"See, the conqu'ring hero comes!
Sound the trumpets, beat the drums!
Sports prepare, the laurels bring,
Songs of triumph to him sing!
"See the god-like youth advance,
Breath the flutes and lead the dance!
Myrtle wreaths and roses twine,
To deck the hero's brow divine.
"See! the conqu'ring hero, &c."

Presently the troops were dismissed by the

Duke, marching back to barracks with bands playing, whilst all that remained of the facsimile of Ching-Ching-Hanghoo-Funky-Bung, was left to the curious inspection of the crowd.

———

CHAPTER XX.

DESCRIBES THE CLEVER MANNER IN WHICH JOEY PUMPS WHEEDLES TWO PEA-SHOOTERS OUT OF MRS. SWAPS FOR DOLLY'S SAKE.— AND THE GRATEFUL RETURN MADE BY DOLLY FOR JOEY'S KINDNESS. — INTRODUCES MRS. RUMBALL, AND HER BAND-BOX.

OWING to the lamentable illness of the Genera,—for which Dick and Dolly were answerable! and for which they ought to have been very sorry—the embarkation was postponed until the next morning.

This delay gave the boys an opportunity of paying last visits to their friends and acquaintances, and sweethearts, in the number and prettiness of which last they beat all the boys in the town hollow.

Like their "elders in the army," the School of the Regiment captured all the pretty girls, to the great envy and chagrin of the civilians.

Besides his mother and other relations, Dolly Swaps had numerous friends, acquaintances, and "dear ones" of the tender sex to visit, and pass through the painful ceremony of saying "goodbye."

As Dolly was by no means sure that he should be able to sustain his fortitude under the trying ordeal, he took his new chum, Joey Pumps, with him to "keep up his pecker," Joey being, as he said, of such an unsurpassingly lively temperament, that it would puzzle "Old Nick" to squeeze up a drop of water, even in the very corner of his eye, where Joey was.

In this Dolly showed the wisdom of his choice; for Joey not only kept up a shower of jokes, and accompanied them with a due proportion of chaff and winks, but he relieved Dolly of much exertion, and diverted any display of the "namby-pamby" by doing all the hand-shaking and kissing—the latter a dozen times over—with the sweethearts.

"And now, Joey," said Dolly, when the last "gal" had been disposed of, "I must go and say good-bye to my mother. I'll introduce you."

"Ah!" observed Joey, with an envious sigh. "It's well to be yer, Dolly, to hev a mother!"

"I don't know that, Joey," returned Dolly, doubtfully. "It ain't always a convenient thing to have a mother, especially when yer very young and can't dodge her when she wants to slap your 'right-about-face'—you know what that is, Joey?"

"It's yer chaps happellation fur a feller's 'posterity,' has hit's called, ain't hit?" queried Joey.

"You're right," returned Dolly, who was too polite to give his new chum the orthodox pronunciation of the word.

"Well, I wouldn't mind takin' that from a genuine parient, Dolly, I thinks. I gits it wus than that from Mrs. Rumball, what ses as she's as good as a mother to me. Hit's some kind o' sattisfackshun to git hit 'ot from yer hone flesh an' blood, as the saying is, wen yer deserves hit."

"Well, perhaps it is," returned Dolly, "but I

was jolly glad when I got out of short frocks, though. A fellow's 'right-about' isn't so easy to tingle when he's got his trousers on; and it seems as though fortune specially favours me in that particular, as my trousers, somehow, are always baggy in that quarter."

Joey, no doubt, would have made a characteristic and suitable reply, but at that moment they stopped at the door of the residence of Mrs. Swaps.

Mrs. Swaps, who was a little widow, with little stiff curls hanging at each side of her face, and had a nose very much the shape of Dolly's, kept a little toy-shop just opposite the north gate of the barracks.

We will not attempt to enumerate the hundreds of playthings that were displayed, in artfully alluring profusion, in Mrs. Swaps' shopwindow, and hung about the door; the reader, no doubt, knows quite as much about what such shops contain as we do.

"Look here, Joey," whispered Dolly, "mother's awfully leaky about the waterworks; she cries at nothing, almost, and she'll be sure to give way when she sees me. But there's one thing, mother's very firm about not letting me get my hand on, although she's very fond of me, and that's a pea-shooter."

"What's that fur, Dolly?" returned Joey. "There's no 'arm in hevin' a shooter, is thur?"

"Mother thinks there is, because the General won't have them in the school if he knows it. Every chap bought one of mother once, and, somehow, the peas shot about at such a rate that the General said his eyes were in danger,"—giving Joey a nudge and a wink—"and he gave mother such a wigging, that she's afraid to let any of us look at a shooter, almost."

"Yer wants a shooter, I s'pose, Dolly; that's what yer a-drivin' hat, ain't hit?"

Dolly nodded and winked.

"Two shooters, Joey; one for you and one for me. They may come in useful on the voyage. See?"

"I ain't a noo-born'd puppy, Dolly," returned Joey, "has I knows on. I b'lieve has I've got my heys hopen! I knows what yer wonts. Yer wonts me to take hadwantage of yer mother's hemotion hat a-loosin' 'er darlin', ter wheedle the shooters hout on 'er?"

"That's just it, Joey! Mind you come it strong!"

As Dolly had predicted, his little mother did "give way" directly her eyes fell upon her hopeful son.

Mrs. Swaps began to cry, using her apron to conceal her tears.

Dolly looked at Joey, as much as to say—

"I told you so, Joey."

Then he added, aloud—

"Don't do that, mother. I want to introduce you to a young friend of mine, who is going to Gib., and whose friendship I highly value. Mother—Joey Pumps. Joey Pumps—my mother."

Mrs. Swaps was too much occupied with her apron and her tears to respond to this introduction; but Joey, taking off his cap, made a most elaborate bow, saying—

"'Ow do yer do, mum? I'm proud to make the hacquaintance hof so distinguish'd a lady. has Dolly's mother. Cheer up, ma'am. Wot's the use of turning hon the waterworks like has that! Why, lor bless yer," giving a sly wink at Dolly, "I'm quite has little has yer Dolly, an my mother hasn' cried a bit!"

"Your mother must be very hard-hearted, then, I'm afraid," sobbed Mrs. Swaps behind her apron.

"'Ard-hearted!" exclaimed Joey. "Not a bit of hit! 'Er 'art, for wot I knows, is has soft has a rotten pear! But it ain't a case o' 'art hat hall. She knows has how I'm hable to take care o' myself wherever I goes an' hin wotever circumstances I may be placed. 'An so she's quite heasy about my going!"

"But, my Dolly's so little!" sobbed Mrs. Swaps.

"Little! Lor, my dear creetur! jist yer take that 're pinnyfore away from yer putty heys an' look hat me."

Mrs. Swaps lowered one corner of her apron, and took a timid glance at Joey, who placed himself in the most advantageous attitude for the scrutiny he could assume, by standing with his legs open, his hands stuck deep into his trousers-pockets, and his "bowler" stuck on one side of his head, and a knowing look on his face.

"Wot do yer think o' me?" asked Joey, with a broad smile.

"You are little," said Mrs. Swaps.

"Ain't I!" returned Joey, with a laugh. "An' yet," he added, triumphantly, "my mother ain't afeared to trust 'er honly hoffspring to roam alone to the huttermost parts o' the hearth!"

"Are you the only child then?" asked Mrs. Swaps, taking down the other corner of her apron and regarding Joey with some shade of interest.

"My mother never told me I wasn't, ma'm," said Joey, giving Dolly a sly look out of the corner of his eye. "Theers a hexample for yer ma'm! Yer jist take my word for hit, hif yer Dolly's little, 'e's quite hable to take kear hon himself! An' hif 'e ain't, I promises yer as *I'll* do that for yer! There!"

"You are very kind," said Mrs. Swaps, brightening up a little at the confidence Joey's assurance inspired her with, "and I am very much obliged to you, I'm sure."

"Don't mention hit, ma'm," said Joey, offhandedly; yer quite welcome. An' now it's time has we wos bringin' this hintervoo to a close, I think. The longer we're about hit, the wus 'll be the partin' scene. Hif there's anythink yer wants ter say to Dolly private, I'll retire *per tom.*"

"You needn't go," returned the grateful Mrs. Swaps. "I've nothing to say you mayn't hear. There's nothing more as I can do for you, Dolly, is there? I made up the last pair of socks as you wore out, and gave you another shirt to make your kit good. I've sewed on all your buttons over again to make them extra strong for tumbling about more on board ship, and I've put double patches on all your trousers behind."

"Those things are all right, mother," said Dolly, looking at Joey to prepare him for the coming crisis. " I want nothing more in that way."

"Is it anything from the window, Dolly, you want?"

"Yes, mother, it is. I—I—want two shooters!"

"Dolly!" exclaimed Mrs. Swaps, elevating her hands, and looking at her son reproachfully.

"Stop a minnit, ma'm," put in Joey; "before yer hadwances any hobjecshuns an' breaks his art with a unkind refoosal, jist listen to me. I knows hall about wot yer've got ter say—about the General's nerwosness as ter peas. But I assoors yer hon my honner has a gen'l'm, we're hup to no larks, an hony wants ter while away the tea-deeam of the woyage. We wants them shooters fur a pertickler purpose. Hif I can satisfir yer hon my honner has a gen'l'm that that pertickler purpose ain't in no way konneckted with the General, hony as regards 's comfort, yer won't say no, will yer?"

"I'm under an obligation to you for your kind offer to watch over Dolly," returned Mrs. Swaps, "and on the conditions you name, you shall have the shooters."

"Done!" exclaimed Joey. "Now, wot do yer thinks we wonts them shooters fur?" he added, bending forward, and looking impressively at the little widow.

"I can't say, of course," she said.

"Why—ter shoot porpusses with!"

Mrs. Swaps was about to reply, when she was arrested by a peculiar noise from Dolly—a noise such as one makes when a drop of tea has "gone the wrong way"—followed by a twisting of the body, and a gradual slipping to the floor, where the contortions and convulsions continued.

The widow—poor innocent creature—was greatly alarmed, and, rushing round the counter, inquired tremblingly—

"Dolly! Dolly! What is it? Is it a fit? Oh, dear, dear!" continued Mrs. Swaps, catching hold of Dolly, and proceeding to slap his back, like babies are treated when seized with a choking cough.

"Don't yer trouble yerself about 'im," said Joey, coolly. "There ain't much the matter with 'im, I knows. He'll come to, hall right, presently."

Here, Joey, seizing the opportunity of Mrs. Swaps' back being turned towards him, stuck his tongue in his cheek, and squinted in a most excruciating manner.

It was quite a minute ere Dolly recovered, and then, not daring to look even in the direction of Joey, he sighed—

"I'm better now, mother—don't distress yourself."

"But what was it?" asked Mrs. Swaps, anxiously.

"I wouldn't had wise yer to bother 'im, ma'am," said Joey, persuasively. "'E can't tell yer. I'm offen took in that 'ere mysterous way, myself, an' I allers prefers a-bein' lef alone to come to gradooal."

It took all Joey's persuasive powers, however, to ease Mrs. Swaps' mind, and when at length she became a little cool, she said—

"I didn't know as you could shoot porpoises with a pea-shooter, Master Pumps."

"Why, yer see, ma'am," returned Joey, "I mus' say as it ain't a fac as is generally known. But there's lots o' things as even *I* don't know, an' I ain't surpris'd at yer not knowin' that. We lives an' learns, Mrs. Swaps, yer see!"

Mrs. Swaps was not quite satisfied, however.

She couldn't understand how porpoises could be shot with a pea out of a shooter, and, not being in a position to dispute with Dolly's friend, who certainly asserted what he said with great confidence, she returned to the charge on a different tack.

"But what do you want to shoot porpoises for?" asked Mrs. Swaps.

But Joey was quite equal to the occasion, and replied with great promptness.

"To take the Gen'ral by surprise."

"By surprise!" exclaimed the widow. "How?"

"That's the best part of it, mum—that is. Yer see, the Gen'ral's werry fond o' fish for his breakfast, an we're a-goin to perwide 'im with some porpuss steaks. If that ain't konklusive, ma'am, that we ony want them shooters for the Gen'ral's comfort, I shud jist like to know wot is?"

Joey finished this "clincher" standing on tiptoe, with his body bent forward, and beating time to each word, with his finger in the palm of his hand.

The attitude was altogether so impressive, and the intention so kind towards the General, that Mrs. Swaps was fairly conquered, and presented Dolly and Joey with a pea-shooter each.

Then came the parting scene,

Mrs. Swaps again let on the water-works, confided Dolly to the safe keeping of Joey, kissed them both, and hastily retired into her little parlour to indulge unseen in her emotions.

Alas! Mrs. Swaps little knew the indiscretion she had committed in giving up those pea-shooters.

It was not till many months had elapsed, that the uses to which those simple and playful instruments had been put, reached her ears.

The proceedings of Dolly and Joey, on reaching the street, were of the most astonishing character.

These proceedings were the more astonishing as they consisted almost of dumb show, and yet, to Dolly and Joey, they were, no doubt, highly intelligible.

They consisted of doublings and twistings of the body, and much rolling from side to side on the pavement, accompanied by a spluttering noise from the lips, like laughter hard to be suppressed.

This symptom was attended with distended cheeks.

For a moment or two, the paroxysms would cease, but only to break out again with renewed violence, on catching a glimpse of each other's faces—a glimpse, taken with great slyness and caution over the shoulder, as they leaned for support back to back.

How long these extraordinary proceedings might have lasted, it is not possible to estimate, but they were brought to an end in a very summary and, as far as Joey was concerned, a most disagreeable fashion.

Standing on the pavement just opposite the barrack-gate, was an old lady of very stout proportions, with a fat red face, very blotchy and pimply, and wearing at this moment anything but an amiable expression.

She looked dreadfully cross, and worried, and hot.

She was dressed in very simple and primitive costume.

Her bonnet was a black straw of the coal-scuttle age, and her ample person was entirely enveloped in an old-fashioned cloak of a plaid pattern, and woollen material.

This garment did not reach to within a foot of the ground—a very pleasing arrangement to sightseers, as it afforded them an unobscured view of the lady's slender ankles, and well-filled white stockings.

She held in her hand a large white band-box, and was staring, evidently in great astonishment and displeasure, at the eccentric movements of Dolly and Joey.

"If won on 'em ain't that Joey Pumps, too!" she murmured. "Drat 'im—the young monkey!"

Just then, Joey overcome by the intensity of his feelings, leaned his back against a lamp-post, and, sinking down muttered languidly—

"Oh lor! Oh dear! I be 'orf agin!"

Joey had scarcely commenced his laughing fit, when the lady, apparently no longer able to control her indignation, dropped her band-box, seized Joey by the waist-band of his trowsers, and, lifting him up said, as she shook his little body, like a dog would a rat—

"Drat yer! Yer a putty chap to go cuttin' sich capers as this, ain't yer? Eh? Yer young monkey. Wher her yer bin all day—eh? Wher her yer bin to, eh, yer young wagabone? I'll teach yer for to go a galivantin' hoff an leave me an Rumball to do yer work, and find our ways 'ere as best we might! I will! How do yer like that? Likewise that? Likewise that? and thurs a lot mor for yer!"

The last expressions were the accompaniments of a series of smacks administered with much vigour and science on various parts of Joey's anatomy.

"Oh lor!" was Joey's mental exclamation as he felt himself suddenly grasped from behind, and lifted up. "Oh lor! if I ain't in the claws o' Dolly Rumball! I knows the grip! Ah, blest if I ain't!" he added, as Mrs. Rumball began to address him. "It's no use a strugglin', I may just as well take my whackin' quiet."

But Joey found that to be impossible on this occasion. Mrs. Rumball, whether caused by absence of mind, or passion that rendered her more than usually energetic, "laid it on" with a will, that caused Joey to loudly protest.

"Come, I say, Dolly, yer needn't be savage hover hit! What hev I done to ketch hit 'otter than usual? That'll do, I tell yer! I say, Dolly —Dolly Swaps, come an' give 'er a touch in the wind! Oh! oh, lor'—yer hold savage!"

Mrs. Rumball had commenced by banging one ear with her left hand, and then, changing, banged away at the other ear with her right hand.

From Joey's second ear, Mrs. Rumball continued operations lower down, by popping Joey's little body under her arm, and slapping away at his "posterity" at a rate that induced him to appeal to Dolly Swaps for assistance.

Nor did Joey appeal in vain to his new-found chum.

Dolly was quite alive to the peril in which Joey was placed, and his only reason for not attacking the irate old lady at once was that he was undecided what tactics to put in force.

Should he approach behind and pull her backwards? She seemed, from her bulk, as though she would "topple" easily, and come down with effect. Or, should he have a pop at her nose with his pea-shooter?

The latter mode was more to Dolly's mind.

"It would be such jolly practice," thought Dolly; "but I haven't any peas! Bother it!"

Dolly would have rushed into his mother's shop for some (Mrs. Swaps kept the requisite ammunition for the use of the shooters), but there wasn't time.

The old lady was "going it" at a tremendous rate, and poor Joey was singing out frantically; so Dolly, in the emergency, looked about for a bit of stone or pebble, and found something that suited his purpose better, and which would prove effective without causing much pain.

It was a rotten pear.

Seizing this with a feeling of exultation, Dolly inserted one end of the shooter into the soft, decayed part—like a cheesemonger does his scoop into a cheese—and placed this end, nicely charged, to his mouth, just as Joey called upon him for aid.

The next moment several things happened in rapid succession.

The rotten pulp flew out of the shooter direct into the old lady's eyes, with astonishing force.

The old lady screamed, threw up her arms (when Joey fell to the ground like a shot bird), tottered a step or two, and sank backwards on to the band-box.

There is no necessity for stating the fate of the band-box, nor that of the fashionable bonnet within it, and which Mrs. Rumball had purchased to come out strong in at Gibraltar, and show the natives the latest fashion.

It was not the first time that Mrs. Rumball's eyes had been filled with some foreign and objectionable substance, and Joey, who had a vivid recollection of the interesting process of clearing them on one memorable occasion, was delighted to witness it a second time.

When Joey discovered by what means he had been rescued from the hands of Mrs. Rumball, and observed that lady squatting on the band-box, busily and angrily engaged in clearing the pulp from her "sightless orbs," that young gentleman, suffering as he was in his knees, from their contact with the ground in dropping, once more made a support of the lamp-post to aid him in slipping down during the limping effect of "gone orf agin."

And, indeed, to have witnessed Mrs. Rumball at work on this occasion was no slight treat, and many who did witness it declared it was the richest thing they had ever seen, and they would never forget it as long as they lived!

"Drat the beastly stuff!" cried Mrs. Rumball, who found it very difficult to get rid of it, as, when she thought she had thrown some away, it came back again attached to her fingers, and refilled her eyes. "Drat the beastly stuff! I I do b'lieve I'm the most unfort'nit creeter as ever was!" (Strange—but the General thought so, too.) "Hev I cum all the way from bootiful Devon to be served like as this! I thort by comin' away as I should hev no more o' this sort o' thing; but I declar to Heaven it's—drat the stuff!—wus!—hever so much wus! An' I wonner wheer that Rumball is? He's allers away wen I'm hovertook like as this! Drat 'im!"

Much more said Mrs. Rumball, but necessity compels us to close the scene.

Mrs. Rumball at length succeeded in clearing her eyes, getting on her feet, and picking up the crushed band-box.

The latter she held up, and gazing at it sadly, yet with anger agitating her bosom, muttered—

"I'd a rather had my heyes blinded fur hever than I'd a seen this! It's dreffel wexin'! The bonnet cost me two-pun-ten, an' eighteen pence for the box; an' now, look hat it!"

"Yes, indeed!"

Mrs. Rumball, in looking at it, wept!

Joey Pumps and Dolly Swaps, in looking at it, were much affected with an opposite emotion.

These two young gentlemen, had not Sergeant O'Shehe come upon the scene and taken Mrs. Rumball to his own quarters in the nick of time, would, as they ultimately declared, have died of laughter!

And then we should not have had the pleasure of their company on the voyage to Gibraltar!

Thank goodness they lived!

—

CHAPTER XXI.

THE EMBARKATION FOR GIBRALTAR.—HOW MRS. RUMBALL GOT ON BOARD.—THE MYSTERIOUS DISAPPEARANCE OF GENERAL SHOOT.

ON the morning of the embarkation of the School of the Regiment for Gibraltar, a scene was presented which will not soon be forgotten by hundreds of the men and the inhabitants of Bangfire.

Let the reader realise in imagination the following scene.

In the east square of the barracks, drawn up in two ranks, accoutred in full uniform—hairy busby, blue cloth tunic, ammunition-pouches, and carbines—are the boys of the school.

In front of the boys, also in full uniform—looking very smart, but a little shaky and white for all that—stands Sergeant O'Shehe, reading from the General Order-Book.

At a few feet from the Sergeant, dressed in a uniform which, if not new, shows no trace of its recent saturating with the fire-engines, or black mark in that quarter which had been subjected to assault with the aid of Mrs. Macnamarrow's frying-pan, stands General Shoot.

The General is standing well forward, as a soldier should, on the fore part of his feet, at attention, with his sword held in his left hand, and the plumes of his cocked-hat fluttering in the gentle breeze.

The General's face is somewhat paler than usual (owing, no doubt, to the exhausting effects, physically and mentally, which followed on the late events); and the noble outlines are greatly marred by puckers about the eyes, and a very austere expression.

The General, in fact, is portentously frowning upon the boys while the Sergeant reads.

The verandahs are crowded by men of the regiment; and the gates and approaches to the square are crowded by curious and excited inhabitants of the town.

At one side of the square, and not many yards from the boys, stands a forage-waggon loaded with trusses of hay.

On the summit of these trusses, with his "bowler" rakishly-cocked, his hands (as usual) in his pockets, and his legs wide apart, stands Joey Pumps, contemplating the scene below as though it had been got up for his special edification.

In another part of the square, with four horses ready hooked to the shafts, is a large baggage-waggon, containing the kits of the boys.

Not many paces in rear of the General, at attention—this time not decorated in cocked hat and tunic, nor carrying a carbine, but listening as attentively as though he perfectly understood what the Sergeant was reading—was "Pomp."

Over this picturesque scene pours down a flood of sunshine, brightening the gay uniforms, glinting on the sword-bayonets of the boys, and turning the undulating folds of the Colours of the School of the Regiment into waves of golden silk.

As the Sergeant reads, the boys feel ready to break into hearty laughter; but the eagle eye of the General is fixed upon them, and they do their utmost to refrain—as long as they can.

Joey Pumps, however—who, at any rate, has not the slightest fear of the General, and who is, at all times, accustomed to indulge his emotions—"goes off" whenever anything that is read particularly tickles his fancy.

There is a great deal of suppressed amusement, too, amongst the soldiers, as those nearest can catch what is said, and pass it on to the others.

This is what the Sergeant is reading :—

"Commandant's Office,

"———, 18—.

'General Orders for the Guidance of the Boys of the School of the Regiment

A
—
7
—

No. 8,888.

"The School of the Regiment being about to embark for Gibraltar, the General Commanding deems it necessary to issue the following instructions for the guidance of the boys, and which are to be scrupulously complied with. Any infringement with any or either of them will meet with the severest punishment.

"1st.—It having been reported to the General that, on inspecting the kits of the boys last evening, a mischievous weapon, called a pea-shooter, was discovered in the possession of Adolphus Swaps (artfully concealed up the sleeve of his regimental jacket) by Sergeant O'Shehe—the General being thereby led to— to—to—smell a rat——"

"Tut, tut, tut!" here interrupted the General, impatiently (Joey Pumps doing a delighted laugh). "What are you reading, sir? Let me see it!"

The General, snatching the book, and glancing at the words, said—

"'Suspect, sir,'—'suspect that'—Plain as the nose on your face, sir! No more like 'smell a rat' than I'm like 'smell a rat!' Be careful, sir!"

The Sergeant resumed—

"—'Led to suspect that other boys may have succeeded in concealing one of those offensive weapons in their kits, or about their persons, would just advise such boys to keep it concealed, or—or—or' ('What beastly writing this is!' thought the Sergeant, trying, in vain, to decipher the next important words.) "I can't read it, boys" he said, aloud, "but I will 'take a shot' at what it means, It means this —if one of them—those—confounded pea-shooters is found on any one of you, he'll just get it 'hot.' I needn't tell you what that means. 'A nod's as good as wink to a blind——'"

"Don't be a fool, sir!" growled the General. "You'll have everybody laughing in a minute. Go on, sir, and get it over!"

"The fool that wrote it, General," murmured the Sergeant, "had better go to school again. I think——"

"Why, confound your impudence, sir! That's my writing!" exclaimed the General, indignantly. "What the devil do you mean? But, there—get on, sir! get on! It's no use wasting words on an ass!"

The Sergeant, feeling very hot, resumed, and as the remaining clauses were short, he got on more rapidly.

"2nd.—The boys will parade in full dress every morning one hour before breakfast, for inspection and drill.

"3rd.—As sea-sickness will not be permitted, under any circumstances, it will be useless to plead that fanciful malady as an excuse for absence from parade.

"4th.—Any boy pleading sickness will be immediately sent to the mast-head, and kept there until he is well.

"5th.—No roaming into the hold of the ship, climbing the rigging, getting into the boats, or fishing for sharks, porpoises, or whales will be allowed.

("Ha, ha, ha!" laughed Joey. "Well, I'm blowed! I should jest like ter see a whale hon thet voyage, werry much!")

"6th.—Practical joking, called 'larking,' is strictly prohibited.

("Loo-or!" cried Joey, sarcastically. "You don't say so!")

"7th.—These regulations to be read out by Sergeant O'Shehe each day at morning parade.

"JOACHIM SHOOT,

"General Commanding the Garrison."

When the Sergeant had finished, the General said :—

"And now, boys, you know what you have to do, and what you have not to do. If you don't do what you have to do, and do what you have not to do, you know what you have to expect— that's all! And now we'll march. Steady. Fours right! Ready, the band there! To 'The girl I left behind me!' Shoulder arms! Column —Right wheel! Quick marr-ch!"

A tap of the drum to mark the time, the rattling quickstep struck up by the band, and our Boys in the Army stepped off to hearty, resounding cheers, and cries of—

"Good-bye, boys!"

"Good-bye! Good-bye!"

"Keep up your reputation at Gib.!"

The scene, as they marched through the town, was very exciting.

The pavements of the road leading from the barracks to the arsenal gates were thronged with spectators, who cheered loudly, whilst, to render the occasion still more lively and impressive, the boys accompanied the band with their voices, singing the words of the celebrated song of farewell.

Joey Pumps put on Dolly Swaps' busby, giving Dolly his "bowler" in exchange, and, persuading Gunner Oilrag to give him a mount on his shoulder, marched by the side of the school, looking a very conspicuous object, and making himself generally agreeable and useful by winking alternately at the General and the ladies, who waved their handkerchiefs from the windows, returned the cheering, and beat time to the singing and music.

And thus everything went on smoothly, without obstruction, until the place of embarkation was reached in the arsenal, when it was found that the passage to the gangway of the steamer —a narrow deal plank—from the slip was blocked up, and seemed likely to be blocked up for some time.

This obstruction was no less a personage than Mrs. Rumball and her "traps."

The latter, which consisted of innumerable boxes and bundles of all sizes and shapes, and one immense feather bed tied up in a beautiful patchwork quilt, were piled about the shore end of the plank, as though Mrs. Rumball intended that no one should get on board but herself.

If such were indeed her intention, Mrs. Rumball had paid dearly for her selfishness.

At this moment the old lady was standing in the middle of the plank, unable to return or move forward.

Mrs. Rumball was in a dreadful fix.

Mrs. Rumball had surveyed the narrow and dangerous bridge for some time before she had screwed up her courage to trust her precious person to its safety, and then only on the assurance of a sailor that there was no other means of her getting on board, unless she were slung on board like they did horses, with a band across her stomach, and hoisted up from the yardarm by a rope attached to the band.

Mrs. Rumball declared she would brave any danger rather than submit to such inhuman treatment.

Accordingly, Mrs. Rumball made the venture, got by slow degrees—her heart in her mouth all the time—to the centre, where, the plank beginning to vibrate with her weight, she immediately stuck fast, expecting every moment to be precipitated into a watery grave.

At the moment the General came up, Mrs. Rumball was uttering the most piercing screams, whilst several of the sailors were leaning over the side of the vessel, contemplating her perilous dilemma with much satisfaction.

"Bless my soul!" exclaimed the General, irritably. "Why don't the old fool go one way or the other?"

It happened that Joey Pumps was at hand to answer this question.

"For a werry good reason, General," said Joey, with a chuckle; "'cos she can't. I knows Dolly's ways well, and she'll stick there till she's made to stir her stumpses."

As this seemed a self-evident fact to the General, and as he was in no humour to be kept waiting there by a timid old woman, he at once threaded his way amongst the boxes and bundles, and proceeded cautiously along the plank until he reached the screaming lady.

"Be quiet!" said the General, sharply. "It's no use making that row. Get on, ma'am—get on!" giving her a push.

"Oh! o-o-h!" screamed Mrs. Rumball, in greater terror than ever. "Yer brute, you! Yer hunfeelin' wretch! Do yer want to drownd me?"

"Drown be hanged!" returned the General, impatiently, "Get on, I tell you. Why do you stand there blocking the way?"

But the General only produced screams and abuse.

Mrs. Rumball was not to be got out of the way in that manner.

What was to be done?

After a few moments' perplexed thought, a bright idea flashed into the General's brain.

He would carry her across!

The next moment, without pausing to consider the stupendous and hazardous nature of such a task, the General seized her round the waist, and, with an Herculean effort, lifted her across his shoulder.

This feat, as a matter of course, met with its due share of laughter and applause, which increased, as Mrs. Rumball, who decidedly objected to such a forcible and indelicate mode of transit, screamed and kicked about her legs in a most energetic and fractious manner.

This kicking had not entered into the General's calculations at all, and he scarcely had mounted Mrs. Rumball, when he heartily wished he had let her alone.

It took all the General's strength and balancing ingenuity to maintain his equilibrium.

But he had got Mrs. Rumball on his shoulder, and he was bound to do one of two things—carry her across, or—drop her into the Thames!

To add to his embarrassment, the General suddenly found the plank vibrating to an alarming extent, and heard a small voice saying,—

"Old 'er tight, Gen'ral. I'm honly a testin' the hextent hof yer skill! Ha, ha! Oh, lor, Dolly, I've a seen yer in some jolly fixes, but never one as took my fancy like this 'ere!"

Joey had been unable to resist taking advantage of the General's and Mrs. Rumball's perilous position, to exercise his tantalising propensities, hence his presence on the plank, which he was working like the treadle of a sewing-machine.

How the General raved and swore must not be written!

He threatened Joey with every kind of punishment he could think of, but the more he raved and threatened, the more Joey worked his treadle and indulged in ironical chaff, and which ended as everybody expected.

The General, unable to longer contend successfully with Joey's treadling and Mrs. Rumball's kicking, gave up the struggle by allowing the lady to glide—if we may so express the movement—off his shoulder, and descend with graceful rapidity into the muddy river!

The scene that followed was certainly very exciting, but we cannot describe it.

The efforts made to rescue Mrs. Rumball, the time it took, and the difficulty that was experienced in getting her limp and saturated body on board, and gently laid on her own feather bed (the largest bunk being too small to take her), and the distress of the ever-affectionate Rumball, we must leave to the reader's imagination, to be enjoyed at leisure.

And now occurred a mysterious circumstance.

When the bustle and excitement attending the rescue of Mrs. Rumball had subsided, a certain important individual was found to be missing.

It was the General!

What had become of him?

No one had seen him go ashore, nor could he be found on board!

Had he jumped overboard and committed suicide?

Hardly! The General was not quite such a fool as that!

But he was not in any of the bunks or cabins of the ship; he was not in the hold—so far as could be seen—nor was he at the mast-head!

Then where was he?

We have a picture in our "mind's eye" which may, if described, tend to throw some light on the mystery.

We are in the hold of the vessel—or the lowest deck.

Scattered around are sundry barrels and bales, and articles of lumber.

The place is almost dark, and smells damp and fusty.

What is the matter there, in the centre of the deck?

There is a trap-door partly open, from which appears the head of a man and his hands.

The man is evidently in a fix.

The trap is firmly pressed down, so that, struggle as he may, he cannot extricate himself.

Kneeling and pressing on the trap, is a boy in the uniform of The School of the Regiment.

Who is this boy? And who is this man?

The latter, is certainly General Shoot—we recognise his face. Besides, there on the deck is his cocked-hat!

The boy, we will swear, is none other than our old acquaintance—Dolly Swaps!

See how he grins!

CHAPTER XXII.

THE VISION INTERPRETED.

As the reader will scarcely be satisfied with the bare presentation of the picture we drew—from mental vision—at the close of the last chapter, we will interpret it for his gratification and proper understanding of the incidents which follow.

The General, as a matter of course, was in a terrible rage with Joey Pumps for the latter's performance on the plank, whereby the General was placed in an awkward dilemma—so awkward, indeed, that to save himself from a ducking, he was compelled to sacrifice the life of a lady.

It is true, the lady was not a female of any great importance.

Socially, she was nothing more than a common cook.

Mrs. Rumball was neither slender, young, nor beautiful. Wasn't her face red and blotchy?

She possessed, too, what the General considered a " devil of a temper."

In fact, Mrs. Rumball, in the General's estimation, was a most unfascinating and objectionable person, and he wondered how the deuce it was that his old friend, General Pyefield, came to recommend her as cook to such a superior school as the School of the Regiment!

He did not care a dash for Mrs. Rumball *as* Mrs. Rumball, but he cared for Mrs. Rumball in connection with his reputation as a brave man.

The General felt, instinctively, that he would be accused of selfishness in allowing his cook to fall into the Thames.

It would be useless, he felt, to throw the blame on Joey Pumps, and yet that young imp was certainly the cause of the catastrophe.

Under these painful circumstances, will the reader be surprised to learn that the General vowed to be revenged—muttered through his clenched teeth, too!—on Joey?

The General vowed to be revenged on Joey for the jeopardy in which he had placed his reputation for gallantry and bravery, but he made up his mind to go about it in a very sly and systematic manner.

The revenge should be ample, but must be safely accomplished.

He wasn't going to rush at it, like a bull at a gate!

Catch him at that! He would wait patiently his opportunity—and it soon came!

It was not until Mrs. Rumball had been rescued—laid with great care by pitying hands on her feather-bed—that these thoughts agitated the mind of the General.

He had been as anxious as any about the condition of the lady, and had descended to the lower deck, in a corner of which, just outside the boys' berths, the feather-bed had been hastily made up, where he paced to and fro in great mental anguish, making constant inquiries as to the state of the interesting patient, whose moans and screams at times were something dreadful to hear.

It was whilst thus engaged that the General had the curiosity to approach the bulkhead, which separated the berths and Mrs. Rumball's bed from that part of the vessel, amidships, where the hold was.

There was a small square hole in the bulkhead, and through this the General peeped.

But he had scarcely placed his eyes to the aperture, when he started as though he had been shot, and a thrill of excitement shook his frame.

With his eyes almost starting from their sockets, and his heart beating rapidly, the General looked again.

With the feeling of revenge the General was cherishing in his heart, the sight which met his gaze was enough to make that heart of his beat with agitation, and send the hot blood coursing at double-quick speed through his veins.

Leaning over the edge of the hold, gazing intently into the gloomy depths, was the object of the General's deadly hatred—Joey Pumps!

What Joey was gazing at the agitated General could not, of course, see.

It was enough, however, that the daring young imp was gazing at something, and that his little person was so disposed that only a slight kick would precipitate him below.

Joey was kneeling on the edge of the hold, with his " posterity " well exposed, and exactly facing the General.

"Oh!" breathed the General through his parched lips: "There's the foul traitor! What a splendid position! Just a very little touch on his rear prominence, and the vile wretch—the insidious viper—would be over and break his cursed neck!"

The spirit of evil was busily at work with the General at this moment.

There was no one about, so far as the General could see, to witness the deed.

"Do it!" whispered the evil spirit. "What a fool you would be to neglect such a splendid opportunity! Just look at his 'right-about-face'; it's enough to tempt an angel!"

"I'll do it!" murmured the trembling General, "if I can only get at him!"

With that he began examining the bulkhead, to find an entrance.

At first he could discover nothing but the square hole, and it was beyond dispute that he could not get through that.

But presently he spied a sliding panel.

With an exclamation of exultation, yet trembling like an aspen leaf, the General silently drew it aside, and peered eagerly through.

Yes, there, still in the same position, was the disturber of his peace of mind—the callous young detractor from his reputation!

Ah, Joey Pumps! If you had but known who it was that, at this awful moment, was creeping up behind you, with intention the most foully murderous, we bet our fortune that, not you, but the General, would have been the one to topple down that gloomy pit!

Nerving himself for the desperate attempt, the General stepped through the open panel— not a jingle of his spurs nor a rattle of his sword startled the echoes of the semi-dark place, as he glided with elfin tread towards his unsuspecting victim!

A few strides and the General's toe was within easy reach of Joey's "posterity!"

Once more the General cast an apprehensive look around.

No one was near—the coast was clear.

No sound was heard save the voice of conscience!

But weak was that voice; for the next instant the toe of the General's boot came into contact with Joey's person.

There was now the sharp jingle of a spur, a shrill cry of "Oh, lor!" and Joey disappeared.

The General lingered for a moment to catch the thud of Joey's fall, but all was silent, save a distant splash, as though a cat had been thrown into a well.

"He's dropped into the bilge-water," muttered the General. "If he's not drowned, the rats will be sure to kill him. Thank goodness! there's one of my tormentors gone! And I'm safe!"

If the General had seen the little face peeping through the panel during the perpetration of this tragedy he would have had serious doubts on the matter of his safety.

The General had no sooner passed through the bulkhead, closed the panel, and left the berths, than the panel was again slipped back, and Dolly Swaps, leaping in, rushed to the edge of the hold, and looked eagerly down, crying—

"Joey! Joey! Where are you? I say, Joey!"

But there was no reply.

"Blow'd if I don't think the General's done for him!" muttered Dolly. "The murdering old scoundrel! Who'd have thought that he'd have gone and done such a thing as this? Joey! Joey!"

But still Joey gave no response.

"I must go down and have a look for him," said Dolly. "If he's dead the General will have to swing for it!"

There was a rope-ladder, quite perpendicular, by which a descent could be made into the hold.

Down this went Dolly with the quickness of a monkey, and began looking about him.

The place was gloomy, and there were barrels, bales, and other articles of lumber scattered about, and there was a close and fusty smell.

Dolly concluded that he was on the lowest deck, immediately above the ballast and bilge-water.

In this he was confirmed by peeping down the open trap-door, from which came the fusty smell he had noticed.

"By Jove!" exclaimed Dolly, "I wonder if Joey has tumbled through this? Joey! Joey! I say, Joey Pumps. Ho-igh, there! Are you there, Joey!"

"Why, I shud rather think I wos, too!" replied a familiar voice, that made Dolly's heart jump for joy. "An' hit's about as queer a place as hever I got hinto hall of a suddint! Talk about hackeraback dodges, Dolly, jumping through make-b'lieve windies hon the stage,

and bein' fired hout hoff a cannin, ain't nothin' ter this go!"

"Then you're not hurt, Joey?"

"Not a bit hon it. Hit's jolly soft down 'ere— feels has though I was luxooriatin' in batter-puddin' afore it's biled."

"More like black-pudding, I should think, Joey," said Dolly, with a laugh.

"I ain't pertickler, Dolly, as long as I can get hout on it, some time or nuther. Hit ain't ekel to a feather-bed, an' I'd reether not take hup my permanent repose hin it! I'd just like to shet the cove hin 'ere as played me the dirty trick, that's hall!"

"I can tell you who it was, Joey," said Dolly.

"Yer ken! Then that cove'll wish as 'e had'nt been never born'd, Dolly! Who's the gen'l'm, now?"

"Come out first, and then I'll tell you, Joey."

"Excuse me, Dolly, my friend, but I perfers 'earin of hit down 'ere. It ain't heverybody as knows 'ow to get hover Joey Pumps, an' the cove as toppled me inter this, has 'is 'ed screwed hon the right way! I 'ont leave the scene hoff my disgrace, Dolly, till I've a heered the willan's name, an' 'atched my revenge!"

"You'd never guess who it was, Joey," said Dolly. "What do you think of it's being the General?"

"Why, as I wouldn't giv' 'im credit for being so sharp," returned Joey, calmly.

"Well, it was then! I saw him do it!"

"Oh, yer did—did yer? Then hall I ken say is it'll be a bad look-hout for the Gen'ral, Dolly! Blow 'is cheek! I wonder wot 'e did it for, now?"

"To murder you, Joey, I could tell that from the look of his eyes, and what he said after he kicked you over."

"What did 'e say?"

"He's dropped into the bilge-water. If he's not drowned, the rats will kill him. Thank goodness, there's one of my tormentors gone! And I'm safe!'"

"Oh! that's wot 'e sed, wos it? Werry good, Gen'ral—werry good! We'll have a reckonin' presently! So 'e thinks himself safe, Dolly, does 'e?"

"That's what he said!"

"Don't yer think as he'd be safer down 'ere Dolly? You can't see me winkin', but I'm a doin' of hit."

"By jingo!" That's not a bad idea, Joey!" exclaimed Dolly. "But how are we to get him in?"

"Yer kin do it jist as heasy as I got the pea-shooter, Dolly. Just go an' tell 'im as you knows what he've been up to, an' as you've a found my dead body. Swear as you'll peach hon 'im if 'e don't come and 'elp yer bury me. Hif I kin only git 'is legs down a little way, blow me hif 'e shall get 'em hup agin; see Dolly!"

"I see. What a lark it will be," chuckled Dolly. "I say, Joey, if we can get him in, we'll take him off to Gibraltar—eh?"

"Reether, my dear!" returned Joey, with a responsive chuckle. "Hoff yer goes, an' do yer best for yer defunk friend!"

Leaving Joey Pumps to await in his dark, wet, and unsavoury prison the moment of his revenge, we must turn our attention to the meeting of the General and Dolly Swaps.

The feeling of satisfaction experienced by the General at the thought of having got rid, in such a clever manner, of one of his tormentors did not last long.

He had scarcely reached the deck, and had time to reflect on what he had done, than he began to repent of it.

What had he done?

Taken the mean advantage of a poor little boy, whilst the little fellow's back was turned towards him, by kicking—actually kicking!—him head-first into the hold of the ship!

All around him was bustle and excitement.

Apart from the commotion caused by the mishap to Mrs. Rumball, the excitement of the boys in getting their kits aboard, and safely stowed away in the hammocks allotted to them below—there was a regiment of the Line, the "fighting 33rd," just embarking for Malta, and the splendid band of the Artillery, which had played it from the Red Barracks, was still playing on shore.

But none of this diverted the thoughts of the General.

All he could see was the tragedy that had been enacted below!

All he could hear was the splash of the little body in the bilge-water.

Over and over again was presented to his mental gaze the naturally innocent position of Joey as he knelt on the edge of the hold, and gazed pensively (it appeared so now to the General) down!

Over and over again that splash, like a cat thrown into a well, splashed as it were in his ears!

Oh, to think that he—a General—could so have given way to his temper at the innocent pranks of a little boy, as to have kicked that little boy down the hold of a ship!

Innocent, harmless, indeed, seemed Joey's pranks now!

"Why, now I come to think of it," thought the General, "I was quite as bad when I was a youngster—quite! Dear me! it requires some such shock as this to remind one that he was once a boy—I—I," with a sobbing kind of sigh, "I'll interfere no more with the boys' tricks! If I could only undo that kick!"

What should he do?

Go down the hold and see what had become of the dear little fellow?

But there were so many persons about, and his proceedings would be the subject of remark!

Just as the General's feelings had reached this stage, and he was debating what to do, his eyes fell upon Dolly Swaps who, to his surprise, immediately tipped him a sign that he wanted to speak to him.

Apart from this familiarity, there was an expression in Dolly's face which seemed to say, "Come here, my boy, I just want to talk to you a bit! You're in for it—Come on!"

Nor was the General mistaken.

Dolly felt that he had the General in his power, and he was resolved to "lead him a dance."

"I'll just bring down his dignity a peg or two, and frighten the life out of him, for all the wackings he's given me!" said Dolly, with a malicious chuckle.

The General's heart leapt into his throat, and he turned pale and trembled.

Had Dolly Swaps made a discovery?

The General drew forth his handkerchief to wipe the perspiration that was fast gathering on his face."

"Ain't he in a sweat?" thought Dolly.

The General, looking cautiously about him, to see that there were no inconvenient listeners, approaching, saying:—

"What is it, Master Swaps?"

"What is it!" said Dolly, with well-assumed indignation. "You know what it is well enough, General! It's Joey Pumps! I didn't think that you would have gone and done such a thing!"

"Wha—wha—what thing?" stammered the General.

"What thing! That's good, that is! Why you've gone and murdered Joey Pum——"

"Hush! hush!" said the terrified General. "Mind what you're say——"

"Oh, but I saw you do it, you know!" retorted Dolly. "It's no use backing out of it! I saw you kick Joey into the hold!"

"S-i-s-h" S-i-s-h!" continued the General; "People may hear you!"

"Why did you go to do it, General?" asked Dolly, putting his hands in his pockets, and opening his legs, in imitation of Joey.

"I did it for a lark—only a lark!"

"Well, I'm blest!" cried Dolly. "If that ain't better and better! Fancy kicking a chap down a hold for a lark! And you, too, as is so down on us when we're up to anything!" added Dolly, shaking his head. "That ain't fair-play, you know, General!"

"I—I—won't interfere with you again" said the General, humbly.

"I don't think you will," returned Dolly, significantly. "You'll be hanged!"

"Then is—is—is——?" stuttered the poor General.

"Joey dead? Dead as a flounder, General!" said Dolly, coolly.

"Good Heavens?" groaned the General, mopping the streaming perspiration off his face. "Here's a terrible thing!"

"You're right, General. You're in a mess and no mistake! You've often threatened to shoot me, you know, and now I could hang you! But, just look here. I won't, on one condition."

"What is it?" asked the General, eagerly.

"That you'll just cancel those rules and regulations about our larking and that."

"I will," replied the General, "I quite intended to before I went on shore."

"Very good! Mind no backing out! And now if you'll come down, I'll help you to bury the body. You must come," added Dolly, as the General hesitated. "I can't do it by myself! I'll go first to put the chaps and the sailors off the scent—see General?"

Scarcely knowing whether he was walking on his head or his feet, the General presently followed Dolly, which young gentleman he found waiting for him by the ladder which led into the hold.

He could hardly believe that what had happened was reality.

"Oh, that would turn out to be hideous dream!" he thought, as he stood for a moment contemplating the rope-ladder by which he had to descend.

But he was recalled to himself by the voice of Dolly from below.

"Now General, down you come! You've got another place to go down before we come to the body! Turn round and come down backwards. That's it. Mind your spurs. Oh lor!" chuckled Dolly to himself, "Just to think as I should have the General following me like a blessed dog with its tail between his legs! Here we are," he added aloud as the General stepped off the ladder, "we shall have to go down there," pointing to the open trap. "That's where the body is!"

The General contemplated the hole like a man stunned.

Could it be possible that *he* had to go down *there?*

Suddenly a thought struck him.

Was it, after all, a trick the young rascal was playing upon him?

But Dolly, who had anticipated the doubt, here struck a match, and kneeling down, held the light in the hole, saying—

"See, General!"

The General, with an indescribable, sinking feeling, bent over, and there—Oh, Heavens!—was the body of poor little Joey in the black, slimy bilge, apparently lifeless!

Oh, the agony of that moment!

"He may not be dead, you know, General, though he looks like it," said Dolly, in a solemn whisper. "You get in—it ain't deep—and examine him, and if he is alive you can hand him up to me."

The chance of Joey being still living brought a thrill of hope into the General's breast, and tremblingly requesting Dolly to keep on lighting matches, he sat on the edge of the hold with his legs hanging in, and then, turning over on his stomach prepared to let himself down.

It was trying work, for the General could boast of a tidy "corporation," and he was hampered with "kicking-straps," and pretty tight "over-alls," and he still wore his sword.

Now had arrived the exciting moment.

It was Joey's turn to act.

"Was he ready?" was Dolly's inward question.

Rather. Joey had been watching for the General's legs with the patience of a cat waiting for a mouse, and they had no sooner got into proper position, than Joey sprang up and seized them, and began tugging away with all his might.

But the General, though taken by surprise, did not prove a very easy prey.

The moment he felt his legs seized, that moment he knew he had been "done!" and he fought for liberty with desperate determination!

Pressing his stomach and elbows on the deck with what force he could muster—for there was nothing to cling to—he set his legs in motion with a rapidity and wildness that literally led Joey a kind of flying dance, which he afterwards described as "the mud-larker's dance."

Joey was flung about in all directions (for he wouldn't leave go) at such a rate that he began to think his arms would be jerked from their sockets.

Beginning to despair of pulling the General in, he called upon Dolly for aid—

"I say, Dolly, jist giv 'im a push hup there, will yer! His legs 'air a-going of hit like winkin! Punch his nose! Tread hon 'is 'ands, or somethin! 'Es a shakin me inter fiddle-strins!"

The General would have called for assistance, but, shamed at his position, held his tongue.

He would struggle to the last!

And he did, but it was useless!

Dolly didn't tread on his hands, or punch his nose, as Joey, in his extremity, had suggested, but he lifted the first, and playfully tweaked the latter, until the General gradually slipped back, and then Dolly, letting the trap-door fall upon him, knelt on it in high glee.

"How are you getting on, Joey?" called out Dolly.

"Is he kicking much now?"

"Werry little!" replied Joey. "'Is legs is givin hup!"

The General, now feeling that his chance was hopeless, began shouting loudly for aid,

"Ah, would yer? cried Joey. "No yer don't!"

These words were accompanied by a last vigorous pull, and the General, unable longer to retain his hold, dropped into the bilge with a heavy splash!

The trap-door shut with a bang, but the next moment Dolly had it again opened, saying hastily—

"Where are you, Joey? Where's your hand!"

"Ere yer air, Dolly," said Joey.

A desperate tug or two, and a few wriggles, and Joey was dragged up, smothered from head to foot with black slimy mud, and looking anything but in suitable condition for a drawing-room party.

"Good-bye, Gen'eral," said Joey, facetiously; "opes as 'ow you'll henji yer noo quarters! Hif the rats don't kill yer, ye'll be shure ter be starved ter def! Ta! ta!"

Bang went the trap-door, aad the General was left to the horrible darkness and his own sweet reflections.

CHAPTER XXIII.

THE DEPARTURE.—MRS. RUMBALL SEES AN AWFUL GHOST.—THE SERGEANT GOES MAD AGAIN.

IT is needless to inform the reader, after the perusal of the last chapter, that the mysterious disappearance of the General remained a mystery for some hours.

The troops had embarked, and every article of baggage had been got on board, and yet the General did not turn up.

It was very strange, but it was impossible to keep the steamer waiting, and so the moorings were cast off, and, as the majestic vessel slowly steamed away, with her head down the Thames, the band played that heartstirring tune of farewell, "Auld Lang Syne."

As long as the steamer was in sight of the band and the spectators, the strains of the tune and cheers were kept up, the latter being heartily responded to by those on board, Joey Pumps and Dolly Swaps, who seemed to be in most astonishing good spirits, doing enough for half a dozen big men.

Indeed, long before the vessel got a quarter of the way down the river, the conduct of those two young gentlemen attracted particular attention.

Dolly, having considered it advisable that Joey should change his clothes, to avert any suspicion that his otherwise muddy appearance might create, had lent him a suit of his regimentals.

The fit had turned out exact.

There were the short-legged trousers, with the bagginess behind, beautifully patched; there were the short sleeves of the jacket, leaving the arms bare nearly from the elbows; there, jauntily cocked, was the forage cap; and so they paraded the deck arm-in-arm, giving way to sudden attacks of laughter, and making the most extraordinary faces at each other, especially whenever the mysterious disappearance of the General was mentioned. They looked as much like twin brothers—especially when viewed from behind—as two peas are alike.

And what was very strange, no one could get out of them what it was they were laughing about; not even Dick Everett could elicit more information than a mysterious continuation of points towards the deck, accompanied by winks and idiotic laughter.

Sergeant O'Shehe—who was looking wild and haggard, after a long and disappointing search for the General—tackled them in various ways, from wheedling to boxing their ears, but all in vain.

Dolly and Joey kept as close as oysters.

It was midnight before the mystery was solved.

By that time, the mighty steamer had passed the Nore and had begun to roll a bit, to get herself ready, as it were, for the heaving and rolling of that uneasy customer—the Bay of Biscay.

All was quiet, save the regular working of the monster engines, the hollow rumbling noise made by the revolving screw, the monotonous wash of the briny sea on the vessel's prow, the whistling of the night-wind through the rigging, and the slow tread and low conversation of the watch on deck.

The moon was at the full, but behind swiftly moving clouds, dodging the steamer, and taking shy peeps at her big black hull as it laboured onward through the heavy waters, dodging and peeping as though she knew there was a "lark" brewing on board, and would presently burst with startling violence.

All was quiet below, and, with the exception of two persons, and a few who were already feeling "queer" from the motion of the vessel, all were sleeping, the soldiers stretched on the deck on blankets, the sailors and Our Boys in hammocks.

The two persons exceptionally alluded to were the General and Mrs. Rumball.

As regards the General, it would have been a surprising incident had he been able to sleep under the distressing circumstances in which he was placed.

In darkness—his person covered with black slime—a horrible stench—rats disporting over him—a dreadful sensation in the stomach from the rolling of the vessel—how was it possible he could sleep?

After the first shock was over and he had succeeded in gaining his feet, the General had instinctively begun feeling for the trap-door to try and push it open to make his escape.

But he felt in vain!

He groped about and felt and felt again, and pushed, and again pushed, but—it was no go!

And so he continued groping and feeling, and pushing, and moaning and groaning and swearing, until the rolling of the steamer, and the rolling of himself in the black, muddy slush, told him that he was at sea.

At sea!

What an awful predicament he was in!

Were those young imps going to leave him to die?—to perish miserably in that miserable place?

It seemed like it, for hours had passed and not a voice—not a footstep had reached his straining ears!

It was midnight—not that he knew it, for ages have seemed to have passed since his incarceration—and the General knew by the constantly increasing roll of the vessel that she was getting into deeper water—rapidly making for the bay of terrors—Biscay!

The General felt that if he could not effect his escape, or was released before entering the bay, he would never leave it alive!

The idea of his dying there and his body becoming food for the rats was too horrible to contemplate.

He must make another attempt to find the trap!

His strength was almost gone, but he tottered to his feet and, as well as he could for the rolling of the vessel, began feeling for the trap.

This attempt lasted some time, and the General was again on the point of giving up the search and resigning himself to despair, when, exerting all his strength for a last vigorous push, the trap opened.

It was only an inch or two, however, but that was enough.

With an indescribable feeling of joy, the poor General knew that with the aid of his sword which, fortunately, he had kept buckled round his waist, he could fully open the trap.

He unsheathed it, and in another moment he was free to pass up.

But this was rather a difficult feat to accomplish.

The days when the General was a slim and practical gymnast had long since passed.

He had to draw himself up, and his hands were slippery with slime!

But it must be done!

He had had quite enough of that place, and he did not want to call for assistance. He wanted to get out unobserved, for he had a plan in his head.

He would creep quietly to Mrs. Rumball and crave her assistance.

Surely she would assist him.

Unbuckling his sword and putting that out first to rid himself of an encumbrance, the General tried his luck.

It came, but it was only after a tremendous amount of struggling, puffing, and grunting, ungainly antics, and the splitting of his overalls at the knees and right across the rear.

But, no matter, he was out; and, buckling on his sword, and putting on his cocked hat, which he found on feeling for his sword, the General groped his way to the rope-ladder.

Up this he went, but only to find that the hatch had been put on.

This caused another struggle, and a one-handed one, too, as he was obliged to hold on to the ladder at the same time as he pushed away the hatch.

He succeeded at length in lifting it sufficiently to get his head through, and grasping the edge of the hold, he drew himself out, the keen edge of the heavy hatch scraping the back part of his body from the shoulders to his calves, and nearly cutting his feet off.

"And now for Mrs. Rumball," thought the General, after he had shaken himself together.

Through the square hole in the bulkhead already mentioned, the General could see the glimmer of a faint light.

"That's fortunate," he muttered; "having a light, she will be able to see me, and I shall not have the trouble of waking her, and entering into a tedious explanation. It's very fortunate!"

Very, indeed, as the General soon found!

We have already said that Mrs. Rumball's feather-bed had been placed in a corner in the space between the berths and the bulkhead.

As Mrs. Rumball could not be called upon to enter on her professional duties (contrary to Joey Pump's expectations) until her arrival at Gibraltar, this spot was considered the most private and out-of-the-way that could be found for a lady, and who had brought her husband with her, too.

A screen of blankets had been rigged by the sailors around Mrs. Rumball's bed, and a more snug and cosy corner than was thus improvised could scarcely have been desired for the purpose.

But at the moment the General applied his eyes to the hole, the following scene met his gaze.

Mrs. Rumball, deeming her temporary domestic domain free from sudden intrusion or vulgar gaze, had drawn the screen aside and left her couch exposed with all its innocent contents and arrangements.

Mrs. Rumball, who was already at that stage when the horrible sensation of sea-sickness may be said to be at its worst, that is, the feeling of deathly sickness without being able to relieve the stomach—was partly sitting up in bed, the upper part of her body reclining against her pillows, and the lower part—her legs—drawn up nearly to her chin.

Mrs. Rumball had been told that this was the best attitude to assume under the agony of sea-sickness, as the pressure of the knees helped to keep corpulent stomachs from "wobbling about" with the roll of the ship, and was very graceful at the same time.

Mrs. Rumball was looking dreadfully ill. Never was there a countenance that exhibited such a woe-begone and prostrate appearance, framed as it was, too, in a lily-white night-cap, with a magnificent border.

In one hand Mrs. Rumball held a bottle of brandy, which, of course, was quite excusable under the circumstances!

By her side was Mr. Rumball, in much the same position and condition.

On a box by the head of the bed burnt a night-light, the glimmer of which shed "a pale and misty radiance around."

As the General looked, Mr. Rumball slowly opened his eyes, and rising gently on his elbow, cast a sly glance, first at the face of his better half, and then at the bottle of brandy.

"I wonner is Dolly asleep *this* time," thought Mr. Rumball. "I'm preshus bad! I'm sure as a drop of that 'ud do me good. But it is busted 'ard work to get it; she do keep it so 'orful tight! I mus' try or I shall die!"

Mr. Rumball then very cautiously stretched forth his arm towards the bottle, and was in the act of taking it from Mrs. Rumball's fingers, when it was suddenly whisked aside, and Rumball fell hastily but silently back on his pillow.

"Bother 'er!" was Mr. Rumball's mental exclamation.

"Hit won't do, Rumball!" said the weak voice of his wife. "I seed wot yer was hup to, though yer didn't think as I did! Hits no use a pretendin' to be asleep. Yer ain't bad, an' yer only want to deprive me on it for yer own greedy hinside!"

"Dolly," simpered Mr. Rumball; "ow can yer! Yer *knows* as I'm feelin' orful sick!"

"Shet up, drat yer! Hif yer was a-dyin', yer shudn't hev a drop! An yer knows why—a-leavin' me expoghed ter hevry danger hever since we lef bewtifool Devon. I wish I was there now!"

Mrs. Rumball ceased talking so suddenly that Rumball was induced to rise once more on his elbow, and take a look of inquiry at the unkind partner of his bosom.

To his astonishment and alarm, Mrs. Rumball was staring at something with widely-opened eyes and mouth, apparently fearfully terror-stricken.

Her face was almost blanched, and her whole frame shook as though she had been suddenly transported to the Arctic regions in her slumbering costume.

"Wot in the world is it, Dolly?" asked Rumball, in a low and tremulous tone. "Wot is hit yer sees? Don't stare like that! Dolly, my darling, yer frightens me!"

"Wot is hit?" returned Mrs. Rumball, her teeth chattering and her body still shaking. "I—I—believe as I see the—the—devil hisself," with a shudder, "a-lookin' hat me through thet theer hole, Rumball!"

"Never, Dolly!" exclaimed Rumball.

"I *did*, Rumball—I swears hit!"

"Couldn't, Dolly!" returned Rumball, who was now in as great a tremble as his wife. "I never heard o' the—the—devil peeping, like playful babbies, through holes an' round corners. Yer mus' hev been dreamin', Dolly! Yer all of a shake, like. Let me 'old the bottle fur yer," he added, kindly, and stretching forth his arm.

The next moment, lightning flashed from his eyes as the back of Mrs. Rumball's hand fell heavily across them, and as he fell back on the pillow, he heard a voice, saying—

"Take thet, now! Hif yer comes thet agin, Rumball, I'll smash the bottle hon yer nose—theer! Yer unnerhan' tricks——"

Again Mrs. Rumball stopped suddenly, and again the terror-stricken look came over her face, and the trembling increased.

This time her gaze was fixed on the slowly-moving panel, which was being pressed back by a pair of hands—hands, too, as black as a negro's.

What, in the name of all that was dreadful, was coming in?

In another moment, Mrs. Rumball's eyes saw appear a head with a general's cocked-hat!

The face was as black as night, with white rolling eyeballs, giving it a most fiendish expression.

Mrs. Rumball, paralysed with fear, sat staring with the blood stagnant in her veins; and her heart, for all the good it was in the way of beating, may just as well have been at the mast-head, exposed to the cooling influence of the midnight breeze.

To add to her terror, the owner of the head, at this moment, put his finger on his lips, as though to caution silence, and a voice thus addressed her in a low hoarse whisper—

"Si-s-h! Don't be frightened, Mrs. Rumball, I'm the General—General Shoot. I want your assistance. I-I-I'm in a devil of a mess; I've been imprisoned in the lower regions——"

As the General was speaking, he advanced gradually into the bunk—as we must call it—his black, muddy uniform, and sword; but the words "lower regions," had hardly escaped his lips, when Mrs. Rumball found her tongue, and, uttering a piercing shriek, she—forgetting her sea-sickness—leapt out of bed and, dashing aside the other blanket which divided the boys and men's berths from hers, rushed in exclaiming—

"The devil! the devil!"

The commotion which followed was one of those scenes of mixed incidents which we have long since given up the attempt to describe fully.

Our Boys, the soldiers, and sailors were aroused to a fear of some terrible calamity having overtaken the ship, in two ways.

The first was by the screams of Mrs. Rumball, and the second was by Mrs. Rumball's body.

As the sailors and boys were in hammocks slung at each side of the deck, and the soldiers were lying on the deck with their feet to the centre, it was impossible that Mrs. Rumball in her frightened state, and in the dark, could steer a clear course.

It was inevitable that she should come into collision with one, and trip over the other.

Accordingly, Mrs. Rumball, screaming terrifically "The devil! The devil!" rushed full-butt against the first hammocks, rebounded, fell on the deck, picked herself up, but only, the next moment, to trip up against a sleeping warrior and pitch headlong on to the next, nearly crushing the life out of the poor fellow, apart from nearly frightening him to death.

In this manner Mrs. Rumball progressed—a mad career that was quickly to be followed by another equally mad—the career of Mr. Rumball.

Mr. Rumball no sooner caught sight of the black General than, reiterating the cry of "The devil! The devil!" off he started on the tracks of his wife.

Soon the greatest confusion prevailed.

Boys, sailors, soldiers, groping and floundering about in the dark, demanding what was the matter, with Mr. and Mrs. Rumball—being unknown voices—vociferating the name of the evil one, formed a veritable pandemonium.

The confusion and alarm were increased by Joey Pumps.

That young gentleman, who never lost his coolness, had been coiled up in a corner on a blanket, next to Mrs. Rumball's berth and, on the first outcry, he had crept on his hands and knees and peeped in to see what was up.

Joey's sharp eyes falling on the General, he saw at once what had happened.

"Oh lor!" chuckled Joey. "'Ere's a go! Oh, my heye! I'm blow'd hif the Gen'ral ain't got loose an' Dolly hev took 'im fur the devil! Oh, lor!—I be orf agin;" he added, sinking down and giving way to a delicious fit of laughter.

Presently, as he came to himself, he muttered:

"I wish Dolly Swaps was 'ere, hit 'ud do 'is art good!"

"What's it all about, Joey?" asked a voice close to him.

"Is that Dolly Swaps?" asked Joey.

"Yes. What's going on?"

"Jist take a peep hin ther', Dolly," said Joey.

Dolly did, and almost screamed with astonishment and delight.

"I wonder how the General got out, Joey?" asked Dolly, when he could speak calmly.

"Thet 'ere's mor' 'n I kin tell, Dolly, but theer 'e is, and 'e looks as frightened as a wild Hogibbaway Injun."

At this moment a wild-looking fellow staggered into Mrs. Rumball's berth.

It was Sergeant O'Shehe in his shirt, with hair dishevelled, and a pale, scared face.

As his eyes fell upon the General, looking misty, yet palpable, in the faint radiance of the night-light, the Sergeant's face grew paler still; and, clapping his hands to his head, he stood glaring in horror-struck silence at the awful vision.

The vision thinking there was now a chance of being heard, and the true state of the case discovered if it only spoke cautiously—spoke:

"Don't be alarmed, Sergeant; I'm only the General. I'm in a deuce of a mess. I've been imprisoned in the lower regions——"

The next moment the Sergeant, followed by screaming yells from Dolly and Joey, was off, exclaiming:

"The devil, by Heaven! In a general's cocked-hat!"

"What an unlucky devil I am!" muttered the poor General, despairingly, as the frightened Sergeant disappeared. "What am I to do?"

"You'd better go back to where you've come from, General," said Joey Pumps. "I'm blow'd hif yer haint been an' gone an' done hit now! Yer've drov' hevrybody mad, and hif they ketches yer they'll tear yer ter pieces! Yer'd better hev stayed in them lower regions, an' had patience ter be let hout. Go back agin' and I'll make hit all right!"

By this time there was a most extraordinary scene on deck.

Everybody except the watches had turned out undressed, and were running to and fro, standing in groups round Mr. and Mrs. Rumball and the Sergeant, and some had climbed into the rigging, all waiting to see his Satanic Majesty emerge from the forecastle hatchway, sporting a General's cocked-hat.

Officers as well as men were present, the former endeavouring to get to the bottom of the commotion.

The three authorities who had seen the vision agreed substantially in one particular, that the devil had on a cocked-hat, though each differed in minor particulars.

Mrs. Rumball, besides the cocked-hat, had distinctly seen a tail dragging on the deck, and had heard it making a rattling noise.

Mr. Rumball hadn't seen the tail, but had seen two immense eyes flashing fire, which seemed to scorch him as he jumped out of bed and fled.

The Sergeant had not noticed the tail either, and thought Mrs. Rumball must be mistaken.

He had, however, seen the fiery eyeballs, and cloven foot, and, indeed, but for that, and the fact that the vision had distinctly told him that it had just come from the lower regions, he could have sworn that it was the ghost of the missing General.

The officers, putting "this and that" together, came to the conclusion that the supposed devil was none other than the General himself, turned up from some mysterious corner.

Having come to this conclusion, they retired to dress themselves for the purpose of going below to fathom the mystery.

At this moment, Joey Pumps and Dolly Swaps came rushing on deck, apparently in a great state of fright, exclaiming:—

Dolly.—"Here it comes; Here it comes! Look out!"

Joey.—"Save yerselves, heverybody! Hup the riggin'!'

"What confounded rubbish are you reading now? If you don't conduct yourself properly, you will be reduced."—See page 73.

Dolly.—"It's got it's sword drawn, and is cursing and swearing awfully!"

Joey.—"Hup the riggin', I tells yer, hif yer don't hall want to be killed!"

These cries and warnings produced the desired effect, and, in a minute, the nearly naked crew, soldiers, and boys, swarmed into the shrouds; many who had never been to sea before, actually making their way into the fore, main, and mizzen-tops, for the steamer was ship-rigged to carry full sail if necessary.

It was a peculiar sight to see the moon shining on the hundreds of white, fluttering shirts, and the deserted deck.

It looked as though all the ship's company had had a wetting, and had taken this novel course of getting into the rigging to dry their linen.

All eyes were eagerly directed to one spot—the hatchway, from where the devil was expected to come on deck.

Presently, amidst a murmur of excitement, appeared the cocked-hat, then the black face, then the shoulders, then the waist, then the legs, and the devil stood revealed in the full dress of a General!

His majesty, too, seemed to be in a devil of a rage.

Rolling his dreadful eye-balls, and waving his sword at the white people in the rigging, the figure exclaimed, savagely—

"You lot of idiots! You miserable fools! Hang it! can't you tell the difference between a General and the devil?"

Immediately the spell was dissolved, and a roar of laughter, led off by Joey Pumps and Dolly Swaps, resounded over the midnight sea.

———

CHAPTER XXIV.

DESCRIBES WHAT HAPPENED BEFORE READING THE RULES AND REGULATIONS.—HOW DOLLY SWAPS PUT A PLUG IN THE GENERAL'S THROAT AND A SHOT IN THE GENERAL'S EYE, AND THE CATASTROPHE THAT FOLLOWED.

OF course, the two mysteries were now solved.

The manner in which the General had been trapped soon became known, as also the cause of the peculiar conduct of Joey and Dolly.

These two young gentlemen became installed at once into the position of heroes, and became the pets of the crew and the soldiers.

Dick and the rest of the boys became prouder than ever of Dolly, and considered it no disgrace on them for Joey Pumps to swagger about the deck in the uniform of "The School of the Regiment."

Dolly related, with great unction, to Dick and the others, over and over again, the manner in which he made the General go down to bury the supposed dead body of Joey, and he laughed, enough to crack his sides, at the promise he extorted from the General not to interfere again in their larks.

"I wonder what the General will do, Dolly?" laughed Dick, as they sat at the rough table below at breakfast, soaking some ship's-biscuit in their tin of cocoa.

This question was answered by the Sergeant in person, who at that moment entered the berths, dressed up as though for parade, but looking very wan, and evidently suffering from sea-sickness.

He tried, however, to look stern, and throw as much sternness into his voice as possible, as he placed his hand on Dolly's shoulder, saying—

"This way, my joker. Come!"

"What's the matter, Serjeant?" asked Dolly, winking slyly at Dick.

"It's the masthead for you—that's what's the matter!"

"What for?"—innocently, and a grin going round the boys, the state of whose stomachs permitted them to sit at the table.

"No questions, but off you go," said the Sergeant, imperiously, "and thank your stars it's not from the yard-arm you are hanging!"

As Dolly, who rather liked the idea than otherwise of going to the masthead, rose to follow the Sergeant, the latter, looking round the table, said, sharply—

"Parade this morning on the quarter-deck after breakfast, to hear the Regulations read; and mind," glancing round, and elevating his voice, "that every mother's son of you is present, or—it's a bad look-out for you it'll be!"

Dolly Swaps, after some trouble, succeeded in reaching the maintop, where he had not been long perched, when he was joined by Joey Pumps.

With a grin and a knowing wink, Joey produced his pea-shooter and a black lump of something.

"What's the black lump, Joey?" asked Dolly, looking at that and the shooter without a smile,

"Ony a bit o' putty and blacklead, Dolly," replied Joey, with assumed demureness.

"Oh!" returned Dolly. "What's it for?"

"Only ter shoot porpusses, Dolly."

Here the two looked at each other with extreme gravity for a few moments, and then gave way to a series of facetious chuckles.

Leaving these two to enjoy the sport of shooting the porpoises, if such was their little game, we must descend to the quarter-deck where, a few minutes later, the boys assembled to answer to their names, and hear the Regulations read by the Sergeant.

The General, though he felt very ill from sea-sickness, and was looking very seedy, had determined to set an example to the boys, by showing them how he could do his duty under difficulties.

The General was not only seedy in himself, but seedy in his uniform.

The latter had been hastily dried, and the mud beaten out, followed by a vigorous brushing, but still it was a uniform no longer handsome.

It was irremediably stained, and that was vexing to one whose great point was that a soldier on parade, or off parade when dressed, but especially on parade, should look clean and smart.

But it couldn't be helped now.

Having been shipped off to sea in such an unexpected manner, it was, of course, the only uniform the General had, and so he resolved to make the best of it, as, indeed, he had resolved to make the best of his position.

So, putting as good face on it as he could, the General had forced himself on deck.

The steamer had now got into the Bay of Biscay, and the weather being rough, she rolled and pitched considerably, rendering it very difficult for anyone but a sailor to keep his legs.

Nevertheless, the parade took place in full dress, with carbines.

Many of the boys felt deadly sick, and could hardly obey the words of command.

Some felt qualmish, and only a few were well enough to enjoy the scene.

Those on board—notably the Jack Tars—who were well enough to put in an appearance, stood and lounged about, looking on with great expectation in the way of amusement.

The Sergeant, with the Regulation written out and posted on a board, stood in front of the boys, awaiting the General's order to begin.

The General, who had great difficulty in balancing himself, and maintaining that upright position so essential to a soldierlike appearance, and was also feeling too ill to trust himself to speak, was impatiently waiting to catch the Sergeant's eye to give him a dumb sign to proceed.

But the Sergeant was in the same fix as his General, and kept his eyes glued to the board, only too glad to postpone the moment when he should have to open his mouth.

The eyes of all the boys were fixed on the General, and he knew it.

Presently he caught a smile on the face of Dick, Tom, and Bob.

"The young rascals think I'm in a fix," he thought, "but I'll just show them that I'm *not.*"

Goaded, as it were to begin, the General was about to order the Sergeant to read, when something struck him on the point of the nose, causing him to start with a motion so violent as nearly to destroy his equilibrium.

With the sudden sting of pain, the General clapped his hand to his tingling organ, on the front of which he felt something sticking.

Carefully removing the foreign substance with his finger and thumb, the General gazed at it in astonishment, and then slowly scanned the features of the boys with a fierce and heavy frown.

The General had been struck on the nose—and a splendid shot it was, too—by a small black ball, which, although he didn't know it, had left the black mark of its impact.

Not a smile could the General see on any face, and the only indication he could detect of the incident having been noticed, was that of Dick Everett, Tom Sheppard, Bob Jones, and a few others, biting their lips.

"There's a pea-shooter about here, somewhere," snarled the General, addressing the Sergeant. "I thought I told you, sir, to examine their kits—eh, sir?"

"I did, General——" began the Sergeant, with the feeling of something rising in his throat.

"Silence, sir! When I give an order, sir, I——hang it, there's another shot!" suddenly cried the General, pulling out his handkerchief and holding it to his face, and staggering about with pain and the motion of the vessel.

"Wh—where, sir?" asked the Sergeant, in a faltering voice, making a staggering effort to approach the General.

"Where, sir! In my eye, sir! That's where!" yelled the General, followed by a good deal of suppressed laughter from the boys and spectators. "By heaven, sir! I——"

The General stopped, and holding his arm to protect his face, cast his eyes aloft to the maintop.

He had suddenly recollected that he had ordered Dolly Swaps to be located in that spot,

and that possibly the shots came from that quarter.

The General was right.

"I thought so!" he cried savagely. "Come down out of there, you young vagabond!"

The reply was a grin, and another shot, that passed into the General's open mouth, and, lodging in his throat, caused him to rush to the side of the vessel, and perform an energetic and involuntary operation, before he could get rid of the unsavoury plug.

Everybody was now in a state of side-splitting laughter.

The General's position was most ridiculous.

Nor was the Sergeant's much better.

Sea sickness, like gaping, must be catching, for Sergeant O'Shehe had no sooner caught sight of the General's predicament, than he was seized in like manner, and sought relief—as was the proper place for a good soldier—by his General's side.

And now followed a most exciting scene.

To the astonishment of everyone, he had no sooner got rid of the plug from his throat, than the General, his face inflamed with rage, rushed off the quarter-deck, mounted a water-barrel, from thence stepped into the chains, and, before he could be prevented, had commenced climbing the shrouds of the mainmast.

"By Jove!" cried Dick, "if he isn't after Dolly.

This was true, and well Dolly knew it!

The General had reached nearly half-way, when a cry of consternation arose from the spectators.

The General's hold had suddenly given way, and the next moment he was observed hanging head downwards, held by his spurs to the ratline!

The immediate cause of this was a well-directed shot in the General's other eye, delivered by Dolly Swaps.

"Well, I'm blow'd!" cried Joey Pumps, with a chuckle, as he saw the effect of the shot. "Hif 'e ain't has pretty a hobject as hever I see! That wur a stunnin' shot, Dolly, that wur! Yer gettin' quite 'spert at it."

"Do you think he looks anything like a porpoise, Joey?" asked Dolly.

"Now don't, Dolly!" pleaded Joey. "Don't go for to make me go orf, hup 'ere. I ain't a bird as can fly from this 'ere perch, yer know, an' I don't want ter hend my days till hall the fun's hover! Oh, lor, don't 'e look has though 'e carnt 'elp hisself!"

Then, addressing the General, Joey continued—

"I say, Gen'ral, ow'll yer describe yer present sensasherns wen yer coms ter write yer diary? Ses yer, 'I hed the rollin' sea hon top o' me an' the wessel hunnerneath; an' I seed 'unnerds o' gibberin' deemon hall around, an' I was hall hupsy-down an' topsy-turby, and wibbelly-wobbelly; an' I heerd dreffel noises hin my heers, an' my nose hit swelled hout.' Hullo, Dolly, jist look hat the Sargint; ain't 'e jist a feedin' the fishes! I say, Sargint," added Joey, in a shrill voice, which set all the boys screaming, in spite of their sick feeling, "that's kontrarey to the regellashuns, yer know, that is! an' hon the quarterdeck, too! I say, chaps, yer kin relieve yer feelins soon as yer like, now! Hif the bigwigs carnt 'old hout agin hit, wot's the little uns ter do? Oh! ah! I hunnerstans hall about hit, my fine feller," continued Joey, as the Sergeant looked and shook his fist at him, angrily. "

shud feel jist the same, hif I wos yer! He, hi! Oh, lor, wot a rumpus yer've made, Dolly, hall through some bits o' putty an' blacklead!"

"It's wonderful, Joey!" replied Dolly, with a grin. "There they go to get the General down."

This was true.

As a matter of fact, the General had scarcely dropped and hung by his spurs to the ratlines, when a rush had been made to rescue him from his perilous position.

Officers, sailors, and soldiers all vied with each other in rendering assistance.

But the task was not so easy of accomplishment.

The General, of course, was suspended outside the shrouds, and, as he hung with his head downwards and his vision had become dim from the rush of blood into his eyes, and his brain was in a general state of obfuscation, he was incapable of aiding the efforts of his rescuers.

What was to be done?

The General was suspended in a very awkward place; he was very heavy, and he might slip through their fingers in lifting him off, or cutting the ratlines to free the spurs.

As in this contingency the poor General, having ·his heaviest end downwards, would assuredly plunge into the bay, a rope was at length lashed round his body, passed over the yard-arm of the mainsail, and in that manner he was hauled up and swung on board.

It was two or three minutes before the General, who was placed in a sitting position, lost the deadened sensation in his head, and blinding feeling in his eyes, sufficiently to recall what had happened to him.

Then, uttering a groan of disappointed rage, he cast his eyes instinctively towards the maintop, and catching sight of Dolly's grinning face, he muttered—

"A sovereign to the man who will catch me that young villain!"

This was not a difficult feat to perform for a Jack Tar.

Dolly, though nimble enough on terra-firma, and very smart in the gymnasium, was not at home in a ship's rigging, and had quite as much as he could do to keep his hold in the maintop at the rate the steamer was rolling, was easily captured and, along with Joey, triumphantly handed over to the General, who, in the meantime, had regained his station on the quarter-deck.

"There they be, yer honour," said the Jack who had effected the capture, "I thought as they was chips o' the same block like, and nothing much to choose atween 'em, you'd just like to settle accounts with both."

This was a supreme moment of gratification for the General, and yet fraught with embarrassment.

He was burning to punish Dolly and Joey in the most effectual and telling manner, but was puzzled what course to adopt.

The General had swooped upon them as an eagle swoops on its prey; but, as he held them at arm's length, glaring upon them with a malicious scowl, they looked so little, so utterly insignificant, that it seemed almost an act of cowardice to chastise them.

"I only wish they were men," thought the General, "I'd sink the dignity of my rank and take them 'one up and one down,' and spoil the regularity of their impish features."

The scene now was an interesting one.

As Dolly and Joey stood, each with one of the General's hands on his throat, pretending to look as demure and shy as though they were about to be decorated for an act of valour, they became the focus for a hundred pair of laughing eyes, and a hundred features expanded upon them in a broad grin.

The question which each asked himself was, "In what manner will the General punish them?"

The General was debating this question in his mind.

He could box their ears, but that would not have a lasting effect. Dolly had already been punished in that manner, and it had proved unavailing.

It would be *infra dig.* to take them across his knees, and subject their "right-about-face" to the rapid application of his hand.

Suddenly a thought struck him.

He would test the resistibility of their skulls by collision—in other words, he would knock their heads together to see how they would like it.

The next instant was heard a succession of sharp detonating sounds, like the snapping of a gun-cap, as the General brought the heads of Dolly and Joey together, closer than they had ever been in life before, and with a force that seemed to arouse within them a thousand cannon roars, and kept a continual light before their eyes, like flashes from a thousand guns.

Dolly afterwards said that the sensation was like a sham-fight on Bangfire Common, without the expenditure of an ounce of powder.

The General having once commenced, seemed· as though he could never leave off operating, and kept it up at a fine rate until everybody, at length, expected to see the boys' brains flying over the deck.

How much longer the General would have kept it up, had he not been interrupted in a very singular manner, it is impossible to say.

Joey Pumps, whose skull had never experienced such a number of stunning cracks—not even from the rolling-pin of Mrs. Rumball—endured them until he considered he had had quite enough, and then began to give tongue in his usual protestive manner.

"Now, then, Gen'ral, that'll do. D'ye 'ear? Yer agoin' hon hit like Mister Bones o' the nigger methodists.* Stop it, I tells yer. Yer'll wish yer hadn't done so much hon hit."

Here Joey yelled with an energy that touched a sympathetic chord in a lady's bosom.

That bosom was Mrs. Rumball's.

At that moment Mrs. Rumball, whose state of ·internal suffering was almost unendurable, and who felt, like many have felt before her, that she could submit to be thrown overboard with perfect indifference, had dragged her almost lifeless body from the fo'castle hatch on deck to try the effect of some fresh air.

Mrs. Rumball's beautifully-rounded person was enveloped in very scanty apparel, which consisted only of her nightdress and petticoat, a pair of bare legs, and a voluminous nightcap.

This slight costume was not adopted by Mrs. Rumball from her belief in the questionable taste of the assertion that "Beauty unadorned is adorned the most," but from a perfect indifference as to whether she were adorned or not.

Mrs. Rumball was far too ill to care about the

* Joey evidently meant to say "Melodists."

quantity and nature of the garments she had on at this moment; but, to her everlasting honour be it said, Mrs. Rumball was not too ill to attend to a cry of distress.

As she emerged into the fresh air a cry of this description fell upon her ears.

It was a voice, too, she had heard often before. Pausing a moment to listen, Mrs. Rumball murmured—

"Thet's Joey's woice. I'll swear! Somebody mus' be whackin' 'im!"

Where was the poor little fellow?

Mrs. Rumball's eyes, which a moment since were languid almost to death, seemed to flash into life as they glanced around in search of her adopted Joey.

Mrs. Rumball's searching glance ended on the quarter-deck, where she beheld a sight that almost dried up her blood with horror, and filled her soul with indignation.

"Good Heavin!" cried Mrs. Rumball, "he's a beatin' theer poor little brains hout!"

The next moment, amidst the greatest astonishment and amusement, Mrs. Rumball staggered, from the rolling of the vessel, off to the rescue, exclaiming—

"A-done! a-done, yer brute! Agh! Leave 'em alone, do!"

The General, hearing the strange noise, looked up, and seeing with horror from whom it emanated, cast about for a place of refuge.

The General had a perfect dread of encountering ladies of the Mrs. Rumball class—he could encounter anything but a virago.

Just behind him was the saloon skylight, and at the far end of this the Captain's private entrance into his cabin.

Down this the alarmed General dived with the speed of thought, and succeeded in closing the hatch just as Mrs. Rumball scrambled upon the quarter-deck.

"Whur is he? Whur is the base wretch?" cried Mrs. Rumball, looking around for her intended victim.

"'E's gone, Dolly," said Joey, "wanished down the skylight. Yer too late fur wengence."

"Drat 'im!" cried Mrs. Rumball. "Hit's well fur 'im I didn't git my han's hin 'is 'air—the brute! I'd a giv' 'im knockin' hout my Joey's brains! I hallows noboddy to whack my Joey but myself, an' so I lets hevrybody know," she added, looking around significantly. "Yer grinnin' lot o' jackonapses! Come hon, both hon 'e."

The latter speech was addressed to Dolly and Joey, who were squatted on the deck rubbing their aching pates.

Much as the latter had suffered at the General's hands, they soon had reason to regret their rescue at the hands of Mrs. Rumball.

As that lady spoke she stooped forward, and, turning Dolly and Joey over on their faces as though they were two pieces of dough, took one in each hand by the seat of his trousers, and, amidst the convulsive laughter of the spectators, staggered off with her prizes.

The adventures that Dolly and Joey went through, the hairbreadth escapes they had for their lives, from this moment, until they found themselves safely deposited in Mrs. Rumball's berth, were something wonderful in their character.

Imagine a tipsy milk-maid with a pair of well-filled milk-cans yoked across her shoulders, staggering beneath their weight between the walls of a narrow street—imagine the swinging and swaying of the cans, with an occasional collision between them, and frequent terrific smashes and dashes against the walls,—imagine this, reader, and you will have a faint idea of the progress of Dolly and Joey in the hands of Mrs. Rumball as she rolled from side to side of the rolling vessel.

Dolly's and Joey's heads not only came into contact with each other with a force that beat the General's efforts all to "fits," but threatened to be smashed to bits, or pounded out of all shape by frequent knocks and bumps against the masts, and other articles that strewed the vessel's deck.

In such imminent danger appeared Dolly's and Joey's brains of being scattered about, that the sailors and soldiers thought it wise to interfere to prevent such a catastrophe.

But when some of them made the attempt they came to the conclusion that, if they wished to gain their end, they had better leave her alone, for Mrs. Rumball used the luckless boys as though they had been a pair of dumb-bells, or war-clubs, swinging them about her head, and scattering her assailsnts like nine-pins.

Mrs. Rumball carried all before her, bumped Dolly and Joey down the forecastle hatchway, staggered with them through the men's berths until she reached her own, when, dropping them on the deck, she sank back on her feather-bed exclaiming—

"Thank Heavin, they're safe!"

Having thus seen Dolly and Joey in a place of safety, beyond the immediate reach, at any rate, of the General's unslaked vengeance, we must return to the quarter-deck and describe what transpired after the triumphant retreat of Mrs. Rumball.

The General, who was determined to carry out his programme of reading the rules and regulations, no sooner saw the coast clear than he appeared on deck, trying to look as dignified and unconcerned as though he hadn't beaten an ignominious retreat before a lady, and turned tail like a low-bred cur.

The interest in the proceedings had in no way diminished, on the part of the sailors and soldiers, on the disappearance of Mrs. Rumball and Dolly and Joey from the arena of fun.

Everybody was curious to witness the further progress and ending of the ceremony.

Both the General and Sergeant were still very ill, and looked very white about the "gills," but there was a stern and stubborn look about the former that spoke well in favour of his endurance, whilst there was a lack of spirit and energy—a limpness as it were—in the Sergeant's bearing that rendered it doubtful whether he would hold out to the end.

Besides the General, the Sergeant, and the boys which formed such conspicuous objects on the quarter-deck, there were assembled the captain and officers of the ship, and many of the officers belonging to the troops on board.

These were watching the General somewhat critically, a fact of which the General was aware, and he was determined to uphold his dignity and authority.

Knowing what was to be read out, he was the last person who would venture to give way to the prostrating effects of sea-sickness.

He had been sick already it was true; but that, as everybody could have seen, was purely unavoidable on his part.

Who would not have been sick if he had had a plug stuck in his throat?

Many persons are sick when a pill sticks in their throat, and his plug was quite as nauseous as a pill.

Thus reasoned the General.

Assuming his most dignified manner and tone, the General, coughing once or twice to clear his throat, thus addressed the Sergeant—

"Begin, sir, and read loudly and distinctly!"

Sergeant O'Shehe, inwardly wishing the General and the reading were "at the devil," also cleared his throat, and, holding up the board, began in a shaky voice—

"'Rules and Regulations to be observed by the School of the Regiment on board ship, viz. :—

"'Memorandum.

"'General Shoot being desirous of showing himself a man of his word in regard to the promise he made to Dolly Swaps to no more interfere with the la—la—' ("Hang it !" muttered the Sergeant, hesitating, "it is!") and then continuing aloud, 'larks of the boys for his kindness in helping him to bury—bury—the—the—de—de,' ("Bless my soul!") 'dead body of—Joey——'"

Here broke forth a simultaneous tittering from the boys and the officers on the quarter-deck, whilst the General stood staring at the Sergeant astounded.

The Sergeant, not receiving a check from the General, continued—

"'Joey Pumps hereby directs the clauses relating to the possession of pea-shooters and larks generally to be cancelled. In fact the more larks they have, especially with—with—pea—pea.' ("Hanged if I don't think the General's gone mad!") 'pea-shooters, the better the General will be—be—pleased—the—'"

At this point the Sergeant was pulled up by loud laughter, and the voice of the General thundering in his ears—

"Silence, sir! what confounded rubbish is that you are reading, sir? Are you mad, sir—eh? what?'

"It's—it's," stammered the Sergeant, "it's in your own handwriting, General."

"That's a lie, sir!" retorted the General, vehemently. "You're getting a systematic liar, sir! What——'

"I beg your pardon, General——"

"Si-lence, sir!" roared the General. "Will you keep that confounded tongue of yours still, sir? Hang it! sir—"

"Here's the board, General," again interrupted the Sergeant, holding it forth, and trying to look at his officer with offended dignity; "you can see for yourself, sir."

This was such confounded presumption on the part of Sergeant O'Shehe that, for a few moments, the General regarded his non-commissioned officer as though the latter had suddenly been transformed into a new species of gorilla.

Then advancing, his lips livid with passion, the General placed his face and fist as close to the Sergeant's face as he could without actually touching it, and was on the point of growling out some terrible threat when a deeper roll of the vessel than usual caused him to pitch forward with his nose against the Sergeant's buttons, and the next instant they both rolled on to the deck, followed by renewed laughter.

"Dolly ought to be here to see this fun," thought Dick.

Dolly wasn't far off, as it happened.

If Dick at that moment had cast his eyes aloft to the mizen-top, he would have seen that young gentleman and Joey Pumps gazing down at the scene in much enjoyment, and would have observed a large piece of something attached to a string dangling a few feet from the top.

What that something was we shall see presently.

The General's temper underwent no improvement in consequence of his ridiculous tumble, nor did the nether portion of his uniform.

When the General regained his feet, an alteration in the shape of the seat of his trousers had taken place.

The fracture, which had occurred in his struggle to get out of the trap, and which had been hastily closed by the captain's servant, was observed to have given way, and was now reopened—a chance which his shirt tail had taken advantage of to escape, and was seen fluttering in the breeze.

Unaware of this graceful addition to his soldier-like appearance, the General, taking care not to fall this time, turned on the Sergeant, who had got up without an accident, and said fiercely—

"You ungainly fellow! You've no more steadiness in your legs than—than—a—a—young chicken, sir! If you want to tumble, sir, go below and tumble, and don't choose the quarter-deck to make a fool of yourself—and me!"

"I—I—beg your pardon, General," stuttered the Sergeant, placing his hand to his mouth to conceal a smile, which, even in his agitation and the sick state of his stomach, he could not repress at the sight of the General's fluttering tail, "I—I—thought it was you——"

"Silence, sir!" snarled the General. "Be careful what you say, sir! What are you grinning at? Take your hand down, sir, and stand at attention, before a general officer! I say, sir, you ought to belong to the awkward squad, sir! The awkward squad, I say! D'ye hear?"

"Yes, Gen——"

"Silence, I say! Don't 'Yes General' me, sir! If you can't maintain a more soldierlike deportment than you exhibit now, you shall have an hour's setting-up drill every day, sir! Give me the board, sir, and let me see who has dared to put down such rubbish. This is an imitation of my handwriting, sir!" continued the General, with a growl; "the work of one of these mischievous rascals! Of what use are you, I should like to know, sir, if you can't prevent such tricks as this?—eh, sir?"

"I—I—can't see everything that goes on, General," pleaded the Sergeant.

"Then you ought to see, sir! What's the use of having eyes, sir, if you don't make use of them? You know what the young rascals are, sir, and you should watch them—watch them, sir! Keep your eyes open, sir! Why didn't you discover this before reading it out here, sir?"

"I—I—was too unwell, General, to——"

"Then you have no business to be unwell, sir, and allow it to interfere with your duty! I wonder you're not sick on parade, sir! Read the clauses about sea-sickness, and mind you attend to them, as well as the boys, sir!"

The Sergeant, whose sickness was each moment increasing in intensity, took the board, and, facing the boys, began reading in a very faint voice whilst the General stood close to his shoulder—

"'Clause 1st—Sea-sickness is strictly prohibited.

"'Clause 2nd—Any boy pleading that avoidable complaint——'"

At this juncture the piece of something that had been dangling from the mizzen-top on the end of a piece of string, was suddenly let down by Dolly Swaps, who arrested its descent just as it arrived under the noses of the General and the Sergeant.

As this bit of something happened to be a large piece of fat pork, in a horribly putrid state, the effluvia was excessively offensive, and the effect upon the General and Sergeant was almost instantaneous.

They both recoiled from the tainted morsel as though they had been shot, began sniffing and puffing, pressing their hands to their stomachs, and making the most hideous faces, indicative of excessive nausea.

General.—"God bless (hic) my (hic) soul! Poof—ugh—this (hic) is horri (hic) ble! Ugh—ugh!" ending in a frantic rush to the vessel's side.

Sergeant.—"Poof—poof! (hic) pshaw (hic) Oh Lor (hic) Lord! Oh, Lord! Oh!—O—h!—O——" ending, like the General's emotion, in a transgression of the order prohibiting sea-sickness.

The sight now presented by the General and Sergeant in the relief of their overcharged feelings, with the former's protruding linen flapping to the wind, was so exceedingly ridiculous, that it was greeted with shouts of convulsive laughter from the quarter-deck to the fo'castle.

Many there present thought it impossible that they could laugh more.

But they were mistaken.

Suddenly a little figure, followed by a black Newfoundland dog, glided across the quarter-deck, and approached the suffering General.

The little figure was Dolly Swaps.

The dog was our old and clever acquaintance, "Pomp."

Before his little game could be prevented, Dolly caught hold of the General's flying tail, and shaking it, said coaxingly—

"Seize it 'Pomp'! Seize it then! That's a good dog!" added Dolly, as "Pomp" promptly obeyed. "Pull it then! Tug away! Si-s-s-s! Shake it, good dog!"

It would be impossible to depict in sufficiently graphic language the screaming uproar which followed this last grand idea of Dolly's, or the fix in which the General once more found himself.

What with his sickness urging him one way, and "Pomp" pulling another, it was about as embarrassing a predicament as could well be conceived.

The struggle ended in "Pomp" gaining the day, that is, the shirt gave way, and "Pomp" went capering about the deck, tossing his white trophy triumphantly in his mouth.

How the boys got off the quarter-deck they have but a misty recollection to this day.

But there was a great deal of tumbling and rolling, tripping up with carbines, spasmodic laughter, and a loud voice uttering annihilating denunciations behind them, accompanied by fire-buckets, mops, marline-spikes, and sundry other articles flying above their heads, the latter ceasing not until the last boy found himself scuttling for his life down the fo'castle hatch.

CHAPTER XXV.

THE GENERAL DISPATCHES SERGEANT O'SHEHE IN SEARCH OF A PAIR OF OVERALLS.—RECORDS THE SUCCESS WHICH ATTENDED THE SERGEANT'S EFFORTS.

As will be imagined, the General, after this last trick, retired to his cabin as quickly as possible.

He was now in an awkward fix.

Unless he could borrow a pair of trousers, he would be unable to make his appearance in public.

"Confound the young devils!" muttered the General. "I could manage to go without a shirt, but what am I to do for overalls?"

He determined to consult the Sergeant, and he sent for him.

The General had taken off his fractured overalls, and, when the Sergeant entered, he was seated on a cabin-stool in his bare legs and tunic.

"A nice mess I'm in now, ain't I?" growled the General, as O'Shehe entered.

"I'm afraid you are, General!" said the Sergeant. as he saluted, and came to a stand at the position of attention.

"Afraid! You can see I am, sir!"

"Ye—yes, sir," returned the Sergeant, feeling a sensation akin to laughter agitate his nervous system.

"Then answer to the point in a soldierlike manner," snapped the General. "What the devil am I to do?"

"I don't know, General," returned O'Shehe.

"Don't know? Then you ought to know, sir! After getting me in this cursed fix——"

"Beg pardon, General. I—I—don't think—"

"Silence, sir! Hang it, will you keep to the point, and answer my questions! Your confounded tongue goes like a clapper! I can't go on parade like this, can I!—eh?"

"No, General."

"A pretty half-and-half fool I should look, should I not, sir—eh?"

"Yes, General."

"You can say 'Yes, General' to that, quickly enough," growled the General, casting a scowl on the Sergeant.

"It's an awkward costume, too, General, to appear before the ladies in," ventured the Sergeant.

"What's that to you, sir?" thundered the General. "Will you confine your remarks to the regimental part of the business? What am I to do, sir? Tell me that."

"I—I—I'm afraid you'll have to keep your cabin, General," returned the Sergeant, hesitatingly. "And I—I—almost think it's the best place for you, sir!"

"What, sir!" roared the General. "What's that, sir? Th—th—the best place for me, sir? Confound your cursed impudence, sir! Why may I ask, sir, do you think this is the best place for me? Do you insinuate that I cannot take care of myself, sir? Eh, sir, is that what you mean?"

"No, General," returned the Sergeant, "I—I—don't mean that, sir, but those boys are such dare—devils——"

"Then you do mean that I can't take care of myself, sir! Allow me to tell you, Sergeant O'Shehe, that, for a Non-Commissioned Officer you've got the devil's own cheek, sir! How dare you talk to me—me, sir—as though I were only a little boy—eh, sir?"

"I didn't intend——"

"Silence, sir! Allow me to impress on your dense mind, sir, that I *can* take care of myself, and what is more, I *will* appear on deck! If I can't go on deck *with* trousers, I'll go on deck *without* trousers, sir! D'ye hear that, sir?"

"Yes, General."

"Then go and borrow me a pair, sir."

The Sergeant shook his head doubtfully.

"I don't think there's a pair on board, General, large enough——"

"Go and *look* sir! Confound you, sir, don't stand there, 'don't thinking!'"

"Are you *very* particular, what sort of overalls, General?"

"How can I be particular, sir? Beggars can't be choosers, can they? I don' care so long as they are decent. The stupid ass!" muttered the General irritably, as his Sergeant closed the cabin door. "Rather than those young rascals should have it all their own way, now that they have got me on board, I'll look 'em up, if I have to go about with bare legs!"

Sergeant O'Shehe proceeded on his mission,

Naturally, he tried his luck, first amongst the officers of the ship, and the officers of the regiment that were on board, but his efforts in those quarters were unsuccessful.

There wasn't one amongst them with a corporation half the size of the General's.

"Why don't you put a patch on the stern, Sergeant?" asked the Captain of the steamer; "that would be better than no breeches."

"Couldn't do it, sir," said the Sergeant, shaking his head; "I'm nothing of a tailor"

"Go to the ship's tailor," returned the Captain.

But it was no go.

The Sergeant went and got his reply—

"Tell the General to patch his own stern, and go to the devil!"

The Sergeant then went round the crew and the soldiers, but met with nothing but rude jokes and laughter.

The bos'n was the nearest man to the General's size, but he'd see the General scuttled first before he'd lend him anything to cover his bare poles, and *then* he wouldn't."

"What the deuce am I to do?" muttered the Sergeant, at the last repulse. "There seems to be no pity for the General amongst the lot on board. I'm afraid to go back without a pair of some sort."

"I ken put yer hup ter a dodge, Sergeant, hif yer likes."

The speaker was Joey Pumps, who had watched the Sergeant's efforts with much interest, and had waited the moment of his failure to come to his assistance.

"I ken," continued Joey, seriously, as the Sergeant looked down on the little imp with a lofty glance of suspicion. "I knows wheer to put me 'and hon has bootifool a pair o' trousers has hever yer seed. They's jist the werry thing for the General."

"Are you sure?" asked the Sergeant. "Mind —don't you come any nonsense with me!" he added, sternly.

"'Onner bright, Sergeant!" returned Joey, with a wink. "I means what I ses, and ken do wot I ses!"

"Well, where are the trousers?"

"Yer'll stan' my fren', will yer, hif I'm found hout?"

"Certainly, and so will the General, too. I promise you that."

"I honly wants yer to hanser fur yerself, Ser-jint. Yer see hit's honly hout o' konsiderashun for yer has I does it. Yer sweers yer'll stick ter me?"

"I do, Joey. I shall be only too glad to do so."

"Werry well, then. Hall ye've got ter do, is jist ter put yer 'ead hinside theer, an' yea'll see the 'bags' 'angin agin the boards."

"In there!" exclaimed the Sergeant. "Why, that's Mrs. Rumball's crib!"

The Sergeant's tone and looks were suspicious again all at once.

"I knows hit is," said Joey, coolly, and giving the Sergeant another of his knowing winks. "Yer jist look hin. Do hit quiet, fer poor Dolly's—Dolly Rumball, I mean—jist got inter a sweet doze, an' it wouldn't be good fur yer 'elth to wake 'er hup neither!"

The Sergeant hesitated for a few moments.

Apart from his fear of his possibly bringing upon his head a full share of Mrs. Rumball's abuse, if not something more tangible, he had a natural delicacy in intruding, unbidden by the lady herself, into a lady's chamber.

Many ladies, he knew, had an insuperable objection to being suddenly intruded upon by one of the opposite sex.

The ladies had manifold and good reasons for this objection, and the Sergeant was of too gallant a nature himself to disregard a lady's feelings, unless he were compelled to do so under the stern call of duty.

Did the duty he was upon now justify him in entering upon the retirement of Mrs. Rumball at this moment?

The General wanted a pair of trousers.

He—the Sergeant—had tried everywhere to get him a pair, but without success.

He—the Sergeant—was informed, on good authority, that there was a pair of suitable trousers in Mrs. Rumball's sanctum.

Query.—Would he be justified in getting those trousers at any risk?

Would the General approve of the forcible abduction of those trousers?

The Sergeant pictured to himself the General's bare legs, and came to the conclusion that the General *would* justify the surreptitious act.

"Then it's a case of duty before gallantry," thought the Sergeant, "and so, here goes!"

Sergeant O'Shehe then gently drew aside the blanket, and peeped in.

Mrs. Rumball's crib being, from its situation, unavoidably dark, Mrs. Rumball was compelled to keep a nightlight burning day and night.

By this faint light the Sergeant was enabled to see that Mrs. Rumball was in bed, and, as Joey Pumps had said, appeared to have fallen into a sweet slumber, with a bottle of brandy, as usual, held in her hand.

By her side was Rumball, also asleep, and was at that moment dreaming that he had, also, a bottle of brandy in his hand.

The Sergeant having satisfied himself that the worthy couple were asleep, looked about for the trousers.

But he could not see any garment that bore a resemblance to a pair of suitable overalls.

Hanging against the bulkhead was an article of wearing apparel, of scarlet flannel, belonging to a lady, and which, from the ornamentation of white silk in a fancy pattern, which ran round the bottom of the legs, the Sergeant made out to be Mrs. Rumball's drawers.

These, surely, were not what Joey alluded to!

They would not suit the General at all!

Of couse Joey meant a pair of Rumball's trousers; but then, the only pair he could see was a pair that Rumball had on, and which he had got into bed with, being too ill, no doubt, to undress himself.

The Sergeant, beginning to fancy that he had been imposed upon, withdrew his head, and whispered—

"I don't see anything there, Joey, but a pair of Mrs. Rumball's drawers—eh?"

"Well, Sergeant," returned Joey, with a grin; "that's them!"

"Why, what the deuce;—do you mean to say that the General's to wear Mrs. Rumball's drawers?"

The Sergeant spoke indignantly, and was utterly astounded to hear Joey reply, cooly—

"Why in course I does! Ken 'e hev anythin' as is more sootable. I shed like ter know?"

"What;" exclaimed the Sergeant, opening his eyes. "Do think what your saying; my boy! I'm speaking of a lady's drawers—do you understand? I said drawers—*trousers*, you know!"

"An' I mean drawers—*trousers*—myself."

"Look here," said the Sergeant, suddenly catching Joey by the throat. "I'll give you ten seconds to explain your meaning—if you can—and if you can't I'll choke you! In what way are those trousers suitable for the General?"

"Why, 'ell look jist like a French gen'ral, won't he?" said Joey. "Them furrin sodgers likes scarlet cloth, yer knows, an' plenty o' room ter set down hin! An' hif there ain't lots o' that in Dolly Rumball's trousers, besides being a jolly sight puttier than the Frenchies, then yer ken choke away! You'd better collar 'em while the're wissable, Sergeant," added Joey, persuasively. "You won't hev such another chance hif Dolly wonce gits 'em hon agin. They're jist clean, an' she won't take 'em orf hunder a month ter wash, Jist konsidder hit, now,"

The Sergeant did consider it.

It wasn't such a bad idea after all.

"They are not exactly the thing," thought the Sergeant; "but upon my soul, he might go further and fare worse. I can but try him. I *will!*"

Having come to this conclusion, he removed his grip from Joey's throat, saying—

"If I consent to take them to the General, will you slip in and take them?"

"Not hif I knows hit!" returned Joey. "Yer mus' take the whole of the respons-hab-ility o' priggin' 'em, Serjint, an' yer'd better do hit afore she comes to."

The Sergeant, finding Joey was firm, came to the conclusion that he must accomplish the burglarious deed himself.

Would he not enter a lion's den, or go through fire and water for the General?

Certainly?

Then what was Mrs. Rumball to risk in comparison to those dangers?

Nothing!

Before venturing upon the risky job, however, the Sergeant looked for some weapon of defence in the event of Mrs. Rumball suddenly awaking and thinking it necessary to have a fight for her property.

In a corner was a tar-bucket and brush.

Just the very thing!

Seizing the brush, and placing the handle between his teeth, after the manner of the midnight robber and assassin, the Sergeant once more drew back the blanket, and began cautiously to approach the scarlet object of his desire.

All that was wanting to render the moment blood-curdling and thrilling was a little weird, ghastly stage-music.

Softly trod the Sergeant until he had crossed the sanctum, and was in the act of putting forth his hand to grasp the trousers.

At this moment he was arrested by a movement on the part of Mrs. Rumball, accompanied by a deep sigh—almost a groan—and the murmur of words.

"Oh dear, dear! Drat 'im! croo'l wretch! Ter go—fur—to—beat—thur—poor—brains—hout!"

Mrs. Rumball was talking in her sleep, and evidently witnessing over again the cruel banging together of Dolly's and Joey's heads by the General.

The Sergeant stood ready with the tar-brush, but Mrs. Rumball's murmured words dying away into a snore, he replaced the handle between his teeth, and reached down the trousers.

He then drew his handkerchief from the breast of his jacket, spread it on the deck, rolled up the precious trousers in a bundle, placed it in hastily, did it up, and was on the point of slinking off, when Mrs. Rumball awoke with a start and sat up, staring at the misty intruder, little imagining that he was walking off with her fancy trousers.

It would have been better for Mrs. Rumball had she continued to dream; for, she had scarcely opened her eyes ere they were closed again in a very extraordinary fashion, and as she opened her mouth to scream she felt something enter it with a rush, and remain there.

This was the tar-brush.

The Sergeant, fearing discovery at the moment he had the purloined trousers under his arm, made use of the means he had provided for his protection in such a contingency.

With the quickness of a man accustomed to the sword exercises, he dexterously slopped the tarry brush first in one eye and then the other, then popped it in her mouth, and there leaving it sticking, decamped with his prize.

Though we feel sure the reader must feel much sympathy for Mrs. Rumball at this cruel treatment, and would like to learn how she bore her her sufferings, at once, yet we must first return to the General, who, it will be remembered, has been sitting all this time in his cabin without his trousers, and is anxiously awaiting the reappearance of the Sergeant.

In less than three minutes after his successful raid upon Mrs. Rumball, the Sergeant entered the General's presence, slamming the door behind him, and running in the bolt with an energy and evident trepidation that caused the General to exclaim, irritably—

"Bless the man—what's all that fuss about?"

For reply, the Sergeant pointed to the bundle under his arm, placed his fingers on his lips, and said in a mysterious whisper—

"S-i-s-h! Don't make a row just yet, General! I don't want to be bowled out! He—he—he!—there'll be the devil's own shine presently!"

Why—wha—what do you mean?" asked the General, astounded at this conduct of the Sergeant's, which, in his opinion. was not only extraordinary but decidedly familiar—confoundedly familiar!

"Why, I've got the trousers, General," returned the Sergeant, with another chuckle! "but

I had to prig 'em! I don't think the lady will be in a fit condition to follow me yet, though—ha—ha!—as I've stopped her eyes and mouth—ha—ha!—with a tar-brush! Such a go, General!" added the excited Sergeant, beginning to open the bundle.

"Stop, stop!" cried the General. "What do you mean by 'prig 'em'—'lady'—'tar-brush?' Do you mean to say that you have had the—the—impudence to steal a pair of trousers in *my* name, and from a lady? Speak, sir, if you can, without grinning!"

"I couldn't help myself, General," replied the Sergeant. "If I couldn't get 'em by fair means, wasn't I obliged to get 'em by foul?—and from anybody? I knew you were so hard up that you wouldn't mind taking the responsibility of my act! Stop till you see 'em. There, General!"—rising, and spreading open the scarlet trousers. "They are rather short in the legs, but there's plenty of room elsewhere, and you'll look like a French General."

Perhaps the General was never so much surprised in his life as he was at this moment.

At any rate, his face turned the hue of the trousers, and he stood staring at them—aghast!

At length he found breath to stammer—

"Why — why—up-on — my — soul, they—they're a pair of *lady's* trousers! You villain! How dare you play off such a joke on *me*, sir?"

"It's no joke, General, upon my——"

"No joke, sir! What?—have you the audacious impudence to tell me that you expect me to wear a pair of woman's drawers—and a confounded flaming colour like that—eh?—What?"

"It's the only thing in the ship, General, I could get, and you'll pardon me, sir, but I think they are better than bare nature, or, as the poet says, 'beauty unadorned,' in your case. Besides, General, you said you were not particular."

"Bless my soul!" cried the General, "here's a pretty fix! Did you ask the Captain of the steamer?"

"I did, General."

"And his officers?"

"I did, General."

"Did you try the officers of the 33rd?"

"Every one of 'em, General, but there is no one but has a waist like a wasp! I tried all the sailors, but met with nothing but impudent remarks."

"And pray," said the General, "to whom do these outlandish things belong? From whom have you 'prigged' them, as you express the fact of your theft?"

"A lady, of really no consequence, General—Mrs. Rumball."

"Good Heavens!" wailed the General. "This is worse even than I anticipated! The last woman in creation I would have had such an act practised upon! Oh! you ass!—you idiot!—you—you—Here, give them to me!" snatching them from the Sergeant's hand, frantically rolling them up and flinging them at his head. "Be off with you! Out of my sight, you vagabond!"

This was followed by the enraged General aiming sundry rapid kicks at the Sergeant, who, to avoid them, hopped and dodged all round the cabin with the scarlet trousers in his hand, the sight of which only acted on the General's temper like a red rag on a bull's.

As this was a game the General could not keep up for any length of time, he presently became exhausted, and sat down panting and clenching his hands and teeth with passion.

The Sergeant, as anyone might be led to suppose he would not have done, did not take advantage of the General's exhaustion to escape.

"He'll be calmer presently," thought the Sergeant, "and then, perhaps he'll listen to reason."

And this proved to be the case.

The General, after a few minutes, looked up and eying the Sergeant, said in a half-subdued, half-menacing tone—

"Are you going to take yourself and those brutes of trousers off?"

"I beg you will listen to me, General," replied the Sergeant. in a respectfully insinuating manner. "There can be no harm in your wearing these in your cabin. There isn't a pair of trousers to be had in the ship for love or money, and these will be better than going bare-legged. You can slip up on deck at night for a litle fresh air, and nobody will see you; and when we arrive at Gibraltar, I will go ashore and get you a proper rig out. It's only the thought of wearing such a thing that isn't exactly pleasant. Just try them on, General."

To tell the truth, the Sergeant was secretly delighted at the fix in which the General was.

He had got him to a certain extent at his mercy, and he resolved to make him pay for all the abuse he had heaped upon himself, in making him look and feel as ridiculous as possible.

Consequently, the Sergeant inwardly chuckled in the anticipation of seeing the figure the General would cut in the scarlet "bags."

But it was much easier to say "Try them on," than actually to accomplish it.

The General, at first suspecting that he was being quizzed, looked suspiciously at the Sergeant, but, seeing nothing but a look of imperturbable gravity on the non-commissioned officer's face, directed his gaze at the scarlet trousers.

"I suppose I had better try on the beastly things," ruminated the General, as he half-shyly stretched forth his hand and took them from the Sergeant.

Having taken them, the General began turning them about and examining them, like a crow would an object put up for the purpose of scaring it.

"How the deuce am I get into them?" he muttered. "Hanged if I can tell which is the front and which is the back of the things! There's a slit both sides! And I don't see any buttons about! Do you understand the make of them?" he asked, looking up at length at the Sergeant.

The Sergeant, who was standing bolt upright at attention in a corner of the cabin, apparently looking on with respectful gravity, but in reality feeling ready to explode like an overcharged "gazogene," replied with difficulty—

"I—I'm as innocent as a baby, General, about the construction of 'em. I've never had more to do with that sort of garment than seeing my sisters' flying on a clothes-line, filled out with wind, and then I never could understand how they got into 'em."

"Then how the deuce do you think I should know anything about them?" snapped the General.

"You've had a greater experience of life, General, than I have, and——"

"I've not had experience in the shape and cut

of such things as these," growled the General·
"Just take yourself off, sir! Begone, or I shall
be tempted to run you through!"

The General looked so much as though it
would take but a little extra provocation to induce him to make use of his sword for that
purpose, that the Sergeant considered it the
wisest plan to make himself scarce, and, accordingly, retired with extraordinary despatch.

But it was only for a short distance.

Sergeant O'Shehe was determined to see how
the General looked in Mrs. Rumball's trousers;
and so, instead of leaving the saloon, he drew
one of the dining-chairs beneath the cabin ventilator (a kind of venetian shutter), and, having
adjusted the latter to suit his line of vision,
peeped through.

Never before did the Sergeant witness a sight
so entertaining, and one that caused him such
side-splitting agony.

Just as he looked through, the General was in
the act of pulling on the drawers.

He had discovered that the waist was drawn
in and tied by a piece of tape.

This let him into the secret of how the drawers
were to be held up when on, and the General had
at once proceeded to insert his legs.

He succeeded in inserting one leg, and was in
the act of inserting the other, when he lost his
balance by a sudden roll of the steamer, and fell
backwards with a crash that nearly stove in a
panel of the cabin, and made his head ring
again.

"Curse it!" he growled, as he sat up and
rubbed the back of his head. "This is enough
to make a saint swear! Curse everything and
everybody, I say!"

To prevent a second tumble, the General got
in the other leg whilst sitting on the floor, and
then, getting on to his knees, cautiously rose to
the perpendicular, drew up the drawers to his
waist, and stood swaying to and fro, surveying
himself in a long strip of looking-glass that was
let into one end of the cabin.

"Good Heavens!" groaned the General. "Oh,
lord, lord! I'm a most ridiculous-looking
object, I must say? What the devil *am* I to
do?"

The General certainly *was* a most ridiculous-
looking object; and it was no wonder the Sergeant laughed till it became necessary to hold
his sides, as though he had the colic.

From the waist, down to a few inches below
the knees, the General presented the appearance of a huge scarlet balloon, of such a deep
colour, that made his scarlet tunic look pale in
contrast, whilst the calves of his legs showed
up like pure white marble pillars.

As the General, with a mingled look of vexation at his appearance, turned to survey himself
from different points of view, ejaculating at each
glimpse, "Oh, Lord!" "Good Heavens!" "Bless
my soul—worse and worse?" the Sergeant's
sense of the ridiculous increased to such a pitch
that, holding on to the ventilator to prevent himself falling, he fairly roared with laughter.

The Sergeant would probably have continued
several minutes to thus enjoy himself, but he had
scarcely been imprudent enough to give audible
vent to his feelings, when there resounded
through the saloon a fearful crash, and he found
himself lying on his back on the floor.

The General, hearing the noise, and catching a
glimpse of a face, had hurled one of his boots
through the ventilator.

CHAPTER XXVI.

HOW MRS. RUMBALL RECOVERED, AND HOW
THAT LADY PUNISHES THE INNOCENT FOR
THE GUILTY IN RESPECT OF HER TROUSERS.

To return to Mrs. Rumball.

Sergeant O'Shehe had no sooner decamped
with Mrs. Rumball's drawers under his arm,
than Joey Pumps popped in to see what was
going on.

The sight he saw vividly reminded Joey of
other days.

Mrs. Rumball, he saw, was once more in a
dilemma.

"But, Oh lor!" murmured Joey, as he sank
down to go through the usual process of getting
"limp." "I never see 'er hin sich a mess has
this! I be orf agin!"

Tar is naturally, in its property of sticking,
vastly superior to treacle.

The smell and taste also, are much more disagreeable.

Mrs. Rumball found this out very quickly.

What nasty stuff had got into her eyes, or
what had been thrust into her mouth, Mrs. Rumball at the moment could not imagine.

Indeed she hadn't time to imagine.

She felt that she had been blinded by some
sticky substance, and that, if she didn't pull
something out of her mouth she would be
choked.

In accomplishing this, Mrs. Rumball, unhap-
pily, nearly choked her husband.

So imminent was her own danger, and so
hastily and energetically did Mrs. Rumball
snatch the tar-brush from her mouth, and dash
it away, that Mr. Rumball, who happened to be
snoring at the moment with his mouth wide open,
awoke in great alarm with something sticking in
his throat.

This was the tar-brush.

Unconscious of the jeopardy in which she had
placed her husband's life, Mrs. Rumball, gasping
for breath, pitched herself head foremost on to
the feather-bed and commenced a series of frantic rollings and kickings, that strongly reminded Joey Pumps of the playful antics of an
elephant.

The manner in which she threw her arms
about, lay on her face and kicked, and then turned
on her back and kicked, was something wonderful to behold.

Here again, in her struggles to gain her sight
and breath, Mrs. Rumball more than once placed
Mr. Rumball's life in serious danger.

Before Mr. Rumball—who could see—could
gain his feet, his blinded and choking wife had
rolled over him thrice, and once lay upon his face
so long and so heavily that he was obliged to
use his teeth before he could succeed in dis-
lodging her.

In truth, the struggles of Mr. and Mrs. Rumball on this occasion would almost fill a volume
to relate.

It was not until they had covered themselves
and the sheets of the bed with tar, and had been
several times sick, that all danger of being choked
had passed away.

But even then their powers of speech were very
limited.

A great deal of tar still clung about their
tongues, mouth, and lips, rendering articulation
extremely difficult.

In addition to this sudden impediment in her
speech, Mrs. Rumball's eyes were still closed.

Had this not been the case she would have been able to see a host of grinning faces around her.

It must be here mentioned that the hubbub had been heard by Dolly Swaps, who, being anxious that such an unprecedented sight should be witnessed by Dick Everett and the rest of the chaps, had quickly given the hint of what was going on, and in two or three minutes, all who were not rendered *hors-de-combat* by sea-sickness, had crowded into the berth.

Their promptness in responding to Dolly's call met with its reward.

Scarcely a moment passed from the time they entered that the boys were not "in fits."

The fun was, indeed, overpowering.

When Mrs. Rumball could at length get out a few intelligible words she addressed them to her husband, as she sat in the middle of the bed rocking herself.

Rumball was leaning in an exhausted state against the bulkhead, removing the tar from his mouth with the corner of a sheet.

"Rumball."

"Yes, Dolly."

"Wot—hever hev 'appened?"

"Hit's tar, Dolly."

"I knows that—don't I smell hit?"

"Yes, Dolly."

"Then where did hit cum from, Rumball?"

"Hum!" ejaculated Rumball. "That's good, that is!"

"Wot do yer mean, now?" asked Mrs. Rumball, sharply, scenting some kind of personal accusation.

"Why, for to go to dab a beastly tar-brush in yer heys an' mouth like that, and then dab it hin mine."

"I didn't do nothin' o' the kind, Rumball!" exclaimed Mrs. Rumball, indignantly.

"Who did then, Dolly, hif yer didn't? Come, now!"

"Who did? 'Ow shud I know? I expec as yer did hit yerself, Rumball," retorted Mrs. Rumball; "ter get hat the bottle o' brandy."

"Nonsense, Dolly! Yer don't know wot your talkin' about."

"Nonsense, is it? I tells yer I woke hup, an' seed someone a pokin' about, and then my heys was blinded an' my mouth filled, an' I b'lieve 'twas yer, Rumball!"

"Rubbish," returned Rumball. "I say yer've bin dreamin', Dolly, or had the nightmare, or hev bin a walkin' hin yer sleep agin."

"Drat 'im! Ony 'ark at the wretch!" cried Mrs. Rumball, spreading forth her arms. "I happeals to hevry boddy 'ere present whether I'd go fur to blin' my own heys and stop my own mouth with a beastly tar-brush? Are it likely, now?" she added, in a tone between a sob and a whine.

"No, certainly not, Mrs. Rumball," said Dick, winking at his chums. "You're being grossly deceived. Put down the brandy-bottle, Rumball; it isn't fair to take the mean advantage of your wife in that manner."

"Wot's that?" cried Mrs. Rumball. "Rumball a-drinkin' the ony drop I hev ter kep orf the sickness? Oh, yer willan!" she added, passionately, and clenching her fists. "I only wish as I cud get hat yer! Yer'll git hit, when I clears my heys!"

"Hit's no sich thin', Dolly!" exclaimed Rumball, indignantly. "I ain't near hit! Hit's a 'liberate attempt o' them boys ter set yer agin me

an' take away my character. Take my word for hit, Dolly."

"Never, Rumball!" returned his wife, melodramatically. "Never! Hit ain't the fust time yer've tried ter deprive me of the bottle, an' hit won't be well for your blessed 'air and face hif I finds any of hit gone! I ony wish my heys was clear!"

As this was a state of vision that Joey Pumps, from an interested motive, wished to see accomplished as speedily as possible, he retired and presently returned with a small bottle.

"Look 'ere, Dolly," said Joey, bestowing a wink on the grinning company; "I'll soon let daylight inter yer peepers. 'Ere's some ile," putting the bottle into her hand; "an' hall yer've got ter do, is ter rub hit hin like Billy-o. Yer'll soon ketch sight o' that derceivin' ole man o' yers. There's summat else to, Dolly, has yer've got ter learn."

"Wot dreffull thin' is hit, Joey?" asked Mrs. Rumball, faintly, as she commenced to oil her eyes. "There surely can't be nothin' wus than Rumball a-stealin' my drop o' sperrit?"

"Oh, much wus, Dolly?" returned Joey, favouring the boys with another wink.

"Don't tell me thet, Joey!" said Mrs. Rumball, still more faintly. "Wot hever are hit?"

"Wait till yer gits yer heyes open, an' kin see fur yerself. I'm afraid as yer'll go halmost mad."

"Good Heavin, wot are hit?" murmured Mrs. Rumball, fairly trembling in her anxiety to regain her sight.

No one present but Joey knew of the fate of Mrs. Rumball's drawers, and so, full of the importance of his knowledge, and chuckling in anticipation of the fun he was about to create, Joey stood in his favourite attitude, with legs stretched open, and hands deep in his trousers-pockets, awaiting the restoration to sight of his friend and protector.

"Now, Dolly," said Joey, as Mrs. Rumball at length cleared her eyes sufficiently to render objects about her pretty plain. "Now, Dolly, prepare yersef fur a horrible rewelashun. Yer've been shamefully robbed!"

"Is—is hit the brandy, Joey?" asked Mrs. Rumball, apprehensively.

"Wus than thet, I told yer, Dolly, didn't I?" said Joey.

"Yes, Joey."

"Wot are hit yer prizes most on 'arth, barrin' myself, Dolly? Ain't hit yer scarlit trousers?"

"Oh, Good Heavin! Don't tell me as they be gone, Joey!" exclaimed Mrs. Rumball, now trembling visibly.

"Jist look behind yer, Dolly, that's hall!"

Mrs. Rumball did so, and lo! the spot where erewhile hung the pride of her heart—her scarlet drawers—was blank!

The colour—though the change could not be seen for tar—forsook Mrs. Rumball's face. She felt awfully pale, and her heart almost ceased beating!

Mrs. Rumball's ample bosom—after the first stunning shock—heaved with the intensity of her emotion.

This dreadful agitation lasted quite a minute, and then Mrs. Rumball gave deep utterance to these words—

"I sees thro' the base trick now! The wretch wot stole my trouses put the tar-brush hin my heyes an' mouth! Joey—tell me that willian's name!"

Joey shook his head, as he replied, gravely—

"I hardly likes ter tell yer, Dolly."

"Joey," cried Mrs. Rumball, "I hinsists!"

"Hit's werry 'ard to be deceiv'd in one yer loves an' hev always trusted—ain't it?"

"Hit is, Joey. But whether hit's won I loves an' trustes, an' whether hit's won I dosn't love an' trustes, I'll be rewenged hon 'im fur stealin' my trouses!"

"Then wot does yer say, Dolly, ter treachery by the pardner o' yer buzzom?"

"What—Rumball!"

"Why," cried Joey, imitating Mrs. Rumball's indignant tone, "why didn't I see 'im take the putty things orf the nail? Didn't I follow 'im ter se wot 'e was a going ter to do with 'em? An' didn't I see 'im sell 'em for arf-o'-pint o' sperrit ter the Capt'n of this werry ship? Look at 'im, Dolly, an' tell me hif 'e ain't a guilty struck man!"

"Oh, Joey Pumps!—You malicious little imp!"

Certainly, if ever a man looked "struck,' that man was Rumball, but it was with astonishment at such a deliberate accusation.

Mrs. Rumball looked a combination of indignant, reproachful, angry daggers at her husband, and was preparing to snatch her revenge, when Rumball, stretching forth his arm, said in an agony of appeal: "Dolly, listen ter me afore yer lets hout! Hev I or hev I not been reposin' by yer side fur the larst hour an' a arf? Wasn't us—fur a hour afore that—us two orful sick together? Then 'ow cud I hev stole yer trouses w'en asleep? Yer knows as I likes too well ter see yer in 'em to sell 'em fur arf a pint o' sperrit——"

"Oh, Rumball—Rumball!" interrupted Joey, reproachfully, "that's a werry hartful and insinnevating speech, but it won't do, yer know! Now yer konfess as yer stole them trouses, an' got drunk on the sperrit, an' don't know what yer sayin'. Come now—yer'll sleep hall the better fur hevin' a heasy konshince!"

"Joey," said Rumball, appealingly, "hev mussy hon me, an' don't commit perjury——"

But Rumball's appeal was suddenly cut short by Mrs. Rumball rushing upon him, exclaiming—

"I'll mussy yer, yer willan! I'll teach yer ter sell my trouses, I will!"

With these words, Mrs. Rumball seized her husband by the hair, and bore him to the floor, where, sitting across his body, like a man on horseback, she alternately slapped, thumped, and scratched his face, and bumped his head against the boards, amidst the screaming laughter of the boys, and the encouragement of Joey Pumps.

Rumball yelled as only a man could yell under such circumstances, and the more he gave tongue, the harder his wife pitched into him.

Mrs. Rumball was like a tigress that had been robbed of her cub, and Rumball's cries were music in her ears.

In the midst of the hubbub, Dick Everett found time to ask Joey—

"Did he really prig the drawers, Joey?"

"Not a bit on hit!" grinned Joey. "But, yer see, old Rumball jest wanted liv'nin' hup a bit. He was gettin awful slow and glumpy!"

At this answer, Dick started off laughing afresh, and communicating it to Tom Sheppard, Harry Smith, and Bob Jones, it soon spread, and the laughter was quickly redoubled.

"Then I suppose the Captain is about as innocent as Rumball, Joey?" laughed Dick.

"Jolly sight hinnocenter, hif anything," said Joey. "But the Cap'n must hev his share o' whackin', or hit 'on't be fair ter Rumball."

Then approaching Mrs. Rumball, he said—

"Don't 'zaust yerself, Dolly, hover one on 'em. Remember as the Captain o' the wessel ain't no better nor he ought ter be, an' 'e's got the trousers. Yer'd better try an' get 'em afore 'e makes 'em a berfday present to 'is hone wife."

This was simply adding fuel to the fire.

The idea of another woman sporting her trousers, was unbearable to Mrs. Rumball.

Mrs. Rumball required no further stimulating to seek out the Captain and his hussy of a wife, and, her blood being now fairly up, she gave Rumball one or two finishing bumps, and rushed for the deck.

The boys made way for her, and followed her with such loud shouting and laughter, that long before she emerged from the fo'castle hatchway, dozens of the sailors and soldiers had gathered round, wondering what was up.

As Mrs. Rumball's tarry-decorated person became fully revealed, she was greeted by demonstrative shouts and laughter.

Heedless of this, however, and thinking only of regaining her stolen trousers, Mrs. Rumball pushed and fought her way towards the quarter-deck.

But when abreast the funnel, a catastrophe happened which temporarily stopped Mrs. Rumball's career.

At this moment Sergeant O'Shehe, fresh from his discomfiture in the saloon, was also approaching the funnel, and, catching sight of Mrs. Rumball rushing towards him in full mad career, came to the conclusion that she was after him as the purloiner of her property.

"Here's a go!" thought the Sergeant, coming to a sudden stop. "What am I to do?"

Looking about for a place of shelter, he dropped on his knees behind the funnel, just in time for Mrs. Rumball to trip over his projecting feet, and fall with a force that did more damage to her nose than the deck.

So eager was Mrs. Rumball, however, to get at the Captain, that her eagerness was superior to the pain, and, scrambling up, off she went, and shot down the saloon-stairs like a meteor.

It so happened, at this moment, that the Captain was engaged in a lively conversation with several officers at one end of the saloon, the subject being the fun created by the reading of the "Rules and Regulations."

The Captain was a little fellow, and seemed to be in high glee over the recollection of the General's misfortunes.

"Never saw anything so well timed, gentlemen, as the moment when the dog was set at the fluttering shirt-tail. Ha, ha, ha! I was a rum dog myself when I was a youngster, but, 'pon my honour——Hallo!"

This exclamation was caused by the sudden appearance of Mrs. Rumball.

At the Captain's exclamation, all eyes turned in the direction he was looking, and stared in astonishment at the rapidly-approaching tarry figure.

"Who is it?" said the Captain.

"It's that woman that interfered to prevent the General beating out the boys' brains, if you remember," observed an officer.

"What's the matter, I won——?"

The Captain's question was cut short by one

screamed ont by Mrs. Rumball, who at this moment had reached the group.

"Where's the Cap'n?"

"I am the Captain," said the little man. "What is it, my good creature? What can I do for you?"

"Yer the thief, are yer?" cried Mrs. Rumball, flying at the Captain and seizing him by the collar. "Give 'em hup, you willain! Give 'em hup, or I'll shake the life hout of yer!"

"Bless my soul!" cried the astonished Captain. "What do you mean? I—I—don't understand you! Leave go, confound you!"

"An' konfound *yer*, too; thet's wot I ses, yer little sneakin' robber. Give 'em hup! Give 'em hup, I tells yer!"

"Robber! Give them up!" exclaimed the Captain, who was now very red in the face, and was being pretty roughly handled by Mrs. Rumball. "I protest! I don't know what you mean! There must be some mistake. Explain yourself."

"Mistake!" screamed Mrs. Rumball. "On'y 'ark hat the mean little wretch, arter sneakin' inter my cabin, an' stealin' the on'y thin's has I prizes, and corst me twenty-severn an' four three fardens, with two-an'-six hextra for the trimmin'! On'y 'ark hat 'is sayin' hit's a mistake. Ugh—yer thievin' wretch! Give 'em hup, or I'll drag yer hon deck an' hexpose yer ter hevery boddy! Yer ought ter be hung from the masthead! Give 'em hup—drat yer!"

Not only was the poor little Captain surprised at all this, but the officers, who were standing around gazing at the scene with feelings in which pity for the victim and amusement were mixed.

"Gentlemen!" cried the Captain, piteously, whom Mrs. Rumball had now pinned against one of the cabins—the very cabin in which was the General, and who was now in a profuse perspiration, and stood trembling in the scarlet trousers. "Gentlemen, I protest to Heaven I do not know what this violent woman means! I've not stolen anything——"

"Wot!" here yelled Mrs. Rumball, bumping the unfortunate Captain's head against the cabin. "Hev yer the himpudence ter say as yer didn't sneak inter my bedroom an' steal my scarlet flannel drawers—which it makes me blush ter name—orf the nail an' wark orf with 'em, ter make as a berfday presint ter yer thin' hoff a wife? Hey? Will yer hev [bump] the cheek [bump] ter say [bump] as yer didn't [bump, bump]—hey!"

"The woman's mad!" cried the Captain. "For Heaven's sake, take her off, gentlemen. She'll beat my brains out!"

Indeed, it had become very evident that, unless he were rescued, the little captain, who was powerless in Mrs. Rumball's hands, would suffer grievous bodily harm.

A concerted attempt was, therefore, made to deliver him from his perilous position.

But this was not accomplished until after a great deal of resistance on the part of Mrs. Rumball.

The maddened lady was at length torn from her victim, and conveyed back to her own domain by the arms and legs, face downwards, like a drunken and fractious soldier, squealing at a frantic rate, and followed by roars of laughter and loud clapping and cheering from the boys, sailors, and soldiers.

But no one enjoyed the discomfiture of Mrs. Rumball more than two persons—her husband and Sergeant O'Shehe.

"If ever I sport a crest," chuckled the Sergeant, "it shall be Mrs. Rumball's head, with a tar-brush sticking in her mouth!"

CHAPTER XXVII

MRS. RUMBALL AND SERGEANT O'SHEHE MEET UNDER PECULIAR CIRCUMSTANCES, AND REMAIN FOR A CONSIDERABLE TIME IN A STATE OF PAINFUL SUSPENSE.

"Now, we're all ready to hoist at a moment's notice, I think?"

"Yes, and the sooner the Sergeant makes his appearance the better."

The speakers were Dick Everett and Tom Sheppard.

These, with nearly the whole school, are grouped around, and in the vicinity of the mainmast, awaiting the denouement of a little plot against Sergeant O'Shehe.

The time is midnight.

The moon is shining brilliantly.

The steamer is still rolling heavily on the long swelling billows of the Bay—a circumstance that is a source of much satisfaction to the boys, who have determined to send the Sergeant to the end of the yardarm for disobedience of orders.

At a council of war, called by Dick Everett shortly before out-lights, it had been unanimously decided, that Sergeant O'Shehe having twice succumbed to sea-sickness, whilst on duty on the quarter-deck, had been guilty of disregarding the clause prohibiting indulgence in that "preventable" complaint, and had in consequence rendered himself amenable to the punishment laid down for its infringement.

The punishing clause plainly set forth, that any one pleading sea-sickness as an excuse for absence from parade, would be sent to the masthead, and kept there until he got well again.

The Sergeant, it was freely acknowledged, had not absented himself from parade; but, on the other hand, no one could deny that he had been sick *on* parade, and as he had no business to be sick at all, it was considered that he came within the meaning of the clause.

"Not that it matters much whether he does or not," said Dick. "If he don't deserve to go to the masthead, we'll split the distance and send him to the yardarm."

The moderation of this sentence was received with murmurs of admiration and satisfaction, and under the leadership of Dick, who enlisted the services of a couple of old tars, the proper tackle for the purpose was rigged, and everything made ready to carry out the punishment.

They knew where the Sergeant was, and momentarily expected his appearance.

The Sergeant had been summoned by the General to his cabin on a very important matter.

"I'm nearly suffocated in this beastly hole," growled the General, as the Sergeant entered. "What chance is there of getting a walk on the quarter-deck for an hour without being interrupted?"

"Capital chance, General. It's bright moonlight, 'tis true, but there's nobody about but the watch and the man at the wheel, and they won't bother themselves about you."

"And that—that—beastly creature, you stole those confounded trousers from," faltered the General. "So, there's no fear of—of——"

"Her twigging you, General? Ha, ha! I shall be much surprised to see her on deck before we reach Gib., sir. She's nearly had her legs and arms wrenched off in being carried, spread-eagle fashion, to the guardroom—I mean her den. There's no fear, General—take my word for it!"

Though thus positively assured that he could venture up with safety, it was not without much misgiving, and great inward trepidation, that the General followed the Sergeant from the cabin, and peered out of the saloon hatchway to look cautiously about him.

As the Sergeant had said, however, the coast was nearly clear, and everything looked calm and private.

"The moon's confounded bright," whispered the General, "and if that woman only gets one eye on deck, she'll be sure to see her trousers. You'd better keep sentry, go to the foot of the ladder, and give the alarm if any danger threatens."

Though well hidden themselves, the boys saw the whole of what was going on, and they were rather taken in to see the Sergeant take up a stationary post, by deliberately seating himself on the companion-ladder leading to the quarter-deck.

Had their presence there not been for a certain purpose, they would have given way to their feelings at the absurd appearance of the General, as he paced the deck.

This was no time for laughing, however.

The question was, how long would they have to wait for the passing of the sergeant?

Could nothing be done to lead him into the snare?

These questions were discussed in whispers, but as it was considered that they couldn't make a move with safety, it was decided to wait the Sergeant's time.

But things were brought to a crisis much quicker, and under exciting circumstances that they did not anticipate.

This was through the agency of Joey Pumps.

That young gentleman had no sooner caught sight of the General in the scarlet drawers, than an idea flashed into his head.

With an inward chuckle, Joey crept noiselessly away, and, in less than a minute made his appearance in Mrs. Rumball's crib, and startled Mrs. Rumball from a fitful slumber by an unceremonious poke in the ribs.

"Wot's the matter now?" cried Mrs. Rumball, with a little scream.

"Look 'ere, Dolly," said Joey, abruptly; "look up, quick, an don't go for to make none o' your blessed rows. I'm Joey Pumps. Does yer know me, Dolly?"

"Yes, Joey," replied Mrs. Rumball. "Wot hev 'appened now?"

"Hit's the woice 'o natur agin," murmured Joey. "She allers knows me under any cirkum-stances."

Then he added aloud—

"Dolly, I know wheer yer scarlet trousers is."

"Yer do, Joey?" said Mrs. Rumball, opening her eyes eagerly.

"Yes. The're perambulatin' the quarterdeck at this blessed minnit on the General's body."

"Good grashus!" cried Mrs. Rumball, breath-lessly. "Then hit wheer that dreffel Gen'ral as stole 'em?"

"Hif 'e didn't prig 'em, Dolly, 'e've got em' hon, an' now's yer time to hev a fight for 'em."

"Yer're sure, Joey, as yer ain't deceived?"

"Cum an' look for yerself, Dolly. I don't wan't yer to believe me!"

The chance of regaining her lost trousers was too precious to be thrown away, and Mrs. Rumball hastily arose, tremblingly put on her petticoat, and deliberately putting a pillow over Rumball's face, lest his snoring should reach the General's ears and scare him away, passed through the berth, and took a peep towards the quarter-deck.

"Yes, there, sure enough, was the General, stalking about as brazen as brass in the lost trousers.

The next moment she was flying along the deck.

But quickly as Mrs. Rumball flew, there was an individual who flew quicker.

That individual was the Sergeant.

Mrs. Rumball's white figure had no sooner emerged into the moonlight than it had been twigged by the Sergeant, and her intention divined.

How Mrs. Rumball had discovered that the General was taking a midnight refresher, the Sergeant had no time to speculate upon.

He only knew that such was unmistakeably the case, and that he had his duty to perform.

"Here she comes, by Heaven! Quick, General, —down you go!"

Having uttered these words, the Sergeant, without looking to see that his warning had been heard, rushed forward, and caught Mrs. Rumball in his arms.

As this was an embrace entirely unsought for on the part of Mrs. Rumball, and one which, at the moment she didn't desire, she protested against it in the most forcible manner in the form of kicks, struggles, and loud declamations.

But the Sergeant was resolved to risk his life, if necessary, in the protection of the General, so he stuck to Mrs. Rumball like wax, and the struggles became most terrific.

Suddenly they both fell heavily to the deck—a mishap caused, we're afraid, by Dick's foot getting somewhere between their legs, and the next moment several boy-figures seemed to be very busily engaged around the persons of the writhing couple.

Then, from the midst of the commotion, arose a clear voice—

"Haul—ho! Heave away, boys! That's it!"

Now might have been observed what, to the uninitiated, would have seemed an extraordinary phenomenon.

The bodies of Mrs. Rumball and Sergeant O'Shehe rose from the deck and gradually ascended until they reached within a few feet of the yardarm, where they remained swaying to and fro, distinctly outlined in the rays of the moon.

This phenomenon was followed by wild shouts, and still wilder dancing, from the boy-figures on the deck.

It was a weird, wild, exciting, stupendously grand scene—one that was never before witnessed in the Bay of Biscay!

" Bravo, General !" cried Joey. "That's a joily clever dodge, that is ! Go it ! Hold on Dolly ! Hold tight, Rumball ! Ha ! ha ! ha !"—See page 92.

CHAPTER XXVIII

HOVERS FOR A TIME OVER SERGEANT O'SHEHE
AND MRS. RUMBALL.—THEN DESCENDS TO
GENERAL SHOOT, AND DESCRIBES HOW HE
GOT FIXED IN A TUB; HOW HE GOT OUT OF
IT, AND FURTHER DESCRIBES OTHER INTER-
ESTING MATTERS.

WE must now mount on the wings of imagination, hover for a time around Mrs. Rumball and
Sergeant O'Shehe, and then descend and look
after the General and another personage, who,
though a cowed husband of the henpecked
order, it will be seen, possibly, had a little spirit
left in him—we mean Rumball.

For a few moments Mrs. Rumball and the Sergeant couldn't make out what was happening to
them.

They felt themselves in motion, but whether
the steamer had made a sudden plunge and
was going down stem first, or had leaped out of
the water, they couldn't tell.

Something very extraordinary had happened,
that was evident.

The deck, sails, masts, the water and the
moon seemed to be all mingled together, and
to be moving about in the most eccentric
manner.

One moment the deck appeared to be under
them, the next the sea; and then the scene again
changed, and they were apparently floating over
the moon.

Amidst all the changes of scene, the latter
sensation — floating—was the most palpable,
and, not being able to conceive how they could
be in that buoyant condition without having
wings, they felt greatly alarmed, and clung to
each other with, if possible, a closer embrace.

Neither dared, for a minute or two, to speak—
scarcely to breathe.

Mrs. Rumball thought of the spirits that carry
off persons bodily (as she had done on one
memorable occasion at Garrison House Academy),
and, closing her eyes, to shut out the unnatural
aspect of things around her, she clasped the
Sergeant's neck with such force, as to lead
that individual to imagine that he was being
strangled.

Close to the Sergeant's ear was Mrs. Rumball's mouth, and, as she hugged him, she murmured—

"Good grashus—this is drefful! Wot-hever
hev 'appened now? Air hit a norrible dream,
or am I bin carried off by them sperrits? Hit
feels like one o' them orful dreams as I hev arter
eating' coocummer fur supper—like as hif I was
flyin', with a cow arter me, ony there ain't no
cow, or as hif I was jumpin' orf a bottomless
press-i-pis! Oh!—o-h! O-o-h! I—I—I-'m-
a-be-in'—cho-o-o-ok'd! Rum-um-ball—wheer—
air—ye-er-er? Dr-rat—yer!"

These cries were being caused by vigorous
efforts on the part of the Sergeant to prevent
himself being choked.

It had suddenly flashed across his mind what
had happened, and, at the same moment, he
became painfully conscious of what would
happen if he permitted Mrs. Rumball to clasp
his neck in the ardent fashion she was doing
much longer.

He should be choked as sure as fate!

Already he felt that he was nearly black in
the face, and that his eyes were protruding from
their sockets.

The Sergeant was, however, in a fix.

Mrs. Rumball was a powerful woman, and,
being moreover dreadfully frightened, she was
clasping him with all the strength with which
her fear impelled her.

The Sergeant felt it would be like getting his
head out of the jaws of a vice; but life was
sweet, and Mrs. Rumball was nasty!

Had Mrs. Rumball been young and pretty, he
might, perhaps, have been content to breathe
his last in her fair arms; but there was no
denying the fact that Mrs. Rumball was an
exceedingly unpleasant person, and the Sergeant
was resolved not to be choked by her.

So, after a little fumbling, he got his hands
round her throat and began the contracting
pressure which caused Mrs. Rumball to cry out
in the manner described.

"Take your arms away from my neck, then!"
gurgled the Sergeant. "You're choking me!"

"Mur-murder! Murder!" cried Mrs. Rumball.

"Confound you," growled the Sergeant, "I—I
—will murder you if you don't leave go. If
you don't be quiet and keep cool we shall
both be killed! Be quiet, you beastly old
hag!"

Fortunately, for the Sergeant, these last words
had a magical effect in loosening Mrs. Rumball's
embrace.

They recalled her, as it were, from heaven to
earth.

She never had submitted, under any circumstances, to be called a hag by anyone, and she
wouldn't now!

The next moment the Sergeant felt Mrs.
Rumball's arms drop from his neck, and the next
he felt her knuckles drop on his face, accompanied by scratches, and loud denunciations in
the shape of—

"Yer wile wretch! Yer willain! Take that!
I'll 'ag yer, I will!"

As bad as this alteration of circumstances
was, it was preferable to the embrace of Mrs.
Rumball, in the Sergeant's opinion, as it enabled
him to use his tongue to call for assistance.

But, although he called out lustily, he met
with nothing but mocking laughter and jeers,
which he knew, and could see, came from the
boys of the School of the Regiment.

The latter were dancing about the deck like
so many imps.

'Twas in vain the Sergeant threatened what
he would do if they didn't let them down!

'Twas in vain he pleaded for the same end!

His threats and pleadings had no more effect
upon the boys than they had over the wild waste
of waters over which he and his fellow-victim
were swinging.

And there he was, lashed to Mrs. Rumball,
with that lady subjecting him to personal violence
and abuse, swaying in mid-air, the sport of the
boys—a victim to his heroic defence of the
General!

Why doesn't the General come to his assistance? or cause assistance to be rendered him?

"He doesn't care a fig, so long as he's safe!"
almost sobbed the Sergeant, "and everybody
below seems deaf, except those cursed scamps,
and yet we're making row enough! This old
cat won't leave an inch of skin on my face!
The confounded rope, too, is cutting me in
two!"

There was an excellent reason why the General
didn't come to the Sergeant's assistance.

He couldn't.

He was in a fix himself.

The General was, at this moment, seated in a tub, with his knees closely pressed against his nose, and as firmly fixed and helpless as the Sergeant himself.

The General's predicament occurred in this way.

Although he was not altogether unprepared for the alarm given by the Sergeant, announcing the approach of Mrs. Rumball, the General was, nevertheless, so anxious to get out of the way with all possible despatch, that in ducking his head to dart down the saloon steps, he, unfortunately, ran full butt against the roof of the hatchway, staggered, fell backwards from the roll of the vessel, rolled over and over until he finally passed under the rail of the quarter-deck, and two seconds after found himself sitting in the steward's "washing-up" tub, so firmly jammed that he was utterly incapable of getting out again.

"Bless my soul," cried the General, with a savage wail, and casting a frightened, apprehensive glance in the direction he expected to see that dreadful terror — Mrs. Rumball — approach — "Bless my soul, here's a confounded misfortune! What in the deuce has come to my luck, I don't know? If that woman catches me in this fix, I'm done for! What a fool I was to be persuaded by that ass, O'Shehe, to put on these cursed trousers! Fixed in a common tub!" continued the General, almost crying with vexation. "Upon my life, it's a most ridiculous position to be placed in!"

"Ha, ha, ha! Oh lor, I be orf agin!"

Turning his head quickly as these sounds met his ear, the General's eyes fell upon a little fellow leaning against a water-barrel, and gradually sinking to the deck in a state of exhaustive laughter.

It was Joey Pumps.

The General knew Joey only too well, and he glared at the laughing imp with fierce hatred in his glance.

The General was ready to burst with anger, all the more so, that he was painfully conscious he cut a most ridiculous figure.

He tried to look as dignified as his helpless position would permit, whilst he watched Joey go through his paroxysm of laughter to limpness.

"Oh lor! oh dear!" sobbed Joey, as he partially recovered and sat up looking at the General. "I be gettin' weaker an' weaker hin the pint o' givin' way ter larfin'! I've hed sich a lot hon hit durin' my short lifetime, an' hits a gettin' wus and wus hevery day I lives, that I'm putty sure as I carnt stan' much more hon hit! I—I—say, Gen'ral—ha—ha!—I—I—seed yer git inter—ha—ha—ha!—that 'ere fix! I see yer butt yer 'ed agin' the doorway theer an'—ha—ha! Oh lor!—See yer go a rolly-polly—hover-an'-hover till yer fixed yer hend hin the tu—u—u—ub! Ha! ha! oh! oh! oh lor, oh lor! oh dear! I—be—o—o—rf agin!"

The General looked so comical as he sat there doubled up in the tub, with his knees to his nose, the scarlet drawers, and his scarlet, angry face, staring up in the bright moonlight, that Joey, being again overcome, both at the appearance and the recollection of the way in which the General had got into his fix, fairly rolled over and over on the deck in hysterical laughter.

In this state Joey was stumbled upon by Dolly Swaps, who, on demanding to know the cause of his chum's emotion, was languidly pointed to the General in the tub.

Dolly could hardly believe his eyes.

It seemed altogether too good a joke that the General could be fixed there in a tub.

But it turned out to be a solemn fact, and Dolly immediately determined to take advantage of the General's helpless position to indulge in a little chaff.

"By jingo! General," said Dolly, looking down with a delicious chuckle, "you are in a fix this time! However did you manage to get in there? I'm blow'd if you don't look a more sublime figure than the statue of your celestial friend, Ching-Ching-Hanghoo-Funky-Bung, after its head was blown away!"

The General said nothing, but he thought a wicked thought.

He thought that nothing would afford him greater pleasure at that moment than to strangle his tormentor.

"I will, too, said the General to himself, "if I can only get my hand upon him!"

The latter was not beyond the bounds of probability.

Dolly was standing within a few inches of the General's right hand, and the least diminishing of the distance between them would place Dolly in the General's power.

Dolly was on the verge of a great danger.

The next moment Dolly leaned forward, and, looking into the General's face, said facetiously—

"I say, General, can't you get out? Oh lor! Oh! Oh! Murder! Murder! Help! Help!"

With the quickness of thought the General had seized his opportunity, and before Dolly had the slightest idea of the General's intention, he was writhing in the latter's grasp.

The General would certainly have carried out his threat, too, had not Dolly's cries brought Dick and his chums to the rescue.

Dick at once took in the "situation," and resolved to have further fun.

After Dolly had been with much difficulty rescued from his perilous position, Dick, first making a sign to the chaps to keep quiet, turned to the General.

Assuming a tone of sympathy, he said—

"I am sorry to see you in such an awkward fix, General. I won't ask you how you got into the tub, but will do my best to get you out. If you will give us your hands, a good tug or two will do it."

Then taking, with Tom Sheppard, the General's right arm, he directed Bob Jones and Harry Smith to take the left arm.

"Now," said Dick, "we must pull together. Ready—present—fire!"

The next instant the four operators were lying on their backs on the deck.

But what become of the General?

Had they succeeded in pulling him out of the tub?

Not a bit of it!

They had simply reversed the position of the tub.

The latter, which had been under the General, was now on top of his back, and the General was resting on his head and his knees.

"Oh, lor!" said Joey Pumps, who had recovered sufficiently to watch the interesting operation,—"Oh, lor, if 'e don't look like a jolly big snail with hit's shell on hit's back!"

This remark of Joey's was followed by a lot of tittering.

But it was no laughing matter for the General, and he would doubtless have been suffocated had not Dick ordered him to be reversed again.

Dick, who had been perfectly aware of what would happen—knowing that the General, being much heavier than the tub, would not come out unless the latter were fixed to the deck—again addressed the General—

"We shall not be able to get you out that way, sir, I'm afraid, You're wedged in tighter than I thought. Shall I call for more assistance?"

"No, no, no!" replied the General, hastily. "I don't want everybody in the ship to see me in this disgraceful dilemma! I want to get back to the cabin without the Captain and officers seeing me!"

Dick knew that well enough.

The General, he concluded, would long since have called loudly for assistance had he not been too sensitive on the point of personal exposure.

Sensitive people, it is well known, will endure the most excruciating pain in silence and patience, rather than be subject to public ridicule.

The General was, unfortunately for himself, an exceedingly sensitive man—in fact, it has never been our fortune to have met with a more sensitive man than General Shoot.

His fear of being exposed to the ridicule of the Captain and other officers on board on this occasion was, we think, very excusable.

Just think a moment.

He had on a pair of lady's drawers of a flaming scarlet colour—a pair of drawers, too, that had been stolen from the cook by the boys of the School.

This in itself was enough to make him shrink from being exposed to the gaze of persons of his own social standing, and the General had already cut a most ridiculous figure on the quarter-deck in open daylight.

It would have been bad enough to have been caught taking an airing in the flannel drawers; but now that, through his own fear and awkwardness, he had got stuck fast in a tub, he felt that he could endure any bodily pain, short of being reduced to death's door, to get back quietly to his cabin.

But where was the watch?

Why did they not interfere?

Well, the officer of the watch was on the bridge, and the men on deck, and all were keeping a good look-out.

They all saw what was going on, and rather enjoyed it than otherwise.

Trust a Jack Tar for not spoiling good sport!

The General saw the officer of the watch, and he determined to appeal to him to keep the affair to himself.

But the General was destined to be singularly unlucky that night.

His extreme sensitiveness not only brought about the exposure he dreaded, but nearly cost him his life.

"Well," said Dick, "if you have such an objection to being seen by the officers, there is only one way that I can think of for getting you out, I think it will be effectual."

By Dick's direction, the tub was slipped along the deck—some pulling at the General's legs, some pushing at his shoulders—until it was brought under the starboard shroud of the main-mast.

"Now," said Dick, "for a rope."

The General pricked up his ears.

A rope! What in the world did they want a rope for?

The now excessively nervous General watched the proceedings of the boys with a queer feeling about the region of the heart.

He saw them procure a rope, pass it through the ratlines near the maintop, and make a slip-knot at one end. What on earth did it all mean?

The General was not left long in doubt.

"Now, General," said Dick, approaching with the slip-knot; "just keep steady whilst I adjust this round your neck."

"Wha—what do you mean?" asked the General, falteringly.

"We are going to try the effect of opposite forces, General," said Dick, gravely. "With the rope round your neck, some of us will haul you upwards, whilst some will hang on to the edge of the tub and pull it downwards. So, between the two physical appliances, you and the tub *must* part company. Don't you see?"

"See? Yes, the General did see with a vengeance!

"Why, good Heavens!" he cried, turning pale at the bare idea. "Do you intend to hang me?"

"No, certainly not, sir," returned Dick, coolly. We intend to get you out of the tub. Hold your head ready, if you please, General."

"I—I—won't submit to such——"

Before the General could finish, Dick clapped the noose over his head, crying—

"Haul away! Quick!"

The next instant the rope tightened, and the General, with a choking sensation, and divers colours floating before his eyes, felt himself slowly rising, when suddenly there arose a piercing scream and a yell, followed by a loud splash in the sea, cries of alarm from the boys, and a general rush to the side of the steamer.

What had happened?

Mrs. Rumball and Sergeant O'Shehe were floundering in the sea!

As Dick had fastened, as he thought, the rope securely which held the couple in suspense, this catastrophe was totally unexpected by himself and chums, and there immediately followed a general commotion.

Cries of alarm and excitement were raised by the boys and the watch.

"They'll be drowned!"

"Where's the end of the rope?"

"They're sinking! They're sinking!"

"Man overboard!"

The latter cry came from the watch, and was repeated until the deck swarmed with sailors, soldiers, and officers, all eager to assist in saving life.

At the first cry of alarm the officer of the watch had ordered the engines to be reversed, and, by the time the men had got the deck, the steamer was almost stationary.

Fortunately the boats was not required.

Dick, with Tom Sheppard, Bob Jones, and Harry Smith, had retained sufficient coolness to look for, and secure the end of the rope, before it had time to run out of the block, and in a less time than it takes to write it, Mrs. Rumball and the Sergeant were hauled in, and were lying a couple of saturated helpless heaps on the deck.

At this moment, the Captain of the steamer, who with other officers had rushed on deck at the cries of alarm, pushed his way through the crowd asking——

"What is it? What is the matter? Anyone drowned? Ah, who are these?" as he caught sight of the insensible forms on the deck. "Why, one is the Sergeant in charge of the boy soldiers, and the other is—eh?—that person who—who—accused me of stealing her drawers! —eh!—eh!"

"Yer right, Cap'n," said Joey Pumps. "Them's the werry identikle individools, an' I kin tell yer 'ow they got inter sich a jolly mess hif yer likes."

"How did it happen?" asked the Captain, appealing more to the men around him than to Joey, but who replied promptly—

"Yer see Dolly was told that Gen'ral Shoot was the won as prigged her drawers, an' not yerse'f, Cap'n. She wer' furder told that the Gen'ral hed 'em hon an' wes 'ramblin' the deck a showin' hon 'em off, bein' about as proud on 'em as a peacock is of his tail. So orf she cuts like anythink to pull em orf, an' she would, too, I kin tell yer, hif the Sergeant had'nt run hup agin 'er, an' stopped 'er! Then somehow they fell ter the deck, an' w'en they was a strugglin', them young rask'ls," pointing to Dick and the others, "gets a rope roun' 'em an' auls 'em hup ter the yard harm ther', an then—I konfesses hit honnerable, as I ain't no wish ter konseal my share hon hit—I went ter hev a look hat the knot as was tied in the hend o' the rope as 'eld 'em, an' somehow, it cum undun, an' down they goes slap inter the biiin' oshun!"

"Bless me!" cried the Captain, who had listened to Joey's explanation with great impatience. "I shall be glad when these boys are out of the ship; their tricks are outrageous! Where's the General?"

"Hif some of yer'll hev the goodness ter step a one side," said Joey, "yer'll find the gentl'man hisse'f."

Here at last came the exposure the General dreaded!

After what he suffered, had it come to this?

Yes, there was no getting out of it!

There was an irresistible burst of laughter as the poor General was opened to view, which the Captain, who could not help sympathising with the victim, tried in vain to suppress.

The laughter increased too, rather than otherwise, at the process of extricating, at the Captain's order, the General from his ridiculous fixture.

Thankful, however, for his release, and only too anxious to hide his chagrin within the protecting limits of his cabin, the General was hastening off, when he felt something seize him from behind, and heard a voice exclaim—

"Stop, you thievin' willain! Them's my Dolly's drawers, I'll swear!"

The voice was Rumball's, and Rumball himself was in an uncommon state of mental excitement, or rather elevation of spirits.

It will be remembered that Mrs. Rumball, in her hasty exit from her berth, covered her husband's face with a pillow to smother his snoring.

This method of obtaining silence nearly ended in Rumball's sudden suffocation.

On awakening however, and recovering his breath, he spied the brandy-bottle, which his wife had unintentionally left behind her.

Rumball seized this prize with a deep chuckle, and did such ample comforting to his feelings for past and present injuries, that he soon became the jolliest fellow alive, and after a good sing and dance all to himself, and finding there was no more brandy to be got out of the bottle, he tottered on deck to look for his Dolly.

The first thing that he caught sight of, after elbowing his way through the crowd, was his wife's scarlet trousers on the person of the retreating General, and then he had acted as has been just described.

But the persecuted General's patience had now passed all bounds, and, turning upon his tipsy detainer, he seized him by the throat, and flung him, with a savage oath, violently away, and presently regained his cabin.

The General went one way, Rumball another.

The latter was sent sprawling on the top of his wife, who, with the Sergeant, was undergoing the process of restoration.

Tipsy as he was, Rumball, on getting on his knees, recognised the person of his insensible Dolly.

He remained for a few moments gazing on her damp form with stupid amazement.

What had happened?

Was his Dolly dead?

Had the loving wife of his bosom gone and left him—left him to live alone in this wretched world?

Rumball had scarcely asked himself the latter question, when a voice said in his ear—

"Hits hall over, Rumball! Poor Dolly's gone!"

Rumball, whose very blood seemed to turn into ice at these words, threw up his arms spasmodically, and cried in a voice between a sob and the yelp of a hyena—

"Gone! Ho, good Heavin! An jist as I'd found her scarlet trouses!"

———

CHAPTER XXIX.

THE SCHOOL OF THE REGIMENT ARRIVES AT GIBRALTAR.

WE open this chapter upon a scene very opposite in its character to any we have witnessed in the Bay of Biscay.

Let the reader imagine himself on board.

We have left the Bay and have just entered the Straits of Gibraltar.

We have left rough weather, and rolling, and tossing, and sea-sickness far behind us, and are now calmly steaming within three miles of the Spanish shore.

The weather is deliciously calm and beautiful.

A slight breeze scarcely ruffles the glistening waters, which, rolling idly towards the land, break so gently on the beach as scarce to mark it with a silver fringe.

Along the shore extends a range of gentle swelling hills, and within their recesses may be seen numbers of white buildings dazzling the eyes in the afternoon sun, and rendered more conspicuous by the dark and luxuriant foliage of the woods and groves.

Occasionally the line of beach is interrupted by small fishing-villages, distinguished by the masts of the little craft belonging to them, and a few scattered whitewashed cottages.

The heat of the unclouded sun is tempered by the refreshing breeze.

The motion of the vessel is almost imperceptible as she glides through the sunlit waters, and the decks are crowded by idlers and others contemplating the novel and fascinating panorama.

On the quarter-deck are promenading or lounging the officers of the ship and troops, some engaged in pleasant chat, some silently enjoying the ever changing prospect, others taking a closer view, through telescopes, and commenting on the aspect.

The soldiers and Our Boys in the Army, just dismissed from afternoon parade, and looking "spic and span," in their scarlet and blue uniforms and white belts, are scattered over the vessel in picturesque attitudes and groups.

Sergeant O'Shehe and Mr. and Mrs. Rumball are conspicuous objects, and divide with the brilliant scenery the attention of officers and men.

These three are located on the fo'castle.

Mr. and Mrs. Rumball are seated on a coil of rope, looking fully recovered from sea-sickness and the misadventures they have experienced, and reminding those who contemplate them of a couple of full fledged, fat, happy turtle-doves.

The Sergeant, exceedingly smart and fresh looking, save a few scars on his face,—the healing marks of Mrs. Rumball's nails,—is leaning his graceful form on the hatch, and bending over the now serene couple.

Stay—there is a slight disturbance in the breast of Mr. Rumball—he is not *quite* serene.

Since their fearful adventure, the Sergeant and Mrs. Rumball have become great friends.

They would no more now think of tearing each others' faces than they would of "flying,"

They are very gentle and considerate with each other. Mrs. Rumball, in fact, not yet knowing that it was he who stole her trousers, has been bestowing many tender glances on the bold Sergeant; and Mr. Rumball doesn't quite like it.

He is getting slightly jealous, is Rumball, and casts a glance now and then on "that 'ere milantery dandy," as he mentally calls the Sergeant, that is not exactly dovelike in its expression.

Mrs. Rumball, however, is quite unconscious of this, and sits drinking in the Sergeant's words (he has been to Gibraltar before, and is explaining the striking points of the scenery as they pass onward), as though they savoured of her favourite beverage—gin—which she hasn't tasted since she left old England, brandy having been recommended as the best antidote to sea-sickness.

Occasionally Mrs. Rumball sighs, and mentally murmurs—

"Wot a elegant man he is! I wish as I 'adn't scradged 'is poor face!"

Joey Pumps and Dolly Swaps are in the maintop, enjoying the scenery, and themselves, after their own fashion—taking alternate shots with the pea-shooter (putty-balls), at Dick Everett, and a number of the boys, who are grouped below listening to an old Sergeant of the 33rd, who s giving them some particulars respecting the famous Rock they are now so rapidly approaching.

The only really unhappy man on board is the General.

He is seated in his cabin, morose and lonely.

The Captain of the steamer, and many other officers, have made friendly advances, and of-

fered their profound sympathy in his misfortunes; but he had repelled their advances, and snarlingly refused to be comforted.

The General has not only been reduced to a pair of lady's trousers, but he has lost his cocked hat and tunic; the former he knows went overboard on the night he got fixed in the tub, the tunic has vanished—how, he does not know, though he shrewdly suspects that someone has pushed it through the port in his cabin, with the view to sending it to join the cocked hat.

How is he to get on shore? he asks himself.

He must manage to get a suit of some kind from the town—he will send Sergeant O'Shehe ashore to procure it; and then he can disembark decently, and endeavour to keep the story of his misfortunes from the Governor of the Rock.

The latter might be done with a little manoeuvring.

All on board, with the exception of the boys, the Sergeant, Mr. and Mrs. Rumball, and Joey Pumps, were going on to Malta, and there wouldn't be time for the story to get wind through those on the departing steamer.

The Sergeant he would take his oath, on the pain of being reduced to the ranks, to keep his mouth shut.

The boys, he thought, wouldn't bother themselves to proclaim what had happened—they had had their little jokes, and that was all they cared about.

At any rate, he would promise them, through the Sergeant, not to punish them for what they had done, if they would only keep their tongues still, and turn over a new leaf at Gibraltar.

As for Mr. and Mrs. Rumball, if they only hinted at what had taken place, he would throw them off the east side of the Rock, when, unless they became transformed into monkeys, they would become food for the sharks of the Mediterranean.

The General was actually fast becoming an infamous character.

He was already a robber, and now he deliberately contemplated murder.

The last, and certainly not the least dangerous personage he had to deal with, was Joey Pumps; but he would attach Joey to his own person, put him in a livery of blue cloth and silver buttons, and thus secure his silence.

Having thus given a general description of things, and elucidated the General's plans, we must return to the group around the old 33rd Sergeant.

The latter, who had been stationed at Gib., as he called the Rock, no less than three times, and was, consequently, well acquainted with it, had been giving Dick and his chums a glowing acount of the last, and what is called the "Great Siege of Gibraltar."

"That was a siege, my lads, I can tell you," continued the Sergeant. "It lasted from July, 1779, to March, 1783, and then the combined Spanish and French fleets and armies couldn't take it from us, although they peppered the fortress, on one occasion, with no less than one thousand two hundred pieces of ordnance—all firing together.

"The Rock is the strongest fortress in the world, isn't it Sergeant?"

"Well, I should say it was. At any rate, the fortifications are amongst the most formidable, and the value of the Rock to England has induced the Government to maintain the defences in such a state of formidable perfection as to render the place impregnable. The fortifications, which are not constructed on any particular system, may be classed under three heads.

"1st.—A sea wall, with a system of 'curtains,' 'flanks,' and 'bastions.'

"2nd.—Retired batteries, armed with the heaviest ordnance in commanding positions, but scarcely discernible from the sea, and comparatively safe from the fire of the shipping.

"3rd.—The galleries, excavated out of the solid rock."

At the latter information there was a chorus of "Oh's!" in astonishment from the Sergeant's young auditors.

"It's a fact," continued the veteran. "The galleries were excavated out of the solid rock during the siege, to bring a flanking fire to bear on the approaches to the Rock. They commanded the North Front, 'Neutral Ground,' and part of the bay.

"Every spot from whence a gun can be brought to bear is occupied by cannon, which oftentimes quaintly peep out of the most secluded nooks, among geraniums and flowering plants, while huge piles of shot and shell, some of enormous size, and stowed away in convenient places, screened from an enemy's fire, but all ready for use."

"It must be a formidable place, indeed!" exclaimed Dick.

"It is," returned the Sergeant. "Have you any idea what part of the Rock you will be stationed on?"

"Not the slightest," replied Dick.

"Well, there are several places on the Rock where you young monkeys could be put out of the way of mischief!"

"So I suppose," said Dick, laughing. "Are there more than one barrack there?"

"More than one!" exclaimed the Sergeant. "Why, let me see," beginning to count on his fingers. "There is the 'Casemate,'—'Town Range,' — 'Hargreaves,' — 'South,'—'Rosia,'— 'Buena-Vista,' — 'Windmill-hill,'—'Europa,'— 'Bravery,'—and 'Defensible' barracks; besides casemated barracks along the whole of the line wall front (chiefly occupied by Artillery), small barracks in the Moorish Castle, and wooden huts, lately erected on the North Front.

"There is also a small barrack for a detachment stationed at Catalan Bay, a small village on the eastern side of the Rock, ensconced in a sandy bay, and occupied principally by Genoese fishermen."

"There are plenty of them, then, certainly," observed Tom Sheppard. "Which is the most out-of-the-way, do you think, Sergeant?"

"Europa. That's beyond the Naval Hospital. That is the general hospital for the whole of the garrison, as well as the seaman. From the married quarters at Rosia—better known as 'Misery Hole'—a path leads over Camp Bay to the hospital, and from there you get through the Buena Vista Barrack, across a slight bridge over a tremendous ravine, to Europa Pass, and thence by the Devil's Bowling-green to Europa."

"We should be pretty well isolated there, Sergeant, eh?" laughed Dick.

"Yes. But there are other points where you might be put, and be pretty well cut off from civilisation, too," returned the Sergeant. "There's the Rock Gun, or Wolf's Crag, at the north summit, 1,250 feet high. The upper signal station in the centre, 1,255 feet high; and

O'Hara's Tower at the south end, 1,408 feet high. If you get on either one of those stations, you'll be as near the clouds as anyone could wish you to be to lessen your opportunities of getting into mischief."

"'Necessity is the mother of invention,' you know, Sergeant," observed Dick; "and I should'nt be surprised if our wits got sharpened at the same time as our appetites, for it must be jolly bracing on the top of the Rock."

"Yes; and the view will repay you for your isolation—at least till the novelty wears off. The signal-station, for instance, is situated on the central eminence of the Rock. There is a stone building there, with a tower, from which the Straits are watched and the movements of shipping reported. The range of observation from that elevated spot is so extensive that vessels can be reported, on a calm day, when 40 miles distant from the Rock.

"From there is visible the whole of Gibraltar Bay, the opposite coast of Spain, the Ronda Mountains, the Sierra Nevada, and a portion of the tract of country between them, the blue waters of the Mediterranean, the Atlas Mountains in Africa, Ceuta, the convict station of the Spaniards, Apes' Hill, and the coast of Barbary.

"A few feet below the town, facing the westward, is a battery of four cannon, from which the morning and evening guns are fired as a notice for the opening or closing of the fortress gates."

"By jingo!" said Bob Jones. "It's almost like a vast and rocky prison!"

"It is, so far as getting off the Rock without permission is concerned," returned the Sergeant.

"Are there no places of special interest on the Rock?" asked Dick.

"Oh, yes! The whole natural construction of the Rock is interesting. But what will please you boys the most, I expect, will be the caves, of which there are several. The most celebrated are St. Michael's and Genista, Martin's, Fig-tree, Monkey's, and Poca-Roca.

"The largest is St. Michael's, 1,100 feet above the sea-level. The entrance is small, but within is a species of lofty hall, 220 feet long by 70 high, supported by stalactite pillars, which, when lighted up, have a most beautiful effect. I've penetrated many hundreds of feet into the cave, and have descended a long series of smaller caves, Their actual extent, however, is unknown."

"Well, I should think we might find a little excitement in exploring that cave, at any rate," said Dick. "Anything else, Sergeant?"

"Well, I suppose the galleries are the great sight of Gibraltar. There is no excavation in the world, for military purposes, at all approaching them in conception or execution. They are divided into two ranges, the upper and lower, the latter being partly under cover and partly open. The upper range contains two magnificent halls, St. George's and Cornwallis.

"Then there is the Moorish Castle—a very interesting old place that is, and must have been a most formidable structure before the time of artillery. You'll find it, even now, riddled with shot-marks—the honourable scars of the siege. But come, here we are," broke off the Sergeant, suddenly. "Here's Carner's Point, and we are just entering the Bay of Gibraltar. Come forward and catch a glimpse of the Rock as we enter."

This was so, a fact of which everyone on deck

seemed to be aware, as many were rushing forward, and the officers had got ready their telescopes to catch the first sight of the celebrated Rock.

It was a noble sight, and there was not one of our boys who did not open his eyes and gaze in wonder at the romantic scene.

As the steamer entered the bay, the last rays of the setting sun fell upon the bastioned rock, which, bristling with cannon, and stretching far into the calm waters, lay like a lion (to which its form bears some resemblance) resting in the consciousness of its strength.

On the opposite side of the Strait, not more than fifteen miles across, rose the huge Abyla, elevating his head to the very clouds; and between these gigantic heights, known to the ancients as the Pillars of Hercules, rushed the waters of the Atlantic, with a mighty current into the Mediterranean.

Across the bay, facing the western front of the fortress, were seen the white buildings of the Algueziras, backed by a range of beautifully-formed hills, which gradually lessened as they receded from the shore.

A few men of war lay at anchor in the harbour, while the number of mercantile vessels from the various parts of the Mediterranean gave animation to the scene, and attested the value to England of the important fortress.

As the steamer came to an anchor, a boat put off from the shore, and an aide-de-camp of the Governor slipped on board, bringing orders that the School of the Regiment was not to disembark till the morning, when it was to march to, and take up temporary quarters in, the Moorish Castle, first parading in the Alameda Gardens for the inspection of the Governor.

The probable arrival of the School by the steamer had been notified to the Governor by General Shoot, and arrangements had been made accordingly.

The presence of the General on board was not, of course, mentioned by Sergeant O'Shehe, nor by anyone else—the Captain of the vessel, considering that he was not responsible in any way, and the General being "in the sulks," having given orders to his officers to keep quiet, and let him get out of his scrape as he best could.

At the request of the General, the officers of the 33rd had also maintained silence.

Whether this was a wise course or not to pursue on the part of the General, will presently be seen.

The boys, who were eager to land, were greatly disappointed at the disembarkation being delayed until the morning, but they were somewhat compensated therefor by the romantic night-scene which they beheld from the deck.

As the sun sank below the horizon, the signal gun—placed about midway on the long, sharp ridgy summit of the Rock, whose rugged outline was distinctly indented against the deep azure of the heavens—gave notice of his disappearance.

The echoes of the surrounding crags and rocks returned the report with long-continued reverberations; while the drums and bugles of the different regiments replied by sounding the retreat.

At this well-known signal, Our Boys could hear the several guards along the wall line being turned out—the cries of "Guard turn out!" and the rattle of rifles being distinctly conveyed across the water to the steamer.

To the retreat of the sun succeeded one of those radiant moonlights which throw such an air of inexpressible beauty over the scenery of Southern climes.

The moon, rising from behind the giant Rock, touched its crags and pinnacles with her silver rays, which glancing far beyond the deep shadows of the mountain, fell upon the taper masts of the vessels riding in the Bay, and sparkled in the foam of the distant waves which broke gently over the long protecting points of the rocky shore.

No sound disturbed the stillness of the night, except the occasional challenge of the sentries, and the slight splash of the rippling waters, as they dashed against the sides of the boats and shipping.

Such was the romantic nature of the scene presented to the wondering gaze of Our Boys in the Army, on this the first night of their arrival at Gibraltar.

CHAPTER XXX.

THE PARADE IN THE ALAMEDA GARDENS.—THE EXTRAORDINARY PEOPLE WHO DODGED ROUND THE GOVERNOR.—EXPLANATION.—THE GENERAL, AND MR. AND MRS. RUMBALL BEING CONSIDERED MAD, ARE TAKEN TO THE CIVIL PRISON.

WE now raise the curtain upon another of the varied scenes which mark the course of the events of our story.

The place is the Alameda Gardens on the Rock.

The time, two hours after morning gun-fire—six o'clock.

Under the young rays of the sun, strong enough to be gloriously bright, but, as yet, not too hot, the School of the Regiment is drawn up, in full dress, awaiting the appearance of the Governor of the Rock, General Sir Gentle Sharpset.

Whilst awaiting the Governor, the band of the school, formed into a circle, is playing various airs, to which hundreds of spectators—consisting of representatives of several nations,—amongst which are Jews from Barbary and the Levant, Greek Islanders, Sardinians, Sicilians, Neapolitans, Genoese, Portuguese and Spaniards, with a few Turks and Armenians, the former distinguished by their turbans, and the latter by their high mitre-shaped caps—drawn together by the unusual sight of the boy soldiers, are listening with considerable pleasure, and are expressing their feelings in the language and gestures characteristic of their various nationalities.

The Alameda Gardens, which are planted in terraces with trees and shrubs, and show a great profusion of flowers and vegetation, of which the geraniums are the most noticeable, are the favourite resort of the inhabitants, who crowd thither to listen to the music of the military bands, which play twice a week during the year.

Never before had the beautiful walks been crowded at such an early hour of the day; but, on this occasion, the inhabitants have been drawn together by a spectacle unusually novel in its character.

All are eagerly awaiting the arrival of the Governor.

There is no one there present awaiting this event with greater eagerness than Sergeant O'Shehe.

The Sergeant is in fine form, and struts about in the full consciousness that he is the focus of admiration, as he has hidden the scars made by Mrs. Rumball's nails with flesh-coloured court plaster.

He looks, too, on the boys, with a glance of proud admiration.

"They look well—very well!" is his occasional mental comment. "Capital! Never saw them look better! Never, by Jove! Hope everything will pass off all right?"

Presently, the Governor, accompanied by his staff—all on foot—makes his appearance. The Sergeant orders the band to cease playing, and form up on the right of the boys; then he rings out the word of command—

"T' hun! Pre-zen 'rms!"

These motions are splendidly executed, and the Sergeant takes up his position in front of the parade, standing rigidly to attention.

The Governor, a prim-looking man, very thin, with sharp-looking eyes and features, returns the salute, releases the Sergeant from his position, and requests that he will accompany him during the inspection.

Then, with methodical slowness, the inspection is made, Sir Gentle only finding occasion to make a longer stop than usual at one boy—that boy being, as the reader can see, Dolly Swaps.

This is not to be wondered at, as we know that Dolly's personal peculiarities are at all times, whether in full dress or undress, sufficiently conspicuous and marked to attract particular attention.

In fact, Dolly, on this special occasion, has set himself out to make an impression, and he can see that Sir Gentle is very much struck.

Dolly stands with his carbine all awry, his stomach compressed as though someone were tickling him in that sensitive region, his mouth half-open, and his busby falling on one side, looking very rakish and tipsy.

As Sir Gentle looks at Dolly, in doubt as to whether our little friend is silly or is acting in a disrespectful manner, Sergeant O'Shehe eyes him—Dolly—as though he could jump down his throat, and inwardly swears to give him two dozen on the "right-about-face" when they got to quarters.

At length the inspection is over, Sir Gentle has stepped to the front, and is about to address the boys, when he is arrested by great commotion.

The crowd suddenly opens, and three figures —three most extraordinary-looking figures, wild-looking, gesticulating violently, two of them shouting, "Thief! Thief! Stop thief!"—rush forward at headlong speed towards the astonished Governor, and commence dodging around him.

These three figures are at once recognised by the Sergeant and the boys as General Shoot and Mr. and Mrs. Rumball.

The General, of the three figures, was (to go back to the past tense) the most extraordinary-looking, and almost convulsed the boys with laughter.

To begin from his nether parts, the General's feet were encased in Wellington boots with spurs, the tops of which, reaching to about half-way up his calves, left a space of flesh between them and the bottom of Mrs Rumball's scarlet drawers, the embroidery on which was now displayed to great advantage.

The General was minus his tunic, and, consequently, had the upper part of his person clothed in a white shirt.

To complete the oddity of the General's appearance his head was crowned with—well, not his cocked hat, because we know that went overboard in the Bay of Biscay, but a hat—the most dissipated, rakish, most disreputable hat imaginable.

This hat had once been a "topper" of respectability, upright, with a sleek, shining face, that cast a bright radiance around, and beat the sun all to fits; but now it was dingy, low-looking, and crushed—crushed to the brim, which was split from the top, as flat as a pair of bellows.

We won't describe any part of the costumes of Mr. and Mrs. Rumball, save to say that, the latter had on a full-bordered white night-cap, and the former was bareheaded.

Did not the Sergeant's conscience smite him when he saw the wretched condition to which the General was reduced?

It did—and with good reason.

For this reason we must retrace our steps—a course, too, that is necessary, in order to connect the events of this story and render them intelligible.

It will be remembered that having lost his regimental tunic and cocked hat, the General had conceived the plan of sending the Sergeant on shore to procure a coat and hat, of any shapes, so long as they were decent in appearance, to enable him to go ashore.

"I don't care what shape or contour they are," said the General to the Sergeant, as the latter stood in the cabin about the time of morning gun-fire, "so long as they are clean. D'ye hear?"

"Yes, General!"

Sergeant O'Shehe was standing as stiff as a ramrod, trying to make believe by an assumption of great gravity of manner and attentive demeanour, that he had more respect than ever for the General under the trying nature of his circumstances, and couldn't possibly raise a smile at the ridiculous figure he was cutting.

"Mind, don't go to any of the officers or people on board. I don't want to be brought into contact with any of them. Just slip quietly ashore and slip quietly back again. D'ye see?"

"Yes, General?"

"Now, don't make a bungle of it!" continued the General, with a premonitory scowl and growl, "d'ye hear."

"Yes, General!"

"'Yes, General?'" repeated the General, with a snap. "You say 'yes, General,' like some confounded parrot! I'll bet a five-pound note you go making a mess of it! You'd better not, I can tell you! A pretty fool you've made of yourself and me too, during the voyage" glancing at the scarlet drawers—"haven't you?"

"Yes, General!"

"Yes, Gen—er—al!" returned the irritated gentleman, with a snarling drawl, "and if the truth was known you're highly delighted about it, ugh! Leave the cabin, sir, and go and do what I tell you, and just take my advice and don't make any mistake, or the deuce take me if I don't reduce you to the ranks!"

Sergeant O'Shehe left the cabin and the saloon to carry out the General's orders and indulge in a little private chuckling.

In accomplishing the latter the Sergeant experienced no difficulty whatever, but he found the former impracticable.

It was no use attempting to get ashore until the gun had signalled for the gates of the fortress to be opened—he knew that and waited.

But when the gates were opened he was told that none could leave the steamer until the quarantine officer had admitted them to *pratique*, and, when the latter had been given, lo and behold it was too late to go ashore and return before the steamer would start!

Here was a pretty dilemma!

The boys had packed up their kits, transferred them to one of three boats that had been sent to take the School ashore, and the boys themselves were paraded at the gangway ready to enter the remaining boats.

What was he to do?

"The deuce take the General," muttered the Sergeant, as he hastily walked to and fro in front of the School, slapping his leg with his whip, and biting his moustache, "how I am to get him a coat and hat now I'm blest if I know! He'll have to go on shore as he is—that's all about it?"

But, fortunately for the Sergeant, a pair of sharp ears happened to catch what he was muttering.

Those ears belonging to Joey Pumps.

"Don't be down on yer luck, Sarjint," said Joey. "If yer comes with me I kin put yer in the way o' getting what yer wants. I kin, an' no gammon," he added, as the Sergeant eyed him with a suspicious look, "there's a bran-noo coat an' 'at o' Rumball's down hin the burf, as I've laid hout to put hon when he goes ashore. Rumball hev made hup his mind to cut a orful swell, but them togs is too fine fur 'im. Jist the werry thin's fur the Gen'ral"—with a wink—"come hon."

Should he take the advantage of this opportunity.

The Sergeant stood for a few moments revolving this perplexing question in his agitated mind.

There were two or three unpleasant contingencies to be apprehended from a second prigging.

Mr. Rumball would be almost sure to kick up a row when he missed his property.

The General would run the risk of being sent to prison for wearing articles of clothing which he knew to have been stolen—at least, the Rumballs would swear that he knew.

He himself might be served in the same manner for stealing such articles.

"But there," he mentally exclaimed, "Hanged if I care what happens! I'll chance the luck!"

And he did.

He saw the coast was clear, for Mr. and Mrs. Rumball were busily engaged at that moment in superintending the safe transfer of the feather-bed from the ship to the boat.

He descended to the berth, and, in a few minutes returned, with Mr. Rumball's best coat and silk hat, tied up in a sheet and darted to the saloon.

Here he untied the purloined articles and then slipped into the General's cabin.

A look of intense relief came over the wretched General's features, as the Sergeant entered, and he almost smiled as he said—

"So you have succeeded—eh, Sergeant?"

"Yes, General. They're quite new—hat and coat—never been worn before."

"Coat and hat!" cried the General, with changing countenance. "Haven't you got a pair of trousers?"

Here was a go!

"Confound it all," thought the Sergeant, "I forgot all about the trousers! I—I—You never said anything about trousers, General," he stammered aloud.

"Never said anything about trousers!" shouted the General, turning purple with rage. "What if I didn't sir? Hadn't you common-sense enough to know that I wanted them? Why, I should look a greater guy than ever with a frock-coat and hat, and those cursed scarlet drawers! You consummate idiot!"—shaking his fist close to the Sergeant's nose—"I knew you'd make some confounded bungle over it! Wasn't there plenty of trousers where you bought the coat and hat?"

"Yes, General,"—this aloud—and then to himself, "By Jove, I never told a bigger lie than that! But in for a lamb, in for a sheep."

"'Yes, General.' That's all you can say, you —you—Good Heavens, I don't know what to call you bad enough! Get out! Curse you—get out!"

Here the infuriated General, picking up the topper, shied it with all the force he could muster at the Sergeant's head.

A quick "duck," however, avoided the shot, and the next minute the General was alone with his passion, and the coat and hat, on the latter of which he vented his fury, by kicking it about the cabin as though it were a football.

The Sergeant had no sooner made his escape from the cabin than he rushed on deck, got the boys into the boats, and pushed for the shore, leaving the General and the Rumballs to get off the best way they could.

As it happened, there was not much time for the latter.

The steamer was only waiting for the Rumballs and the General to get into the boat to start.

The Captain had sent to hurry the disembarkation of both parties, but there seemed to be a hitch somewhere.

Neither of them would make an appearance on deck.

What was the matter?

The truth is, Mr. and Mrs. Rumball had missed the coat and hat, and were making an awful row about it below, and the General was in an awful "stew" in his cabin.

After his rage had somewhat cooled down, he came to the conclusion that there was no help for it but to put on the coat and hat, get on shore the best way he could, and complete his costume by buying a pair of trousers.

Accordingly he tried the hat, and again lost his temper.

The hat was too small, and it took all the General's strength to force it on his head, and then it was so tight, and made the skin smart to such a degree, that it felt as though his brow was compressed by a band of red-hot iron.

But if the General's temper was tried in fixing the hat, it was doubly so in putting on the coat.

Both the General and Mr. Rumball were stout men, but the latter, unlike the General, was very short in the arms and very narrow across the shoulders, and the consequence was that the General, before he could get it on, split the coat all down the back; and even then it was so cuttingly tight under the arm-pits that he found it an utter impossibility to get his arms straight down by his sides.

"Good Heavens!" almost sobbed the General, looking at his elegant reflection in the glass, "if this isn't enough to drive a man mad, I should like to know what is?"

And, indeed, he prowled about the cabin like a madman, unable to summon up the courage to leave it.

But the moment came at length when he was obliged to do so or go on with the steamer to Malta.

The Captain sent a peremptory message to both parties, and a scene ensued that gave the crew and the men of the gallant 33rd something to laugh at until they reached Malta.

Looking like a man that had just robbed a hen-roost, and was trying to avoid observation, he slunk up the saloon-steps on to the quarter-deck, where his appearance was greeted with much tittering, while Mr. and Mrs. Rumball were being greeted in a similar fashion at the forecastle.

Mr. Rumball, whose weekday habiliments had been packed away in the boat with the other things, now that his best coat and hat had vanished, was bare-headed, and in his shirt-sleeves, and both he and his wife still declaiming loudly at the theft.

As the General, in fear and trembling, approached the gangway, the eyes of Mr. Rumball fell upon the coat and hat and scarlet drawers.

This was a fatal glance for the General.

Mr. Rumball knew his property at a glance.

"Dolly?" he exclaimed, "that's the coat an' 'at an' yer scarlet trousers!"

Mrs. Rumball looked, saw, and, with a yell of rage, rushed at once at the daring thief, followed by Rumball.

Do you suppose the General waited to be clawed by Mrs. Rumball and her husband?

Not a bit of it!

He turned, and made for the saloon hatchway, and, no doubt, would have got safely down, but for one unfortunate circumstance.

In his blind hurry to get down, the General rushed full-butt against the top of the hatch, crushing Mr. Rumball's best silk hat out of all shape, and knocking himself backwards into Mrs. Rumball's arms.

How the General escaped without being torn to pieces is a miracle!

He did, however, and made a frantic rush for the gangway, minus his coat, which his desperate assailants had managed to tear piecemeal off his back.

The chase became exceedingly exciting.

Down the companion-ladder scrambled the General into the boat and made his way to the bows, where he squatted himself and began shouting frantically—

"Pull off! Pull off! Quick! For the love of Heaven, pull off! They'll be in in a second!"

But the men who were at the oars could do nothing for roaring, and the next moment Mrs. Rumball, who had got half-way down, slipped, and fell the other half into the boat, happily for herself, alighting on the feather-bed.

Rumball, fortunately, got in safely, and so did Joey Pumps, the latter individual experiencing great difficulty in doing so, owing to a serious state of limpness, caused by an unusually prolonged disturbance of the risible nerves.

Mrs. Rumball and her husband would, no doubt, have tackled the General, but for a clever bit of generalship, in the boat.

Mr. and Mrs. Rumball were on the feather-bed, and which, being on the top of the boys' kits, and other luggage, was considerably above the sides of the boat,

The General saw this position of the enemy, and, with a promptness that spoke well for his sagacity in taking advantage of the enemy's weak points, commenced to rock the boat with great violence, a movement that gave Mr. and Mrs. Rumball quite as much as they could do to hold on and save themselves from being rolled into the bay.

"Brayvo, Gen'ral!" cried Joey, from whose eyes, from the violence of his peculiar emotion, were rolling big tears. "That's a jolly clever dodge, that is! Go it! Hold hon, Dolly! Hold tight, Rumball! Ha, ha, ha, h-a-a-a! Oh lor! I wish Dolly Swaps was 'ere!"

It was thus that the boat, under difficulties, progressed, till it reached the Old Mole, or landing-place; and the prow had no sooner touched than the General sprang on shore, made for the gate, shot past the guardroom, and away into the town at a tremendous rate.

Quick as he was, however, Mr. and Mrs. Rumfall were quite as quick in their movements, and the General had scarcely passed through the gate when they were at his heels, and then commenced the chase, which ended, as we have seen, in the General dodging his pursuers around the Governor, Sir Gentle Sharpset, at the moment he was about to address the boys.

If Sergeant O'Shehe's conscience did not prick him as he beheld the dreadful predicament of the General, it certainly ought to have done; and perhaps it did, for, as soon as he could recover from the shock which the sight gave him, he exclaimed—

"By Jove, here's a devil of a go! I shall drop in for it, for this!"

The hubbub that followed was very great, and there were but four individuals of the vast crowd of spectators whose features were not expanded in smiles.

These were the Governor, the General, and Mr. and Mrs. Rumball.

"Protect me!" cried the General, catching the Governor by the hips and twisting him about, using him as a shield against the enraged and determined pursuers, as first one made a grab, then the other, "Protect me! For Heaven's sake, don't let them touch me! They'll tear me to pieces!"

"Leave go, you rascal!" cried the astonished and indignant Governor. "What the deuce do you mean by—by—by this outrageous impertinence? Release me directly! Do you know I'm the Governor of the Rock, you villain?"

"And I'm a General!" panted the victim. "I am, indeed! I'll prove it to you, presently, if you'll only have those dreadful persons arrested!"

This passage of words between the Governor and the General was accompanied by fierce invectives and charges from Mr. and Mrs. Rumball, as they did their best to get at the object of their chase.

"Yer thievin' willan, yer've got hon my scarlet drawers, yer hev!" cried Mrs. Rumball.

"He stole my 'at an' coat!" shouted Rumball.

"Only let me git hat 'im!" threatened Mrs. Rumball.

"I'll fight 'im for nothin'!" vociferated Mr. Rumball.

"Git hout o' the way, yer little hinsignificant jack-o'-napes!" at length cried Mrs. Rumball, seizing the Governor by the back of the neck, and shaking him. "Git away, an' let us git hat the thievin' wretch—do!"

Whether the Governor, between his assailants, would have escaped with his uniform in a whole condition, it is impossible to say; but possibly such would not have been the case, had not assistance arrived in the form of several police-men, who speedily released him by "collaring" all three of his tormentors.

But although this placed the Governor out of danger, it did not end the row.

Mr. and Mrs. Rumball protested against this treatment in the most energetic manner, both by voice and physical demonstration—scream-ing, kicking, and struggling with their captors frantically.

The General protested on the ground that he was a General, and that he was the victim of a series of outrageous tricks.

But unfortunately for the General's assertion as to his rank, his present appearance was deci-dedly against him.

"I'm a General—my name's Shoot. Surely that's a name well known to you, Sir Gentle?" said the General, appealingly.

"He must be mad!" said the Governor, turning to his aides-de-camp. "I've heard of Shoot, the famous Artillery General, but it's impossible this extraordinary-looking fellow can be he!"

"No, Sir Gentle," replied one of the officers; "I have met General Shoot, but he certainly is no more like this man than chalk's like cheese."

"I am! I swear I am!" cried the General. "I can bring a witness to prove my identity. There's my Sergeant—the Sergeant of the School of the Regiment—ask him if I'm not?"

The Sergeant, who had expected this, had made up his mind how to act.

He had resolved to deny all knowledge of the General, and Mr. and Mrs. Rumball, too, if ap-pealed to.

His reason for deciding to act thus was ex-ceedingly deep, having been suggested to his mind by the remark of the Governor that the General must be mad.

After all, it was the Sergeant himself who had stolen Mrs. Rumball's drawers, and her husband's coat and hat; and he argued that if the General had been charged with the theft, and prosecuted by Mr. and Mrs. Rumball, he, the Sergeant, would be sure to be bowled out, and sent to prison, as well as the General.

"If it's mad the General's made out to be," he thought, "he'll be put into a lunatic asylum, and the charge will then never be made against him, and then we'll both be safe! By Jove, but that's a fine idea! And it wouldn't be a bad stroke to try and make out the Rumballs mad, too. I should be rid of the lot of 'em!"

This diabolical resolve was the result of almost instantaneous reflection, passing through his brain more like a sudden impression than a chain of reasoning.

So, when the Governor addressed him, he was prepared with an answer cool and prompt.

"Do you know this person, Sergeant?"

"Never saw him in my life, sir, till this minute."

"I thought as much," observed the Governor. "He must be mad."

"He looks very much like it, sir," assented the treacherous Sergeant. "See how he's glaring at us, sir!"

This was true enough.

The poor General, dumbfounded at the auda-ciously cool denial on the part of the Sergeant, was staring at him, with protruding eyeballs, in speechless amazement.

"He's a dangerous madman, evidently," said the Governor. "The poor fellow had better be removed to the Civil prison until his history can be inquired into."

Here was a dreadful pass to come to!

His identity coolly denied, and his madness suggested by his own Sergeant!

Had he been free, he would have rushed at and choked the traitor there and then!

As it was, he began cursing and swearing, and calling the Sergeant all the wicked names he could think of, and threatening him with every kind of punishment.

But this abuse, uttered with the full power of his lungs, and accompanied by a purple coun-tenance, indicative of ungovernable rage, only confirmed the impression of his madness, and the finishing stroke was given to the General's mad state of mind by the Sergeant giving it as his opinion that—

"I believe the other two are mad also, Sir Gentle, and I think the best plan would be to strap them to stretchers and take them off to the Castle. It's out of harm's way they'll be then."

Not only the Governor, but all the officers, the police, and the spectators who were near enough to see and hear what was going on, were quite satisfied that the three were stark-mad, and it would only be doing them a kindness to do as the Sergeant suggested.

So the Governor gave the order, and it was done—after a resistance and a continuation of deafening yells, which none but those who are raving mad *can* make—and the three were carried off, accompanied by Joey Pumps, run-ning from victim to victim, expressing his sym-pathy by sundry chuckles and winks, and advising them to keep up their peckers.

When the excitement caused by this extra-ordinary scene had subsided, the School of the Regiment, which had broken its ranks to enjoy the sight in comfort, was reformed, briefly ad-dressed by the Governor as to the conduct that was expected of it during its stay on the Rock, and then marched, with colours flying and band playing, to their temporary quarters, the Moorish Castle.

CHAPTER XXXI.

THE MOORISH CASTLE.—DICK EVERETT AND CHUMS DETERMINE TO RESCUE THE THREE MAD PEOPLE.—NEW RULES AND REGULA-TIONS.—THE SERGEANT ON FIRE.

THE Moorish Castle, in which our boys had been assigned temporary quarters, is one of the most interesting buildings on the Rock.

History records that the Castle was built in the days of bows and arrows and battering-rams, and must have been a most formidable structure before the time of artillery.

Indeed, although the old castle was finely bat-tered at during the sieges when cannon were used, the Tower—a square, massive structure—riddled with shot-marks, still stands.

The Castle is one of the oldest buildings in

Spain, supposed to have been commenced by the Moorish Chief, Tarik-Ibn-Zeyad, in the year 711, but was not completed until 725, by Abul Hazez—as the Arabic inscription over the south gate records.

Gibraltar is said to have been first known to the Phœnicians, but there is little doubt that it was not inhabited until the Mahommedan invasion of Spain.

Tarik landed on the Rock in 711, hence it was that the castle had a Moorish origin.

Gibraltar, it is believed, derives its name from a corruption of two words—Gebal-Tarik, or Mountain of Tarik.

The Rock has undergone many vicissitudes of fortune.

In 1086, it was in possession of the Caliph Yusefben-Taxfin, and at this time the Spanish Moors, unable to contend with the forces brought against them by Alfonso of Castile, implored aid from Africa.

This was granted, and a powerful Moslem army was sent into Spain, which soon wrested the country from their weaker brethren.

During these strifes, Gibraltar was, for a time, in possession of both parties.

In 1161, the primitive fortifications constructed by Tarik, were largely increased by Abd-l-Mumem-Ibn Ali. They became most formidable, and afforded great facilities for succouring the neighbouring towns.

In 1309, the Rock was, for the first time, exposed to a regular siege, and taken by Ferdinand IV., of Spain, after it had been in the hands of the Moors for 598 years.

It was retaken by the Moors in 1333, but reverted to the dominion of the Christians, in 1462, when the Duke of Medina Sidonia wrested it from the Moslem dynasty, which was rapidly drifting to its final dissolution.

The Moors held Gibralter altogether for 726 years, and it may be described as their first landing-place, and their last point of departure from Europe.

Up to this time, Gibraltar had sustained eight sieges, and was to sustain many more before it remained finally, as at present, in the hands of the English nation.

In 1598 the last relics of the Moorish race were removed from Spain, and the Rock was under the dominion of that country until 1704, not, however, without witnessing some obstinate struggles—once owing to a deperate attack by corsairs.

Through all these hundreds of years of almost constant strife, the mighty castle held its own—and the remaining walls, and fragments of arches, &c., still show of what a massive construction it formerly consisted.

As gunpowder was invented, the attack came from the present North Front, and as the walls on this side were comparatively thin, its defenders built it up inside with a tough concrete called "tapia" and the Tower, as it now stands, is almost solid—a square shaft, in which is a wooden staircase, is the only hollow, with the exception of a deep tank or well, which opens from the rooms at the top.

The staircase leads out on to a terrace running round the North and West faces of the Tower, from whence a splendid view is obtained; and on the same level are the only rooms now in the Tower, called the "Moorish General's" rooms.

A great portion, inside the walls, has been devoted to officers' quarters and barracks.

Inside the walls also is the civil prison.

It was within the walls of this ancient and warworn castle—in the rooms of the Tower—that the School of the Regiment took up its quarters.

The rooms had been furnished in the usual military style—iron bedsteads with straw beds, coarse sheets, blankets, and rags, movable tables on iron trestles—all exactly the same as the rooms of the school-house had been furnished in Bangfire Barracks.

Bangfire Barracks.

"Why !" said Dick Everett to Tom Sheppard, and several others of his chums, who were lounging on the terrace, contemplating the view. "Why, Bangfire Barracks and the jolly old school-house, seems to my imagination to be awfully distant, as though they had existed only in a dream—so sudden is the change, and so utterly unlike the old place is everything here."

"Yes," returned Tom. "The change certainly does give one that impression. I can scarcely realise it."

"We are all alike in that respect," said Bob Jones. "But it strikes me there is another individual who can scarcely realise the sudden change," he added, with a knowing smile.

"Ah! You mean the General, Bob, I suppose?" said Dick, with a laugh, in which they all joined.

"Just so, Dick."

'By jingo!' exclaimed Harry Smith, "it's about the rummest set out I ever came across!'

"Yes," returned Dick. "I wonder what the General would have said, if anyone had told him that, in a few days after reading those rules and regulations to us on the morning we embarked, he would be confined within the walls of the Moorish Castle as a dangerous madman?"

"He would have called that one himself mad," observed Tom.

"What a complication of mishaps it's been,' said Dick.

"For which the General has only to thank his own ungovernable temper," said Harry.

"And the persevering attention of Dolly Swaps and Joey Pumps," laughed Dick.

"You just leave those honoured names alone, master," said Dolly, who came up at the moment, pipe-claying his gloves with a sponge. "You just mind they don't come down on you. You ain't everybody," added Dolly, winking at the others. "Nor you don't always succeed in what you undertake."

Here Dolly made a comical grimace.

"Just explain yourself, Dolly," demanded Dick, holding up his fist threateningly, "or I'll pummel your ugly little carcase into a jelly, and pipe-clay that dirty nose of yours."

"Ugly little carcase!" cried Dolly. "That's what I call precious cheeky. Why, I'm a perfect model—everybody knows that," assuming an elegant attitude by standing knock-kneed, putting his left hand, on which was the wet pipe-clay'd glove to his nose, and completing the graceful pose by a terrible squint.

"Oh, you get more perfect every day," said Dick, amidst a chorus of laughter. "But don't think you are going to get out of answering my question. In what have I ever failed, my little beauty? Come—out with it!" added Dick, catching Dolly by the collar of his shirt—for Dolly, like most of the boys, was dressed in his overalls.

"Why you couldn't get the General out of the tub, you know you couldn't," said Dolly—an allusion that caused a general and spontaneous burst of laughter.

"I should have done so, however," said Dick, when he could make himself heard, "if that young scamp of a Joey Pumps hadn't let go the rope which held up Mrs. Rumball and the Sergeant to the yardarm. At least, he should have either come out of the tub, or been hanged!"

"There's an 'if' in it, after all, Dick," retorted Dolly. "Now, my friend Joey and myself did succeed in all we attempted, and if it hadn't been for our inventive genius, what fun would you all have had, I should like to know? Why, if it hadn't been for us two, you wouldn't have seen the devil in a cocked-hat—nor the General hanging by his spurs from the shrouds—nor the General breaking the rules and regulation by being sick—nor Pomp tugging away at the General's shirt-tails—nor the General sporting Mrs. Rumball's scarlet drawers—nor——"

"The General knocking your wooden-heads together," suddenly cut in Dick, with a serio-comic quietness of manner that turned the laugh at once against the boasting Dolly.

"Well, I'd rather have a hard skull than a soft one," returned the imperturbable Dolly, nodding his head and winking significantly at Dick. Be off, now, Dick!"

This exclamation was caused by a sudden rush of Dick, who, forcing the sponge out of Dolly's hand, vigorously therewith pipe-clayed his face.

"There, you young cheeky beggar," said Dick, when he had released the spluttering Dolly, "if you wash that pipe-clay off your ugly phiz, I'll turn you up and warm you rightabout—mind that!"

"Dick," said Dolly, in a melodramatic voice, and looking at him with one eye, the other being closed with pipe-clay, "Dick I'll never consent to wear a mask unless the time comes when I I can't look anybody straight in the face without blushing? And that time——"

"I shed be werry sorry to see cum, Dolly," said the voice of Joey Pumps, who at this moment stepped on to the terrace. "When yer takes ter blushin', Dolly, fren' o' my art, Joey Pumps 'll cut yer! Thur!"

As Joey said this he came to a stand with his legs wide apart, one hand in his trousers-pocket, the other pointed at Dolly, his head bent sideways, his lips and brow puckered into a frown of the deepest severity.

"Joey," returned Dolly, in a solemn tone, and with a solemn face, bending forward and placing his hand with the wet pipe-clayed glove over his heart, "Joey, 'fren' o' my 'art, don't be afraid; you never shall see it!"

"Dolly, swear hit!" said Joey, with a roll of the eyes, and a sepulchral tone.

"Joey, I will I so help me—the General's cocked hat!"

"Dolly, yer makes yer fren' as 'appy as 'e kin be unner the most fearful forebodin's! Not about the blushin', Dolly, but wot's likely ter 'appen atween the three mad 'uns."

Joey had no sooner alluded to the General and Mr. and Mrs. Rumball than the boys gathered round him clamouring for the news.

"What's the matter, Joey?"

"What's up?"

"Anything going on?"

"Stand back, chaps," cried Dick, "and give Joey a chance to speak. Go on, Joey," added Dick, when he had cleared a space.

"I shed jist think as sumthin' air agoin' hon, too!" said Joey. "Hif there's a bit o' the Gen'rl lef' when they goes inter the cell ter-morrer—I shall be wery much surprised, that's hall!"

"Is Mr. and Mrs. Rumball pitching into him, then?" laughed Dick.

"I shud rather think they wos, too; hat enny rate, Dolly Rumball is, a good'un, an' no mis-sake! It's like as this, I foun' hit hout, yer see. Being wery hint'rested hin their fate, I pokes about till I diskivers the cell whur they's confined. Thur was a 'ole hin the door with little bars akross, an' a sentry a slow marching afore hit, but I tips 'im a wink an' 'e grins an' let me look through, an'—oh, lor, hif the sight I see didn't make me go right orf agin! Ho, ho! ha, ha! oh lor! he—he—he!"

"What did you see, Joey?" asked Dick, impatiently.

"See! Why, wen I fust look hin they was a sitting one hin each corner, looking at each other like cats as is jist agoin' ter fight, wen, all of suddint, Mrs. Rumball she ses somethin' as the Gen'ral 'e didn't seem ter like, and then 'e growls hout somethin' back, an' hup she jumps an' begins ter tug away his scarlet trousers, an' then ther' wasn't jist a jolly row nether! Oh no, hin course not! Dolly pulled an' screamed, an' the Gen'ral he roars an' fought like mad, an' hif the sentry hadn't a called the guard an hinter-fered, why, the Gen'ral 'ud a bin sitting nakid hon the cold stones pretty quick! Oh lor, oh dear! I be orf agin!"

The recollection of the narrow escape the General had from his person coming into contact with the cold floor of the cell was too much for Joey's risible endurance, and, as he sank to the ground in a collapse of laughter, his example was followed by the boys, and they all rolled about as though they had been seized by a fit.

"I don't know what will become of the poor General," said Dick, when they had recovered. "He's had the most extraordinary run of ill-luck that any man could have in such a short time. That was a rum notion of the Sergeant's to declare that he did not know him, and suggest that all three were mad."

"Well, they certainly looked as though they were mad, Dick," observed Tom Sheppard; "but unless the Sergeant is mad himself, I can't understand his motive for acting as he has."

"Nor I," remarked Bob Jones. "He'll get into trouble over that, I expect."

"Oh, he must have a motive," said Dick, "for wishing to pass them off as mad. He wants to keep them in confinement for some reason or another; and I tell you what has just come into my head, chaps."

"What?" "What?"

"Let's hear, Dick."

"Why, I suppose if he has a motive for confining them, he will want to keep them confined as long as possible—eh?"

"Yes. Yes."

"To be sure."

"No doubt, Dick."

"Then what do you say if we try and help them to escape?"

"Bravo!"

"Yes. It will be a jolly lark."

"And the Sergeant will be baulked."

"Just so," assented Dick. As the Sergeant

hasn't taken us into his confidence,"—with a wink—"we don't care a straw for his motive—eh?"

"No! No!"

"Hang his motive!"

"So I say," laughed Dick. "We'll just turn round and befriend the General! I put it to the vote—isn't it a jolly shame that a general officer should be treated like that by a sergeant?"

Loud laughter and cries of—

"It is!"

"An awful shame!',

"It isn't as though we did it?" cried the little boy with the squeaky voice—a naive remark that the boys fancied amazingly, and increased the laughter.

"That's a very sharp little boy," observed Dick, "and I'm glad he can distinguish, at such an early age, between what the boys of this celebrated school have a right to do, and what outsiders have not a right to do; for to suit our purpose, and be consistent, we must look upon the Sergeant, in this matter, as an tsider—eh?"

"Oh, certainly!"

"Anything you like, Dick!"

"Besides," cried the little boy with the squeaky voice, encouraged by Dick's patronising approval of his last effort, "we can't do without Mrs. Rumball. Who's to cook our rations?"

"Oh! to be sure!" cried Dick, amidst another roar of laughter. "That little boy wouldn't like to go to bed with a terrible vacuum in his 'bread-basket.' That's a very happy thought, youngster, if we don't look after our interests, who will?"

"Nobody!"

"Hear! hear!"

"The School of the Regiment to the rescue!"

"Hurrah!"

"Then we'll try it on to-night, boys. Joey Pumps will show us the cell. In the meantime, I'll think over how it is to be done."

"Now, boys, attention here!"

This was uttered in the well-known voice of the Sergeant.

He had come on the terrace suddenly, and so occupied had been the boys in listening to Dick, that his presence took them completely by surprise.

They became instantly silent, and stood wondering whether the Sergeant had overheard their little plot.

But whether he had or not, the Sergeant made no sign, but having once more claimed their attention, he began—

"Listen boys, whilst I read you the new Rules and Regulations. It's under my charge you'll be for the future."

As the Sergeant gave out this intimation, he paused and looked round with a very impressive nod, and a significant purse up of the lips, adding—

"I suppose you all understand what that means? If you don't, I'll just enlighten you. It means paying off old scores, and begad, I intend to pay them off, my beauties, with compound interest. It's soldiering you'll have to do here, and no mistake! It's at the top of the Rock you'll all go, when the place is ready for ye. And so help me ten men and a donkey, it'll be many a long day before you come down again. It's nothing but drill you'll get from gun-fire to gun-fire!"

Here the Sergeant nodded his head again with great impressiveness, and Dolly Swaps took the opportunity to ask—

"Shan't we be allowed to go down into the town, Sergeant?"

"Devil a bit of it, my dear Dolly!" returned the Sergeant, ironically.

"I don't think that's fair, Sergeant," said Dolly, "Anybody would think that we're no better than the monkeys."

"I don't care a button, Dolly dear," replied the Sergeant, sarcastically, as a laugh ran round at Dolly's remarks, "what anybody thinks. Up you'll all go, and up you'll all stay, and so help me ten men and a donkey, it's wishing you never played tricks on Sergeant O'Shehe, you'll be, before you come down again!"

"Oh! I dare say we shall——"

"Silence and listen. I've got it all written down here, and by-and-bye it will be stuck on a board, and hung up somewhere, and I'll come in and read it every morning. Now—

"'1st.—Every boy will turn out one hour before gun-fire, make his bed, wash and dress by gun-fire, ready for drill."

"'2nd.—To preserve the health, and keep the boys lively and in good spirits, each boy will take a tablespoonful of brimstone-and-treacle every morning before he gets out of bed.'"

"The jar will be kept on the shelf in the middle of the room," said the Sergeant; "and," he added, with a smile of grim satisfaction, and a significant nodding of the head, "I'll see to the mixing and taking of the health and spirit sustainer myself; and, so help me ten men and a donkey, if I don't feed you till it's always grinning you are, and ready to leap about like young rabbits, so light 'll be your spirits!"

At the reading of this sweet rule, and the announcement of the Sergeant's intended personal superintendence at each mututinal administration, the astonished boys expressed their feelings in various ways, some—the youngest— turned pale; some felt faint and sick at the very idea, and turned a pale blue; others opened their eyes, stared at the Sergeant, and wondered whether he had gone mad again. Dick, Tom, Harry, and Bob looked highly amused, whilst Dolly set everybody in a roar by placing his hands on his stomach, turning up the whites of his eyes, and pulling a doleful face, and uttering a deep groan.

"It's a pain you'll be getting in your belly in reality, my dear Dolly," grinned the Sergeant. "And I flatter myself"—looking round on the others—"that old scores will be paid off before I've done with you." Now listen again—

"'3rd.—Drill from gun-fire to breakfast.'

"'4th.—Drill between breakfast and dinner.'

"'5th.—Drill between dinner and tea.'

"'6th.—Drill between tea and evening gun-fire."

"'7th.—After gun-fire an hour will be allowed to clean accoutrements; then roll-call, and then bed.' And I tell you what," added the Sergeant, emphatically, and in a regretful tone. "If I could prevent you snoring, so help me ten men and a donkey, I would. But listen—only let me hear a blessed whisper between bed-time and morning gun-fire, and it's a double dose of the health mixture I'll give every mother's son of you, and a basin of piping hot tea to work it off, so that it shant't interfere with the drill! Talk about polishing off old scores," added the Sergeant, amidst a general roar of laughter.

"Why, what th —— what the dickens——Where does this smoke come from?" stammered the
sergeant.—See page 97.

"Oh, so help me ten men, but I'll show you nicely how to do it! Now listen to the next clause:—

"'8th.—Sergeant O'Shehe has the power to alter any of the foregoing rules, if he thinks that circumstances require it.' Which means," explained the Sergeant, "that I can do what I like, and make you do any blessed thing I like. For instance, if I think it'll punish you more to keep you in bed all day, instead of keeping you at drill, why, I'll keep you in bed. Not that I'm ever likely to think that, mind you," added the Sergeant, as he fancied he observed signs that such a course would not be considered much of a punishment. "But if ever I do, it's nothing you'll get all day but the health mixture!"

"In that case," cut in Dolly, followed by shouts of laughter; "we should be more out of bed than in it, Sergeant."

"It's witty you are, my dear Dolly," returned the Sergeant, facetiously; but it's astonished you'll be at yourself, when I've got you into good health! You'll be so smart with your tongue that I shall have to play a good deal, I am thinking, on the 'right about.' And talking of that reminds me that I promised you, in my own mind, a couple of dozen for the elegant attitude you took on parade before the Governor this morning. Come here, my dear, continued the Sergeant, opening his left arm invitingly; "put your head through there, and remember, if you make use of those pretty teeth of yours, so help me ten men and a donkey! I'll draw the blessed lot of e'm! Come!"

There was no getting out of it, and so Dolly submitted, and in another minute he was sitting on the stone floor in the rear of the Sergeant, feeling very hot and tingling, as though a blister were drawing away at his "right-about."

The Sergeant then resumed the reading of the new rules.

"'9th.—The cooking will in future be done by the boys.' It's not a blessed bit or drop you'll get to eat or drink if you can't do it," remarked the Sergeant. "Mrs. Rumball's gone mad (an ironical laugh), and if you don't begin to do for yourselves, you'll never know how to cook. It's not babies you must be, to be fed by a stupid old woman."

Could Mrs. Rumball but have heard the Sergeant say that, and have been in a position to return the compliment!

But never mind, the injured and persecuted lady was avenged—amply avenged in another minute.

"'10th.—A "roster" will be kept (a sniff) of twenty (sniff, and a remark, 'What the deuce is it smelling?') of the biggest boys for cook (pooh!) Where can the deuced smell come from? and there's smoke, too!" turning round and seeing no fire, though he was enveloped in smoke), and cook's mate——'"

Here the Sergeant, feeling something burning him behind, clapped his hand to his "right-about," and drew it away again with the exclamation—

"Bedad, but it's on fire I am! Oh, Lord! Oh, oh! It's burning to death I am! Oh, oh! What'll I do?"

The cause of the Sergeant's distress may be easily explained.

As Dolly sat on the stones behind him, cooling the burning sensation in his "right-about," he happened to raise his eyes to the same part of the Sergeant's person, and observed that the seat of his overalls were covered with a black, shiny patch.

This patch, on closer inspection, Dolly found was composed of tar, and looked freshly done.

The Sergeant had evidently been sitting on some tarry article on board the steamer, and was probably unaware of having done so, or, if aware of it, he thought it was hidden by the tail of his tunic, perhaps.

Whether or not, Dolly spied it, and he immediately resolved to try an experiment.

"By jingo!" thought Dolly. "I wonder if that would catch fire? It would warm him for warming me! Blow'd if I don't try it!"

Dolly hadn't a light, but, catching the eye of Joey Pumps, he tipped him a sign that he wanted to speak to him.

"I say, Joey," whispered Dolly, just go and get me some matches."

Joey, smelling a lark from Dolly's manner, winked, and departed on his errand, returning in less than a minute with a box of "Stand-stickers."

Then, getting on his knees, and cautiously approaching the Sergeant, Dolly struck a match and applied the blaze to the tarry patch.

The first try was a failure, and so was the second, but the third, to his great joy, succeeded, and, in a few seconds, the seat of the Sergeant's overalls was burning fiercely and brilliantly.

The Sergeant's agony, as fire began to make itself felt through the trousers, made itself apparent in loud cries of pain, and most astonishing and ungainly antics.

To get his flesh away from the fire he twisted himself first one way and then another, and rushed round the terrace, bent backwards, trying to pull away the seat of his trousers with his hands.

But his efforts were useless.

His agony was heartrending, and called forth much sympathetic advice.

"Jump into the tank, Sergeant!"

"Take off your overalls, Sergeant!"

"Rub yourself againt the wall and smother it!"

"Sit down on the stones, Sergeant!"

"Shall I beat out the fire with a mop handle, Sergeant?"

But efficacious as each of these remedies promised to be, the Sergeant either wouldn't, or couldn't, adopt either.

It will not have been forgotten that there existed a well, or tank, in the centre of the Tower opening from the rooms.

This happened to be half-full of water, and it was into this the Sergeant was advised to jump.

As the Sergeant did not take the advice, he perhaps thought that it was better to suffer temporary pain than to be drowned.

To have taken off his overalls would, to say the least, have been extremely inconvenient.

To have rubbed himself against the wall would have had an extremely ridiculous appearance.

To have sat on the stones would not have put out the fire, and cooled his burning pain; whilst the application of a mop-handle would only make his seat warmer than before.

So the burning victim, eschewing all these remedies, at length darted from the terrace, down the staircase, and rushing like a madman across the yard, dropped into a tub of water (which stood under a spout close to the cook-house door), in which he sat, feeling greatly relieved, and contemplated by the sympathetic glances of the boys, who had considerately followed him, to be at hand in case their services should be wanted.   ..

CHAPTER XXXII.

RELATES HOW GENERAL SHOOT MADE AN IMPORTANT CONFESSION. — DESCRIBES A ROMANTIC RAMBLE UP THE ROCK.

As the incident in the last chapter occurred just after dinner, and as it was too early for our boys to go to bed, they determined, the Sergeant not being now able to prevent them, to take a ramble up the Rock.

This was a very natural thing to do, under the circumstances in which they were placed.

They had just come from England, and everything around them was novel. The Sergeant had enough to do to look after himself. There was no drill going on, and so they were at liberty to enjoy themselves.

"Being the senior," said Dick, "and not yet arrived at that period of life when most people forget they have ever been boys, I give you all leave to go up the Rock. But," he added, imitating the Sergeant's manner, "it's better be keeping out of mischief you'd be, or, so help me ten men and a donkey, I'll be down on your right-abouts like——"

"A thousand of bricks," cried the squeaky tone of the little boy.

"No, youngster," returned Dick with a deep frown, and a deep voice, "like a thousand of cat's claws! Mind now, don't go losing yourselves, breaking your worthless necks by tumbling down ravines, and over precipices, or allowing the monkeys to take you prisoners!"

"Shut up, Dick," said Dolly, who was busily buttoning his jacket, "go and talk to your grandmother."

"I tell you what it is, Dolly," returned Dick, suspending the operation of brushing his overalls, and shaking his brush at the facetious youngster, "I've come to the conclusion that you are not safe to be at large, and I've a great mind to have you confined with the General and the Rumballs."

The reply to this was a wink, a disgraceful action toward his superior, that brought Dick's brush flying at Dolly's head, but which, missing his aim, lodged with great force on the nose of an individual who happened at that unlucky moment to be entering the room from the terrace.

This invidual's name was O'Doo, having Michael for a Christian name, and glorying in the rank of Corporal in the 67th Regiment of the Line.

"The divil take the brush!" cried the Corporal staggering with the blow, and clapping his hand to the injured organ. "It's a pretty specimen of a nose I'll be getting prisintly! That's twice this blessed day, once with the fist o' that cursed mad creature, and once with a brush. Bad luck to ye, wherever ye are, that flung it! That isn't what the brush was served out to ye for, was it?"

"It wasn't intended for you, Corporal," said Dick. "I'm very sorry."

"Sorry!" returned the Corporal, looking at Dick with a half-angry, half-comical expression

"It's mighty fine to be sorry after ye've done it. It's just a wink ye might hev tipped a fellow that it was coming."

Corporal O'Doo was an individul whose physical development came under the description " short and stout," and on removing his hand from his nose, that also was seen to partake of the same nature, being, in addition, at this moment, red as a rose.

"Look here, boys," continued the Corporal, rubbing the hot point of his nose, "who's the senior among ye?"

"I am, Corporal," replied Dick.

"Thin as the Sargint's met with an accident," winking at Dick, "it's this letter I'll get ye to take to the Governor, Sir Gentle Sharpset. It's from the mad chap that swears he's a Gen'ral."

"Oh, indeed, said Dick, with a laugh. "Does he seem to be mad now?"

"Mad! It's raving, he is! An', bedad, for that matther, so is the three of 'em. I niver met with three madder, nor three puttier-looking ca-rakters. It was fighting and swearing like Kilkenny cats, they was, till I was obliged to separate 'em."

"So bad as that, eh?"

"Bedad, it was, I thought the ould woman would hev skinned the Gin'ral of his scarlit breeches, which she swore was hers; and the other fellow was at him about a coat and hat, which he swore he stole, until I put the Gen'ral into a cell by himself. It's a little quieter he seems, now, an he's writ this letter to the Governor, wid some paper an' ink he bothered me into gettin' from the guardroom."

"All right, Corporal," returned Dick, taking the letter. "I don't know yet where the Governor's quarters are, but I can find them, I've no doubt. Leave it with me."

"The quarters is easy enough to find," said the Corporal. "It's anybody 'll tell ye where's the Convent in Southport-street. It's afther promoting me, the Gin'ral's goin', for doing him the favour," he added, with a wink, as he left the room.

The letter that had thus fallen into the hands of Dick was half a sheet of foolscap, folded into the shape of a cocked hat, and addresssd in the well-known hand of the General to the Governor, Sir Gentle Sharpset, with the word "Immemediate," in large letters in one corner.

"There's no mistake about it being the General's note," said Dick, holding it aloft for the inspection of the boys as they crowded around. "I wonder if he thought of his own lost cocked-hat, when he folded this, this shape."

"Don't waste time speculating about the General's thoughts," put in Dolly Swaps. "The proper question is, "What are you going to do with it?"

"Why, take it to the Governor, of course," returned Dick. "What else do you think I should do with it, Dolly Swaps the mighty?"

"Open it," said Dolly, promptly.

"Dolly!"

As Dick uttered this exclamation, he threw himself into a melo-dramatic attitude, expressive of inexpressible astonishment, and stood gazing in gloomy sorrow at Dolly.

"It's all very fine, master Dick, to pretend to be shocked," said Dolly, "but you know you are going to open it."

"Presumptious prophet," cried Dick, breaking into a laugh. How knowest thou that?"

"I saw it in your eyes, Dick," said Dolly.

"Right you are, my dear Dolly. I wouldn't do it though, were the General not mad, you know. I must look after the reputation of the school, however, and there's no knowing what a person may say about us in moments of insanity. We may not consider it fit to send, and, in that case, may deem it advisable not to send it, or to substitute another."

This was received with ironical laughter, and impatient demands to go on reading.

The letter being unsealed, Dick unfolded it and read—

"'The Civil Prison, Moorish Castle, 2 p.m.

"'DEAR SIR GENTLE,—Now that I trust sufficient time has elapsed to have allowed the natural irritation, which my conduct of this morning caused you, to subside, may I request that you will be good enough to pay me a visit? I can, I assure you, convince you that I hold the rank of a General Officer of Artillery, and that condition to which you saw me reduced was caused by a series of mishaps over which I had no control, I am not mad—upon my soul I'm not; and, if you will only come, you will find me now perfectly quiet, and as sane as yourself.

"I am, my dear Sir Gentle,
"'Yours sincerely,
"'JOACHIM SHOOT,
"' General Commandant of Bangfire Garrison, and the School of the Regiment.'"

"Well, chaps," said Dick, when he had finished. "I must say that he doesn't write at all like a madman. Nothing could be milder; and I tell you what, if we allow this letter to go, we shall only have our fun of releasing him this evening spoiled, to a certainty. That won't do, you know!—eh?"

This was affirmed by cries of—

"Of course it won't!"

"Certainly not!"

"We can't be done out of our good intention!"

"We're bound to release him ourselves!"

"Here, here!"

"Then the question is," said Dick, "shall we keep back the letter or write another?"

This was responded to by clamorous voices, expressing difference of opinion.

"Yes, yes; write another."

"No, no; keep back this one. What good will it do to make him out madder than he is?"

"A great deal of good," cried the squeaky-voiced youngster. "We don't want him interfering with our larks!"

"Hear, hear; well said!"—and much laughter.

"If he's mad, we don't need to release him. Let him stay where he is."

"Now, listen," cried Dick. "I think I agree with the young squeaker. I have a plan, just jumped into my head. I think we can get on very well without the General. As he is believed to be mad, we had better keep him mad; and, I think, by releasing him, we can convince the General that he is madder than he thought himself, or one of the most diabolical monsters that ever breathed."

"How? How?"

"What's the plan?"

"Oh, it's very simple!" responded Dick. "We must defeat our own project at the last minute. It's easily done, I think. Just listen. In the first place I'll write another letter for this, that will rather astonish the Governor. In the second place, the Governor shall send a private note to the Sergeant of the Guard over the prison, to allow the mad people to escape, as he has discovered that they are not mad, and wishes the affair to be hushed up. That letter will be delivered by me, and I'll take good care that the arrangements for the escape are intrusted to me. See?"

"Good! Good!"

"Capital!"

"First-rate idea!"

"Go on, Dick. What else?"

"Why," continued Dick, "in the third place, the Governor must receive a note to the effect that a plot is on foot to release the mad people, and advise him to take precautions to thwart it. When I read the letter I'm going to write in place of this, you'll see that the Governor will be only too eager to prevent the escape. And now I'll write it."

Dick then got a sheet of foolscap paper and pen and ink, and set to work to concoct the letter, a process over which he experienced a good deal of interruption, owing to the impatient curiosity of his chums, who would insist upon peeping over his shoulders, or getting on to the table to read it upside down and sideways.

It was accomplished at length, however, and then Dick read it out.

"'Civil Prison, Moorish Castle.

"'SIR,—The horrible thought of being considered mad, and the still more horrible fear of, perhaps, being permanently confined as an incurable lunatic, are more dreadful to contemplate than death itself. I would rather be dead than incarcerated within the pitiless walls of a lunatic asylum, and, therefore, I have resolved to make a confession.'

"How does that read so far, boys?" Dick paused to ask—a question that was followed by lively cries of—

"Jolly!"

"First-rate, Dick!"

"That'll do. Go on, Dick!"

"'This confession is very short,'" continued Dick; "'but methinks you will say it is plenty long enough! I must confess then—start not, my dear sir, if you can help it—that I was seized with a desire to slaughter, at one blow, as many British soldiers as it was possible to do.

"'This was, you will say probably, a diabolical idea. So it was, sir, but it was irresistible, and I thought long and deeply as to how I could accomplish it. The thought—long in coming—came at length, and the plan, you will say, probably, was worthy the diabolical idea. I determined to construct an infernal machine and have it placed in the hold of the first troopship leaving England.

"'This was not a new idea, but it struck me as being the most effectual means I could adopt for my purpose, and so I adopted it. I made the infernal machine (I won't describe the mechanism, lest others should be tempted to do evil), contrived to have it conveyed on board the ship that has just arrived with the School of the Regiment, by passing myself off as a General Officer.

"'I had no accomplices.

"'As I had no desire to sacrifice my own life, I regulated the mechanism to run down between Gibraltar and Malta.

"'That mechanism is at work now, and in forty-eight hours from this the machine will explode, and five hundred British soldiers and seamen will be blown to atoms, and the noble steamer will strew the ocean with a million chips!

"'I have further to confess that I am a

Spaniard—reared in England—and that I fully intended to place infernal machines in every convenient nook and corner of Gibraltar for the purpose of blowing the English off the Rock, and restoring that great and important fortress to my nation. I have done! I am prepared to die!

"'I beg to subscribe myself, sir,

"'Your most obedient servant,

"'DON SYLVIO DE POCO DE DIABOLO,

"'alias GENERAL JOACHIM SHOOT.'"

It is needless to say that the reading of Dick's letter was followed by roars of laughter much delighted capering, and comments of approval.

Dolly Swaps, however, wasn't quite satisfied.

"It's a capital letter, Dick," remarked Dolly, "but you have made one mistake, and omitted one important explanation."

"What's the mistake, Dolly."

"Why, you say that the ship will be strewed over the ocean in a million chips. Considering the ship is an *iron* steamer, I should like to know how the *chips* will float? I've got you there, Mister Dick!" chuckled Dolly.

"I haven't said anything about floating, Dolly—eh!"

"No, but you meant it."

"Well, never mind, my able critic," laughed Dick. "The Governor will be too horrified to notice that. What's the omission?"

"You haven't accounted for Mr. and Mrs. Rumball chasing the General, and accusing him of stealing a coat and hat and a pair of scarlet drawers."

"Ah, right you are, Dolly; that can be added in a postscript."

Dick sat down, and hastily writing the postscript, remarked—

"'P.S.—I must explain the conduct of those two persons who chased me, and who have been put down, in consequence, as mad. Thinking to destroy my identity ere disembarking, I cast my General's uniform overboard, first stealing a coat and hat, and a pair of scarlet drawers (the only kind of civilian trousers I could find aboard). These I had no sooner put on than I was discovered by the owners, and chased on shore.

"'As this was a very natural thing to do, you will see that those poor people were, and are, anything but insane.

"'Now my conscience is easy!

"'D. S. de P. D.'"

"That will be better," said Dolly, patronisingly, "I don't know what you'd do without me, after all, Mister Dick."

"I don't know, indeed, Dolly," said Dick. "You are my right hand now, I must own, and you're not so soft as you look."

"Thank you for stale news," returned Dolly. "Hadn't you better intrust your right-hand man to take the letter?"

"We'll take it together, Dolly; but there's plenty of time. Some time this evening will do, after our ramble over the Rock."

The boys then sallied forth, and dividing themselves into "chum" parties, began an exploration of the fortress.

One of these parties consisted of Dick, Dolly Swaps, Tom Sheppard, Bob Jones, and Harry Smith, and this party we must accompany.

As Dick and his chums wished to reach the summit of the Rock, they did not waste time by lingering to view the prospect from every fresh point of observation, or rest in every shady nook, from which, occasionally, peeped an enormous gun, backed up by a huge pile of shot.

The temptation to do so, however, was great, as the sun was pouring its rays on the compact limestone, or grey dense marble, of which the Rock is composed, with an almost tropical temperature, rendering the flower-strewed paths and flower-crowded nooks very inviting.

Though Gibraltar has traditionally held the title of a barren rock, yet the clematis, geranium, aloe, and rose run wild; and the myrtle, locust-tree, the wide-spreading bella-sombra, a great variety of cactus, the vine, fig-tree, olive, almond, orange, and lemon are present in various localities.

"That looks a retreat fit for a princess," observed Dick once, as they passed a nook shaded from the sun, and filled with geraniums in full bloom. "Fancy a couch of geraniums!"

"And all for nothing!" exclaimed Dolly. "Only fancy what a bed of geraniums would cost in England. Why, the lowest price they ask outside the Arsenal-gate at Bangfire, is a penny a pot, and then they're little better than weeds!"

"Here we are at the Galleries, I expect," said Dick, as a laugh, caused by Dolly's matter-of-fact speech, died away.

This was the case.

They had reached the entrance to the Upper Batteries, excavated out of the solid rock, and were at once admitted by an old gunner who was on duty.

Greatly astonished and delighted were they at the sight of the vault-like passage, with the muzzles of the heavy guns protruding through the embrasures—frowning, as it seemed, a perpetual and silent caution to the coveters of the Rock to keep at a respectful distance.

To gaze through the embrasures at such a height made them feel giddy, and almost took away their breath.

"By jingo," exclaimed Dolly. "I shouldn't like to fall down there! I expect it would be a case of smash, and done for it, Dick!"

"Rather!" laughed Dick. "How small everything looks at that depth."

"And yet," observed a Gunner, who was engaged in rearranging the contents of a "portable magazine," which stood in rear of one of the guns, "and yet what do you think of several gunners being blown clean out of that very embrasure you're looking through on to the Lower Lines and Inundation?"

"Do you mean to say that ever happened?" asked Dick.

"I do!" replied the Gunner. "It's a great many years ago now—1830. Experimental practice was being carried on to show the effect of grape-shot on the Inundation—that's an artificial sheet of water, traversed by ditches and palisading, forming part of the lower defences; you can see it there—and the road to the Bay Side Barrier. A gun was pointed at the target, and the detachment went to the next embrasure (the one you're standing at), where there was no gun, to see the effect of their shot."

"The gun was fired, and some burning piece of wad must have blown back, and somehow, never known, ignited the contents of a 'portable magazine' near. The men, with the exception of the one who fired and the one who gave the order to fire, were blown out."

The boys could not help shuddering at this fearful tale, and stepped back from the embrasure almost involuntarily.

"It makes a fellow feel queer, only to think of it—don't it?" said Dolly, with a shiver. "I hope I shall never be blown out!"

"If ever you are," observed the gunner, winking at Dick, "there is only one way to save yourself."

"How is that?" asked Dolly, innocently.

"You must hang on to the muzzle of a gun by your eye-lashes," replied the Gunner, raising a laugh at Dolly's expense, and who, for once, being fairly "caught" had nothing to say.

From this place—the Union Galleries—they passed on to Willis's Batteries, a perfect network of formidable batteries commanding the Spanish Lines and Neutral Ground.

Here they found more to wonder at, and heard another wonderful story of how a shot from one of the Spanish batteries during a siege, entered one of the embrasures in the "Princess Amelia" battery, and, striking four men, cut off seven legs among them.

"That's a problem for you, Dolly," observed Dick. "How many legs did each lose?"

"Why, two legs each, all but one, to be sure," returned Dolly.

"But which one was that?"

"How should I know, gaby?" retorted Dolly.

"Then you don't know everything, you see, Dolly," returned Dick.

"Perhaps you can tell us, Mister Dick," observed Dolly, winking at Tom Sheppard.

"You'll be as wise as myself, if I do, Dolly," said Dick, giving him a sudden jerk under the chin, that made him bite his tongue.

Chaffing in this manner, the party left Willis's Batteries, and ascended to the "Rock Mortar" —the highest piece of ordnance on the Rock.

Here the gunner in charge had to tell them that even at the height of over 1,200 feet, the Rock Mortar was several times dismounted by the Spanish fire.

Just below this was the "Rock Gun Battery," originally built and armed before there was any road to it, the guns being dragged by hand up the Rock on a sledge.

From this battery the first gun is fired of the Royal Salute on Her Majesty's birthday.

From the Rock Gun Battery they now made their way along a romantic pathway, almost at the very summit of the rock, and arrived at a point which had more interest for them than anything they had seen.

This was the "Upper Signal Station."

The interest consisted, not so much at finding themselves at this elevation above the sea, and from which commanding position such a varied and extensive view is obtained, but in the fact that this was the spot in which the School was to be quartered.

Even now the military artificers were busily at work, preparing one large room in the stone tower for the accommodation of the boys, a room for Sergeant O'Shehe, together with a cooking and sleeping domain for the person or persons engaged to cook.

"According to the new rules issued by Sergeant O'Shehe, we are to do the cooking ourselves," observed Dolly, to the sergeant superintending the work.

"I don't know anything about rules," returned the sergeant. "I am doing just what I'm ordered to do."

After a long inspection of their new and romantic quarters, they examined the battery of four cannon which is situated a few feet below the tower, and from which the morning and evening guns are fired.

Then, after a good tuck-in of bread and cheese, supplied by the Sergeant of the Signal Station, Dick and his chums descended to the "Union Galleries," inspected the two magnificent halls of St. George's and Cornwallis, in the former of which they learnt the Governor would hold a grand banquet that evening, and from thence returned to the Moorish Castle.

CHAPTER XXXIII.

DICK AND DOLLY DELIVER THE GENERAL'S LETTER TO THE GOVERNOR AT THE BANQUET. —THE EFFECT UPON THE GOVERNOR AND PARTY.

DICK, in carrying out his programme, had intended to deliver the General's (new) note at the Governor's palace soon after tea, in order that Dolly and he might indulge in a ramble through the town; but the fact that the Governor would be present at a banquet in one of the great halls of the subterranean batteries induced him to remain in the castle.

"We can have a ramble through the town some other day, Dolly," observed Dick.

"That will be a long time to come, Dick," returned Dolly, pulling a long face, "if what the Sergeant says is true—that, when we are once at the top of the Rock, we shall have to stick there till we return to England."

"Oh, he couldn't have meant to imply that, Dolly. Besides, if it is to be so, we must find a way of getting down without leave, I am rather glad than otherwise, that the banquet is to come off in the gallery; the Governor will be nearer, and there will be a chance of my plan working with greater certainty. We must deliver the letter at the banquet."

"By jingo!" exclaimed Dolly, hugging himself and making a chuckling grimace, "won't the Governor open his eyes!"

"And everybody else, too, I expect, Dolly," said Dick with a quiet laugh.

"When shall we take it, Dick?"

"After the dinner, when the wine is going."

There was not a boy in the school, as will be guessed, that did not feel greatly excited at the carrying out, and possible result, of Dick's scheme.

That the game was getting very complicated, and that great issue hung in the balance there was only one feeling.

As the whole school could not be present at the delivery of the note, the wonder of the Governor—how he would look, what he would say, and what he would do there, were points and contingencies that were unceasingly talked over, and witnessed in imagination, until the time came for Dick and Dolly to depart on their errand.

It was past ten when the two bold adventurers presented themselves at the entrance of the subterranean batteries, and requested permission to proceed to the banquet-hall to deliver a letter to the Governor.

This, after a rigid questioning by the sentry, was granted.

Though the moon shone with great brilliancy, showing up clearly and distinctly the Bay of

Gibraltar, the Lower Line, the Neutral Ground, and the Spanish Lines, and causing the embrasures of the warlike tunnel to appear like so many moons from the interior, the whole length was lighted by many branched candelabra, fixed to the sides, and was further illuminated by Chinese lanterns of variegated shades and patterns, suspended from the rocky roof, and studded on the breeches of the great guns.

The scene was very fairy-like, but as Dick and Dolly neared the great hall the scene became more fairy-like still, whilst numerous powdered and gorgeously-liveried servants were incessantly passing to and fro from the banqueting-room.

There were a couple of sentries guarding the entrance, more as a matter of form, and to add to the picturesque effect, than from any precaution against danger.

There is no spot on the Rock more secure against danger, perhaps, than the subterranean galleries.

To say the truth, Dick and Dolly were somewhat awed as they contemplated this scene, and the audaciousness of their mission seemed now to assume terrific proportions, though neither would acknowledge it.

"I say, Dolly," whispered Dick, "how do you feel?"

"All right, Dick," returned Dolly, winking, with a desperate effort to appear at his ease. "How do you feel?"

"Oh, cool as a cucumber, Dolly. Let's go in. Come on."

They had no difficulty in passing the sentries, and, proceeding through the vestibule, lined on each side with a perfect forest of the most exquisite flowering plants, over which a soft radiance was thrown from hundreds of tastily arranged Chinese lanterns, Dick accosted one of the gorgeously apparelled servants and made known his errand.

The great man, at first, gave himself great airs, and threatened to have them turned out for their presumption, but at length—knowing that he was only blustering—pretended to condescend to deliver their request for an immediate interview.

Presently the flunky returned, saying curtly—

"Follow me!"

"Now for it, Dolly," whispered Dick.

The next moment they were within the spacious hall, ablaze with light and the dazzling uniforms of some two hundred officers of the Army and Navy.

As their gaze fell upon this grand and imposing assemblage, they both felt—as Dolly afterwards lucidly described the feeling—"all over somehow—jolly rummy."

"We must put a good face on it now, Dolly," again whispered Dick. "We'd better march up to the Governor as though we were on duty. It will look more respectful."

Then, in a loud voice, which attracted immediate notice, Dick cried—

"T'shnn! Forward! Quick—mar—r—ch!"

As Dick and Dolly, erect as telegraph-posts, and looking neither to the right nor the left, marched with automaton-like steps up the hall, they were the centre of two hundred eyes—eyes which stared at them in open wonder, not unmixed with indications of amusement.

But, apparently unconscious of the notice they were attracting, Dick and Dolly proceeded until they were abreast of the Governor, when Dick gave the commands—

"Left wheel! Halt! Eyes front!"

"Bless me!" cried the little Governor, putting up his eye-glass, and staring at the boys with a puzzled expression, whilst the officers at that end of the table contemplated them with considerable curiosity, "what is the meaning of this?"

"Letter, please sir, from the madman," said Dick, holding forth the epistle.

"What madman?" asked the Governor, mechanically taking the letter, and turning it over and over, evidently at a loss to understand the meaning of it.

"The man who calls himself General Shoot, sir."

"Hem! The idea," said the Governor, turning red in the face from annoyance, "of bringing a letter from a madman at such a moment as this! James," turning to the great flunky, "conduct these boys out again!"

But Dick wasn't going to be turned out in that fashion, now he had gone so far, if he could help it, and he said quickly—

"The letter is of great importance, sir."

With an impatient gesture, the Governor intimated to the flunky to wait, and then hastily opened the letter.

The result was beyond anything that either Dick or Dolly had imagined.

The look of annoyance with which the Governor had commenced reading, gradually altered, as he perused, to one of blank amazement.

At length, with a pale face, and in accents that were visibly agitated, he exclaimed—

"Gentlemen! Gentlemen! This is one of the most horribly diabolical crimes I have ever heard of! Admiral," he added, excitedly, to the Admiral of the station, who was seated at his right hand, "you must start one of the gu—gu—gun-boats after the troop-ship that left for Malta this morning! At once! There's not a moment to be lost! A man, whom I took to be insane, and had confined in the Civil Prison, confesses here—in this letter—that he has concealed an infernal machine in the hold of the steamer, for the purpose of destroying the whole of the troops on board!"

"Good Heavens!" exclaimed the Admiral. "You don't say so!"

"I do, indeed!" returned the agitated Governor. "The man says he's a Spaniard, and came to the Rock for the purpose of setting infernal machines in all directions to annihilate us all, and restore the Rock to the Spanish nation!"

The excitement which followed this news, with the expressions of horrified indignation at the enormity of the crime, was too great to be described.

So great, so stunning, indeed, was the exciting effect, that not one had the coolness to reflect, or ask himself the question, as to whether the letter was the production of a madman or not.

The effect of the diabolical confession was overpowering.

There was not a mind but what saw in imagination the air filled with, and the ocean strewed by, hundreds of human arms, legs, and heads, rising and falling in a ghastly, mutilated medley, amidst a terrific outburst of flame and smoke, and the splintered hull of the steamer.

In the confusion neither the Governor nor

any one else thought of questioning Dick and Dolly.

The banquet was brought to a sudden end.

The naval and military officers returned, filled with the apprehension that a most tragic calamity was about to happen to their ships and quarters, but long ere they had reached them, the signal for the "Blazer" gunboat to get up steam and proceed on an important mission was fired from the battery at the Signal Station, and the little but swift vessel had departed.

There is no use hiding the fact that Dick and Dolly were very much "flabergasted" at the result of their mission, and, for a time, wished they had not gone so far.

"But who would have thought the Governor would have acted like that, Dick?" said Dolly, as, a few minutes after the banquet had broken up, Dick and Dolly found themselves sitting in a shady nook of the Rock, overlooking the Moorish Castle and the bay.

"Why, if you come to think of it, Dolly," replied Dick, "it's a very natural thing to do, I made the supposed Spaniard say that the machine would explode in forty-eight hours from the writing of the confession; and so there is just a chance that the gunboat may overtake the steamer in that time."

"Oh, lor! oh dear!" said Dolly, hugging himself in his favourite manner, and giving vent to a series of low chuckles. "I say, Dick, what a go it is! I never dreamt there would be such a rumpus! Why, it will get into all the newspapers! Oh, lor, what a jolly lark it will be!"

"The Governor, and Admiral, and the General won't consider it much of a lark," laughed Dick. "It never struck me that I was going to create such an excitement. It will soon be found out, Dolly. As soon as the 'Blazer' overtakes the steamer, the hoax will be discovered, and also the indentity of the General."

"And then 'up goes the donkey,' Dick, eh?" said Dolly. "And, I say, won't the Sergeant drop in for 'coco'—Oh, lor!"

Here Dolly, carried away by the depth of his feelings, fairly doubled up his little model of a body, and rolled about in an ecstasy of delight.

"I say, Dick," cried Dolly, suddenly recollecting himself, and breaking off his physical manifestations. "How about releasing the General? Will you try that on now?"

"Yes, most decidedly, I think our best policy is to release him, and get him quietly stowed away somewhere until the return of the 'Blazer'; otherwise he will stand a chance of being torn to pieces by the excited mob as he goes to be examined before the magistrate to-morrow."

"Do you think he will be examined then, Dick, to-morrow?"

"I should think so," replied Dick.

"Then, of course, you won't have him arrested as he's escaping, as you intended, Dick?"

"Of course not. We must let the Sergeant into the secret too," added Dick. "He will be only too glad to get the General out of the way now! and the sooner we set about it the better. Come along."

They then emerged into the glorious moonlight, and, in a few minutes, were recounting to their chums the unexpected success their schemes had met with.

Never before, we may venture to assert, had the rooms of the old Moorish Tower echoed to so many boyish voices, raised in exclamations of surprise, delight, and merry laughter.

CHAPTER XXXIV.

AN INTERVIEW WITH SERGEANT O'SHEHE.— THE ESCAPE OF THE GENERAL. — AND SUNDRY INCIDENTS CONNECTED THEREWITH

WE must now pay a visit to Sergeant O'Shehe.

The last time we had the pleasure of gazing upon the gallant Sergeant, we contemplated his figure as it rested in a tub of cold water, in which he had dropped in great haste, to quench the flames that were consuming the seat of his overalls, and to cool his scorched person.

The relief he experienced from that measure was, we are justified in saying, very great—a cessation of pain, though only of a temporary character, for which he was very grateful.

Though the bathing process was very soothing, the Sergeant could not sit there, for several reasons, until the fire was extracted, and so, after a reasonable time, he arose and went to his room—a small apartment in one of the boys' rooms in the Tower.

Here he spent the rest of the day in great agony of mind and body.

The former he could not assuage, but the latter he managed in some degree to lessen by a process that was very simple and cooling.

As the Sergeant's overalls were always a tight fit—for the purpose of developing the graceful outlines of his figure—he had not a pair loose enough behind to suit the soreness of his flesh, so he cut away entirely the seat of the pair that had been burnt, and pinned over the vacant space a round piece of linen—a piece cut off one of the coarse linen sheets of his bed.

Thus the pressure on the afflicted part was not only avoided, but a gratifying degree of coolness secured.

"It's not a very handsome patch, certainly," muttered the suffering Sergeant, a grin like a spasm moving the muscles of his face, as the General's appearance in the scarlet drawers of Mrs. Rumball involuntarily flashed into his mind; "but it will do to walk up and down here with. If I am obliged to leave the room, I must put on my top coat. It will look rather funny to be wearing an overcoat in this hot place, but I must swear I have the ague."

The Sergeant found this patching arrangement to answer admirably, as he walked about the room—for he couldn't sit—in great mental disquietude.

His conduct towards the General was preying upon his conscience, and he felt, that could he undo what he had done with only the loss of his stripes, he would do it.

"Yes, that I would, willingly, mortifying as such a degrading come-down would be," he muttered, as he walked about; "but, the penalty would be worse than that! Transportation at the very least! I must have been mad myself to have ventured upon such a course! Bless my soul, only fancy me declaring in the most brazen manner that I never clapped eyes on the General till that minute! Tit, tit, tit! Good Heavens! The more I think of it, the more astounded I am at the infernal nature of my cheek! Good—gra—ci—ous!—not only swearing I didn't know him, but actually suggesting that he was mad! Good lord!"

The Sergeant not only gave verbal expression to his mental torture and astonishment, but indulged in various physical gestures eloquently expressive of his mental state

Thus he would occasionally clap his hand to his forehead, give himself a terrific blow on the breast, or stop suddenly in the middle of the room, place his arms akimbo, and stare blankly at the wall or floor—stunned at the measureless amount of his "cheek,"

"Then, to make matters worse," continued the Sergeant, "those young rascals—may the devil fly away with that Dolly Swaps, for setting fire to me!—talk about releasing him! And they will, too, if they can! Here am I disabled, and can't do anything to prevent 'em! If it wasn't for the transportation part of the business I'd confess and have him released, but I can't stand the thought of being a convict! What *am* I to do?"

But the Sergeant's good angel had not deserted him, as he had begun to think, in his hour of need.

As he continued his perambulations, muttering and pondering, a thought as to how he might be able to countercheck the boys flashed brightly into his brain.

"That's it, by Jove!" he exclaimed.

That all the boys were out rambling over the Rock, the Sergeant was aware of, and as he made the exclamation, he slipped out of his room, proceeded to the Terrace, and whistled to attract the attention of the sentry, who was on duty over the Civil Prison.

"What is it, Sarjint?" asked the sentry, approaching the Terrace and looking up.

"Who'll be on sentry from ten to twelve o'clock to-night?" asked the Sergeant, in a low tone.

"Mesilf sure. Whoy?"

"I want you to keep a good look out on this side of the prison," returned the Sergeant. "The boys of the school talk of releasing the madman to-night."

"The devil they do?" exclaimed the sentry.

"Yes; and I want you to nail them in the act—see?"

"It's as plain as a pike-stiff, Sarjint, an' as 'asy to do as kiss me hand."

"Keep dark. Don't say a word about it to anybody, mind! D'ye hear?"

"Not aivin to the corp'ral of the garred?"

"Not even to the corporal of the guard!"

"Roight it is thin, Sargint. It's darrak enaf I'll kape."

The Sergeant chuckled, when he regained his room, at the thought of having laid a trap to checkmate the boys, but ere midnight he had reason to regret the precaution he had taken.

The time passed slowly away for the Sergeant, boxed up in his little room, and almost tired to death with incessant walking.

The afternoon and evening passed away, and nothing occurred to relieve the monotony of his solitary walk but the merry voices of the boys in the farthest room—for the boys kept as far away from the Sergeant's quarters as possible—until the signal reverberated from the Signal Station to get the "Blazer" under steam.

"What's the meaning of that?" he exclaimed, hastening to the window and looking toward the Signal Station, from the summit of which he could see four clouds of white smoke floating away, looking silvery under the rays of the moon, and showing out distinctly against the blue sky. "Something important has happened," he muttered. "It's only on emergencies that the four guns are fired like that. It's a signal to the fleet, too, if I forget not."

The Sergeant was not left long in doubt as to what had caused the unusual signal.

Presently, at the moment Dick and Dolly returned, he heard the wild shouting and laughter of the boys, the cause of which he in vain strained his ears to catch, by protruding his head from the door of his room.

In a few minutes he heard footsteps approaching, and drew back his head; and he had scarcely resumed his walk when Dick and Dolly entered.

"I thought as much," said the Sergeant, assuming a severe tone, casting a severe look on Dick and Dolly, standing with the white patch to the wall, and trying to assume his usual dignified bearing. "You've come to tell me what the signal's about, I suppose—hum?"

"Yes, Sergeant," replied Dick; "I'm sorry to say we've got you into an awful mess!"

The Sergeant's heart gave a great thump against his ribs as he heard this, and then sunk, metaphorically speaking, into his boots, but he tried to speak with indifference.

"Got *me* into a mess, Everett? Ah! What is it?"

"At least, you will be in a mess," said Dick, "unless we can do something quickly. The identity of the General will be discovered within two or three days."

"Bla—bla—bless my soul!" stammered the Sergeant, loosing his dignified manner as suddenly as falls a house of cards. "How?"

"You heard the signal guns, of course?"

"Of course. Yes."

"Those signals were for the gunboat, 'Blazer,' to get up steam and overtake our troopship—the 'Orontes.'"

"Pro—pro—ceed," said the Sergeant, in a weak voice. "Wha—wha—what was the 'Blazer' sent after the—the—the steamer for?"

"Take it coolly, Sergeant," replied Dick. "It's just this way. The General managed to get some paper and ink from the Corporal c. the guard over the prison, and wrote a note to the Governor, asking for an interview, and declaring that he could prove his identity with General Shoot."

"How—how did you know that?" interrupted the Sergeant.

"I opened the note, and read it," replied Dick, "and not liking it—thinking it was too tame altogether—I kept it back, and concocted another, in which the General confessed that he had placed an infernal machine in the hold of the steamer for the purpose of blowing up all the troops on board. That the machine was wound up to explode between Gibraltar and Malta, and that within forty-eight hours of the time he was writing the note the explosion would take place. Dolly and I delivered that note to the Governor just now, whilst he was at a banquet, and you never heard such an awful row as it has caused."

"Heavens above us" cried the astounded Sergeant, with a wail of despair, "You've ruined me! Lord! Lord! Lo——'

"'Elp me ten man an' a donkey! hit's all hup with yer, Mister Sarjint! Yer'll be"—a sound with the mouth, supposed by the facetiously inclined to express being hanged. "Hit's a just retribution hon yer, yer know, fur stealin the scarlit trousers, the coat an''at, and swearin' as the Gen'ral was mad! Hit is, so 'elp me ten men an' a donkey hif it 'aint?"

The speaker was little Joey Pumps, who had followed in the steps of Dick and Dolly.

Distressed as the Sergeant was, the sight of Joey, and his taunting words—taunting words from the very imp that had led him into temptation!—so incensed him, that he looked about for something to throw at his tormentor.

In doing so, the Sergeant thoughtlessly turned round, and exposed the white patch on the seat of his overalls—an inadvertency of which he immediately became aware by a ringing laugh from Joey, and the words—

"Oh, lor! Oh, dear! Look! Look!"—pointing with his finger—"Wot a jolly big blister! Oh—O—O—Oh! Oh, lor—I be orf agin!"

As Joey sank to the floor to get limp, the Sergeant made a rush at him, and but for the timely interposition of Dick, the young gentleman would have fared badly.

"Leave him alone, Sergeant," said Dick, placing himself between them, "there's no time for that sort of thing. Drag him out, Dolly," added Dick, "and let him get limp outside."

Then addressing the Sergeant, he said—

"Look here, Sergeant, the only way to get out of the scrape, is to assist the General to escape——"

"Escape!" cried the Sergeant. "Oh, lord. lord, it's too late!"

"How?" asked Dick.

"I've put the sentry on the watch!"

"Never mind," said Dick, "I'll make that all right. Just listen to my plan. I've a note here from the Governor to the Corporal of the guard, to let the mad people escape—leaving traces to show that escape was not connived at. You must procure a woman's dress for the General, be at the gate of the Tower—outside—ready to disguise him, and conduct him into the town, and get him safely stowed away for the night. The next evening, just before gun-fire, he must be passed through the gate and conducted into the cork woods, and concealed there until the supposed danger is passed, for the General must be made to believe that his life will not be safe until the return of the 'Blazer.' D'ye see?"

The Sergeant did see, and, such was the state of his mind, that he consented to aid the escape. Indeed, there was no proposition, however daring, the Sergeant would not have consented to at this moment.

There was no time to be lost.

The Sergeant put on his top coat, and, forgetting the pain of his burn in his mental excitement and anxiety, passed through the gate of the Tower, and proceeded to procure the required dress for the General.

In the meantime Dick went to the Corporal of the guard, and presented the fictitious note of the Governor.

It ran thus—

"Sir Gentle Sharpset authorises the Corporal of the guard over the Civil Prison to connive at the escape of the three persons confined on the supposition of their being mad. They are not mad.

"The Convent.
"——18—."

"Bedad, but I can't make it out," said the corporal, shaking his head, and looking bewilderingly at the note. "If they're not cracked, why can't the Governor let 'em out dacently, shure—thro' the gate?"

"It's just this way, Corporal," said Dick. "The Governor's ashamed of having made such a mistake, and he wants to get them out of the way, and have done with the awkward affair.

They'll simply escape, and the Governor won't trouble himself to have them arrested. See?"

"There may be somethin' in that," replied Corporal O'Doo. "But it ain't for me to question the Governor's orders, I suppose It's quare though, upon me conshince!"

Corporal O'Doo then gave orders to the sentries to see "nothin' that is goin' on," giving particular directions, at the suggestion of Dick, to the Irish sentry who had been forewarned by Sergeant O'Shehe.

"Mind, Pat," said he. "It's the man in the scarlet drawers as'll drop out of the windy above ye, but it isn't seein him ye must be. D'ye hear, now?"

"I hear corporal, an' I'll attind' to me orders. It's only wan of 'em as'll come out up there?"

"Yes, Pat."

All went well.

The preparations for the escape were made with great despatch.

The General at first was very stubborn, declaring that the Governor should come in person and release him—he wasn't going to be treated like a common person.

"Allowed to escape, indeed!" growled the General, indignantly. "It's like Sir Gentle's confounded impertinence! I won't escape!"

"But don't you remember what I've told you about the infernal machine, Gen——?"

"Hang the infernal machine!" almost foamed the General. "What has the infernal machine to do with me?"

"A great deal, General," said Dick. "If you don't escape now, the Governor and all the troops in garrison will hardly be able to prevent you being torn to pieces to-morrow by the people."

It was some time, however, before the infuriated General could be made to see his danger and consent to escape.

A few minutes later the sentry saw a rope lowered from the window of the cell, followed presently by a broad figure in scarlet and white—the General with his scarlet drawers and white shirt.

"It's a bright bewty ye air," muttered the sentry, eyeing the General, as the latter stood shivering in the night wind that was blowing rather strongly off the Bay. "A quare looking customer, entirely!"

Scarcely had the sentry made these mental comments, when he heard a smothered scream, and some exclamations of fear, and, casting his eyes to the window, he saw another figure in white, with a nightcap with a huge border, laboriously and cautiously backing out and commence letting itself down.

This figure was Mrs. Rumball, in great mental distress and physical pain, the former being caused by a dreadful fear of falling, and the latter by the scraping of the skin off her knees and knuckles against the wall.

"Who the divil may ye be now?" murmured the sentry, approaching and looking suspiciously at the strange figure. "It's no buzziness ye hev there. Shure an' it was only wan I wor told had to come. I'll be gittin' into thrubble, I'm thinkin', if I don't stop ye. Git back, bad luck to ye! Git back wid yez!" he said aloud, at the same time giving Mrs. Rumball's hinder part a smart prick with his sword-bayonet. "Git back wid——"

The sentry's sentence was cut short by an agonised scream, and, to his astonishment, he saw the figure descend, like an immense white ball, and alight on the head of the General, who was standing immediately beneath.

———

CHAPTER XXXV.

FOLLOWS SERGEANT O'SHEHE IN SEARCH OF A DISGUISE, AND RECORDS THE LUCK HE MET WITH.

WITH the exception of Dick and his chums, we can safely assert that everyone connected with the night's proceedings was in a tolerable state of bewilderment.

Corporal O'Doo was bewildered at the conduct of the Governor, and had it not been for the habit drilled into him, in common with every British soldier, of yielding obedience without asking questions as to whether an order is just or unjust, sane or insane, he would have hesitated ere acting upon the instructions conveyed in the note.

The Corporal would have made extensive queries—and the cat would have been out of the bag.

The General was bewildered—more bewildered, perhaps, than ever, for, since his imprisonment in the hold of the steamer, he had been in state of bewilderment of more or less density.

He had begun to think that he was not—could not be—General Joachim Shoot, of the Royal Artillery, at all; that, if such a person had ever existed, it must have been in his imagination. ¢

Never, perhaps, has there been a case where a person has been the victim of so many untoward circumstances—all having their mainspring in the General's sensitiveness; for was it not his sensitiveness on the score of his reputation for gallantry that induced him, in an unfortunate moment, to kick little Joey Pumps down the hold of the steamer?

And it was from that moment that his misfortunes began.

Let the reader reflect upon all that has happened to the General on the voyage, and since, on the basis of the General's sensitiveness—combined with great obstinacy of character, and the possession of an awfully irritable temper and unsociableness of disposition, when it will be found the various events were only such as might have been expected.

Mrs. Rumball was bewildered, though, perhaps, her mental condition may be more accurately described as a state of concentrated passion at the treatment she had received.

Mrs. Rumball was in a state of strained fury; swelled out, as it were, like a balloon.

If the pressure of Mrs. Rumball's passion could have been gauged, like steam in a boiler, it would have been found something more than a thousand pounds to the square inch.

Mr. Rumball is too insignificant to bother about.

But, of all the victims, we think that, as the Sergeant passed out of the gate to procure a disguise for the General, the poor Sergeant was the most bewildered.

As he got into the road which led towards the town, and saw how deserted it was, and realised how quietly the town lay sleeping in the moonlight—for not a human voice could be heard, not even a dog "baying the moon"—it struck him what a wild-goose errand he had come upon.

"'Pon my soul," he muttered, as he went mechanically forward; "now I've come out, I don't know where the deuce I'm to get a lady's costume from! All the shops are shut. I don't know any private people on the Rock. What I'm to do, I don't know! The General *must* be got safely away. I never was in such a cursed mess in my life! I'd steal the clothes if I could see any! Good lord!" sighed the Sergeant. "I feel the most miserable devil that ever lived! I've a great mind to go back and blow my brains out! A touch of the trigger, a bang—and I should be out of my misery!"

But it was evident that, as the Sergeant continued walking at as rapid a pace as the state of his burnt person permitted, he had not arrived at the proper mental pitch to summarily disturb the natural formation of his own brains.

Perhaps he had a hope—a scarcely defined impression, say—that some luck would turn up and, therefore, that the scattering of his brains might as well be deferred till all hope was gone.

At any rate, whether this were the case or not, he had scarcely entered the first street when his ears caught the sound of voices, emanating from a dirty-looking shop, the door of which stood partly open.

The Sergeant stopped abruptly, and his heart began beating rapidly.

What was the cause of his agitation?

He had came upon an open, second-hand wearing apparel emporium!

A candle burnt within, and the Sergeant could see some garments through the partly open door.

What should he do—walk boldly in? or listen to what the persons within had to talk about at such a time of night?

Two or three minutes would not make much difference—he would listen.

The conversation, apparently, had not proceeded long, for he heard a voice say, with a Jewish accent and snuffle—

"Come, come, Master Cupidsh, you must tellsh me vats vor you vantsh zish niggersh vig an de gownsh an shawl—shelp me you mush! He! he! he!"

"He! he! (a racy kind of chuckle). It wone do, Massa Simon; Cupid get 'um ears pulled hoff, an' 'um back warmed wid 'um tick hif 'um split. He, he, he!"

"Supposh I guesh, Cupidsh—eh? He, he!"

"'Pose you do, Massa Simon, you nebber tell 'um! He, he, he!"

"I knowsh—shelp me, I dosh, Cupidsh! Missy Jennie Sharpshet, de Governorsh shistersh, ish goin' to elopsh mid the Senor Don Juan de la Vega Grey de los Brabones—eh, Massa Cupidsh? Thatsh sho—eh? He, he!"

"He, he, he! Lub de Lord! I'm bressd hif Massa Simon you done know ebberyting! You berry debbil 'imself! Ha, ha!—he, he, he! 'Ow you fine it out, Massa Simon?"

"Mushn't tell shecrets, Cupidsh—mushn't tell shecrets! He, he!"

"Hoh, hoh! Bresh 'um! Wot else you know Massa Simon—eh? He, he, he!"

"He, he! Missey Jennie ish goin' to dresh ash womansh niggersh, and past de gate ash lovely black woman—eh? He, he!"

This was followed by a great deal of chuckling from both, and many exclamations of delighted astonishment, either real or pretended, from the negro—the latter, as the Sergeant (who had now got one eye round the door) could see, being a boy dressed in a dark livery —a jacket with three rows of plated buttons, trousers, a white neck-tie, and a topper with a silver band and side-strings.

"Ven Missey Jennie go, Cupidsh—eh ?"

By this time, the information involved in this question had become a matter of considerable importance with the listening Sergeant.

So desperate was the necessity to which he was reduced of procuring a suitable disguise for the General, that, as the conversation developed, the Sergeant had sufficiently caught its meaning to have started an idea in his throbbing brain.

Here was evidently a lady bent upon throwing herself into the arms of her lover at great personal risk and inconvenience, not to say disfigurement.

The lady was going to transform her lovely visage into the likeness, the semblance of a benighted negress, to enable her to transfer her blooming person—possibly buxom and blooming person—into the legal custody of a husband.

It was a stupendous example of the power of love ; but the Sergeant, in these few moments, had resolved that the lady should not blacken her person or her character.

The lady in question was the Governor's sister, and the Sergeant saw—or fancied he saw —his opportunity of killing two birds with one stone.

He should be enabled to secure the escape of the General (which was only to be a temporary measure, of course), and do the Governor a personal favour at the same time.

Would he not, by preventing the Governor's sister making, so to speak, an ass of herself, prevent the misguided and love-blinded lady from bringing disgrace upon the family name ?

Not a doubt of it ; for certainly this Don must be personably objectionable to the Governor, or there would be no need for this clandestine move on the part of his sister.

The lady might never forgive him for spoiling her black little game ; but the Governor would, and also would use his influence with the General to obtain his forgiveness in that quarter.

Here was a splendid idea.

The Sergeant fairly trembled with feverish excitement as the issues of this idea fastened themselves on his brain.

His plan was to substitute the General for the lady.

This must be accomplished by pouncing on the negro boy—or "tiger"—and compelling him, on pain of revealing the plot to the Governor if he refused, to deceive the Don, passing off the General as his lady-love.

The time fixed for this intended elopement was, therefore, of vast importance to the Sergeant's scheme.

Its success depended upon the moment.

The "Blazer" would return within three or four days, and if the General could not be got out of the way before then, why all the plotting to bring things right would only end in making things more wrong than ever, as far as the Sergeant was concerned.

The boys, of course, wouldn't care a fig which way it ended.

The reply to the Jew's question came, and with it a load of anxiety was removed from the Sergeant's mind.

"He, he, he !" chuckled Cupid. "Massa Simon seem berry coorus 'bout it—eh ? As Massa Simon know so berry much, 'pose 'um guess wen 'um go ? He, he, he !"

"I don't know everythingsh, you she, Cupidsh," returned the Jew, in a simpering tone. "How can I tell when de lady go—eh ? He, he !"

"Taught Cupid do Massa Simon dar ! He, he ! 'Pose 'um tell 'um wen Missey go, Massa Simon no split ? Heh ?"

"No, no, Cupidsh ! What for Simonsh spLtsh —eh ? I vill keep ash dark ash pitsch ! Shelp me !"

"Den um go morrow night, He, he !"

"Shelp me, you don't shay sho ! What time they gosh, Cupidsh ?"

"Jist afore de gun-fire. Missey, she go tro de gate as Cupid's big sisser. He ! He ! Hah ! hah ! Bressed fine lark ! Oh, yas ! Heh ? He, he, he ! Ough-a-a-h !"

Here the old Jew, whose eyes the Sergeant could see, shone with cunning twinkle, rubbed his dark, skinny hands and chuckled in apparent sympathy with the easily-pumped Cupid.

"You *swar* you no split, Massa Simon—eh ?" asked Cupid, in a tone as though he thought he hadn't been quite wise to let out the secret of his mission.

"Shelp me, I do, Cupidsh !"

"Den I take de tings an' go, Massa Simon, Missy Jinny wonner wha de debbil I got to ! He, he !"

———

CHAPTER XXXVI.

DESCRIBES IN WHAT MANNER THE GENERAL WAS DISGUISED, AND HOW HE LOOKED IN HIS NEW CHARACTER.

As Cupid was speaking he began wrapping up in a cotton gown of a pattern flowery and gorgeously-coloured, an equally gorgeous shawl, a nigger's wig, and a white veil—a square piece of Brussels net, edged with lace—a pugaree to form a turban.

"Dis wail berry good idea, Massa Simon. He, he !" laughed Cupid. "Nobboddy see dat ma big sisser face ony brack wid de burn cork—eh ? He, he !"

"Splendish idea, Cupidsh ! Shelp me, it tish. He, he ! You big shister vill look like von bridsh—shelp me, she vill ! I must shay double prish for thatsh idea, Cupidsh—eh ? He, he !"

"'Pose Massa Simon charge wat um like. Cupid no care a fig—bress'd if um do ! He, he, he !"

At this moment the Sergeant drew back his head, and, precipitately retiring, concealed himself in the shadow of a doorway a few yards up on the same side of the street, a precaution he had scarcely adopted when Cupid, with a bundle under his arm, emerged from the Jew's shop, and turned in the same direction.

Though Cupid could not see the Sergeant, the Sergeant could see Cupid.

Both were chuckling—Cupid at the thought of the fun, the Sergeant at the thought of "doing" Cupid.

As Cupid passed, rolling like a ship at sea, and chuckling as though he had the hiccup, the

Sergeant peeped round, followed him with his eyes till he had turned the corner of the street, and then followed him with his body, treading very quietly on tip-toe.

At the corner of the street the Sergeant came to a halt, and again made use of his eyes, when he made out that the still chuckling Cupid had crossed the main road, and was proceeding to climb the rock, apparently as a short cut to a path which led in the direction of the subterranean batteries.

This proved to be the case.

Cupid gained the path, and then continued his way upwards until he became invisible behind an angle of the rock, which cut the path and caused it to turn off abruptly at right angles.

Wondering what in the world Cupid was up to, knowing that the Governor's palace did not lie in that direction, the Sergeant left his point of observation, and presently found himself watching Cupid's movements from the point of the Rock.

These movements considerably aroused the curiosity and astonishment of the Sergeant.

Cupid, instead of pursuing the path, edged off and entered a nook in which stood a huge gun, and passed behind the pile of shot.

"I wonder what the deuce he is up to?" muttered the Sergeant. "He must be going to hide the things behind the shot. That's it, for a guinea! The things are to be kept there till to-morrow night, and the Governor's sister is to go there to dress. I'll soon see!"

The nook was not many yards off, and, in less than two minutes, he had crept quietly up and was peeping round the pile of shot.

The sight that met his gaze was amusing enough to bring a grim smile on the Sergeant's face.

Cupid had unrolled his bundle, and, curious, apparently, to try the effect of the fit of the disguise, he was in the act of putting on the gown.

As he got his arms into the sleeves, which were about as shapely and full as a couple of pillow-slips, whilst the voluminous skirt rested on the ground and completely hid his person, Cupid indulged in a series of chuckles and remarks.

"He, he! Bress'd if de gown aint big 'nuff fo' ma ole gan-mod-der, an' she big as lelliphunt a'mos! He, he, he! Be gum, woan Missey Jennie look berry 'ansom fig're! De Don, 'um die ob lub. Hoh! he! he!"

Here Cupid, who had taken off his topper, tried on the wig.

"Bress ma sou', 'um to big! Moighty mus too big! He, he! Nebber mind, 'um mus do now—all de better pras. 'Pose 'um try on de wail now? Se 'ow dat look on nigger, Cupid."

The next moment Cupid had thrown the square veil over his woolly headgear and the gown, and then commenced a series of grotesque actions.

At one moment Cupid affected the shy and timid bride; at another, a bride of haughty and contemptuous demeanour; another moment he became a giggling, frivolous bride, giving herself too conscious airs of the light in which she regarded the change from a virgin to a married state of existence.

Cupid, indeed, indulged in endless variations of graces and airs, and had commenced to wind up with a dance when he was arrested, with one foot in the air, as completely as though he had been turned into stone.

The negro's eyes had, at that moment, fallen on the figure of the Sergeant, creeping round the pile of shot.

As such an interruption was utterly unexpected by Master Cupid, he was not only astounded but greatly alarmed, and with good reason.

Cupid had been over and over again impressed by his mistress with the necessity of great caution in carrying out his delicate mission, and he had sworn to her over and over again that he would not indulge in any nonsensical act that would imperil its success.

But here he was, caught in the act of breaking his most solemn oaths!

The game was all up!

He had been and gone and done it!

He had betrayed his mistress!

These reflections passed through Cupid's mind with lightning rapidity, and equally rapid was his next movement.

Glaring one moment at the intruder with his black-and-white frightened eyes, the next, Cupid turned and fled.

But not far.

Unfortunately for his desire to escape, the cotton dress was too long, and Cupid had scarcely taken two steps when he fell to the ground in a heap, and the Sergeant had seized him, and clapped one hand over his mouth, pressing the other against the back of his head.

Cupid was thus rendered speechless, but not entirely helpless.

If Cupid couldn't make use of his tongue, he could of his arms and legs, and he began instinctively fighting and kicking, struggling and twisting about his body as a cat will when objecting to being held up by the poll.

"It's no use kicking, my animated piece of ebony," said the Sergeant. "You can't get away if you kick till doomsday, I've got you too tight, my black Cupid. You hear? I know your name. I know all about where you've been, what you've been doing, and what you and your mistress are up to! You'd better be quiet and listen to what I have to say. If you don't, I'll split and tell the Governor! Ah, that's it!" added the Sergeant, as Cupid, taking in the purport of his captor's words, ceased his struggles. "You mean to keep quiet—eh?"

A muttered sound, which the Sergeant supposed was meant to reply in the affirmative, came from beneath his hand, but he didn't remove it until he had given him another caution.

"Mind, if you make a noise I'll dash your brains out with one of these shot."

Cupid, squatting on the ground, with the veil still over his head, let out a deep respiration as the Sergeant's hand was removed from his mouth, and then looking up said, in a tone which showed that he had regained his coolness—

"'Ow de debbil you know all 'bout Cupid, 'an wat 'um bin up to?"

"Easy enough, my Cupid," replied the Sergeant. "There's not much mystery about it. I overheard all your conversation in old Simon's shop. Just listen. This disguise is intended for the elopement of the Governor's sister to-morrow night. I don't choose that she shall elope. I choose that a friend of mine shall take that lady's place, dressed as your big sister, and

I choose that you shall help to deceive the Don. See, my Cupid?"

"Bress me soul!" ejaculated Cupid, throwing back his bullet-shaped head, with an intelligent chuckle. "Me see dat well 'nuff. But, lub de Lord, Cupid get 'um back skin'd like de eel, if 'um do dat! Dat nebber do! He, he, he!"

"Am I to tell the Governor, Cupid?" asked the Sergeant, significantly.

"No, dat nebber do, nutner!" said Cupid. "Ma swar dat nebber do! Bress'd if Cupid know what de debbil to do—'um get skin'd bof ways. He, he!"

"Better to disappoint the lady, Cupid, than have her intention exposed. She can elope another night. See, my Cupid?"

"'Pose she can, too. Yas, dat do prase. Wha' Massa sodjer want Cupid do—eh?"

"I want you to disguise my friend. Have you got the stuff to black his face?"

"Yas. Got ebberyting reddy. When Massa want 'um do it?"

"Presently. Just stay where you are; and, mind, my Cupid," added the Sergeant, threateningly; "if you are not here when I return, it's something more than skinned you'll find yourself when I catch you."

Rejoicing in his success in obtaining a splendid disguise for the General, Sergeant O'Shehe hastened back to the Castle, feeling pretty sure that Cupid would not take to himself wings and fly away.

He would rather get his "rightabout" skinned for disappointing his mistress, than for causing her exposure. "No, no, I've got him safe enough. By Jove!" he muttered, with a chuckle. "But that will be a first-rate disguise. I wonder how the escape is getting on? I hope they——"

What the Sergeant was going to say, was cut short by a piercing scream, which caused him to stop abruptly and listen with an uncomfortable feeling of apprehension.

"What's up?" he murmured, as the scream was followed by others quite as piercing, and with which were now mingled shouts, and voices as of much confusion. "Something gone wrong, by Jove! Hang it, what a nuisance!"

The commotion still continuing, the Sergeant could no longer endure the suspense, and, expecting to witness something dreadful, he entered the gate, and the first thing that met his gaze was a group of soldiers, and the boys standing round some object from which was being emitted the screams he had heard.

As the screams apparently came from a woman, the Sergeant concluded that the woman was none other than Mrs. Rumball.

"Confound her!" he muttered, savagely. "What the devil has she been up to now! Kicking up such a row at this moment!"

The Sergeant, feeling his heart at this moment filled with hatred at Mrs. Rumball, pushed through the crowd, and there, on the ground, sure enough, was the detestable creature.

Mrs. Rumball, too, was uttering the most awful groans and moans, and rolling over and over like an animated bundle of rags.

"What is it? What the deuce has happened?" asked the Sergeant, trying to make his voice heard amidst the din.

The sentry who had caused all the mischief, happened to be standing near the Sergeant, and, hearing the question, replied—

"Bedad, Sergeant, but it was nothing worse than the prick of a pin, an' the ould creature's makin' as much row about it as though she wor kilt outright."

"Prick of a pin? Where was she pricked with a pin? Who pricked her?" asked the Sergeant, impatiently.

"'Twas mesilf shure as did it, Sergeant, but it wor only jist the prick wid the beyonit behind, as she wor comin' down the rope from the windy. Twor only won as I wor tould wor to come down—that mad chap there wot's broke his blissed neck trou her. Bad luck to him—it's mad he his himsilf!"

This exclamation was caused by the Sergeant darting away like a man suddenly struck frantic.

There was good reason for this wild proceeding.

If the General had been killed, he, the Sergeant, was done for.

Trial by "drum-head" court-martial on the spot, and death by shooting would be the certain consequences!

Stunned with apprehension, and caring little whom he upset, the distracted Sergeant darted through the circle, flinging men and boys aside like so much chaff, and, darting again into another group, that was gathered around the prostrate form of the General, cast himself on his knees, demanding in anxious tones—

"Is it dead he is? Oh, lord, lord!—Is he dead?"

With the exception of the corporal of the guard, his group was composed of Dick Everett, Tom Sheppard, Bob Jones, Harry Smith, Dolly Swaps and a few other boys.

"Oh, no, he's all right, Sergeant," said Dick. "He's only stunned, I think—a little bit knocked out of time like, by Mrs. Rumball falling on his head. He'll come to in a minute; keep calm."

"Thank goodness!" murmured the Sergeant, with a sigh of relief. "It's an awful piece of business as it is, without having the Gen—"

"Si-s-h. Mind what you're saying, Sergeant," whispered Dick, giving the Sergeant at the same time a gentle reminder by a dig in the ribs. "You'll betray the plot, if you arn't cautious. Have you got the disguise?"

"Yes," returned the Sergeant, in a whisper.

"Where is it?"

"Outside the Castle, behind one of the guns."

"Why didn't you bring it in?"

"I couldn't. It's not an ordinary disguise, and can only be put on outside."

"Then you must cover him with your topcoat when he comes to, and we must lead him to the spot. Is it far?"

"Not five minutes' walk."

"All right. The sooner he comes to the better. We couldn't have a better opportunity than whilst everybody's attention is taken up with Mrs. Rumball."

The mishap that had befallen the General by the body of Mrs. Rumball depriving him of temporary consciousness was, as it happened, a fortunate circumstance to the furtherance of getting him properly disguised, in the manner provided by the Sergeant.

That this was the case will be seen presently.

It was not until after a good sousing with cold water, and a vigorous shaking, that the General recovered sufficiently to be half-led, half-carried from the Castle yard to the spot where Cupid was awaiting the return of the

Sergeant with the person whom he had to transform into a black angel.

As the sentry at the gate had had his instructions about the escape, the party had no difficulty in passing out, leaving behind them Mrs. Rumball and her groans, the latter of which were gradually attracting all the soldiers within the Castle walls.

The Sergeant, however, did not care a fig what became of Mrs. Rumball, so long as he succeeded in getting the General safely out of the way.

It was not till he had got clear of the gate, and was well on the road to the rendezvous, that he began to breathe freer than he had for some time.

He saw now the goal of safety within his reach, and he longed to see the General transformed into a sable Hebe—not that the General was destined to become a black waitress, or to occupy the post of cup-bearer to the gods (as did Hebe) or mortals, in his translation, but the Sergeant, at the moment could think of no other mythological lady or goddess.

Nor was it likely that the General, if he continued in his present misty and unsteady state, would be in a condition to wait on anyone with intelligence and grace.

In addition to being in a state of partial obfustication, as to what was passing around him, the General's knees had lost their power of maintaining their usual mode of elegant progression, and the consequence was a series of eccentric movements, and gave much trouble to his supporters.

An enemy would have pronounced the General drunk—a word that would have saved us the foregoing elaborate explanation of his condition, if we had only thought of using it.

In this manner the party proceeded until it turned the angle of rock, which afforded a glimpse of the nook where Cupid awaited its approach in state.

We use the word " state " advisedly.

As our friends turned the corner, they came to a dead stop, staring at an object which filled them with wonder.

"What in the world is it?" said Dick at length.

The circumstance was such as perfectly justified this expressive mode of asking a question—used only when something momentarily unexplainable confronts us.

Cupid, who could never keep still for any length of time, but was compelled to seek for something to occupy his attention and make that time pass pleasantly, finding his present position rather monotonous, had turned his attention to producing an effect that would not only afford him occupation and amusement, but would considerably astonish the Sergeant and his friend on their approach.

To this end, Cupid got a tolerably long and stiff twig, which he stuck in the vent of the gun.

On the top of this twig he then stuck his " topper."

Next, Cupid adjusted about his body the flaring cotton gown, put the shawl across his shoulders, and the nigger's wig on his own woolly pate.

Around the wig he wound the pugaree, until he had produced a voluminous turban.

Over this Cupid placed the flowing veil, and then clambered along the gun until he reached the muzzle, across which he seated himself,

looking a most astonishing mysterious apparition in the moonlight, chuckling unceasingly, his body vibrating like the surface of the ground under a succession of earthquakes.

As our party came to a stand, and Cupid saw the effect he had produced, he added to it by putting a finger in each side of his mouth and stretching it to its full extent, a process that disclosed the whole of his white teeth, and gave a ghastly grin to his black features.

" It's Cupid," said the Sergeant.

" Cupid? who's Cupid?"

" A young nigger," replied the Sergeant. " The tom-fool has got on the gun with the General's disguise."

" Disguise!" cried Dick. " What, in Heaven's name, sort of disguise is it?"

" A nigger's and a first-rate one it is too. The General won't ever know himself, and so I'll take my oath nobody else will."

" Oh, lor!" here exclaimed Joey Pumps, who having left Mrs, Rumball to her fate, had followed in the wake of the party. "'Ere's summat like a lark hon 'ere, I hexpecs! I mus go forred and kontemplate that putty-looking gen'l'm."

Accordingly, Joey ran on ahead, and, long before Dick and the others had come up with the " groggy " General, he had gone " orf agin," and was limp as a dead flat-fish.

Nor were the others in a much better condition a few moments after reaching Cupid.

The sight of the veiled, grinning imp, was so comical—specially when the costume was viewed as that provided by the Sergeant for the disguise of the General—as to be overpowering, and they all yelled with laughter.

" Good gracious!" said Dick, almost sobbing with risible emotion, this beats all I've come across yet! I-I-ha-h-a !—ca-ca-ca-n-scarcely ha-ha-a-a—realise it! Oh-o-oh dear, dear! Oh-o-o-h!"

Here Dick went off into another paroxysm, followed by the rest—Dolly Swaps being so much overcome, that he sank down by the side of Joey Pumps, and became equally as limp as his special friend.

But not one of them laughed more than Cupid himself, who, after endeavouring in vain to maintain his seat, toppled to the ground, where, for some time, he rolled about, a strange-looking heap, giving way to gurgling chuckles of the most extraordinary kind.

It was some minutes before the party had attained a sufficient degree of calmness to see about the decorating and enrobing of the General, but this was not accomplished without many interruptions in the form of spasmodic laughter.

The process of effecting the disguise was rendered somewhat difficult, owing to the helpless state of the General, and yet, had he been in a mental condition to know where he was, it is highly probable that the process would have been rendered much more difficult, if not impossible.

With all the General's desire to escape from the supposed evil consequences of Dick's letter, it is open to doubt whether or not he would have calmly submitted to be disguised in such an extraordinary manner.

We express this query from our foreknowledge of subsequent events.

But we must not anticipate.

As regards the process of transformation, it was accomplished as follows—

"Drat 'em!" exclaimed the jealous Rumball. "Give me the torch. I'll do it!"—See page 122.

No. 9.

The General—whose impression of outward things was about as clear as if he were in a dream, in which the senses and limbs are alike paralysed—was dragged behind a pile of shot and seated on a bed of geraniums.

In this position he was held, whilst, in the first place, the cotton gown was passed over his head, his arms put into the sleeves, and the skirt decently adjusted over his scarlet drawers.

Then followed the blacking operation.

This was effected with burnt cork—produced by Cupid, who had provided it for a similar operation on his mistress.

Particular attention was bestowed on this part of the performance.

It was, of course, absolutely necessary that the General should look as much like the character of a female negro as possible, and to secure this desideratum it became evident that, not only must there be not a pin's point of white flesh showing, but that the General's face must show no sign of hair.

"It's easy enough to black his face," said Dick, when the fitting and adjusting of the gown had been satisfactorily completed; "but how about the moustache? We haven't a pair of scissors. Has any one a knife?—a penknife will do."

Dolly and Joey Pumps having elected to witness the interesting proceedings from a point which would afford an unobstructed view, had mounted the pile of shot at one side and lay on their stomachs, peering over the top, and resting on their arms.

As no one had come provided with either scissors or knife, the difficulty was solved by Dolly.

Dolly, after setting fire to the Sergeant's overalls, had put the box of matches in his trousers-pocket.

This box Dolly now produced, saying—

"You'd better singe 'em off, Dick. Here's lots of matches."

"You're a perfect genius, Dolly," said Dick, as he took the box amidst a burst of laughter. "Horses' coats are reduced by singeing, and I don't see why the General's moustache shouldn't be safely taken off in the same way. Here goes at any rate," added Dick, striking a match and deliberately applying the flame to the moustache, which at once blazed up, diffusing a pleasant smell of burnt hair.

This attempt was so satisfactory that the operation was repeated until nothing remained of the General's hirsuite appendage but two patches of black stubbly bristles, like a well-used scrubbing-brush.

"That won't be noticed," observed Dick, "when his face is properly blacked. Now for the burnt cork, Cupid."

"Stop a bit, Dick," said Dolly. "You haven't done all the singeing yet."

"What do you mean, Dolly?" asked Dick.

"You must singe the hair off his head," replied Dolly, "to make the wig fit properly,"—a notion that was received with a burst of laughter.

"By Jove! you're right, Dolly!" exclaimed Dick. "It won't do to have a misfit nor any straggling hairs about. We must imitate nature as closely as possible," he added, still shaking with laughter.

The further operation of singeing off the poor General's hair was then performed by Dick, amidst much laughter, smoke, and smell.

Nor was there much, if any, pain inflicted, as the operation was performed in as close an imitation of singeing a horse as possible—a certain patch of hair was allowed to blaze for a few moments, then blown out, and the place rubbed by Dick, and so on.

Then followed the process of imparting the nigger complexion, which was done thoroughly over the scalp as well as the face.

That the General's appearance at this stage was somewhat peculiar will be readily believed.

From the neck downwards he was a mass of gorgeously-flowered cotton gown, whilst his head presented very much the appearance of one of the black cannon-balls close at hand, with the exception that it had a pair of ears—sticking out like a butterfly's wings—and was rather more animated by having a nose, mouth, and a pair of eyes.

The resemblance of the back of the head, however, was perfect, and called forth many expressions of admiration.

After this artistic piece of work had been duly contemplated and criticised, and such additional rubs of burnt cork added as were considered necessary to insure "one harmonious whole," the wig was very carefully put on and adjusted.

Then the pugaree was wound round by Cupid—who understood his part of the programme well—until a magnificent turban was the result.

The effect was now not unpleasing.

The wig and the white turban had considerably softened the bare, unfledged look of the General's face and scalp.

"That ain't so bad," said Joey Pumps, approvingly. "He'll pass werry well for a nigger gal 'e will, wen 'e's got the wail hon. I never could tell the difference atween a male and female black hif hit wasn't for the way they dresses! That's hit—Hoo—o—ray!"

This demonstrative exclamation of approval and satisfaction was caused by Dick casting the veil over, and then standing with one hand on his left hip, his body drawn upright, and his right arm extended over the head of the transformed General—the whole attitude being expressive of proud satisfaction at triumph over an exceedingly complicated and trying task for an amateur costumier.

In fact, the artistic effect was admired for several minutes, and then it became a question what was to be done with the General?

"Do you think it will be safe to leave him here all day to-morrow, Sergeant?" asked Dick.

"There's no occasion to do so," replied the Sergeant. "We can put him in the magazine here. He'll be safe enough there."

This was a capital idea.

The magazine referred to was a recess in the rock—artificial—where powder would be stored when the gun was in action. It was, of course, bomb-proof, and had a bomb-proof door.

No place could have been found better suited for their purpose, and when the Sergeant had procured the key, the General was lifted and placed within, and the door closed.

——

CHAPTER XXXVII.

THE PROCEEDINGS OF THREE LITTLE IMPS.

WE omitted to mention that there was one individual left behind to keep company with the

General, not, however, for the purpose of cheering the General in his loneliness, but for the purpose of keeping him, the individual, in safety.

That individual was Cupid.

The Sergeant was, just now, in a very suspicious mood, engendered by his nervousness under the circumstances in which he was placed.

His nervousness rendered him anxious that there should be no hitch in the programme he had laid out for insuring the escape of the General.

Although he felt pretty confident that Cupid, not for his own sake (for that little darkie would, in any case, be sure to catch "coco") but for the sake of his mistress, keep dark, the Sergeant wisely considered that it would be as well to place his sable assistant out of the reach of temptation.

Cupid had already given striking evidence of a restless and eccentric disposition; and there was no knowing what might happen if he were allowed the free use of his legs and tongue, therefore it was that Cupid was locked up in the magazine, where, for some hours, he occupied his time in, metaphorically speaking, momentarily blowing up the cause of his captivity—Sergeant O'Shehe.

But, although he knew it not, Cupid had two sympathising friends, and who had determined to return and keep him company.

These two friends were Joey Pumps and Dolly Swaps.

It was shortly after gun-fire, about four o'clock in the morning, that Cupid's sympathisers emerged from the Castle gate.

Not together, however, but singly.

They had a special reason for adopting this course of procedure.

It was to lull the suspicion of Dick and his chums as to what was going on.

Joey Pumps was the first to slip out, and proceed by a roundabout way to the nook, and hide himself behind the pile of shot.

A few minutes later, Dolly Swaps—with his trousers-pockets and seat, and the breast of his undress jacket, bulged out to an extent that completely distorted the outlines of his usually graceful figure, and his forage cap bulged up at the crown, and so tightly strapped under his chin that his cheeks and eyes protruded as though he were · on the point of choking—waddled through the gate, and, observing the same caution as Joey, presently slipped behind the pile of shot, and joined his chum.

"I say, Dolly," said Joey, with a wink and a chuckle, "Wot hev yer got? Yer seems to hev grow'd hout o' shape hall of a suddint!"

"Do you think my mother would know me just now, Joey?" asked Dolly, assuming an attitude that would have been graceful but for the bulges and protuberances already mentioned.

"Why, I 'ardly think as she would, Dolly," replied Joey, scanning his friend with a critical glance. "I 'opes as it ain't a permanent disfigermen, cos yer see as I'm hanswerable fur the safety an' elegance of yer pusson!"

Here the facetious friends indulged in a considerable amount of mysterious chuckling.

"Look here, Joey," said Dolly, when this ceremony had been indulged in to a proper extent of time, "I'll begin with my forage cap. There you are," he added suddenly, taking off his cap and allowing a large Spanish onion to fall to the ground.

"That ain't so bad, Dolly," said Joey, winking. "Look here."

Here Joey whipped off his cap, and shook out something which fell to the ground with a dull "squash."

"What is it, Joey," asked Dolly. "It looks queer."

"It's a pancake," replied Joey.

"Pancake! If anybody had asked me, I should say it was a dirty bit of paunch," said Dolly, turning up his nose.

"I'm surprised at yer, Dolly," returned Joey, affecting a look of indignation, "Hit's pancake, made by Dolly Rumball 'erself."

"I didn't know Mrs. Rumball had got over her wound, Joey," said Dolly; "I thought she was too sore to move."

"Yer don't know that ere lady as well as I do, Dolly," returned Joey, again winking, "Don't yer know as she wos put hin the Sarjint's bed?"

"Yes."

"An she wouldn't let the Sarjint cum hin hon no account?"

"Yes."

"Well, wot wos 'er little dodge, does yer think?"

"I don't know, I am sure."

"Yer knows as she ast fur flour an hegs doesn't yer?"

"Yes, I know that."

"An' sugar?"

"Yes."

"An' milk?"

"Yes."

"An' a big basin, an' a spoon, an' a fork, an' a lot o' fat, and a frying-pan."

"Yes, and lots of other things which she called medical comforts," said Dolly, with a knowing wink,"

"Just so," returned Joey," with great gravity, "This 'ere cove's nat'ral purtector, knowed 'zactly wot wos good fur that ere wound, or sommat else," added Joey, with a significant wink.

"Her stomach?" suggested Dolly.

"Well," returned Joey, "konsidderin' as she hadn't nothin to heat fur I don't know ow long, I guess as her hinside wos as huncumfurtable has 'er houtside, an' so she manoovered fur the hetcetrers to make 'er fav'rite dish. I knowed wot she wos hup to pretty well, I kin tell yer"—a wink—"an has we'd agreed ter git wot we could in the way o' wittles, fur hour fren Koopid hin theer,"—jerking his head in the direction of the magazine—"I jist keep my heye hon 'er. Oh lor, didn't she hev just a jolly tuck hin, neither!"

"Did she?" asked Dolly.

"She jist did, too! She made such a jolly lot, has I thort has she'd never a-don fryin an heatin! I'm blowed hif she did'nt heat till she could a-touched hit wit 'er finger!"—putting his finger into his mouth—"And wen she lef' hoff theer wos only won lef hon the plate, an thet wos becos hit wosn't quite done! Oh lor, Dolly! I sez ter myself 'hif this eer Gibberhalter aint giv yer a nappitite then I'm blowed. Yer greedy ole thin, I'm quite ashamed hon yer!'"

"And this is the pancake, I suppose?" said Dolly.

"Right yer air, Dolly!" said Joey. "An' I 'opes has frien' Koopid 'll be habel ter gerdest hit, thet's hall!" nodding his hend and winking.

"Is that all you've got, Joey?" asked Dolly.

"'Ceptin' these," returned Joey, putting a hand in each pocket, and pulling forth two large bones, which he held up to Dolly's astonished gaze. "Thur real leg o' mutton 'uns," he added, nodding his head impressively.

"But there's no meat on 'em," said Dolly. "What's the use of them?"

"They're full o' marrer though," returned Joey, staring hard at Dolly. and trying to maintain a grave countenance; "an' wen fren' Koopid's cleared thet hout, 'e ken hev the bones ter play with!"

As this remark was followed by another wink, the conversation between the two caterers for Cupid was interrupted for the space of two minutes by more mysterious chuckling, accompanied by sympathetic motions of their bodies.

When this ceremony was over, Joey said—

"Wot hev yer got 'sides the hinyan, Dolly?"

For reply, Dolly unbuttoned the breast of his jacket, and pulled forth something wrapped in a piece of paper, which, on placing it on the ground and opening it, proved to contain sundry scraps of meat and fish, pieces of plain pudding and carrot, and nubs of spongy turnip.

"Hit's a great wariety, but hit don't look werry tempting," said Joey, shaking his head gravely as he poked his finger about amongst the pieces. "I'm feared as Koopid ain't peckish enough fur this 'ere, fren' Dolly."

"It's better than nothing, anyway," returned Dolly; "and it's as good as you've had sometimes from Mrs. Rumball, Joey, ain't it?"

"A jolly sight better, Dolly!" said Joey, opening his eyes, and giving his head a slow movement, a kind of half-shake. "Many's the time I've had nothin' but tater-peelin's, wich I've had to cook mpself on the sly in the boilin' water, wen Dolly Rumball was washin'."

"Ah!" ejaculated Dolly; "the peelings didn't taste very nice, I should say."

"Rather soapy, yer know, Dolly, in course, and jist a trifle too much flavor'd with sody. But has yer observed jist now, hit wor better than nothin, an' hif I hadn't bin kontented with that, I should a bin hobliged to go without. Wat hev yer got in yer pockets?"

Dolly, who was kneeling over the paper of scraps, silently put his hand into his right pocket, and then, instead of producing any of the contents, pulled a wry face, exclaiming—

"Oh—o-o-oh! I say, Joey, here's a go! Ain't I got into a mess!"

"Wat is it, Dolly?" asked Joey, much interested. "Hegs?"

"You've jist guessed it, Joey—four on 'em all to smash!"

"Biled?"

"No—raw!"

"Oh, lor! That's hunfortnit, that is, for Kupid, an' orful huncomfert'ble fur yer. Never mind, Dolly, bring hout the shells an' mix hin, 'e won't mind hif 'e's peckish. Turn yer pocket hinsidehoutard. Thet's hit," added Joey, as Dolly, after diving his hands into the mass of broken shells and slimy yolks and white, in rather a gingerly manner, as though the process was altogether disagreeable, did as Joey had suggested. "Squeedge the pocket now, it'll hall 'elp."

With this advice Dolly complied, returned the pocket—nicely "squeedged"—wiped his hand on the rear part of his trousers, and then essayed to empty the left-hand pocket.

"I expect this is almost as bad, Joey," observed Dolly. "Yes—I'm blest if it ain't!"

"Wat are hit? Bread?"

"No—potatoes."

"Taters?"

"Yes, and all to a smash," said Dolly, pulling forth a handful, and squeezing it till it oozed between his fingers like so much paste. "It don't look very nice, does it?"

"The taste's the thin' to go by, Dolly, I hexpect hit's better than hit looks. I don't suppose Koopid 'll hobjec. Hin with hit."

This, after three or four dives amongst the mashed potato, Dolly succeeded in doing, leaving only a thin crust, as an extra lining to his pocket, and then producing some salt and pepper, screwed in separate bits of paper, from his boots, added it to the collection of trifles, and then proposed to take the delicate and appetising refection to the no doubt starving Cupid.

"But there ain't no bread," observed Joey, "Wat's thet in the seat o' yer trousers?"

"Never mind now, Joey," returned Dolly, "You shall see presently. Come along. Take up the victuals."

"Stop a bit, Dolly," said Joey, without attempting to shift his position—a cross-legged one on the ground. "I've got somethin' to purpose, first."

"What is it, Joey?"

"Koopid are a 'brudder,' 's well 's a fren, ain't 'e?"

"Of course."

"Then I purposes has we shows hit by makin' of hourselves black. Hit'll be a delicate komplemen to Koopid, an' 'll please the Gen'ral too, I hexpect. Wat do yer say?"

"I think it's a capital idea, Joey," said Dolly. "And the General won't be so frightened to see all black faces about as he would half-and-half, if he comes to."

"Right yer are, Dolly," returned Joey, "Ere's the burnt cork," picking up some pieces that had been unused in the process of transforming the General—"Where's the matches? I'll do yer, and then yer can do me."

"What do you want matches for? Are we to singe each other?"

This was asked by Dolly in a tone as though he thought his friend and colleague were coming it rather too strong, and he gave his friend a look of unqualified admiration, as he replied—

"In coorse? Why, has we ain't got no wigs, mus'n't we look has much like niggers has we can?"

"Oh, all right," returned Dolly. "I'm not particular. I don't suppose it'll hurt much—only, if I'd known it. I would have brought a pair of scissors."

"That wouldn't do, Dolly, that wouldn't," returned Joey; "scissors 'ud cut too close, an' wouldn't look nattral. It's the short, kerly wool has we wants ter himertate, an' nothin' 'll do that better than the singein'. Yer can hoperate hon me fust. Go a'ead."

The process of blacking and singeing then commenced by Dolly taking the initiative, and, in less than a minute, Joey's locks were in a blaze behind.

"Oh, lor, how it does flare up!" cried Dolly "What——"

"Blow hit hout, quick!" exclaimed Joey "Oh, lor! Oh, dear?"

It happened, however, that this was more easily said than done.

Alarmed at Joey's energetic cries, Dolly puffed and puffed away, but the blaze was obstinate.

"It won't go out!" cried Dolly, who was half-smothered with the smoke that arose. "What have you been doing to your hair?—it crackles and smells just like fried fish!"

Puff—puff—puff, from Dolly.

But it was no go.

The flame and smoke only seemed to increase in power and density, and had not Joey, who could stand the pain no longer, rolled on the ground and, by means of his hands and "bowler" succeeded in putting out the conflagration, not only his hair, but his scalp would have been nicely frizzled.

In spite of the pain which he saw his bosom chum was suffering, and which ought to have elicited his sympathy, so curious were Joey's movements as he rolled and wriggled on the ground, and fought to put out the blaze, that Dolly was nearly convulsed with laughter, and as Joey sat up rubbing his poll, with a rueful countenance, Dolly could scarcely articulate.

"Wha—ha, ha!—what is the mat—he, he, he!—ter with your ha—ho—ho—o—ah—a—h!—hair, Jo—o—ey?"

"Why," returned Joey, looking up with a half-grin on his face. "It's drippin'!"

"Dr—dr—dripping!" yelled Dolly.

"Ye—ye—yes," said Joey, beginning to be affected with Dolly's emotion. "Thinkin' has I'd make my 'air look smart an' glossy, I prigged some o' Dolly Rumball's drippin' has she fried the blessid pancakes with, an' rubbed hit hon—oh, lor! o—o—oh—dear—I be orf agin!"

To describe the excess of laughter which here followed, and the awful state of limpness to which our little friends were reduced would be impossible.

CHAPTER XXXVIII.

WHERE DOLLY FOUND CUPID, AND WHERE DOLLY AFTERWARDS FOUND HIMSELF.

SOME time elapsed before either Dolly or Joey was in a condition to perform or submit to the process of singeing; nor would Joey present his poll to undergo the finishing touches until he had taken the precaution of rubbing away as much of the dripping, by the aid of grass and geraniums, as he could.

The operation was successfully performed, however, at length, and then, being perfectly satisfied with their appearance, they prepared to enter the magazine, to the relief of their friends.

This was effected without much difficulty.

The key had been hidden by the Sergeant amongst the geraniums, and, as the locality was known to Dolly, he soon found it; and, after a few vigorous pulls, the heavy door yielded and they passed in, closing the door behind them.

"Hit's jolly dark, ain't it?" said Joey. "Hev yer got the candle, Dolly?"

"Of course," replied Dolly; "I've got a bit in my jacket-pocket. Just light a match while I get it out."

After some fumbling, the candle was lighted, and Dolly, holding it up, looked around for the occupants.

The first object that met their gaze was the General, occupying the same position in which he had been placed some hours before—seated with his back against the rocky wall.

"'E ain't moved a hinch," said Joey, as Dolly held the candle as close to the veil as he could without setting it on fire; "an' 'e's has hunken-shus has a noo-born'd nigger baby hoff whur 'e his. 'E little knows 'ow pretty 'e looks!"

"He's fast asleep, I think," said Dolly. "He's breathing precious hard."

"Never mind 'im, Dolly," returned Joey; "where's Koopid?"

This question was asked by Joey, because, although his eyes had roamed around the magazine, not the least sign could he discern of his negro friend.

Cupid was nowhere visible.

The magazine was not large—about four yards square.

Two sides—one on the right hand, and one facing the door—were fixed up with racks, divided into compartments like huge pigeon-holes.

In each of these holes was a large flannel cartridge, being the charge for the gun outside, and weighing fifty six pounds.

With so many powder-beds confined in so narrow a space, a lighted candle was not exactly the thing to explore it with.

But our young friends had no though of the danger which was so near at hand, or, if they had it did not trouble them.

They set about their search for Cupid, as though the powder were not made to explode and blow such little carcasses as theirs to "impalpable atoms."

Joey, who carried the candle—Dolly carrying the grub—held the flame close to the immense powder cartridges, peering in the triangular corners of the pigeon-holes (the cartridges were round, and the holes square), as though he expected to find Cupid crammed into one of the small spaces, which were hardly large enough to accommodate a sixpenny doll.

"I can't think whur 'e's got to," observed Joey, as he peered about unsuccessfully. "I wonder hif 'e's made hisself hup inter one o' them cartridges! I'd blow him hup if I know'd wich un!"

"Climb on the top of the racks, Joey," said Dolly. "He must be here somewhere, unless he's made his escape through the key-hole."

To accomplish this, Joey stuck the candle in one of the corners of a pigeon-hole, and prepared to climb.

As he was in the act of mounting, a black head, with a pair of staring eye-balls, appeared over the top of the rack, and a voice, which told of extreme terror on the part of the owner, said—

"Bress ma soul! Who de debbel 'um you?"

"Hullo!" exclaimed Joey. "Ham dat you, Koopid? 'Ow de debbil you get hup dar hin de dark—ugh?"

Here Joey put his hands akimbo on his hips, and made a comical grin, by opening his eyes and showing his teeth, as he had seen the street-niggers do, at the same time throwing back his head to obtain a good glance at the sable object of his address.

"'Ow de debbil you tink 'um get up? Tink Cupid no got 'ans and feet—ugh?"

"Bress hif dis nigger know 'ow you got hup,'

replied Joey; "but 'um tink yah better kum down."

And Cupid did come down with a vengeance.

Before Joey could finish his sentence, he experienced a feeling as though he had been struck blind and his neck broken, and to his bewilderment he found himself on the floor of the magazine, with a vague idea that the roof had fallen in on his head.

The next moment, however, he felt himself relieved of the pressure, and, on opening his eyes, he saw Cupid standing with the candle held at arm's length, staring at the cartridge with a horrified countenance and trembling in every limb.

"Wot's hit hall about?" said Joey, sitting up and addressing the frightened Cupid in a grumbling tone. "Wot did yer cum down hon a feller like as that fur—eh?"

"Ho—o—o—h! Dis drefful dam putty ting! muttered Cupid, with chattering teeth. "Lub de Lord, in nudder min't 'um all bin blow to de debbil!"

"Wot do yer mean?" said Joey, sharply.

"Look dar whar 'um candle burn de big powder-bag?" returned Cupid, pointing to a black spot on the flannel of the cartridge, against which Joey had fixed his candle.

"Well, but yer needn't a cum down on a feller's nut like as that," said Joey. "Why didn't yer sing hout as the blessid thing was ketchin' fire?"

"Lub de Lord—Cupid too berry much frighten!—'um no want be blow to de debbil jis yet—ugh?"

"It's all right, Cupid," said Dolly, who until this moment had been too much overcome with laughter to speak. "We're Joey Pumps and Dolly Swaps, come with grub for you. Come and pitch into it. There's no danger now."

So great, however, was the shock that Cupid had received that several minutes elapsed before he was calm enough to listen to the explanation of the cause of the presence of his friends, and smack his lips over the anticipated luxurious repast they had prepared for him.

The repast in question, however savoury it might really be, was, as the reader knows, not very inviting to the eye.

But Cupid was hungry from long fasting, and no sooner had the paper been spread open on the floor, and the contents revealed, than he commenced operations by fishing up piece after piece and popping it in his capacious mouth at a rate that called forth the silent admiration of his gratified entertainers, who expressed their appreciation of the scene by sundry gestures of the hands, winks, elevations of the eyebrows, and other signs too numerous to mention.

More than once the faces of Dolly and Joey exhibited looks of alarm as the starving Cupid appeared to be on the point of choking from a too rapid loading of his black muzzle.

Happily, however, he got through the process without any serious injury, and, having cleared the lot, even to the last scraping of mashed potato, Cupid, for the first time, looked up with a broad grin, saying—

"Bress de lord fo' dat grub. 'Pose Cupid um starve, you no brin' um suffin' to eat. He, he, he!"

"Could you eat any more, Cupid?" asked Dolly.

"'Pose um eat blessed lot, mo hif um hab it, but wha um cum from—egh?"

Without reply, and with great gravity, Dolly rose to his feet, and commenced a process that made Cupid open his eyes. and sent Joey Pumps into a fit of limpness.

What this process was we must leave to the imagination of the reader—a process he will have no difficulty of mentally conceiving when we mention that Dolly's motions and manipulations were all directed towards removing something from the seat of his trousers, which something, when brought to light, proved to be half a two pound loaf of bread, and which, having been popped in its hiding-place almost as soon as it had left the baker's oven, was considerably compressed, and as heavy as lead.

This piece of preserved bread Dolly smilingly held out to Cupid, saying—

"There you are, old fellow. It's brand new, and almost as hot as when it left the oven. What do you turn up your nose for?"

This question was called forth from a look of disgust, which showed itself pretty plainly on Cupid's face, as Dolly stood presenting the tempting morsel.

The fact is, that although a nigger, and he had a pretty strong stomach, as he had just manifested, there was a point at which Cupid's internals were capable of feeling a slight degree of sensitiveness.

This point had been reached on the offer of Dolly's new bread.

Not that, although it had been compressed into a heavy, indigestible lump, it was objectionable to Cupid on that account; but he did not at all approve of the place where Dolly had concealed it.

So Cupid replied, whilst eyeing the bread with a look of disgust on his expressive face—

"Cupid berry 'ungry, but um no eat bread um take hout ob de back hob um trousers."

This reply, with the look of disgust which accompanied it, so tickled Dolly's fancy that, first dropping the bread, he next dropped himself, and in a short time had become as limp as Joey.

As Cupid could never look on gravely, where laughing was going on, he soon forgot his disgust, and joined in, making the magazine echo again with his chuckles.

And now followed some proceedings which, but for a timely interference, might have ended if not in actually blowing the rock itself into the Mediterranean, at least in blowing a considerable piece into its blue waters, and certainly annihilating the three imps with General Shoot.

But these proceedings deserve another chapter.

CHAPTER XXXIX.

MORE PROCEEDINGS OF THE THREE LITTLE IMPS—A STRANGE "WALK ROUND"—GENERAL SHOOT'S TERRIBLE AWAKENING.

DOLLY, Joey, and Cupid were three restless beings, who were never happy or satisfied unless they were engaged in some exciting proceedings.

They would no more have been content to sit down and suck their thumbs, as some boys are, than are birds content at being confined in cages.

The interior of the magazine was not a particularly lively place—on the contrary, it was a particularly dull, grim, and gloomy place.

It had not been constructed with the view of providing amusement for Dolly, Joey, and Cupid, and so those little individuals set about creating amusement for themselves.

And Joey Pumps hit upon a grand idea.

After the outburst caused by the bread incident, the excitement had flagged until Joey started his idea.

"This'll never do, this won't," observed Joey. "The cannel'll be hout soon, an' we shall be lef' in the dark. I purposes has we makes cannels nef hour hone."

"How, Joey?" asked Dolly.

"By makin' a lot o' devils, an' wen won goes hout ter light anuther. See, Dolly?"

"First rate!" cried Dolly. "There's plenty of powder!"

"Wha' 'um call debbils?" asked Cupid.

"We'll soon show yer," replied Joey. "'Elp this covy git hout won 'o them bags, Dolly. That's the style!" added Joey, as, after some hard tugging, he and Dolly succeeded in pulling one out of its pigeon-hole and standing it upright against the rack.

"Now fur a jolly big un ter begin with."

But we must contemplate the process of "devil"-making through the medium of General Shoot's eyes, as that individual saw it in a light that rendered the process particularly thrilling and awe-inspiring.

The General, it will be remembered, was placed in the magazine in a state of unconsciousness brought about by the contact, under peculiar circumstances, of Mrs. Rumball's body on his head.

The General had been unconscious during the ceremony of transforming his person into the similitude of a female of the African race, and up to the present moment he had remained unconscious of this peculiar alteration in his outward man, and of the elegant attitude in which he had passed the night—so great had been the shock to his brain.

But the moment was at hand when he was to be restored to sensibility, slowly, as it proved, but surely and impressively.

Like one recovering from a trance, the General's eyes slowly opened—opened upon a misty light of a faint, flickering character, that rendered objects around him indistinct and confused, yet presenting certain outlines that were very curious to look upon, and which afforded ample scope for mental speculation.

The first object that became palpable, after a minute's stare, was the flame of the candle, but burning as though it were in a fog.

Close upon this became visible moving shadows which, though lighted up by the dim rays of the candle, appeared to be ridiculous forms of human beings—ridiculous from being black as coal and lacking the human features.

These figures, in the General's eyes, seemed like nude persons, yet possessing neither eyes, nose, nor mouth, busily engaged at some work over which they were bending—the light of the candle casting their moving shadows on the walls and roof.

The reader will understand that these phenomena were simply caused by the semi-transparent fabric of the veil through which the General was gazing, and which, whilst it served to partly conceal the General's elegant make-up, rendered the movements of Dolly, Joey, and Cupid misty and mysterious.

These movements were unaccompanied by any palpable noises, for the simple reason that the three imps were too busy in giving subsistence and form to little "devils," by dipping out from the cartridge the powder, a handful at a time, mixing it into adhesive consistency with large supplies of spittle, and then adding them to the body of the big "devil."

The General continued to look and listen, but nothing could he see beyond the misty, shadowy forms, and nothing could he hear but hard breathing, and short sounds as of persons spitting at a tremendous rate.

The General could not, however, connect these sounds with any special source—he heard something, but what he knew not.

"This seems very strange," thought the General when he had looked and looked again, and listened for several minutes. There must be something the matter with my eyes or else I must be asleep."

Here the General mechanically raised his hand to test the state of his vision by rubbing his eyes, but stopped short gazing at them in astonishment.

"Bless my soul!" he murmured. "What's this? My hands seem black as pitch! And what's this on my arms?"

The General's eyes had fallen upon the pillow-slip sleeves of the gaudily-flowered cotton gown.

"What the deuce has happened now? Let me collect myself. Where was I——?"

Before he could finish the query, the General's eye fell upon the shawl which covered part of his arms, and in elevating the latter to make sure that he was not really dreaming, the ample and graceful proportions of the body and skirt of the gown became fully revealed.

All this seemed plain enough, and yet everything was misty only a few inches beyond his nose.

"God bless me!" he muttered, breaking into a profuse perspiration, as a dreadful thought rushed into his mind—"I—I—I'm not really mad? Is this singular costume real? or is it the fantastic creation of a distorted brain?"

At this moment the General felt an itching sensation on his upper lip, and putting up his hand to rub it, his fingers came against something rough and stubbly—not unlike the surface of rough sand-paper.

"Good Heavens! what in the world's the matter with my lip? Why—why—yes!—so help me Heaven, it is! My moustache is gone! *Where* in the devil am I? *What* in the devil's name has happened? I *must* be mad!—and this extraordinary transformation is all fancy! I have heard of mad people imagining the most extraordinary things about themselves. One, I remember, used to fancy he had been decapitated by Saladin himself at the time of the Crusades, and was condemned to carry his own head perpetually under his arm. They gave him a football with a face painted on it to carry out the idea, and in moments of forgetfulness he used to kick it about. There is something the matter with *my* head, I do believe!"

The General felt the pressure of the nigger's wig and turban, but apart from that he felt a pricking sensation all over the scalp—the pressure of the wig on the singed bristles of his own luxuriant locks.

Naturally he essayed to allay the irritation by rubbing or scratching, when his fingers came into contact with the folds of the turban, and with a fresh fear at his heart, he began feeling the change that had taken place in the shape of his head.

"This is most extraordinary!" murmured the General. "Is it fancy or is it reality? My head seems to have increased to double the size it was! Dear me—what's that?"

This question was elicited by the General's fingers coming into contact with the bristles of the nigger's wig, and he received an answer to his question much quicker than he anticipated.

The General had no sooner felt the prickly wig than, like one whose hand had suddenly come in contact with the hot handle of a poker, he withdrew his fingers hastily, and, in so doing, pulled off the wig and turban.

His look of astonishment, as his gaze fell upon these articles of head-gear, was profoundly great.

"Bless my soul!" he murmured again. "This is getting more and more extraordinary! Why, this looks like a negro's hair and a turban, as I have seen the native dress in the East. I am afraid this is getting unexplainable except on the hypothesis that I'm gone off my "nut," as a state of madness is vulgarly termed. Yes, that must be it " shaking his head sadly. "I've gone cracked—there's no doubt of it!—I'm as cracked as a piece of old china! How strange that my delusion should take this shape! Fancy me imagining that—that I am dressed in a gaudily-flowered cotton gown, a loud patterned shawl, with a negro's hair and turban—movable, too, that's the best of it! Me—who have always had such a hatred of the negro race!"

The General, profoundly astonished—hopelessly bewildered—sat for a minute contemplating the wig and turban, as they lay in his lap.

"The delusion's perfect," he murmured. "My hands are—or seem so—black as any negro's, and I dare say my face is the same. Yes—I thought so! Black as jet!" he added, squinting in such a manner as enabled him to catch a glimpse of his nose. "Well, it's no use—"

The General's sentence was nipped in its formation by a sudden shout, the first distinct noise that had reached his ears, and which caused him not only to start and prick up his ears, but to palpitate violently at the heart—a palpitation that increased as he listened to sounds which for a time led him to imagine that he was not only "cracked," but was "cracked," and in the "lower regions!"

The sounds that produced this state of body and mind were as follows :—

"Hoo-a-roar! Brayvo—thet's a jolly devil, thet is!"

"Won't he flare up, hey?"

"Ray-ther!"

"Pose 'um put um goin'—ugh?"

"Pose 'um do, Koopid—ugh? Pose we sets hit agoin' an' haves a dance roun' hit—ugh?"

"Pose um do? Cupid dance like de berry debbil! He-ah! He-ah!"

"We'll hev 'a walk round." I'll make a jolly un, an' yer kin boff jine hin the korus."

"That will be jolly fun, that will!"

Here fell a sudden silence, followed by total darkness.

The candle had been blown out, and the General, in the place of the flame, could see a bright spark moving about like a glow-worm on the move. It was the glowing wick of the candle.

Watching intently, suddenly a bright light sprang up, followed by a peculiar hissing noise, and numerous sparks, radiating from a centre, and falling in graceful showers around, developed before the General's gaze.

This was followed by a sudden movement on the part of the three figures—dim-looking still, for the General was still under the veil—and a voice saying—

"Now, then, for the walk round. That 'eer devil'll fiz fur I dono 'ow long. Mind, I'll sing the hair and yer two'll holler the korus. Hoff we goes, yer niggers!"

And stamping and capering, and making the most awful grimaces, the three started, going round and round the flaring "devil," singing—

"Darkies, 'eer's a debbil hob a go!
[" Korus! "]
Ho! Ho! Yah! Yah!
Ho! Ho! Yah! Yah!
"De debbil burn fur de nigger, ho!
[Hall tergedder! "]
Bah! Bah! Yah! Yah!
Bah! Bah! Yah! Yah!
"'Eer we goes hall roun' about!
[" Shout yer niggers! "]
Ma! Ma! Yah! Yah!
Ma! Ma! Yah! Yah!
"'Eer we goes, like debbils shout!
[" Hout wid de korus! "]
Goo! Goo! Yah! Yah!
Goo! Goo! Yah! Yah!
"See dat nigger ober dare!
[" Rattle 'um out! "]
Ho! Ho! Yah! Yah!
Ho! Ho! Yah! Yah!
"See um squat without 'um 'ar!
[" Louder dis time! "]
"Boo! Boo! Yah! Yah!
"Boo! Boo! Yah! Yah!
"Dat nigger um wunce a gen'ral bold!
[" Now den fur hit! "]
He! He! Ho! Ho! Yah! Yah!
He! He! Ho! Ho! Yah! Yah!
"Now um loss um wool, um catch um cold!
[" Louder than hebber! "]
Bow! Wow! Yah! Yah!
Bow! Wow! Yah! Yah!
"Hoh, dat gen'ral we orful sell!
[" Debbil hob a row dis time! "]
Ho! Ho! Yah! Yah!
Ho! Ho! Yah! Yah!
"Hif de debbil ketch um 'e'll make um yell!
[" Mor debbil hob a row dan hebber! "]
He! He! Yah! Yah!
He! He! Yah! Yah!

Never before was a "walk-round" performed under such peculiar circumstances.

The din created by the singing, and stamping, and shouting of the "ko-rus," was deafening; whilst each moment the light from the burning "devil" increased in intensity, until all around seemed like a fiery furnace.

The smoke, too, began to fill the place, and, as it reached the General's nose, he exclaimed—

"Powder! Good Heavens!—where am I? Surely the infernal regions can't be worse than this! Pooh! I'm being smothered!"

So dense had now become the smoke, that the General could indeed scarcely breathe.

With an effort he rose to his feet, and, in flinging his arms wildly about, displaced the veil.

Gracious Heavens! what a terrifying sight was that, that was suddenly revealed!

Still singing, dancing, and yelling, in spite of the fast-thickening smoke, were three imps, as black as night, going round, what seemed, a miniature volcano.

"Volcano!"

Infinitely more terrible was that hissing, fiery-like fountain!

But a moment it took the General to see where he was, and comprehend the awful character of the danger which threatened his existence.

With a glance, almost as quick as the lightning's flash, he saw the great flannel bags reposing in their pigeon-holes—each bag a sleeping mine!

In the centre of the floor burnt and hissed away, the mountain of powder—the infernal place all aglow with the weird glare, and the sparks shooting upwards, and then falling gracefully to the floor, like myriads of fire-flies!

Imagine this awful fountain of fire, each moment increasing in power, as the base of ignition became broader, sending forth its fiery stream, and throwing off its sparkling meteors in dangerous proximity to the cartridge-loaded racks,—imagine this, and you will guage the nature of the General's feelings, as, with almost paralyzed limbs—his brain seemingly dead, yet fully impressed with the awfulness of the situation—he groped his way to the door, and sought to free himself.

An age seemed to pass as he felt for the bolt—yet it was only a moment.

A moment and the door flew open—outwards.

Another moment revealed to him several forms.

One of these—a man—he recognised, stretched forth his arms, and fainted.

The persons whose arrival was so opportune were Sergeant O'Shehe, Dick Everett, Tom Sheppard, Bob Jones and Harry Smith.

The immediate cause of their presence at so early an hour of the day will be explained presently; and indeed we must leave them whilst they are setting matters with the General, and introduce the reader to new scenes, but which had a most important bearing upon the events of our story.

CHAPTER XL.

A CHAPTER CONTAINING FOUR SCENES.

SCENE I.

[A bedroom in the Governor's palace. Present: the Governor in dressing-gown and slippers, and Simon the Jew. Time: half-an-hour after morning gun-fire.]

GOVERNOR [speaking indignantly and looking at Simon as though he could annihilate him].—"What's that, you old rascal? My sister going to elope disguised as a negress? Why, you must be mad!"

SIMON [stretching forth his hands, elevating his shoulders, and speaking energetically].—"S'help mine Got, itsh true, Shir Shentle! I swearsh it by the blessed book of Mosesh. Mish Shulia hash arranshed to pash through the gatsh dish bleshed night mit Cupidsh to shoin de Don at ɷe Spanish linsh."

GOVERNOR [somewhat shaken by Simon's

earnest manner].—"It can't be true. Where did you get your information?"

SIMON [assuming more confidence from the Governor's manner].—"I did get it from Cupidsh, Shir Shentle. He come to my shopsh dish blessed night and took away de dishguise, he did, s'help me! What for you tink me come hif it no true, Shir Shentle? Itsh true, s'help me! and I tink only of de dishgrace."

GOVERNOR [much impressed with the Jew's manner and fair way of reasoning, perambulates the room in great agitation, and then, suddenly seizing Simon by the collar, drags him from the room, saying]: "Come with me. I'll confront you with my sister! If she denies it, as I feel convinced she will, by Jove, I'll hang you!"

SCENE II.

[Miss Julia Sharpset's bedroom.—Julia, a fat, plain-looking lady of fifty, is seated in dressing-wrapper before a glass, having her grey locks brushed by a negro girl, Lilly].

JULIA [a cross look on her face].—"What can have become of that brother of yours, Lilly? I'm afraid he'll ruin all by his foolish tricks. If he does I'll—I'll—skin him alive, I will!"

LILLY [making a grimace unseen behind Miss Julia's head].—"An' serb um right too, Missy Julia. Cupid de biggest little fool as hebber wos, he spoil de fun——"

[Interruption.—Enter Sir Gentle Sharpset, looking much excited, and dragging Simon by the collar. Approaches Miss Julia.]

GOVERNOR [panting from his exertion].—"Julia, this fellow informs me that you intend passing the gates this evening, in the disguise of a benighted negress, to join that infernal Spanish Don. Is that true?"

JULIA [very savagely and very red in the face].—"True? Certainly not! Simon's a liar. Oh, you bad, wicked old Jew! I'll tear you to pieces!"

[Tableaux:—Julia rushes on the old Jew, begins to pulls his hair and excoriate his face, whilst Sir Gentle begins to haul him from the room, making frequent and energetic use of his right foot and knee to the Jew's hinder part. Lilly looking on in a state of exuberant delight.]

Result:—Old Simon, much torn, battered, and bruised, is ejected from the palace, considering himself an old fool for his pains, and wishing he had let the matter alone.

[Final Scene in Julia's Bed-room.]

GOVERNOR [breathing heavily from his exertions].—"The old villain, that will teach him to come here with such a ridiculous tale as that! It is not true, Julia—eh?"

JULIA [reproachfully].—"Gentle—what do you take me for? To ask such a question!"

GOVERNOR [waving his hand].—"Your reproach is deserved, Julia. I ought not to have asked such an absurd question. I beg your pardon. Where's Cupid?"

JULIA [taken aback at the question, and showing more agitation than she had shown before].—"Cu-Cu-Cupid. I'm sure I-I-don't know. Why do you ask?"

GOVERNOR.—"The black scamp did not bring my hot water at gun-fire this morning. That's all."

JULIA.—"The lazy fellow!"

[Exit the Governor, suddenly struck with the

coincidence of his sister's agitation at the mention of Cupid's absence, and the story of old Simon of Cupid's presence at his shop during the night.]

Result:—Resolves to hunt up Cupid, and keep an eye upon his sister's movements.

SCENE III.

[Governor's bedroom on the Governor's return from his interview with his sister. Is in the act of commencing his toilet, when a knock is given at the door, and on a summons to enter, an aide-de-camp makes his appearance in a flurry.]

AIDE-DE-CAMP.—"Beg pardon, Sir Gentle, for appearing at so early an hour, but I have just been informed that Don Silvia de Diabolo has escaped."

GOVERNOR [aghast].—"What? That villain escaped?"

AIDE-DE-CAMP.—"Yes, and by your orders, so I'm told."

GOVERNOR [thunderstruck].—"By my order? What are you talking about, for Heaven's sake?"

Here the Aide-de-Camp, without replying, steps back to the door, put out his hand and says—

"Step this way, Corporal O'Doo."

Enter the Corporal, holding a paper in his hand, anc coming to attention, salutes the Governor, and remains stationery.

Now the Aide-de-Camp takes the paper, and presents it to the astonished Governor.

It was the letter written by Dick, ordering the connivance of the corporal of the guard to the release of the mad people.

Governor reads—feeling like a man in a dream —and then exclaims:

"Good Heavens! This is not my writing! This is a forgery, and "addressing the frightened Corporal, "You acted upon this?"

CORPORAL O'DOO.—"Yi—Yi—Yis, Gin'ral."

GOVERNOR [hastily].—"Who brought it to you?"

CORPORAL.—"Wan o' the yang sodger buoys, sir. The wan as took the letter from the madman as called himself a Gin'ral."

The Governor and the Aide-de-Camp looked at each other at this news. The former spoke.

"There is something wrong here, Captain Richards."

AIDE-DE-CAMP.—"Evidently, Sir Gentle: This letter has been forged by the boy who delivered that letter from that diabolical criminal to your Excellency at the banquet last night."

GOVERNOR.—"And how do we know that that infernal letter was not a forgery?"

AIDE-DE-CAMP [shrugging his shoulder].—"I should not be surprised, your Excellency. Had I not better have the escaped men captured, and the boy arrested?"

GOVERNOR.—"Certainly, certainly! Good Heavens! Yes. Have the whole Castle and town searched! away!"

[Exit AIDE-DE-CAMP and Corporal O'Doo to hunt up the escaped criminal.]

It was this that had caused the Sergeant, Dick, and those who had taken an active part in the escape, to qake fflight and rtsh to the magazine for concealment. As will be imagined, they were considerably alarmed at the state of affairs, brought about by the agency of the three imps, but, after a time, they succeeded in extinguishing the "devil," and restoring things to order. Great difficulty, however, was experienced in inducing the General to consent to carry out the programme for his escapr through the Spanish lines. This way accomplished at length, by working upon his fears, persuading him that it was only a temporary necessity, and reducing him to passive indifference by sundry doses of brandy, procured by Cupid, who was the only one who could venture to show himself. The search proved abortive.

SCENE IV.

[Time.—An hour before evening gun-fire. Place.—An inner guardroom of one of the forts of the Spanish Lines. Present.—Senor Don Juan de la Vega Grey de los Brabones, perambulating the room, engaged in conversing with an attendant. The latter just entered. Conversation translated into English.]

DON.—"Ah, Pepe!—what news?"

PEPE.—"Good, Senor. The English lady is readp."

DON.—"Haye you seen the lady yet, Pepe?"

PEPE.—"Senor—I have. The lady is now in the magazine, fully disguised as a negress."

DON.—"The magazine."

PEPE.—"The magazinr behind the gun. The lady has been ill at the thought of such a dreadful disguise. Much brandy she has taken to restore her."

DON.—"Ah, that's good! The more brandy the better! The lady will be fit to come?"

PEPE.—"Quite. The lady is now on the move, attended by the boy Cupid."

DON.—"Then see that the lady passes the Lines in safety, and have her conducted hither."

[Exit Pepe.]

From the foregoing scencs the reader will have no difficulty in divining the course of events.

The object of the old Jew—Simon—had in so artfully worming out the purpose for which Cupid wanted so singular a disguise, was to make the best use of it he could with a view to pecuniary reward.

The reward he received has been duly recorded.

The result of this information was to put the lady—Miss Julia—on her guard, and so postpone her elopement to a more favourable season, and she would have given due notice to her lover, the Senor Don Juan de la Vega Grey de los Brabones, but for one circumstance—the absence of Cupid.

What has become of her srusty messenger Miss Julia knew not; and she freely promised that young African an unlimited amount of cane.

Being unable to communicate with the Don, that faithful lover, of course, was faithful to his appointment and, as we have seen, was anxiously waiting the approach of his bride-elect.

The Governor, in spite of the energetic denial his sister had given the statement of the Jew, had had his suspicions aroused by his sister's manner, and the unaccountable absence of Cupid (whom he could not find), that all was not exactly as it should be, and he resolved to watch, with a party of soldiers, the gates of the Spanish lines, and pounce uopn the conspirators against the honour of his name.

For this purpose, he took up a post of observation behind the garden-hedge of a cottage, a short distance from the Lines, about an hour before evening gun-fire.

The Governor had a dozen soldiers with him —enough, he considered, to enable him to capture the Don, as well as the erring lady.

He had not taken up his position long when he was considerably surprised to see approach, in two and threes, the whole of the boys of the School of the Regiment, and lounge about tho pass into the Spanish Lines.

From their restless manner and eager way of talking it became evident to the Governor that there presence there was caused by something unusual.

"What can be the meaning of it ?" thought the Governor. "These boys are evidently expecting the appearance of someone or something. It's very strange !"

Our boys *were* there waiting the appearance of someone.

That someone was the General.

They had been made acquinted by Dick with what was going to happen, and had swarmed to the Lines to witness the fun.

Neither of the parties—the Governor, the Don, and the boys, had long to wait.

Scarcely half an hour had elapsed when a simultaneous shout from the boys announced the approach of the disguised General, accompanied by Cupid, the Sergeant, Dick, and the other boys, with Dolly Swaps and Joey Pumps walking in the rear, arm-in-arm.

Scarcely had they made their appearance when the Governor, greatly bewildered at the look of things, gave the signal, and in a few moments the concealed soldiers had leapt the hedge and surrounded them.

Utterly astounded at this unexpected move, Sergeant O'Shehe, giving vent to a despairing howl broke through through the cordon of soldiers and fled, whilst Dick and the others, seeing that the game was "up," ducked and dodged to escape, leaving the General in the hands of the soldiers.

The Governor, scarcely understanding what had happened, gazed at the disguised figure before him, endeavouring to trace in its black face the familiar lineaments of his sister.

Failing to do this, he was about to address the General, when he was checked by the figure suddenly exclaiming—

"Hurray ! Gen'l Shoo for ever ! Who cares? Hurray !"

"Bless my soul !" exclaimed the Governor, "This is the escaped prisoner ! Take him back to the prison ! Stop," he added, as four of the soldiers, who had seized him, holding him belly downwards by the arms and legs, were moving off. "Stop ! Let me give the villain something for his trouble."

The next moment the Governor, who carried a stick in his hand, began belabouring the General's "right-about" at a rate that caused him to fairly roar with pain.

All this had not passed, however, without being observed by the Don, who, imagining that it was his lady-love who had been thus pounced upon by the Governor, and whose precious person he was so mercilessly chastising, became, naturally, greatly enraged, and being determined not to be thwarted, hastily summoned his party, together with all the soldiers composing the Line Guard, and rushed to the rescue.

The scene that followed was very exciting.

With a wild cry the Don pounced upon the Governor and hurled him many paces away, and then attacking the four soldiers who held his supposed struggling and yelling "love," succeeded in making them drop their captive.

What a moment of seraphic triumph was this !

With another wild cry—a cry of exultation—the Don seized the body of the General, threw it across his stalwart shoulders, and leaving his followers to cover his retreat, carried off his lovely prize to the protecting shelter of the Spanish Lines.

CHAPTER XLI.

THE CAMP IN THE CORK-WOOD—JEALOUSY AND REVENGE.

ABOUT seven miles from the Rock, and in Spanish territory, there is a wood of cork-trees, many miles in extent, and possessing scenery of the most picturesque and varied character.

Through this wood runs a broad river, on the left bank of which, beneath the branches of the fine old cork-trees, we come upon the School of the Regiment.

Our Boys are encamped, and the scene is a most pleasing one.

Pitched here and there—more with a view to effect than soldierlike order—are several white, bell-shaped tents, contrasting pleasantly with the deep green of the surrounding scenery.

It is mid-day.

The sun is pouring on the cork-tree forest its fiercest rays, but tho shade is cool and refreshing notwithstanding.

The boys are engaged in various ways.

Some are busily employed in polishing the buttons of their jackets, pipe-claying gloves and belts, and otherwise overhauling their uniforms and accoutrements.

One party—consisting of the latest joined—is being drilled by one of the senior boys, under the eagle-eyed glance of Sergeant O'Shehe, who is moving about with anything but a pleasant look on his face.

This may be accounted for from the fact that the Sergeant, owing to pressing circumstances, had no time to change his trousers, on the seat of which he was compelled to place the linen patch, before accompanying the school on the present expedition.

Standing apart, some distance from the rest, is a tent.

In front of this tent is a cooking apparatus, in the shape of a huge iron camp-kettle suspended from a tripod over a fire—the fireplace consisting of stones formed into a square, and fed with wood, the dry branches of the cork-trees.

In this camp-kettle is simmering the mid-day meal for the boys, which consists of soup concocted from salt meat and preserved vegetables.

This preparation is being superintended by Mrs. Rumball, who looks very red, hot, and greasy, and bad-tempered.

Near the cooking-apparatus to Joey Pumps, busily engaged, with shirt-sleeves tucked up, at a large tub, washing up plates and basins, and trying to make-believe that he very much likes the job.

Standing looking on at the interesting process, and enlivening it with pleasant conversation, is Dolly Swaps.

"Well, I must say, Joey," said Dolly, looking at his friend admiringly, "you do that sort of thing first-rate."

"Why, yer see, Swaps," returned Joey, who had arranged to address Dolly by his surname to prevent a possible clashing with the pet cognomen of Mrs. Rumball, "I ort ter be fust-class hat it, konsiderin' as I've bin hat it putty nigh hever since I wos born'd. I flatters myself has I kin wash an' dress chiny with any chap of my own size, hage, an' hexperance."

"So I should think, Joey," said Swaps. "How you get the grease off in cold water, I can't think. I couldn't do it."

"Hit's hall practice, Swaps," returned Joey, "an' genus. I kin do more with cold water than a many can do with 'ot. I just dashes hin the basin—like as this—wobbles hit roun', hout's with hit, swish goes the dishclout, an' the thing's done!"

"But how do you get the polish on, Joey?" asked Swaps.

"Heasy has hanythink, that his. Wen the crockery's gone through the washin' and dryin', I piles 'em hup, an' then I takes my pocket-ankercher, takes 'em wun hat a time, breathes hon 'em, an' then works away. But hif the polish don't cum ter my satersfacshun, I just spits hon 'em a bit, an' thet does hit hat wonce. Thet was my hone hinwenshun that——"

Joey's speech was cut short by a dishclout lodging on his mouth, aimed unerringly by Mrs. Rumball.

"Come, I say, Dolly!" cried Joey, wiping his mouth with his bare arm. "Wot's thet fur, now?"

"Shet hup," returned Mrs. Rumball, savagely, "an' git hon with yer work. Wen do yer think as them plates an' basins'l git done? Git hon, do or I'll ketch yer hup an' duck yer hin the tub."

"I wos a gittin' hon, wasn't I?" retorted Joey. "Yer'd no bisness ter bring crockery inter camp. They don't hev chiny plates an' basins wen they goes ter war, I knows. Hit ort ter be tin crockery—Ah!—yer gettin savage, air yer!"

This remark was elicited from Joey by the unsuccessful flight of a wooden ladle, hurled with great force at his head by his impatient mistress.

"Sawage! I'll break hevery bone hin yer body, yer haggerawatin little himp, I will, hif yer don't shut hup!" shouted Mrs. Rumball. "Wot with yer cheek, and this 'ere camp bizness allers a cookin', with snakes an' mosa-keetos a frightenin' and bitin' one continual, hit's enuf to drive a body mad. Drat the lot of hit I ses, I wish as I hadn't lef' bootiful Devon!"

"Well, it's not my fault, I s'pose Dolly, are hit?" returned Joey. "I didn't want yer to leave bootiful Devon, did I? An' I'm not aware as I'm hans'erable for snakes and moss-kateers, am I? No toads, nor frogs ni-ther, has I knows hon. Nor bulls, I don't think. Nor——Ah!"

Joey had good reason for making this exclamation.

Mrs. Rumball, goaded beyond endurance by Joey's tantalising language, had made a sudden dash at him.

Joey, who was well skilled in the art of dodging, and was quite accustomed to such attacks as this, essayed to evade the threatened onslaught by slipping under Mrs. Rumball's upraised arm.

Joey, tripped, and fell at Mrs. Rumball's feet, and, the next moment, he felt himself seized by the seat of his trousers, and plumped into the tub of water, where he was dipped and rinsed about as though he were nothing better than a dirty rag, and, finally, flopped on the grass like a mere saturated sponge.

"Hit serves me right fur lettin' 'er ketch me, that does," said Joey, sitting up, and clearing his eyes of the greasy water. "I wos werry orkard to trip like thet. Fair's fair yer know, Swaps. Hif I hadn't tripped, Dolly would yer see, and bit's werry likely has she'd pitched inter the tub. That is jist 'ow we gits hon. Sometimes it's Dolly as gits the best on it, an' sometimes hit's me. I say, Swaps, 'eres the Sarjint a commin' fur 'is snack hout o' the kittle with Dolly."

This remark was accompanied by a wink, which, being returned by Swaps with a knowing grin, indicated that the circumstance was one of peculiar interest.

"I say, Swaps," continued Joey, yer'd better get clear, or yer'l be noweer wen the bust comes."

"You'd better get out of the way too, Joey," returned Swaps. "Or you will be in the same place, eh?"

"Oh, it wouldn't 'urt me now I'm wet, Swaps," replied Joey. "Besides, yer see, I wants to see 'ow they looks wen they goes up!"

"Take my advice, Joey, and get out of the way. Here's off at anyrate. I don't want to be scattered over the forest."

As Dolly uttered this, he turned his steps in the direction of a group of his companions, standing near a tree at the extremity of the camp.

This group consisted of Dick, Tom, Bob, and Harry, and a lot more, and Mr. Rumball.

The latter individual was resting with his shoulder against the tree, his arms folded across his breast, one leg crossed over the other, and a gloomy frown on his puffy face.

Mr. Rumball's attitude and facial expression denoted that his heart was filled with bitterness, and that he had arrived at a point of fierce resolve.

There was a dogged, determined look on his pallid face that was very shocking to contemplate.

What was the matter with Rumball?

What had occurred to transform his usually genial countenance into one worthy only of a fiend?

The fact is, Rumball was jealous of his Dolly and Sergeant O'Shehe.

So jealous, indeed, was Rumball that he had made up his mind to murder them both.

Not without mature deliberation had Rumball come to the conclusion that he was justified in sending those two mortals out of the world.

The offence was great and unpardonable.

This was the third day the School had been in camp, and for two days had Mrs. Rumball entertained the Sergeant at luncheon.

Two consecutive days had Dolly given Sergeant O'Shehe a basin of soup from the camp-kettle before dinner-time.

This, in itself, would not have constituted a very heinous offence, but for one circumstance that accompanied it, and had been patent to all the boys.

Dolly wouldn't allow Rumball to have a drop?

Rumball could not get a chance of even dipping in a spoon and licking it.

Indeed, when Rumball had approached on the second day with the resolve to have his share, Mrs. Rumball had licked him!—licked him over the head with the wooden ladle!

Rumball couldn't stand that!

Rumball *wouldn't* stand it!

He swore he wouldn't, and the boys called him a brick, and backed him on.

But Rumball was puzzled how to be revenged.

He couldn't challenge the bold and hated Sergeant to a duel with either pistols or swords. Rumball had never fired a pistol in his life, and he knew no more how to handle a sword than a goose.

He didn't consider it fair terms to fight with fists, as the Sergeant was nearly twice his size and his arms as long in proportion.

So Rumball was puzzled in what manner to take his revenge, until a plan was suggested by Dick.

"Look here, Rumball," said Dick, who had come upon the outraged little man, brooding alone in the dark recesses of the Cork-wood forest, "I know what's up with you, old fellow. You want to punish the Sergeant for stealing Mrs. Rumball's affections."

"I do!" replied Rumball, in a hoarse, hollow tone. "I *do!*"

"But you don't know how—eh?"

"I don't! I wish I did!"

"Then I can tell you, old boy."

"Then tell me, an' I'll hever bless yer."

"Wouldn't you like to punish them both?"

"Hif I thort has Dolly was has bad has the Sargint——"

"Why, of course she is," interrupted Dick. "Any woman that would give away our soup like that, must possess a shaky character——"

"Stop!" cried Rumball, stretching forth his arm, and shaking with agitation. "Do—do—do yer think has she—Dolly—hev gone furder then—then—*soup?*"

"Certainly, I do!" returned Dick, unhesitatingly. "Further than soup? Why, Rumball, where's your eyes? Why, didn't you see her, yesterday, put her arms round his neck and kiss him?"

"The false—the hindecent hussey!" cried Rumball. "She ain't fit ter live! I'd blow 'em both inter hatems, hif I could!" he exclaimed, fiercely.

"Then you shall," said Dick. "We'll blow them up at the very moment they are drinking the soup to-morrow. I'll tell you how we'll do it. To-night we'll dig a hole beneath the camp-fire, put a lot of powder in, and cover it up with earth. Then we must make a concealed train of powder from the fire to one of the trees, and, at the right moment, set it off, and up they'll go, soup and all. Won't that be a stunning revenge, eh, Rumball?"

Rumball thought it would be, and agreed to it.

That night, Dick and his chums prepared the mine

At the silent hour of midnight the hole was dug and filled with cartridges.

A train of cartridges, buried about two inches in the ground, was laid from the mine to the tree, against which the wretched-minded Rumball was now leaning—wretched in mind, not because his conscience smote him at the foul deed he contemplated, but wretched in thinking of the cause which necessitated the blowing up of his Dolly—the Dolly who had hitherto been heart-proof against the fascinations of the opposite sex.

After many trials and temptations, Dolly had fallen so low as not only to give away the boys' soup to a stuck-up Sergeant, but actually put her arms around the Sergeant's neck.

Rumball would rather have had a thousand pins stuck in himself, than that Dolly should have bestowed her favours on the Sergeant.

If Rumball, however, had felt any degree of compunction of conscience at that moment, at the thought of blowing up his Dolly, there were those at hand, whispering evil spirits, to inflame his mind, and work him up to the desired pitch.

"Look, Rumball," whispered Dick. "Look at Dolly actually squeezing the Sergeant's hand."

Rumball, with the lowering look deepening still more on his face—looked.

Mrs. Rumball's hand was close to the Sergeant's.

Rumball would not be sure that his Dolly was actually squeezing the Sergeant's hand—but, Dolly's hand was near the Sergeant's—there was no mistake about that!

That was quite enough for Rumball!

Dolly's hand had no business to be near any man's hand but his—Rumball's!

"Do you see, Rumball?" again whispers Dick.

"I do!" returned the wretched man, in a stage whisper.

"See how she smiles on him," said Dick, making a comical grimace at his chums.

The latter were nearly bursting with laughter.

Rumball could not speak for excess of jealous indignation, but breathed heavily, and his look was blacker than thunder.

Dick, though finding it hard work to keep calm, spoke again.

"She's taking awful care of him, Rumball. See, she's actually putting in some salt whilst he holds the basin!"

Then came other whispering voices to Rumball's ears.

"The brazen thing!"

"Shameless hussey!"

"Fancy her feeding him like that, and giving Rumball none!"

"It's too bad," here added Dick. "And, by Jove!—if she isn't actually tasting it for him! I didn't think it had gone so far as that!"

This was the "last straw."

Rumball could endure no more.

"Give me the light!" he said, with stern determination.

Dick put a piece of touch-paper in his hand, saying—

"There you are, Rumball. Here's the train," pointing to a piece of blue paper, the tag of a cartridge, which showed through the ground. "Quick!"

Rumball cast a final glance at the guilty pair.

They were smiling at each other, and looking as jolly as possible.

The next moment Rumball applied the match, folded his arms, leaned against the tree, and, with a melo-dramatic glance at the victims of his just revenge, awaited the result.

The result was something terrific.

A few moments of hushed expectation followed.

Then there ran along the ground a stream of fire.

Rumball never even shut his eyes.

Suddenly there was a loud explosion; the air became darkened by scattered pieces; the scattered pieces began to fall around.

At Rumball's feet fell two heavy bodies—plump—plump.

Rumball, startled, cast his eyes on the ground and there—what did he see?

Good Heavens!—Two heads!

One was his Dolly's; for the huge cap and border graced the decapitated head still.

The other was the Sergeant's, with the forage-cap still on, and the face black with gunpowder.

Rumball's face turned deathly white, and an indescribable fear fell upon his heart as, paralysed with horror, he gazed upon the ghostly objects.

Then a voice broke the dreadful charm.

"Rumball, you've done it now, and no mistake! You've committed a double murder! You'd better cut!"

Mr. Rumball awoke to the full enormity of the crime he had committed, and, casting around a fear-filled glance, he disappeared in the depths of the forest.

CHAPTER XLII.

DESCRIBES WHAT FOLLOWS THE BLOWING-UP OF MRS. RUMBALL AND THE SERGEANT—HOW THE FORMER " BLEW UP " THE LATTER, AND HOW THE LATTER TURNED A WONDERFUL SOMERSAULT.

RUMBALL fled, and had no sooner got to a safe distance than Dick and his chums gave way to their pent-up laughter.

Had Rumball known that he himself had been really victimised, the dread that filled his soul, and gave extra impetus to his legs, would have changed to indignation against those who had imposed upon him.

If Rumball had not been so intent upon watching the soup flirtation between his Dolly and the Sergeant, and had glanced into the branches of the tree against which he was leaning, he would have seen, most likely, a couple of heads, the fac-similes of those the objects of his jealousy.

These heads had been manufactured and finished off by Dick, with the aid of Dolly Swaps and Joey Pumps.

The get-up was very simply accomplished.

Some white shirts had first been rolled up into a couple of bundles to the size of human heads.

This had been done by Dick, and then he had enlisted the services of Swaps and Joey.

To Swaps had been intrusted the duty of slily procuring one of the Sergeant's forage-caps.

The genial task of purloining one of Mrs. Rumball's voluminous caps had been assigned to Joey.

Each had performed his task most successfully, and then the bundles had soon been transformed, by the aid of burnt wood and blacking, into tolerable fac-similes of Mrs. Rumball's and the Sergeant's heads.

These heads had been placed in the tree, and, at the right moment, one of the boys—Dawson—had mounted, and remained perched, ready to let them drop.

As we have seen, the trick had proved most successful.

Rumball, as had been anticipated, was too bewildered and horror-struck to notice the deception.

All he could realise were the mutilated heads of his victims—actually lying, blackened and ghastly, at his feet; and, shocked to the point of sickening fear, he had bolted.

"That's one of the best tricks we've had," observed Dick, when he had recovered from the over-powering laughter into which the incident had thrown him. "I never—ha—ha! saw a fellow look so awfully horrified and frightened in my life!"

"Nor have I ever seen a fellow run faster, Dick," said Tom Sheppard, wiping the tears from his eyes. "I wonder when he'll pull up?"

"Never, I should think," remarked Dawson, "Rumball from henceforth will be a second edition of the Wandering Jew! Ha, ha—h—a—a!"

"But, I say, boys," here cut in Swaps, though his voice was weak from exhaustive laughter, "we'd better see after the Sergeant and Mrs. Rumball, hadn't we?"

"It's about time we did," said Dick.

"I hope they are not really hurt," observed Tom Sheppard, "or our little game will be spoilt."

As the safety of Mrs. Rumball and the Sergeant was necessary to the carrying out of another part of the programme, Dick and his chums were somewhat anxious as to the result of the blow-up.

As the boys reached the spot where the explosion had occurred, they found their victims sitting up, apparently uninjured, though both were black in the face, and seemingly much bewildered.

They were several yards apart, a distance that had not been caused by the force of the explosion, but an involuntary effort to get as far away from the danger as possible.

Fortunately for themselves, they had not met with the fate of the great camp-kettle, and its contents.

The former, at this moment, was nicely lodged in the branches of a tree, bottom upwards, and such of the contents has had not been spilled in the ascent, were now strewing the grass beneath.

Joey Pumps was seen leaning against the tree, in an extreme state of limpness, having "gone orf agin" at least three times, since the blow-up.

According to a preconcerted arrangement, the boys separated into two parties, one led by Dick, and the other by Tom Sheppard, and surrounded the victims.

Dick's party took the Sergeant, and Tom's, Mrs. Rumball.

Dividing this into two scenes, we take first, that enacted by Dick's party.

"I say, Sergeant," said Dick, approaching, and assuming a serious tone. "This is a pretty fine thing—eh? I hope you're not hurt."

"Hurt!" returned the Sergeant, who was wiping his eyes with his handkerchief. "I tell you what, you confounded rascal, I'd just like to put you and the whole school in a magazine, and get rid of the lot of you. So help me ten men and a donkey, I would."

"Why, what do you mean, Sergeant?" returned Dick, opening his eyes in astonishment. "You don,t think—— ?"

"That you had anything to do with the blow-up?" growled the Sergeant. "I do! so help me ten men and a donkey, I'd swear it! Though I didn't see you do it, I know deuced well you're at the bottom of it!"

"Then you'd perhaps swear wrong, Sergeant," said Dick.

"Wrong;" said the Sergeant, incredulously. "Why not, Sergeant?"

Looking at Dick for a few moments, to note the expression of his countenance, the Sergeant said—

"You're not in the habit of telling lies, Everett. If you will tell me who did do it, I'll believe you."

"I won't tell you who did do it, Sergeant," returned Dick; "but I'll refer you to Mrs. Rumball."

"Mrs. Rumball!" exclaimed the Sergeant. "Do you mean to say *she* did it?"

"Well, I didn't actually see her put the powder on the fire, but,—there, I'll say no more. I have given you a hint, and if you can't profit by it, that's your look-out."

The Sergeant was considerably puzzled.

Did Everett *know* that Mrs. Rumball had served him this beastly trick? or was he only gammoning him?

What reason could Mrs. Rumball have for wishing to blow him to atoms?

The Sergeant couldn't think of any feasible reason.

'Twas true he had served Mrs. Rumball a shabby trick in making her out mad; but he had explained and expounded the circumstances under which he had done so, and Mrs. Rumball had assured him of her forgiveness.

She had proved the latter in many ways.

"If I really thought she did do it," muttered the Sergeant, "I'd——"

Here the Sergeant was startlingly interrupted; but we must see what Tom's party were doing around Mrs. Rumball.

Mrs. Rumball was squatted on the ground, busily engaged in tenderly feeling her black face, and filled with the fear that her beauty had been spoiled for ever, and was rocking herself and moaning and groaning as the boys surrounded her.

"I call this a great shame," said Tom, "to blow you up like this, Mrs. Rumball. He ought to be ashamed of himself, and you so kind to him too."

Tom winked at his chums as he said this, but there was no reponse to his sympathetic speech from Mrs. Rumball.

She was evidently still too frightened to listen to the voice of sympathy.

Tom waited a few moments, and then spoke again to the same effect.

But still Mrs. Rumball was silent.

"This won't do," thought Tom. "She takes no notice of me. I wonder if Joey Pumps could make any impression. I'll try."

Tom beckoned to Joey (who was still seated against the tree) to approach.

In obedience to the summons, Joey came up slowly, dragging his limp legs, and looking thoroughly done up.

He brightened up, however, as Tom whispered the nature of the service required of him.

"Ah," said Joey; "Dolly'll be sure ter lissen ter the woice of natur. Just see now."

Joey dropped on his knees by the side of his protectress, and said—

"Dolly."

"Yes, Joey.

Joey looked up and winked, as much as to say—"I told yer the woice o' natur 'ud do it."

"Don't give way Dolly—yer ain't 'urt."

"Air yer sure, Joey?"

"Quite."

"What, ain't my feeters blowed hall away?"

"Lor, no, Dolly; yer're hall right, I tells yer. Cheer hup."

Mrs. Rumball, much relieved in mind, looked around her, and said—

"O, it's too bad o' yer boys ter serve a body like as this. Yer might a——"

"Stop a bit, Dolly," put in Joey. "Jist don't yer go a blamin' the hinnercent."

"Why, didn't one o' these boys do it, Joey?" asked Mrs. Rumball, looking at Joey in astonishment.

"Jist as if *they* 'ud do sich a crool thing as that, Dolly!" exclaimed Joey.

"Who were hit then, Joey? He's a bad 'un who hever 'e wos."

"An' a fren too, Dolly," said Joey, shaking his head, sadly, "One as you've bin so kind to. Can't you guess?"

"Not—not—the—the—the——"

"Sargint? Hif hit wasn't, Dolly, why, I'll jist stan an let yer do what-hever yer like ter me. Yer shall dip me hin the tub—whack my nut with the rollin-pin—yer shall dab me with hall the dirtiest dish-clouts, 'ot or cold—yer shall bile me hin the camp-kettle, and I won't dodge yer a bit, or cry nout! There!"

Mrs. Rumball was not a woman given to reason before she acted.

Mrs. Rumball was a creature of impulse, always acting, whether right or wrong, on the spur of the moment.

At the suggestion of the Sergeant being the person who had conspired to take her life by gunpowder or had blown her up for the purpose of spoiling her complexion, Mrs. Rumball felt the blood rush into her face with angry indignation.

To be deliberately injured by the man she had given soup to, and whacked her own husband for, was base ingratitude indeed!

Mrs. Rumball would have instant revenge!

"Joey," said Mrs. Rumball, hastily rising to her feet. "Yer 'oodent give me leave ter do hall that hif yer didn't speak troo. Where his the willan?"

Joey pointed to where the Sergeant was surrounded by Dick and his chums, and the next moment Mrs. Rumball had broken through, and, to the Sergeant's astonishment, he saw two big fists being shaken in his face, and a fierce, blackened face, partly shaded by a huge cap-border, above him, and heard a voice screaming in his ears—

"Yer hold wiper! Yer willan! Yer cock-roach! Yer—yer—I doan know what ter call yer bad enuf, ter go fur to try an' ni'late me with gun-powder! Yer wiper, I say! I've a good mind ter pummle yer hugly face ter a mummy, I *hev!*" added Mrs. Rumball, approaching her formidable fists each moment closer to the Sergeant's face.

"Come, I say, my good woman," cried the Sergeant, shrinking back; "just take your common greasy fists out of *my* face, if you please! What do you mean by saying I blew you up with

"Hallo, Dolly, my dear!" said the Sergeant with a chuckle, "is that you? I've got you trick-players in a fix at last."—See page 134.

powder? It was *you* that blew *me* up! You blotchy-faced old toper!"

The rage of Mrs. Rumball was something fearful to behold as she heard the accusation, and heard herself called—yes, there was no mistake about it!—"a blotchy-faced old toper!"

For a few moments her astonishment struck her dumb and motionless.

For a few moments Mrs. Rumball glared at the audacious Sergeant as though he were mad, and then, looking about for a weapon, caught sight of the soup-ladle, seized it and turned upon the "wiper."

The latter, however, had made up his mind not to be knocked and stirred about like soup in the camp-kettle, and before Mrs. Rumball could reach him he had sprung to his feet and was beating a retreat.

Taking the relative length of Mrs. Rumball's and the Sergeant's legs, and other conditions, such as stoutness and activity, into consideration, the chances that the Sergeant would outstrip Mrs. Rumball were, cerainly, two to one; and nobody expected that the chase would end otherwise.

But the race is not always to the most active legs.

And it happened so in this case.

It was a peculiar circumstance that turned the race against the Sergeant.

He had not proceeded many yards when he felt a sudden coldness behind, and hastily feeling with his hand for the cause, he found that the patch at the seat of his overalls had given way, and was flopping in the breeze!

"Confound the thing!" muttered the Sergeant. "I can't run with that exposed to everybody! I must go backwards!"

Hastily scrambling up the loosened patch, he turned his with his face to his pursuer, and holding his hands behind, commenced an ungraceful retreat—a retreat that soon brought Mrs. Rumball's ladle about his head, and elicited screams of laughter from the boy

Mrs. Rumball made the most of er advantage, and followed the Sergeant, who dared not take his hands from the patch—until a fortunate accident put an end to his misery.

The Sergeant backed until, unconscious of his proximity thereto, he had reached the river and escaped further belabouring with the ladle, by turning a graceful somersault into the sparkling water!

CHAPTER XLIII.

MRS. RUMBALL RIDES TRIUMPHANTLY INTO CAMP ON HER RETURN FROM AN EXPEDITION IN SEARCH OF HER HUSBAND.

"Look! Look!"

"Here's a go!"

"Hurrah! Mrs. Rumball riding on the horns of a bull!"

"Bravo!"

These cries came from the boys of the School.

It was evening, and the boys, having finished all duty—such as drills, ball-practice at targets, &c.—in the mysterious absence of Mrs. Rumball, were congregated round the cooking-tent and fire, busily engaged in making their own tea.

This was no hardship.

They were rather pleased at it than otherwise, and whilst occupied with their work they had kept up a lively conversation on the incidents connected with the blowing up of their respected cook, and equally respected friend and instructor Sergeant O'Shehe—wondering and speculating what had become of the former, when, to their astonishment, the object of their anxiety rode into their midst in the manner described.

The mysterious disappearance of Mrs. Rumball from the camp was caused by her resolve to give a villain and intended murderer, not only a taste of her mind, but a taste of her hands and nails.

Soon after the Sergeant had been rescued from his involuntary bath, and Mrs. Rumball, satisfied at the punishment she had inflicted upon him, had retired to the privacy of her tent, Joey Pumps entered, and approaching her in his familiar way—taking care, however, to keep the camp-table between them for fear of any sudden desire upon the lady's part to pull his nose, box his ears, or perform any other kind of operation tending to hurt his feelings—said—

"I say, Dolly, yer had yer revenge hon the Sargint—eh?"

This was accompanied by a wink, but Mrs. Rumball, setting down a glass which Joey had caught her in the act of draining of a soothing draught of brandy, made no reply, though as she wiped her lips she cast a suspicious glance sideways at her youthful interrogater.

Joey remained a moment or two keenly watching the mood of his "purteckter," and then said—

"Wot are yer sulky about, Dolly? Yer've had yer revenge, yer know. Ain't the licker good?"

Does yer want ter be skinned, Joey?" asked Mrs. Rumball softly—for her.

"Well, I ain't a eel as I knows hon', Dolly. I'm a rum fish, I dare say, but I ain't a eel."

"Yer'll get skinned hin a minnit, heel or no heel," replied Mrs. Rumball, significantly, "hif yer don't take yerself orf."

"I ain't a goin' till I've heased yer mind, Dolly."

Mrs. Rumball at this opened her eyes, saying—

"What does yer mean now?"

"Nutthin, hony has I made a mistake jist now."

"Mistake?" said Mrs. Rumball, wonderingly.

Joey, nodding his head, and thrusting his hand into his pocket, replied—

"An orful mistake!"

"Wot were it?" she asked.

"Hit wasn't the Serjint as blowed yer hup, arter hall!"

"Then who was it, Joey?"

"Hit was a man—a bad man—has wos jealous o' yer, Dolly."

"Jealous o' me, Joey?" exclaimed Mrs. Rumball, elevating her hands and opening her eyes incredulously. "Never."

"Yes. 'Cos has yer give the soup ter the Serjint."

"Not Rumball, Joey?" said Mrs. Rumball, turning crimson with anger.

"That's the man, Dolly," nodding his head, impressingly.

"An' hit was Rumball has blowed us hup, was

hit?" asked Mrs. Rumball, significantly—and hotly.

"Hit wos. Does yer want me to take my hoath, Dolly?"

"No, Joey. I wants yer to take me to 'im."

"I carn't, Dolly. Rumball hev hooked it—cut and run inter the forest ter 'ide hisself. Hif yer wants 'im yer mus ketch 'im."

Mrs. Rumball did want "him," and was determined to find him.

Mrs. Rumball, however, bottled her wrath (which became all the hotter and fiercer the more she thought of the diabolical deed) until a fresh dinner had been cooked, and then, taking the soup ladle, she stealthily left the camp, and started in search of her husband.

Mrs. Rumball's search proved successful.

After long wandering through the forest glades, she discovered the would-be murderer in a tree, where he had been compelled to ascend to save his own life.

Mr. Rumball, his brain filled with the vision of the ghastly heads of his wife and the Sergeant—Mr. Rumball feeling horror-struck at the frightful deed his jealousy had led him to commit, fled on and on into the gloomy depths of the forest—fled on until he came to the bank of a large pond.

Here, in his misery, he halted, gazed at the dark surface of the gloomy pool, and had just made up his mind to plunge in headlong, and put an end to his misery in this world, when his ears were assailed by a loud roar, and the heavy trampling of feet.

Looking round, Mr. Rumball saw approaching at full speed, the foam dropping from its mouth, its breath puffing from its distended nostrils, and its eyes flashing with angry fire—a Spanish bull!

In a moment, Rumball, forgetting all about committing suicide, dashed frantically towards the cork-tree, made a desperate jump at one of the lower branches and succeeded in clambering up, just as the infuriated Toro had got one of his horns within an inch of his person.

Here Mr. Rumball stuck until the bull, feeling indignant that the object of its wrath would not come down to be gored, reluctantly moved away, and even stuck there until after the animal had taken itself off.

"There's no trusting them bulls," murmured Rumball. "He may come back, an' I'll stick up here till it gits dark."

It was not long after the bull had gone off before Rumball heard footsteps below, and looking down he saw a sight that gave him a dread-shock, and caused him to exclaim—

"Good heavin! hit's—hit's Dolly's sperrit!"

Not so, Rumball; it was Dolly's body, with soup-ladle in hand.

Mrs. Rumball heard her husband's exclamation, too, and looked up.

Both, equally struck at the strange encounter, gazed at each other in silence—Mr. Rumball wondering whether it was the ghost of his Dolly or not, and Dolly trying to find words to express the fulness of her indignation.

At length Mrs. Rumball's tongue loosened.

"So!" she spoke, in ominous tones, and placing her arms akimbo. "So it's thur yer are, yer willian, is it?"

"Dolly," said Rumball, in trembling accents, "his hit yer poor sperrit?"

"Sperrit!" answered Mrs. Rumball, flourishing the ladle. "Jist cum down, yer bad-minded, blood-thursted, gunpowdered-busted wretch, an'

I'll let yer know whether I be a sperrit or not! Cum down, yer willain!"

Now he knew that Dolly was really in the body—soup-ladle and all—his courage revived, and he determined to take advantage of his position (he knew Dolly couldn't get at him), and make friends if he could.

"Dolly," said Rumball, "won't yer furgiv' me?"

The reply was a flourish of the ladle and the angry demand—

"Cum down, yer wretch!"

"Dolly," returned Rumball, "I wouldn't hev' blown yer hup hif yer hadn't give the soup ter that stuck-up Sergeant."

"Drat the Sergeant and you too! will yer cum *down*?" cried the angry Dolly.

"Not unless yer ses yer'll furgiv' me, Dolly."

"Furgiv' yer? Never, Rumball, till I've broke yer blessed 'ead!"

"Then I *won't* cum down!"

"Then I'll stay 'eer till yer drops, Rumball!"

How long that might have been it is impossible to conjecture.

Mrs. Rumball meant what she said, and placed her arms akimbo, and planted her legs with firm determination to carry out her threat; but she had scarcely assumed this position when the bull suddenly made its appearance, and before Rumball could offer any warning, Dolly was lifted between Toro's horns and borne off.

Rumball—the wretch!—sat perched in the tree, actually chuckling at the clever manner in which Toro had taken Dolly out of the way, watching the figure of his wife as, with outstretched arms, minus the ladle, making the forest ring with her screams, she was carried along at mad gallop, and until she got finally out of sight.

Then Rumball descended an retraced his steps to the camp, chuckling all the way, and muttering—

"I'm blest if she ain't got into a fix *this* time—He! he! *I* won't 'elp 'er."

Mrs. Rumball certainly was in a fix.

By the time she had reached the camp, the fear of being tossed had caused her to hold on by the bull's horns, and though the animal tried its utmost to dislodge his heavy burden, it found it impossible to do so.

The excitement that ensued was uproarious.

Mrs. Rumball screamed—as, indeed, she had not ceased to scream since her elevation—the bull roared, the boys shouted.

The animal, bewildered by the noise, tore round and round the camp, each moment getting, if possible, more angry.

This continued for several minutes, the boys favouring Mrs. Rumball with sundry remarks and advice.

"Hold tight, Dolly!"

"Keep fast—the bull will be tired first!"

"Don't be frightened—you're all right!"

"If you leave go you'll be gored!"

"It's as good as going to the circus!"

The finishing stroke was at length given by Joey Pumps.

That individual had said nothing, but he had been trying hard at doing something.

Joey had been dodging about after Toro, trying to catch his tail.

At length he succeeded, and he brought about a most extraordinary *denoûment*.

No sooner did Toro feel the dragging weight behind, than, frightened still more at the ad

THE SCHOOL OF THE REGIMENT.

ditional appendage, he gave an extra roar, charged through his tormentors, and, making straight for the river, plunged in—Mrs. Rumball at his head, and Joey at his tail.

Leaving the reader to imagine the exciting scene that followed the rescue of two such important personages as Mrs. Rumball and Joey Pumps, we will begin a new chapter, and treat of topics that ought to have been mentioned before.

CHAPTER XLIV.

A SHORT CHAPTER, BUT NECESSARY TO BE READ, TO ENABLE THE READER TO CONNECT THE COURSE OF EVENTS.

WE must now return to the events that occurred after the Spanish Don had carried off the disguised General under the delightful impression that it was his (the Don's) lady-love.

The Governor, Sir Gentle Sharpset, was considerably astounded at the audacious conduct of the Don, and declared that he would despatch a British regiment to effect a recapture of the diabolical conspirator—the wretch who had placed an infernal machine in the hold of the British troopship.

He would effect the recapture, and settle with those who had contrived the escape afterwards.

The first thing the Governor did on returning to his palace, was to despatch an aide-de-camp, with orders for the 67th Regiment of the Line to get under arms, to be supplied with thirty rounds of ball cartridge, and hold itself in readiness to march at a moment's notice.

This order spread like wildfire through the garrison and town, and which, together, with the daring and clever manner in which the escape of the supposed infernal-machine monster was accomplished, caused great excitement.

Great was the speculation as to whether the Spanish Government would oppose the entrance of an armed British Regiment into the Spanish territory.

The infernal-machinist had confessed that he was a Spaniard, and therefore, the inference was that the Spanish authorities would not give him up—especially if the villain was really an agent of theirs.

The Governor, however, knew what he was about.

He knew that he could not send an armed force into Spain without the permission of the Spanish Government, under the almost certain risk of provoking a war.

So, Sir Gentle set to work to ask permission.

The telegraph was put into requisition between Gibraltar and Madrid, and in less than two hours, and desired leave to enter the Spanish Lines was granted.

"That will save a great deal of bother," observed the Governor to his aide-de-camp, as they were standing together in the official office of the Palace. "Take the order for the 67th to march at once, providing rations for seven days."

The aide-de-camp left the room to carry the order, but in less than five minutes he again entered with a newspaper in his hand, and advancing to the Governor said:—

"Read that, Sir Gentle!"

The Governor, wondering what fresh horrors he was doomed to hear of, took the paper, and read the following in the "Times":—

"MYSTERIOUS DISAPPEARANCE.—A mystery in the sudden disappearance of the well-known Artillery Officer, General Joachim Shoot, is just now exercising the minds of the officers and men of the Bangfire garrison, and the civil inhabitants of the town.

"The General's name is well known as the projector of the novel idea of establishing a school in connection with the gallant regiment of which he is commandant. The idea was to train up the sons of soldiers in the military profession, with a view to supplying the ranks from the youth so trained. The scheme, which, for a long time, met with opposition from the commander-in-chief, was at length allowed to be tried.

"With what degree of success, our readers will guess, when they learn that, so outrageously did the boys conduct themselves (even going so far, it is reported, as to burn a Chinese Pagoda, which the General had had erected in the Repository Grounds, and subsequently to chastising the General most severely on the recumbent part of his person with a frying-pan, the General being unable to help himself at the moment), that it was considered advisable to transfer them to Gibraltar, to subject them to the martinet discipline maintained on the Rock garrison.

"It appears that the General himself resolved to see the school safely on board the troopship. He accordingly accompanied it from the barracks, was seen to go on board, and was even seen on the quarter-deck during the embarkation of the 33rd regiment, which was proceeding to Malta.

"From this time the General suddenly disappeared. Although close search was made, he could not be found in any part of the steamer, and it was supposed that he must have gone on shore—the school having been safely embarked before the regiment—and returned to the barracks.

"This supposition was not verified however. It was found that the General had not returned to his quarters, had not been observed to leave the Arsenal; and from that moment he has never turned up.

"There are those belonging to the garrison who shrewdly suspect that the General will turn up at Gibraltar, and prove to have been the victim of the boys of the school; whether such will prove to be the case we shall learn in due time, as a steamer has been despatched to, if possible, reach the Rock before, or as soon as, the troopship 'Orontes.'

"In the meantime, and until some definite news is heard, no doubt, the General's friends and the public will experience a considerable amount of anxiety and suspense."

As the Governor read the paragraph, he turned hot and cold—cold and hot, alternately, and when he had finished it, he looked and met the eyes of the aide-de-camp.

Neither spoke for a moment, and then the Governor spoke first:—

"What—what do think of this, Saunders?"

"That that infernal-machinist is—is——"

The aide-de-camp nodded his head impressively, being afraid to utter the name.

"So do I!" nodded the Governor, in return. "The madman, conspirator, and the General, are —must be—one and the same person!"

"No doubt of it, Sir Gentle. He has somehow become the—the——"

"Victim of the boys!" said the Governor.

"My opinion exactly, Sir Gentle!"

"I can't understand how he could have got into such a mess," said Sir Gentle. "I—I don't see that I am to blame for what has happened—of course, not before—but since his arrival at the Rock. Why, you said yourself that——"

"He wasn't General Shoot?"

"Yes—in the garden the morning the school arrived."

"How could I be expected to recognise him in that absurd costume, Sir Gentle?"

"True. How he got reduced to such a state is a mystery."

"It is. And if you remember, the Sergeant declared emphatically that it was not General Shoot, and even suggested that the man was mad."

"I remember."

"And those two singular persons who were chasing him?"

"Just so."

"The whole affair——"

"Is the work of the boys, and the Sergeant—no doubt about it?" interrupted the Governor. "I must find out the whole scheme. I will ride up to the Castle, and parade the school."

As the Governor spoke, he reached forth his hand to the bell-rope, to summon his groom to saddle his horse, but, ere he could pull it, a naval officer entered.

It was the Captain of the "Blazer" gunboat.

"Well," said the Governor, addressing the Captain. "Answer my question shortly. Did you overtake the 'Orontes?'"

"Yes, Sir Gentle. We came up with her quicker than we expected—found she had broken her shaft and was disabled.

"You didn't find an infernal machine on board?"

"No, Sir Gentle."

"What did you find out?"

"That it was all a hoax."

"And that the supposed madman and conspirator was General Shoot?"

"So it is supposed."

"The supposition is correct. It *is* General Shoot, and, may I be shot if it isn't the most extraordinary affair I ever heard of. A nice dance I—all of us—have been led!"

Here the Governor began walking to and fro, recapitulating the circumstances in an excited, angry manner.

"Just think, gentlemen. The General dressed in the most ridiculous costume, is chased by two vulgar persons into the gardens, and uses *me* for a doging-post. Naturally annoyed, I have the three of them arrested. One declares he is the General—General Shoot, and appeals to the Sergeant in charge of the school to prove his identity. The Sergeant denies all knowledge of him, and suggests that he is mad. You, Saunders (who know the General) cannot recognise him—and no wonder. Convinced that the three are mad, I have them confined in the civil prison. The same night, two young scamps bring me a note at the banquet, purporting to be a written confession of the man who called himself General Shoot, that he is not General Shoot, but a Spaniard, who has concealed an infernal machine in the hold of the troopship. Thereupon I despatched the 'Blazer' gunboat in chase. The next thing I hear is that the supposed monster has escaped—an escape actually connived at by the Corporal of the Guard, under a forged note purporting to come from *me*. Then comes the most astonishing thing of all. For certain reasons, I have occasion to watch the pass into the Spanish Lines, having been informed that a certain person—not the General—might attempt to escape into Spain, disguised in the costume of a negress. What do I discover? That the person so disguised is the supposed monster of the infernal machine! Then, just as I am recapturing him, he is pounced upon by the Senor Don Juan de la Vega Grey de los Brabones, and carried off! Gentlemen!" wound up the Governor in a highly theatrical tone, and stretching forth his hand in a theatrical manner, "I have no wish to shock your ears by using strong language, but—if this affair does not exceed everything I have ever heard of in impudent audaciousness, then may I be——!"

The officers quite agreed that it did, and that, therefore, there was no likelihood of the Governor meeting the fate he had suggested.

The Governor then, with his aides-de-camp, mounted their horses, and galloped to the Castle, where we will precede them.

The sun had not yet set, and the boys, after witnessing the stoppage and rescue of the disguised General, had returned to the Castle, and were now assembled on the terrace.

Amongst these were Dick, Tom, Bob, Harry, Dolly and Joey Pumps.

Dick and his chums, now that the game was up, had resolved to face it out, and take such punishment as the Governor thought proper to award them.

"We have had our lark, chaps," Dick had said, "and we won't be cowards enough to run away. We shall live to lark again another day!"

The Sergeant, however, frightened out of his life at the non-success of the scheme he had laboured so hard to accomplish, sought the protecting help of Mrs. Rumball, and that lady, after allowing herself to be persuaded that having her confined as a lunatic was for her ultimate comfort and good—so soft was her heart—forgave him, and allowed him to hide in her apartment.

This was the position of affairs when the Governor started for the Castle.

The approach of the party was quickly twigged, and, simultaneously, all the boys gathered round Dick and the others who had been most prominent in the late transactions, in a state of subdued excitement.

The game was up now!

There would soon be a reckoning!

Dick and his chums, however, seemed calm enough.

"Mind, chums," said Dick, "we must tell nothing but the truth."

As Dick spoke, the Governor, with his suite galloped into the Castle-yard.

Drawing rein, Sir Gentle looked up to the terrace, saying—

"Where's the drummer?"

"Here, sir," answered the little fellow, looking down.

"Beat for the school to fall in!"

"I thought that would be it," said Dick, as the little fellow took his drum and descended to the courtyard.

Scarcely had the last tap of the drum died away when the boys were already in two ranks, standing at ease.

"Where's the Sergeant?" demanded the Governor.

Nobody knew.

"He must be found," said the Governor. "Send the Corporal of the Guard to find him."

An aide-de-camp having given orders to this effect, the Governor called the school to attention, and then scanning the front rank, ordered Dick and Dolly to step forward.

Looking sternly at them, he said—

"You are the boys who brought me the letter at the banquet?"

"Yes, sir," said Dick.

"That letter was forged?"

"Yes, sir."

"By whom?"

"Myself, sir."

"Had you any accomplices?"

"No, sir."

Here the squeaky-voiced little boy cried out —"We all knew about it, sir."

"Hem—so I suppose'" muttered the Governor, and then asked aloud—

"Who forged that note to the Corporal of the Guard?"

"I did, sir," said Dick.

"Hem! You appear to have been the ringleader?"

"Yes, sir."

Dick's manner was very candid and open, and there were those present who felt themselves favourably impressed thereby.

Even the Governor's manner perceptibly softened as he said—

"Come, now, just tell me all you know of the whole affair."

This was just what Dick wanted.

If he could only succeed in impressing the Governor with the ridiculousness of the General's adventures, he felt that he should have done a great deal to soften the punishment that he and the whole school richly deserved.

Dick, therefore, commenced the recital, and with such good effect that, by the time he had got to the stealing of Mrs. Rumball's drawers he had the Governor unable to open his lips for fear of giving way to uncontrolled laughter, whilst the officers of his suite were seen cramming their pockethandkerchiefs in their mouths for a like purpose.

This state of suppressed laughter continued until the description of the transformation of the General into a negress, and the mistake of the Don in supposing the General to be his lady-love, when the laughter burst forth and became general.

Dick took good care, in speaking of the Don and his lady-love, not to mention the lady's name, a delicate piece of consideration for the Governor's feelings that told wonderfully in Dick's favour in the mind of Sir Gentle.

The laughter was further increased by Rumball at this moment leaning over the terrace and screaming forth—

"'Ere 'e his, Gov'nor! 'Ere's the Sarjint! I've a found 'im!"

It was impossible to resist the comicality of the situation, and the courtyard rang again with volley after volley of laughter.

The Governor, suspecting that the Sergeant was in some way acquainted with the intended elopement of his sister, and had prevented it, ascended and held a private interview with him, very much to his—the Governor's—satisfaction.

The sentence pronounced was that, as the General had been carried off mainly through the instrumentality of the Sergeant and the boys, they should find him.

The march of the 67th was, therefore, countermanded, and the School of the Regiment sent into Spain, with strict orders not to return without the General.

The School, with camp equipment, provisions, ammunition, Mrs. Rumball, and the Sergeant, was sent off the same night.

The reader will doubtless think that, taking into consideration the fact that the School of the Regiment was despatched in search of the missing General, the boys were taking it very coolly.

When we introduce the boys in camp, they had already been out the third day and were discovered instead of looking for the General, playing pranks, on Mr. and Mrs. Rumball and the Sergeant, and had formed, apparently, a permanent encampment.

This stationary position was due to the Sergeant.

When, on the first day, the store waggon was unloaded, and the tent pitched, the Sergeant had formed up the boys and thus addressed them—

"Look here, boys. Here we are, free as birds in the beautiful cork-woods, and, between you and me and the gate-post, I intend to stay here as long as convenient."

This announcement elicited loud cheers.

"I'm glad you like the idea," continued the Sergeant. "But let me tell you that one reason I have for it is that, for some time at least, you'll be out of harm's way and temptation."

Much laughter.

"I mean it. Here's nothing but trees and grass and this river, and it isn't many tricks you'll find to play here, and as I don't intend you shall pass the time like a lot of babes in the wood, sleeping all day and night, and covering yourselves with leaves, so help me ten men and a donkey," the Sergeant continued, amidst much laughter, "it's some real campaigning I intend you to have. I'll teach you to be soldiers. It's up in the morning you'll get for a bathe in the river. Then it's some drill I'll give you. Then it's some breakfast, from that estimable woman Mrs. Rumball will come next, and she'll be as good as a mother to you."

"I 'ope has she'll serve yer hall better than me then, chaps—that's hall."

This speech came from Joey Pumps, and who, happening to be standing incautiously close to the Sergeant, received a sudden kick which sent the little fellow flying until his course was stopped by a cork-tree, the bark of which rubbed the "bark" off his nose.

"Then," continued the Sergeant, "after breakfast, there'll be more drill, with ball-practice at a targit that I'll chalk on a tree. Then dinner, and then more drill, and then tea, and then drill again, just like I intended to give you at the Signal Station on the Rock——"

"Except the brimstone and treacle," put in Dolly, followed by much tittering.

"Exactly," said the Sergeant, "except the 'health-sustainer,' and more's the pity. You see, coming off in a hurry, I hadn't time to think of everything. But I'll promise to try and think of a substitute. If I can't, why, you see, it's at the Signal Station we'll be by-and-bye, and then we'll make up for lost time. I'll double the dose for a week or two. And now you know what you have to do, I'll break you off."

"But when are we to look for the General, Sergeant?" asked Dick.

"Look for the General? Oh, that depends upon circumstances. You see, I don't know where to look, and so the General must take his chance. I'm not going to put myself out of the way for the General. If he comes in my way, why, I'll bring him back. If he doesn't come in my way, why he'll have to stay where he is, and all I hope is that he's in comfortable quarters. And now go and put your tents square, help Mrs. Rumball get the cooking-tent ready, get the rations out of the store waggon, and give the horses some corn and water. T'shun! Right face! Break off!"

As far as the Sergeant could, he had carried out his programme in the way of drill; but, as we have seen, he could not prevent the boys playing tricks.

Even in the midst of the forest they had found out a way to amuse themselves.

"There's no getting over them at all," muttered the Sergeant, as he was washing the black off his face, caused by the springing of the mine beneath the camp-kettle. "I'll be off out of this, and march them to the ruins of El Rocadillo. That's the place for them!"

The Sergeant kept his word.

In the evening, about an hour before roll-call, the boys were considerably surprised to hear the drummer beat the "fall in."

Dick and his chums were lounging on the grass in the front of their tent as the rattle of the drum awoke the echoes of the forest.

"What's up now, I wonder?" said Dolly Swaps.

"Oh, one of the Sergeant's surprises, I expect, Dolly," replied Dick.

"Nothing like excitement, I say," said Tom Sheppard. "Come on, chaps, let's fall in, and see what it's all about."

In another minute Dick found that it *was* one of the Sergeant's surprises, and not an unpleasant one by any means, though the Sergeant intended it should be otherwise."

"Look here, boys," began the Sergeant, when they had formed up, "I'm going to give you a treat, a reward live for the blowing-up you were good enough to favour us with to-day. I'm going to march you to the ruins of El Rocadillo, and let you sleep out for a night under the cold moon for a change. There's no grass there, nothing but sharp stones to sleep upon, and, so help me ten men and a donkey, I hope you'll all like it! And mind—just listen to this—every time there's a lark, I'll march you to some outlandish place, and sleep you out all night. The next time, it won't even be stones you'll sleep upon, but, so help me ten men, if I won't pick out the softest, dirtiest, and stinkiest boy I can find for you! And mind this, it's ready for parade you'll have to be at the usual time before breakfast, with not a blessed stain on your uniforms, and buttons and brasses bright enough for me to see my face in. I'll teach you to play tricks, my beauties! We'll march in five minutes in full dress, with rifles and ten rounds of ball ammunition. Right face! Break!" and

Five minutes later, the boys, with the band at their head, playing "Sally come up," marched from their encampment.

We know of few things more charming and romantic than a march by moonlight, with stirring music to enliven the way.

This night-march to "Our Boys" was romantic from its complete novelty.

They were in Spain, tramping to a quick step, through a wood—a wood rendered mystic by the patches of moonlight on the springy turf, that guided their footsteps through its sombre, sylvan recesses.

Where they were going they knew not, beyond the name, but that did not trouble them, and they sang and laughed and talked in a manner that convinced the Sergeant they enjoyed the sudden turn-out, rather than otherwise.

Whilst the boys marched and sang, and the band played, the Sergeant tramped along, with a short pipe in his mouth, puffing away with great enjoyment.

After halting twice to rest, they emerged from the forest, and immediately came in sight of some picturesque ruins, perched upon an eminence, evidently the remains of an ancient castle, as, indeed, they were, the castle having been built, it is supposed, in the days of the Phœnicians.

Now it was that the Sergeant's voice was heard above the strains of the band.

"To the ruins! Right wheel! Forward!"

Ten minutes' marching brought them into the midst of the moss-grown and ivy-mantled remains—the scattered and broken skeleton of a once enormous castle.

———

CHAPTER XLV.

THE MIDNIGHT BIVOUAC IN THE RUINS OF EL ROCADILLO.—THE MYSTERIOUS NOISE.—THE DISCOVERY OF THE GENERAL.—THE MYSTERIOUS FLOOD. — THE CAUSE EXPLAINED. — SHOWING HOW SERGEANT O' SHEHE PAID OFF OLD SCORES.

OF all that once mighty structure, nothing seemed to have retained its original shape and form but the strong, squat, square-looking tower —resembling very much the tower of the old Moorish Castle of the Rock.

All around was sublime decay—fallen creeper-covered walls, and massive moss-layered stones, some half-buried in the *débris*, others piled up in tumbled confusion, and as the boys entered the moonlit ruins, a peculiar feeling pervaded each mind—a feeling as though they had entered some ghostly region the clouds.

The band had ceased instinctively, for the strains had a weird, unnatural sound, and the echoes seemed to die away in a succession of wavy wails.

Instinctively the boys dropped their merry tones to tones subdued and awe-struck.

Was this where they had to bivouac under the cold moon?

This question passed in low murmurs from one another.

That this was so, they were not left long in doubt.

The Sergeant, delighted at the impression the ghostly ruins had made, commands—

"Ho—lt!"

How hollow the familiar command sounded!

"Front!"

This seemed to be answered by a spirit voice, so long and mournful was the echo.

Now the Sergeant began addressing them in ironical tones, and it seemed as though a restless evil spirit were gibbering and chaffing at them.

"Look here, my beauties. This is the place you'll have to slumber in to-night. It's a delightful place, take my word for it. So help me ten men, if it's ghosts any of you are particularly partial to, it's here you'll find 'em! There's a splendid variety of sleeping nooks and corners—hardly damp enough, I'm afraid—but blessed hard and cold. There's nice, comfortable, slimy chambers beneath, called dungeons sometimes, where any of you are quite welcome to take your night's lodging! Play tricks on me, is it? So help me ten men, but you'll wish you hadn't before I've done with you! This is nothing to what I'll find for you next time. And now go and pick out the softest places, and may you all sleep like tops. He, he! Right-face! Break!"

Late as it was, tired as were the boys, they overcame the feeling of the supernatural with which the ghastly ruins inspired them, sufficiently to scatter in twos and threes, and explore.

It would take a long time to describe the gloomy nooks and corners and weird places they found, and wondered at in awe-struck whispers.

By degrees the boys sought out the most convenient places to take up their night's abode, and huddled together in groups for companionship.

One of these groups consisted of Dick and his chums.

They had selected for their sleeping-place a mossy nook, close to the old tower, which screened them from the direct rays of the moon.

How long Dick had slept he knew not, but he was suddenly awoke by a peculiar cry—a cry as of despair, emanating, it seemed—for he listened attentively and heard it repeated—from the ground beneath him.

Dick was not chicken-hearted, but at such a time and place the cry sounded, literally, so unearthly, that he felt his blood "creep," and after a bit he touched Tom Sheppard.

"What is it, Dick?" asked Tom, subduing his voice, as he felt a pressure of Dick's hand, and saw his finger placed on his lips to impress caution.

"Do you hear anything, Tom?"

Tom listened.

"Do you mean that unearthly sound?"

"Yes."

"What do you think it is, Dick?"

"Someone a prisoner in one of the dungeons. I have been listening a long time, and I believe it is a man confined below."

"Shall we try and find out, Dick?"

"Yes. Be cautious: wake Bob and the others, and we'll all go together."

This was affected very quietly, and, full of suppressed excitement, the search began.

They seemed like ghosts themselves, peering into nooks and corners of the weird ruins in the moonlight, and trying to find an entrance to the lower part of the tower.

At length they descended a long flight of slippery stone steps and, at the foot of the well-like depth, they came opposite a massive stone door, a slab which proved to be nearly twelve inches thick.

Here the cries seemed to be more distinct.

"It's in here, boys," said Dick. "I feel sure. Can't you discern the cries plainer?"

"Yes," said Tom, "but we shall never get that stone door open."

"We must try. Let us all push tagether. Steady—all together—now!"

The first effort just moved it.

Then they tried again and again.

Presently it yielded to their combined pressure, groaning on its now unused hinges.

Nor will the boys forget the thrill of horror which seized them as, with a sound betwixt a sigh and a groan, the heavy door went "home," as though fixed on a spring, as they got inside and heard the vast iron bolts slipped in their sockets outside!

For a few minutes they remained horror-struck and speechless.

"This way! This way! For Heaven's sake! Come and put out this slow match!" cried a woeful voice.

The next moment, by the faint glimmer of a streak of moonlight which entered the dark place through an aperture near the ceiling, they saw a figure seated on a barrel, tied hands and feet,

A slow match (a soft rope impregnated with saltpetre) was set in the bung of the barrel, slowly burning.

Approaching the figure with cautious footsteps, they gazed for a moment, and then came a simultaneous shout—

"*It's the General!*"

Yes, it was the General, and for once, feeling awfully glad to see a few of the faces of the boys of the school.

The extent of this gladness will be understood, when it is stated that the General was seated on a barrel of powder, and secured in such a manner as precluded all chance of his liberating himself.

The General, however, had not been able to shift his position, and for many hours, how many he was quite unable to say, the slow match had been gradually burning—getting nearer and nearer with snail-like certainty, the powder that had been destined to blow him, with the old tower, into countless atoms!

The reader will have no difficulty in guessing who could have consigned the General to a death accompanied by elements of such devilishly-refined torture.

It was the disappointed Senor Don de la Vega Grey de los Brabones.

Scarcely had the Don discovered the way in which he had been duped, than the fate of the General had been decided.

He swore a terrific oath that within eight-and-forty hours, not an atom of the General as big as a pea should be in existence to deceive him—the Don—or anybody else in like manner.

So the night following his capture found the General seated on the barrel of powder, reduced once more to his costume of Mrs. Rumball's scarlet trousers, and minus his turban and wig.

The astonishment of Dick and his chums at making this discovery overcame, for a time, the horror they felt at the sudden closing of the stone door—the horrible thought it engendered of being buried alive—and, despite the tragic elements of the situation, they could not repress a grin at the comic appearance of the General.

In the semi-darkness, the General's black head and face, white teeth and staring eyes, white shirt and drawers—the latter looking black—could just be discerned.

By these outward indications alone could they have recognised that the individual seated on the barrel was none other than the lost General—for his voice was strangely altered.

How feeble and husky was now the once ringing and sonorous tones of the General, as he said imploringly—

"For Heaven's sake, put out the slow match!"

There was no mistaking the agony of that appeal, nor was there any mistaking the imminent necessity for making it.

Another minute, and the slow match would have touched the powder.

"For God's sake, be careful!" added the General, as Dick dropped on his knees to remove the match.

Dick could not see but, there might be some grains of powder on the floor of the dungeon under the bung of the barrel, which even a spark shaken from the slow match in removing it, might ignite.

The removing of the match was a moment of indescribable suspense to all!

Not daring to breathe, lest even the slight fan of his breath should detach a spark, Dick cautiously took the match between his left finger and thumb, and holding his right hand open beneath the glow-worm-like blaze, to catch a falling spark, gradually withdrew the end from the bung-hole, and carried it to the opposite side of the dungeon.

Here he carefully placed his foot on it and, in a tone that betrayed the relief he felt at the removal of the danger, exclaimed, followed by a simultaneous cheer from his chums—

"There! Thank Heaven, that's done!"

Yes—that danger was averted, but there was another, now that they were free to think, which they had to confront, and which, perhaps, was scarcely of a less awful nature.

They knew that unless they could force open the stone door, a fearful death was, almost surely, in store for them.

That of being buried alive.

"Yes," said Tom Sheppard, "but that's only getting over one danger to confront another, Dick. If we can't open the door of this black hole, we must expect death in a slower, but equally certain form."

"That's true, Tom," returned Dick. "But we must have a good try for liberty. As soon as we have released the General, we will try our luck.

As Dick was speaking, he was already busy unfastening the General's cords, and in a few minutes, with the aid of Tom and the others, the General was free, and resting against the wall of the dungeon, thankful, but exhausted.

"Now!" cried Dick. "For the door!"

But where was the door?

Its whereabouts was nowhere to be found!

They felt the walls all over, but not a bolt nor hinge, nor anything indicating the presence of a door could be discovered.

Nothing but the stones of which the dungeon was built—cold and damp—could be found.

"It's evident the only way of opening the door is from the outside," said Dick, as they consulted together as to what could be done "and unless we can make ourselves heard—we know a voice can reach the ruins—and a lucky search can be made, there's nothing for it but to starve here to death!"

"Mind what you're saying, Dick, will you?" said Dolly Swaps, giving a shudder. "Don't!"

"It's no use mincing matters," Dolly, or trying to shut our eyes to the inevitable. If we can't make ourselves heard so as to be found, I say—deliberately—we're doomed! Now then, altogether."

This was followed by a shout that caused the old dungeon to ring like a belfry.

Again and again went up that shout, but there was no answering response.

"Our efforts seem fruitless, Dick," said Tom Sheppard, as they paused once to listen. "We are booked?"

"We mustn't give in whilst we've any power in our lungs, Tom," returned Dick. "It is not morning yet you can see by the ray of moonlight through the hole up yonder. A thorough search is sure to be made when we are missed. We must keep on shouting."

"Yes," put in Dolly, "and if all comes to all—that is if the shouting produces nothing but shouting—we can only give up and live as long as we can on the General!"

A groan from the latter indicated that Dolly's remark had been heard but not appreciated, and a simultaneous titter was the result.

"Once again," cried Dick. "One—two—what's that?"

This pause and question was caused by a sudden sound as of falling water in the dungeon—not a splash-like fall, but a continuous stream.

"Water!" cried Bob Jones. "I've got a dose of it on my head. It comes from the ceiling, I think.

This, on close examination, was discovered to be the case.

The water was rushing in through a hole at the top of the wall close to the roof!

Steadily—like a stream from a pump!

Was this a new danger?

It must be, for in a few moments the floor of the dungeon was covered—the water covered the soles of their boots!

It was indeed a new and equally awful danger to contemplate to being starved to death.

A speedy death by drowning!

A death by drowning confined, without the slightest chance of escape, between four stone walls!

But, even at this moment, Dolly Swaps must have his joke.

The General, it will be remembered, after his release, had been left to rest himself and recover from his exhaustion, sitting with his back against the wall.

As Mrs. Rumball's trousers, consisting as they did of scarlet flannel, were not waterproof, the water had begun to penetrate that part on which the General was sitting, and he was making strenuous efforts to gain an upright position, but without success.

Dolly took compassion on him, saying—

"You chaps shout away whilst I help the General. I'm afraid he'll catch cold in his 'right-about.'"

The reader will, perhaps, think that this was an unseasonable moment in which to joke—that it savours, perhaps, of the unnatural.

But what the strains of the band are to the soldiers marching into action, the encouraging words of the officer to his men in the battle, so is a joke or a cheerful word in a moment of supreme anger.

It tends to revive the spirit, keep up one's sinking courage, and encourages to fresh exertion—and fresh exertion must always bring fresh hope.

Dolly, though he felt the desperateness of their position as much as any of his chums, and was only a little fellow, knew the value of a cheerful word.

Dolly, was, too, as the reader must have discovered after such a long acquaintance with him, something of a philosopher.

We know more than one little fellow who is always as cool as a cucumber—some may call it "impudence," "cheek,"—never frightened, never disconcerted, who could no more give up, or knock his brains out against the wall in sheer despair, under the circumstances in which we find Our Boys, than soar like the eagle into the very face of the sun.

Dolly's joke did good service—it caused a laugh, and revived the spirits of his chums.

"You are worth your weight in gold, Dolly," said Dick.

"I wish I was bigger then, Dick," returned Dolly, in a tone that caused another laugh.

"You are plenty big enough, Dolly," said Dick, "for my purpose."

"Your purpose, Dick? What scheme have you in your head?"

"Do you see that hole where the moon shines through?"

"I understand," said Dolly divining Dick's thoughts. "You think I might manage to get through it—eh?"

Just so," said Dick. "We can make a 'pyramid,' I think, that will take you up there. Tom, you go down as base, Bob Jones will go next, then Harry, and then myself, to be able to talk with Dolly."

The water by this time had risen above their ankles, and Dick's plan was eagerly agreed to.

If Dolly could only get through or succeed in attracting attention they would be saved.

"That's a good idea of yours, Dick," observed Tom, as he went down and planted his head firmly against the wall. "Up you all go."

In two minutes more, the pyramid, or ladder, was complete, and Dolly had got his head opposite the aperture.

"Do you think you can get through, Dolly?" asked Dick.

"I might by taking some stones out, Dick," returned Dolly. "They seem loose en——"

"What's the matter? What did you stop so suddenly for, Dolly?"

"S-i-s-h—Be quiet, Dick, I hear a noise!"

A few moment's silence, and then Dick whispered:—

"So do I! What is it? Can you see anything?"

"I can't see any one, and I don't know what the noise is, but it sounds like somebody pumping."

"Pumping! How odd! Can't you possibly get your head out, Dolly?"

"Not without taking away some stones."

"How far can you see? Where does the hole look out upon?"

"The hole seems to be on a level with the ground; but there's a wall in front, and I can't see beyond that."

"The noise is still going, isn't it?"

"Yes—regular as clockwork."

"Try a shout."

Dolly, placing a hand each side of his mouth, gave a regular triple "view—hallo!"

As the echoes died away—partly outside and partly in the dungeon, a low chuckling sound was heard, followed by muttered words, interspersed with short laughs.

"What is that, Dolly?" asked Dick, curiously.

"Some one chuckling," replied Dolly

"Nonsense!"

"It's a fact, Dick."

"Call out to him, Dolly."

Dolly, craning his neck as far in the hole as he could, cried—

"High, there! High!"

Listening intently, there came the sounds of muttered words, accompanied by more chuckles, and the noise of pumping more vigorous than ever.

"Can you catch the words, Dolly?" asked Dick.

"Some of them."

"What are they?"

"Why, whoever it is, says we may call away as much as we like, he'll see us blow'd first before he'll let us out."

"What a brute!" replied Dick. "Who can it be?"

"I don't know; but the voice seems familiar to me."

"Try again, Dolly."

This time Dolly sent forth a piercing whistle, and then shouted—

"I say! High there! Why don't you answer?"

The response to this was another prolonged string of chuckles, with louder pumping than ever.

"It's no go," said Dolly. "The beggar, whoever he is, only chuckles and pumps away faster than ever."

"Get down, Dolly," said Dick, "and let us talk it over."

"This is the rummiest go that ever was," said Dolly, as they resumed their feet, standing now up to their knees in water. "There's someone pumping in the water, and seems very happy over it, too!"

"Good gracious!" exclaimed Tom Sheppard. "What an infernal monster he must be! Fancy, a fellow deliberately pumping for the purpose of drowning us!"

"It's a fact, I believe," said Dick. "I heard the pumping noise and the chuckles quite plain. Who can it be?"

"Someone who can speak English," said Dolly, "that's certain. I heard him say he'd see us blow'd first before he'd let us out, as plain as possible."

"It's queer," said Bob Jones.

It was queer.

The situation, despite its gravity, had its comic aspect.

The notion of some fellow pumping away like a steam-engine, and chuckling over his murderous work, was too ludicrous to be resisted, and they gave way to a long and hearty burst of laughter.

"A thought has just entered my mind," said Dick, when he was in a condition to speak. "I wonder if it's the Sergeant?"

"I hardly think so," observed Tom. "What can he know about the contrivances of the place?"

"It is just what it would delight him to do," returning Dick. "He knew where he was bringing us, and perhaps he's better acquainted with the secrets of the ruins than you suppose. However, we must have another try to find out who it is. It won't do to be drowned like mice in a trap if we can help it. Dolly, you must get as many stones out as you can, and, if this chuckling pumper won't help us, you must squeeze through, and bring the chaps to the rescue."

Once more the pyramid was raised, and Dolly set to work removing the stones.

"Fortunately, Dolly, being in full dress, had his sword-bayonet to work with, and which, being flat, proved a capital tool to get between the stones.

It was tiring work for Dolly, but he poked and scraped away with a will, all the time hearing the chuckling outside, and the regular monotonous pumping.

It was tiring work for Tom Sheppard too.

Tom, being the base of the pyramid, his legs were immersed in the water, and he was not only getting numbed, but getting awfully tired with the weight of his chums.

"How are you getting on, Dolly?" asked Tom.

"I've got one stone nearly out," replied Dolly.

"Look sharp, old chap. I can't bear this much longer. The water's nearly touching my nose, and you kids are precious heavy."

"We'd better rest for a bit," said Dick, "and I'll take 'base' next time."

"Oh, lor!" said Dolly, as he flounced into the water, which was now nearly up to his waist. "That's jolly refreshing after that mason's work. I'm awful hot!"

"And I'm awful stiff," said Tom. "My back feels as though it would never come straight again."

"Another five minutes will do it," remarked Dolly. "I only want to get out one stone; I think I shall be able to get through then."

After a few minutes' rest, the pyramid was again formed, Dick this time taking the base.

Dolly resumed his work with such energy, that, within the time named, he had detached the stone, the welcome fact being announced by a triumphant cry from Dolly, and the heavy, well-like splash of the stone in the water.

Then Dolly essayed to get through.

To do this, however, he found he had miscalculated the breadth of his shoulders, narrow as they were.

Clutching the outside edge of the hole, Dolly, by a mighty pull, got his head clear, but his shoulders stuck in the aperture, and Dolly found himself in a fix, trying in vain to move either forward or backward.

"Bother it!" muttered Dolly Swaps. "Here's a fine go! Blest if I ain't stuck as fast as a rusty nail! I say, Tom—Tom!"

"Hullo!" came the hollow sound of Tom's voice.

"I'm stuck fast! Give me a pull, will yer?"

"Can't you move one way nor the other?"

"No!"

The next moment Dolly felt a vigorous tugging at his legs; but a sound caught his ears at the same time that caused him to look up quickly.

That sound was a chuckle.

And the chuckle came—yes, surely it did! Could Dolly believe the evidence of his eyes? Did it come from the Sergeant? Was it the Sergeant?"

Yes, it was—the Sergeant seated on the top of a low wall that surrounded the tower—the Sergeant seated there with a short pipe in his mouth—the Sergeant working away at an iron ring attached to a long chain, the chain attached to a projecting lever in the wall of the tower—the Sergeant coolly smoking, and pumping, and chuckling.

Dolly was so astonished that he called out—

"Hold hard, Tom! Here's such a go!"

Then, addressing the Sergeant, he said—

"I say, Sergeant, do you know what you're up to, eh?"

"Hallo, Dolly, my dear!" replied the Sergeant, with a chuckle. "Is that you?"

"I guess it is, ra—ther," returned Dolly. "I say, do you know there's a lot of us here, and that you're pumping the blessed place full!"

"I do, Dolly," returned the Sergeant, with another exquisite chuckle.

"What—do you mean to say you're going to pump us to death?"

"That all depends upon circumstances, Dolly."

"Circumstances! What circumstances?" cried Dolly, opening his eyes.

"If the water holds out, Dolly. He, he!"

Here a voice came from the dungeon—

"What's the news, Dolly?"

"News!" shouted Dolly. "Jolly rum news, I can tell yer. Blest if I don't think I'm dreaming!"

"What is it?"

"Why it's the Sergeant sitting on the wall, smoking his pipe, and pumping away like anything."

This was followed by exclamations from within, and then Dick's voice.

"Tell him the water's up to our necks"

"Do you hear that, Sergeant? The water's up to their necks," said Dolly.

"Is it, Dolly?" replied the Sergeant, coolly. "Then I suppose it will soon be over their heads, eh?"

"Come, I say, Sergeant!" said Dolly, who now felt really alarmed. "You don't mean to say you intend to drown us, eh?"

This question seemed to gratify the Sergeant mightily, for, chuckling with great unction, he replied—

"I told you my turn would come some day, Dolly. Ha, ha! I've got you trick-players in a fix at last; and so help me ten men and a donkey, I intend to pay off old scores now I've got the chance. I'll drown you off like a lot of surplus puppies. Ha, ha! You've played your last tricks on Sergeant O'Shehe, my beauties! He! You see I know the ins and outs of this place, my dear Dolly! I've been here before, my sweet boy! You're in a little hole where more important personages than trick-playing young scamps have been pumped to death. I didn't expect such good luck when I brought you hear; but now I've got you in there, so help me ten men and a donkey I'll keep you there! You'll never be discovered!"

As the Sergeant finished, he coolly resumed his smoking, and continued his pumping as though he really meant what he said.

Dolly stared at him as though he thought he was gazing at a madman.

Did the Sergeant *really* intend to drown them, or was he only carrying out a joke to its greatest extent to frighten them?

The wretch *couldn't* intend to drown them, surely!

The idea was too monstrous to be entertained.

Dolly tried him again.

"Come, I say, Sergeant, let us out; I'm stuck fast, and the others will be drowned in another minute."

Puff—puff—puff from the pipe.

Pump—pump—pump.

"Sergeant, I say, let us out!" (beseechingly)

"'How would you like it?" (pathetically). "What's a few tricks to get offended about?" (coaxingly). "Don't bear malice against a few kids! Let us out, Sergeant—do!

Puff—puff—puff.

Pump—pump—pump.

"Oh lor!" thought Dolly, as he came all over in a cold persiration. "I believe he *does* intend to murder us! What am I to do? I'm stuck fast, and I could do nothing but tumble back into the water if I wasn't. I have it! The General! I say Sergeant," said Dolly aloud, trembling in his eagerness, "who do you think you'll drown besides us?"

"Don't know, nor care, my dear Dolly!"

"The *General*!"

"Gammon, Dolly!"

"It's a fact upon my word it is! We found him here, sitting on a barrel of gunpowder!"

"It won't do, Dolly! He! he!"

"It's a fact! It is indeed!"

"If it is, Dolly, I'm rather glad of it. The General's been a devil of a nuisance, and I shall be glad to get rid of him!"

Dolly was thunderstricken.

"Oh, lor!" thought Dolly. "He means cold-blooded murder, and no mistake! I say, chums," called Dolly, in a husky voice.

No response.

"I say Dick—Tom!"

Still no response.

"Oh!" groaned Dolly, "I believe they're all dead!"

As Dolly said this, a mistiness came over his eyes.

The figure of the Sergeant became dim—dimmer!

For a moment Dolly fancied himself back again in his little mother's little toy-shop in Bangfire, with Joey Pumps, wheedling for pea-shooters and then—all became a blank!

When Dolly Swaps came to himself, his circumstances were greatly changed.

The first thing he noticed, and which made Dolly blink his eyes, was a great light.

Then came forward, winking and blinking, and bowing and scraping—at least, so it seemed—a number of skeleton artillerymen—skeletons with only a back-bone, and a black hairy head.

Besides these curious things, was a number of forms lying, or crouching about the light, some in white with pale faces.

Near the light were two large figures.

One was a grim-visaged fellow, calmly smoking a short pipe, and looked like someone he had seen before under terrifying circumstances.

Dolly shuddered involuntarily as he looked at the figure.

The other figure was strange and incomprehensible, being in keeping with the mystic scene.

The head of this figure was crowned with what seemed to be a Spanish sombrero, very wide in the brim, from the edge of which dangled a lot of little black balls.

The figure's shoulders were graced by a Spanish cloak, on the legs were Spanish breeches, and top boots of Wellington pattern encased his feet and calves.

This figure had a round face, devoid of hair, and whilst holding its hand to the blaze, gazed at Dolly with a baleful glance—stared at him as though it meant mischief.

In a minute after Dolly opened his eyes, this mystic scéne resolved itself into the following:—

The bright light was a huge camp-fire.

The skeleton artillerymen, with only a back-bone and a hairy head turned out to be rifles, with busbies stuck on them, the said rifles resting against a wall.

The figures lying about and crouching by the fire proved to be the boys of the school, some sleeping, some warming themselves at the blaze.

The grim-looking figure, smoking his short pipe, showed up unmistakably as Sergeant O'Shehe.

The strange and incomprehensible figure remained strange and incomprehensible still.

Dolly couldn't make head or tail of him.

Dolly had no sooner made out all this, than he came out with one of his characteristic speeches.

"I'm blest if this ain't a rum go!"

"Hullo, Dolly!" cried the voice of Dick at his elbow. "You've woke up, eh?"

"Am I?" said Dolly, opening his eyes.

"It looks like it," returned Dick, with a laugh.

"I should like to be sure of that, Dick," said Dolly, getting on his elbow, and looking round: "The last thing I remember is that I was squeezed jolly fast in a hole, and that the Sergeant was pumping you and chums to death."

"It's all right, now, Dolly. The Sergeant was only making believe to drown us, though I must say he carried the joke rather too far. He was only just in time to save us."

"Ah!" muttered Dolly, nodding his head significantly at the Sergeant. "Only just in time, were you, old patched breeches? All right! That was one to you. Stop a bit!"

"The Sergeant thinks we shall have had enough of practical joking, Dolly, after that lesson."

"Does he?" said Dolly, with affected simplicity. "Who is that rum figure in the Spanish rig, Dick?"

"The General."

"He wasn't drowned, then?"

"It doesn't look like it, eh?"

"Is he cracked, Dick? He looks queer about the eyes."

"Quite gone off his head, Dolly, and no wonder, either."

"How?"

"We suppose the fright of being fastened to the barrel of powder must have affected his brain. He did nothing but mumble all the time the water was deepening, and when the water was let out, and the General was brought to light, he began storming, and calling upon Mrs. Macnamarrow to take off his cocked hat and scarlet drawers. Declared he couldn't go to a field-day without them, and threatened to send her into the maintop till she got rid of her sea-sickness."

"Poor fellow!" said Dolly. "He's thinking of what happened on the voyage, and is confounding one thing with another. He looks like a melancholy brigand. How did he get those outlandish togs?"

"The Sergeant found them in this part of the ruins, and, between me and you and the gate-post, I'd rather the General sported the romantic costume than myself. He's done nothing else but scratch himself since he has got warm!" added Dick, shrugging himself.

"I see—tenants in previous possession?"

"Thousands!"

"I hope he won't come near me!"

As Dolly spoke, the General, who had never taken his eyes off him from the moment he came to, suddenly crept towards him, his look deepening to one of extreme mystery, and said in a low, mysterious voice—

"Have you seen my cocked hat ?"

"Humour him," whispered Dick.

"Yes," said Dolly, "lots of times."

"Ah !" muttered the General. *Where* did you see it last ?"

"On the mast-head."

The General, considering a moment, shook his head slowly, saying—

"No, you're wrong ! It was when Mrs. Macnamarrow was cooking it in a frying-pan on the top of my burning pagoda—eh ?"

CHAPTER XLVI.

RESTORATION AND EXPLANATION—SERGEANT O'SHEHE, HAVING AN OPPORTUNITY OF DISPLAYING HIS BRAVERY, COMES OUT STRONG.

"QUITE RIGHT," returned Dolly, "I remember you had invited me and your friend Ching-Ching Hango-Funky-Bung to supper."

"That's a lie !" suddenly thundered the General, seizing Dolly by the throat. "By Jove, sir ! by Jove, I'll——"

Here the General was seized by the collar by the Sergeant and forced into a sitting position again over the fire, where he continued muttering and glaring at Dolly.

"So you've come to life again, my dear Dolly, have you ?" remarked the Sergeant with a grin, resuming his smoking.

"No thanks to you, Sergeant !"

"All thanks to me," returned the Sergeant, nodding his head impressively. "I could have drowned the blessed lot of you had I liked. But you see I didn't like. I hope it will be a caution to you, my dear Dolly, not to play tricks off on Sergeant O'Shehe. Here's a nice specimen of what you've, amongst you, brought a fine intellect to," giving the General a kick in the ribs that made him shrink away. "So help me ten men you'll not get off so easily next time."

"I think I could name someone," said Dolly, significantly, "who had something to do with bringing about the General's present state."

"Suppose you hold your chatter and go to sleep, Dolly dear, eh ?" returned the Sergeant. It's just three hours to daybreak, and it's turn-out then you'll have to do, to march back to camp at daybreak."

"You'd better get what rest you can, Dolly," whispered Dick. "We shall have a long march before breakfast. I shall have something to say to you as we march along. Good night !"

"Good night, Dick !"

Though Dolly's couch was only the cold ground, and his pillow his busby, he was soon off into the land of dreams.

Tired people, as a rule, sleep soundly—sleep without rocking.

This was the case with our embyro campaigners.

The boys were, in truth, physically and mentally exhausted.

Apart from the long evening's march, they had all been turned out to assist in the rescue of Dick and his chums and the General.

Then there had been much tramping to the cork-wood for fuel to make a huge fire for drying the uniforms of those who had been nearly drowned.

Thus the boys were thoroughly tired out and

slept like tops; and no time seemed to have passed when the sharp rattle of the drum reverberated through the ancient ruins at the cold grey time of the morning, announcing the *reveillé.*

The boys had scarcely opened their heavy eyes, and pulled themselves shiveringly together, when the beat of the drum was followed by the sharp, peremptory voice of the Sergeant—

"Now then, boys. Turn out ! Pull yourselves together ! You've just two minutes to fall in ! Laggers will be left behind !"

Then followed a great tumbling and bustling about putting on busbies, hurriedly buttoning of tunics and hunting for rifles at the same time.

Scarcely two seconds, instead of two minutes, seemed to have passed as the drummer beat the "fall in."

It was run and scurry to get into line, but all were up to the mark except Dolly, who, it was observed, was busily engaged near the embers of the fire fumbling away at the breast of his tunic, with his back turned to the parade.

"Now, Dolly Swaps !" cried the Sergeant, who was standing in front of the parade, waiting to give the necessary word of command. "There you are—as usual—behind everybody else !"

"Coming, Sergeant !" cried Dolly, "I'm only buttoning my tunic to prevent my getting a cold on the chest."

A titter passed through the ranks as Dolly, the next moment, came running up still fumbling away at his tunic, and took his place in the front rank.

Then the Sergeant proceeded—

"T'shun ! Eyes right—dress !"

Here the Sergeant took his place at the right, and scanned the front rank.

"All in line except Adolphus Swaps. Breast too far advanced. Back yet. More still. Now your face and busby's out of line ! Up ! Breast too far forward again."

The fact is it was utterly impossible for Dolly to get into line, and for a good reason.

That reason the Sergeant soon found out.

"Confound him !" muttered the Sergeant, suddenly marching up and confronting Dolly. "Ah ! I see !" he said aloud, poking the little fellow in the breast with his stick. "Got a chest complaint—eh ? What's the matter, Dolly dear ?"

"Where, Sergeant ?" asked Dolly, innocently, whilst many heads were put forward trying to get a glimpse of him.

"There, my dear. There ! There !" poking him at each word in the chest. "You're bigger in the chest than ever you were in the 'right-about' this morning ! What's the matter, Dolly ?"

"Perhaps my chest has expanded, Sergeant, after being squeezed in the hole."

"I should like to see that phenomenon, Dolly," said the Sergeant, ironically, followed by an audible titter. "Unbutton !"

"It's too tight, Sergeant," replied Dolly. "Better leave nature alone."

"I'm curious," said the Sergeant. "I'll unbutton it for you, Dolly."

Suiting the action to the word, the Sergeant began unbuttoning—each button coming unfastened with a pop.

With each "pop" the breast of Dolly gradually opened out, revealing something of a scarlet hue.

"Hullo ! my robin red breast," exclaimed the Sergeant, beginning to pull something forth.

"Hul—lo ? (pull.) Why ! (pull.) What ! (pull.)

Well, well! (holding up a scarlet article of lady's wearing apparel, and continuing amidst loud laughter.) So help me ten men and a donkey if it isn't Mrs. Rumball's scarlet trousers! May I ask what my dear Dolly wanted with Mrs. Rumball's trousers in his bosom?" he, added banteringly.

"To keep his bosom warm!" returned Dolly, with affected simplicity.

"Oh!" exclaimed the Sergeant, as Dolly,s remark elicited fresh laughter. "Oh! Are you warm behind, Dolly— eh?"

"Quite, thank you, 'Sergeant," returned Dolly, imperturbably.

"Sure, dear Dolly?'

"Quite?"

"Dolly, I'm sorry to doubt your word," said the Sergeant shaking his head; but I'm strongly under the impression that your 'right-about' sadly wants warming! We'll try. Now! Right-about face!"

Round went Dolly, and next moment he received an impression on his "right-about" from the Sergeant's toe, that sent him flying into the arms of his covering file.

"Up you get, my Dolly," continued the Sergeant. 'T'shun! Front! Steady—hands down by the side, my dear," he added, sarcastically, as Dolly came to the "front" holding his "right-about" with one hand as though he felt a pain in that region, and was trying to soothe it. "We'll just try it once more, Dolly——"

"But I'm quite warm, Sergeant," hastily said Dolly. "I'm awful hot—I am, indeed!"

"Nothing like making sure, Dolly dear," returned the Sergeant, with affected gravity. "For fear you mistake your own feelings, we'll just try it once more. Now! Right-about-face!"

Round again went Dolly; but if the Sergeant thought he was going to have it all his own way he was mistaken.

Dolly at that moment thought of a dodge.

"If I can only catch his foot I'll give him a toppler!"

With this dodge in his mind, Dolly, as he went to the "right-about," glanced round, and just as the Sergeant's foot rose he turned with the quickness of lightning, caught it in both hands, and with another dextrous movement placed it over his shoulder, and commenced backing his enemy.

As the Sergeant had now only one leg to stand upon, he was at Dolly's mercy.

He had to choose between two alternatives—to stand still and sustain a heavy fall on the back of his cranium, or to hop about backwards on one leg.

Apparently the Sergeant thought the latter, though it detracted from the usual gracefulness of his movement, was preferable to a fractured skull; for giving way to Dolly's pressure, he went hopping backwards along the front line, shouting forth terrible retribution on Dolly's head, and eliciting the undisguised amusement of the boys.

After a little "chaff" at the Sergeant, whilst in this position, Dolly suddenly slipped his leg off his shoulder, let it fall to the ground with a shock that nearly dislocated the knee, and then, as the Yankees say, "made tracks."

Dolly's legs, however, were much shorter than the Sergeant's, and he quickly fell a captive to the latter, and felt what it was to get a warm tanning from a stick before he was again permitted to "fall in."

"It's only a 'lick and a promise' that, my Dolly," observed the Sergeant. "It's fine times when we get up to the Signal Station on the Rock, my dear. As Mrs. Rumball will be glad of her trousers, you can carry them across your shoulders—they'll keep your whole body warm. Now we'll be off," he added, addressing the grinning boys. "Number from the right. Steady. Number in sections of fours. Steady. Right of section—prove! Left of sections—prove; Steady. Fix bayonets! Shoulder-'um! Fours—left! Shoulder-'um. To the tune of "The School of the Regiment." * Quick mar—r—ch!"

And in the grey of the morning Our Boys left the ruins and stepped out for the camp, accompanied by two conspicuous figures—Dolly Swaps robed with Mrs. Rumball's scarlet drawers, and the demented General in his new Spanish costume, strutting along by the side of the Sergeant.

. . . .

Scene in the camp.—Sunset the same evening. An alarm has been given that an attack is about to be made on the camp by brigands. To meet it, the Sergeant has divided the School into three divisions. Two of these—one under the command of Dick Everett and the other under Tom Shepherd—has been despatched to outflank the enemy. The third division under the command of the Sergeant himself, is posted in a circle round a large tree. In this circle, and behind the tree, stands the Sergeant. In the distance are heard rifle shots.

"By jove!" cried the Sergeant. "They're at it! Can any of you see the smoke? For the reasons I gave you just now, I mustn't look round the tree! You see, it 'ud never do for a general to expose himself. What would the troops be without a general? I'm in the same position as a general. If I was shot it 'ud be a bad look-out for you all! Good Lord!—how they are going it! Is any of the dear boys shot?"

"Can't say, Sergeant," said Dawson. "There is so much smoke and we are too low down—kneeling, you know. Can't you look round a second?"

"I can't, by Jove! Wheu—u—gh! Do you hear that? Wasn't that a volley! So help me ten men, but it reminds me of the battle of the Alma! Oh! oh! What the deuce was that?"

"Only some shots from the brigands, Sergeant, against the tree," said Dawson. "They're coming nearer?"

"Coming nearer? You don't say so?" cried the Sergeant, getting as close to the tree as he could, for fear of a stray shot should touch him. "What'll I do boys? I—I don't want to be shot for your sakes! Good Lord!" (more rattling of shot amongst the trees.) "It's getting blessed hot!"

"Our boys are running, Sergeant," cried Dawson. "Can't you step out and rally them?"

"Running? The cowards!" exclaimed the Sergeant. "By Jove! it'll serve 'em right if they get all shot! Oh! oh! Good Lord! It's shot I am! Oh! oh! So help me ten men, it's done for I am!"

"What's the matter, Sergeant?" asked Dawson, in a voice of affected concern, whilst the other boys' faces were on the stretch with broad grins—for they all knew what had happened.

"Oh, the cowardly villains!" groaned the Sergeant. "It isn't fighting fair they are!"

"What do you mean?" said Dawson.

* This song, which was composed by Dick Everett, will be given before the conclusion of the story.

"What is it I mean? Oh! oh! Lord! It's firing with small shot they are! They've riddled me 'right-about,' and it's as full of holes as a sieve; Oh! carry me off the field. It's wounded mortally I am!"

"Nonsense, Sergeant," said Dawson, who with his chums was nearly choking with suppressed laughter. "I—I don't (chuck-chuck), se—e (a choke and splutter)—e a—any blo—blo—blood! Take your hands away (chuck-chuck), and see—e (chuck) if there's any go—o—re on them."

Mechanically complying, the Sergeant brought his hands to the front, and there, to his horror, he saw that the palms were covered with what his frightened imagination took to be the life's blood which had a minute ago circulated through his seat of honour.

"The Lord save us!" cried the Sergeant, in a faint tone of despair and alarm. "It's bleeding to death I am!"

We pause in the midst of describing this thrilling scene, to inform the reader that the blood which the "small-shot" of the enemy had drawn from the Sergeant's "right-about," had oozed forth in the nature and consistency of liquid blacking.

Though this liquid compound was now flowing —as he imagined—from the Sergeant's person, it had only a minute since been propelled from the rifle of Dolly Swaps, the said Dolly having been perched behind a tree, in waiting for what is known amongst the most accomplished marksmen as a "pot-shot."

"I'm afraid you're right, Sergeant," said Dawson, seriously, and in a pitying tone.

"Do you think so?" asked the Sergeant, falteringly.

"I do," returned Dawson. "The blood is awfully black, showing that it has come from a great depth!"

During the progress of these remarks, anxious questions, and momentous replies, we must observe, parenthetically, that at the moment the Sergeant was wounded, Dawson had made a preconcerted sign to Dick and Tom Shepherd that Dolly had accomplished the sanguinary task intrusted to him, and that, therefore, the two divisions began to close in around the tree in straggling order, kneeling down, firing, reloading, firing again, like troops retreating and hard-pressed by the enemy.

Dick, indeed, and several of the ringleaders had hastened up at Dawson's sign, and had stood most interested spectators of the Sergeant's alarm—Dick all the time winking hard at Dawson, and making signs for that by no means unwilling individual to "pile on the agony."

But as the Sergeant gave a dreadful groan in responce to the awful verdict pronounced by Dawson, Dick deemed it time for himself to "put in a spoke."

Suddenly Dick put himself into a very warm, puffy, and excited state, and rushing in front of the wounded man, began a series of spasmodic exclamations.

"For Heaven's sake, Sergeant, get out of that!" cried Dick, loading his rifle in a great flurry. "Save yourselves! The enemy are upon us in overwhelming numbers!"

This was apparently confirmed by a sharp volley and a great rattling of bullets (seemingly) amongst the branches of the trees, and followed by the fluttering down of a lot of leaves.

"I can't move!" moaned the Sergeant, who had once more placed his hands behind him, and was supporting himself in an exhausted condition against the tree.

"Can't move!" cried Dick. "Why, what's the matter?"

"It's wounded I am!" moaned the Sergeant.

"Wounded! Where?"

"Me—me 'right-about'! The cowardly unsoldier-like devils are firing with small-shot, and it's winged me they have behind!"

Here came another volley, more rattling of bullets, and more falling of leaves.

"If you don't come away," cried Dick, presenting his rifle and letting fly at an imaginary foe, "you'll be captured! What shall we do without a leader?"

"The devil take them!" exclaimed the Sergeant. "It's up in the tree I ought to have been all the time. That would have been the place for me to have conducted the battle! But I'm done for! So help me ten men and a donkey, I wish that infernal General had been——"

"Come!" cried Dick, hurriedly. "You'll be captured as sure as a gun! Here they are! Bugler," shouted Dick, "sound the retreat!"

The next instant the notes of the bugle rang out, and like a lot of frightened rabbits away scampered the boys, firing at random, and exhibiting every sign of bewildered terror.

"Farewell, Sergeant!" shouted Dick. "If you won't come, we must leave you to your fate! To the trees!" added Dick, waving his arms to the boys. "Each one get under cover! Quick with it!"

Left to his fate!

As the ominous words fell upon the Sergeant's ears, his fear and agony of mind broke forth in the form of great drops of perspiration, and he cried—nay screamed—

"Halt! Halt! Is it like that you'd forsake me? Would you leave me to be taken prisoner by a lot of dirty Spaniards? Do you call yourselves British boys to be frightened and leave your wounded commander stuck against a blessed tree like this? Oh! So help me ten men and a donkey, but I'll be down on you for this! I'll flog you all round and confine you to the barracks—woods, I mean," he added as an irresistible burst of laughter greeted this mistake. "Oh, you cowards!"

Suddenly, at a sign from Dick, the firing ceased.

"There, Sergeant," cried Dick, from behind his tree, whilst there appeared nearly as many heads, peeping from behind as many trees as there were boys, all watching the preceedings with delighted faces, "they've ceased firing. Now's your time! This way! Make a rush for my tree!"

"What are they doing?" asked the Sergeant, who was loath to run any risk, "I mustn't expose myself, d'ye see, for your sakes. It's a very compromised position I'm in. Fancy a general being wounded and his troops cutting away and leaving him in the hands of the enemy, when it's behind his troops he ought to be, out of harm's way, and seeing that every mother's son was doing his duty! What are the cowardly Spaniards up to?"

"Nothing just now," said Dick. "They've got behind trees like ourselves. Just give a peep for yourself.

As Dick had said, the enemy had stationed themselves behind trees, but that enemy's force had dwindled down to two—Dolly Swaps and Bob Jones—each standing with rifle at the "present," ready to "let fly," whilst at the moment

Confronting the Sergeant was Rumball, his arms crossed defiantly on his breast.—See page 129.

No. 11.

Dick spoke Joey Pumps came from behind a tree, for he had been dancing about and constantly on the point of "goin' orf" through the thick of the fierce fight, and assuming his favourite attitude, took up his stand a few yards in front of the Sergeant, tipping the latter a wink of encouragement as he did so.

Joey did more, for he took up the conversation.

"Now, Sarjint," said Joey, encouragingly, and as though he were the man and the Sergeant the boy. "Try a peep. Hit's all right. There's no one ther as'll 'urt yer!"

It must not be supposed that the Sergeant, in cautiously advancing his head to "try a peep," was enabled to do so from the reviving influence Joey's encouraging manner had on the Sergeant's courage. Joey was much too insignificant an atom, a kind of human flea that was only worth catching and crushing when he became too troublesome, for the Sergeant's notice just now.

The Sergeant was suffering too much from his wound, and his mind was too much exercised about his personal safety for Joey's words to nip his sensative feelings at this moment.

The Sergeant was quite conscious that Joey was there, but he was to much preoccupied with himself or to feel the drift of Joey's words, or reflect upon the peculiar circumstance of Joey's fearlessness in exposing himself to the bullets of the enemy, whilst he, the Sergeant, was slinking and trembling behind a tree.

It was with a considerable amount of eager expectation, a smile of exquisite enjoyment on his expressive features, that Joey watched the Sergeant's head slowly feel its way, as it were, to get one eye round the tree.

So excited was Joey as the Sergeant's head got nearer and nearer exposure, that he bent forward his body, keeping both hands in his pockets, whilst his eyes opened to their full extent, and fairly shone in anticipation of the fun.

As the Sergeant's forage-cap projected, followed by a bang, and the Sergeant drew himself back with a start, giving utterance to the shock his nerves had sustained in the short exclaimation— "The Lord save us! but the devils are watching me like a blessed mouse!" Joey burst out with an exquisite laugh.

"Ha! ha! ha—a—h! a—a—e—ah? Oh, lor! ha! ha—Oh, dear! I say Sar—jint, yer 'ed wor putty—ha! ha—a—h—nigh blowed orf then, eh? Ha! ha—a—a—h! Oh, lor! wasn't hit? Try a peep t'other side. Lor bless yer, don't be afeared —jist look 'ow *I* stans hit! Jist fancy a little fellow like me——"

There was a good deal of chuckling and demonstrations of amusement amongst the boys at the scene that was being enacted, but the scene that followed was so rich in its comic elements that many of the boys were speedily reduced to a state of limpness that had never been surpassed by Joey Pumps, whilst so much damage was done to the sides of others by distention from internal pressure caused by a mighty agitation of the risible nerves, that for days after a soreness was experienced, which was productive of much inconvenience.

From the signs of amusement around him, the Sergeant had began to suspect that he was the victim of another trick, and this, together with Dolly's barefaced chaff, had begun to arouse the Sergeant's indignation.

The Sergeant was conscious that he had not exhibited his courageous qualities to great advantage, nor favourably demonstrated his fitness to take an army into action nor bring it out again,

and with this consciousness came a feeling of chagrin and wounded pride. If a man's courage will not always stand the sticking-point, he does not like, nevertheless, to be found out; or, if a man is not fit to lead armies, though he says he is, he usually has a particular objection to having his boasting disproved.

This was just now the Sergeant's state of mind, and he was on the point of rushing upon Joey, when he was arrested by scathing words—words uttered in mocking, tantalising, sarcastic intonations—uttered with an incisive scornfulness worthy of Mephistopheles, uttered by a short, stout man, confronting the Sergeant with his arms crossed defiantly on his breast, in an attitude strikingly like the images of Napoleon Bonaparte.

"Ha, ha, ha! Yer a putty commander, ain't yer? Ha! ha! Yer a brave indiwidool, I don't think—e—h? Ha, ha!"

Thus abruptly accosted, the surprised Sergeant turned his gaze from Joey and turned it upon the individual who had thus the daring hardihood—presumption—cheek—to beard him to his face, and that astonished gaze fell upon the scornfully bursting figure of—yes?—

Rumball!

Talk about being dumb-founded, thunderstruck, knocked off one's mental equilibrium—any one at that moment might easily have upset the Sergeant with a puff of tobacco-smoke!

"Hah! look away," continued the mocking voice of Rumball, to whose words Joey Pumps beat slow time with his head, to show his emphatic approval. "Coward! Ha! H—a!"

"By Heavens!" cried the Sergeant. "Wha—wha—what the devil do you mean? You—you common—common grease-butt!"

"What I ses," retorted Rumball. "Coward Ha-a-ah!"

"So help me ten men!" almost foamed the Sergeant. "I never was so insulted in me life! Look here," he yelled, shaking his fist at the grinning Rumball. "If you don't take off that bladder of lard body of yours in a brace of shakes I'll—I'll make your flat nose flatter than it is!"

Rumball, like the Sergeant, was extremely sensative about his figure: he considered his physical proportions perfect in size, shape, and contour, and nothing aroused his anger more than any disparaging comparison thereto.

Rumball's anger was aroused at the Sergeant's greasy comparisons "grease-butt," "bladder of lard," but Rumball had no great reserve of vituperative language. Rumball wanted to retaliate in the most effective manner, but for a moment felt at a loss what to say, and was about to fall back upon the word that had called forth the Sergeant's offensive personalities—"Coward," when another word leapt, as it were, to his assistance, and he hurled it with withering scorn in the Sergeant's teeth—

"Soup!"

At this suggestive word the Sergeant turned almost black in the face with rage, and a succession of personalities commenced—the Sergeant waving his arms and Rumball still standing with his arms defiantly folded—that caused Joey Pumps to once more seek support against a tree to facilitate the limping process, and sent Dick and the whole School into "fits."

"Pigmy!"

"Soup!"

"Blubber-bag!"

"So—up!"

"Bludder-bug!" beginning to mix and confound his similes.

"Yah! So—o—up!"

"Blugger-butt!"

"Soup! Soup!"

"Ladder-blard!"

"Ugh! So—up! Soup! So—o—o—up!"

"Brease - blag! Glutter - buck! Begger-blud!"

"Yah! Yah! So—o—up! So—so—soup! So—o—up! Soup! Yah! Soup!"

Here the Sergeant, mad at the continued iteration of the one word launched at him with merciless scorn, and finding that he was getting hopelessly bungled with his own sentences, took up his opponent's cry—

"Soup to you!"

"Yah; Soup! So—o—up!"

"So—o—up to you—you blatter-sug! Go and get some soup! Ha, ha!"

"So I ken," defiantly.

"No, you kin't. Your wife won't give you any! Ha! ha!" with sarcastic triumph.

"Won't she? Ha! ha! That's hall you knows about hit! Yer won't get no more, I knows that! He! he!"

"Go and get some soup!"

"Sharn't! Who thought as 'e was wounded wen hit was ony blackin' as was fired? Yah!"

"It's a lie! you bragger-bag!"

"Hit ain't! Whoever seed black blood? Yah——!"

How long this war of words—these insulting, aggravating taunts—would have continued without coming to hotter outlets of their wrathful feelings, in the form of blows, like many other climaxes we have had the pleasure of describing, must be placed in the category of conjecture.

But at this moment Rumball's mouth—to speak vulgarly—was "shut up" in the most summary manner by a back-handed blow from the convex side of the iron soup-ladle, accompanied by the words—

"Shet hup, drat yer! Yer gunpowder busted willan! Wot do yer mean by haggerwatin' of the Sergeant like as that, with his precious gore a comin' from 'im like ennythink? Be orf with yer," bringing the ladle down with a sounding crack on the back of Rumball's head. "Be orf with yer, I ses, and don't show yer blessed face in camp this night, or——"

Here, as Rumball had not attempted to move away—not because he wouldn't, but because the blow with the ladle had so stunned his faculties that he couldn't—Mrs. Rumball commenced a perfect rain of blows, that may be said to have brought her husband to his senses, for he very wisely took to his heels and "bolted."

And now ensued a further novel and exciting scene.

Whilst still the boys were in their convulsions, the voice of the Sergeant rang with stentorian tones through the camp—

"Drummer!"

"He—he—here, Sergeant!"

"Beat the 'fall in.' Quick!"

Quickly as he could the astonished drummer got his drum and commenced rattling away at a rate that brought the boys to the "fall in" before the "beat" was over, the Sergeant's threat of sleeping them out for the night in some outlandish and uncomfortable spot recurring to each mind.

The Sergeant, with a fierce, resolute look upon his face, was in his place ready, and the instant the drummer ceased he gave out these words of command, rapidly—

"T'shun! By the right—dress! Shoulder-um! Pre—sent—um! Should—er—um! Sup—port—um! Should—er—um! Or—der—um! Fix swords! Should-er—um! Port—um! Charge-swords! Should-er—um! Slope—um! Shoulder—um! Order—um! Unfix—swords! Slope—um! Order—um! Should-er—um! Number off from the right! Number in sections of four! Fours—right!"

All these motions were gone through with a precision that, whatever the Sergeant's personal characteristics and peculiarities were, certainly did credit to his drilling abilities, and when the boys had made the last formation, the Sergeant thus addressed them—

"Look here, boys, I told you what I'd do every time you got up to a lark. If I remember correctly, I said I'd march you to the softest, dirtiest, stinkiest bog I could find, and let you take a sweet nap in it, and, so help me ten men and a donkey, I'm just going to keep my word! You see, I don't know where there's a bog, but we'll just go on a march of exploration at the double, and may I be—ahem! If I don't keep you at the trot till we find one! I'll take the play out of ye, my beauties, before it's done with you I am. You'll find out what Sergeant O'Shehe's made of before we part. Now; trail—um! At the double —mar-r-ch!"

As the band couldn't play at the double, the fifers placed their fifes under their arms, the drummers secured their drums (the time first being given on a drum), and away they went, the Sergeant doubling at their side, and keeping them up to the mark thus—

"Now then, heads up!—keep up the pace! No lagging there! Dolly Swaps, if you don't keep up, I'll keep you at it for a week! Ugh!—a pretty looking soldier you are! What's the matter with your busby that it's bobbing about like a barrel at sea? I'll——"

"It won't keep on, Searg——"

"Si-lence! Head of column, right wheel—forward! Left wheel—forward! Right counter-march! Keep at that. By Jove! I'll give you enough of it, my beauties. I'll take the puff out of you first, and then find a convenient bog for you. So help me ten men, but it's shake the lark out of you I will!"

It would take too long to describe all the movements, the wheeling, the countermarchings round trees, and marchings over rough ground (at the double the whole time) the Sergeant put the boys through.

Suffice it to say that he led them a pretty dance and—not being able to find a bog—he doubled them back to camp in such a state of puff they had never before experienced.

"By Jove!" chuckled the Sergeant, as they came to the halt, blowing like so many animated pairs of bellows, "it'll be a few days before you'll think of larking, I'll bet! Eyes right—dress! Now, mind, it's up for drill you'll all be in ten minutes after the beat of *reveillé*, clean as new pins, or, so help me ten men, it's look out for squalls you may. To the right face—break!"

CHAPTER XLVII.

THE DEATH, BURIAL, AND RESURRECTION OF RUMBALL.

BEFORE taking Our Boys back to the Rock, it's our melancholy duty to record the thrilling incident set forth at the head of this chapter.

It must be short, and we hope it will prove sweet—we refer to this chapter.

There is no denying the fact that in taking the puff out of the boys with the long double through the woods, the Sergeant, for once, succeeded in taking the lark out of many—not all—for the night, at any rate.

There were those to be found who were ready and willing, even an hour after midnight, to be up and doing mischief; and these consisted of the sleepers in Dick's tent.

It was an hour past midnight when Joey Pumps might have been seen, by the aid of the silver light of the moon floating in space at her usual distance from the earth, creeping into Dick's tent.

We mention the above recorded fact about the non-divergence of the moon from her accustomed path because, taking into consideration the dreadful tragedy that was about to happen, we wonder she didn't drop on to the spot and put a stop to it !

But the moon went shining on and took it all very calmly.

In two seconds after Joey had crept into the tent, its inmates had been aroused, and, sitting in their camp blankets, were listening to this reply of Joey's to Dick's question as to " What was up ?"—

" Why, hit's this," said Joey, assuming his usual attitude, and—the little imp !—a delighted smile on his face, " Rumball's a-goin ter commit Dolly-cide, an' I want yer hall to see 'im do it ! "

" Dolly-cide ! " said Dick, " what's that, in the name of goodness ? "

" Why, don't yer know, Dick ? Susan-cide, there—now ? "

" Oh, suicide ! " returned Dick, with a laugh, in which all joined. " What is he going to do that for, Joey ? "

" Why, I heerd im say to isself, has 'e was a-stridin hup an down unner the trees, hin the moon, as 'e wasn't goin to stan' bein knocked about with the ladle fur that Sarjint no more. 'E ses hif 'e aint wuth no more than bein stirred about with a ladle, 'e 'ed better a jolly sight be de-funk."

Here Joey was interrupted by some rather loud laughing and a remark from Dolly Swaps—

" Oh lor ! what's he goin to do the deed with, Joey ? "

" I done know, Swaps," said Joey, " I seed 'im creep inter Dolly's tent an prig 'er brandy bottle from unner 'er piller. I hexpecs has 'e wants ter git tight fust afore 'e can see 'is way clear as to whether hit shall be drownin, pison, or rizor. But jist look 'eer, chaps, hif yer wants to see hit, yer'd better cum hat wonce, and cum quiet. I'll take yer ter the tree whur Rumball's kontemplatin hon hit, an then I'm a-goin ter ackquaint a lady has is hintrested hin the *brandy*" (with a wink). " Cum ! " added Joey, theatrically.

Joey led the way, and in two or three minutes Dick and his chums, rather scantily clad, having only on their overalls and shirts, were stationed behind a tree, contemplating the jealous and suicide-resolved Rumball work himself up to the desired pitch.

Rumball seemed to be in a state of great mental depression, for each time he applied the bottle to his lips and sipped, the poor fellow heaved a deep sigh and murmured—

" Hah ! 'Ow 'appy I cud be with Dolly, with share an' share alike o' the bottle. Hit used to be so hin days o' yore, Hin them days," shaking his head sadly, " afore that milentary dandy stepped hin atween us. Hah ! (sigh) ha ! h-a-h ! d-e-a-r ! "

" He's awfully far gone," whispered Dick to his grinning chums.

It was a most melancholy exhibition of spiritual depression, for the more Rumball sipped, the more loudly despairing he got.

But, fortunately for the sensitive feelings of the unwilling spectators of his great sorrow, and fortunately for himself, Rumball was speedily put out of his misery.

Rumball had raised the bottle to his lips for the fourth time, when a figure scantily clad, like the rest, with a red face, framed in a huge white cap-border, and a deadly fire in the eyes, plainly distinguishable in the moonlight, and with a soup-ladle in its hand, glided stealthily beneath the cork-tree aisles ; and approaching the sighing man, first snatched the bottle, and then, waving the ladle above his head, brought it down with a cruel thud that brought him to his knees with a deep groan.

" Thur ! " cried the figure. " Take that, yer thievin' willan ! Drat yer ! What, yer *won't* leave my bottle alone, eh ? Thur, thur, thur ! "

As each exclamation accompanied a crack with the ladle, Rumball's feelings were so hurt that he cried plaintively—

" Oh, Dolly, Dolly, don't ! oh, don't ! Yer don't know *what* yer doin' ! "

" Don't I ? Drat yer, don't I ? I ain't sich a fool as that comes to, yer brandy-stealin' willan ! Hif yer don't get hup an' take yerse'f hoff, I'll jist beat yer pig's 'ead ter a mummy. Now ! "

As the last word was accompanied by another crack with the ladle, Rumball sprang to his feet and, confronting Mrs. Rumball with folded arms, said, in a deeply-thrilling, sonorous tones—

" Ah ! strike away, Dolly Rumball—strike away, I ses. You'll be orful sorry for hit ere the sun's a-rizzen a hour. Ere the sun's a rizzen, the hunhappy man, has hev been the pardner of yer faithful buzzum—I mean the faithful pardner o' yer unfeelin' buzzum—will seize to hev hexhisted."

" An good riddence, too, I ses," said Dolly, holding up the bottle to the moonlight. · "The sooner yer goes the better. Thur's quite arf-o'-pint hon hit gone, drat yer ! "

" Then, Dolly,"—in faltering accents—"far'-well, far'well—for he——"

The latter word was never finished, for Mrs. Rumball suddenly flourishing the ladle, the sight had such an effect upon his nerves that Rumball turned and fled, whilst, dratting her husband in no measured terms, the exasperated lady returned to her tent.

At the close of this affecting scene, a sudden chorus of laughter rose from behind the tree where Dick and his chums had been stationed, and the voice of Dick was heard saying—

" Come on chaps, after Rumball. This way ! "

If Rumball sped on like a stiff breeze, Dick and his chums, in another instant, sped after him like lightning, and not two minutes had elapsed when Rumball was "collared" and brought up panting with this exclamation—

" Now, Dolly, car'nt 'yer let me die hin peace ? "

"It's not Dolly, old fellow," said Dick! "we're your friends come to save you."

"Hah!" sighed Rumball, dropping into his melo-dramatic tone, and the attitude he had of late adopted to show the melancholy and lugubrious state of his mind—the Napoleon Bonaparte attitude.

As Rumball uttered that expressive exclamation, he also slowly shook his noble head, as a sign of his despair of his wild-looking friend being able to save him either from Dolly or his own suicidal hand.

"I wouldn't sigh if I were you, Rumball," said Dick, winking at his chums. "If you will listen to me you shall yet be happy."

"Hah!" exclaimed Rumball.

"Yes, I mean it, Rumball. Wouldn't you like to win back Dolly's heart?"

Rumball heaved a deep sigh again slowly, and sadly shook his head, rolled his gloomy eyes at the boys and said—

"I should! I should, but——"

"You think it's impossible, eh?" interrupted Dick.

"I do!"

"I don't, Rumball. Just listen. Instead of really committing suicide, suppose you make believe you do so, eh?"

Rumball looked at Dick with questioning eyes, as though he didn't quite see the drift of Dick's proposition—as, indeed, he did not.

"This is what I mean, Rumball. Don't you know, if you were really to make away with yourself, Dolly would be awfully grieved?"

"I don't!" replied Rumball, with an approach to savageness in his tone, and a savage gleam in his eyes. "I'm blest hif I does!"

"She would, though," said Dick. "The Sergeant told me a story of a similar case to your own. I will tell you if you like."

"Do," said Rumball, mournfully.

"In the regiment of the——there were two young officers in love with the same lady," Dick said, commencing his story. "Evelyn Warncliffe was the accepted suitor, and married the lady much to the chagrin of Richard Dawson, who lost no opportunity of secretly annoying his brother officer, and got reports spread casting dishonour and disgrace upon Evelyn. Warncliffe's young wife, believing the reports, flirted with Dawson, to make her husband jealous, the same as your wife did, and Evelyn and Dawson became deadly foes, the same as you and Sergeant O'Shehe.

"Things went on. Evelyn began to be looked upon with some suspicion by the rest of the staff, and at last he called his foe out to a duel. The General, with several other officers, were on the ground. All was arranged, and at the moment the officers were about to fire, a young and beautiful lady rushed in between them. She threw herself at her husband's feet, and asked him to forgive her. She knew, by the means he took to defend his honour, that he was innocent of the base reports, and Dawson got kicked out of the army. Now, if you were to challenge the Sergeant, Mrs. Rumball would do the same."

"No she wouldn't," answered Rumball.

"You're wrong, Rumball. It's always the case that, when two people—say man and wife, like you and Dolly—have led a life of squabbling, and one 'kicks the bucket,' the other is always sorry for having been so unkind. Now, Dolly, has banged you so much of late—especially with that ladle—that if she thought you had killed yourself over it, she'd break her heart. See Rumball?"

"By jingo!" exclaimed Rumball, suddenly brightening up, and a hopeful tone taking the place of the lugubrious. "That's not a bad hidear! I sees wot yer mean now!"

"That's it, Rumball. You must pretend to be dead, and we will bury you—only make-believe, you know—with military honours."

"Don't carry it to fur, yer know—heh?" said Rumball, uneasily and somewhat suspiciously.

"No, no, of course not. You needn't be afraid of being buried alive, old fellow," said Dick. "But whatever happens—whatever Mrs. Rumball may say or do in the first shock of her feelings—you must keep quite still—not even breathe—until you are in the grave, and Dolly thinks she is seeing the last of you. That'll be the moment she will be most affected, and then you must come to life, throw your arms round her neck, and do the loving and forgiving husband. That will restore your connubial happiness, and be ever so much better than really killing yourself, you know, eh?"

"By jingo, yer right!" said Rumball, whose face was now radiant with joy and smiles. "I don't mind sayin' has I didn't like that hidear o' cummittin' sueyside, but I wor drove to kontamprate hit. Lor', why I feels has jolly has possybill!!"

"Very well," said Dick. "You stay just here and sleep, and in the morning we must find you dead. Then we'll cover you up with a sack and carry the sad news to Mrs. Rumball. See?"

"Hall right!" returned Rumball, with a chuckle.

"Good night, then. Now, mind you play your part well."

Rumball, chuckling to think how nicely he should entrap his Dolly into favouring him with a return of her affection and esteem, and picturing in his mind's eye the happy life he should thereafter lead with the partner of his bosom, stretched himself on the greensward beneath a tree, murmuring, ere sleep fell upon his happy spirit—

"Dear Dolly 'll be sure to share the bottle with me then!"

The dew had not been evaporated by the morning sun, when Rumball was awoke from seraphic dreams by the beating of the reveillé, and Rumball knew that the first act of the drama that was to unite the severed tie between him and his Dolly was close at hand.

Scarcely had the last rat-tat of the drummer been given, when Dick stealthily approached with a sack, a couple of pieces of bath-brick and a box of blacking.

"Now, Rumball," said Dick, beginning to rub together the pieces of bath-brick, "I'm going to make you look as much like a corpse as posssible. This brickdust is to rub over your face to make it look yellow, like parchment you know, as your skin is too rosy, especially about the nose, to pass for a dead fellow. See?"

"I sees," chuckled Rumball, who, by the bye, was rather shivery from exposure during the night.

"The blacking's to mark you under the eyes, and on the lips, to give the proper look of decomposing, as though you were turning off rapidly. See?"

"I sees," again chuckled Rumball. "Yer a deep 'un, yer are, master Dick! He! he!"

"Ain't I?" laughed Dick, "and now I'm ready."

And without ceremony, Dick grasped Rumball by his hair, and commenced rubbing the brick-dust on his face.

"That's capital!" exclaimed Dick. "Just the very colour! Now for the blacking!"

Here Dick's attention was attracted to a murmuring, plaintive voice, saying—

"Oh lor'! I shall go orf hin a minute."

Dick looked up to see Joey Pumps leaning with his back against a tree in readiness for getting limp with proper and becoming gracefulness, whilst, behind other trees in the vicinity, he caught sight of a host of grinning faces.

The news of the latest lark had been disseminated through Dolly Swaps, and this was the result.

Dick shook his fist at the faces slily, behind Rumball's back, and then finished his painting.

"Now, lie down and compose your features," said Dick. "That's it! Bravo! I'm blest if you don't look as genuine and nasty-looking a dead body as I have ever seen, Rumball! Do you think you will be able to keep your countenance?"

"Oh, I'm safe!" chuckled Ramball.

"Very good."

Dick then covered the body over with the sack, removed all traces of the brickdust from the grass, and, picking up Joey Pumps, who had passed into a state of limpness, and throwing the afflicted boy across his shoulders, departed to impart the sad news of her husband's death to Mrs. Rumball.

Mrs. Rumball was already astir, engaged in the absence of her assistant Joey Pumps, lighting the cooking-fire and talking to herself in muttered angry tones—

"Drat 'im! the young himp; he allers away now, a-leavin' me to——"

Here Mrs. Rumball, hearing a confused hum of voices, looked up, and was astonished to see herself almost surrounded by the boys of the school, and Dick close to her, all trying their hardest to look frightened and concerned.

"Well I never!" said Mrs. Rumball, testily. "What's the matter, as yer all hall comes roun' a body like this, a-pulling them long faces? I'd begin a-crying, the whole lot hon 'e, hif I was yer!"

"It is a crying matter, Mrs. Rumball," said Dick, gravely. "We have sad news for you."

"Wot?" returned Mrs. Rumball, stopping to look at Dick.

"Yes; very bad news," said Dick.

"Hit's that Joey Pumps, then!" said Mrs. Rumball. "I know'd has 'e'd come ter a bad hend. I allers sed has——"

"No, it's not Joey," interrupted Dick. "It's Rumball. There is—something has happened to him——"

"Oh, drat 'im, I ses! I sh'ud be glad ter 'eer has 'e'd a-broke 'is neck or summot helse, for stealin' of my drop o' brandy—that I shud!"

"Well, Mrs. Rumball," returned Dick, "you have your wish. We've just found him—dead!"

As Dick uttered this dread word, Mrs. Rumball at first seemed a little agitated, and turning slightly pale; but the next moment, she said with a sneer—

"Pooh! No, 'e aint dead! 'E aint got the sperrit ter kill 'isself! 'E's only shammin'. Jist yer show me where 'e his, an' I'll soon wake 'im hup!"

As Mrs. Rumball spoke, she picked up her favourite instrument of chastisement, the soup-

ladle, and, admidst the suppressed amusement of the boys, followed Dick to where the body was lying.

As Dick tenderly removed the sack from Rumball's face, and revealed the pale, yellow features with the darkened eyes and lips, Mrs. Rumball was fairly staggered, and stood gazing at the altered countenance in silent horror, whilst the depth of her emotion was evidenced in the laboured rising and falling of her ample bosom.

Mrs. Rumball was evidently much shocked—or appeared so.

But after the lapse of a minute her emotional symptoms underwent a sudden change; the heaving of her bosom subsided—subsided quicker than the heaving waves of the ocean after a storm, and still gazing at the rigid, discoloured face, she said, coolly—

"It's 'is hone fault, ewerry bit hon hit! This comes o' stealin and drinkin my drop of sperrit,"

"No, Dolly, yer wrong," said Joey Pumps, who had recovered sufficiently to be present and assume his favourite attitude. "Rumball hev a done susancide. Rumball was jealous, Dolly—that's wot 'e was. That konplaint hev cum out now 'e's a gone—just see ow yaller 'e is."

"More fool 'e, then, Joey, hif 'e's a gone an killed 'isself for that," returned Mrs. Rumball. "Hif I thort 'e had, I'd just give 'im a touch with the ladle for being such a hass-"

Now Mrs. Rumball had come to view the body of her husband with the express intention of giving it an enlivening touch with the ladle, not believing for a moment that he was really dead.

Mrs. Rumball (although the allusions made by Rumball to his probable sudden decease with his farewell words had come across her mind when Dick announced to her the finding of Rumball's body), as we have seen, would not give him credit for having the pluck to take his own life! but when the face of her husband met her gaze, evidently bearing unmistakable signs of dissolution—of decomposition, Mrs. Rumball altered her opinion.

Rumball was dead—there was no mistake about it; therefore it was useless to test him with the ladle; but, though abandoning her intention on that point, Mrs. Rumball had a good mind to use the ladle for another—to express her practical contempt for him in his being fool enough to get jealous and commit suicide over it.

Mrs. Rumball was angry now, and Joey saw that she was, and as Joey had no particular objection to see Rumball get a sounding crack, he encouraged Mrs. Rumball's half-formed resolution.

"I would, too, Dolly, hif I was yer," said Joey, "'E desarves to get hit—don't he chaps?" added Joey, winking specially at Dolly Swaps.

Joey's appeal met with a unanimous verdict—

"Of course he does!"

"He's shown himself a coward!"

"So insulting, too, to. Mrs Rumball!"

"Yes; I'm sure she's never given him real cause for jealousy."

"Certainly not!"

"It was only his selfishness to want all the soup!"

"His body ought to be burned instead of being struck with a ladle!"

As the reader will have no difficulty in imagining, Rumball's state of mind whilst listening to this heartless confabulation over his supposed dead body was the reverse of serene.

Instead of being looked upon as a martyr to his outraged feelings, as he ought to have been, here was everybody considering him a fool, regarding his body with pitiless contempt, sympathising with his wife, and backing her up in her wish to use the ladle about him, even in death.

"Oh lor!" thought Rumball. "I'm a goin' to ketch a plumper, I knows, with that theer ladle! An' I've a got to keep still unner hit, too, an' make believe has I carnt feel hit! Oh, lor! I wish has I 'adn't shammed bein' dead!"

Dick, perhaps, was the only one present who had no wish to see the ladle put to such use at the present moment. He wanted his programme to be fully carried out, to witness the scene at the grave.

"He will hardly be able to receive a blow without betraying himself," thought Dick, "and that will spoil the rest of the fun. I don't think I would maltreat his body, Mrs. Rumball, if I were you," he added aloud. "It will do no good."

But the remarks made by the boys had worked up Mrs. Rumball's feelings to high-pressure indignation against her husband, and nothing short of physical intervention would now have prevented her venting that indignation through the medium of the ladle, and so she cried—

"Won't hit! Hit'll do me good! Drat 'im, fur to go an' aspurge my karakter by a killin' hoff 'isself! Thur!"

The next instant there occured three incidents —the descent of the ladle on Rumball's nose—a deep groan—and a roar of laughter.

Dick, who had seen that Mrs. Rumball was bent on using the ladle, and had endeavoured to stop it in its descent, dropping on his knees on hearing the groan, hastily recovered Rumball's face with the sack, and whispered—

"Keep still! Bear it as well as you can!"

The groan given by Rumball had reached other ears besides Dick's, and those ears were Mrs. Rumball's—a groan that caused her to turn pale, drop the ladle, and stand staring at the sack which hid her husband's body.

"Confound it all!" thought Dick. "She's heard it, and can't make it out. I must gammon her. What is it, Mrs. Rumball?" asked Dick, approaching her, and speaking in a low tone. "You look as white as a ghost!"

"I—I thort has I 'eeerd a—a gr—groan from the—the body!" returned Mrs. Rumball, trembling. "Did yer?"

"How can a dead man groan, Mrs. Rumball?" asked Dick.

"I—I cud swear I 'eerd *somethin'* !" asserted Mrs. Rumball.

"Nonsense, he's as dead as a nail. If you heard anything, it must have been his spirit, to reproach you for your unnatural conduct. Fancy striking his dead body with a ladle!"

From that moment a great change came over Mrs. Rumball's feelings and demeanour.

Mrs. Rumball's soul was struck with remorse, and putting her apron to her eyes, she began weeping bitterly, and would have thrown herself on the dead body, uncovered the now dear face and bathed it with her tears, but that Dick arrested her in time, and pursuaded her to retire to her tent.

It was fortunate for the success of Dick's scheme that it was so, for had Mrs. Rumball removed the sack, she would have witnessed a suspicious sight—the phenomena of a corpse crying, and its nose bleeding at the same time.

With the exception of the Sergeant, who was rather glad than other wise, Rumball's death, we must suppose, was a source of deep sorrow to everyone, for during the day everyone (Mrs. Rumball excepted being ashamed to look it in the face) went over and over again to take a last look at the body.

Dick, having represented that decomposition was rapidly increasing, the Sergeant gave permission for the funeral to take place an hour before sunset, and with military honours.

Accordingly, at that time, the procession was formed in the following order.

First came a small section of boys with arms reversed, as an escort. Then came the band, with drums muffled, playing the "Dead March in Saul."

Behind the band came the corpse, as there was no coffin, carried in a blanket, by six boys, three on each side, and there being no pall, the body was reverently covered with Mrs. Rumball's scarlet trousers, which, in the emergency, had been produced by Dolly Swaps, and willingly permitted by Mrs. Rumball.

As Mr. Rumball had not been a military man, and had, therefore, no boots and spurs, sword, carbine, or busby, which could be placed on his body, his nightcap, stuffed with hay to make it stand, and Mrs. Rumball's ladle were artistically arranged on the scarlet trousers, and very pretty they looked.

Behind the body, as chief mourner, came Mrs. Rumball, in the impossibility of procuring mourning, dressed in her simple everyday clothes, with her best white cap—the border sticking out like the feathers of a white fantail pigion—shaking her head in great dejection, and holding a teacloth, which Joey Pumps had kindly washed and pressed—by sitting on it—to her eyes.

As Mrs. Rumball had never habituated herself to use pocket-handkerchiefs, she was glad of any rag on the present melancholy occassion.

By Mrs. Rumball's side walked Joey Pumps, with one hand in his pocket and occasionally applying a cloth to his eyes, with a large Spanish onion inside to make his eyes water, but without success.

At intervals, Joey might have been seen burying his face entirely in the cloth, and each time a staggering about the legs might have been observed, and it was shrewdly guessed that these symptoms indicated that Joey would have "gone orf," but for one circumstance—there was no post or tree for him to lean against.

The chief mourners were followed by the rest of the boys, also with arms reversed! and, in this order, the procession proceeded with a slow step, to the solemn strain of the band.

The Sergeant brought up the rear.

The scene at the grave was very impressive and picturesque.

The boys were formed into two ranks, facing inwards, like a lane, for the body to pass through. As the latter ceremony was being performed, the boys rested on their arms reserved, looking towards the body,

Then they were called to attention by the Sergeant, and, after again reversing arms, were marched to the grave, the escort, or firing party, being formed up in open order. The order was then given to rest on arms reversed. The body was lowered into the grave (a very shallow one, owing to the shortness of time in which to make a proper one) blanket, scarlet trousers, nightcap, and ladle. Mrs. Rumball knelt at one end, and Joey at the other, and then Dick Everett read the service.

All this looked very pretty in the golden rays of the setting sun.

Everybody was delighted with the ceremony, even including Rumball himself, except when the earth was dropped in, some of the boys throwing in clay balls that hurt him considerably.

But Rumball didn't care much for that; what occupied Rumball's thoughts and rendered him happy was the prospect—the *certain* prospect—of being reconciled to his Dolly.

Dolly was kneeling at Rumball's head, and Rumball could hear Dolly's sobs, and murmured expressions of regret, sorrow, and remorse, at having ill-used him in life.

" I do wish as I hadn't 'it 'im so with thet ladle ! " Rumball heard her say once, distinctly.

" Ay ! " thought Rumball, " poor Dolly's orful penitent ; but I musn't let hon yet. I mus' try 'er, an' she'll cum hout like gold a-tried hin the ovin ! "

The moment came presently, and in a manner that considerably startled Rumball's nerves.

Rumball being thoroughly unacquainted with the ceremonies of military funeral, was unprepared for the firing over his grave. Dolly, having once more given utterance to an endearing phrase, Rumball was on the point of throwing off his death-like disguise, when the following commands arrested his attention, delivered in the sonorous voice of the Sergeant—

" Escort—'T'shun ! Present-'um ! Shoulder-'um ! With blank-cartridge—Ready ! Fire three volleys in the air ! Pre—sent ! "

Bang !

At the first volley Rumball's head popped up, with eyes protruding wildly.

Bang !

At the second volley Rumball hastily raised himself on his elbow, wondering what was up.

Bang !

The third volley brought Rumball to a sitting posture, feeling himself all over to see if he had been riddled with bullets.

" My goodness ! " cried Rumball. Wha—what's the—the matter ? "

Above the laughter which greeted Rumball's bewilderment, he heard a familiar voice, saying—

" Ah, wot's the matter hindeed ? "

" Dolly ! " cried Rumball, holding forth his arms, " my darling, cum ! "

And Dolly accepted the loving invitation—seizing the ladle, she screamed—

" Drat yer ! So you've bin a purtendin' hall the time, hev yer ? I've a wasted all my tears an' groans hon yer fur nuthin ? hev I ? Take thet —an' thet—an' thet ! "

In the fight that followed, the solemnity of the scene was totally destroyed, and leaving the couple to come to an amicable understanding—if possible—the Sergeant thoroughly disgusted at this last trick, marched the boys back to camp, kept them at drill for two hours, and then took them for another double through the cork-woods.

————

CHAPTER XLVIII

FROM CORK-WOODS TO THE GOVERNER'S PALACE. THE CEREMONY OF ENDEAVOURING TO IDENTIFY THE GENERAL.—AT THE SIGNAL STATION.

WE open this chapter on a scene of excitement. The School of the Regiment, having found General Shoot, is marching him back to the Rock in triumph.

The fortress on each side of the Landport Gate is literally crowded with red-coated and blue-coated English soldiers—troops of the line and artillerymen.

The causeway which leads to the Gate, and inside the Gate, are thronged, and almost blocked up by hundreds of curious spectators,

Soldiers and civilians are equally excited about the return of the School, for, though Our Boys had not been long at the Rock, they had already earned for themselves a fair amount of fame, fully sustained the reputation they had gained at home—as they had been recommended to do on the morning they marched, with colours flying and band playing from Bangfire barracks.

The whole story about the General, and the daring manner in which Dick and Dolly Swaps had delivered the now celebrated letter to the Governor at the banquet, were well known, and there was an irresistible curiosity to see the School return to the Rock, bringing with it the now celebrated General.

The soldiers, especially the artillerymen, felt proud of their boy comrades, and were prepared to give them a laughing, noisy welcome.

The success in finding the General had been officially communicated to the Governor by the Sergeant as under—

Camp in Cork-woods. Sunday morning, — 18—

SIR,—I have the honour to inform you that we, myself and the boys of the School of the Regiment, have succeeded in accomplishing the object for which your Excellency despatched us so hurredly from the Rock, viz., to find General Shoot. We have found him, and I beg to make the following report of our proceedings—

" On the first day not knowing where to look for the General, I decided to encamp, and wait to see what luck would turn up, and so ordered the boys to pitch tents, assist Mrs. Rumball to get out the rations, and get up the cooking-tent, etc. ; first giving them a devil of a ' dressing ' for the tricks they'd been up to with the General and your Excellency, and told them, now that I had them all to myself in the beautiful cork-woods, it wouldn't be well for their health if they tried to come any of their larks on *me*.

" Directly the camp had been formed, I set them at drill, and kept them at it till roll-call, and it was glad they were to go to sleep that night. The next morning, as the General had not come in, and wasn't present to answer his name, I decided to stay where we were till he did, and give the boys a lesson in campaigning. The way I drilled them from morning to night beats the devil himself ; and not a blessed chance did they get for larks. The second day and night passed quietly, but on the third day the young devils did me. All this time, when I thought I'd cured them of playing tricks, they had been artfully preparing a mine under the camp kettle, and, hang me, if they didn't spring it, just as Mrs. Rumball and myself were tasting the quality of the soup. No lives were lost, but I punished the rascals by marching them to the ruins of El Rocadillo and sleeping them out all night.

" It was fortunate I did so, for there I found the General, and was enabled to punish the ring-leaders at the same time. Some of the boys, in peking about the ruins at night, got into the water-dungeon, where they found the General stripped, all but his shirt and the scarlet trousers, seated on the top of a powder-barrel, with a slow match burning in the bung-hole.

"Watching the young rascals go in, I thought I'd just pay off old scores for the General, your Excellency, and myself, and I slipped the bolt, and pumped away (not knowing the General was there) like blaz—like a steam-pump, till they were like a lot of drowned rats. I beg to submit that that was throwing cold water on their tricks with a vengeance.

"It didn't have the desired effect, however, I'm sorry to say, for they commenced their tricks the next evening. I regret to state that when the General was brought to light, I found that his brain was turned, and all that he could re-member was that he had lost his cocked hat. Being almost naked I procured a Spanish costume—found it in the ruins—and dressed him; but though he is clothed, he is still not in his right mind.

"I have nothing more to report, but beg to state that we shall return to the Rock on Monday morning, when I trust that, taking into considera-tion the clever manner in which I recaptured the General, and that I didn't stay even to change my overalls, though they have an ugly patch on the seat, I trust your Excellency will be pleased to consider that I have done my duty.—I have the honour to be, Sir, your most obedient, humble servant,   DENNIS O'SHEHE,

"Sergeant in charge of the School of the Regiment."

The Sergeant was too modest to say any-thing about the surprise on the camp, and the brave manner in which he had acted.

On the receipt of this report, at the style of which he scarcely knew whether he was offended or amused, the Governor gave orders that the school was to be marched to the Palace, and the General and the Sergeant brought before him, that the former might be identified by an officer who had just arrived from England to make inquiries respecting him.

The Spanish lines, which are indicated by a long row of white sentry-boxes, are visible from the Landport Gate, and the passing of these boxes by the boys was waited for, as the reader will imagine, with considerable impatience by the soldiers on the ramparts, and the miscella-neous crowds that thronged the gate and the causeway.

At length the colours were seen flying, and as the head of the column appeared at the gate of the lines, a buzz arose from the spectators, as the excited exclamation was uttered by each lip—

"Here they come!"

And then followed many remarks as the boys marched over the neutral ground, and gradually neared the fortress.

The interest of the soldiers on the ram-parts was displayed in such observations as these—

"They're stepping it out pretty lively."

"Yes, they seem brisk enough."

"What tune is that they're playing?"

"Can't make out yet."

"I don't see the General."

"You don't expect to see him in uniform, do you?" with a laugh.

"I forgot that. Isn't that the Sergeant—O'Shehe?"

"It must be—though I don't know him."

"What is that bringing up the rear? Oh! I see—it's the store-waggon. There are two persons in it."

It was not till the boys had passed the neutral ground, and had reached the causeway that the order of the procession could be de-fined.

The band, of course, came first. Immediately behind them, marching between Dick and Tom Sheppard, was a figure dressed in Spanish costume—sombrero, cloak, breeches, and top-boots.

This queer-looking figure was rightly conjec-tured to be the General, who became an object of much merriment and many jokes. The occu-pants of the store-waggon were seen to be a female and a boy.

These were Mrs. Rumball and Joey Pumps, Dolly showing up conspicuously in her volumi-nous white cap, and Joey standing behind her in his favourite attitude, his handsome features beaming with a most engaging smile, and his eyelids (each alternately) dealing out patronising winks.

Rumball, dragging on his weary steps, and looking very hot and miserable, shuffled on be-hind the waggon.

At the left of the band swaggered the Sergeant, who, but for one drawback, would have felt supremely happy. He was only too conscious that the patch on the seat of his overalls completely marred his soldierlike ap-pearance, and as he marched along to the inspiring tune of "One Saturday Night I lost my Wife," and listened to the uproarious cheer-ing of his fellow-soldiers and the admiring clamour of the civilians, he muttered—

"This is splendid! Glorious! I should be as proud as a king if it wasn't for that d——patch!"

We must pass over, for lack of abilty, to describe it, the excitement that attended the boys as they marched through the town, and bring before the reader the scene of identifying the General.

This took place in the magnificent banquet-ing-room of the Governor's palace, known as the Convent.

This noble room is enriched with the shields of arms, flags, mottoes, &c., of illustrious persons connected with Gibraltar, and of all the Governors of the fortress of upwards of a cen-tury and half past: the gorgeous stained glass in some of the windows shows the Royal Arms, the arms of Gibraltar, &c.

CHAPTER XLIX.

AT THE SIGNAL STATION.—NEW ARRIVALS.—SHOWS HOW MORE THAN ONE PERSON GOT MIXED UP, IN THE MIXING OF THE "HEALTH-SUSTAINER."

IN this noble room the Governor and a number of officers awaited the entrance of the General; the audacious pranks of Our Boys and the ex-pected return of the unfortunate officer being the subject of amusing conversation.

"You are well acquainted with the General, are you not?" said the Governor to the officer who had been sent to look the General up, in the course of conversation.

"Know him intimately, Sir Gentle."

"Then you think you can identify him?"

"I would recognise him under any circumstances. I could *not* be mistaken."

"Egad!" returned the Governor with a laugh, "I'm not so sure of that. There is no knowing but that those young rascals may have prepared a trick for us. Don't be positive until you have indisputable proof. I've ordered him to be placed amongst a lot of other persons dressed as Spaniards, and of the same build, to afford a good test."

"I have no fear, Sir Gentle, of failing," returned the officer, confidently. "If the young rascals deceive me, they'll deceive the devil—that's all I can say!"

In a few minutes after this conversation, the door of the banqueting-room was thrown open, admitting a rush of excited persons, pushing and jostling Sergeant O'Shehe, who was endeavouring to march into the august presence of the Governor, in order, including several stout individuals with old-fashioned sombreros, like black carriage umbrellas, or monstrous mushrooms turned upside down, cloaks of the bravo order, great baggy knee-breeches, and wearing Wellington boots.

The confusion was so great, however, that the Sergeant had great difficulty to get in himself, let alone his improvised Spaniards, and it was only after a great deal of loud talking, shoving, and adjusting, he, at length, got his men formed up for inspection.

Then, turning to the Governor, and tipping a splendid salute, he reported—

"All ready, Sir!"

"You *have* the General here, *have* you, Sergeant?" asked the Governor, putting on a severe and threatening frown.

"He *is* here, Sir, and *no* lies!" said the Sergeant, emphatically.

"I know Sergeant O'Shehe," said the officer, "well, and I am sure he would not tell a premeditated falsehood."

"I would not, indeed, Captain Nipper," said the Sergeant, earnestly, "unless I was forced to it. It's glad I am to see you, Captain, though sorry to meet under such painful circumstances. You don't see me as soldierlike looking as I could wish, and I hope you will excuse the big patch on me overalls, on me 'right-about.' Duty——"

"Never mind that!" interrupted Captain Nipper, hastily, as a tittering began to make itself heard. "I will pick out the General."

The Captain then proceeded, amidst a breathless silence to inspect the rank of Spanish "dummies," beginning at the end where stood Mrs. Rumball, with a scarlet bundle under her arm.

Rumball was one of the dummies, and the old lady had forced herself in, with the intention of assisting in the identification, in the event of a hitch in the proceedings.

The Captain scanned each one narrowly, pausing at the General.

The excitement of the spectators at this was almost at fever heat, being all the more burning from being suppressed.

Had Captain Nipper "spotted" the General? No!

The Captain, slowly shaking his head, passed on, and the excitement increased, for there was not one in the crowd who had not seen the General march in with the boys; whilst grinning at the Captain's inability to recognise the General were Dick, Tom Sheppard, and many others, standing near the door.

When the Captain had come to the last of the row, he repassed the dummies again in review, again stopping at the General.

"You seem undecided, Nipper," said the Governor, smiling.

"Dear me!" exclaimed the perplexed officer. "I should not like to swear that this is the General! He is much altered if it is!"

"Hem! I thought you could recognise him under any circumstances! Test his voice."

"Have I the pleasure of speaking to General Shoot?" asked Captain Nipper, looking the General closely in the eyes.

But there came no reply; the eyes of the General only seemed to glitter, as they met the Captain's gaze.

"His intellect is quite gone," said the Captain, "if he is the General. If not the General, this man is simply a fool. The General was never a fool, except when he was drunk, and then he had the most fishy eyes I ever saw in any man when in so degraded a state."

"Hem! Is there no——"

Here the Governor was suddenly interrupted by the energetic voice of Mrs. Rumball, the lady having lost all patience at the slowness of the proceedings.

Unrolling the scarlet bundle, Mrs. Rumball held out the celebrated trousers, saying, sharply, to Captain Nipper—

"Wot a stoopid yer air! I'd a 'dentified 'im hin arf the time! Let 'im put hon my scarlit trousers. 'E stole 'em wunce an' wore 'em, and ruined 'em too, has 'eve busted hout hall the gores and seams, and wore 'em threadbare."

But Mrs. Rumball was here interrupted in her turn by an indignant voice—a voice that Mrs. Rumball never heard now without its acting on her temper, and rousing it a thousand times quicker than having her nose held to a revolving grindstone could do.

It was the voice of Rumball.

"Dolly—yer jist leave the room! This ain't no place ter come a-showin' yet scarlit trousers! For shame—and afore the Governor, too!"

It would be impossible to depict the withering look of astonishment and fierce anger which this speech of Rumball's drew upon himself, from his wife.

For a moment Dolly gazed at her daring husband, speechless with overswelling anger, and then, with a scream, she darted upon the presumptuous man, knocked off his sombrero, seized upon his hair, bore him to the ground, and hammered the floor with the back of his head as as though she were driving in an obstinate nail.

But as such conduct as this could not be permitted in the presence of the Governor, Mr. and Mrs. Rumball were unceremoniously dragged from the room, and summarily taken to the lock-up, there to settle their little difference.

When quietness had been restored, the Governor completed the question which Mrs. Rumball had interrupted—

"Is there no mark by which you can identify him?"

"I don't see one," said Captain Nipper, shaking his head. "I remember the point of the General's nose used to be a fiery red—we used to call him 'Congreve,' from the resemblance the tip had to the colour of a lucifer-match—but now it's a pile pink, at least this man's nose is, and it's not so swollen as was the General's. If this *is* the General, I can only account for the reduction in colour and size to his being unable to procure either of his favourite beverages—port and brandy. What a pity it is this man has lost his senses——"

But here occurred an incident of the most startling nature. An incident of so stupendously startling a nature that, had a shell suddenly burst into the midst of the assembled persons, those immediately round the General could not have started back with greater surprise and consternation depicted in their looks and actions.

Suddenly the supposed lunatic stepped forward, and placing his fists under the nose of Captain Nipper, exclaimed—

"Is it? Has he lost his senses? You villain! You liar! You skimping, miserable rogue! I'm in the habit of getting drunk, am I? My nose is like the head of a lucifer-match, is it? The tip has lost its fiery colour, has it? It's pink, is it? Is *that* pink (blow on the eye). Is that fiery? (blow on the other eye). What colour is *that?* (tap on the nose). Does *that* help you to identify me? (blow on the mouth—the Captain backing and trying again to defend himself). You rascal! You villain! Am I General Shoot—eh? (blow). Eh? (blow). What, do you recognise the General's voice—eh? (blow). Eh?"

"Yes, yes! Oh, Lord! Take him off—he'll kill me! He's murdering me!"

That the identification of the General was brought about in an entirely different manner to what had been expected, the reader will not require to be told. It was as surprising as unexpected, and as there was now no denying that they had at last got the right man, the Governor hurriedly caused the room to be cleared of spectators, and then proceeded to pacify the much-imposed-upon, much-injured General.

*   *   *   *

The scene is transferred from the Governor's palace to the signal station. The time is the day after the ceremony of identifying General Shoot, the hour night—just after roll-call.

The place is the room fitted up as a barrack-room for the boys of the School of the Regiment.

The room is circular, and ranged round the room are the narrow beds of the boys. There being no gas, the room is lighted by candles, but there is sufficient light to discern what is going on. The circular room is very lofty, and within a couple of feet of the ceiling, fixed in the whitewashed wall, is a square piece of wood, whitewashed like the wall.

Reaching to this piece of wood from one of the beds, immediately under it, is a ladder, or pyramid of the boys. The summit of the pyramid is crowned by the figure of that most elegant and artistic of modern perfect little models—the renowned Dolly Swaps.

We have described Dolly's figure so often, that it must be perfectly familiar to the reader by this time, so we will leave his figure alone just now, and merely observe that Dolly's refined and elegant outlines, on this occasion, were not veiled in a manner that would have been permitted on parade.

Dolly's beautifully modelled legs were not encased in the baggy trousers—not that that, we must candidly own, in any way detracted from the gracefulness of his limbs—Dolly's usually elegantly fitting jacket was lying on one of the beds below. Dolly, in fact, was not dressed in uniform, and, if it hadn't been for the protecting drapery of his shirt, Dolly's per-fect little model of a body would have appeared to those gazing at him from beneath as it had many times appeared to his mother in the innocent days of his infancy.

Slight as was this costume, Dolly appeared to be perfectly indifferent to the gaze of his chums. Dolly was too well modelled to be ashamed of his figure, and, as at that moment his airy costume allowed him to feel cool and comfortable, he was perfectly happy and contented.

All the more happy and contented, perhaps, that he, with his chums, was up to mischief.

The boys had suddenly had their curiosity aroused as to whether the piece of whitewashed wood served the purpose of stopping up a hole that passed through the wall, and had an outlet in the room that had been appropriated to Mrs. Rumball.

In the latter lady's apartment was a square hole near the ceiling, and which seemed, from the position of the two rooms, to strongly suggest such a desirable circumstance.

We say "desirable," because the boys, having a regard to the state of Mrs. Rumball's health, thought that if the communication could be re-established, it would materially assist in aiding a necessary ventilation.

"You see, boys," Dick had observed, whilst they were at breakfast that morning. "Mrs. Rumball's room is very small and close—not room for a mouse to jump across, hardly—and if she doesn't live in a pure atmosphere, she'll be ill. See?"

Dick's observation had been answered by a good deal of laughing, and an assurance on the part of Joey Pumps, who was present, that such would certainly be the case, as the room was awful stuffy, and he was sure that Mrs. Rumball would be eternally grateful for the thoughtful attention.

But as Joey had concluded this assurance with a wink, we cannot be sure that he was in earnest. At any rate, Dick proposed that after roll-call that evening, there should be a court of inquiry on the subject, and see if anything could be done to enable their respected cook to breathe something besides the noxious vapour that entered her room from the cook-house.

Now, taking into consideration that the latter department was at the other end of the building, and consequently some distance from Mrs. Rumball's sanctum, it is difficult to conceive the logic of the reason that Dick had adduced for his humane intention towards its occupant.

But Dick always gave a reason of some kind, and whether it were a good or a bad reason, it was always a matter of supreme indifference to his chums. It was enough for them to know that Dick always had the good of the respected administrators of the School in view, when he proposed to accomplish anything on their behalf, and they always backed him up in his philanthropic efforts.

In accordance with the resolution above mentioned, after roll-call, sentries had been posted at the room-door, inside and outside, as was usually done on important occasions, and the court of inquiry began.

That there was not a boy in the room who was not interested in the proceedings need scarcely be said. Many were grouped at the foot of the pyramid, others stood or sat on their beds, some had climbed to the bread-shelf that crossed the centre of the room, amongst the latter being Joey Pumps; all gazing with as much interest and excitement at the airily clad figure of Dolly Swaps, as though that individual had been a newly-discovered comet; and, indeed, with more interest.

Dolly had scarcely reached the pinnacle of the pyramid, and had given a tap or two at the wood, when he cried out—

"Well, what do you make of it, Dolly?"

"It's hollow, Dick, and no mistake!"

This important intelligence was received generally with exclamations of satisfaction, and a self-satisfied remark from Joey.

"I know'd hit! Didden I tell yer so, Dick?"

"What more do you make of it, Dolly?"

"It's a door, Dick. There's a little wooden button to it, and it has hinges, and it opens inside; but you can't see it from down there, it's all so plastered with whitewash."

This information elicited more cries of satisfaction, and another remark from Joey—

"Oh, *I* know'd it! *I* ain't a bit surprised—*I* ain't!"

"Can you get it open, do you think, Dolly?" asked Dick.

"Easy, Dick; I only want a knife to scrape away the whitewash, and the thing's done!"

This was glorious news, and produced a loud cheer, whilst Joey Pumps threw up his cap, exclaiming—

"Hooroar! *I* knowed hit!"

As a knife was an instrument easily procured, one was quickly passed up to Dolly, who lost no time in making use of it. In two seconds the dry whitewash that filled up the chinks of the door began to fall in filmy clouds.

The work progressed rapidly and satisfactorily. Dolly had cleared away the whitewash from the button edge of the door and around the button, and was proceeding to tackle the top, when his labours were brought to a sudden close.

At this moment there came a cry of alarm from the inside sentries, and the boys scattered like so many mice.

Those on the shelf dropped on the table like so many monkeys, and made for the beds, for most of them were in the same kind of airy costume as Dolly. The pyramid rapidly collapsed, Dolly coming down with a scramble on to a bed with such haste as caused him to perform a somersault from thence on to the floor, with an action so graceful that his perfect model of a body was fully displayed to the admiring gaze of his chums, and with a force that nearly broke his neck.

Scarcely had the boys scattered to their respective beds, and had assumed attitudes and looks of careless repose and innocence, when the door flew open, and in stalked Sergeant O'Shehe, followed by a couple of lads dressed in plain clothes—that is, "civilian togs."

Though it was so near "out-lights," the Sergeant had not doffed his uniform, and he looked once more the beau-ideal of a soldier, the objectionable patch having disappeared from his overalls, and otherwise looking as tight as a well-stuffed sausage, and as straight and bright as a new pin.

The Sergeant's carriage was very imposing and awe-inspiring as, advancing into the centre of the room, he came to a halt and cast a searching glance around.

A few moments of this piercing scrutiny, and then the Sergeant spoke.

"Hem! It's all quiet and innocent enough you look, but so help me ten men if I don't think you've been up to something!"

"Why, Sergeant?" asked Dick, who had hastily taken a boot off the rack over his head, seized a polishing brush from his kit, and was polishing away in the most business-like manner.

"Why?" returned the Sergeant. "Is it blind you think I am? There's half of you snoring away like pigs in the most unnatural positions! There's the other half of you sitting on the beds looking as if butter couldn't melt in your mouths. There's Tom Sheppard there, gone to bed with his overalls on. There's yourself polishing a clean boot without blacking. There's——"

Here the Sergeant paused abruptly, as something white under the foot of the bed caught his eye. The something white seemed rolled in a ball, with a pair of beautifully modelled feet and calves in full view. As this object caught the Sergeant's eye, he stepped to the foot of the bed on tip-toe, and, amidst a suppressed tittering from the boys, snorers included, the latter having suddenly looked up as the Sergeant's voice suddenly ceased—the Sergeant stooped gently forward, took a firm grip of the tail of what proved to be a white shirt, and firmly drew forth the white bundle, which, now gracefully unfolding, resolved itself into the elegant form of Dolly Swaps.

Dolly's presence under the bed was due to the bewildering effect of his somersault. Dolly, not having been able to collect his scattered faculties in time to get between the sheets, had hastily taken refuge under the bed, and doubled his beautifully modelled person into such a compass as he thought would enable him to escape the Sergeant's evident gaze.

Dolly being found out, sat looking with assumed demureness at the Sergeant, whilst the Sergeant, half bent forward, remained looking down at Dolly. Dolly and the Sergeant were now the focus of many eyes—those of the lads who had accompanied the Sergeant watching the couple with evident interest.

After a few moment's silent contemplation of each other, the Sergeant began nodding his head in accompaniment.

"Hoh! hoh! master Dolly, it's you, is it!"

"Yes, Sergeant," returned Dolly, in a demure tone, "it's me."

"Hem! and may I ask how it is that my Dolly chooses to repose his artistically and delicately-modelled form under the bed, instead of preserving it from exposure between the sheets? —um?"

"You may, Sergeant," said Dolly, with assumed innocence.

"Then, begin, Dolly."

"You haven't asked the question yet, Sergeant," returned Dolly, with a gravity that brought forth little hisses and gurgles from his chums, caused by suppressed laughter.

"Hoh!" returned the Sergeant again, nodding his head with slow impressiveness. "That's it, is it? The handsome Dolly in a chaffing mood, is he? Very well, then, so help me ten men and a donkey, I'll let Dolly feel that Sergeant O'Shehe's in a *chafing*—or perhaps I'd better call it a *slap*-up mood, or, if I may be allowed to correct the definition, I ought to call it a slap-down mood. So help me ten men, but it's no modesty my Dolly has in him at all! Isn't it ashamed you feel, Dolly, at being undressed, and your beautifully-chiselled figure exposed to the gaze of a couple of strange young gentlemen ?"

"I don't think I do, Sergeant," replied Dolly, with imperturbable gravity.

"Then I'm sure Dolly won't mind Sergeant O'Shehe affording the young gentlemen a more extensive view of his perfectly-modelled form. It's a sight they won't see every day. Turn up, Dolly. Come to the arm that's many a time lovingly encircled Dolly's tender frame. It's ready, Dolly," added the Sergeant, gracefully opening his left arm, and bestowing a sweet smile on Dolly. "Come!"

It was not the first time that Dolly had received a similar loving invitation, but it was the first time it had been given when the thick seat of Dolly's trousers was not present to intervene between the Sergeant's hand and Dolly's "right-about," and for once Dolly's sensitive feelings rather shrank from the too close contact. And Dolly would have given the Sergeant a chase for the unusual treat but for one important consideration—his anxiety to continue the court of inquiry.

So Dolly arose and, much to the seeming amusement of one of the "young gentlemen." with a red head, gravely inserted his head in the Sergeant's bent arm.

"It's a splendid figure you are, Dolly," said the Sergeant ironically, as he gazed on Dolly's linen veiled "right-about"; "but now I come to look closely into it, I don't think it's quite perfect in shape. To my thinking, Dolly, it wants a little more chiselling—a little more rounding of the out-lines !"

"Look sharp about it, Sergeant, please," said Dolly.

"And why would I, Dolly?" asked the Sergeant. "Mayn't a man of taste look as long as he likes at a beautiful work of art?"

"I wouldn't advise you to, in my case, Sergeant."

"Oh! Why, Dolly?"

"I'd rather not say, Sergeant."

"Just gratify me, Dolly—for once."

"I'd much rather not, Sergeant."

"Then I'll hold you till you do, Dolly."

"Don't force me, Sergeant!" (in a warning tone).

"You'd better out with it, Dolly!"

"Then—then—well, I took a large dose of the health-sustainer, just before tea."

If Dolly had been a red-hot poker, the Sergeant couldn't have dropped him quicker than he did, with the exclamation, followed by a perfect yell of laughter from the boys.

"The Lord save us! I wouldn't have touched you with a pitchfork, if I'd known it!"

Whilst the laughter was subsiding, Dolly, chuckling at the clever manner in which he had saved an assault on his unprotected "right-about," jumped up, and slipped into bed, where he remained chuckling and enjoying the scene which followed.

The Sergeant paused a minute for quietness, but the laughter still continuing, he cried, in his stentorian tone—

"Si—lence! Look here, boys—so help me ten men, I'm ashamed of you!" and continued, followed by increased laughter—"Instead of laughing at the indecent scamp, it's making him leave the room you ought to be. It's nothing to laugh at. So help me ten men, but it's a nice introduction for the two young gentlemen here,"—pointing to the new comers—"that's come to join the School for the purpose of instruction. And it's real young gentlemen they are, too, let me tell you," nodding his head as though that circumstance was of overwhelming importance. "One is the son of a parson, and nephew of a great general, and the other is the son of a great doctor, and, so help me ten men, if you don't drop your larks and mend your manners, I'll get the one to preach to you, and the other to doctor you with the 'health-sustainer.' They're good-looking boys, and they look good boys."

As the Sergeant was speaking he turned to look at the objects of his adulation, and as his gaze fell upon the countenance of the young gentleman with the red head, he stopped abruptly—gazing in astonishment, and evidently disconcerted, for the Sergeant's gaze had fallen upon the young gentleman's countenance at a moment when the eyes had lost their straightforward look.

When the Sergeant found his speech, he said, with a deep frown on his brow—

"I thought it was a young gentleman you were, but so help me ten men if you wasn't squinting at me! Look here my beauty," continued the Sergeant, with a warning nod—"and the other can take the hint at the same time—you'll find that Sergeant O'Shehe's not the one you can squint at with impunity! Gentleman or no gentleman, so help me ten men, if you come any of your larks with me, you'll find there's some 'health-sustainers' that'll take the larking out of you—in double-quick time, too! There's a big barrel of it Mrs. Rumball and myself are going to mix between us, and you'll find it strong, I can tell you!"

Here the Sergeant's voice was perfectly drowned by a burst of laughter spontaneous and hearty, in which the "young gentlemen" joined with great gusto.

"You may laugh now, the whole lot of you," cried the Sergeant, elevating his voice, and added, giving his head frequent nods of impressiveness, "but so help me ten men, it's no laughing matter, you'll find it by-and-by. I'll not only stuff you here with the 'health-sustainer,' but I'll do what a bandmaster of my acquaintance did with a lot of wicked young devils of drummers and trumpeters."

As the Sergeant paused here to give a look around to notice the effect his mysterious allusion had upon the boys, Dick said—

"Don't keep us in suspense, Sergeant. What did he do?"

"What did he do!" chuckled the Sergeant. "He did this, master Dick. The young scamps were a thousand worse than you boys in the way of larks, and the bandmaster thought of a plan to take the larks out of 'em, and, so help me ten men if he did not do it nicely! The bandmaster prepared a jorum of the 'health-sustainer,' chuckling to himself all the time over the fun he would have; and when it was ready the bandmaster went to the drummers and trumpeters, and he says, 'Would you like to go for a pic-nic, my dears?' 'We would,' said the drummers and trumpeters. 'Ye shall,' said the bandmaster, kindly. 'Hurrah!' shouted the drummers and trumpeters. The bandmaster, laughing to himself all the time, hired a drag with a splendid pair of spankers, and took the innocent drummers and trumpeters to the picnic. The young drummers and trumpeters bowled away in the drag, waving their caps, blowing their drums—I mean their trumpets, and looking very happy. But, so help me ten men, it wasn't happy the drummers and trumpeters looked when they came back!"

Here the Sergeant paused again to enjoy a chuckle over the remembrance of the fun, his one eye twinkling like a star.

"Go on, Sergeant," said Dick. "How did the drummers and trumpeters look when they came back?"

"Look! You know what colour is the colour of a cooked cod-fish, master Dick?"

"Well, I think so," returned Dick, with a little laugh.

"Then it was just that colour they looked about the gills. You see, the bandmaster gave the drummers and trumpeters a blow-out of treacle pudding—at least, they thought it was treacle pudding, and it was the 'health-sustainer'" (a wink), "and begad, there wasn't one of them trumpeters could blow a little puff even on the trumpet, and not a blessed drummer was able to lift a drumstick!

"Oh!" continued the Sergeant, amidst a storm of screaming laughter. "So help me ten men, but it's worse I'll serve the blessed lot of you than the bandmaster served the wicked drummers and trumpeters!"

"Mind *that* now!," added the Sergeant, as he backed towards the door, looking about on the floor to see that his retreat was not intercepted by any stray foreign articles. "Find the younger gentlemen beds, master Dick, and they'd better look sharp and get into 'em. It'll be out-lights in five minutes. I'm off now to see to the mixing of the 'health-sustainer,' and, so help me ten men, Mrs. Rumball and myself'll attend on you to-morrow morning, just ten minutes before gun-fire, with a ladleful for each, and a basin of smoking hot tea!"

As the Sergeant backed out of the door, nodding his head significantly, he was followed by the most uproarious laughter.

The disappearance of the Sergeant was the signal for a general uprising, and a rush at the "young gentlemen," who were surrounded in less than ten seconds, Dick Everett acting as spokesman.

"You're the first new blood we've had since our arrival at the Rock," said Dick, "and your joining was quite unexpected. It was not very polite of the Sergeant not to introduce you by name. Whom have we the honour——?"

"Jist yer stop that kind o' langwidge, Mister Dick. Hit ain't sootible ter them. I kin tell yer."

The speaker was Joey Pumps, and if Joey had not taken a prominent part in the scene we have just described, it was because he had been too much flabbergastered by the sudden appearance of the two "young gentlemen."

During the scene Joey had remained with his back against the wall, staring at the "young gentlemen," as though he were gazing at an unnatural phenomenon; and it was only when Dick had begun to address them, that Joey had found his tongue.

"No, hit ain't," continued Joey, as he met Dick's laughing face turned towards him. "*I* tell yer hit ain't."

"Why, what do you know about them, Joey?" asked Dick, winking at the new-comers.

"What does I know about them? Oh lor! wot a question to arst. I say, somebody, jist stan' agin me ter 'old me hup, I shall go orf in a minit. Wunners'll never seize! Why, I just as soon a hexpected ter see the sun, moon, and all the 'lestial bodies drop hinter the blessed room,

'has my old chums Tom Pyefield and Jerry Jones! Oh lor! I be orf agin!"

But scarcely had Joey mentioned the names of the "young gentlemen," when there arose a simultaneous shout of pleasure, followed by a clapping?

"Is Joey really right?" asked Dick. "Are you two Tom Pyefield and Jerry Jones, of Garrison House Academy?"

"We are," replied Tom. "But I'm sure we were quite unprepared for such a reception as this. I suppose you are indebted to Joey Pumps for our names being known to you?"

"You suppose right," said Dick, holding forth his hand for a shake. "We are indebted to Joey for your names, and you may be sure, your larks too," added Dick, with a merry laugh. "But how is it that a couple of young gentlemen come to join the School of the Regiment?"

"That's easily explained," said Tom. "We heard of your school for the first time when the Rumballs left Garrison House to join you, under the recommendation of my uncle, General Pyefield, and as Jerry and I thought we should like a change, we petitioned the General to get us transferred. For certain reasons," added Tom, with a meaning look at Jerry, "the General didn't need asking twice—eh?"

"I should think not, Tom," chuckled Jerry.

"I understand," said Dick, with a laugh, in which all the boys joined. "I should have been just as compliant as the General, I think."

"And now we are here," said Tom, "and are likely, I hope, to spend a long time together, we —Jerry and I—want you to understand that there must be no social barriers to our comradeship. We want to be comrades and chums, pure and simple. Your life must be our life, without distinction; your larks, our larks; heart and soul we must be one. What do you all say?"

There was something very taking in this straightforward declaration, and Tom's appeal was answered by loud cries of—

"Bravo!"

"That's the style!"

"You'll do!"

"Three cheers for Tom Pyefield and Jerry Jones!"

Not only three cheers were given, but three times three cheers, and so heartily given, that the two heroes of Garrison House Academy had no reason to doubt the sincerity of their welcome.

When the excitement had somewhat subsided, Dick said—

"You're just in time for a couple of beds. Two of the boys went on the sick-list to-day, and you can have theirs for the present. After 'out-lights' we'll have a quiet chat. The Sergeant will be here in a minute to take the candles away."

"He doesn't give you a chance, then, of getting a light in the night?" laughed Tom.

"So he imagines," returned Dick, with a wink. "We have a little job to accomplish before morning's gun-fire, and you shall see that we won't work in the dark."

Scarcely had Dick spoken when the Sergeant entered with a good deal of puff and clatter, saying in a blustering tone:—

"Now, then, out lights—bed—bed—away you all go!—Quick with it! And mind, don't let me hear a whimper from any mother's son of you, or, so help me ten men, I'll bring round the health-sustainer at midnight instead of gun-fire! All in! Come, young gentlemen," addressing Tom and Jerry, "look sharp and slip off those overalls of yours! Things are done to the minute with me! This is none of your make-believe military schools, I can tell you; and gentlemen or no gentlemen, you'll have to keep up to the scratch!"

Here the Sergeant, waiting till Tom and Jerry had turned in, blew out one candle—there were only two—and holding aloft the other, took a final look around, and seeing that each bed contained a form, took the other candle and left the room.

"Be quiet for a few minutes," said Dick, in a low tone, "he may come back suddenly. I'll give the signal for 'blinds,' when I think it all right."

In the meantime Dick slipped out of bed, and creeping over, took a seat on Pyefield's bed.

"What do you think of the Sergeant?" asked Dick.

"He's a character, certainly," laughed Tom.

"A regular rum 'un, and no mistake," said Jerry.

"Yes, you're right, he's a rum character. I can tell you what he is in a few words. He's a regular 'bounce,' thinks no end of his soldier-like appearance; is a 'Tartar' in the way of drill; boasts a good deal of his bravery, but has no more pluck in him than a mouse; and he's a tolerably educated Irishman, but often lets out a bit of strong brogue when he's excited; he's a great liar, and lastly, he drinks like a fish when he can get the 'lush' on the cheap."

"Does he do much in the whacking line?" asked Jerry.

"Not now. He used to try it on when the school was first opened, but he likes drill best by way of punishment. I think the only one that gets touched up on the 'right-about' occasionally is Dolly Swaps. That's the little fellow that furnished the scene between himself and the Sergeant, when you came in?"

"A cool little 'card,' I should think," laughed Tom.

"Yes. There's no one can chaff the Sergeant so quietly and effectively as Dolly. I think you'll like him."

"I'm sure I shall," said Tom.

"And I'm sure I shall," echoed Jerry. "I say, Dick, what's the meaning of being touched up on the 'right-about?'"

"On the rum—ty—tum—tight—o," laughed Dick.

"I might have known that, too," said Jerry, joining in the laugh.

"I guessed that was the meaning," observed Tom; "but I cannot understand one thing. What is this 'health-sustainer' the Sergeant seems to be always threatening you with?"

"Brimstone and treacle."

"What!" cried Tom, in astonishment. "Ha, ha! You don't mean to say that he doses you with that, like Mrs. Squeers at Dotheboys Hall—eh?"

"No," returned Dick. "He hasn't tried it on yet. It's a new notion he's got into his head, and I think it's only a notion—a fancy that by holding the threat over us, we shall be more cautious in the way of larking."

"Of course you wouldn't stand being dosed?" said Tom.

"Stop till he tries it!" laughed Dick.

"He'd better not try it on me!" said Jerry.

Here Dick felt himself digged in the ribs, a dig that was followed by the voice of Dolly Swaps—

"I say, Dick, isn't it time to resume the court of inquiry. I've got the candle and the matches all ready."

"Dolly," returned Dick, with pretended severeness, "I've a great mind to keep you in bed during the inquiry."

"What for, Dick?"

"For getting out of bed without orders."

"Shut up, Dick; you know you couldn't get on without me."

"I'll get Joey Pumps."

"Not available," returned Dolly. "Joey was carried on to the landing, just before 'out-lights,' limp as a drowned puppy."

"Poor little Joey!" laughed Tom. "What good fun he was at Garrison House!"

"And so he is here," said Dick. "Joey and Dolly are bosom-friends, and go hand-in-hand together."

"Like a couple of good little boys," said Dolly.

"Is there a lark on?" asked Jerry.

"Not exactly a lark at present, but there's no knowing what it may lead to. You shall see what we're up to. I think we can venture to begin."

Then pausing for a few moments, Dick suddenly called out—

"Blinds!"

The next moment there followed a rustling sound, accompanied by the creaking of iron bed-steads, then much whispering. The latter continued two or three minutes, and then suddenly ceased, but was followed by the low voice of Dick—

"Number one?"

"Ready!"

"Two?"

"Ready!"

"Three?"

"Ready!"

"Four?"

"Ready!"

"Five?"

"Ready!"

"Six?"

"Ready!"

"Outside sentries?"

"Posted!"

"Inside?"

"Posted!"

"Candle?"

"Ready!"

"Light up!"

In compliance with this order, Dolly Swaps struck a match and lit the candle—the latter medium of illumination being a short piece of "dip," stuck into a potato by way of candle-stick.

By this light the meaning of the foregoing questions and replies was seen in the six windows of the room being closely darkened with bed-rugs, fastened round the sashes by forks. By each window stood a couple of boys. At the door stood a couple more—all in the airy uniform of a white shirt.

"You see we do our larks by system here, Pye-field," observed Dick. "Each window is told off to a couple of 'blinders,' and they will stand there to snatch down the 'blinds' in case of alarm. Then there are the sentries, six in

Slowly rising from the mixing-pan was a strange, unnatural figure.—See page 159.

No. 12.

number. At night-time two are posted at the top of the Sergeant's staircase, where, if they hear any movement on the part of the Sergeant like leaving his room, they give the signal by pulling a string held by each outside sentry by a couple of taps, and I can tell you it would take a sharper fellow than Sergeant O'Shehe to catch us napping."

"That is capital!" said Tom. "You were up to something when we came in with the Sergeant, weren't you?"

"Yes. The court of inquiry you heard Dolly Swaps speak about. We are going to resume it now. You shall see some more of our system of working. Sentries!"

At this word, the inside sentries put their hands to their foreheads at the salute, and kept them in that position, until Dick gave the next word of command—

"Telegraph!"

At this command one of the sentries gave a single, low tap on the door. This was immediately acknowledged by a low tap from outside.

Almost immediately following this last came two sharp taps from the same side, which were no sooner heard when one of the sentries, giving another salute, said—

"Report!"

"Well?" asked Dick.

"No enemy in sight."

"Good! Pyramids!" said Dick.

And, much to the surprise and amusement of Tom Pyefield and Jerry Jones, a number of boys, including Tom Sheppard, Bob Jones, Harry Smith, Dawson, and two or three smaller ones, scrambled to the bed beneath the wooden door, and began making a pyramid.

One after the other, like a lot of monkeys, up they went, Dolly Swaps' beautiful figure ascending last, with a knife in his mouth.

"Now, Dolly," said Dick, "quick about it."

"All right, Dick," called down Dolly. "I'll have it open in a brace of shakes. If I don't, so help me ten men I'll submit my 'right-about' for a couple of dozen."

Whilst Dolly set to work with the knife, Dick explained to Tom and Jerry what was going on.

"We think there's a hole there that leads into Mrs. Rumball's sanctum; and, as we consider the old lady's crib rather confined and stuffy, we're going to ventilate it for her," said Dick, looking at Tom and Jerry with an expression of comic gravity.

Tom and Jerry chuckled, and the former said—

"How kind of you! What a pity Dolly isn't aware of how hard her young friends are labouring in her behalf—eh?"

"That would never do," laughed Dick. "She might object to it. Some persons are too proud to accept favours—ha! ha!"

And now let us ascend and join Dolly.

That indefatigable individual set to work at clearing the whitewash from the chinks with an energy and skill that proved him to be, not only a perfect little model of a figure, but a perfect model of a little workman.

In less than three minutes he had scraped and picked away the whitewash, and had commenced to push open the door.

In effecting this, Dolly was very successful; rather too successful, in fact, as the effect not only nearly cost him his life, but the human bricks composing the pyramid a number of compound fractures of the arms, legs, and craniums

When Dolly began to push, the door only yielded a little at the top, the bottom remaining an obstinate fixture.

"Bother the thing!" muttered Dolly. "It's stuck at the bottom, and the blessed thing won't move."

"Mind what you are about, Dolly," said the boy on whose shoulders Dolly was standing. "If you push like that, you will have us over."

"I must push, mustn't I?" returned Dolly, savagely. "How am I to get it open, if I don't? Look out, pyramids!" added Dolly, in a tone of warning. "I'm just going to give the blessed door a jolly hard push. Now—ugh! Oh!"

Collecting himself for this "jolly hard push," Dolly, having respect to his balance, went at it with all his strength.

The jolly hard push was perfectly successful, for the door not only yielded, but yielded with a suddenness that let the beautifully-modelled upper part of Dolly's body into the hole.

This unexpected departure from the perpendicular, as a matter of course, affecting the steadiness of Dolly's perfectly-modelled legs, and which, pressing outwards against the shoulders of the top pyramid, destroyed the equilibrium of the structure, and all in a moment, to change a word or two of a line of a certain affecting nursery-rhyme—

"Down came pyramid, Dolly, and all."

The fall was great, and at first there was anything but mirth at the mishap, as visions of broken necks, heads and limbs rushed into the minds of those who had been looking on.

But as the pyramids became unlocked from the clasp of each other's legs, and got up smiling, they were greeted with ringing bursts of laughter.

The laughter continued until someone suddenly cried out—

"Where's Dolly Swaps?"

No one could tell?

There were sounds as of something floundering, scratching, puffing, and blowing, but where those sounds came from was a mystery.

That those sounds came from Dolly everyone seemed certain.

As under the beds suggested itself as the most likely locality in which Dolly might be found—there being no other they could think of—every boy dropped on his hands and knees, and began a voyage of exploration.

But still, no Dolly was forthcoming.

But just as this disappearance of Dolly was becoming a serious mystery, the mystery was solved by Dolly himself.

We must inform the reader that Dolly, as the pyramid of which he was the apex gave way, dropped into a large cast iron receptacle, known in military circles as the coal-box.

As these boxes are large enough to swallow up and hide half-a-dozen such insignificant little boys as Dolly, and as Dolly had dropped into about six inches of small coal, Dolly's mysterious disappearance, and the mysterious sounds, will now cause no surprise.

Dolly's discovery was made in this way.

After a minute's floundering about, half-blinded and choked with the small coal, Dolly managed to sit up, to clear his eyes and mouth of the black dust.

Even in this position, the top of Dolly's head was not visible, and so his chums dropped, as we have said, on their hands and knees to explore under the beds.

It was whilst they were thus invisible that Dolly succeeded in clearing his eyes, and got up to announce his safe arrival at the mouth of his coal-pit.

But Dolly was so staggered at the disappearance of his chums that he was obliged to hold on to the edge of the pit, to prevent himself again being precipitated to its coal-dusty depth.

Dolly could hear voices, but did they proceed from his chums?

Where were Dolly's chums?

"Oh, lor," murmured Dolly. "There must be something up."

Then, unable longer to endure the suspense, Dolly sang out—

"Hie! Hie! Chaps—where are you? Hie! Hie!"

At the sound of the familiar voice, the boys knew that Dolly had turned up somewhere, and they came skipping from under the beds like a lot of rabbits, each one as he appeared sitting up to catch a glimpse of the whereabouts of the lost little model.

But as Dolly's figure, by floundering in the coal-dust, had lost its original whiteness, it was not in a state to render it immediately perceptible, so Dick, who was one of the first to appear, called out—

"Where are you, Dolly?"

"Here I am, Dick! Can't you see? In the coal-box?"

We know from experience, and doubtless the reader has experienced the same, that one of the pleasantest sensations that can be felt by us poor mortals, is a sudden and unexpected removal of a weight of deep depression from the mind.

This was exactly the sensation our boys experienced on the unexpected discovery of Dolly in the coal-box. Though Dolly's besmeared and black appearance was calculated to arouse commiseration rather than mirth, we must charitably suppose that the joy of finding Dolly alive and well overcame the more gentle and tender emotion, for Dolly's appearance was greeted with loud and convulsive laughter.

"It's all very well to laugh, grumbled Dolly, when he could get in a word, and was in the act of climbing out of the coal-box, "but I'll take my Davy that not one of you would feel inclined to gibber if he had tumbled into the beastly box!"

Somehow, this reproving speech of Dolly's didn't tend to bring his chums to their sober senses, but, acting as one's finger-point frequently does in the ribs of a ticklish person, sent the boys rolling in most extraordinary and ungainly motions on the floor.

These convulsive motions, and the laughter which accompanied them, lasted some time, for Dolly looked so funny, and stared at his black little model of a figure so lugubriously, and protested so reproachfully at the unseemly mirth, that his chums could not control, all at once, either the convulsive motions or the laughter.

They ceased at length, however, and when Dolly had received a full measure and running over of sympathy from all, and had received offers to wash him back to a state of marble purity, and everyone had offered to lend him a clean shirt—all of which kind offers Dolly politely refused—the court of inquiry was again resumed,

Dolly, none the worse for his adventure in the coal-box, ascended the pyramid and entered on his course of investigation.

We can assure the reader there was as much interest felt by the boys in Dolly's venture as the people of England felt at the starting of the late expedition to the Arctic regions, and his return was looked for with as much anxiety and curiosity.

Would Dolly succeed in discovering a Northwest passage into Mrs. Rumball's torrid regions? —we cannot call them frigid regions, because we know that the object of discovering the passage was to find the way of ventilating Mrs. Rumball's room.

When Dolly had got safely into the aperture, and another piece of candle had been provided, lighted and passed up to him, he proceeded in his work of discovery.

The first discovery made by Dolly was, that the wall was about two feet thick, and that the hole terminated, not as he had fondly hoped, in affording a bird's-eye view of Mrs. Rumball's room, but in affording a view of a blank wall opposite the hole with a space between, the said space being occupied by a spiral flight of stone steps.

"By Jove!" muttered Dolly. "This blessed tower has double walls, and these stairs lead to the top, I shouldn't wonder. What am I to do now?"

Dolly reflected a minute as to whether he should go forward, or return and tell Dick what he had already discovered.

As Dolly had a full share of the romantic in his disposition, and liked being the hero of singular exploits, the former—to go forward—had the greatest fascination for him, and Dolly decided to venture on.

"It looks jolly gloomy up the steps," thought Dolly, " but I don't suppose there's anything to hurt a little chap like me. I don't care if the candle lasts."

As Dolly spoke, he dropped on to the steps immediately under the hole, and began to ascend, looking by the yellow light from the candle thrown upon his besmeared face and shirt, and on his dirty bare legs and feets, like a little imp making its way from the lower regions to take a view of the outer world from the summit of the great Rock.

Though Dolly was thus alone in the close gloomy space, he did not feel particularly nervous, but continued to mount, wondering where the hole could be that opened into Mrs. Rumball's sanctum.

At length Dolly reached the top of the steps, and found himself at an aperture that led on to the summit.

Placing his candle on a step, Dolly gave a peep to see that the coast was clear. The moon was shining, and Dolly could see that there was ho human occupant of the signal tower. Nothing was there but the tall, tapering flag-staff, against which the wind—always pretty stiff at this elevated region—made a low humming noise as it swept over the Rock.

Though Dolly, lightly clad as he was, felt the chilling influence of the night-breeze, he stepped forth, and advanced to the parapet to take a view of the prospect.

It was a magnificent sight in the moonlight.

On one hand, far—far—below, the town with the zigzag wall fortifications, the Moorish castle, like a defiant old giant, the bay with its numerous ships, the opposite coast of Spain, the Rondo mountains, the Sierra Nevada; on the other hand, the Atlas mountains, in Africa; Ceuta, the convict station of the Spaniards; Apes' Hill and the coast of Barbary—between the latter and the Rock rolled the Straits, with here and there a steamer or sailing vessel bowling along—all this, with the battery of four cannon at the foot of the tower, from which the morning gun was fired, lay before Dolly's gaze, a vast, picturesque, glittering panorama!

Beautiful as was the scene, however, Dolly stayed not long to contemplate it, for the wind up there having no particular respect for our little favourite, blew at him, and treated him very coldly, making his shirt-tails flutter, and his nicely, modelled figure shiver, till his teeth began to clatter together.

"I can't stand this," muttered Dolly. "I'll go down and bring up Dick and some of the others."

In two or three minutes, Dolly had his black little face looking down upon the boys in the room, and a general cry arose—

"Here's Dolly!"

"Why, Dolly," cried Dick, "where have you been?"

"Top of the tower, Dick."

"Top of the tower! How did you get there?"

"On my legs," returned Dolly, with a wink.

"Come, no gammon, Dolly," said Dick. "What have you been up to so long?"

"Why, it's just this, Dick," said Dolly. "I suppose I must tell you chaps all about it, though I've a good mind not to, for your laughing at me just now."

"Go on, you tantalising young beggar," said Dick, shaking his fist.

"Well," said Dolly, chuckling, "I've made a great discovery. I can't see a hole into Mrs. Rumball's room; but there's a flight of stone steps leads right up on to the top of the tower!"

This intelligence was received with a great many exclamations of—

"Oh, I say!"

"How Jolly!"

The news almost took away their breath.

"You don't mean it, Dolly?" said Dick.

"I do, though," returned Dolly. "And I want you and some of the chaps to come up."

There is no need to describe how quickly a pyramid was raised, and how Dick, with Sheppard, Smith, Dawson, Tom Pyefield, Jerry Jones, and several others, soon found themselves gazing at the wondrous scene from the tower top we have just described.

The boys were delighted—nay, more—they were entranced.

"Yonder is the coast of Africa," said Dick. "How I should like the School to go there, to have lots of adventures!"

This sentiment was echoed by all.

There was something very fascinating in the idea of penetrating great Africa—the land of romance, mystery, and stirring adventure, to the minds of Our Boys.

"I should like to have some real fighting," said Dolly. "Fancy pitching into the wild Moors and Arabs! By Jingo!"

"Talking of fighting the Arabs," said Tom Pyefield, "reminds me of poor Charley Wilder. Doesn't it you, Jerry?"

"Yes, indeed, Tom. I was thinking of him as you spoke."

"Who is he?" asked Dick. "One of your chums at Garrison House?"

"He was," returned Tom. "But he was killed falling down a steep cliff in France. He left us to join a French military school. Charley used to write to us, telling us how eagerly he looked forward to joining a French regiment at Algiers to fight the Arabs. But he little thought he should meet his death in the manner I have said."

"How did it happen, Pyefield?"

"I believe it was trying to reach a flower, which a young French girl expressed a wish to possess. Charley declared she should have it, and succeeded in reaching it. But the moment he had plucked it he felt the roots of the bush he was clinging to giving way, and he knew he was lost. 'I am going, Adele!' he cried. 'Nothing can save me; keep the little flower for my sake,' as he spoke, he, with a mighty effort, flung up the flower, which fell at Adele's feet, and the next moment Charley had vanished."

"Poor Charley!" said Jerry. "He was a good fellow, and a splendid chap for larks."

Jerry's bit of sentiment was so naively expressed and was so touching, that it called forth some laughter, and they were on the point of returning, when Dick called attention to some sharp flashes of light—like flashes of summer lightning—which could be distinctly seen on the African coast, in the direction of the Spanish convict-station.

"I wonder what the flashes can be?" said Dick. "Lightning?"

"They are too quick for lightning, I think," said Sheppard. "They seem to me more like gun-flashes."

"By Jove! I believe they are, too!" cried Dick, "What's up, I wonder?"

It was very evident, from the flashes which now came in quick succession, that something was "up" across the straits; that a cannonade, though the reports could not be heard, was going on, but the cause of it was a mystery.

Dick and his chums could only look on and wonder.

They little suspected, however, as they gazed at the red flashes, that a terrible conflict was passing between a fierce party of Moors and a body of Spanish soldiers, and that the School of the Regiment would, ere many hours, be despatched to the scene, and pass through dangers and adventures to their hearts content.

But, between the scene we are describing and the marching of the School into Barbary, occurred one or two incidents which we must not leave unchronicled, and one of which occurred ere ten minutes had passed.

Now that they were out on a voyage of discovery, it was resolved not to return to their room without having a search for the hole supposed to overlook Mrs. Rumball's sanctum, and, for this purpose, it was necessary to descend the steps beyond the aperture leading to their own domain.

Whether or not success crowned their efforts, we shall see presently. In the meantime we must shift the scene to the torrid regions of Mrs. Rumball herself.

The living-space allotted to Mrs. Rumball was not of large dimensions, and its size may be easily calculated by stating that Mrs. Rumball's feather bed, pressed up to half its natural width to fit a narrow military iron bedstead, occupied one-third as it stood across one end of the room.

It will be remembered that Mrs. Rumball brought an innumerable number of boxes, of all sizes and shapes, with her to Gibraltar, containing a miscellaneous collection of articles absolutely necessary, as Mrs. Rumball declared, for the use of a lady of her heavy build and standing.

These boxes occupied the two sides of the room—leaving the fire-place open—and were piled up in an alarming state of tottery and shaky equilibrium, nearly to the ceiling. The boxes looked each moment as though they had a good mind to topple over, crush their owner, and put themselves out of their misery and uneasy standing in life.

The wall over Mrs. Rumball's head was occupied by a deep, wooden shelf—like a deal box with the top and bottom knocked out, and leaving only the framework.

This frame-like shelf had two partitions. One part was stuffed with plates and dishes, knives, forks, and spoons, bread, broken meat, and sundry other items, and two or three wet dishcloths, and one of Mrs. Rumball's dirty caps. The other part was, save a bed-rug spread on the bottom, at this moment empty, but when Joey Pumps felt inclined to forget the cares and anxieties of this mortal life in sleep, he was permitted by his adopted mother to make use of it as a bed-chamber.

As Joey was not at this moment occupying his place of repose, we must suppose that he had not yet recovered from the state of limpness in which he was recently carried from the boys room.

Some four or five feet over this shelf and sleeping apartment was the square hole which was the object of Our Boys' anxious search. From this hole to the centre of the ceiling was a curious arrangement of rope-gear. A stout rope was passed through a heavy iron staple, with both ends caught up, and fastened, apparently, in the hole itself.

What purpose this arrangement had probably served will presently be demonstrated—and also for what purpose it was presently used.

The available space in the centre of this unique apartment was occupied by two individuals engaged in concocting an unpleasant-looking compound in a large earthenware pan.

These individuals were Mrs. Rumball and Sergeant O'Shehe, busily occupied in mixing the long-threatened "health-sustainer."

Yes, there was no mistake about it!

There was Mrs. Rumball with her sleeves tucked up to her dimpled elbows, her voluminous cap in full bloom, her face radiant with pleased anticipation, and all aglow with good spirits—there was a bottle of brandy and two glasses on one side of the boxes—there was Mrs. Rumball, working away at the mixture with her ladle, whilst the Sergeant, with a short pipe in his mouth, was taking up the brimstone from a canvas bag, a handful at a time, and dashing it in the treacle as Mrs. Rumball gave him directions.

The Sergeant seemed to be enjoying the process too, for, as he stood with his back to the fire (Mrs. Rumball didn't think the place too close for a fire) like a true Briton, he indulged in remarks between the puffs from his pipe.

"It's getting pretty strong now, Mrs. Rumball eh—? He, he!"

"Ah!" exclaimed Mrs. Rumball, ceasing from her labour to take a refresher from the bottle, and then pouring out a glassful for the Sergeant. "Ah! it's gettin' hon, Sarjint, but it ain't arf stron' enuf yit! I likes to see the yeller hin hit. I'd give 'em hall brimstun hif I 'ad *my* way—drat

'em! I wudn't give the young willans *no* treacle, I wuld'nt! I'd work thur blessed hinsides hout for 'em, I wud! That's what I'd do!" added Mrs. Rumball, taking up the ladle. "Put hin anuther 'andful, Sarjint."

"*All* brimstone wouldn't have the desired effect, I'm afraid, Mrs. Rumball," observed the Sergeant, shaking his head. "It wouldn't pass out of the system, I'm thinking, and then it's having a lot of cases of spontaneous combustion we'd be! Begad, every boy that got near a light would burst into flames? I——"

Here the Sergeant abruptly paused in the flow of his fiery language, Mrs. Rumball at the same moment stopped her ladle, and each looked at the other with surprise strongly depicted on their faces.

"Wot wor that, Sarjint?" asked Mrs. Rumball, suspiciously. "I heard a noise o' sum kind a'most like a turkey a-gobblin'."

"I heard it, too, certainly, Mrs. Rumball, but can't say what it was!"

"It ain't none o' them boys a 'idin' hin eer, I 'opes?"

"No, no," returned the Sergeant, "I left them all in bed, and came straight here. Besides I've locked the door."

"Locked the door!" exclaimed Mrs. Rumball, almost turning pale. "Wothever did yer go to do *that* fur! S'pose has 'ow thur shud be sum o' them sperrits 'eer—has I had enuf hon hit bootiful Devon; carnt say I likes 'em no-ow—I shud be that shaken has I cudn't let myself hout!"

As Mrs. Rumball was speaking, she was sidling to the door, and hastily unlocking it, rushed on to the landing, demanding in loud tones "Who wos pokin' about *thur?*" and then hastily retreated, and banged the door behind her.

"Never lock the door agin, Sergint, hon *me*," said Mrs. Rumball, emphatically, resuming the ladle and the stirring. "I don't like hit. Put hin anuther 'andful, please, an' let hus get hon with the mixin'."

The Sergeant saw that Mrs. Rumball's dignity had been somewhat touched by his impolite act of locking the door, and fearing an unpleasant interruption to the harmony of the mixing proceedings, he attempted to restore her good humour by putting in a larger handful of brimstone than usual, and making a little joke.

"I don't think we need be afraid of more than *three* spirits present here at this moment—he! he!"

"What d'yer mean?" asked Mrs. Rumball, stopping suddenly.

"Why, you and me, and—he, he! the *brandy!* See, Mrs. Rum—"

Here the Sergeant was made to cut Mrs. Rumball in half, or rather her name, by similar sounds to those that had caused them uneasiness a minute ago, whilst Mrs. Rumball again suspended her mixing, this time with a mixed look of fear and anger on her face.

"Now, I shud jist like ter know wot thet there noises *air*, Sarjint. They wos hin the room this time, I'll swear! Hif I thort as yer was hup ter hanny nonsince with *me*, I'd jist as soon give *yer* a dose o' yer mixter has look hat——"

We have heard of interruptions, unexpected climaxes, and *denouments*, which, in their power of creating surprise, are considered equal, if not superior, to claps of thunder, the bursting of shells, the springing of mines, etc.; but we feel confident that neither of these terrible things, nor all of them combined, would have been sufficient to create the degree of surprise that, at this instant almost bereft Mrs. Rumball and the Sergeant or their senses.

As Mrs. Rumball was addressing the Sergeant, with the ladle full of the "health-sustainer," ready to cram into his mouth, her anger each moment increasing, she was suddenly struck on the face with a heavy irresistable blow, that in an instant sent her flying backwards. An instant later the Sergeant was sent with tremendous force into the fireplace, with his good eye plastered up with a dose of the "health-sustainer," that had been ejected from Mrs. Rumball's ladle at the moment of her sudden overthrow.

Mrs. Rumball had been thrown into a sitting position against her bedstead, from whence, after somewhat recovering from the shock she had sustained, she began to look about her for the cause. In the dim consciousness that was dawning in Mrs. Rumball's brain, there was a germinating idea that her upset was due either to the Sergeant's fist, or to an earthquake that had suddenly uprooted the Rock.

But before this idea could be confirmed either way, Mrs. Rumball's eye fell upon an extraordinary object floating about the centre of the room.

This object seemed to Mrs. Rumball to be something between a half-naked young sweep, and half-dressed young devil, fluttering with an impish grin, waving arms, and kicking legs, over the pan of "health-sustainer."

Mrs. Rumball's conjectures as to the nature of this vision, as she sat and stared in awe at it, ran wild.

Was it a devil?

If so, what had it come for?

Had it come owing to the mixing of the "health-sustainer?"

Had it come because it had smelt brimstone? or because it considered it wicked to give brimstone to little boys?

At this moment these queries seemed to be answered in the affirmative from two circumstances.

A blue light, giving a hellish appearance to every object, suddenly burst forth, and the devil began to address Mrs. Rumball.

"Mrs. Rumball," said the devil, who was still floating gently about, hovering over the pan of "health-sustainer." "Mrs. Rumball, you're a wicked old woman! Did yer think I wasn't watching what you and Sergeant O'Shehe were up to? I've heard every word you have said, and devil as I am, I'm shocked at you! You'd give the boys nothing but brimstone, would you? Why, you're more cruel than the Sergeant—he would give them a little treacle to soften the taste!"

"You wicked old wrotch, I've a great mind to make you take this panful all at once! But I will be merciful to you this time, if you will promise to give more treacle than brimstone?"

"Oh, dear, dear!" moaned Mrs. Rumball. "I wish has I'd never seed the blessed brimstone. Oh! dear——"

. "Answer me, woman," cried the devil, sternly. "Will you give them more treacle than brimstone, or not?"

"I'll give 'em nothin' but treacle!" said Mrs. Rumball, with another moan, "if you'll only go!"

"Very good," returned the devil. "But just one word before I go! Mind, if you break your word, I'll give you such a stirring and a poking

about when I get you down in my place as will make you——"

But here the supernatural visitant vanished—not as spirits are said to do, through the floor or window, door or ceiling, but as a devil would naturally do where brimstone was present—vanished into the pan of "health-sustainer!"

CHAPTER L.

IN WHICH TOM PYEFIELD INAUGURATES HIS ENTRY INTO THE SCHOOL OF THE REGIMENT BY A GRAND IDEA.—SHOWS HOW THE SERGEANT HIMSELF AND MRS. RUMBALL GOT MIXED UP WITH THE "HEALTH-SUSTAINER."—AND HOW THE FORMER (THE SERGEANT) AND THE LATTER (THE "HEALTH-SUSTAINER".) GOT BLOWN TO—TO—TO—WELL, LET US SAY THE—WINDS.

THERE is no doubt, whatever, that Sergeant O'Shehe and Mrs. Rumball cooly thought they were going to have it all their own way in the preparation, &c., of the "health-sustainer."

Those highly zealous and energetic administrators to the School of the Regiment very coolly imagined that, all they had to do was to procure the brimstone and treacle, mix the imflammable substance and uncrystallisable syrup together until they had a combined power considerably above the necessary proof, and administer the cooling preparation to the boys.

There is no doubt that the Sergeant and Mrs. Rumball had indulged in beatific visions respecting the administering of that health-sustainer, and the subsequent consequences in the internal system of the boys.

The Sergeant and Mrs. Rumball saw themselves in the boys room, with the pan of health-sustainer and two five-gallon tin of smoking-hot tea, side by side on the table, flanked by a couple of piles of white basins.

They saw the boys, one by one, slink out of bed, ruefully approach, and stand with open mouth, to be crammed with a large ladleful of the sustainer, lick the ladle clean, and return to bed with a basin of hot tea.

The health-sustainer and tea having been duly taken, the Sergeant and Mrs. Rumball foresaw the inevitable consequences, in pale faces, loss of appetite, qualmish feelings, griping sensations, and hurried movements.

The Sergeant pictured the boys on parade, with two-thirds of them asking permission to fall out—a permission which he heard himself ironically refusing, and over and over again he had chuckled to himself in a congratulatory manner at having hit upon the dodge to take the larking out of the boys.

But, as we have already seen, the Sergeant and Mrs. Rumball had fallen into a similar miscalculation to the personage who counted her chickens before they were hatched. The worthy couple had discounted the effects of the health-sustainer before it was administered.

Neither Mrs. Rumball nor the Sergeant in their innocent confidence of being able to administer the sustainer without let or hindrance from the boys, imagined for a moment that an interposer, a deliverer on behalf of the latter young innocents, would appear at the early stage of the mixing, in the shape of a little devil—a real little devil, too, for Mrs. Rumball had seen it floating over the pan of sustainer, had heard it speak, and finally had seen it vanish *into* the pan of sustainer!

The Sergeant would have seen it too, but for one circumstance that had interfered with the clearness of his vision—his best eye had been filled up with a dose of the sustainer, and the Sergeant was wrathfully engaged—sitting in the fireplace—removing the objectionable compound.

With the vanishing of the little devil, Mrs. Rumball sufficiently recovered from her fright to scramble up, seat herself on the side of her bed, and contemplate the state of affairs.

Although the devil was gone, the room was still in a state of blue illumination, and what was more, the room was pervaded with a highly sulphurous smell—a smell that was very convincing to Mrs. Rumball, even had she not been able to believe the evidence of her own eyes, that a devil certainly *had* been there.!

"Drat it!" exclaimed Mrs. Rumball. "I shall be choked in a minut! (cough) Hit's the fust time I hever bin so close to one hon 'em, an' I 'opes has it'll be the larst! Though they kin float about, and looks werry light, the thins kin 'it dratted 'ard, 'an they leaves a beastly smell behind! I mus' hev a drop ter (cough) keep me from choking. I shudn't wonner hif the dratted thin' hev vanished with the bottle!"

Mrs. Rumball made the latter remark because she had cast her eyes in the direction of the spot she had last seen the bottle, but could see nothing of the kind there now. Thinking it possible it might be the blue glare that was still in the room, and which rendered things indistinct, Mrs. Rumball advanced to take a closer view, and then exclaimed angrily—

"Yes, hit is gone too! Drat hit, hit might hev left me a drop, knowing as I shud be choked with hit's beastly brimstone! Dr——"

Mrs. Rumball's furthur angry declamation was cut short by a glucking sound—the sound as of someone drinking from a bottle—a sound that was very familiar to Mrs. Rumball's ears, and—her mouth too.

Casting a searching glance around, the thought flashing into her mind that she might catch the devil after all, in the act of glucking her brandy—her eyes fell upon a fat figure, squatted in a corner with its head thrown back, and holding her bottle in an elevated position to its mouth, into which the brandy was gluck-glucking at a tremendous rate.

This figure was Rumball.

That sneaking individual had been concealed under the bed all the time, watching the process and progress of mixing the sustainer, with the necessary intervals of refreshment, and no sooner had the little devil upset the presiding geniuses of the pan, and scattered confusion and bewilderment around, than Rumball crept from his hiding-place, seized the bottle, retreated to his corner, and began deliberately to gluck it dry.

There is no doubt, either, that he would have succeeded, had not Mrs. Rumball caught him in the act.

"Rumball!" she exclaimed. "I might a know'd hit! Drat yer! Thur! And thur! Get unner hout o' my sight! do! Drat 'im! Hit 'ud be hal the same hif I was a-dyin'! The greedy hold willin!"

Mrs. Rumball not only settled off her husband's baseness with her tongue, but this time, having no ladle, she touched him up with the toe of her boot in such an effectual manner, that Rumball

was glad to creep once more under the bed, where he remained groaning with pain, and coughing and wheezing over some brandy that had "caught" him in the throat.

By this time the Sergeant had succeeded in clearing his eye of the dose of "health-sustainer," and had managed to stagger to his feet. It must be remarked that the Sergeant, up to the present moment, was in entire ignorance of the real state of his overthrow. Not having seen the little devil knock over Mrs. Rumball, for the simple reason that the contact of the little imp with Mrs. Rumball was simultaneous with the jerk that impelled the ladle of "health-sustainer" in the Sergeant's eye, he was under the impression that he had been subject to a sudden and treacherous assault by the irate lady, and he got up with the intention of giving her a bit of his mind.

The Sergeant was conscious of the strong smell of brimstone, and the light in the room had a peculiar shade; but these circumstances he attributed to the brimstone that had got up his nose at the same moment that his eye was filled, and the still blurred and dim state of his sight.

Ignoring these things, the Sergeant's eye wandered in search of Mrs. Rumball, and fell upon her as that lady was in the act of taking a gluck or two from the bottle.

This added to the Sergeant's anger.

"Well, so help me ten men," cried the Sergeant, "If that isn't what I call the height of coolness, Mrs. Rumball!"

"Wot do yer mean?" asked Mrs. Rumball, as she gulped down the last gluck.

"Mean!" returned the Sergeant, indignantly? "why if you don't call it cool to fill a man's eye with the 'health-sustainer,' knock him into the fire-place when you've bunged it up, and then stand there tipping up the bottle over him, then, so help me ten men *I* do! May the devil fly away——"

"Shet hup!" suddenly cried Mrs. Rumball, looking apprehensively at the mixing-pan. "Don't talk about them drefful thin's Sarjint, or we shell hev that devil back agin! An' I've hed enuf hon 'im fur one night!—Drat 'im!"

It will be comprehended that, as the Sergeant hadn't seen the devil, he was utterly at a loss to understand Mrs. Rumball's infernal allusion, and so, staring at her, he muttered.

"Drunk! Case of 'blue devils!'"

"Hit was blue at the larst, an' black at fust!" replied Mrs. Rumball, mistaking the Sergeant's words, "an' wich yer might a seen fur yerself. It wos a weary little devil, too, an' I shudn't a-thort has it cud a-knocked hus bof down!"

"So help me ten men!" thought the Sergeant; "she is mad." Then added aloud, "Knocked down by a devil! What *are* you talking about, Mrs. Rumball?"

"Cum now." returned Mrs. Rumball, setting at the Sergeant with her arms akimbo, in a kind of I-dare-you-to-say-you-didn't manner, "Does yer mean to say as yer *didn't* see that little devil?"

"Of course not!" replied the Sergeant. "I have not seen any devil. I don't know what you're talking about, and I don't think you do, yourself, Mrs. Rumball!"

At this barefacedly expressed disbelief of the Sergeant in Mrs. Rumball's veracity, Mrs. Rumball stood petrified with asonishment—but only for a couple of moments, and then she fired up.

"Wot!" exclaimed Mrs. Rumball, still standing with her arms akimbo, in one hand firmly grasped the neck of the bottle. "Wot, are hit cum to this? Wot, arter the black thin' a-comin' bang hin' my face, and a-knockin' me down till I werry nigh broke my back agin the bedstead, an' brought fire flashes hin my heys—arter hit a-knocked yer down an' filled yer heye with s't'ainer, an' then I see hit a-floatin' about the room, grinning an' callin' of me names an' a-threatenin' to stir me hup wen it got me at its place, an' then breakin' hout inter a blue fire, an' wanishin' with a screedge hin the pan! Wot, arter that am I to be called a liar?"

"Pooh, pooh!" said the Sergeant. "That's all fancy, Mrs. Rumball. That blue kind of light is only from the brimstone. See, its burning in the hearth-stone, and everything looks blue."

This was a staggerer for Mrs. Rumball.

Mrs. Rumball could not deny it, and she was casting about in her mind for some argument that should justify her assertion, when, happening to look in the direction of the mixing-pan, her eyes and mouth suddenly opened, and pointing with her disengaged hand, she gasped—

"Thur! Thur! Lo—lo—look!"

The Sergeant did look, and he had no sooner looked than he too opened his eyes and mouth, and stared aghast.

And the sight they saw was enough to make anyone look aghast, and shake the strongest nerves.

Slowly rising from the mixing-pan, was an object which, at first, was undefinable shape, but, as it gradually developed, it exhibited a pair of arms, the hands of which began groping about as though feeling for the edge of the pan.

That this was the object of the strange figure's search was soon made evident, for it had no sooner found it than a leg—proving that the object was either a being of flesh and blood, or something bearing the extremities of a human or supernatural form—began to put itself over the edge of the pan, and feel about for a footing.

The latter was found on the box on which the pan rested, and then the leg was followed by another leg, which found a footing by the side of its fellow leg.

Thus far, the figure could be recognised as of human model; but, in other respects, it bore no resemblance to the ordinary outward aspect of a human being. Its whole frame—from head to foot—was enveloped in a thick, sticky, slimy coating of the "health-sustainer." If the figure had features they were hidden behind the "sustainer."

Still, utterly at a loss to account for the strange presence, and scarcely believing the evidence of their senses, Mrs. Rumball and the Sergeant continued to watch its movements.

That those were slow and uncertain, was evidently attributed to two causes—the figures eyes were crammed with the "health-sustainer," and couldn't see, whilst the same slimy composition rendered its hold extremely slippery.

The figure now began to develop a most extraordinary appendage.

This was a tail—and a tail growing out of the middle of its back.

This was not the natural locality for a tail.

That whisking, frisking, expressive, wagging appendage, the Sergeant and Mrs. Rumball knew was usually attached to the lower end of the spine.

What was this nasty, shiny-looking thing?

It couldn't be a monkey—at least, not one of the monkeys inhabiting the Rock, for they had no tails.

Then what could this thing be?

Was it, after all, the little devil seen by Mrs. Rumball?

As the figure's movements continued, these questions became more and more difficult of solution, for as it reached the floor, and began groping about, the tail seemed to have no end.

Go where the figure would—make what twistings and turnings it would—the end of the tail would not come out of the pan.

Never had Mrs. Rumball and the Sergeant seen such a long tail as this.

Mrs. Rumball and the Sergeant were bewildered, and not only bewildered, but shocked and terrified, and as the slimy, unnatural thing, groped about, stretching forth its slimy arms, spluttering and groaning, it took them all their time to dodge and skip out of its way.

Mrs. Rumball's terror was, at length, brought to a climax.

In spite of her active endeavours to avoid contact with the loathsome creature, the latter caught her gown, and Mrs. Rumball, in stepping back, tripped one foot against the other, and fell, and the next instant, with deafening screams, she was rolling over and over in the monster's grasp, and being firmly entwined in his tail which still kept coming out of the pan.

If the reader by this time has guessed, or, has a strong suspicion that this unknown, and unnatural monster—to Mrs. Rumball, and the Sergeant—was none other dangerous creature than the celebrated Dolly Swaps, the reader's guess or suspicion will be correct.

The slimy thing *was* Dolly Swaps, and Dolly had, literally, through his ambition to assume the supernatural character of an inhabitant of the lower regions, got himself into a devil of a mess.

It happened in this way.

Of course, the adventurous party of boys in search of the hole in the wall of Mrs. Rumball's room, succeeded in discovering it. It was just one half turn of the spiral steps below the hole leading from their own room, and, consequently proved that Mrs. Rumball's room was not exactly in a line therewith.

But this did not matter, and they resolved that it should not hinder their endeavouring to establish a free ventilation for Mrs. Rumball. By-and-by that was to be, for, just as they found the hole, they found it necessary to stop the ventilation for the present, with their bodies, in watching the process of mixing the health-sustainer, an interesting proceeding they certainly had not anticipated seeing, for all the school had looked upon the Sergeant's threat as something more to work upon their terrified imaginations, and make them good boys, than something tangible to work upon their insides.

At first, the exploring party could not credit the evidence of their eyes, and thought they saw a funny vision before them, or had health-sustainer on the stomach, and were suffering with nightmare.

But as the vision passed not away, the more they looked and listened, the more they became convinced that what they saw and heard, was only too ridiculously real, and, now and again, they gave utterance to those mysterious sounds which had so alarmed Mrs. Rumball.

The mixing of the sustainer—not the sustainer

itself—was the most delicious sight they had ever looked upon. It was gratifying too, to think that the Sergeant, after all their tricks upon him, was more sweet upon them than they imagined.

But for all that, Dolly Swaps was of opinion that it would not do to allow the mixing to proceed, and proposed a novel method to put an end to it, by stirring up and knocking down the mixers.

The rope-gear, that has already been mentioned, had been used in days gone by, as a stay to the flag-staff on the tower—passing from the staple in the ceiling, along the winding steps to the staff.

Some of this rope was still left in the hole, and Doll'ys proposition was, that he should be tied round the waist, and swing out of the hole into the midst of the mixers.

"And, as I'm black after being in that coal-box," whispered Dolly, "they'll take me for a floating devil. It'll be the jolliest lark out."

"I wouldn't be mixed up in it if I were you, Dolly," said Dick.

"Oh, I don't care," said Dolly, "it'll be a bit of fun; only, mind, Dick, don't you go letting go the rope, as I don't want to drop into the health-sustainer. That would be worse than the coal-box, that would you know, a jolly sight!"

"All right, Dolly," returned Dick, gravely, "get ready."

Dolly was not two minutes getting the rope fastened round his waist, and then, whilst Dick held one end, Dolly shot out of the hole, and into the midst of the sustainer-mixers, with the velocity of a falling star—though Dolly did not look so brilliant—with the terrible results described.

The vanishing of the floating devil into the pan was brought about by the weakening effects of excessive laughter, on the part of Dick, and this laughter was brought about by two circumstances—the scene which followed the upsetting of Mrs. Rumball and the Sergeant, and the fact that it would be impossible to haul the floating Dolly back again.

Small as Dolly was, he was much to big to get through the staple, and even if he could have been pulled through, he must have been dashed with considerable force against the wall. And so, what with the comicality of Mrs. Rumball, and the Sergeant's bewilderment, and the fix Dolly was in, Dick laughed till he no longer had strength to hold the end of the rope, and which slipping through his hand, let Dolly, at the right moment, vanish into the sustainer, the rope itself slipping out of the staple and coiling into the pan.

This latter circumstance will account for the tremendous tail.

With these necessary explanations, we must return to the scene of the unequal and terrific struggle between the slimy, long tailed monster, and Mrs. Rumball.

As the Sergeant observed that this monster was something that could be felt, and that the immeasurable tail was something the shape of a rope—as it didn't show the least indication of tapering—he began to suspect that he and his mixing partner had been made the victims of another "lark," and that the supposed monster, or floating devil, was none other than the perfectly modelled body of Dolly Swaps, temporarily concealed beneath a coating of the health-sustainer.

This suspicion having entered his mind, the Sergeant's coolness returned, and the modus operandi by which Dolly had effected his infernal transformation quickly suggested itself. It had been done by the rope gear. The boys had left their room—of course by the usual door—found the spiral steps and the hole, caught him and Mrs. Rumball at the mixing process, and Dolly by aid of the rope, had done the floating devil.

The Sergeant saw it all; but he was not angered, nor vexed, nor annoyed.

Not a bit of it.

On the contrary, the Sergeant was highly pleased at the splendid winding up—or rather letting down—to Dolly's bit of devilment, and as he thought of the mess Dolly had dropped into, he felt so greatly tickled that murmuring, "So—so—help me ten men; but ha—ha—h-a! but it beats the ha—ha—pumping affair at the ru-ru-ruins all to fi-fi-fits! Ha—ha—ha—h-a-a—ah—yah—e-e-e—yah—a!" The Sergeant fell back on Mrs. Rumball's bed, and fairly yelled and screamed with laughter.

This laughter was echoed from the hole in the wall; but happily for the carrying out of an idea that was started in the brain of the new-comer—Tom Hyefield—was not heard by the Sergeont, owing to that individual being too much occupied in a similar manner.

The laughter, too, was echoed from another quarter of the room, at first in hollow sounding vibrations, and then the faint but perfectly natural notes under the circumstances.

This laughter came not, as may perhaps be conjectured, from Rumball, and which indulgence would have been perfectly natural certainly—but from a no less important individual than Joey Pumps.

Now Joey, instead of having retired to rest after his fit of limpness in the chamber allotted to him—the compartment on the shelf in the hole—had slipped into one of Mrs. Rumball's boxes, and deliberately made a bed of Mrs. Rumball's best silk gown, and Sunday-going white cap.

From this receptacle, Joey, whilst stretching his limbs on his silk and muslin couch, had contemplated the whole of the proceedings through an inch of the open lid.

In this luxurious position, Joey had thoroughly enjoyed the varied incidents of the sustainer-mixing tragedy, and enjoyed them in security, and without having had to shift his position or to suffer any inconvenience in the way of an interruption in his respiratory organs, until the monster had seized Mrs. Rumball, and began to coil "its" dreadful tail around her.

Then it was that Joey, being temporarily overcome with the first symptoms of a fit of limpness, had subjected himself to a possibility of being smothered, and so putting an end to his distinguished career by letting down the lid of the box.

But as Joey had no wish to be smothered, and wished very much to watch the progress of the struggle between the monster and Mrs. Rumball, he made a great effort to overcome the subtle power of the limping fit, and succeeded so far as to be enabled to lift the lid, roll out of the box, and support his weak body against it.

From this position Joey watched the terrific struggle, and made appropriate remarks and comments, though in a somewhat spasmodic manner,

"Oh, lor! Oh, dear!" murmured Joey, plaintively. "Hif I done beer hit hu-hup agen go-o-oin orf this time, I—I—he, he, he!—ha-a-ah!—I—I shall never cum right agen! O—O—oh—lor—oh, d-e-a-r!"

Here Joey had to shake himself to prevent a thorough collapse, and then, addressing the Sergeant, who was reduced to a state as bad as his own, he observed in a weak, squeaky voice—

"I—I say, sarjint—did—yer—he-ver—he, he-e—see anyfing tu ekel this? Di-di-did—yer? I never did! Oh, lor!—that's—sumfing—li-iike a tail *that* his! Oh, lor!—I done b'leave has hit'll *hever* cum hout o' the pa-pa-pan! Ha, ha, ha a-a-a-a-ah!"

Here Joey began to slip slowly to the floor, articulating in gasps—

"I—I'se a-go-in orf! I—I—say—sar-jint"—faintly—"I—I—never thort—h-h-has I—I—he, he!—shud, he—he, hever—see—*yer*—a-getting—*limp*? O-O-h, I'se a-goin!"

And Joey, who could no longer support his vitally exhausted frame, sank gracefully to the floor, and went "orf" into one of his limpest of limp conditions.

This state of things could not last for ever, and presently the Sergeant recovered sufficiently to silence Mrs. Rumball's screams, and calm her fears, by explaining the true nature of the supposed reptile, and giving her ocular demonstration of its harmlessness by cutting off its tail, and addressing the aminated part that was left—Dolly Swaps himself—

"So help me ten men, but it's a beautifully bronzed model my dear Dolly is at last! It's uncertain I am though, my dear Dolly, whether you look best in the pure white marble, or not! I'll have to contemplate you a few days before I can decide. Look here, Dolly, since you seem fond enough of the health-sustainer to take a bathe in it, you shall have a bath every morning for a week! D'ye hear that, now?"

"Yes!" replied Dolly, who appeared much subdued! "but I'd rather not, thank you."

"I dare say that," chuckled the Sergeant; but your fate's sealed, Dolly. It's a dip in the health-sustainer you'll get every morning for a week, my dear!"

"Won't you touch up my 'right-about' at once, and have done with it, Sergeant?" asked Dolly.

"Not if I know it, Dolly my dear, in its *present* state! We'll wait till your clean, Dolly, and *then* we'll manage the touching up between us. And now, march back into your room, and get into bed *just as you are!* D'ye hear that, now!"

"Yes, Sergeant."

"Don't forget it, Dolly! Never mind dirtying the sheets! Now go, my dear, for it's this lady I have to attend to. I'd take you back myself, Dolly, and have a word or two with the other beauties (for I know how the floating devil came about), if it wasn't for the lady. But just give Sergeant O'Shehe's love to 'em, and inform them they'll have the pleasure of hearing from him first thing in the morning, as he promised, with the health-sustainer and the hot tea. Good night, Dolly, it's your mother I'd like to see her little model of a boy at this minute! Good night, Dolly, and don't forget to get between the sheets as you are! Sweet repose to you, Dolly!"

Whilst the Sergeant remains to attend to Mrs. Rumball, and to a fresh bottle of brandy which the much-tried lady produced, we must take the reader to witness another scene, and hear the outlines of another plot, having for its object the perpetration of a dreadful deed, and the wholesale taking of the health-sustainer.

Let us follow Dolly Swaps.

That sustainer-besmeared little model proceeded in obedience to the Sergeant's reiterated commands, to get between the sheets, but—not his own sheets.

Certainly not!

"He shall have a bathe in the sustainer himself," muttered Dolly, as he descended the steps. "I'll just get between *his* sheets, and then we shall see what his beautifully-modelled figure looks like in a coating of bronze!"

And so Dolly, instead of proceeding to his own room, proceeded to the Sergeant's, and turning down the bedclothes, deliberately got into bed, and commenced to roll and rub about in much the same manner that a dog will roll and rub about on the grass after a swim.

Dolly did this so effectually that, not only the sheets, but the pillow was thickly coated with the sticky "sustainer," and Dolly turned out at least ten shades ligher of hue than when he turned in.

Dolly then adjusted the bedclothes, and, after squeezing all the "sustainer" he could out of his hair, and spreading it, as an additional coat, on the pillow, returned to his room, and reported in what manner he had obeyed the Sergeant's orders.

This brings us to the hatching of the plot.

Dolly's return was welcomed with loud shouts of laughter and a considerable amount of chaffing, but Dolly's "report" was received with "roars" and endless caperings, and the chaffing was turned into praise at his forethought, and the delight Dolly's chums experienced at the anticipated appearance of the Sergeant in the morning almost amounted to delirium.

But to this anticipation was presently added another, which drove them stark mad.

"Dick and chums," said Tom Pyefield, "I've an idea. May I ventilate it?"

"Only to glad for you to, Tom," laughed Dick. "What is it?"

"It's this," returned Tom, with assumed modesty, "I am anxious to inaugurate my, and Jerry's, advent into the School of the Regiment by an act that will show that we take an interest in keeping up the reputation—the deserved reputation of the school for mild and innocent larking!"

Here the modest speaker was encouraged by kindly laughter and cries of—

"Go on, Pyefield."

"Out with the idea."

"It's this," continued Tom, "we must get rid of that 'health-sustainer.'"

"How? How?"

"I propose that, when the Sergeant has returned to his room, after the soothing of his feelings, with Mrs. Rumball, over the brandy, we enter Mrs. Rumball's room, take the 'sustainer' by basinsful—not inwardly, of course—and pass them through the ventilators into our room."

"It can be done easier than that, Pyefield," said Dick. "The Sergeant is sure to go to bed stupidly drunk, and so is Mrs Rumball, and all we have to do will be to walk into the room, and carry of the 'sustainer,' pan and all."

"All right," laughed Tom. "I am not particular how it's done, so long as it is done. And now tell me, is it easy to get at the gun from which the morning signal is fired?"

"I daresay it can be done with a little manœuvring," said Dick. "We shall only have to dodge the sergeant in charge of the battery. He makes a round of inspection about midnight, and doesn't again turn out till gun-fire. What's your little game?"

"Only to put the 'sustainer' into the gun, and give the whole of the inhabitants of the Rock a taste of it!"

Tom Pyefield had no sooner ventilated his idea than it was received with a burst of approval, and it was resolved unanimously to carry it out.

"It's the idea of a 'master of arts,'" said Dick, with a laugh. "It's your first idea, Pyefield, and I must congratulate you at having hit upon a very taking one. But, whilst we are about it, we may just as well improve upon it."

"All right," said Tom. "What do you suggest?"

"That we blow the Sergeant away with his health-sustainer."

"You don't mean *literally*, of course, Dick?" said Tom, joining in the laugh which followed Dick's remark.

"Not quite," replied Dick, "but I think we can make everybody believe for a time that such is really the case. It can be done in a very simple manner. All we have to do, when the Sergeant has staggered to bed, is to prig his jacket and overalls, boots and spurs, cut them into small pieces, and ram them in the gun with the 'health-sustainer.'"

Here Dick was interrupted with loud laughter and delighted exclamations.

"But that is not all," continued Dick, when he could be heard. "To make it appear that a human body has, apparently, been rammed into the gun and blown away, we must have flesh and bones as well as pieces of uniform. That can be done by getting a piece of raw beef from the cookhouse store, and cutting it into bits. The bones we shall find on our bread-shelf here, and in Mrs. Rumball's room. To simulate the Sergeant's hair, we can cut up his busby, and dip these pieces in the health-sustainer to give them a ghastly and blood-stained appearance. See?"

Dick's chums thought they did see, and no mistake!

It would be a tremendous improvement on the original idea

It would be the best lark they'd had yet!

"It's a very good idea," said Dolly Swaps; "but it strikes me there's just one little drawback to its complete success, mister Dick."

"What is that, Dolly?" asked Dick.

"Where will the Sergeant himself be all this time—eh, Mister Clever?"

"In his room, Mister Wiseacre," laughed Dick. "We must lock his door. Or perhaps I may think of another plan of keeping him out of the way. I never half do things, Dolly."

"Where there's a will there's a way," observed Pyefield. "The thing can be done; but I do think your improvement can be improved upon still, Dick."

"We may as well bring the idea to perfection, Pyefield," said Dick. "What's the further improvement?"

"Why, as the Sergeant had not more to do with mixing of the 'health-sustainer' than his assistant, I think it would be only just to blow Mrs. Rumball away with him. Suppose we cut her up and ram her in the gun with her fellow-conspirator?"

As no one could see any objection to this proposition, and it seemed only fair that, as the worthy couple had shared in mixing the "sustainer," they should share in the blow out, it was unanimously approved of amidst much laughter, and other lively demonstrations, showing the pleasure it afforded the boys to do so.

Having now decided that the Sergeant and Mrs. Rumball, with the "sustainer," were to be blown out of the gun, the ringleaders dressed themselves, and made such preparations as they could pending the retirement of the Sergeant from Mrs. Rumball's jovial company to his sweet —and sticky—repose.

Dolly Swaps was sent up again to keep a watch on the progress of brandy drinking in Mrs. Rumball's torrid regions, with a caution not to try the flying-devil dodge, however greatly tempted he might be to do so.

As the cook-house store was easily enough to be reached and entered without encountering "objectors," Dick and two or three others very soon made their way thereto, and returned therefrom bearing a good sized piece of beef, a loin of mutton, and a couple of shin-bones.

The latter, which had a little meat on them, it was thought might be taken for the Sergeant's shin-bones, and the bones of the loin of mutton —stripped of meat—for Mrs. Rumball's ribs. To cut up the meat and separate the loin-bones was all they could do to forward preparations until the retirement of the Sergeant, and so, until that desired moment, they had to rest content with an occasional report from Dolly Swaps as to how things were progressing in the torrid regions.

It was one o'clock before the Sergeant retired to his room, undressed in the best manner he could, and got into bed. One minute afterwards he was snoring heavily, and five minutes later, his jacket, overalls, boots, busby, and spurs were in a fit condition for being rammed in the gun.

It took a longer time to get the "health-sustainer" from Mrs. Rumball's torrid-regions, and prepare it for the gun. But this was accomplished at length—the "sustainer" being put into a pillow-slip, and carefully tied up at the mouth.

Then by the aid of Joey Pumps—though he was in a state of partial limpness all the time— a gown of Mrs. Rumball's was procured and cut up; and one of Mrs. Rumball's handsomest caps —not cut up, of course!—got ready for the blow out.

Then followed the ramming of these items in the gun, which already had the cartridge in it for morning gun-fire. As the sergeant in charge had gone his round of inspection and had retired for the night, no difficulty was experienced in this operation, and the gun was crammed to the muzzle.

From that moment till gun-fire was perhaps the most impatient time the boys had ever experienced. But there can be no doubt that the moment of gun-fire *was* the most exciting that they had ever experienced.

To observe the scattering of the Sergeant and Mrs. Rumball effectively, the roof of the tower was selected for that purpose, and there was not a boy absent. The winding steps were reached in the usual way—by pyramids, the last bricks being hauled up by aid of sheets tied into ropes.

It was a glorious morning.

The sun was rising above the tips of the Rock golden and rosy, as though it were smiling on the deed that, in a short time, would fill the good people of the fortress with horror.

The sergeant in charge and the gunner were in readiness to fire—the former to give the word of command, and the latter to pull the lanyard.

The moment came, by the Sergeant's watch, which he held in his hand, it was four o'clock, the hour of gun-fire.

"Fire!"

Instantly the report was followed by a rushing sound, and what seemed a flight of birds.

The sergeant and the gunner were dumbfounded and so were the inhabitants of the Rock.

But the first two to be almost driven into fits were a couple of women of the —— Regiment, who an hour later were busy in the manipulation of dirty shirts, &c., over receptacles containing soap and hot water.

In rushed a fifer of the regiment, in a state of excitement, exclaiming—

"I say, there's such an awful go! What do you think? Lots of bits of uniform, and buttons, bits of a woman's gown, and a cap, bones and pieces of flesh, and hair, all covered with blood, have been picked up in the town, and about the batteries. It is rumoured that the Sergeant and the woman-cook of the School of the Regiment have been murdered by the boys, cut up into bits, and blown out of the morning gun! I'm going up to the Signal Station to see."

With that the fifer bolted, leaving the women sick with horror.

CHAPTER LI.

THE MYSTERY OF SERGEANT O'SHEHE AND MRS. RUMBALL.—DOLLY SWAPS AND JOEY PUMPS TURN QUEEN'S EVIDENCE, AND EXPOSE THE MURDERERS.—THE SCENE AT THE GOVERNOR'S PALACE.—THE SCENE AT THE SIGNAL STATION.

WE can safely assert that never, since the great burning and destruction of the Spanish fleet at the siege, had the troops in garrison and the inhabitants of the Rock been thrown into such a state of horrified excitement as that caused by the supposed murder of Sergeant O'Shehe and Mrs. Rumball by the boys of the School of the Regiment.

At first the shower of pieces of meat and bone, bits of uniform, and brass buttons, items of Mrs. Rumball's gown, and the bespattering of the streets and houses with the health-sustainer, caused only unbounded surprise and astonishment, and conjectures as to what it really all meant, and where the pieces of flesh, bloodstained bits of uniform and cotton dress, and gory pieces of scalp could have come from.

The pieces of various kinds were picked up by the score, and many were the opinions and theories propounded regarding the phenomena, but one theory only is worth recording.

This theory was broached by an old soldier, who stated his belief that a whale had been drawn up into the clouds by a waterspout on he coast of Greenland, that the whale had been wafted from thence to the Rock, where the temperature being higher than it is in the frozen regions, the great fish had thawed internally, and its skin not being sufficiently tough to stand the extra pressure, had burst, and that this was the result.

The old soldier supported this theory by a parallel case which he witnesed in New Zealand. In this instance a whole tribe of natives—men,

women, and children—had been sucked up to the clouds by a whirlwind, and nothing was heard of them for a week, when as he was marching with his company past the Volcano of Tongarero, the blessed lot of them began to drop from a black cloud right into the crater, and then, being vomited up again, they walked off as though nothing extraordinary had happened.

But, unfortunately for the old soldier's theory, he was puzzled to account for the whale having discharged pieces of uniform, with artillery buttons, a couple of boot-heels with spurs attached, pieces of cotton gown, and a lady's nightcap of enormous size and peculiar shape. So the old soldier had to "shut up."

But presently the real state of the case became known, doing away with all theories, and causing a thrill of horror to pass through every frame, and ending in a general rush to the Governor's palace.

The awful news was brought from the Signal Station by two trustworthy individuals—Dolly Swaps and Joey Pumps.

Shortly after the gun was fired, Dolly was seized with a troubled conscience at having taken part in so horrible a crime, and suddenly determined to turn Queen's evidence—go to the General and make a clean breast of it.

Dolly, with tears in his eyes, mentioned his dreadful mental condition to Joey Pumps, who was immediately struck with remorse, and resolved to turn Queen's evidence with his friend Dolly, and also make a clean breast of it.

In order to show the reality of his remorse in an equal degree to Dolly, Joey begged his friend to besmear his face and hands with some of the "health-sustainer" that still adhered to his friend's person—a petition with which Dolly feelingly complied.

Then, mournfully telling Dick and their chums the determination to which their uneasy consciences had driven them, Dolly and Joey, with very long faces, set off to carry it out, at a running pace.

The first persons they met was a group of soldiers, standing at the gate of the Moorish Castle, and who, seeing the blood-besmeared boys approaching in such a wild hurry, all excitedly demanded what was the matter.

"Matter!" exclaimed Dolly, halting and speaking in horrified tones. "Blood—murder is the matter! The boys of the School of the Regiment have murdered the Sergeant and Mrs. Rumball, cut their bodies up in pieces, and fired them from the morning gun! Don't stop us, we're going to the Governor to make a clean breast of it."

And before the bewildered soldiers had time to express their horror at the fearful tale, the two informers started off again at the double, until their career was stopped, as they entered the town, by a second lot of excited persons, to whom they communicated the sickening news.

From here till their arrival at the Governor's palace, the unhappy boys were accompanied by an ever-increasing crowd, vociferating, declaiming, and gesticulating their overpowering indignation and horror.

The Governor, Sir Gentle Sharpset, had already been informed of the extraordinary phenomenon and, half-dressed was discussing the subject with a number of excited officers, including General Shoot in the reception-room of the palace, when Dolly and Joey, followed by the clamouring inhabitants, crowded into his presence, and all speaking at once, began to announce the particulars of the dreadful tragedy, exhibiting at the same time the various pieces of the mutilated remains of the bodies and the clothing the victims had worn.

At least, two dozen pieces of the Sergeant's uniform, and as many of Mrs. Rumball's gown were deposited on the large table, together with many pieces of ghastly, gory-covered flesh, and clotted bits of hairy scalp. To these were added Mrs. Rumball's ribs and cap, several brass buttons, the heels of the Sergeant's boots, with the spurs on, and, to complete the catalogue of sickening items, one person triumphantly deposited the Sergeant's shin-bone.

All this, with the blood-stained appearance of Dolly and Joey, was almost too much for the sensitive nerves of the Governor, who, begging that the windows might be opened, was supported in the arms of two of the officers, in a fainting condition.

As it was expedient, however, though the ghastly collection of pieces was proof overwhelming, to interrogate Dolly and Joey as to particulars, the Governor, throwing off his faintness, demanded silence.

This was readily obtained, as there was not one in the room who was not morbidly curious to hear what Dolly and Joey had to say.

"Is this true?" asked the Governor, looking at Dolly.

"Ye—ye—yes, sir," answered Dolly, in a quaking voice.

"I shud think it was, too!" put in Joey.

"What was the boys' motive for committing so dreadful a crime?" was the Governor's next question.

"They didn't want to take the 'health-sustainer,' sir," replied Dolly.

"'Health-sustainer?'" repeated the Governor, opening his eyes in a puzzled manner. "What in the world is 'health-sustainer,' my boy?"

"Thet's the Sargint's name fur hit, that is," Joey hastened to explain. "But hit's wot I calls 'brimstun an' treak'l.' Yer knows it, Guv'nor, has I hexpec yer muther used ter dose yer well with hit wen yer was a un'ealthy little kid. Yer reckollecs—like this, yer knows."

Here, Joey, much to the astonishment of the General, the disgust of many, and the amusement of a few, put his arms across his stomach, doubled up his body, and pulling a wry face, began rolling about in imitation of one in great pain from an internal dose of "health-sustainer."

"Yes, sir," said Dolly. "It's brimstone and treacle."

"But that's a very 'armless and sweet medicine," observed the Governor, "and nothing to commit murder about."

"Hoh, wasn't hit though?" said Joey, suddenly resuming his perpendicular, and nodding his head solemnly at the Governor. "Hit's 'armless wen took hin moderrashun, but yer'd hev 'mitted murder hif yer'd a thort has yer was goin' ter take hit hin sich dollups has the Sargint threat'nd 'em. Why, 'e was goin' ter feed the chaps on nutthin helse! They was ter hev hit hif they ony winked hor smiled, an' them chaps his given ter smilin', they his. They was ter hev 'ad a dose bon hit this mornin' afore gun-fire, an' the Sargint and Dolly Rumball wus ter bring hit roun' with a basin hof 'ot tea ter take arter it. That was a putty thing ter look

forrard ter, wasn't hit, Guv'nor! Why," continued Joey, amidst much tittering, for Joey's naive words and actions overcame, for the moment, the feeling of horror at the awful tragedy, "the chaps wud soon a' bin reduched ter nutthin helse but brimstone and treak'l!"

"It's quite true, sir," said Dolly, "what Joey says, and as we wasn't going to be brimstone-and-treacled like that, we cut up the Sergeant and Mrs. Rumball in bits, and put them in the morning gun, and we put in the health-sustainer as well, sir, and blew it all out!"

The sensation this announcement caused was very great, and many murmurs of horror went forth, and many hands were uplifted to express the same feeling.

"Then much of this blood-looking stuff is—is—"

"The health-sustainer, sir," said Dolly. "There's a good deal of it about the boys as well, sir, as we had a dreadful struggle over the mixing pan!"

"This is the most astounding atrocity I have ever heard of!" exclaimed the Governor. "I will proceed to the Signal Station, and personally investigate the circumstances. In the meantime, let all these evidences of the mutilation be carefully preserved."

"Quite right," said Joey, approvingly. "Yer carn't be *too* keerful hov the bits, an' I'd hev' em put hunner a glass shade hif I was yer—they'll bring no hend o' munney, by'n-bye!"

From the palace, we must now precede the Governor and the excited crowd to the Signal Station, where preparation had been made by the boys in anticipation of the Governor's arrival.

In the first place, as there was plenty of the health-sustainer about, the boys besmeared with it their faces and shirts as evidence of the dreadful nature of the struggle that had taken place; and, when this had been accomplished to their satisfaction, Dick and the leading boys held a council of ways and means to get the Sergeant and Mrs. Rumball out of the way.

"Because, you see," said Dick, "the longer they are invisible the longer will be kept up the supposition of their murder."

"And the longer the lark," said Jerry.

"Just so, Jerry. Now, who has any plan to suggest of getting the murdered persons out of their rooms?"

"Couldn't we get them both down to St. Michael's Cave?" said Tom Sheppard.

"Not unless we carried them, I'm afraid," laughed Dick, "and I'd rather not tackle Mrs. Rumball, thank you."

"I think it could be done without carrying them," said Tom Pyefield.

"How, Tom?"

"Rouse up the Sergeant, assume a great state of consternation, and tell him that Mrs. Rumball has committed suicide in the cave. He'd go off then by the run, I expect."

"It's a good idea, Pyefield; but you forget one great obstacle."

"What is that?"

"Why," said Dick, followed by great laughter, "that the Sergeant's overalls are now scattered in pieces over the Rock! And the Sergeant's a man who never likes to make his appearance out of uniform. Besides, if he were seen the murder mystery would explode."

"What do you propose then, Dick?"

"I scarcely know what to propose," replied Dick. "They must be concealed in the tower somewhere, and I think there's nothing for it but to seize the Sergeant in his bed, and carry him off to the winding-steps between the walls."

"That may be done with the Sergeant, but how about Mrs. Rumball?"

"We must try and coax her to the same place; but, if we can't succeed in either case, we must just lock their doors and let the affair take its chance.

It was then unanimously resolved to see what could be done with the Sergeant, and they were about to proceed to his room to reconnoitre when their plan was frustrated by the sudden appearance of the Sergeant himself.

But, before recording what followed his appearance, we must account for that unexpected circumstance.

It was considerably past midnight when Sergeant O'Shehe left the refined society of Mrs. Rumball and staggered to bed. As the Sergeant had been enjoying the hospitality of Mrs. Rumball, in the shape of helping that lady to empty a bottle of brandy, it happened that his vision was so blurred and every object in his room looked so much like another in colour, that he could not—and did not—distinguish the sudden alteration in the hue of his sheets and pillow-case. To the Sergeant, the health-sustainer looked so much like the sheets and the sheets so much like the health-sustainer, that he couldn't tell "t'other from which;" and, after a struggle to get out of his uniform—in the course of which he performed various movements entirely contrary to those laid down in the drill-book, scrambled into bed and there slept till gun-fire.

Now, the Sergeant had made a resolve that, to set his boys a soldierlike example, he would always turn out so as to be dressed by gun-fire. He wasn't going to let the gun wake him; he, so to speak, would wake the gun.

The Sergeant, too, wanted especially to be up in time this morning. He had promised himself, and Mrs. Rumball, and the boys a treat in the shape of administering a dose of the "health-sustainer," and the Sergeant liked to be a man of his word—unless it suited him to be otherwise, such, for instance, as when he made a rash promise under spirituous influence.

This morning, the Sergeant had allowed the gun to steal a march on him.

"So help me ten men!" he exclaimed, hastily sitting up; "if that isn't the gun, and here I am in bed, when it's serving out the 'health-sustainer' I ought to be! I promised Mrs. Rumball I'd be ready to the second, and there she's, I expect, waiting for me with the hot tea! But I'll soon put matters right. I daresay the young devils are laughing in their sleeves, thinking that I'm 'done.' But, so help me——What the deuce is this?" he added, abruptly, suddenly catching sight of his stained shirt, for he had got his legs out of bed. "So help me ten men if it's not covered with the 'health-sustainer' I am! May the devil fly away with me, if it's not all over me! And, begad, it's all over the sheets, too, and the pillow-case! How did I get in such a mess as this, I wonder? I'll take me oath that, except the dab I got in me eye with Mrs. Rumball's ladle, I never touched the blessed stuff last night!"

Considerably puzzled, the Sergeant stopped to ruminate.

"It may be that," he continued, presently. "It looks as though I had taken a dose of it without knowing it, and, so help me ten men,

but it must have been a devil of a strong dose, too, from the mess I've made! If it's a trick of Mrs. Rumball's, putting it in the brandy, 'pon me soul it's a beastly dirty trick! But I'll soon find out. I'll dress and have a talk to her about it."

But the latter was easier to say than to do.

"Where the deuce is my overalls?" he muttered, angrily, as he looked about the room and could see no signs of them. "I'll take me oath I was dressed when I left Mrs. Rumball's! I remember undressing here, too; but may I be—— if the blessed things ain't gone, an' me jacket and cap, too! It's me best overalls, too, for the other's are with the regimental tailor, having a new seat put to 'em! Here's a blessed mess I'm in!"

He was, indeed!

Without a uniform, how could he leave his room?

In his present state, how could he face Mrs. Rumball?

It was impossible he could appear at parade in his bare legs and shirt!

Besides, even if he could have braved the laughter of the boys in such a costume, he would have preferred doing so in a clean shirt, and face, hands, and legs free from the sticky and unwholesome-looking "health-sustainer."

A change of linen he could have readily managed, but there was no chance of a wash in his room. That could only be had in the lavatory, or out of a bucket, and he would have to expose himself to reach the former or obtain the latter.

For some minutes the Sergeant fairly danced about the room in a paroxysm of rage, swearing as only a man in such a fix can swear.

But by degrees the Sergeant cooled down, and resolved to take the affair philosophically.

"It's no use swearing and putting myself in a fury about it," he muttered. "Me things are gone, and I can't show up without 'em! Where they're gone to the devil only knows, and until he condescends to tell me, I'll stay in bed. The boys may drill themselves for all I care! Begad, they're quite able to do it, and drill the Governor too, and the General, or any mother's son of 'em! I'll turn in, and take it easy!"

The Sergeant accordingly "turned in," but not to "take it easy!"

He had scarcely drawn the sheet up to his chin, when it flashed into his mind that his present predicament had been brought about by the boys.

"Begad, it's just like one of their tricks!" he exclaimed. "The young villains have done me! But, so help me ten men, I won't be done!

"The rascals shan't have the laugh of me! I'll go to their room and dash in amongst 'em, and get me things out of 'em by hook or by crook! I'll frighten the life out of the young beggars! They've never seen the thundering passion I can get in yet, and so help me ten men if it won't be worse than a dose of the health-sustainer to 'em!"

It was a desperate resolve, but the Sergeant was in a desperate fix—could scarcely be in one more desperate—and so, flinging off the bed-clothes, he sprang out, seized his sword and carbine, and, in less than a minute, was in the midst of the boys, who, as they beheld the wild figure armed in such a formidable manner, scattered right and left, some hastily diving under tables and beds.

"Look here, boys," shouted the Sergeant, flourishing the sword, and holding aloft the carbine, "it's an awful passion I am! I'm in that passion that I'm dangerous! See here's me sword and here's me carbin, the one's as sharp as a razor, and the other's *loaded*, and, so help me ten men and a donkey, if you don't produce me overalls and jacket, and stockings, and forage-cap, I'll cut you all to pieces and then blow your brains—I mean I'll blow your brains out *first*, and then cut you to pieces *afterwards!* Dick Everett, where's me overalls? Come, no lies, or you'll be the *first* victim!"

There was a general titter as the Sergeant made this demand and uttered this dreadful threat, and every boy looked at Dick, waiting for his reply, with a broad grin.

"It would be difficult to point out the exact spot where they are, Sergeant," said Dick, demurely. "I saw them cut up into pieces this morning, and blown out of the morning gun, so they're in various parts of the Rock at this present moment!"

The Sergeant's appearance at this information, as he stood with the sword elevated in one hand and the carbine in the other, gazing at Dick with wide-open eyes, was a most delicious picture—the utterly flabbergastered, thunderstricken man.

For a minute he was too overcome to speak, and then he burst out with—

"What!—me best overalls cut up and *blown* out the *gun*, do you say?"

"Yes, Sergeant," said Dick, "and your shell-jacket, and forage-cap, and busby and boots."

Here the Sergeant, without changing his attitude, mechanically repeated the words after Dick.

"And me shell-jacket, me forage-cap, and me busby, and *boots!*"

"The fact is, Sergeant," continued Dick, "we blew you and Mrs. Rumball, and the 'health sustainer' out of the gun this morning. We murdered you both, cut your bodies and things into small pieces, filled a pillow-slip with the 'sustainer,' and rammed them into the gun, and I don't believe there's a spot on the Rock that is not covered with yours and Mrs. Rumball's mutilated remains and *blood*."

The Sergeant was flabbergastered and thunder-stricken at the first part of the news, but, at the second part, he began to think that he had lost his senses.

A great change came over him.

From a roaring mad passion he suddenly dropped to the gentle demeanour of a lamb. Gently laying the sword and carbine on the table, he lowered himself till his "right-about" found a resting-place on the foot of a bed, and then he began to pinch himself, gently to feel his arms and legs, murmuring—

"Is it awake I am, or is it dreaming I am? Oh, so help me ten men, but I must be dreaming!"

"No, you're not dreaming, Sergeant," said Dick. "You're as wide-awake as ever you were in your life. Just listen, and I'll tell you how we did it. It's the best joke out. First of all, we determined to get rid of that 'health-sustainer,' by blowing it out of the gun. Then it was proposed to make believe we had blown you out of the gun as well. Then it was suggested that, as Mrs. Rumball was quite as bad as you, if not worse, she should also be blown out of the gun. So we decided to do it. Of course, to make the joke as real as possible,

we wanted something to represent real flesh and bones. The 'health-sustainer' did capitally for your 'gore,' so we cut up some raw beef and mutton, and got some bones to represent shin-bones and ribs. For hair, we cut up your busby. Then we cut up your overalls and jacket and things, and Mrs. Rumball's gown—her cap we kept complete—dipped the pieces in the 'sustainer,' and rammed them in the gun, and then watched them go, from top of the tower. Isn't it a capital joke?" added Dick, with assumed innocence.

As Dick was recipitulating the *modus operandi* of the double murder, and disposal of the remains, the Sergeant sat looking fixedly at him, with his hands resting on his knees.

The things was so monstrously extravagant, that Dick proceeded, the Sergeant came to the conclusion that he was simply "chaffed," and he said, with a return to his usual manner of speaking—

"So help me ten men, but it's the daring cheek you have, Dick Everett, to stand their taking the rise out o' me! Look here, Master Dick, if you go 'pulling' my 'leg,' so help me ten men, I'll go pulling your ears for you—mind that, now."

"I'm not taking the rise out of you, nor pulling your leg, Sergeant," returned Dick. "It's a fact. Dolly Swaps and Joey Pumps have gone to the Governor to report the commission of the murders, and to spread the news generally. I expect the Governor and the whole town will be here directly. By Jove! and here they come, too," added Dick, as the sound of many voices was now plainly heard.

"You'd better hide yourself in the stairway leading to the top of the tower, Sergeant," said Dick. "You'll be safe enough there. There's the first of the crowd, and I can see the Governor's cocked hat."

This was so, and the Sergeant, only too glad to have a place to retreat to, rushed off, and shut himself in the refuge suggested by Dick.

"That's one out of the way," cried Dick. "And now for Mrs. Rumball."

There was no time to be lost, and Dick followed by several of his chums, rushed to Mrs. Rumball's room.

Mrs. Rumball was invisible, but in her place was Mr. Rumball, seated on the feather bed, with a bottle of brandy to his mouth, his head being well thrown back, and the bottom of the bottle turned up to the ceiling, like the larger end of a telescope.

"Where's your wife, old fellow?" asked Dick, advancing, and giving Rumball a dig in the stomach that brought the bottle away from his mouth with a jerk, deluging his neck and breast with brandy.

"Oh, lor!" cried Rumball, putting one hand to his corporation. "What did yer do that for, Master Dick? Yer've made me spill a whole lot of it, an' hit aint hoffen, has I now get the chance ter hev a drop!"

"Bother the brandy!" replied Dick. "Where's Mrs. Rumball?"

"She's hall right," said Rumball, with a knowing wink and a grin.

"What do you mean by 'all right?'"

For reply, Rumball pointed downwards to the feather bed immediately under him.

The spot where Rumball was sitting was much more elevated than the rest of the bed, and had the appearance of having risen very much in the

Dick rushed to Mrs. Rumball's room, but she was invisible, and in her place was Mr. Rumball, seated on the feather bed, with a bottle of brandy to his mouth, enjoying a brief spell of happiness.—See page 166.

No. 13.

night, like a baker's sponge, nor was the swelling unlike a dromedary's hump.

"I got 'er hunner 'eer."

"Is that hump you're perched on Mrs. Rumball?"

"An' no mistake!" chuckled Rumball. "I got 'er safe enuf hat larst."

Dick and his chums burst into roars of laughter, in which the triumphant Rumball joined with great gusto.

"That's all right," said Dick. "Just keep her there, Rumball, for a bit; but don't smother her."

"No fear o' that," said Rumball. "I kin feel 'er a-breathin' hunner me, just kas hif I was hon a pair o' bellis! An' I wudn't care hif she did smother or—bust!"

As Mrs. Rumball was evidently safely stowed away for a time, Dick and his chums, screaming with laughter, tore back to their room, to take a look out of the window, to see how things were going on; but they had scarcely entered when the "Assembly" was rattled out on the drum.

"Hallo!" cried Dick; "there goes the 'Assembly!' I suppose the Governor thinks the occasion is important enough to call us out under alarm. Here's a go! Tumble down, boys."

The boys, full of excitement, did tumble down, and pretty "pickles" they looked as they emerged from the tower, and began to fall in.

Under the direction of Dick, who had anticipated that the school would be paraded and questioned, the boys had dressed themselves only so far as their overalls and shirts, the latter and their faces being smeared with "health-sustainer."

As they made their appearance, two or three at a time, and took their places in formation, the crowd — which was each moment becoming greater, and closing round the Governor, General Shoot, and many officers, all on horseback—murmured its astonishment.

That there had been a dreadful struggle, and that every boy had a hand in the murder and cutting up of the bodies there seemed little doubt.

This was the conviction of everybody, from the Governor to the raggedest of the little urchins that made part of the excited crowd.

Dolly Swaps, leaving the crowd, fell in with his chums, whilst Joey stood in advance of the Governor, and facing the boys, in his favourite attitude, ready to answer questions, or make any seasonable and apt remarks during the proceedings.

There was a great amount of loud talking in the crowd, and the Governor waved his hand for silence, but which, not being immediately obtained, brought a shrill remonstrance from Joey.

"Si—lence!" cried Joey. "Carn't yer hall shet hup? Don't yer see has the Governor wants ter begin?"

"Get away from there, you young rascal," shouted General Shoot, looking daggers at Joey. "You young flea, you're always poking and hopping where you're not wanted."

"Hullo, Gin'ral!" laughed Joey. "Is that yer, turned hup wunce more? Yer looks putty fresh arter hall you've been through and done and suffered fer yer country. Yer a riglar tough un, yer air, and a knowin one too, I'm

blest hif yer aint! I say, yer did thet shammin cracked splendid. Thet was a knowing dodge, thet wor," shaking his head playfully at the General, "ter git hout of the larks. An', I say, jist didn't yer do thet Cap'en Nipper, neither Oh, no, hin course not!" with a wink. Yer a knowing one, yer air. I knows yer. Does yer 'member 'ow nicely yer did me, wen yer cum behind me an tipped me hinto the 'old of the wessel? I——"

But here Joey's voice was drowned by a greater clamour than ever from the crowd. Several persons who had entered the tower to search for traces of the victims, had just returned and reported that the whole place was covered with blood, and one person exhibited a pair of lady's drawers (no doubt Mrs. Rumball's), the original colour of which—scarlet—was almost entirely hidden by gore!

As these drawers were held up Joey turned to the General, and giving an intelligent wink, shouted:—

"Yer 'member them things, Gin'ral, hey? Dolly Rumball's scarlet trowsers, yer knows."

"For heaven's sake," growled the General, "say what you have to say to the boys, and let us go, Sir Gentle."

"For you to get rid of this young scamp, I suppose?" returned the Governor, sharply. "You should not have made such a fool of yourself, General Shoot, and then you would have had nothing to be sensitive abo——"

"Don't call me a fool, Sir Gentle," said the General, hotly, "I won't stand——"

"You must stand it, sir," interrupted the Governor, "I say you're a——"

"You shall not say anything of the kind, sir——"

"Oh, lor!" laughed Joey. "We're a goin to hev a fight? Thet's right, Gin'ral, don't yer be put down. Go on, pitch hinter 'im!"

But this remark of Joey's recalled the wo great officers to their senses, and the Governor, moving forward his horse, began to address the boys, whilst Joey, instead of staying to listen, slipped away, and darted into the tower, having been struck with a sudden idea.

"Boys," said the Governor, "I cannot believe that, wild as you have shown yourselves, you have been guilty of so horrible a crime as this. I hope for the honour and credit of the British army, your own ease of conscience, your own good name, that this cannot be real. Is it true?"

No response; but many sullen-looking faces.

"I am afraid, from your silence," continued the Governor, "and sullen looks, that you are guilty. Boys, why did you do it?"

"Because they wanted to dose us with brimstone and treacle, and hot tea, sir," said Dick.

"You should have complained to me," returned the Governor, "and not have taken revenge into your own hands. Why," he added, getting up in his stirrups, stretching forth his arm, and speaking impressively, and with considerable emotion, "why, boys, rather than I would have had this awful disgrace brought upon this school and the British army—for it is disgraced through your act—I—I—would have taken the brimstone and treacle for you!"

"But not the tea directly after it, sir?" said Dolly, followed by suppressed tittering.

"Yes! and the tea drinking after! I would,

at any moment, sacrifice my life for the honour of the British army; I would take poison, let alone a dose or two of brimstone and treacle, if I thought that by so doing I could add to the lustre of the British ar——"

But here the Governor's eloquence was suddenly brought to a close by the appearance of an unexpected apparition—the ghost of Mrs. Rumball, looking very hot and inflamed about the face, and covered, like the boys, and the interior of the tower, with the health-sustainer.

But before we record what passed on Mrs. Rumball's appearance, we must explain how it came about that the good lady was able to do so, after having been sat upon by her husband.

The fact is that Mrs. Rumball, having taken more already than she was in the habit of taking, owing to the shattered state of her nerves, arising from the exciting incidents connected with the mixing of the health-sustainer, was so sound asleep that she was unconscious that Rumball had made a stool of her person, and was coolly drinking himself drunk in that position, until he had become too drunk to be cautious in his movements.

Rumball got so jolly, and so defiant, that at length he began to try to "bust" his Dolly by rising and then dropping on her, like a man on horseback at the trot; but Rumball hadn't continued this "bursting" process half a minute, when he felt himself rise for the last time, and in two seconds found his head trying to dive through the floor, with the result of nearly breaking both his skull and his neck.

Mrs. Rumball, who had been thoroughly aroused, and was in the act of tumbling out of bed to add to Rumball's punishment, was suddenly arrested by the entrance of Joey Pumps.

"I'm glad yer be roused hup, Dolly," said Joey. "I be come to tell yer sum noos!"

"Drat the noos!" said Mrs. Rumball. "I'm a goin to kill that willan there! He've bin a tryin to jolt me ter death!"

"Tryin ter!" said Joey. "Why don't yer know yer's ded halreddy, Dolly?"

"No I don't, Joey, an I ain't, neither! I'm live enuf to kill 'im—drat 'im!"

"But I ses yer are ded, Dolly," retorted Joey. "Yer was murdered larst night, cut hup inter blessed little bits, an' blow'd hout o' the mornin' gun!"

"Joey," said Mrs. Rumball. "Yer doesn't know wot yer talkin' about. Hif yer thinks has yer goin' to perwent me bein' rewenged hon Rumball, yer jist mistaken."

"Blow Rumball!" returned Joey. "Yer may kill 'm an' heat 'im fer hall I kears, Dolly. Look eer, where's yer gownd?"

"Gownd?" said Mrs. Rumball, looking at the floor, the bed, and then at herself, without seeing that article of attire. "Joey," she added, in a suspicious tone, "wot hev them boys done with my gownd?"

"Hah! Wot hev they boys done with hit! Why they boys hev cut hup thet gownd, an' blow'd hit hout o' the gun! Thet's wot they've done, Dolly!"

"Drat 'em!" exclaimed Mrs. Rumball, angrily. "Hif I don't jist give 'em a hextra dose o' 'stainer' fur hit, my name's not——"

"'Stainer!' Ha, ha!" laughed Joey. "Where'll yer git the 'stainer' from—eh?"

"Why, there's lot hon hit hin the pan, Joey.

Didn't the Sergeant an' me nearly get killed hover the mixin' larst night?"

"Where's the pan, Dolly?"

"Why, who've a took hit away?" cried Mrs. Rumball, looking at the spot where she had left the pan on retiring to bed.

"Ther boys hev took hit, Dolly."

"An' the 'stainer,' Joey?"

"An' the 'stainer,' Dolly!"

"Then I 'opes has hit'll do 'em good, Joey. I wish has I'd a put more brimstun hin hit!"

"Ha, ha, ha!" laughed Joey. "Why yer don't think has they boys hev bin flats enuff to take the 'stainer' hinside, Dolly—eh? Why they took the 'stainer,' but they took it ter the gun hin a pillow-case, an' popped hit hin, an' blowed hit hout along o' yer gownd, an' best cap, an' the Sarjint's trousers, an' jacket, an' cap, an' busby, an' lots o' bits o' meat and bones, and they've made hevryboddy think has yer an' the Serjint hev bin murdered and cut hup, an' blowed away from the gun. And there's a hawful crowd houtside, an' the Governor and Ginral Shoot; an' there's yer bootiful scarlit trousers hall covered in the 'stainer,' an' bin hexibited has his hall that air left o' yer! Oh, lor! Dolly, I'd jist bolt hout an' let em know whether yer was blowed away or not! 'Eres the ladle, Dolly," picking it up and holding it out. "I'd jist let about me, too, an' especially thet Ginral Shoot, has his the worst o' ther lot!"

Mrs. Rumball was thunderstricken, but she wasn't incapable of action, and she demonstrated it in her usual promptness of execution; regardless of her personal appearance—for Mrs. Rumball, in undressing for bed, had been unable to remove more than her gown—she seized the ladle, and rushed out—presenting the unexpected apparition that had interrupted the Governor's speech.

Immediately there arose a shout of astonishment, whilst those nearest Mrs. Rumball, noticing that the face of the ghost looked inconsistently flashed and angry, and not liking, besides, the look of the ladle, began hastily to back away.

As this movement opened the way easily to the Governor and General Shoot, Mrs. Rumball shot up to the bewildered officers, and setting her arms akimbo before the General, shouted out—

"So yer've began yer hold tricks hev yer? Yer've made b'lieve ter cold-blooded murder me hev yer? Yer've purtended to cut me hup inter bits, an' my gownd an' cap, and yer've had the darin' himpidence ter say has yer blowed me hout of the gun, hev yer? An' where's my scarlit trousers has his hall has his left hon me—heh?"

And before the General could even comprehend the nature of Mrs. Rumball's vituperative address, or step back his horse, the ladle flourished for a moment in the air, and then fell with a terrific "spat" on his right eye.

This was followed by another, and another, accompanied by loud demands for the scarlit drawers; and the General would probably have been ladled to a jelly about the head, had not the crowd and the officers interfered, and carried Mrs. Rumball screaming back to her room, where she was deposited on the floor by the side of Mr. Rumball, who came in for the rest of the ladling.

As one of the supposed murdered individuals

had turned up, it was natural to infer that the other was somewhere whole in the body, and could be found if a diligent search was made.

This the Governor ordered to be made, and several of the officers started to unearth the Sergeant, and with such success that he was brought forth in the state he had sought refuge in the secret ascent to the tower, and placed before the Governor and the crowd, looking and feeling as sheepish and ashamed as a man could do who was exposed to public gaze in his shirt and bare legs, and covered in patches from head to foot with the "health-sustainer."

"Hem! You are Sergeant O'Shehe, are you not, sir?" asked the Governor, as well as he could, with a catching in his throat, and a tremendous effort to keep down the risible muscles of his face.

"Upon my sou—my word, sir," said the Sergeant, in lugubrious tones, and with the tears almost in his eyes, "I wouldn't like to swear that I am *now*. I *was* last night, sir!"

"Hem! How did you come to get in that disgraceful mess?"—sternly.

The Sergeant shook his head.

"I went to bed clean enough last night, sir, and this is the state I got up in!" [Tittering in various directions]. "I've thought since, sir, whether I could have taken a big dose of the health-sustainer without knowing it, or perhaps it was the smell of the brimstone as I was mixing it, that got into my system, and come out in the night through the pores of my skin!" [Laughter behind and in front.]

"You are aware of the practical joke that has been played at your—and—and that vulgar woman's expense, and, to the great alarm of the inhabitants of the Rock, by the boys under your charge?"

"I am, sir, but I didn't know it till it was too late, or so help me ten men—hem!—I'll take me oath they would have done it, sir!"

"So I suppose, and what s the reason you did *not* know what was going on?"

"I don't know, sir," returned the trembling Sergeant, shaking his head again as though the question was quite beyond his ken. "Its usually wide awake enough I am to the young de—— rascals, but they got over me *somehow*, this time!"

"This time!" exclaimed the Governor. "They are always getting over you. I've a great mind to deprive you of the charge of the School, and reduce you to the ranks."

"Don't do that, sir, please," pleaded the Sergeant. "I'd rather be tried by a drum-head court-martial, and shot. I'd never get over the disgrace of losing me stripes. If you will only look over it this time, sir, I'll promise to be down upon the young scamps like a thousand of bricks. I mean, sir, eh—eh—I don't know what I mean, sir, only that I'll be down on 'em in future."

"What can I do with them all, General Shoot?" asked the perplexed Governor.

"I can tell you what to do with them," replied the General, with a growl and a scowl. "Send them on this expedition to Morocco, to co-operate with the Spaniards against the Moors. That will take the pluck and larking out of them, if anything will."

"A very good idea," said the Governor. "They shall go. Boys," he continued, "I am going to punish you most severely for this outrageous trick. General Shoot—your old General—has suggested that I shall send you into Morocco on active service, to fight against the Moors. You are very young to encounter such danger, but the fact is, we cannot put up with you any longer on the Rock, and I have decided to send you. Hold yourself in readiness to march at a moment's notice."

To the astonishment of the Governor and the crowd, instead of causing tears, this sentence was received with prolonged cheering by the boys, who not waiting to be dismissed, broke off, and scampered to their rooms, where they continued shouting and cheering for the rest of the day, and getting ready for the march.

. . . .

The School of the Regiment were not the only military boys who were made glad that day.

The drum-and-fife band of the —— Regiment of Infantry was at practice the same morning, in a large room of the Casemate Barrack when the news reached it that the band was to accompany the regiment with the expedition into Barbary.

This happened at the moment when the stout, pompous-looking drum-major was having a battle with an obstinate young fifer, Jack Piper. Jack was the boy who rushed in upon the two women to impart the news of Our Boys having murdered Sergeant O'Shehe and Mrs. Rumball.

Jack had gone up to the station, as he said he would, and had there witnessed the extraordinary scenes we have lately described—scenes which had made such an impression on Jack's risible nerves, that from that moment he had been in a state of jerky, spasmodic laughter.

The sustainer-smeared boys, the sudden appearance of Mrs. Rumball and her attack on the General, and the comical predicament of Sergeant O'Shehe, were constantly rising before his mental vision, and Jack could neither beat a drum, nor puff out a dozen notes on his fife, without a spasmodic interruption to the regularity of the "roll," or the harmonious flow of the notes.

This morning, the drum-major was teaching the fifer a new and difficult march, which he wanted played that very afternoon in the Alameda Gardens. This, however, seemed impossible of attainment, as the jerky seizures of Jack extended themselves by sympathetic attraction to his comrades, and the result was a complete breakdown of the performance, and a considerable breaking up of the mental equanimity of the drum-major.

The drum-major was getting in a towering passion.

"Come forward, here, Jack Piper, and take your stand in front o' the music. Ye'll jist play the tune tro yerself, widout a blissed jerk, or by the holy piper that piped afore Moses, I'll beat the notes out o' yer wid the drumstick. Now, begin."

"Too, tootle too, te too, too tootle too, tootle tootle te too-o-o-pish-ish-he-e-e——"

Jack had broken down with another jerky attack, and the next moment he felt a bang on his ear, which made his head ring like a drum. And no wonder, it was the drumstick of the big drum.

"Take that, Jack Piper!" cried the drum-major. "P'raps ye'll get out the notes now!"

"Come, I say, Major," said Jack, "that sort of thing won't do, you know. I beg to say that my head's not a big drum!"

"Begad, I'll make a big drum or some other kind o' drum afore I've done with ye, Jack Pip——"

Here the drum-major was interrupted by the

entrance of the orderly non-commissioned officer, who requesting attention, began reading the following order—

"General Order.

"Garrison of Gibraltar, — 18—

"The —th Regiment will hold itself in readiness for active service at a moment's notice. The regiment will be accompanied by both bands.

"Signed GENTLE SHARPSET, K.C.B.

"General and Governor of the Rock."

This news was received with three cheers, and from that moment the practising of the new tune was abandoned.

"Begad," growled the drum-major, "it's not sorry it's on active service ye're going, for ye are getting as bad as them young devils up the Rock.

CHAPTER LII.

DESCRIBES IN WHAT MANNER CERTAIN INDIVIDUALS EMBARKED FOR ACTIVE SERVICE IN BARBARY.

IT was not till the evening of the second day after the incidents attending on the double murder, cutting up, and blowing away of the Sergeant and Mrs. Rumball occurred, that the anxiously-expected order came for the School of the Regiment to embark for Barbary.

It was tea-time, and all the boys were standing round Mrs. Rumball, who was serving out the tea, when the Sergeant, who had managed to get a new uniform, stalked into the room with the General Order-book in his hand.

"Look here, boys," said the Sergeant, in his usual commanding tone, "just put down your basins and listen while I read the general order to you—

"'Gibraltar Garrison,

"'General Order.   —18—.

"'It having been decided by his excellency, Sir Gentle Sharpset, that the School of the Regiment shall accompany the expedition to Morocco to operate against the Moors, the General appointed to command that expedition— General Shoot—desires that the boys be in readiness, in full marching order, to embark with the —th regiment to-morrow morning at six o'clock.

"'The ——"

But here the Sergeant was interrupted by loud cheering from the excited boys.

"Stop a bit, my beauties," said the Sergeant, "before you give way to cheering. It strikes me that some of you will pull a face as long as my arm presently—especially you, my dear Dolly. Just keep your blessed tongue still and listen."

"'The General having regard to the effective appearance and strength of the School, as well as to its character for respectability, orders that the undermentioned persons shall not accompany the School, viz:—

"'Adolphus Swaps, as being too little, and altogether of an unsoldierlike figure.'"

As this unexpected paragraph was read out Dolly's face fell, whilst there arose an uncontrolable burst of laughter.

"What does my dear Dolly think of that?" said the Sergeant, facetiously. "That's you that's so proud of your figure, too! So help me ten men, if I had such a remark made about me in general orders, I go and get shaped properly on a grindstone."

"It's not my fault, Sergeant," said Dolly, followed by splitting laughter; "it's the tailor's. He always would make the seat of my overalls too big."

"Shet hup!" cried Mrs. Rumball, trying to look shocked. "Don't go a-talkin' about that part of yer trouses afore me! I'm ashamed of yer, I am!"

"Then you had better leave the room," said Dolly.

"I will," returned Mrs. Rumball. "I won't stay to hear no sich langwidge!"

Mrs. Rumball, who really only wanted to pay a visit to the brandy-bottle, was walking off when she was arrested by the Sergeant.

"Don't go yet, Mrs. Rumball," he said. "There's a clause here that refers to you."

"What!" snapped Mrs. Rumball; "does yer mean to say has the General as hed the cheek to put me hin his drefful horders?"

"Yes," returned the Sergeant, "he has, and no mistake. Let me go on, please."—(reads):—

"'Joseph Pumps, being possessed of irrepressible impudence and disrespect to General Shoot—'"

"That ain't me, Sergeant," said Joey, calling forth more ringing laughter. "Why lor, I was never himpertinent nor mispectful to anybody hin my life. Nor my name ain't Joseph; it's Joey, wich Dolly Rumball kin prove. Can't you, now?" added Joey, addressing his adopted mother.

"Wich I can, Joey," replied Mrs. Rumball, "has was the won who took yer out of the pump."

"Haut o' the troff, Dolly," corrected Joey, "I don't want yer to proff too much; stick to the truf, and shame the what's-is-name—yer know."

"Drat yer cheek!" cried Mrs. Rumball, shaking her fist at Joey, who threw himself into an attitude indicative of great terror, "I'll——"

Here Mrs. Rumball was stopped by a polite request from the Sergeant to listen to the next paragraph.

"'Mrs. Rumball, being addicted to intoxicating habits, making use of vituperative language, and not being particular whom she knocks about with her ladle, the boys must do their own cooking, and if they cannot, they must starve. Mrs. Rumball is not an ornament to her profession, and not a fit person to hold the responsible position of cook to —'"

The paragraph was never finished, as in the first place the Sergeant's voice was drowned by roars of convulsive laughter, and the indignant interruptions of Mrs. Rumball.

"Shet up!" screamed Mrs. Rumball, confronting the Sergeant, with her arms akimbo. "Ow dares yer read hout such a passil o' bombinal lies. Well, I never! To think has I shed a lived all these years to be akoosed o' tostikatin abits and wertrivitous langwidge, when I only take a little ter make up fur wot I loses in persperin hover the fire, wich it runs from me like water from a duck's back; and never buses nobody cept when I'm put upon, and then I gives it strong! I ain't no horniment ter my perfeshun, ain't I! I ain't fit ter hold the 'ponsible perzishin of cook ter a young scamp, ain't I? I ain't ter go with the school, ain't I. Yer'll just see hif I 'ont, and the wicked, lyin Gen'l 'll see ef I 'ont! I will go, an I'll be a thorn in all yer sides, has yer won't be habil yer git howt! I'll go and pack up, an' I shed jist like ter see the Gen'l try and perwent me! I'll give 'im the ladil hif 'e do; thur."

With this exclamation Mrs. Rumball snapped her fingers in the Sergeant's face, and strode, with offended dignity, from the room, followed by roars of laughter.

"So help me ten men," said the Sergeant, "but it's a devil of a temper she has," adding, in a tone that nearly killed the boys with additional laughter, "it's precious glad I'm not her husband."

Here the Sergeant was so overcome with the comicality of the scene that he sank on to a form, and fairly gave himself up to a good and long laugh.

When calmness was restored, the Sergeant, addressing Dolly Swaps, said—

"It's very sorry I am, my dear Dolly, that we shall be deprived of the pleasure of your charming society· It's yer beautiful figure we'll all miss. But you see you're *not* altogether a perfect model of a soldier, and the Moors might turn up their noses at such small game."

"You had better ask the General to let me go, Sergeant," said Dolly.

"Why, Dolly?"

"Because with your bold front, and my unsoldier-like figure, we should be enough to frighten all the Moors in Barbary.

"Hoh, hoh!" exclaimed the Sergeant, as a chorus of laughter was elicted at this allusion to his anything but conspicuous display of bravery in the Cork-woods; "Hoh, hoh! so my Dolly's in one of his chaffing humours, eh? You haven't had your right-about touched up lately, Dolly, I think—hum?"

"I don't want it touched up, Sergeant," said Dolly.

"Oh, I dare say that, Dolly; you never do. But I want to touch it up."

"You aint fair, Sergeant," grumbled Dolly, affectedly. "When I asked you to touch me up on sustainer-mixing night, you declined."

"I made a promise to do it, though, Dolly, and I believe I gave a good reason for declining. If I don't mistake I believe I said that when your right-about was clean—I mean clean of the health-sustainer (tittering in the room), I'd be down upon it. I could have given you a lick and I promise, but I only gave you the promise, and now come and I'll give you a licking."

"Well, all I know is that it isn't fair," mumbled Dolly, with an expression on his face between a grin and a pout, advancing slowly towards the Sergeant's open arm, "I'll pay you out for it, mind, when we're in Barbary."

"When we're in Barbary, Dolly."

"Yes."

"Didn't you hear me read the general order, Dolly?"

"Yes, Sergeant! but I don't care for the general order. *I shall be there.*"

"So help me ten men, but it's as bad as Mrs. Rumball you are, Dolly. But words are not deeds, my dear," nodding his head. "I've heard of a coach and four being driven through an Act of Parliament, but unless the pair of you, and Joey Pumps to boot, can manage to drive through Sergeant O'Shehe, you'll never see Barbary. Come on, Dolly."

As Dolly advanced to put his head under the Sergeant's arm, there came the rattle of sword-scabbards, and Dick called out—

"Here's the General, Sergeant."

"All right, Master Dick," returned the Sergeant, coolly, "That won't stop the punishment. There's nothing the General would like to see better than a fine touching up of dear Dolly's right-about."

And so it proved.

Just as the Sergeant began to touch up Dolly's right-about, the General and his aide-de-camp entered.

The Sergeant, however, desisted not from his touching up; but Dick, hoping to make him drop Dolly, called out in a sharp, peremptory tone—

"T—shun!"

All the boys sprang up at the word of command, but the Sergeant did not drop Dolly.

"What is the meaning of this disrespect, Sergeant O'Shehe?" demanded the General, in his usual irritable manner (for the General was quite himself again; he had got back his arrogance and temper, and in fact, everything but his moustache and whiskers). "Don't you know I am in the room, sir!"

"Yes, General," answered the Sergeant suspending operations, but keeping Dolly under his arm, "but it's touching up Master Swaps I am, for disrespect to your general order. The young scamp swears he'll go to Barbary."

"Oh, he does, does he?" snapped the General. "Then you are doing me a service, Sergeant. Go on with your touching up."

The General, as is well known, had a great antipathy for three persons—Mrs. Rumball, Dolly Swaps, and Joey Pumps. He was always glad to see either of these individuals in trouble, and he was glad to see Dolly being touched up on the present occasion; so glad that, forgetting the want of respect shown towards him by the Sergeant not calling the boys to attention, he became absorbed in the comtemplation of Dolly's punishment, bending forward and holding his face as near the point of operation as possible to avoid the Sergeant's hand.

It was like old times at Bangfire Barracks to hear the General say:—

"That's it. Lay it on, sir! Give it to him sharp! Faster—faster, and harder! Here, let *me* give him a touch up!"

But, as on other celebrated occasions, when the General was about to take the punishment into his own hands, he was unexpectedly interrupted —not by soot being fired from a gun this time, but in another fashion that was almost equally painful.

When that little innocent individual, Joey Pumps, saw the General enter in the room, he sought refuge from the General's gaze by slipping behind the Sergeant, where he remained in his usual favourite attitude, winking at all the boys he could see, and ready to dart and dodge if found necessary.

In this position, peeping under the Sergeant's arm, Joey caught sight of the close proximity of the General's face to Dolly's right-about. Joey was immediately struck by an idea; so putting his lips to Dolly's ear, he whispered,

"Begin a kickin' hup yer legs, Dolly."

As Dolly knew that Joey would not give such advice for nothing, he let out vigorously, and before the General could bring down his hand on Dolly's right-about, he felt his face being battered and rammed by Dolly's booted feet.

With one eye blinded, and his nose on fire, the General fell backwards, his "seat of honour" coming into contact with a sharp corner of one of the iron bedsteads, and then rolled to the floor.

The row the General made, and the chase he made after Dolly (whom the Sergeant in his consternation had dropped) was something terrible, until Dolly was captured.

Then the General, seizing Dolly by the baggy part of his overalls, and swearing he would pitch him over the rock into the sea, and get rid of him at once and for ever, carried him out of the room. But the General had scarcely reached the passage when he caught sight of Mrs. Rumball descending the stairs; and as the General would, at any moment, rather have faced an unmentionable personage than Mrs. Rumball, he dropped Dolly on to the floor, and trembling with horror, hastily mounted his horse, and flew from the Signal Station at a flying gallop.

Had the General but known what happened to Mrs. Rumball consequent upon his hasty retreat, he would have indulged in some fine chuckling.

At the moment that the General caught sight of Mrs. Rumball, Mrs. Rumball caught sight of the General, and, recalling the insult passed upon her in the General Order, she quickened her movements for the purpose of giving the General a piece of her mind. But the General had dropped Dolly at the right moment and in the right spot —just in front of Mrs. Rumball's feet.

The result was a great come-down, and a fearful collision between Mrs. Rumball's nose and the boards. Of course there followed a tremendous uproar, but, with this we will not deal, as we must hasten to describe the means Dolly Swaps and Joey Pumps adopted to get to Barbary.

Late in the evening Dolly and Joey met in the battery just below the Signal Tower, to hold a solemn conclave upon that serious matter.

"Well, Dolly," said Joey, "hev yer thort of a dodge?"

Dolly shook his head despondingly.

"Can't say that I have, Joey—wot will do exactly."

"Let's 'eer wot yer hev thort on, Dolly?"

"Why, we shall have to stow ourselves somewhere, shan't we Joey?"

"Hin corse we shell. Go hon."

"We're very little, yon see, Joey, and won't take up much space, and I thought we might get off amongst the baggage. If we were put into valises and strapped up, nobody would take us for a couple of kids. But when I came to think of the plan, I saw it would not do. For when we once got strapped up we mighn't be able to get out again just at the moment we wanted. See that, Joey?"

"Hin coorse I do, Dolly. That wouldn't do, that wouldn't. Besides we might get chucked inter the waggon furst, and then we shud hev hall the baggage hon top hon us, an' that 'ud be arkard would'nt it?"

"No. And then again see how we should get pitched about. First into the waggon, then out of the waggon onto the quay, then picked up again, and chucked into the boat, then from the boat on board the ship, and perhaps bundled into the hold. We couldn't stand all that, Joey."

"No, that sort o' travellin wouldn't do hat hall, Dolly. Goodness knows wot state we shud be hin wen we got ter Bar-bary."

"Then I thought of our going to the big drummer of the regiment that is going in the expedition, and getting him to put us in his big drum."

"That 'ud be wus than the t'other dodge, that would, Dolly," said Joey giving his head an emphatic shake. "Wat a row it 'ud be when the drum was a being whacked. Oh, lor, I'd rather be chucked about hin the baggage, I would."

"I think I would too, Joey. Besides, when you come to think of it, it isn't likely the big drummer would have us hanging on to his neck inside his drum. We should be too heavy! besides, we should deaden the sound, and spoil the music."

"Nuther o' them dodges is to be thort hon for a hinstant," said Joey. Hev you hanny huther dodge, Dolly?"

"No, Joey. Have you?"

"Well, I think has I've a got a hideer, Dolly."

"What is it, Joey?"

"Wot do yer think o' gettin' hinside o' Mrs. Rumball's feather bed?"

"But Mrs. Rumball isn't to go either, Joey."

"So the gen'ral horder ses; but does yer think has Dolly Rumball cares for the gen'ral horder?"

"Do you think she'll go, then?"

"I'se *sure* hon hit, Dolly. She've almost packed hup heverythin' but the bed. Wot do yer think of the bed dodge?"

"It would be awfully fluffy inside, Joey, eh?"

"But hit 'ud be nice and soft, Dolly, an' they might chuck us about over hanny-ow, an' we shudn't feel it. An' we shud be putty, safe, too, has Dolly loves her feather bed, an' she'd take jolly good keer not to lose sight hon hit."

"That's all very well, Joey, but we should get the fluff in our eyes, nose, and mouth, and be smothered."

"Well hif yer don't like the bed, wot does yer think of Dolly's big box?"

"That would be just as bad for breathing, wouldn't it, Joey."

"Not hif yer bores 'oles hin hit, Dolly."

"But there won't be room for us, will there?"

"Plenty o' room. Thet's the box has Dolly keeps 'er best clothes hin, an' we shell hev hit jolly comf't'ble hif we gets atween 'er silk gownds, 'an we sharn't be shook'd much. Wot does yer say to hit?"

"I don't mind trying it, Joey, though I hope the blessed box won't be dropped into the sea on the way. It might, you know, and then we should be in a nice fix. See, Joey?"

"Hit carn't be 'elped, Dolly. Yer wants tu go tu Bar-bary, don't yer?"

"Of course I do, Joey."

"An' so does I, an' I ain't goin' tu let the Gen'ral ' do ' me nor more nor Dolly Rumball."

"All right, then, Joey, you'll tip me the wink when there's a chance!"

"Rather, Dolly."

With this the two wicked plotters parted— Dolly to his chums, and Joey to watch Mrs. Rumball's proceedings.

As Mrs. Rumball did not want to be hampered and bothered with too much luggage, she decided to take only a half-dozen boxes besides her feather bed. Mrs. Rumball being of luxurious and refined habits, and possessed of a delicate constitution, that was so frail, indeed, that contact with the bare earth would have withered her up in no time, the feather bed was an indispensable item of luggage.

This bed, and the large box containing her rich and Sunday-going dresses and costumes, Mrs. Rumball left to the last to pack. This being the case, Mrs. Rumball was not ready until an hour before gun-fire, and she kept such close watch over her treasures that Joey began to think that getting in the big box would be no go, and came to the reluctant conclusion that he and Dolly would have to try the valise dodge.

But at length—about a quarter of an hour before gun-fire—Mrs. Rumball went out to look after the mules she had hired the previous night to take her baggage down to the Mole. This step —hiring the mules—had been rendered necessary, owing to an intimation, sent up by the General, that no Government transport would be at Mrs. Rumball's disposal.

Now was Joey's opportunity.

Slipping into the boys' room, Joey gave Dolly the wink, and in less than a minute they were in Mrs. Rumballs room.

"We must be quick about it," cried Joey, opening the lid of the box, and beginning to pull out some of the things with which the box was crammed, and stowed them away in another box that Mrs. Rumball was going to leave behind. "Hin yer get, Dolly," added Joey, when he had cleared out to a sufficient depth.

Dolly was in full uniform ; but as he could not get in with his busby on, he hastily pitched it in the box.

"Wot does yer want that thing for?" said Joey.

"To frighten the Moors, Joey."

"Hall right. Get hin, or Dolly Rumball 'll be back."

Dolly then bundled into the box, when Joey covered him up with one of Mrs. Rumball's silk gowns, and then, slipping in himself, pulled down the lid of the box and snuggled closely to Dolly.

"It's jolly close here," said Dolly. "Have you made the air-holes ?"

"Hall right, Dolly ! yer'll breathe bootiful wen we gits hin the hopen hair. I made the holes last night. Keep quiet."

The further adventures of the School of the Regiment, with the account of how Mrs. Rumball, Dolly Swaps, and Joey Pumps get on board, and what became of the latter, will be related in the Second Part.

Further adventures of the characters of this story will be found in

"OUR BOYS IN THE ARMY."

NOW READY!

IN

❖ PENNY NUMBERS ❖

A VERY

INTERESTING & THRILLING TALE

ENTITLED

"STRAYED ❖ ❖ ❖ ❖ ❖ AWAY."

BY

ERNEST BRENT,

Author of "MILLY LEE," "WAITING FOR THE TIDE," "BETTER THAN BEAUTY," etc., etc.

Splendidly Illustrated with Original Drawings

BY

W. BOUCHER.

To be given away with No. 1

A BEAUTIFUL COLOURED PICTURE.

Published every Monday by the ALDINE PRINTING AND PUBLISHING COMPANY, 9, Red Lion Court, and 11, Gough Square, Fleet Street, London, E.C.